A Thousand Golden Cities

JUSTIN MAROZZI has spent most of his professional life living and working in the Muslim world. A former Trustee of the Royal Geographical Society, he is the author of seven books, including the bestselling *Tamerlane: Sword of Islam, Conqueror of the World* and the Ondaatje Prize-winning *Baghdad: City of Peace, City of Blood*, which was praised by the judges as 'a truly monumental achievement'.

Also in the anthology series

THE ART OF THE GLIMPSE
100 Irish Short Stories
Chosen by Sinéad Gleeson

THE BIG BOOK OF CHRISTMAS MYSTERIES
100 of the Very Best Yuletide Whodunnits
Chosen by Otto Penzler

DEADLIER
100 of the Best Crime Stories Written by Women
Chosen by Sophie Hannah

DESIRE
100 of Literature's Sexiest Stories
Chosen by Mariella Frostrup and the Erotic Review

FOUND IN TRANSLATION
100 of the Finest Short Stories Ever Translated
Chosen by Frank Wynne

FUNNY HA, HA
80 of the Funniest Stories Ever Written
Chosen by Paul Merton

GHOST
100 Stories to Read With the Lights On
Chosen by Louise Welsh

HOUSE OF SNOW
An Anthology of the Greatest Writing About Nepal
Chosen by Ed Douglas

JACK THE RIPPER
The Ultimate Compendium of the Legacy and Legend of History's Most Notorious Killer
Chosen by Otto Penzler

LIFE SUPPORT
100 Poems to Reach for on Dark Nights
Chosen by Julia Copus

OF GODS AND MEN
100 Stories from Ancient Greece and Rome
Chosen by Daisy Dunn

QUEER
A Collection of LGBTQ Writing from Ancient Times to Yesterday
Chosen by Frank Wynne

SHERLOCK
Over 80 Stories Featuring the Greatest Detective of all Time
Chosen by Otto Penzler

THAT GLIMPSE OF TRUTH
100 of the Finest Short Stories Ever Written
Chosen by David Miller

THE TIME TRAVELLER'S ALMANAC
100 Stories Brought to You From the Future
Chosen by Jeff and Ann VanderMeer

THE STORY
100 Great Short Stories Written by Women
Chosen by Victoria Hislop

WE, ROBOTS
Artificial Intelligence in 100 Stories
Chosen by Simon Ings

THE WILD ISLES
An Anthology of the Best of British and Irish Nature Writing
Chosen by Patrick Barkham

WILD WOMEN
and their Amazing Adventures Over Land, Sea & Air
Chosen by Mariella Frostrup

2,500 Years of Writing from Afghanistan and its People

A Thousand Golden Cities

EDITED BY
JUSTIN MAROZZI

HEAD of ZEUS

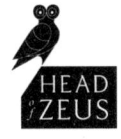

An Apollo Book

First published in the UK in 2023 by Head of Zeus Ltd,
part of Bloomsbury Publishing Ltd

In the compilation, Introduction and biographies © Justin Marozzi, 2023
In the Foreword © Masood Khalili, 2023

The moral right of Justin Marozzi to be identified as the editor of this work
has been asserted in accordance with the Copyright,
Designs and Patents Act of 1988.

The moral right of the contributing authors of this anthology to be
identified as such is asserted in accordance with the Copyright,
Designs and Patents Act of 1988.

The list of individual titles and respective copyrights to be found on page 687–95
constitutes an extension of this copyright page.

All rights reserved. No part of this publication may be reproduced, stored in
a retrieval system, or transmitted in any form or by any means, electronic,
mechanical, photocopying, recording, or otherwise, without the prior permission
of both the copyright owner and the above publisher of this book.

All excerpts have been reproduced according to the styles found
in the original works. As a result, some spellings and accents
used can vary throughout this anthology.

9 7 5 3 1 2 4 6 8

A catalogue record for this book is available from the British Library.

ISBN (HB) 9781803285351
ISBN (E) 9781803285344

Typeset by PDQ
Printed and bound by CPI Group (UK) Ltd, Croydon CR0 4YY

Head of Zeus Ltd
5–8 Hardwick Street
London EC1R 4RG
WWW.HEADOFZEUS.COM

To the poets and writers of Afghanistan.

'Even the highest mountain
has a way to the top.'

CONTENTS

Introduction Justin Marozzi	xi
Foreword Masood Khalili	xvii

Herodotus, *The Histories*	1
Strabo, *Geography*	3
Pliny, *The Natural History*	7
Diodorus Siculus, *Historical Library*	9
Frank Holt, *Into the Land of Bones: Alexander in Afghanistan*	12
Hugh Kennedy, *The Great Arab Conquests*	21
Mohammed ibn Jarir al Tabari, *The History of al Tabari: The Zenith of the Marwanid House*	27
Ferdowsi, *Shahnameh, Book of Kings*	40
Hudud al Alam: Discourse on the Country of Khurasan and its towns	84
Rabia Balkhi, Selection of Poems	87
Khwaja Abdullah Ansari, *Intimate Conversations with God*	91
Mohammed ibn Abd al Jabbar Utbi, *Account of the Alliance of the Sultan with Ilek-Khan, and their Subsequent Estrangement*	96
Farid al Din Attar, Selection of Poems	105
Saadi, Selection of Poems and Stories	110
Rumi, Selection of Poems	116
Marco Polo, *The Book of Ser Marco Polo, The Venetian*	129
Ibn Battuta, *The Travels of Ibn Battuta*	138
Hafiz, Selection of Poems	142
Sharaf al Din Ali Yazdi, *The History of Timur-Bec*	148
Khwandamir, *Habib al Siyar*	153

Ibn Arabshah, *Tamerlane or Timur, The Great Amir*	158
Jami, *Haft Awrang (Seven Thrones)*	163
Alisher Navoiy, Selection of Poems	171
Ruy Gonzalez de Clavijo, *Embassy to Tamerlane 1403–1406*	174
Babur, *Baburnama*	181
Saib Tabrizi, 'Kabul'	226
E. M. Forster, 'The Emperor Babur'	228
Amitav Ghosh, *The Man Behind the Mosque*	234
Mountstuart Elphinstone, *An Account of the Kingdom of Caubul*	252
Alexander Burnes, *Travels into Bokhara*	256
Florentia Sale, *Journal of the Disasters in Afghanistan, 1841–1842*	271
Mohan Lal, *Travels in the Punjab, Afghanistan and Turkistan*	280
William Dalrymple, *Return of a King*	289
Reverend George Gleig, *Sale's Brigade in Afghanistan*	293
General Frederick Roberts, *Narrative of Events in Afghanistan*	297
Gordon Whitteridge, *Charles Masson of Afghanistan*	301
Rudyard Kipling, 'The Young British Soldier' and 'Ford O' Kabul River'	308
Frank Martin, 'Tortures and Methods of Execution'	313
Amir Abdur Rahman, 'The Boundaries of Afghanistan and the Durand Mission'	319
Sir Henry Mortimer Durand, 'Skin of the Donkey, Teeth of the Dog'	323
Robert Byron, *The Road to Oxiana*	333
Eric Newby, *A Short Walk in the Hindu Kush*	350
Rosanne Klass, *Land of the High Flags: A Travel Memoir of Afghanistan*	356
Peter Levi, *The Light Garden of the Angel King*	369
Nancy Hatch Dupree, *An Historical Guide to Afghanistan*	381
S. A. Mousavi, *The Hazaras of Afghanistan*	389
Shaikh al Islam Abu Bakr Abdullah al Waiz, *The Merits of Balkh*	398
Artyom Borovik, *The Hidden War: A Russian Journalist's Account of the Soviet War in Afghanistan*	408
Svetlana Alexievich, *Boys in Zinc*	414

Jason Elliot, *An Unexpected Light: Travels in Afghanistan*	421
Rory Stewart, *The Places in Between*	426
Ahmed Rashid, *Taliban: The Power of Militant Islam in Afghanistan and Beyond*	431
Christina Lamb, *The Sewing Circles of Herat*	448
Khaled Hosseini, *The Kite Runner*	455
Åsne Seierstad, *The Bookseller of Kabul*	463
Justin Marozzi, 'Mutton Stew with the Lion of the Panjshir'	468
Ahmad Shah Massoud, 'A Letter to the People of the United States of America'	472
Alex Strick van Lincshoten and Felix Kuehn, *Poetry of the Taliban*	476
Homeira Qaderi, *Dancing in the Mosque: An Afghan Mother's Letters to her Son*	482
Farookha Gauhari, *Searching for Saleem: An Afghan Woman's Odyssey*	491
Edward Zellem, *Proverbs*	495
Charles Gammell, *Herat: Pearl of Khorasan*	498
Chris Sands and Fazelminallah Qazizai, *Night Letters: Gulbuddin Hekmatyar and the Afghan Islamists who Changed the World*	508
Lawrence Wright, *The Looming Tower: al-Qaeda's Road to 9/11*	518
David Kilcullen and Greg Mills, *The Ledger: Accounting for Failure in Afghanistan*	523
Abdul Salaam Zaeef, *My Life with the Taliban*	530
Anand Gopal, *No Good Men Among the Living: America, The Taliban, and the War Through Afghan Eyes*	544
Atiq Rahimi, *Earth and Ashes*	552
Durkhanai Ayubi, *Parwana: Recipes and Stories from an Afghan Kitchen*	559
Tim Albone, *Out of the Ashes*	566
G. Whitney Azoy, *Buzkashi: Game and Power in Afghanistan*	576
Lalage Snow, *War Gardens: A Journey Through Conflict in Search of Calm*	582
Fawzia Koofi, *The Favoured Daughter: One Woman's Fight to Lead Afghanistan into the Future*	593

Nadia Hashimi, *The Pearl That Broke Its Shell*	608
Qais Akbar Omar, *A Night in the Emperor's Garden: A True Story of Hope and Resilience in Afghanistan*	615
Nadeem Aslam, *The Wasted Vigil*	628
Nushin Arbabzadah, *Afghan Rumour Bazaar: Secret Sub-Cultures, Hidden Worlds and the Everyday Life of the Absurd*	644
Bilal Sarwary, 'The Plane Hit the Tower and all our Lives Changed'	658
Contemporary Afghan Poetry: Nadia Anjuman, Shakila Azizzada, Samay Hamid, Khalilullah Khalili, Masood Khalili, Sayd Bahodine Majrouh, Reza Mohammadi, Partaw Naderi, Somaya Ramish, Roya, Bahar Saied, Roya Sharifi and Farangiz Sowgand	663
Extended Copyright	687

INTRODUCTION

The mountains. That first, heart-stopping sight. However you come to Afghanistan, whether you are threading your way through the Khyber Pass, that ancient pathway of conquerors, or flying into Kabul, the high peaks always dazzle. The very act of entering Afghanistan lifts your eyes towards the heavens. Those serried peaks, dragon's teeth, bewitching curves, line after line of them, singed by the sun, lost in shadow, radiant in snow-white, dissolving one by one into the horizon.

How many visitors, over how many centuries, have been completely smitten by this unearthly panorama? Unearthly because there seems nothing else like it on earth. The late Lebanese historian Samir Kassir wrote of Beirut, the city of his birth, occupying an enviable location 'that seems to have fallen to earth from the heavens'. The same could be said, though on a far grander scale, of the entire country of Afghanistan.

This is not a pretty or picturesque country. Those words are too petty, too small and mundane to encompass the savage grandeur of this mountain kingdom. This is a landscape whose beauty is as soaring as its summits. It transfixed Babur, the sixteenth-century chess-playing conqueror, calligrapher, poet, diarist, gardener and founder of the Mughal dynasty, who came to adore his adopted capital of Kabul. Having seized it in 1504, he doted on it for decades, fortifying it, adorning it with mosques and markets and, above all, laying out numerous gardens in and around it. His favourite, Bagh-e Babur, Babur's Gardens, still stands resplendent in the city on an eleven-hectare sweep of ground tumbling down the western slopes of Mount Sher-i-Darwaza to the foaming Kabul River below.

Babur was a complicated man: Pepys, Tamerlane, Machiavelli and Montaigne rolled into one. In *Baburnama*, his effervescent memoirs which are featured in these pages, he marvelled at Kabul's flora and fauna, counting thirty-two varieties of wild tulips on the mountainsides and admiring the abundance of 'grape, pomegranate, apricot, apple, quince, pear, peach, plum, almond and walnut'. Here too were roses, pistachios, sour cherries and plane trees interspersed with the Arghavan, or Judas trees, that he especially cherished. He thrilled to the many birds and their daily chorus – nightingales, herons, mallards, blackbirds, thrushes, doves, magpies, egrets, waterhens and cranes, the birds of heaven.

Perhaps it is this empyrean setting that encourages speculation as wild as its wind-shredded mountain passes. Lured back time and again to this irresistible country, I have sometimes wondered whether a visiting alien, shocked by its outrageous beauty on the one hand and the terrible destitution and suffering of its people on the other, might posit some form of correlation between the two. 'Our country's landscape is deceptive,' writes the Afghan journalist Bilal Sarwary, a chronicler of recent wars here. 'It is easy to be struck by its beautiful valleys, sharp peaks, winding rivers, and little hamlets. But what presents as a peaceful image hasn't provided ordinary Afghans with any peace. You can't find peace without safety in your own home.' Nor can you eat the view. Of course, there is nothing inevitable about the tragic plight in which Afghanistan has found itself in recent decades, but the physical lure of the place – above all, for successive foreign conquerors – is very real and no mere flight of fancy. All too often the attraction has proved fatal for untold numbers of Afghans on the receiving end of invasions dreamt up by empire-builders on the make.

Afghanistan's physical geography has been a blessing from the heavens, but it has also been a devilishly long-lasting curse. Invaders and neighbours, and especially invading neighbours, have, over the millennia, turned Afghanistan, a Silk Road crossroads for merchants, militaries, pilgrims, gem-dealers, spies, intriguers, travellers and adventurers, into a battlefield of imperial ambition. This is as true of ancient times as it has been of the blood-spattered opening decades of our own century. Well on his way to becoming the Great, Alexander campaigned with savagery here from 329 BC, meting out atrocities and setting the template for future ferocity from other world conquerors. 'May God keep you away from the venom of the cobra, the teeth of the tiger and the revenge of the Afghans,' says a proverb attributed to him, establishing a tradition of foreign, frequently barbaric, invaders deploring the supposed barbarism of the Afghans. Alexander paved the way, less than a century later, for the Hellenistic Greco-Bactrian Kingdom, the Land of A Thousand Golden Cities from which this book takes its title.

When the Buddhist monk Hsuen-Tsang passed through the Kabul River valley in 630, he bore witness to the latest round of conquest, this time by the Central Asian tribe of the Hephthalites, or White Huns. They had put an end to the crumbling vestiges of the once resplendent Kushan Empire, whose princes had by then become Persian vassals. 'There are a million Buddhist monasteries which are in ruins and deserted,' he wrote sadly. 'They are overgrown with weeds and constitute a mournful solitude.'

Hsuen-Tsang was writing on the cusp of the great Arab Conquests which, starting here in the 650s, first brought Islam to the deserts, steppes and mountains of Central Asia. Other empires rose and fell in the wake of the world-changing Arab Umayyads, wresting control over what is today Afghanistan, or at least parts of it. The Tahirids were followed by the Saffarids and Samanids, the Ghaznavids, Seljuk Turks and Ghorids. The Mongol conqueror Genghis Khan blazed an annihilating trail of destruction here in the 1220s, sacking the illustrious northern city of Balkh among a host of cities. Timur, or Tamerlane, Christopher Marlowe's 'Scourge of God', the self-styled Sword Arm of Islam and Lord of the Fortunate Conjunction, brought similar levels of maniacal slaughter here in the 1380s, half a century after another foreigner, Ibn Battuta, the great Arab traveller bar none, had deplored the Afghans for their allegedly aggressive qualities. 'These are a powerful and violent people,' he wrote, 'and the greater part of them highway robbers.'

In more recent times, too, Afghanistan has found itself facing a series of ruinous foreign interventions, foremost among them the British in the nineteenth century, the Soviet in the twentieth, and the American-led in the twenty-first. 'My country is like a poor goat on whom the lion and the bear have both fixed their eyes,' Abdur Rahman, Amir of Afghanistan in the closing decades of the nineteenth century, wrote of the ever-encroaching British and Russians, 'and without the protection and help of the Almighty Deliverer the victim cannot escape very long.'

All this, a prelude to the literary feast that follows, is to demonstrate that the country we call Afghanistan today has long been at the heart of world events. Far from being the 'remote' and inaccessible kingdom of popular, western-centric imagination, it has, more often than not, been absolutely central to world history. Empires have waxed and waned among the jagged summits of the Hindu Kush and Karakoram, trade routes have prospered and declined, faiths have been carried west and east, north and south, while aggressors have launched their brutal assaults and beat their ignominious retreats. Peoples and languages and faiths have met and mixed – and fought – here over thousands of years and the cultural legacy of these encounters has been profound and varied. Quintessentially Muslim today, in different epochs Afghanistan has also been a thriving hub of Zoroastrian, Hellenistic, and Buddhist civilisation. Cities prospered. Bamiyan once echoed to the chanting of Buddhist monks, Muslim Arabs revered ancient Balkh as the Mother of Cities, and mosque-thronged Herat flashed its royal glitter during the Timurid Golden Age. National education may be in tatters today, but a longer view reveals that Afghanistan is also a place steeped in learning. Both Zoroaster and Avicenna taught here.

This is not a history of Afghanistan. It is a celebration of its extraordinarily rich literary heritage, from ancient times and the dawn of prose writing – take a bow, Herodotus – to today's efforts to make sense of the most recent chapters of devastating conflict.

There is tragedy in these pages, to be sure. It could hardly be otherwise, given the persistent cycles of war and violence which have bedevilled the country since the Soviets invaded in 1979. Afghan women in particular, under siege and attack now more than ever, raise their voices with courage, defiance and searing wit, lambasting cruel fathers, hypocritical husbands and brothers, scorning religious bigots and celebrating their own sexuality in death-defying resistance to the patriarchy in a country where writing can be a matter of life and death. There are accounts of ancient and modern incursions, natural histories, geographical surveys, tall tales from high-spirited explorers, spiritual diversions, studies of storied cities, literary criticism, alternately on-the-edge-of-your-seat and hilarious travel writing, biography and autobiography, and a wealth of contemporary fiction from Afghan novelists, many – in another sign of the times – living in exile in Europe and North America.

Among the screeds of prose, there are torrents of poetry here too, for inside every Afghan – man, woman and child – there lurks a poet. Afghanistan is a nation of poets, and verse flows freely, pouring across the country like rivers crashing down from the mountains to irrigate the literary soil. These pages celebrate the classics – Rumi, Jami, Hafiz, Saadi, Rabia Balkhi, Alisher Navoiy, Ansari and Attar among them. Though not all are from today's Afghanistan, each poet is venerated by millions in this multilingual, multi-ethnic nation. That geographical blurring, the reverence for Farsi verse by the 77 per cent of Afghans who speak Dari, or Afghan Farsi – Pashto, second in popularity, is spoken by 48 per cent of the population – speaks to a resonating cultural influence beyond today's borders. And that, too, is a reminder that what we call Afghanistan today has been a part of many empires in its history. Founded as a state by Ahmad Shah Durrani in 1747, the country's borders were not settled until long afterwards, and never without contention. The border between British India and the then Emirate of Afghanistan, known as the Durand Line after the British diplomat who led negotiations over it, was only established in 1893, an enduring controversy which is examined from both Afghan and British perspectives in this volume.

Beyond the classics of Persian, Pashto and Uzbek verse, this anthology also explores more recent poetry. We hear from Khalilullah Khalili, the late poet laureate of Afghanistan, his son, fellow poet and diplomat, Masood Khalili, author of the Foreword, Sayd Bahodine Majrouh, assassinated by militants in 1988, and many more Afghan voices besides. Here the familiar join forces with the unexpected. War-weary mothers mourn their lost sons and lovesick Taliban warriors rail against American and British invaders. More dangerous, in a country where women poets have been killed for their writing, are the verses of young women – like Nadia Anjuman, beaten to death by her husband in 2005, Rahila Muska, who set herself on fire and died in 2010, and all those anonymous authors of the 'lightning flash' *landay* folk verses – who mock their menfolk and howl with righteous rage, pain and despair. These outcries are from darker places, where poetry is not for the faint of heart. But it is not all tragedy and gloom. Far from it. There are also plenty of lyrical verses in this anthology celebrating joy, wine, love and laughter.

Do not think for a moment, whatever Taliban extremists might have us believe to the contrary, that Muslim Afghanistan has always been a place of austerity and sobriety. That is a nonsense. In the words of the poet Mullah Mohammed 'The Riddler', quoted by Babur half a millennium ago in his memoirs – themselves teeming with all manner of wine- and hashish-fuelled revelries, not to mention dreams of dalliances with both sexes:

'Drink wine in the castle of Kabul and send the cup round without pause
For Kabul is mountain, river, city, lowland in one.'

*

Like so many foreign travellers to Afghanistan, I was bewitched on my first visit more than a quarter of a century ago. On the way to my first job as a *Financial Times* foreign correspondent in southeast Asia, I managed to meet the man who had wowed the West, given the Soviets a bloody nose and who was in the process of bewitching much of his country. One of the twentieth century's great guerrilla leaders, Ahmad Shah Massoud was then doing his best to stem the Taliban tide. Although Massoud was a man of war, whose *mujahidin* forces had done more than the Soviets to reduce swathes of the Afghan capital to smoking rubble, he was also a voice of moderation against the forces of extremism and fanaticism. Although much of the interview predictably turned upon military matters, Massoud became most animated when speaking about his love of the Persian poet Hafiz. It was my first experience of poetry as a living force in Afghanistan. Hafiz is one of the greatest, but by no means the only, poet whose verses may be recited by heart from one end of the country to the other.

How different a trajectory Afghanistan might have followed with Massoud in a leadership role in the wake of Al Qaeda's attacks against the US on

11 September 2001 will never be known because he was assassinated by two of its terrorists a couple of days earlier. He became one of the numberless Afghan martyrs killed in a seemingly never-ending war, his face visible across the country today on street hoardings and car stickers paying tribute to the great warrior.

Breaking bread with Massoud in the midst of war was an unforgettable introduction to Afghanistan. I knew then that I would always want to return and have been fortunate enough to do so, enjoying the legendary hospitality which is at the heart of Afghan culture. In the years that followed that meeting, I have returned again and again. Once, I travelled across the country to research a biography in the footsteps of all-conquering Timur, great-great-great-grandfather of Babur. Shukur, an Afghan guide who had lost both parents in a rocket attack on Kabul sixteen years earlier, showed me the desolation – since restored – of Babur's Gardens. Mortars had destroyed much of the park and craters had replaced flowerbeds. Even Babur's tomb, a 'highway of archangels, this theatre of heaven, this light-garden of the God-forgiven angel king', in the words of his epigraph, had been damaged by bullets.

In 2001, three weeks before the Taliban destroyed it with dynamite, I stood on the head of Lord Buddha, one of the two colossal and peerless Buddhas of Bamiyan, who have stared out over this exquisite valley, unfolding beneath them like an emerald prayer rug, for almost 1,500 years. Years later, I returned to make the pilgrimage to Massoud's tomb – subsequently desecrated by the Taliban – high in his beloved Panjshir Valley. Arif, my Afghan friend, and I stood together silently, shivering in the bone-chilling wind, and said our goodbyes to the Lion of the Panjshir. Later still, I worked with idealistic young Afghan men and women who had flocked to join their new, western-backed government, only to see it fold like a pack of cards in 2021 as the West pulled the rug from under its feet, beat another shameful retreat and left its Afghan friends – with far too few honourable exceptions – to fend for themselves.

A Thousand Golden Cities showcases the many facets of the jewel that is Afghanistan. It is an exploration of its history and geography, religion and culture, politics and poetry, sport, drama, memoir and home-grown fiction. Every effort within the bounds of available translations, budget and copyright has been made to bring Afghan voices to the fore. I hope you enjoy reading these literary gems as much as we did choosing them.

Justin Marozzi
September 2023

FOREWORD

In the last half century, the world has been watching a country burning, a nation crying and a generation dying.

That is Afghanistan, a nation whose history of war and peace has been shaped, fortunately or unfortunately, by its very sensitive geography, making it both a corridor for the movement of people and ideas – merchants, travellers, pilgrims, soldiers, religion, trade and philosophy – and a graveyard of conquerors. A nation with an ancient culture and a strong people who have survived 2,500 years since Alexander the Great first crossed it to conquer the world. A country with a history of conquerors and the conquered, of invaders and the invaded, of subjugators and the subjugated, of leaders who have been both visionary and short-sighted, cruel and kind.

From the snorting and whinnying of Alexander's galloping horses to the diesel-fuelled roars of American and NATO tanks, everything that Afghans have seen, felt, lived, realised and learnt, you can find in the book you have in your hands: an anthology of Afghanistan, written by many much-loved writers over many centuries: men and women from Afghanistan, as well as men and women from outside, who so often have fallen in love with my beautiful country.

There is no question that Afghans have seen great reversals in fortune in recent decades. The story of my own family's life, like that of so many Afghans, has been stained with violence and bloodshed. My grandfather was hanged in 1919 by the then King Amanullah when my father, Khalilullah Khalili, was eleven years old. His mother had already died and he was left with nothing. The king ordered my father to leave Kabul and go to a village in the north, where he was not allowed to go to school. But secretly he went to the mullah in the middle of the night and learnt Farsi and poetry, reading Saadi, Rumi and Hafiz. He became a poet at sixteen and the poet laureate of

Afghanistan under King Zahir Shah. He worked in the palace as an advisor and taught the king philosophy and poetry. In 2002, the elderly King Zahir told me in Kabul, 'I learned the alphabet from your father, not of Persian, but of life. He taught me about the spirituality of our culture and I'll never forget it.'

Several generations of my family have now experienced war at first hand. My father was seventy when the Soviets invaded, my son was born during a time of war and now my grandson is a teenager and still the fighting continues. It started in 1979 and for forty-three of my seventy-four years there has been war. When will it ever end?

We Afghans have experienced times that have been sour and times that have been sweet. We have tasted great successes and devastating failures, but we have always survived. Why is that? Mainly, I think, because of our love of three things: faith, freedom and culture.

Let me explain what I mean. To show you the nature of the poor Afghan people and to understand how faith, freedom and culture have been such an essential part of our lives, I would like to share three real-life stories which I experienced during the Afghan–Soviet war between 1979 and 1989.

It was 1985. I was crossing the high mountains of Nuristan in the northeast of the country. While I was climbing a steep mountain with deep valleys and extremely narrow tracks, I saw a penniless Nuristani woman almost blocking the track. She had one hand held up like a beggar and her face was covered with a black cloth. The minute she saw us, she lamented, 'I have just four walnuts in my hand. If you are fighting for the sake of God, take them please. I wish I had more to give you. May God bless you all.' It was an extraordinary moment. 'What a faithful poor lady she is and if God needs another Mary, mother of Jesus Christ, she is the one to be chosen,' I wrote in my diary.

It was 1986. I was a political officer of my party, Jamiat, and an advisor to former President Rabbani. I was also a very close friend of commander Ahmed Shah Massoud, the hero of modern Afghanistan. To mobilise my people against the Soviet invaders, I travelled twenty-three times right across the country – on foot, by donkey and on horseback. The roads and skies were controlled by the Soviets so I had to travel mostly at night from mountain to mountain, river to river, village to village, mosque to mosque and, above all, heart to heart. I always carried a thick notebook in my backpack to write to my wife, Sohailla, about what I saw, heard, felt and touched. Not just about the war, but about how ordinary Afghans lived and suffered in the fires of conflict.

One day during that summer of 1986, I reached a village on the very top of one of the high mountains of the Hindu Kush. Despite the fear of bombardment, I could see a small group of boys aged between ten and twelve sitting under a willow tree. They were being taught Persian poetry by a humble teacher. I got off my donkey. The boys, though surprised, were very happy to see me. After a few minutes, I asked them to write the word *azadi*, meaning freedom. Out of maybe twenty-five or thirty pupils, just two started to write. I asked the teacher why only two of the boys were writing. What about the others? The teacher, with a long sigh, told me, 'Oh, they are all talented boys and they can all write very well, but please be patient, we only have two pencils in the whole class.' At that moment, I appreciated the sheer depth of poverty in my country. My eyes filled with tears. While fathers fight with guns, I told the teacher, their sons struggle with pencils.

It was 1987. After three months of travelling around the country, rallying the people, my donkey and I were both exhausted. One day I saw a poor boy playing with his goat. I asked him what his name was and if he could call his father to spare us a little food. He did not answer. I asked his name again, but still there was no answer. I thought he must be deaf, so I approached him more closely and spoke more loudly. He started crying, 'Oh, please do not kill me. I am a good boy. You killed my father last year. Don't kill me! I am a good boy. I am a good boy!' I immediately told my bodyguards to hide their guns. Then I heard the voice of a lady from a tent close by. She shouted, 'My son is scared of guns. Please hide them. The Soviets killed his father last year in front of him. If you are fighting for the sake of God, I will send you some food.' I was in tears, murmuring to myself, 'May God make this war disappear for the sake of the tears of this innocent boy and his poor mother.'

I hope these three little stories will show the reader how the values of faith, freedom and culture were – and still are – vital parts of the lives of ordinary, moderate Afghans, in war or in peace, no matter how lowly or destitute they may be.

Coming from Afghanistan and now living overseas, like so many of my countrymen and women who have had to flee their beloved country, I'm often asked the question, are the people of Afghanistan as fanatical as the Taliban, Al Qaeda and ISIS? It is tragic but understandable that they should ask this – and for me it is always an easy answer. Definitely not, because, except for several thousand Taliban, Afghans are all Muslims, but we are not Islamists. We are faithful, but we are not fanatics.

Even the most fleeting glance at our past and present culture reveals an encyclopaedia full of great philosophers, poets, writers and artists from the ages, many of whom are rightly and joyfully celebrated in these pages. People who have been intellectually curious in their examination of the human condition, far-reaching in their interests, alive to their culture and fearless in their writing. We have men and women like the poets Rumi, Hafiz, Saadi, Ansari, Jami, Rabia Balkhi, and Makhfi Badakhshi. There is the philosopher

Al Farabi, the physician Avicenna, the polymath Omar Khayyam, the peerless portraitist and artist Behzad, and so many more women poets, writers, singers and artists who taught us love, peace, tolerance, freedom and wisdom. Whether they live in Afghanistan or elsewhere, whether they are male or female, Afghans continue to explore the written and spoken word with boundless energy and imagination.

Let me give you another example. Many years ago, when I was student in Delhi University, I lived in an apartment that was owned by an old Christian lady, Mrs Biswas, who kindly agreed to teach me English, but only on the condition that I would learn the language through the Bible. I thought maybe as a Muslim this was not good. So I asked my father, who was then the Afghan ambassador to Iraq. He laughed and told me:

Be faithful.
Churches, synagogues,
temples and mosques
are lit by one light.
Never fight.

That was the moderate way we were taught by our fathers and teachers. In the mosques, besides the holy book, we were always taught the temperate philosophy of poets like Rumi and Saadi.

You may ask, then, why most of the pages of Afghan history are soaked in blood? Do Afghans love fighting? No, not at all. It is mainly because of our tragic, strategic geography and the lack of visionary leadership that Afghan history is full of blood. People fight not for the love of war but sacrifice their precious lives for peace and prosperity.

Look at the emergence of fanatical groups like the Taliban and their fanatical, alien ideas. Where did they come from? They were armed, trained, and financed by other regional countries. These groups are beyond fanatical in their brainwashed interpretations of Islam. Once I asked a member of the Taliban why they had banned kite flying. He simply said: 'The string of the kite may cut the wings of the invisible angels like Michael and Gabriel.' Can you imagine such nonsense?

I have to tell the readers of this book, it hasn't always been like this. The Taliban are the exception not the norm. Go back a century, and it wasn't like this. Go back sixty years to the reign of King Zahir Shah (1933–73) and you would find him encouraging girls to go to school, to work, to teach, to travel alone with no chaperone, to be ministers, members of parliament, artists, singers, actresses – in short to be active in all walks of life, shoulder to shoulder with men. But fanatics like Taliban have stopped everything.

The second cause for the problems we face in Afghanistan is the lack of honest and visionary leadership. The people have always won the wars of liberation but unfortunately it was thanks to the selfish politicians that they lost the peace.

In the midst of all these difficulties and challenges, Afghans have always taken refuge in culture. If we are fanatical about anything it is in our love of poetry. I will always remember how, during my last night on earth with my dear friend Commander Ahmed Shah Massoud, it got very late and he said to me, 'For God's sake, let us finish with all the politics. I've got the best thing here.' And it was Hafiz, one of his favourite poets. And we stayed up together and read him until three in the morning. Later that day, on 9 September 2001, two days before Al Qaeda's attacks on the United States, he was killed by two terrorists posing as journalists – assassinated in cold blood while I was sitting next to him. Even in the midst of war, one of the last acts of his too short life was reading his beloved Hafiz. This is what Afghans are like. Poetry is as important to us as the air we breathe and the water we drink.

Afghans are no different from any other people in the world in their love of freedom. Yet the Taliban have turned Afghanistan into a prison, especially for women and girls, whose dreams of education, careers and travel they are doing so much to destroy. Our culture is moderate, the Taliban's is fanatical. We want civil law and justice, they believe in neither. They are incapable of government. People want jobs to fill their stomachs, the Taliban keep them starving. Don't make the mistake of expecting Taliban V2.0 to be any different from their first time in charge. A rock stays a rock. But if they are incapable of changing their barbaric rule, then mass political, cultural and social resistance will simply spread all over the country. The Taliban will not last forever. This land of poets and writers will not allow it.

Let me end this poetically political piece with what I always believe: with hope for bringing peace, we live forever. Without it, we die every minute.

MASOOD KHALILI

THE HISTORIES

Herodotus
Translated by A. D. Godley, 1920

Herodotus (c. 484–425 BCE) is widely known as the 'Father of History', but he was also the world's first travel writer, a pioneering geographer, anthropologist, explorer, investigative reporter, foreign correspondent and multiculturalist before the word even existed. He was learned professor and tabloid journalist in one, a man of wit and wisdom with an unfailing eye for fabulous material to inform and amuse, horrify and entertain. *The Histories* was the world's first great prose epic, a compulsively readable masterpiece teeming with tall stories of dog-headed men, testicle-slicing eunuchs, flying snakes and strange sexual customs from foreign parts, alongside the mesmerising narrative of the world-changing Persian Wars. Although Herodotus's writing here smacks of the fantastical with his tales of underground, gold-digging ants (marmots, perhaps?), it is interesting to note that 2,500 years ago he reckoned the Afghans were 'the most warlike' of the region's people.

3.102

Other Indians dwell near the town of Caspatyrus and the Pactyic country,[1] north of the rest of India; these live like the Bactrians; they are of all Indians the most warlike, and it is they who are sent for the gold; for in these parts all is desolate because of the sand. In this sandy desert are ants,[2] not as big as dogs but bigger than foxes; the Persian king has some of these, which have been caught there. These ants live underground, digging out the sand in the same way as the ants in Greece, to which they are very similar in shape, and the sand which they carry from the holes is full of gold. It is for this sand that the Indians set forth into the desert. They harness three camels apiece, males on either side sharing the drawing, and a female in the middle: the man himself rides on the female, that when harnessed has been taken away from as young an offspring as may be. Their camels are as swift as horses, and much better able to bear burdens besides.

4.204

This Persian force advanced as far as Euhesperidae in Libya and no farther. As for the Barcaeans whom they had taken for slaves, they carried them from Egypt into banishment and brought them to the king, and Darius gave them a town of Bactria to live in. They gave this town the name Barce, and it remained an inhabited place in Bactria until my own lifetime.

Notes

1 N.E. Afghanistan. Caspatyrus (or Caspapyrus) is said to be probably Cabul.
2 It is suggested that the "ants" may have been really marmots. But even this does not seem to make the story much more probable.

GEOGRAPHY

Strabo

Translated by Horace Leonard Jones, 1924

> Best known for his *Geographica*, or *Geography*, the first-century Greek scholar **Strabo** (64 or 63–24 BCE) lived in Asia Minor, today's Turkey, and presented his readers with full-blooded descriptions of peoples and places across much of the then known world. His account of ancient Bactria, encompassing today's Afghanistan and parts of Tajikistan and Uzbekistan, includes details of Alexander the Great's bloody conquests in the region. More controversially, it also repeats earlier stories of how the Bactrians, the ancestors of the Afghans, treated their sick and elderly. Readers of a sensitive disposition, look away now!

11.11

As for Bactria, a part of it lies alongside Aria towards the north, though most of it lies above Aria and to the east of it. And much of it produces everything except oil. The Greeks who caused Bactria to revolt grew so powerful on account of the fertility of the country that they became masters, not only of Ariana, but also of India, as Apollodorus of Artemita says: and more tribes were subdued by them than by Alexander—by Menander in particular (at least if he actually crossed the Hypanis towards the east and advanced as far as the Imaüs), for some were subdued by him personally and others by Demetrius, the son of Euthydemus the king of the Bactrians; and they took possession, not only of Patalena, but also, on the rest of the coast, of what is called the kingdom of Saraostus and Sigerdis. In short, Apollodorus says that Bactriana is the ornament of Ariana as a whole; and, more than that, they extended their empire even as far as the Seres and the Phryni.

Their cities were Bactra (also called Zariaspa, through which flows a river bearing the same name and emptying into the Oxus), and Darapsa, and several others. Among these was Eucratidia, which was named after its ruler. The Greeks took possession of it and divided it into satrapies, of which the satrapy Turiva and that of Aspionus were taken away from Eucratides by the Parthians. And they also held Sogdiana, situated above Bactriana towards the east between the Oxus River, which forms the boundary between the Bactrians and the Sogdians, and the Iaxartes River. And the Iaxartes forms also the boundary between the Sogdians and the nomads.

Now in early times the Sogdians and Bactrians did not differ much from the nomads in their modes of life and customs, although the Bactrians were a little more civilized; however, of these, as of the others, Onesicritus does not report their best traits, saying, for instance, that those who have become helpless because of old age or sickness are thrown out alive as prey to dogs kept expressly for this purpose, which in their native tongue are called "under-takers," and that while the land outside the walls of the metropolis of the Bactrians looks clean, yet most of the land inside the walls is full of human bones; but that Alexander broke up the custom. And the reports about the Caspians are similar, for instance, that when parents live beyond seventy years they are shut in and starved to death. Now this latter custom is more tolerable; and it is similar to that of the Ceians, although it is of Scythian origin; that of the Bactrians, however, is still more like that of the Scythians. And so, if it was proper to be in doubt as to the facts at the time when Alexander was finding such customs there, what should one say as to what sort of customs were probably in vogue among them in the time of the earliest Persian rulers and the still earlier rulers?

Be this as it may, they say that Alexander founded eight cities in Bactriana and Sogdiana, and that he razed certain cities to the ground, among which was Cariatae in Bactriana, in which Callisthenes was seized and imprisoned, and Maracanda and Cyra in Sogdiana, Cyra being the last city founded by Cyrus and being situated on the Iaxartes River, which was the boundary of the Persian empire; and that although this settlement was fond of Cyrus, he razed it to the ground because of its frequent revolts; and that through a betrayal he took also two strongly fortified rocks, one in Bactriana, that of Sisimithres, where Oxyartes kept his daughter Rhoxana, and the other in Sogdiana, that of Oxus, though some call it the rock of Ariamazes. Now writers report that that of Sisimithres is fifteen stadia in height and eighty in circuit, and that on top it is level and has a fertile soil which can support five hundred men, and that here Alexander met with sumptuous hospitality and married Rhoxana, the daughter of Oxyartes; but the rock in Sogdiana, they say, is twice as high as that in Bactriana. And near these places, they say, Alexander destroyed also the city of the Branchidae, whom Xerxes had settled there—people who voluntarily accompanied him from their homeland—because of the fact that they had betrayed to him the riches and treasures of the god at Didymi. Alexander destroyed the city, they add, because he abominated the sacrilege and the betrayal.

Aristobulus calls the river which flows through Sogdiana Polytimetus, a name imposed by the Macedonians (just as they imposed names on many other places, giving new names to some and slightly altering the spelling of the names of others); and watering the country it empties into a desert and sandy land, and is absorbed in the sand, like the Arius which flows through the country of the Arians. It is said that people digging near the Ochus River found oil. It is reasonable to suppose that, just as nitrous and astringent and bituminous and sulphurous liquids flow through the earth, so also oily liquids are found; but the rarity causes surprise. According to some, the Ochus flows through Bactriana; according to others, alongside it. And according to some, it is a different river from the Oxus as far as its mouths, being more to the south than the Oxus, although they both have their outlets into the Caspian Sea in Hyrcania, whereas others say that it is different at first, but unites with the Oxus, being in many places as much as six or seven stadia wide. The Iaxartes, however, from beginning to end, is a different river from the Oxus, and although it ends in the same sea, the mouths of the two, according to Patrocles, are about eighty parasangs distant from one another. The Persian parasang, according to some, is sixty stadia, but according to others thirty or forty. When I was sailing up the Nile, they used different measures when they named the distance in "schoeni" from city to city, so that in some places the same number of "schoeni" meant a longer voyage and in others a shorter; and thus, the variations have been preserved to this day as handed down from the beginning.

THE NATURAL HISTORY

Pliny

Translated by John Bostock, 1885

Pliny the Elder (23 or 24–79 CE) was a Roman naturalist, natural philosopher, historian, military commander and friend of the emperor Vespasian. A prolific writer who finished a twenty-volume *Bella Germaniae (The History of the German Wars)*, he is best remembered for his *Naturalis Historia*, or *Natural History*, a prototype for future encyclopedias. He died in his mid-fifties during the eruption of Mount Vesuvius. Here he describes a swathe of Central Asia, encompassing modern-day Afghanistan.

6.23

The greater part of the geographers, in fact, do not look upon India as bounded by the river Indus, but add to it the four Satrapies of the Gedrosi,[13] the Arachotæ,[14] the Arii,[15] and the Paropauisidæ,[16] the river Cophes[17] thus forming the extreme boundary of India. All these territories, however, according to other writers, are reckoned as belonging to the country of the Arii. Many writers, too, place in India the city of Nysa,[18] and the mountain of Merus, sacred to Father Bacchus; in which circumstance[19] originated the story that he sprang from the thigh of Jupiter. They also place here the nation of the Astacani, whose country abounds in the vine, the laurel, the box-tree, and all the fruits which are produced in Greece. As to those wonderful and almost fabulous stories which are related about the fertility of the soil, and the various kinds of fruits and trees, as well as wild beasts, and birds, and other sorts of animals, they shall be mentioned each in its proper place, in a future portion of this work. I shall also very shortly have to make some further mention of the four Satrapies, it being at present my wish to hasten to a description of the island of Taprobane.

Notes

13 Gedrosia comprehended probably the same district as is now known by the name of Mekran, or, according to some, the whole of modern Beloochistan.

14 The people of the city and district of Arachotus, the capital of Araehosia. M. Court has identified some ruins on the Argasan river, near Kandahar, on the road to Shikarpur, with those of Arachotus; but Professor Wilson considers them to be too much to the southeast. Colonel Rawlinson thinks they are those to be seen at a place called Ulan Robat. He states that the most ancient name of the city, Cophen, has given rise to the territorial designation.

15 The people of Aria, consisting of the eastern part of Khorassan, and the western and north-western part of Afghanistan. This was one of the most important of the eastern provinces or satrapies of the Persian empire.

16 This was the collective name of several peoples dwelling on the southern slopes of the Hindoo Koosh, and of the country which they inhabited which was not known by any other name. It corresponded to the eastern part of modern Afghanistan and the portion of the Punjaub lying to the west of the Indus.

17 It is supposed that the Cophes is represented by the modern river of Kabul.

18 The place here alluded to was in the district of Goryræa, at the north-western corner of the Punjaub, near the confluence of the rivers Cophen and Choaspes being probably the same place as Nagara or Dionysopolis, the modern Nagar or Naggar.

19 The word μύρος, in Greek, signifying a "thigh."

HISTORICAL LIBRARY

Diodorus Siculus
Translated by C. H. Oldfather, 1989

> The Ancient Greek historian **Diodorus Siculus** (c. 90–c. 30 BCE), a contemporary of Julius Caesar and Augustus, was the author of the monumental, forty-volume *Biblioteca historica*, a universal history, much of which has itself been lost to history. His work ranges magisterially and eclectically from the age of mythology and the fall of Troy through to the career and death of Alexander the Great and on into early Roman times, ending around 60 BCE. Like Herodotus he takes a great interest in the culture of the non-Greek world, roving from Ancient Egypt, Mesopotamia and India, to Arabia, Scythia and North Africa.

17.82

When this year was over, Euthycritus became archon at Athens and at Rome Lucius Platius and Lucius Papirius became consuls. The one hundred and thirteenth Olympic Games were held.[1] In this year Alexander marched against the so-called Paropanisadae, whose country lies in the extreme north; it is snow-covered and not easily approached by other tribes because of the extreme cold. The most of it is a plain and woodless, and divided up among many villages.[2] These contain houses with roofs of tile drawn up at the top into a peaked vault.[3] In the middle of each roof an aperture is left through which smoke escapes, and since the building is enclosed all around the people find ample protection against the weather. Because of the depth of the snow, they spend the most of the year indoors, having their own supplies at hand. They heap up soil about vines and fruit trees, and leave it so for the winter season, removing the earth again at the time of budding. The landscape nowhere shows any verdure or cultivation; all is white and dazzling because of the snow and the ice which form in it. No bird, therefore, alights there nor does any animal pass, and all parts of the country are unvisited and inaccessible.[4]

The king, nevertheless, in spite of all those obstacles confronting the army, exercised the customary boldness and hardihood of the Macedonians and surmounted the difficulties of the region. Many of the soldiers and of the camp followers became exhausted and were left behind. Some too because of the glare of the snow and the hard brilliance of the reflected light lost their sight. Nothing could be seen clearly from a distance. It was only as the villages were revealed by their smoke that the Macedonians discovered where the dwellings were, even when they were standing right on top of them. By this method the villages were taken and the soldiers recovered from their hardships amidst a plenty of provisions. Before long the king made himself master of all the population.[5]

Notes

1 Euthycritus was archon at Athens from July of 328 to June of 327 B.C. The Roman consuls of 330 B.C. were L. Papirius Crassus and L. Plautius Venno (Broughton, 1.143). The Olympic Games were those of July 328. Diodorus neglected to name the winner of the foot race, who was Cliton of Macedonia, according to Eusebius, Chronikon. By now, Diodorus's chronology is seriously off; it can have been no later than the autumn of 330 B.C., "at the setting of the Pleiades" (Strabo 15.2.10).
2 Curtius 7.3.5–18; *Justin* 12.5.9; Arrian. 3.28.4–7. This country is the highland of Afghanistan, cold in the winter, but neither in the north nor a plain. According to Aristobulus (Arrian. 3.28.6), nothing grew there except terebinth and asafoetida.
3 Curtius's description of these buildings (Curtius 7.3.8-9) is clearer. He compares the roofs to the keels of ships. The houses were partly underground (Plut. *De Fortuna aut Virtute Alexandri* 2.9.340e).

4 Curtius 7.3.10–11, also, mentions burying the plants to protect them and the absence of animals and birds.
5 Alexander wintered there in 330/29 (Strabo 15.2.10).

INTO THE LAND OF BONES
ALEXANDER IN AFGHANISTAN
Frank Holt

> Alexander the Great (356–323 BCE) sits at the very top table of world conquerors alongside two ferocious Asian warlords: Genghis Khan and Timur, or Tamerlane. Both men campaigned with savagery in today's Afghanistan and they did so in the wake of Alexander's ruthless depredations among the deserts, steppes and mountains of Central Asia. In the wake of his victory over the Persian Great King Darius III, leader of the Achaemenid Empire, at the Battle of Gaugamela in 331 BCE, Alexander pressed east first into Persia, then into Bactria, the start of several years of punishing campaigns in the region. In Afghanistan alone he founded or renamed half a dozen cities, including Herat, Bagram, Ghazni and Kandahar, while waging a blood-soaked war against determined guerrilla fighters, ancestors of those Afghans who resisted foreign invaders so determinedly in more recent times.
>
> **Frank Holt** (1954–), professor of history at the University of Houston, is an American archaeologist and author and is considered the foremost authority on Alexander the Great in Afghanistan. *Into the Land of Bones* set the disastrous US-led war in Afghanistan from 2001 in the context of Alexander's much earlier invasion in an entertaining and scholarly account.

Known in antiquity as Bactria, Afghanistan emerged as a danger zone in direct response to Alexander's mounting power throughout the Middle East. From the perspective of the native peoples, Alexander and his followers represented an intrusive, alien culture offensive to local traditions. Alexander was later decried as an "unbeliever" who brought evil to the East and drenched the land with blood. Many Persians rejected Alexander's claims of legitimacy as a liberator; they questioned the sincerity of his efforts to respect Persian religion and to promote a true partnership with local princes. So, as the invaders battled deep into what is modern-day Iraq, and their forces occupied the entire region, Bactria became the refuge of what Alexander called, in turn, a rogue regime that harbored warlords and terrorists. Using rhetoric that still resonates today, Alexander denounced these men as lawless savages, the enemies of civilization. In what he called a new and dangerous world, Alexander warned his followers that these resourceful criminals would continue to exploit differences of religion, language, and culture to rouse attacks against innocent victims. They must be confronted with overwhelming military force, and stopped; their leaders must answer—dead or alive—for their crimes. Not to act was to jeopardize the safety of Greece itself. "This is a noble cause," proclaimed Alexander to his armed forces, "and you will always be honored for seeing it through to the end." Then, backed by unbridled support, the most powerful leader of the time led the most sophisticated army of its day against the warlords of Afghanistan. Ask those ancient Greek and Macedonian ghosts to reflect upon our situation today, and they might feel strangely at home. The old dictum "Plus ça change, plus c'est la même chose" (The more things change, the more they remain the same) ought to be the official motto of Afghanistan.

When in turn the British, Russians, and Americans each seized Kandahar in southern Afghanistan, they occupied a city founded by Alexander himself and still bearing the Arabic version of his name. When U.S. troops charged on horseback against the Taliban strongholds of Mazar-i-Sharif, they rode past the crumbling walls of Alexander's main camp, and the capital of the Greek kingdom that endured there for centuries. When American newspapers printed datelines from Ai Khanoum accompanied by photographs of a Northern Alliance gun emplacement on the heights of this remote village, practiced eyes could see the ruins there of an ancient city where Greek settlers once wrestled in the gymnasium, watched tragedies in the theater, worshiped the gods of their ancestral pantheon, and warred for control of Bactria for nearly nine long generations.

VICTORIES

At Bactra, the Greeks and Macedonians nonetheless got some very good news. The generals who had remained behind near Herat to capture or kill Bessus's ally Satibarzanes now rejoined the army and reported what had happened. There had been a significant battle during which Satibarzanes had paused, taken off his helmet, and challenged any opponent brave enough to fight him in single combat. Old white-haired Erigyius, who shared the Macedonian command with three others (including a Persian, Artabazus), stepped forward and accepted the offer. During the fight, Satibarzanes missed with his spear and Erigyius charged, driving his lance into the enemy's throat and out the back of his neck. Thrown from his horse, Satibarzanes continued to fight though still impaled. Erigyius grabbed the lance and pulled it free, then thrust it forcefully into Satibarzanes's face. The latter could do nothing but help drive it deeper to hurry his death and end his own suffering.

At Bactra, Alexander and his soldiers marveled at the mangled head of Satibarzanes, which Erigyius carried around as a trophy of war. The deed had won the battle and ended the insurrection around Herat, preventing those rebels from reinforcing Bessus as the warlord had planned. The same dramatic news may have been what compelled Bessus to withdraw into Sogdiana in search of other allies, and no doubt it demoralized the Bactrian cavalry, which had counted on Satibarzanes's support. When the Bactrians learned that Alexander had crossed the Hindu Kush, that Satibarzanes was dead, and that Bessus planned to retreat north across the Oxus and abandon Bactria to the invaders, most of the native horsemen simply slipped away to their homes. It could not have been a substantial band that followed Bessus to Sogdiana. At Bactra, Alexander considered these facts and decided to forge ahead as quickly as possible to finish Bessus before the assassin could redress his losses. Acting, of course, as the rightful King of Kings, Alexander appointed Artabazus—the Persian just back from the victory against Satibarzanes—to be the satrap of Bactria. The message was clear: join Alexander's cause, like Artabazus, and receive all the perquisites of the old Persian Empire; or live as outlaws, like Satibarzanes and Bessus, and endure the righteous punishments of the civilized world. No one could be neutral.

The march from Bactra to the Oxus River crossed a harsh stretch of desert that would again test the resilience of the Greek and Macedonian army. The invaders had nearly frozen and starved just a few weeks earlier in the mountains, and now during high summer they had to hike through nearly fifty miles of searing wastes where Anahita's water could not sustain them. Local informants advised Alexander to travel only at night, both to escape the worst temperatures and to navigate the desert by the stars. To keep the journey down to two nights, the king lightened the army's load by leaving its baggage at Bactra in the care of Artabazus. Still, it was a disaster. The sand glowed with heat, mirages danced, and the dry air sucked every drop of moisture from the mouths of the suffering men. Water bags emptied too soon, and discipline failed. Soldiers gorged themselves on stores of oil and wine, only to vomit away what they had foolishly drunk. With growing numbers of men dehydrated or already dead, Alexander pressed forward to the Oxus River and lit signal fires to guide and encourage the troops. Relays of water bearers went back into the desert to assist the weakest stragglers. Unfortunately, many drank so excessively that they had "choking fits" and died. Alexander reportedly waited by the trail, without refreshing himself, to welcome each survivor as he staggered into camp. The political battle to win over the Bactrian people was going well, but the land itself was literally killing the Greeks and Macedonians.

The next obstacle was the Oxus River, the longest and largest in central Asia. As today it defines much of the northern border of Afghanistan, in antiquity it separated Bactria proper from Sogdiana. The region of Sogdiana stretched north to the Jaxartes River (modern Syr Darya); it was attached administratively to Bactria as an extension of the province (satrapy). At his crossing point, Alexander measured the river's width at about three-quarters of a mile. Scholars have long disputed the exact location. In antiquity, the key crossings were located at Kerki, Kilif, Kampyr-Tepe, and Termez. Kerki was probably too far west for Alexander's purposes. Of the remaining possibilities, the importance of Termez in later history (it became a key Islamic trading center) has swayed many to settle upon it. Legends do link Alexander to the founding of Termez, but such associations carry no decisive weight in that part of the world. Termez is certainly a reasonable guess, now with its Friendship Bridge (at times an Orwellian misnomer), but Kampyr-Tepe and Kilif cannot be ruled out as the spot where Alexander first encountered and crossed the Oxus. In fact, Kampyr-Tepe is the only crossing site where pottery has been found that is contemporary with Alexander's reign. The challenge would have been the same at any locale. Bessus had burned all the boats, and the powerful current made it impossible to set pilings in the deep riverbed. In any case, no wood could be found with which to construct a makeshift bridge. The only solution was the age-old practice of fashioning flotation devices by stuffing straw into leather tent covers and water skins. By stitching them tightly, these maintained enough buoyancy to float swimmers lying upon them across the river. The whole operation took five or six days.

During this time, Alexander received fresh intelligence about Bessus's situation. The warlord had not fulfilled his promise to oppose the invaders at the "wall of the Oxus." In fact, with each leg of Alexander's relentless pursuit, Bessus found himself more alone. The man claiming to be Artaxerxes V experienced (ironically and perhaps justly) the same plight as Darius after Gaugamela: he fled, unable to mount a fight, and lost the last of his fretful lieutenants. Word of Alexander's kindness to Gobares, the man who had defected after opposing Bessus's speech at Bactra, encouraged other rebels to slip away to the oncoming army. It was easy, under the circumstances, to favor for the moment Alexander's claim to the Persian realm over that of the retreating Bessus. Warlords tend to pledge allegiance as the occasion warrants, whatever the alleged religious and political crimes of the enemy. This remains Lesson One today: "There are no immutable loyalties or alliances in Afghanistan, whatever ethnic or religious umbrella they may be formed under and however fervent the oaths that seal them." Bessus betrayed Darius, and others revealed themselves willing to betray Bessus in turn.

Alexander could afford, therefore, to send part of his army back home. Some old and unfit Macedonians received their formal discharges on the banks of the Oxus. They would not have been dragged across the desert from Bactra if Alexander had not believed they might be needed to fight Bessus; clearly, the military situation had changed and the king could be charitable. An additional contingent of Greek mercenaries from Thessaly also went home, but they were apparently fired. They may have been held responsible for breaking discipline during the recent desert march and for grumbling about the hardships. Anticipating an arrest instead of a battle, Alexander resumed his march into Sogdiana with almost a thousand fewer men.

Then something strange occurred—if we may believe some of the ancient sources. As the invading Greeks and Macedonians approached a town, its inhabitants surrendered in great celebration. They spoke a degenerated form of Greek and claimed to be the descendants of the Branchidae, a Greek clan that had been deported from Miletus (in western Asia Minor) by the Persian king Xerxes in 479 BCE. They happily welcomed Alexander within the walls of their town, expecting nothing like the so-called liberation they were about to receive. On this sesquicentennial of their exile, the Branchidae learned just how long their fellow Greeks could hold a grudge. Alexander's army decided that the Branchidae were traitors living under the protective custody of the Persians, to whom they had once betrayed a famous temple in Miletus. The Branchidae remained, therefore, enemies rather than friends, criminals rather than compatriots. Alexander and his soldiers plundered the town and butchered every single person. No mercy was shown to the defenseless citizens, not even those begging as suppliants. The massacre was complete. Next, in a spasm of rage reminiscent of the Romans at Carthage, the invaders destroyed every vestige of the town and even leveled the surrounding woods and sacred groves. The stumps themselves were pulled up and their broken roots burned out of the ground. What roused such passions we cannot know. Perhaps Alexander's army needed a bloody catharsis after its recent travails; perhaps the men were spoiling for a fight against anyone in their path; perhaps the king wished to play to the home crowd in Greece after acting so much lately as a legitimate king of Persia. Whatever the reason or reasons, the first atrocity had occurred in a campaign that would soon become a breeding ground for senseless brutality.

Having executed these traitors to the Greek cause, Alexander's attention turned back to the treason of Bessus. A message arrived that three prominent rebels (Spitamenes, Dataphernes, and Catanes) had locked Bessus in chains somewhere in the neighborhood of modern Kitab in Uzbekistan. Having stripped their former leader of all his regalia, the warlords wished to surrender the captive to King Alexander for punishment. Two versions exist of the transfer to Alexander's custody. In one, Spitamenes personally delivered the prisoner bound and naked, led around by a collar and chain. Spitamenes made a little speech on the occasion, professing his loyalty to the memory of Darius, for which Alexander praised him. In the other version, the hero is Ptolemy. This account certainly derives from Ptolemy's own memoirs, written when he became the king of Egypt at the outset of the Hellenistic age. Ptolemy could not resist the opportunity to elaborate at great length—indeed, exaggerate—his role in bringing Bessus to justice. When Alexander learned of Bessus's arrest, the king assigned Ptolemy the mission of riding ahead with a picked force of five thousand men to secure the prisoner. This was Ptolemy's first high-profile command, and he wished to make the most of it. Better to describe himself as the key figure, rather than give that honor to Spitamenes, whose daughter later married the general Seleucus, a political rival of Ptolemy.

Fearing the capricious nature of the so-called barbarians, Ptolemy dashed to the rendezvous lest Spitamenes and the others should change their minds and release their captive. Ptolemy's troops covered the ten-day journey in only four. Sure enough, claimed Ptolemy, the conspirators were having second thoughts. As the invaders approached, Spitamenes and his followers allegedly rode off, leaving Bessus behind in a small village. Ptolemy surrounded the place and ordered its inhabitants to surrender Bessus, which the frightened villagers naturally did, after what had happened to the Branchidae. Informed of Ptolemy's success, Alexander sent instructions on the treatment of the prisoner. Bessus was to be stood bound and naked by the right side of the road on which Alexander would pass. The captive should be wearing a wooden collar as a symbol of his disgrace. A few days later, the king stopped beside the would-be usurper and demanded an explanation of his crimes. All accounts agree that Bessus offered a lame defense: he had taken the title "King of Kings" intending only to pass it, in turn, to Alexander. His long flight belied the excuse, and the penalty would be horrific. First, he was tortured while a herald announced his various evil deeds. Then he was placed in the custody of Darius's brother, Oxathres, and sent to prison in Bactra. There in the coming winter, Bessus would be dragged before a sort of Loya Jirga and literally defaced.

According to Persian custom, the rightful King of Kings should be a handsome man; Darius, for example, had been "the best-looking and tallest of all men." Usurpers, therefore, were brutally disfigured before they were killed, in order to render them thoroughly unfit for the throne they had coveted. Later in Bactra, where Bessus had so recently held his war council under the name Artaxerxes V, the captive's ears and nose were cut from his face. There could be no doubt then which man was king. Alexander appeared before the crowd young and ruggedly handsome. He was clean shaven, short, and muscular, with his head habitually cocked to the left. His hair and complexion were fair; his voice deep and harsh; his eyes clear and tending toward blue. After the death of Darius, Alexander had begun to wear some of the regalia of the Persian kings, notably the diadem, striped robe, and belt. Surely with startling effect, beside him stood Bessus chained and bleeding, a broken man. Lord Byron might have been looking at Bessus stripped of his royal robes and name (rather than thinking of Napoleon) when he penned these lines:

> 'Tis done—but yesterday a King!
> And arm'd with Kings to strive—
> And now thou art a nameless thing:
> So abject—yet alive!

But not for long. In one account, Oxathres presided over the crucifixion of Bessus and the desecration of his corpse. In another, Bessus was strapped between two bent trees and ripped to pieces when the saplings sprang upright. Even the greatest admirers of Alexander felt shock at this savagery. One is reminded of the haunting photograph showing the Afghan president Muhammad Najibullah hung from a traffic kiosk in Kabul after the Taliban captured, castrated, and then killed him in 1996. Victory is the proud parent of vengeance in the wars of Afghanistan.

THE GREAT ARAB CONQUESTS

Hugh Kennedy

Hugh Kennedy (1947–) is a British historian and academic who specialises in the history of the early Muslim Middle East, Al-Andalus and the Crusades. Fluent in Arabic and a Fellow of the British Academy, he was Professor of Middle Eastern History at the University of St Andrews for ten years from 1997 before becoming Professor of Arabic at the School of Oriental and African Studies in London. *The Great Arab Conquests* is a masterful summary of one of the most compelling periods in Islamic history. Here Kennedy focuses on the greatest military challenge the marauding, world-conquering Arabs of the seventh and eighth centuries ever faced: Afghanistan.

The most determined resistance the Arabs faced in the lands of the Sasanian Empire came from the area of eastern Sistan, the Helmand and Kandahār provinces of modern Afghanistan. The campaigns in this area are also interesting because the harshness of the fighting provoked the only full-scale mutiny recorded among Arab troops at this time. The desert areas of southern Afghanistan are a difficult environment for any invading army. The scorching heat is very debilitating and the rugged hills provide endless points of shelter and refuge for defenders who know the area well. This was neither Zoroastrian nor Buddhist territory but the land of the god Zun, whose golden image with ruby eyes was the object of veneration throughout the area. The kings of this land were called Zunbīls, their title proclaiming their allegiance to the god, and they moved between their winter palaces on the plains by the Helmand river and their summer residences in Zābulistān, the cooler mountains to the north.

A Muslim force had raided the area as early as 653–4, when the Arab commander had allegedly poured scorn on the image of the god, breaking off one of his arms and taking out his ruby eyes. He returned them to the local governor, saying that he had wished to show only that the idol had no power for good or evil. The god, however, survived this insult and was still being venerated in the eleventh century, symbolizing the fierce resistance of the people of these barren hills to outside interference. The early Muslims were well aware that this area was a potential route to India, with all its riches, but the Zunbīls and their relatives, the Kabulshāhs of Kabul and their peoples, mounted a spirited and long-lasting resistance to the Arabs, making it impossible for Muslim armies to reach northern India.

It was into this fiercely hostile environment that Ubayd Allāh b. Abī Bakra led the 'Army of Destruction' in 698. Ubayd Allāh himself was a typical example of a man of humble origins who had done very well out of the Muslim conquest. His father was an Ethiopian slave in the city of Tā'if near Mecca. When the Muslims were besieging the town in 630, two years before the Prophet's death, he had proclaimed that any slave who came over to his side would be free. Abī Bakra had used a pulley to lower himself over the town walls and so acquired his nickname, the Father of the Pulley. He married a free Arab woman and their son, Ubayd Allāh, inherited his dark skin colour. His slave origins were exploited by satirists. The family moved to Basra when the town was founded and made large sums of money out of urban development by building public baths. Ubayd Allāh was able to build himself a very expensive house and to keep a herd of 800 water buffalo on his estates in the marshlands of southern Iraq. The conquest of Fars provided new opportunities for making money, and we have already seen him making vast sums from the confiscation of the assets of the fire-temples there. He was, in short, a man of obscure origins and little military experience who made a fortune out of the conquests.

Hajjāj b. Yūsuf, governor of Iraq and all the east, now appointed him to command a Muslim army against the Zunbīl, who was refusing to pay tribute, ordering him to go on attacking until he had laid waste the land, destroyed the Zunbīl's strongholds and enslaved his children. The army was assembled at the Muslim advanced base at Bust. They then marched north and east in pursuit of the Zunbīl. Their enemies withdrew before them, luring them further and further into the rugged mountains. They removed or destroyed all the food supplies and the heat was scorching. Ubayd Allāh soon found himself in a very perilous position and began to negotiate. The would-be conqueror was forced to offer a large sum of tribute, to give hostages including three of his own sons and to take a solemn oath not to invade the Zunbīl's land again. Ubayd Allāh was lavishly entertained by the monarch with women and wine. Not all the Muslims were happy to accept this humiliation and some determined to fight and achieve martyrdom, arguing that Muslims should never be prevented from attacking infidels, and, much more practically, that Hajjāj would deduct the tribute from their salaries, leaving them without any rewards for the hardships they had endured during the campaign.

A few brave souls elected to fight and achieved the martyrdom they wished. Most followed their commander in a desperate retreat to Bust. Only a small number made it, the rest perishing from hunger and thirst. Of the 20,000 men 'with their mailed horses and panoply of weapons' who had set out, only 5,000 returned. It was widely believed that Ubayd Allāh himself was exploiting the situation by commandeering any grain and selling it on to his troops at vastly inflated prices. As the ragged remnants of the army approached Bust they were met by a relieving force bringing some supplies, but many of the starving wretches ate so fast that they perished and the survivors had to be fed slowly with small quantities. Ubayd Allāh himself reached safety but died very soon after. The poets were merciless in their criticism of his incompetence and, above all, of his greed and the way he had exploited his troops to make money.

> You were appointed as their Amir
> Yet you destroyed them while the war was still raging
> You stayed with them, like a father, so they said
> Yet you were breaking them with your folly

> You are selling a qafiz* of grain for a whole dirham
> While we wondered who was to blame
> You were keeping back their rations of milk and barley
> And selling them unripe grapes.

It was probably the most significant setback for Muslim arms since the Arab conquests had begun. Hajjāj in Iraq was determined to seek revenge and seems to have been genuinely afraid that the Zunbīl would attack areas already under Muslim rule: if he was joined by an uprising of local people all of Iran might be lost. He wrote to the caliph Abd al-Malik in Damascus, explaining that 'the troops of the Commander of the Faithful in Sistan have met disaster, and only a few of them have escaped. The enemy has been emboldened by this success against the people of Islam and has entered their lands and captured all their fortresses and castles'. He went on to say that he wanted to send out a great army from Kūfa and Basra and asked the caliph's advice. The reply gave him carte blanche to do as he saw fit.

Hajjāj set about organizing the army, 20,000 men from Kūfa and 20,000 from Basra. He paid them their salaries in full so that they could equip themselves with horses and arms. He reviewed the army in person, giving more money to those who were renowned for their courage. Markets were set up around the camp so that the men could buy supplies and a sermon encouraging everybody to do their bit for the jihad was preached. The expeditionary force became known as the 'Peacock Army' because of the elegance of its appearance.

Despite these preparations, the expedition set in train the only military mutiny in the history of the early conquests, the only time an Arab army refused to go on fighting and turned on its Muslim political masters. All was not as straightforward as it looked. Hajjāj had been struggling for some years to force the militias of the Iraqi towns to obey him and the caliph in Damascus. Sending them on a long, hard campaign could be very advantageous: if they were successful they might become rich and

---

* A measure of 4 litres, the implication being that this was very expensive.

satisfied and even settle in the area. If they were not, then their power would be broken. As commander, he chose one Ibn al-Ashᶜath. Unlike the unfortunate Ubayd Allāh, Ibn al-Ashᶜath came from the highest ranks of the south Arabian aristocracy, being directly descended from the pre-Islamic kings of Kinda. He was also a proud man who did not like being ordered about, and had become one of the leaders of the Iraqi opposition to Hajjāj. Putting him in charge was really offering him a poisoned chalice.

At first all went well. The Zunbīl, who seems to have been very well informed about the Muslim preparations, wrote to Ibn al-Ashᶜath offering peace. He was given no reply and the Muslim forces began a systematic occupation of his lands, taking it over district by district, appointing tax collectors, sentry posts to guard the passes and setting up a military postal service. Then, sensibly, Ibn al-Ashᶜath decided to pause and consolidate, before advancing the next year. He wrote to Hajjāj about this perfectly reasonable course of action and received a massive blast in return. Hajjāj accused the commander of weakness and confused judgement and of not being prepared to avenge those Muslims who had been killed in the campaign. He was to continue to advance immediately. Ibn al-Ashᶜath then called for advice. Everyone agreed that Hajjāj's demands were unreasonable and designed to humiliate the army and its leader. 'He does not care', one said, 'about risking your lives by forcing you into a land of sheer cliffs and narrow passes. If you win and acquire booty he will devour the territory and take its wealth . . . if you lose, he will treat you with contempt and your distress will be no concern of his.' The next speaker said that Hajjāj was trying to get them out of Iraq and force them to settle in this desolate region. All agreed that the army should disavow its obedience to Hajjāj. Ibn al-Ashᶜath then decided to lead them west to challenge Umayyad control of Iraq and the wider caliphate, leaving the Zunbīl in control of his territory and the Muslim dead unavenged.

The mutiny was not a success. Ibn al-Ashᶜath and his Iraqi followers were defeated by the Syrian Umayyad army and crushed. But the story is important in the annals of the conquests: a Muslim army had decided that asserting its rights against the Muslim government was more important than expanding the lands of Islam and that preserving their salaries was more valuable than the acquisition of new booty. We can see the conquest movement beginning to run out of steam.

THE HISTORY OF AL TABARI
Vol. XXIII: THE ZENITH OF THE MARWANID HOUSE

Mohammed ibn Jarir al Tabari

Translated by Martin Hinds

> Most magisterial of the ninth-century Muslim historians, **Mohammed ibn Jarir al Tabari** (839–923) was a prolific scholar who devoted much of his life in Baghdad and beyond to compiling the monumental *History of the Prophets and Kings*. Covering the period from the Creation to 915, its English translation runs into a dizzying thirty-nine volumes, or around 10,000 pages. Alongside Baladhuri's *Book of the Conquests of Lands*, it is one of the key sources for the Arab Conquests of the seventh and eighth centuries and the foundation for the early history of Islam.
>
> Here he describes the events of 709–10, when Nizak, prince of Badghis (northwest Afghanistan), fatally underestimated his Arab ally-turned-adversary Qutayba ibn Muslim, governor of Khorasan and mastermind of the Arabs' Conquests in Afghanistan.

In this year Yazīd b. al-Muhallab conquered the fortress of Nīzak at Bādghīs.

The Reason Why [Yazīd b. al-Muhallab] Conquered [the Fortress of Nīzak]

According to 'Alī b. Muḥammad—al-Mufaḍḍal b. al-Muhallab: Nīzak was staying in a fortress at Bādghīs, and Yazīd watched for a good time to campaign against him and set spies on him. [News] reached him that

[Nīzak] had sallied forth, and Yazīd went to [the fortress] in his absence. [News of this] reached Nīzak, who returned, and [Yazīd] made peace with him on condition that he would hand over to him the treasures that were in the fortress and would leave it with his dependents. [In this connection,] Ka'b b. Ma'dān al-Ashqarī said (*basīṭ*):[287]

Bādghīs—which [is such that] he who occupies its upper part overcomes kings and, if he wishes, may act tyrannically and oppressively—
Is well fortified: No king before [Yazīd] has taken it by guile; [it can be taken] only when it is faced by a vast army of his.
Its fires, viewed from a distance, could be imagined to be stars, in the first third of the night.
When [Yazid] circled round it, their hearts sank until they left it to him to judge, and he decided.
He humbled its inhabitant (that is, Nīzak) after his [previous] greatness [by making him] pay poll tax,[288] [he thereby] acknowledging abasement and oppression.
[1130] A few days thereafter, before which you had revealed grief and oppression,
The Provider gave you that, dividing it among [God's] creatures; and the deprived one is he who is deprived.
With one of your hands you give the enemy poison to drink, while the generosity of the other is ceaseless.
Can the gift and grace of Yazīd be compared with anything other than the Euphrates and the Nile in spate?
When they are at their high points, they are no more generous than he, [even] when they rise above elevated ground and hillocks.
And he said (*ṭawīl*):
My praise for the clan of al-'Atīk is that they are generous in hospitality and noble of origin.

---

[287] On the poet, see above, n. 135. Some of the following verses appear also in Ibn A'tham, *Futūḥ*, vol. VII, p. 225.

[288] So rendering *al-jizā*.

When they make an agreement with one they protect, he occupies an elevated place of safety, securely high and well defended.

He expelled Nīzak from Bādghīs, and Nīzak was in a position which was too difficult for kings to snatch from him,

[A position] soaring beneath the sky, like a white summer cloud from which the rain clouds have passed away.

[1131] Not even the mountain goats reach its uppermost parts, nor birds, save its eagle and osprey.

The children of its people have not been frightened by the wolf, nor have its dogs barked at anything save the stars.

I have desired to encounter al-'Atīk, the possessors of wisdom, made to have mastery, with their riding camels protected,

Just as the son of the soil whose lands are parched desires rain from abundant clouds,

Then, after despair, he is given to drink, to the point where [his land's] conduits cannot cope and the billows [of water] gurgle.

God has gathered together those who were remote from one another, and there have come together groups from many and varied distant places.

[1132] ['Alī b. Muḥammad] said: Nīzak used to glorify the fortress; when he saw it, he prostrated himself to it. Yazīd b. al-Muhallab wrote to al-Ḥajjāj concerning the conquest; Yazīd's letters to al-Ḥajjāj were written by Yaḥyā b. Ya'mar al-'Adwānī,[289] who was a confederate (*ḥalīf*) of Hudhayl. He wrote: "We encountered the enemy, and God gave us the upper hand.[290] We killed some and took some captive, while others took themselves to the tops of the mountains, the bottoms[291] of the valleys, the low-lying fields, and the bends of the rivers." Al-Ḥajjāj asked who it was who acted as Yazīd's secretary and was told that it was Yaḥyā b. Ya'mar. He wrote to Yazīd [telling him to send Yaḥyā to him], and [Yazīd]

---

[289] Caskel, *Ğamharat an-nasab*, register.

[290] Lit. "God gave us their shoulders."

[291] *'Arā'ir*: See the *Addenda et Emendanda* and the learned note in the *Glossarium*.

sent him via the messenger service. Then [this] most eloquent of people came to him, and [al-Ḥajjāj] said, "Where were you born?" He said, "In al-Ahwāz." "And this eloquence?" "I memorized the speech of my father, who was an eloquent man." "Now tell me, does 'Anbasah b. Sa'īd make grammatical mistakes?" "Yes, often." "And so-and-so?" "Yes." "Tell me about myself; do I make grammatical mistakes?" "Yes, you make a barely perceptible mistake. You add a letter and you drop a letter: You [also] say *'inna'* instead of *'anna'* and *'anna'* instead of *'inna.'*" [Al-Ḥajjāj] said, "I'll give you three days. If, after three days, I find you in Iraqi territory, I'll kill you." [Yaḥyā] returned to Khurasan.[292]

[Nīzak's] Perfidy and Why He Was Vanquished

[1205] 'Alī [b. Muḥammad] said: According to (i) Abū al-Dhayyāl—al-Muhallab b. Iyās, (ii) al-Mufaḍḍal al-Ḍabbī—his father, (iii) 'Alī b. Mujāhid, and (iv) Kulayb b. Khalaf al-'Ammī—each mentioned something and I have put [what they said] together [in a single account]; and the Bāhilīs mentioned something, and I have annexed [that] to the report of these [others] and have put it in [with the rest]: Qutaybah left Bukhārā accompanied by Nīzak, who had been alarmed by the conquests he had seen and who feared Qutaybah. [Nīzak] said to his companions and his intimates among them,[514] "I am with this [fellow], and I don't feel safe with him, for the Arab is like a dog: If you beat him, he barks, and if you feed him, he wags his tail. If you campaign against him and then give him something, he is pleased and forgets what you have done to him. Ṭarkhūn fought him several times, and when he gave him tribute, he accepted it and was pleased. He is a dissolute brute. The best thing will be for me to take my leave and return." They said, "Take your leave of him," and, when Qutaybah was

---

[292] A briefer version of this story is given by al-Mubarrad (*Kāmil*, pp. 158).

[512] On him, see Shaban, *The 'Abbāsid Revolution*, pp. 65.

at Āmul, [Nīzak] sought leave of him to return to Ṭukhāristān. [Qutaybah] gave him leave, and, when he left his camp heading for Balkh, [Nīzak] said to his companions, "Hasten," and they went at great speed until they reached al-Nawbahār. He stopped to pray in it and regarded it as a blessing, and said to his companions, "I do not doubt that Qutaybah regretted it when we left his camp with his permission to me and [that] his messenger will at any moment reach al-Mughīrah b. 'Abdallāh, ordering him to detain me. So set up a lookout, and if you see [that] the messenger has passed through the city and has gone out of the gate, he will not reach al-Barūqān before we reach Ṭukhāristān. Al-Mughīrah will send a man, but he will not catch up with us before we enter the Khulm pass." They did so.

[1206] ['Alī b. Muḥammad] said: A messenger set off from Qutaybah to al-Mughīrah with orders to him to detain Nīzak. When the messenger passed [on his way] to al-Mughīrah, who was at al-Barūqān[515]—the city of Balkh being in ruins at that time—Nīzak and his companions rode off and went on their way. The messenger reached al-Mughīrah, and [al-Mughīrah] himself went in search of [Nīzak]. [But] he found that he had entered the Khulm pass, and departed.

Nīzak [now] openly disavowed [Qutaybah]. He wrote to the Iṣbahbadh of Balkh, to Bādhām, the king of Marw Rūdh, to Suhrak,[516] the king of al-Ṭālaqān, to Tūsik,[517] the king of al-Fāryāb, and to al-Jūzjānī, the king of al-Jūzjān, calling upon them to disavow Qutaybah. They responded positively to him, and he appointed the spring as the time for them to join forces and campaign against Qutaybah. He also wrote to the Kābul Shāh, seeking his help, sent to him his baggage and money, and

---

[513] Cf. Gibb, *Arab Conquests*, pp. 36ff.

[514] Reading the variant minhum in preference to muttaham.

[515] Following the destruction of Balkh, "the Arabs built a new town in the locality of Barūqān, two farsakhs from Balkh" (Barthold, *Turkestan*,[3] p. 77).

asked him to give him permission—if he was driven to it—to go to him and receive a safe-conduct in his country; [the Kābul Shāh] agreed to that and held his baggage.

[1207] ['Alī b. Muḥammad] said: Jabghūyah, the king of Ṭukhāristān, whose name was al-Shadh,[518] was weak. Nīzak took him and put him in a gold fetter, for fear that he might stir up discord against him, Jabghūyah being the king of Ṭukhāristān, and Nīzak [one] of his slaves. When he was sure [that Jabghūyah could not cause him trouble], he set watchmen over him and expelled Qutaybah's governor, Muḥammad b. Sulaym al-Nāṣiḥ, from Jabghūyah's territories. [News of] his disavowal reached Qutaybah [just] before the winter, [at a time when] the troops had gone their separate ways; only the people of Marw remained with Qutaybah. He sent his brother 'Abd al-Raḥmān to [the district of] Balkh, to al-Barūqān, with [an army of] twelve thousand [men], saying to him, "Stay there and do not initiate anything. When the winter is over, gather the army and go to Ṭukhāristān (sic); know that I [shall be] near you." 'Abd al-Raḥmān went off and stopped at al-Barūqān, and Qutaybah took his time until, late in the winter, he wrote to Abrashahr,[519] Bīward,[520] Sarakhs, and the people of Herat [instructing them] to come to him. They did so, this being at an earlier time than usual.

In this year Qutaybah fell upon the people of al-Ṭālaqān, according to one of the collectors of historical reports [ahl al-akhbār], and killed them on a massive scale; he crucified them in two straight parallel rows four parasangs long.[521]

---

[516] The *Addenda et Emendanda* point to the form S.hr.b (sc. Suhrab) below (pp. 1566, 1569 of the Arabic text), but Justi is ready to settle for Suhrak (*Iranisches Namenbuch*, p. 292, sub Εατράκης).

[517] Following the *Addenda at Emendanda* and G. Schlegel, *La stèle funéraire du Teghin Giogh*, p. 23.

The Events of the Year
91
(November 9, 709–October 28, 710)

[1218] In this year Qutaybah b. Muslim killed Nīzak Ṭarkhān.[543]

The narrative returns to that of 'Alī b. Muḥammad and the story of Nīzak and Qutaybah's victory over him until he killed him. When there reached Qutaybah those of the people of Abrashahr, Bīward, Sarakhs, and Herat to whom he had written instructing them to join him, he went with [his entire force] to Marw Rūdh, having deputed [at Marw] over military affairs (ḥarb) Ḥammād b. Muslim and over taxation (kharāj) 'Abdallāh b. al-Ahtam. [When news of] the advance of [Qutaybah] into his territory reached the marzbān of Marw Rūdh, he fled to the land of the Furs.[544] Qutaybah arrived in Marw Rūdh, took two sons of his, killed them, and crucified them. Then he went to al-Ṭālaqān, the lord of which stayed put, not fighting him and desisting from him. [In al-Ṭālaqān] were brigands, whom Qutaybah killed and crucified. He appointed over al-Ṭālaqān 'Amr b. Muslim[545] and went on to al-Fāryāb. The king of al-Fāryāb went out to him, submissively, and professing his obedience, and [Qutaybah] was satisfied with that and did not kill anyone there; he appointed over it a man from Bāhilah.

[1219] News of them reached the lord of al-Jūzjān, and he left his territory and went out into the mountains in flight. Qutaybah went to al-Jūzjān, and its people met him, compliant and obedient, and he accepted [that] from them and did not kill anyone there; he appointed over it 'Āmir b. Mālik al-Ḥimmānī. Then he reached Balkh; the Iṣbahbadh and the people of Balkh met him, and he entered it. He stayed in it only one day and then went on, following 'Abd al-Raḥmān [b. Muslim], until he reached

---

[541] See above, n. 499.

[542] See EI², s.v. al-Andalus.

[543] Cf. Gibb, *Arab Conquests*, pp. 36ff.

the Khulm pass. Nīzak had gone off and camped at Baghlān,[546] leaving fighting men at the mouth and the defiles of the pass in order to defend it, and placing fighting men in a strong fortress behind the pass. Qutaybah stayed for [some] days fighting them at the defile of the pass without being able to make any progress against them. He was unable to enter it, it being a defile through which the valley passed, and he did not know of any way by which he could get to Nīzak other than the pass or a desert which would not support the troops. He remained, turning his face to right and left in perplexity, looking for strategems.

['Alī b. Muḥammad] continued: He was in this [dilemma] when there came to him the Ru'b Khan, the king of al-Ru'b[547] and Siminjān,[548] seeking a safe-conduct from him on the basis that he would show him a way of getting into the fortress that was behind this pass. Qutaybah gave him a safe-conduct, gave him what he asked for, and sent with him at night men with whom he got to the fortress which was behind the Khulm pass. They fell upon [the men of the fortress] at night, they feeling perfectly secure [from attack], and killed them; those who survived and those who were in the pass fled, and Qutaybah and [his army] entered the pass and reached the fortress. Then he went on to Siminjān, Nīzak being at Baghlān, at a spring called Fanj Jāh;[549] between Siminjān and Baghlān is a desert that is not particularly difficult.

[1220] ['Alī b. Muḥammad] continued: Qutaybah stayed in Siminjān for [some] days and then went off to Nīzak; he sent his brother 'Abd al-Raḥmān on ahead, and he reached Nīzak. [At this,] Nīzak set off from his house, crossed the Farghānah valley,[550]

---

[544] Which does not make sense in this context; in the *Addenda et Emendanda*, Marquart proposes that we should understand this as bilād al-Gharsh, i.e., Gharshistān, a territory in the mountains to the east of Herat (see *EI²*, s.v. Ghardjistān).

[545] This appointment (together with that of 'Āmir b. Mālik—see the next paragraph) is also mentioned in the account of Ibn A'tham [*Futūḥ*, vol. VII, p. 232].

[546] Two days' journey from Siminjān (Barthold, *Turkestan³*, p. 67).

[547] A town near Siminjān (Le Strange, *Lands of the Eastern Caliphate*, p. 427).

sent his baggage and wealth to the Kābul Shāh, and went on until he stopped at al-Kurz,[551] being followed [all the while] by 'Abd al-Raḥmān b. Muslim. 'Abd al-Raḥmān stopped and took control of the defiles of al-Kurz, and Qutaybah stopped at Iskīmisht,[552] two parasangs away. Nīzak took refuge in al-Kurz, having no way out save in one direction, which was difficult, since it could not be negotiated by riding animals.

Qutaybah besieged Nīzak for two months, until Nīzak's stock of grain became scanty and they were afflicted by smallpox, which Jabghūyah caught. Qutaybah feared the winter, and he summoned Sulaym al-Nāṣiḥ[553] and said, "Go off to Nīzak and use artifice to get him to come to me without a safe-conduct. If he gives you trouble and refuses, give him a safe-conduct. Know that, if I see you and you don't have him with you, I shall crucify you. So work for your own sake." [Sulaym] said, "Write for me to 'Abd al-Raḥmān, [telling him] not to disobey me." [Qutaybah] said, "Yes," and he wrote for him to 'Abd al-Raḥmān. [Sulaym] then went to ['Abd al-Raḥmān] and said to him, "Send men to be [stationed] at the mouth of the pass and, when Nīzak and I come out, let them slip round behind us, interposing themselves between us and the pass."

[1221] ['Alī b. Muḥammad] continued: 'Abd al-Raḥmān sent cavalry, and they were [stationed] where Sulaym instructed them [to be]. Sulaym [now] went off, carrying with him foodstuffs to last for days and loads of khabīṣ,[554] until he reached Nīzak. Nīzak said

---

[548] Two days' journey from Khulm (Barthold, *Turkestan*³, p. 67).

[549] Rendered *Panğ-čāh*, "Schneebrunnen" (rather than "Five Wells"), by Marquart (*Ērānšahr*, p. 219).

[550] As Marquart points out (*Ērānšahr*, p. 220), this Farghānah must have been to the south of Baghlān.

[551] Not even Marquart knows any more about this place.

[552] Rendered thus by Marquart [*Ērānšahr*, pp. 219-20]; if Wellhausen's identification (*Kingdom*, p. 435, n. 1) is correct, it was not far southeast of Baghlān.

[553] In a roughly similar account, Ibn A'tham (*Futūḥ*, vol. VII, p. 226) identifies Sulaym al-Nāṣiḥ as Sulaym b. 'Abdallāh.

to him, "You have abandoned me, O Sulaym." Sulaym said, "I haven't abandoned you, but you disobeyed me and did harm to yourself. You disavowed [Qutaybah] and acted perfidiously." [Nīzak] said, "What is the right thing to do?" [Sulaym] said, "The right thing to do now is to go to him. You have angered him with your contention, and he is not going to leave this place of his. He is resolved to winter in situ, whether he perishes or survives." [Nīzak] said, "Am I to go to him without a safe-conduct?" [Sulaym] said, "I don't think that he will give you one, on account of what [he holds] against you in his heart, for you have filled him with wrath. I think that you should place your hand in his before he is aware of you, and I hope that, if you do that, he will be ashamed and will forgive you." [Nīzak] said, "You think that?" He said, "Yes." [Nīzak] said, "I can't bring myself to accept that. If Qutaybah sees me, he will kill me." Sulaym said to him, "I have only come to advise you to do this. If you do it, I hope that you will be safe and that your position with him will revert to what it was. If you refuse, I shall be off." [Nīzak] said, "Then let us give you lunch." [Sulaym] said, "I suspect that you (pl.) are too busy to prepare food; we have plenty of food with us."

['Alī b. Muḥammad] continued: Sulaym called for lunch [to be served], and [his servants] brought abundant food, the like of which [Nīzak's men] had been unfamiliar with since they had been besieged. The Turks devoured it, and that grieved Nīzak. Sulaym said, "O Abū al-Hayyāj, I am one of your [most] sincere advisers. I see that your companions have been worn out. If the siege goes on for a long time and you stay as you are, I can't be sure that they won't make use of you in order to gain safe-conduct. Set off and go to Qutaybah." [Nīzak] said, "I have never felt safe with him, and I shall not go to him without a

---

[554] Lane (*Lexicon*, p. 697c) defines this as "a kind of food, sweet, well known, made of dates and clarified butter, mixed together."

safe-conduct. My feeling about him is that he is going to kill me even if he does give me a safe-conduct, but the safe-conduct gives me more excuse from blame and more hope." [Sulaym] said, "He has given you a safe-conduct: do you have any doubts about me?" Nīzak said, "No." [Sulaym] said, "So set off with me." His companions said to him, "Accept what Sulaym has said; he would not have said but what is true." So he called for his riding animals and went with Sulaym.

When he reached the steps by which he might descend to the plain, he said, "O Sulaym, whoever may not know when he will die, I [for one] know when I shall die. I shall die when I see Qutaybah." [Sulaym] said, "By no means. Will he kill when you have a safe-conduct?" Then [Nīzak] rode, accompanied by Jabghūyah, who had recovered from smallpox, and Ṣūl and 'Uthmān, the sons of Nīzak's brother, and Ṣūl Ṭarkhān, [who was] Jabghūyah's deputy, and Kh.n.s.[555] Ṭarkhān, [who] was the police chief.

[1222] ['Alī b. Muḥammad] said: When he emerged from the pass, the cavalry left by Sulaym at the mouth of the pass slipped around and interposed themselves between the Turks and the exit. Nīzak said to Sulaym, "This is the first bad [sign]." [Sulaym] said, "Don't think that.[556] The [fact that] these people are staying behind[557] you is better for you." Sulaym went on, together with Nīzak and those who had gone out with him, until they entered into the presence of 'Abd al-Raḥmān b. Muslim, who sent a messenger to Qutaybah informing him [of this]. Qutaybah sent 'Amr b. Abī Miḥ-zam to 'Abd al-Raḥmān [with the message], "Bring them to me," and 'Abd al-Raḥmān brought them to him. Qutaybah imprisoned the companions of

---

[555] Or "H.b.s.," as in Ms P and Ibn al-Athīr.

[556] So understanding *lā taf' al* in the text; Ibn A'tham (*Futūḥ*, vol. VII, p. 227) reads *lā 'alayka*, "don't worry," at this point.

[557] Reading *takhallufu* in place of *tukhallifu* (*pace* the Addenda et Emendanda).

Nīzak and handed Nīzak [himself] over to Ibn Bassām al-Laythī. He wrote to al-Ḥajjāj asking his permission to kill Nīzak.

Ibn Bassām placed Nīzak in his yurt, dug a trench around the yurt, and set guards over him. Qutaybah sent off Mu'āwiyah b. 'Āmir b. 'Alqamah al-'Ulaymī, who removed what goods and people there were in al-Kurz and brought them to Qutaybah. [Qutaybah] imprisoned [these people], pending [the arrival of] al-Ḥajjāj's letter concerning what he had written to him about. Al-Ḥajjāj's letter instructing him to kill Nīzak reached him after forty days.

['Alī b. Muḥammad] said: [Qutaybah] called for [Nīzak] and said, "Do you have any commitment from me or from 'Abd al-Raḥmān or from Sulaym?" He said, "I have one from Sulaym." [Qutaybah] said, "You are lying," and he stood up and went into [an inner chamber]. He returned Nīzak to his prison and remained [indoors] for three days without appearing to the people.

According to ['Alī b. Muḥammad]—Al-Muhallab b. Iyās al-'Adawī: The people talked about the matter of Nīzak. Some of them said, "It is not lawful for [Qutaybah] to kill him," while others said, "It is not lawful for him to let him be." Much was said about this.

[1223] ['Alī b. Muḥammad] continued: On the fourth day Qutaybah came out, sat, and gave permission to the people [to come into his presence]. He said, "What do you think about killing Nīzak?" They held differing opinions: There were those who said, "Kill him," those who said, "You have given him a commitment; do not kill him," and those who said, "We are not sure [that he will not do harm] to the Muslims." Ḍirār b. Ḥuṣayn entered, and [Qutaybah] said to him, "What do you say, O Ḍirār?" He said, "I say that I heard you say that you had given God a covenant that if He delivered [Nīzak] into your hands, you would kill him, and that if you did not do so, [you wished that] God would never help you." Qutaybah sat silently and with downcast eyes for a long time and then said, "By God, if there were to remain of my allotted span no more than three words, I would say, 'Kill him, kill him, kill him.'" He sent for Nīzak and ordered that he and his companions be killed; he was killed along with seven hundred [others].

As for the Bāhilīs, they say that neither [Qutaybah] nor Sulaym gave him a safe-conduct. When [Qutaybah] intended to kill him, he called for him and for a Ḥanafī sword.[558] He unsheathed it, lengthened[559] his sleeves, and executed him with his [own] hand. He ordered ʿAbd al-Raḥmān to behead Ṣūl, and he ordered Ṣāliḥ to kill ʿUthmān, called Shaqrān, the son of Nīzak's brother. He said to Bakr b. Ḥabīb al-Sahmī, from Bāhilah, "Have you [enough] strength [to deal with the rest]?" He said, "Yes, more than enough";[560] there was roughness in Bakr. [Qutaybah] said [to him], "Take these dihqāns."

[ʿAlī b. Muḥammad] continued: When he was brought a man, he would behead him and say, "Begin and keep at it."[561] Those who were killed on that day [numbered] twelve thousand, according to what the Bāhilīs say. [Qutaybah] crucified Nīzak and the two sons of his brother at the source of a spring called Wakhsh Khāshān[562] in Iskīmisht. Al-Mughīrah b. Ḥabnāʾ said, mentioning that in a long piece (ṭawīl):[563]

By my life, what a good campaign by the army that was; it put an end to Nīzak and became lofty [in merit].

SHAHNAMEH, BOOK OF KINGS

Ferdowsi
Translated by James Atkinson, 1814

One name looms largest in the world of Persian poetry: **Ferdowsi** (940–1019/25) is treasured both by Persian-speakers and those who do not know a single word of Farsi. To this day his *Shahnameh* is the epic without equal in Persian literature, the story of Iran from the beginning of the world to the Arab Muslim conquest of the seventh century. Read and revered by Iranians more than 1,000 years after it was written, its cultural importance cannot be overstated. It is credited with saving both the Persian language and the country's pre-Islamic cultural identity. 'The Story of Sohráb' is set in Samangan, today a province of northern Afghanistan.

THE STORY OF SOHRÁB

O ye, who dwell in Youth's inviting bowers,
Waste not, in useless joy, your fleeting hours,
But rather let the tears of sorrow roll,
And sad reflection fill the conscious soul.
For many a jocund spring has passed away,
And many a flower has blossomed, to decay;
And human life, still hastening to a close,
Finds in the worthless dust its last repose.
Still the vain world abounds in strife and hate,
And sire and son provoke each other's fate;
And kindred blood by kindred hands is shed,
And vengeance sleeps not—dies not, with the dead.
All nature fades—the garden's treasures fall,
Young bud, and citron ripe—all perish, all.

And now a tale of sorrow must be told,
A tale of tears, derived from Múbid old,
And thus remembered.—

  With the dawn of day,
Rustem arose, and wandering took his way,
Armed for the chase, where sloping to the sky,
Túrán's lone wilds in sullen grandeur lie;
There, to dispel his melancholy mood,
He urged his matchless steed through glen and wood.
Flushed with the noble game which met his view,
He starts the wild-ass o'er the glistening dew;
And, oft exulting, sees his quivering dart,
Plunge through the glossy skin, and pierce the heart.
Tired of the sport, at length, he sought the shade,
Which near a stream embowering trees displayed,
And with his arrow's point, a fire he raised,
And thorns and grass before him quickly blazed.
The severed parts upon a bough he cast,
To catch the flames; and when the rich repast
Was drest; with flesh and marrow, savory food,
He quelled his hunger; and the sparkling flood
That murmured at his feet, his thirst represt;
Then gentle sleep composed his limbs to rest.

  Meanwhile his horse, for speed and form renown'd,
Ranged o'er the plain with flowery herbage crown'd,
Encumbering arms no more his sides opprest,
No folding mail confined his ample chest,
Gallant and free, he left the Champion's side,
And cropp'd the mead, or sought the cooling tide;
When lo! it chanced amid that woodland chase,
A band of horsemen, rambling near the place,
Saw, with surprise, superior game astray,

And rushed at once to seize the noble prey;
But, in the imminent struggle, two beneath
His steel-clad hoofs received the stroke of death;
One proved a sterner fate—for downward borne,
The mangled head was from the shoulders torn.
Still undismayed, again they nimbly sprung,
And round his neck the noose entangling flung:
Now, all in vain, he spurns the smoking ground,
In vain the tumult echoes all around;
They bear him off, and view, with ardent eyes,
His matchless beauty and majestic size;
Then soothe his fury, anxious to obtain,
A bounding steed of his immortal strain.

    When Rustem woke, and miss'd his favourite horse,
The loved companion of his glorious course;
Sorrowing he rose, and, hastening thence, began
To shape his dubious way to Samengán;
"Reduced to journey thus, alone!" he said,
"How pierce the gloom which thickens round my head;
Burthen'd, on foot, a dreary waste in view,
Where shall I bend my steps, what path pursue?
The scoffing Turks will cry, 'Behold our might!
We won the trophy from the Champion-knight!
From him who, reckless of his fame and pride,
Thus idly slept, and thus ignobly died,"
Girding his loins he gathered from the field,
His quivered stores, his beamy sword and shield,
Harness and saddle-gear were o'er him slung.
Bridle and mail across his shoulders hung.
Then looking round, with anxious eye, to meet,
The broad impression of his charger's feet,
The track he hail'd, and following, onward prest.
While grief and hope alternate filled his breast.

O'er vale and wild-wood led, he soon descries.
The regal city's shining turrets rise.
And when the Champion's near approach is known,
The usual homage waits him to the throne.
The king, on foot, received his welcome guest
With preferred friendship, and his coming blest:
But Rustem frowned, and with resentment fired,
Spoke of his wrongs, the plundered steed required.
"I've traced his footsteps to your royal town,
Here must he be, protected by your crown;
But if retained, if not from fetters freed,
My vengeance shall o'ertake the felon-deed."
"My honored guest!" the wondering King replied—
"Shall Rustem's wants or wishes be denied?
But let not anger, headlong, fierce, and blind,
O'ercloud the virtues of a generous mind.
If still within the limits of my reign,
The well known courser shall be thine again:
For Rakush never can remain concealed,
No more than Rustem in the battle-field!
Then cease to nourish useless rage, and share
With joyous heart my hospitable fare."

The son of Zál now felt his wrath subdued,
And glad sensations in his soul renewed.
The ready herald by the King's command,
Convened the Chiefs and Warriors of the land;
And soon the banquet social glee restored,
And China wine-cups glittered on the board;
And cheerful song, and music's magic power,
And sparkling wine, beguiled the festive hour.
The dulcet draughts o'er Rustem's senses stole,
And melting strains absorbed his softened soul.
But when approached the period of repose,

All, prompt and mindful, from the banquet rose;
A couch was spread well worthy such a guest,
Perfumed with rose and musk; and whilst at rest,
In deep sound sleep, the wearied Champion lay,
Forgot were all the sorrows of the way.

    One watch had passed, and still sweet slumber shed
Its magic power around the hero's head—
When forth Tahmíneh came—a damsel held
An amber taper, which the gloom dispelled,
And near his pillow stood; in beauty bright,
The monarch's daughter struck his wondering sight.
Clear as the moon, in glowing charms arrayed,
Her winning eyes the light of heaven displayed;
Her cypress form entranced the gazer's view,
Her waving curls, the heart, resistless, drew,
Her eye-brows like the Archer's bended bow;
Her ringlets, snares; her cheek, the rose's glow,
Mixed with the lily—from her ear-tips hung
Rings rich and glittering, star-like; and her tongue,
And lips, all sugared sweetness—pearls the while
Sparkled within a mouth formed to beguile.
Her presence dimmed the stars, and breathing round
Fragrance and joy, she scarcely touched the ground,
So light her step, so graceful—every part
Perfect, and suited to her spotless heart.

    Rustem, surprised, the gentle maid addressed,
And asked what lovely stranger broke his rest.
"What is thy name," he said—"what dost thou seek
Amidst the gloom of night? Fair vision, speak!"

    "O thou," she softly sigh'd, "of matchless fame!
With pity hear, Tahmíneh is my name!

The pangs of love my anxious heart employ,
And flattering promise long-expected joy;
No curious eye has yet these features seen,
My voice unheard, beyond the sacred screen.
How often have I listened with amaze,
To thy great deeds, enamoured of thy praise;
How oft from every tongue I've heard the strain,
And thought of thee—and sighed, and sighed again.
The ravenous eagle, hovering o'er his prey,
Starts at thy gleaming sword and flies away:
Thou art the slayer of the Demon brood,
And the fierce monsters of the echoing wood.
Where'er thy mace is seen, shrink back the bold,
Thy javelin's flash all tremble to behold.
Enchanted with the stories of thy fame,
My fluttering heart responded to thy name;
And whilst their magic influence I felt,
In prayer for thee devotedly I knelt;
And fervent vowed, thus powerful glory charms,
No other spouse should bless my longing arms.
Indulgent heaven propitious to my prayer,
Now brings thee hither to reward my care.
Túrán's dominions thou hast sought, alone,
By night, in darkness—thou, the mighty one!
O claim my hand, and grant my soul's desire;
Ask me in marriage of my royal sire;
Perhaps a boy our wedded love may crown,
Whose strength like thine may gain the world's renown.
Nay more—for Samengán will keep my word—
Rakush to thee again shall be restored."

   The damsel thus her ardent thought expressed,
And Rustem's heart beat joyous in his breast,
Hearing her passion—not a word was lost,

And Rakush safe, by him still valued most;
He called her near; with graceful step she came,
And marked with throbbing pulse his kindled flame.

And now a Múbid, from the Champion-knight,
Requests the royal sanction to the rite;
O'erjoyed, the King the honoured suit approves,
O'erjoyed to bless the doting child he loves,
And happier still, in showering smiles around,
To be allied to warrior so renowned.
When the delighted father, doubly blest,
Resigned his daughter to his glorious guest,
The people shared the gladness which it gave,
The union of the beauteous and the brave.
To grace their nuptial day—both old and young,
The hymeneal gratulations sung:
"May this young moon bring happiness and joy,
And every source of enmity destroy."
The marriage-bower received the happy pair,
And love and transport shower'd their blessings there.

Ere from his lofty sphere the morn had thrown
His glittering radiance, and in splendour shone,
The mindful Champion, from his sinewy arm,
His bracelet drew, the soul-ennobling charm;
And, as he held the wondrous gift with pride,
He thus address'd his love-devoted bride!
"Take this," he said, "and if, by gracious heaven,
A daughter for thy solace should be given,
Let it among her ringlets be displayed,
And joy and honour will await the maid;
But should kind fate increase the nuptial-joy,
And make thee mother of a blooming boy,
Around his arm this magic bracelet bind,
To fire with virtuous deeds his ripening mind;

The strength of Sám will nerve his manly form,
In temper mild, in valour like the storm;
His not the dastard fate to shrink, or turn
From where the lions of the battle burn;
To him the soaring eagle from the sky
Will stoop, the bravest yield to him, or fly;
Thus shall his bright career imperious claim
The well-won honours of immortal fame!"
Ardent he said, and kissed her eyes and face,
And lingering held her in a fond embrace.

   When the bright sun his radiant brow displayed,
And earth in all its loveliest hues arrayed,
The Champion rose to leave his spouse's side,
The warm affections of his weeping bride.
For her, too soon the winged moments flew,
Too soon, alas! the parting hour she knew;
Clasped in his arms, with many a streaming tear,
She tried, in vain, to win his deafen'd ear;
Still tried, ah fruitless struggle! to impart,
The swelling anguish of her bursting heart.

   The father now with gratulations due
Rustem approaches, and displays to view
The fiery war-horse—welcome as the light
Of heaven, to one immersed in deepest night;
The Champion, wild with joy, fits on the rein,
And girds the saddle on his back again;
Then mounts, and leaving sire and wife behind,
Onward to Sístán rushes like the wind.

   But when returned to Zábul's friendly shade,
None knew what joys the Warrior had delayed;
Still, fond remembrance, with endearing thought,
Oft to his mind the scene of rapture brought.

When nine slow-circling months had roll'd away,
Sweet-smiling pleasure hailed the brightening day—
A wondrous boy Tahmíneh's tears supprest,
And lull'd the sorrows of her heart to rest;
To him, predestined to be great and brave,
The name Sohráb his tender mother gave;
And as he grew, amazed, the gathering throng,
View'd his large limbs, his sinews firm and strong;
His infant years no soft endearment claimed:
Athletic sports his eager soul inflamed;
Broad at the chest and taper round the loins,
Where to the rising hip the body joins;
Hunter and wrestler; and so great his speed,
He could overtake, and hold the swiftest steed.
His noble aspect, and majestic grace,
Betrayed the offspring of a glorious race.
How, with a mother's ever anxious love,
Still to retain him near her heart she strove!
For when the father's fond inquiry came,
Cautious, she still concealed his birth and name,
And feign'd a daughter born, the evil fraught
With misery to avert—but vain the thought;
Not many years had passed, with downy flight,
Ere he, Tahmíneh's wonder and delight,
With glistening eye, and youthful ardour warm,
Filled her foreboding bosom with alarm.
"O now relieve my heart!" he said, "declare,
From whom I sprang and breathe the vital air.
Since, from my childhood I have ever been,
Amidst my play-mates of superior mien;
Should friend or foe demand my father's name,
Let not my silence testify my shame!
If still concealed, you falter, still delay,
A mother's blood shall wash the crime away."

"This wrath forego," the mother answering cried,
"And joyful hear to whom thou art allied.
A glorious line precedes thy destined birth,
The mightiest heroes of the sons of earth.
The deeds of Sám remotest realms admire,
And Zál, and Rustem thy illustrious sire!"

In private, then, she Rustem's letter placed
Before his view, and brought with eager haste
Three sparkling rubies, wedges three of gold,
From Persia sent—"Behold," she said, "behold
Thy father's gifts, will these thy doubts remove
The costly pledges of paternal love!
Behold this bracelet charm, of sovereign power
To baffle fate in danger's awful hour;
But thou must still the perilous secret keep,
Nor ask the harvest of renown to reap;
For when, by this peculiar signet known,
Thy glorious father shall demand his son,
Doomed from her only joy in life to part,
O think what pangs will rend thy mother's heart!—
Seek not the fame which only teems with woe;
Afrásiyáb is Rustem's deadliest foe!
And if by him discovered, him I dread,
Revenge will fall upon thy guiltless head."

*

Meanwhile the sire of Gúrd-afríd, who now
Governed the fort, and feared the warrior's vow;
Mournful and pale, with gathering woes opprest,
His distant Monarch trembling thus addrest.
But first invoked the heavenly power to shed
Its choicest blessings o'er his royal head.

"Against our realm with numerous foot and horse,
A stripling warrior holds his ruthless course.
His lion-breast unequalled strength betrays,
And o'er his mien the sun's effulgence plays:
Sohráb his name; like Sám Suwár he shows,
Or Rustem terrible amidst his foes.
The bold Hujír lies vanquished on the plain,
And drags a captive's ignominious chain;
Myriads of troops besiege our tottering wall,
And vain the effort to suspend its fall.
Haste, arm for fight, this Tartar-power withstand,
Let sweeping Vengeance lift her flickering brand;
Rustem alone may stem the roaring wave,
And, prompt as bold, his groaning country save.
Meanwhile in flight we place our only trust,
Ere the proud ramparts crumble in the dust."

Swift flies the messenger through secret ways,
And to the King the dreadful tale conveys,
Then passed, unseen, in night's concealing shade,
The mournful heroes and the warrior maid.

Soon as the sun with vivifying ray,
Gleams o'er the landscape, and renews the day;
The flaming troops the lofty walls surround,
With thundering crash the bursting gates resound.
Already are the captives bound, in thought,
And like a herd before the conqueror brought;
Sohráb, terrific o'er the ruin, views
His hopes deceived, but restless still pursues.
An empty fortress mocks his searching eye,
No steel-clad chiefs his burning wrath defy;
No warrior-maid reviving passion warms,
And soothes his soul with fondly-valued charms.

Deep in his breast he feels the amorous smart,
And hugs her image closer to his heart.
"Alas! that Fate should thus invidious shroud
The moon's soft radiance in a gloomy cloud;
Should to my eyes such winning grace display,
Then snatch the enchanter of my soul away!
A beauteous roe my toils enclosed in vain,
Now I, her victim, drag the captive's chain;
Strange the effects that from her charms proceed,
I gave the wound, and I afflicted bleed!
Vanquished by her, I mourn the luckless strife;
Dark, dark, and bitter, frowns my morn of life.
A fair unknown my tortured bosom rends,
Withers each joy, and every hope suspends."

 Impassioned thus Sohráb in secret sighed,
And sought, in vain, o'er-mastering grief to hide.
Can the heart bleed and throb from day to day,
And yet no trace its inmost pangs betray?
Love scorns control, and prompts the labouring sigh,
Pales the red lip, and dims the lucid eye;
His look alarmed the stern Túránian Chief,
Closely he mark'd his heart-corroding grief;—
And though he knew not that the martial dame,
Had in his bosom lit the tender flame;
Full well he knew such deep repinings prove,
The hapless thraldom of disastrous love.
Full well he knew some idol's musky hair,
Had to his youthful heart become a snare,
But still unnoted was the gushing tear,
Till haply he had gained his private ear:—
"In ancient times, no hero known to fame,
Not dead to glory e'er indulged the flame;
Though beauty's smiles might charm a fleeting hour,

The heart, unsway'd, repelled their lasting power.
A warrior Chief to trembling love a prey?
What! weep for woman one inglorious day?
Canst thou for love's effeminate control,
Barter the glory of a warrior's soul?
Although a hundred damsels might be gained,
The hero's heart shall still be free, unchained.
Thou art our leader, and thy place the field
Where soldiers love to fight with spear and shield;
And what hast thou to do with tears and smiles,
The silly victim to a woman's wiles?
Our progress, mark! from far Túrán we came,
Through seas of blood to gain immortal fame;
And wilt thou now the tempting conquest shun,
When our brave arms this Barrier-fort have won?
Why linger here, and trickling sorrows shed,
Till mighty Káús thunders o'er thy head!
Till Tús, and Gíw, and Gúdarz, and Báhrám,
And Rustem brave, Ferámurz, and Rehám,
Shall aid the war! A great emprise is thine,
At once, then, every other thought resign;
For know the task which first inspired thy zeal,
Transcends in glory all that love can feel.
Rise, lead the war, prodigious toils require
Unyielding strength, and unextinguished fire;
Pursue the triumph with tempestuous rage,
Against the world in glorious strife engage,
And when an empire sinks beneath thy sway
(O quickly may we hail the prosperous day),
The fickle sex will then with blooming charms,
Adoring throng to bless thy circling arms!"

    Húmán's warm speech, the spirit-stirring theme,
Awoke Sohráb from his inglorious dream.

No more the tear his faded cheek bedewed,
Again ambition all his hopes renewed:
Swell'd his bold heart with unforgotten zeal,
The noble wrath which heroes only feel;
Fiercely he vowed at one tremendous stroke,
To bow the world beneath the tyrant's yoke!
"Afrásiyáb," he cried, "shall reign alone,
The mighty lord of Persia's gorgeous throne!"

    Burning, himself, to rule this nether sphere,
These welcome tidings charmed the despot's ear.
Meantime Káús, this dire invasion known,
Had called his chiefs around his ivory throne:
There stood Gurgín, and Báhrám, and Gushwád,
And Tús, and Gíw, and Gúdárz, and Ferhád;
To them he read the melancholy tale,
Gust'hem had written of the rising bale;
Besought their aid and prudent choice, to form
Some sure defence against the threatening storm.
With one consent they urge the strong request,
To summon Rustem from his rural rest.—
Instant a warrior-delegate they send,
And thus the King invites his patriot-friend,

    "To thee all praise, whose mighty arm alone,
Preserves the glory of the Persian throne!
Lo! Tartar hordes our happy realms invade;
The tottering state requires thy powerful aid;
A youthful Champion leads the ruthless host,
His savage country's widely-rumoured boast.
The Barrier-fortress sinks beneath his sway,
Hujír is vanquished, ruin tracks his way;
Strong as a raging elephant in fight,
No arm but thine can match his furious might.

Mázinderán thy conquering prowess knew;
The Demon-king thy trenchant falchion slew,
The rolling heavens, abash'd with fear, behold
Thy biting sword, thy mace adorned with gold!
Fly to the succour of a King distress'd,
Proud of thy love, with thy protection blest.
When o'er the nation dread misfortunes lower,
Thou art the refuge, thou the saving power.
The chiefs assembled claim thy patriot vows,
Give to thy glory all that life allows;
And while no whisper breathes the direful tale,
O, let thy Monarch's anxious prayers prevail."

    Closing the fragrant page o'ercome with dread,
The afflicted King to Gív, the warrior, said:—
"Go, bind the saddle on thy fleetest horse,
Outstrip the tempest in thy rapid course,
To Rustem swift his country's woes convey,
Too true art thou to linger on the way;
Speed, day and night—and not one instant wait,
Whatever hour may bring thee to his gate."

    Followed no pause—to Gív enough was said,
Nor rest, nor taste of food, his speed delayed.
And when arrived, where Zábul's bowers exhale
Ambrosial sweets and scent the balmy gale,
The sentinel's loud voice in Rustem's ear,
Announced a messenger from Persia, near;
The Chief himself amidst his warriors stood,
Dispensing honours to the brave and good,
And soon as Gív had joined the martial ring,
(The sacred envoy of the Persian King),
He, with becoming loyalty inspired,
Asked what the monarch, what the state required;

But Gíw, apart, his secret mission told—
The written page was speedily unrolled.

    Struck with amazement, Rustem—"Now on earth
A warrior-knight of Sám's excelling worth?
Whence comes this hero of the prosperous star?
I know no Turk renowned, like him, in war;
He bears the port of Rustem too, 'tis said,
Like Sám, like Narímán, a warrior bred!
He cannot be my son, unknown to me;
Reason forbids the thought—it cannot be!
At Samengán, where once affection smiled,
To me Tahmíneh bore her only child,
That was a daughter?" Pondering thus he spoke,
And then aloud—"Why fear the invader's yoke?
Why trembling shrink, by coward thoughts dismayed,
Must we not all in dust, at length, be laid?
But come, to Nírum's palace, haste with me,
And there partake the feast—from sorrow free;
Breathe, but awhile—ere we our toils renew,
And moisten the parched lip with needful dew.
Let plans of war another day decide,
We soon shall quell this youthful hero's pride.
The force of fire soon flutters and decays
When ocean, swelled by storms, its wrath displays.
What danger threatens! whence the dastard fear!
Rest, and at leisure share a warrior's cheer."

    In vain the Envoy prest the Monarch's grief;
The matchless prowess of the stripling chief;
How brave Hujír had felt his furious hand;
What thickening woes beset the shuddering land.
But Rustem, still, delayed the parting day,
And mirth and feasting rolled the hours away;

Morn following morn beheld the banquet bright,
Music and wine prolonged the genial rite;
Rapt by the witchery of the melting strain,
No thought of Káús touch'd his swimming brain.

    The trumpet's clang, on fragrant breezes borne,
Now loud salutes the fifth revolving morn;
The softer tones which charm'd the jocund feast,
And all the noise of revelry, had ceased,
The generous horse, with rich embroidery deckt,
Whose gilded trappings sparkling light reflect,
Bears with majestic port the Champion brave,
And high in air the victor-banners wave.
Prompt at the martial call, Zúára leads
His veteran troops from Zábul's verdant meads.

    Ere Rustem had approached his journey's end,
Tús, Gúdarz, Gushwád, met their champion-friend
With customary honours; pleased to bring
The shield of Persia to the anxious King.
But foaming wrath the senseless monarch swayed;
His friendship scorned, his mandate disobeyed,
Beneath dark brows o'er-shadowing deep, his eye
Red gleaming shone, like lightning through the sky
And when the warriors met his sullen view,
Frowning revenge, still more enraged he grew:—
Loud to the Envoy thus he fiercely cried:—
"Since Rustem has my royal power defied,
Had I a sword, this instant should his head
Roll on the ground; but let him now be led
Hence, and impaled alive." Astounded Gív
Shrunk from such treatment of a knight so true;
But this resistance added to the flame,
And both were branded with revolt and shame;

Both were condemned, and Tús, the stern decree
Received, to break them on the felon-tree.
Could daring insult, thus deliberate given,
Escape the rage of one to frenzy driven?
No, from his side the nerveless Chief was flung,
Bent to the ground. Away the Champion sprung;
Mounted his foaming horse, and looking round—
His boiling wrath thus rapid utterance found:—
"Ungrateful King, thy tyrant acts disgrace
The sacred throne, and more, the human race;
Midst clashing swords thy recreant life I saved,
And am I now by Tús contemptuous braved?
On me shall Tús, shall Káús dare to frown?
On me, the bulwark of the regal crown?
Wherefore should fear in Rustem's breast have birth,
Káús, to me, a worthless clod of earth!
Go, and thyself Sohráb's invasion stay,
Go, seize the plunderers growling o'er their prey!
Wherefore to others give the base command?
Go, break him on the tree with thine own hand.
Know, thou hast roused a warrior, great and free,
Who never bends to tyrant Kings like thee!
Was not this untired arm triumphant seen,
In Misser, Rúm, Mázinderán, and Chín!
And must I shrink at thy imperious nod!
Slave to no Prince, I only bow to God.
Whatever wrath from thee, proud King! may fall,
For thee I fought, and I deserve it all.
The regal sceptre might have graced my hand,
I kept the laws, and scorned supreme command.
When Kai-kobád and Alberz mountain strayed,
I drew him thence, and gave a warrior's aid;
Placed on his brows the long-contested crown,
Worn by his sires, by sacred right his own;

Strong in the cause, my conquering arms prevailed,
Wouldst thou have reign'd had Rustem's valour failed
When the White Demon raged in battle-fray,
Wouldst thou have lived had Rustem lost the day?"
Then to his friends: "Be wise, and shun your fate,
Fly the wide ruin which o'erwhelms the state;
The conqueror comes—the scourge of great and small,
And vultures, following fast, will gorge on all.
Persia no more its injured Chief shall view"—
He said, and sternly from the court withdrew.

 The warriors now, with sad forebodings wrung,
Torn from that hope to which they proudly clung,
On Gúdarz rest, to soothe with gentle sway,
The frantic King, and Rustem's wrath allay.
With bitter grief they wail misfortune's shock,
No shepherd now to guard the timorous flock.
Gúdarz at length, with boding cares imprest,
Thus soothed the anger in the royal breast.
"Say, what has Rustem done, that he should be
Impaled upon the ignominious tree?
Degrading thought, unworthy to be bred
Within a royal heart, a royal head.
Hast thou forgot when near the Caspian-wave,
Defeat and ruin had appalled the brave,
When mighty Rustem struck the dreadful blow,
And nobly freed thee from the savage foe?
Did Demons huge escape his flaming brand?
Their reeking limbs bestrew'd the slippery strand.
Shall he for this resign his vital breath?
What! shall the hero's recompense be death?
But who will dare a threatening step advance,
What earthly power can bear his withering glance?
Should he to Zábul fired with wrongs return,

The plunder'd land will long in sorrow mourn!
This direful presage all our warriors feel,
For who can now oppose the invader's steel;
Thus is it wise thy champion to offend,
To urge to this extreme thy warrior-friend?
Remember, passion ever scorns control,
And wisdom's mild decrees should rule a Monarch's soul."
Káús, relenting, heard with anxious ear,
And groundless wrath gave place to shame and fear;
"Go then," he cried, "his generous aid implore,
And to your King the mighty Chief restore!"

 When Gúdarz rose, and seized his courser's rein,
A crowd of heroes followed in his train.
To Rustem, now (respectful homage paid),
The royal prayer he anxious thus conveyed.
"The King, repentant, seeks thy aid again,
Grieved to the heart that he has given thee pain;
But though his anger was unjust and strong,
Thy country still is guiltless of the wrong,
And, therefore, why abandoned thus by thee?
Thy help the King himself implores through me."
Rustem rejoined: "Unworthy the pretence,
And scorn and insult all my recompense?
Must I be galled by his capricious mood?
I, who have still his firmest champion stood?
But all is past, to heaven alone resigned,
No human cares shall more disturb my mind!"
Then Gúdarz thus (consummate art inspired
His prudent tongue, with all that zeal required);
"When Rustem dreads Sohráb's resistless power,
Well may inferiors fly the trying hour!
The dire suspicion now pervades us all,
Thus, unavenged, shall beauteous Persia fall!

Yet, generous still, avert the lasting shame,
O, still preserve thy country's glorious fame!
Or wilt thou, deaf to all our fears excite,
Forsake thy friends, and shun the pending fight?
And worse, O grief! in thy declining days,
Forfeit the honours of thy country's praise?"
This artful censure set his soul on fire,
But patriot firmness calm'd his burning ire;
And thus he said—"Inured to war's alarms,
Did ever Rustem shun the din of arms?
Though frowns from Káús I disdain to bear,
My threatened country claims a warrior's care."
He ceased, and prudent joined the circling throng,
And in the public good forgot the private wrong.

From far the King the generous Champion viewed,
And rising, mildly thus his speech pursued:—
"Since various tempers govern all mankind,
Me, nature fashioned of a froward mind;
And what the heavens spontaneously bestow,
Sown by their bounty must for ever grow.
The fit of wrath which burst within me, soon
Shrunk up my heart as thin as the new moon;
Else had I deemed thee still my army's boast,
Source of my regal power, beloved the most,
Unequalled. Every day, remembering thee,
I drain the wine cup, thou art all to me;
I wished thee to perform that lofty part,
Claimed by thy valour, sanctioned by my heart;
Hence thy delay my better thoughts supprest,
And boisterous passions revelled in my breast;
But when I saw thee from my Court retire
In wrath, repentance quenched my burning ire.
O, let me now my keen contrition prove,

Again enjoy thy fellowship and love:
And while to thee my gratitude is known,
Still be the pride and glory of my throne."

   Rustem, thus answering said:—"Thou art the King,
Source of command, pure honour's sacred spring;
And here I stand to follow thy behest,
Obedient ever—be thy will expressed,
And services required—Old age shall see
My loins still bound in fealty to thee."

   To this the King:—"Rejoice we then to-day,
And on the morrow marshal our array."
The monarch quick commands the feast of joy,
And social cares his buoyant mind employ,
Within a bower, beside a crystal spring,
Where opening flowers, refreshing odours fling,
Cheerful he sits, and forms the banquet scene,
In regal splendour on the crowded green;
And as around he greets his valiant bands,
Showers golden presents from his bounteous hands;
Voluptuous damsels trill the sportive lay,
Whose sparkling glances beam celestial day;
Fill'd with delight the heroes closer join,
And quaff till midnight cups of generous wine.

   Soon as the Sun had pierced the veil of night,
And o'er the prospect shed his earliest light,
Káús, impatient, bids the clarions sound,
The sprightly notes from hills and rocks rebound;
His treasure gates are opened:—and to all
A largess given; obedient to the call,
His subjects gathering crowd the mountain's brow,
And following thousands shade the vales below;

With shields, in armor, numerous legions bend;
And troops of horse the threatening lines extend.
Beneath the tread of heroes fierce and strong,
By war's tumultuous fury borne along,
The firm earth shook: the dust, in eddies driven,
Whirled high in air, obscured the face of heaven;
Nor earth, nor sky appeared—all, seeming lost,
And swallowed up by that wide-spreading host.
The steely armour glitter'd o'er the fields,
And lightnings flash'd from gold emblazoned shields;
Thou wouldst have said, the clouds had burst in showers,
Of sparkling amber o'er the martial powers.
Thus, close embodied, they pursued their way,
And reached the Barrier-fort in terrible array.

    The legions of Túrán, with dread surprise,
Saw o'er the plain successive myriads rise;
And showed them to Sohráb; he, mounting high
The fort, surveyed them with a fearless eye;
To Húmán, who, with withering terror pale,
Had marked their progress through the distant vale,
He pointed out the sight, and ardent said:—
"Dispel these woe-fraught broodings from thy head,
I wage the war, Afrásiyáb! for thee,
And make this desert seem a rolling sea."
Thus, while amazement every bosom quell'd,
Sohráb, unmoved, the coming storm beheld,
And boldly gazing on the camp around,
Raised high the cup with wine nectareous crowned:
O'er him no dreams of woe insidious stole,
No thought but joy engaged his ardent soul.

    The Persian legions had restrained their course,
Tents and pavilions, countless foot and horse,

Clothed all the spacious plain, and gleaming threw
Terrific splendours on the gazer's view.
But when the Sun had faded in the west,
And night assumed her ebon-coloured vest,
The mighty Chief approached the sacred throne,
And generous thus made danger all his own:
"The rules of war demand a previous task,
To watch this dreadful foe I boldly ask;
With wary step the wondrous youth to view,
And mark the heroes who his path pursue."
The King assents: "The task is justly thine,
Favourite of heaven, inspired by power divine."
In Turkish habit, secretly arrayed,
The lurking Champion wandered through the shade
And, cautious, standing near the palace gate,
Saw how the chiefs were ranged in princely state.

What time Sohráb his thoughts to battle turned,
And for the first proud fruits of conquest burned,
His mother called a warrior to his aid,
And Zinda-ruzm his sister's call obeyed.
To him Tahmineh gave her only joy,
And bade him shield the bold adventurous boy:
"But, in the dreadful strife, should danger rise,
Present my child before his father's eyes!
By him protected, war may rage in vain,
Though he may never bless these arms again!"
This guardian prince sat on the stripling's right,
Viewing the imperial banquet with delight.
Húmán and Bármán, near the hero placed,
In joyous pomp the full assembly graced;
A hundred valiant Chiefs begirt the throne,
And, all elate, were chaunting his renown.
Closely concealed, the gay and splendid scene,

Rustem contemplates with astonished mien;
When Zind, retiring, marks the listener nigh,
Watching the festal train with curious eye;
And well he knew, amongst his Tartar host,
Such towering stature not a Chief could boast—
"What spy is here, close shrouded by the night?
Art thou afraid to face the beams of light?"
But scarcely from his lips these words had past,
Ere, fell'd to earth, he groaning breathed his last;
Unseen he perish'd, fate decreed the blow,
To add fresh keenness to a parent's woe.

    Meantime Sohráb, perceiving the delay
In Zind's return, looked round him with dismay;
The seat still vacant—but the bitter truth,
Full soon was known to the distracted youth;
Full soon he found that Zinda-ruzm was gone,
His day of feasting and of glory done;
Speedful towards the fatal spot he ran,
Where slept in bloody vest the slaughtered man.

    The lighted torches now displayed the dead,
Stiff on the ground his graceful limbs were spread;
Sad sight to him who knew his guardian care,
Now doom'd a kinsman's early loss to bear;
Anguish and rage devour his breast by turns,
He vows revenge, then o'er the warrior mourns:
And thus exclaims to each afflicted Chief:—
"No time, to-night, my friends, for useless grief;
The ravenous wolf has watched his helpless prey,
Sprung o'er the fold, and borne its flower away;
But if the heavens my lifted arm befriend,
Upon the guilty shall my wrath descend—
Unsheathed, this sword shall dire revenge pursue,

And Persian blood the thirsty land bedew."
Frowning he paused, and check'd the spreading woe,
Resumed the feast, and bid the wine-cup flow!

   The valiant Gíw was sentinel that night,
And marking dimly by the dubious light,
A warrior form approach, he claps his hands,
With naked sword and lifted shield he stands,
To front the foe; but Rustem now appears,
And Gíw the secret tale astonished hears;
From thence the Champion on the Monarch waits.
The power and splendour of Sohráb relates:
"Circled by Chiefs this glorious youth was seen,
Of lofty stature and majestic mien;
No Tartar region gave the hero birth:
Some happier portion of the spacious earth;
Tall, as the graceful cypress he appears;
Like Sám, the brave, his warrior-front he rears!"
Then having told how, while the banquet shone,
Unhappy Zind had sunk, without a groan;
He forms his conquering bands in close array,
And, cheer'd by wine, awaits the coming day.

   When now the Sun his golden buckler raised,
And genial light through heaven diffusive blazed,
Sohráb in mail his nervous limbs attired,
For dreadful wrath his soul to vengeance fired;
With anxious haste he bent the yielding cord,
Ring within ring, more fateful than the sword;
Around his brows a regal helm he bound;
His dappled steed impatient stampt the ground.
Thus armed, ascending where the eye could trace
The hostile force, and mark each leader's place,
He called Hujír, the captive Chief addressed,

And anxious thus, his soul's desire expressed:
"A prisoner thou, if freedom's voice can charm,
And dungeon darkness fill thee with alarm,
That freedom merit, shun severest woe,
And truly answer what I ask to know!
If rigid truth thy ready speech attend,
Honours and wealth shall dignify my friend."

"Obedient to thy wish," Hujír replied,
"Truth thou shalt hear, whatever chance betide;
For what on earth to praise has better claim?
Falsehood but leads to sorrow and to shame!"

"Then say, what heroes lead the adverse host,
Where they command, what dignities they boast;
Say, where does Káús hold his kingly state,
Where Tús, and Gúdarz, on his bidding wait;
Gíw, Gust'hem, and Báhrám—all known to thee,
And where is mighty Rustem, where is he?
Look round with care, their names and power display
Or instant death shall end thy vital day."

"Where yonder splendid tapestries extend,
And o'er pavilions bright infolding bend,
A throne triumphal shines with sapphire rays,
And golden suns upon the banners blaze;
Full in the centre of the hosts—and round
The tent a hundred elephants are bound,
As if, in pomp, he mocked the power of fate;
There royal Káús holds his kingly state.

"In yonder tent which numerous guards protect,
Where front and rear illustrious Chiefs collect;
Where horsemen wheeling seem prepared for fight,

Their golden armour glittering in the light;
Tús lifts his banners, deck'd with royal pride,
Feared by the brave, the soldier's friend and guide.

"That crimson tent where spear-men frowning stand,
And steel-clad veterans form a threatening band,
Holds mighty Gúdarz, famed for martial fire,
Of eighty valiant sons the valiant sire;
Yet strong in arms, he shuns inglorious ease,
His lion-banners floating in the breeze.

"But mark, that green pavilion; girt around
By Persian nobles, speaks the Chief renowned;
Fierce on the standard, worked with curious art,
A hideous dragon writhing seems to start;
Throned in his tent the warrior's form is seen,
Towering above the assembled host between!
A generous horse before him snorts and neighs,
The trembling earth the echoing sound conveys.
Like him no Champion ever met my eyes,
No horse like that for majesty and size;
What Chief illustrious bears a port so high?
Mark, how his standard flickers through the sky!"

Thus ardent spoke Sohráb. Hujír dismayed,
Paused ere reply the dangerous truth betrayed.
Trembling for Rustem's life the captive groaned;
Basely his country's glorious boast disowned,
And said the Chief from distant China came—
Sohráb abrupt demands the hero's name;
The name unknown, grief wrings his aching heart,
And yearning anguish speeds her venom'd dart;
To him his mother gave the tokens true,
He sees them all, and all but mock his view.

When gloomy fate descends in evil hour,
Can human wisdom bribe her favouring power?
Yet, gathering hope, again with restless mien
He marks the Chiefs who crowd the warlike scene.

"Where numerous heroes, horse and foot, appear,
And brazen trumpets thrill the listening ear,
Behold the proud pavilion of the brave!
With wolves emboss'd the silken banners wave.
The throne's bright gems with radiant lustre glow,
Slaves rank'd around with duteous homage bow.
What mighty Chieftain rules his cohorts there?
His name and lineage, free from guile, declare!"

"Gíw, son of Gúdarz, long a glorious name,
Whose prowess even transcends his father's fame."

"Mark yonder tent of pure and dazzling white,
Whose rich brocade reflects a quivering light;
An ebon seat surmounts the ivory throne;
There frowns in state a warrior of renown.
The crowding slaves his awful nod obey,
And silver moons around his banners play;
What Chief, or Prince, has grasped the hostile sword?
Fríburz, the son of Persia's mighty lord."
Again: "These standards show one champion more,
Upon their centre flames the savage boar;
The saffron-hued pavilion bright ascends,
Whence many a fold of tasselled fringe depends;
Who there presides?"

*

When the bright dawn proclaimed the rising day,
The warriors armed, impatient of delay;
But first Sohráb, his proud confederate nigh,
Thus wistful spoke, as swelled the boding sigh—
"Now, mark my great antagonist in arms!
His noble form my filial bosom warms;
My mother's tokens shine conspicuous here,
And all the proofs my heart demands, appear;
Sure this is Rustem, whom my eyes engage!
Shall I, O grief! provoke my Father's rage?
Offended Nature then would curse my name,
And shuddering nations echo with my shame."
He ceased, then Húmán: "Vain, fantastic thought,
Oft have I been where Persia's Champion fought;
And thou hast heard, what wonders he performed,
When, in his prime, Mázinderán was stormed;
That horse resembles Rustem's, it is true,
But not so strong, nor beautiful to view."

Sohráb now buckles on his war attire,
His heart all softness, and his brain all fire;
Around his lips such smiles benignant played,
He seemed to greet a friend, as thus he said:—
"Here let us sit together on the plain,
Here, social sit, and from the fight refrain;
Ask we from heaven forgiveness of the past,
And bind our souls in friendship that may last;
Ours be the feast—let us be warm and free,
For powerful instinct draws me still to thee;
Fain would my heart in bland affection join,
Then let thy generous ardour equal mine;
And kindly say, with whom I now contend—
What name distinguished boasts my warrior-friend!
Thy name unfit for champion brave to hide,

Thy name so long, long sought, and still denied;
Say, art thou Rustem, whom I burn to know?
Ingenuous say, and cease to be my foe!"

    Sternly the mighty Champion cried, "Away—
Hence with thy wiles—now practised to delay;
The promised struggle, resolute, I claim,
Then cease to move me to an act of shame."
Sohráb rejoined—"Old man! thou wilt not hear
The words of prudence uttered in thine ear;
Then, Heaven! look on."

    Preparing for the shock,
Each binds his charger to a neighbouring rock;
And girds his loins, and rubs his wrists, and tries
Their suppleness and force, with angry eyes;
And now they meet—now rise, and now descend,
And strong and fierce their sinewy arms extend;
Wrestling with all their strength they grasp and strain,
And blood and sweat flow copious on the plain;
Like raging elephants they furious close;
Commutual wounds are given, and wrenching blows.
Sohráb now clasps his hands, and forward springs
Impatiently, and round the Champion clings;
Seizes his girdle belt, with power to tear
The very earth asunder; in despair
Rustem, defeated, feels his nerves give way,
And thundering falls. Sohráb bestrides his prey:
Grim as the lion, prowling through the wood,
Upon a wild ass springs, and pants for blood.
His lifted sword had lopt the gory head,
But Rustem, quick, with crafty ardour said:—
"One moment, hold! what, are our laws unknown?
A Chief may fight till he is twice o'erthrown;

The second fall, his recreant blood is spilt,
These are our laws, avoid the menaced guilt."

Proud of his strength, and easily deceived,
The wondering youth the artful tale believed;
Released his prey, and, wild as wind or wave,
Neglecting all the prudence of the brave,
Turned from the place, nor once the strife renewed,
But bounded o'er the plain and other cares pursued,
As if all memory of the war had died,
All thoughts of him with whom his strength was tried.

Húmán, confounded at the stripling's stay,
Went forth, and heard the fortune of the day;
Amazed to find the mighty Rustem freed,
With deepest grief he wailed the luckless deed.
"What! loose a raging lion from the snare,
And let him growling hasten to his lair?
Bethink thee well; in war, from this unwise,
This thoughtless act what countless woes may rise;
Never again suspend the final blow,
Nor trust the seeming weakness of a foe!"
"Hence with complaint," the dauntless youth replied,
"To-morrow's contest shall his fate decide."

When Rustem was released, in altered mood
He sought the coolness of the murmuring flood;
There quenched his thirst; and bathed his limbs, and prayed,
Beseeching Heaven to yield its strengthening aid.
His pious prayer indulgent Heaven approved,
And growing strength through all his sinews moved;
Such as erewhile his towering structure knew,
When his bold arm unconquered demons slew.

Yet in his mien no confidence appeared,
No ardent hope his wounded spirits cheered.

   Again they met. A glow of youthful grace,
Diffused its radiance o'er the stripling's face,
And when he saw in renovated guise,
The foe so lately mastered; with surprise,
He cried—"What! rescued from my power, again
Dost thou confront me on the battle plain?
Or, dost thou, wearied, draw thy vital breath,
And seek, from warrior bold, the shaft of death?
Truth has no charms for thee, old man; even now,
Some further cheat may lurk upon thy brow;
Twice have I shown thee mercy, twice thy age
Hath been thy safety—twice it soothed my rage."
Then mild the Champion: "Youth is proud and vain!
The idle boast a warrior would disdain;
This aged arm perhaps may yet control,
The wanton fury that inflames thy soul!"

   Again, dismounting, each the other viewed
With sullen glance, and swift the fight renewed;
Clenched front to front, again they tug and bend,
Twist their broad limbs as every nerve would rend;
With rage convulsive Rustem grasps him round;
Bends his strong back, and hurls him to the ground;
Him, who had deemed the triumph all his own;
But dubious of his power to keep him down,
Like lightning quick he gives the deadly thrust,
And spurns the Stripling weltering in the dust.
—Thus as his blood that shining steel imbrues,
Thine too shall flow, when Destiny pursues;
For when she marks the victim of her power,
A thousand daggers speed the dying hour.

Writhing with pain Sohráb in murmurs sighed—
And thus to Rustem—"Vaunt not, in thy pride;
Upon myself this sorrow have I brought,
Thou but the instrument of fate—which wrought
My downfall; thou are guiltless—guiltless quite;
O! had I seen my father in the fight,
My glorious father! Life will soon be o'er,
And his great deeds enchant my soul no more!
Of him my mother gave the mark and sign,
For him I sought, and what an end is mine!
My only wish on earth, my constant sigh,
Him to behold, and with that wish I die.
But hope not to elude his piercing sight,
In vain for thee the deepest glooms of night;
Couldst thou through Ocean's depths for refuge fly,
Or midst the star-beams track the upper sky!
Rustem, with vengeance armed, will reach thee there,
His soul the prey of anguish and despair."

An icy horror chills the Champion's heart,
His brain whirls round with agonizing smart;
O'er his wan cheek no gushing sorrows flow,
Senseless he sinks beneath the weight of woe;
Relieved at length, with frenzied look, he cries:
"Prove thou art mine, confirm my doubting eyes!
For I am Rustem!" Piercing was the groan,
Which burst from his torn heart—as wild and lone,
He gazed upon him. Dire amazement shook
The dying youth, and mournful thus he spoke:
"If thou art Rustem, cruel is thy part,
No warmth paternal seems to fill thy heart;
Else hadst thou known me when, with strong desire,
I fondly claimed thee for my valiant sire;
Now from my body strip the shining mail,

Untie these bands, ere life and feeling fail;
And on my arm the direful proof behold!
Thy sacred bracelet of refulgent gold!
When the loud brazen drums were heard afar,
And, echoing round, proclaimed the pending war,
Whilst parting tears my mother's eyes o'erflowed,
This mystic gift her bursting heart bestowed:
'Take this,' she said, 'thy father's token wear,
And promised glory will reward thy care.'
The hour is come, but fraught with bitterest woe,
We meet in blood to wail the fatal blow."

    The loosened mail unfolds the bracelet bright,
Unhappy gift! to Rustem's wildered sight,
Prostrate he falls—"By my unnatural hand,
My son, my son is slain—and from the land
Uprooted."—Frantic, in the dust his hair
He rends in agony and deep despair;
The western sun had disappeared in gloom,
And still, the Champion wept his cruel doom;
His wondering legions marked the long delay,
And, seeing Rakush riderless astray,
The rumour quick to Persia's Monarch spread,
And there described the mighty Rustem dead.
Káús, alarmed, the fatal tidings hears;
His bosom quivers with increasing fears.
"Speed, speed, and see what has befallen to-day
To cause these groans and tears—what fatal fray!
If he be lost, if breathless on the ground,
And this young warrior, with the conquest crowned—
Then must I, humbled, from my kingdom torn,
Wander like Jemshíd, through the world forlorn."

The army roused, rushed o'er the dusty plain,
Urged by the Monarch to revenge the slain;
Wild consternation saddened every face,
Tús winged with horror sought the fatal place,
And there beheld the agonizing sight—
The murderous end of that unnatural fight.
Sohráb, still breathing, hears the shrill alarms,
His gentle speech suspends the clang of arms:
"My light of life now fluttering sinks in shade,
Let vengeance sleep, and peaceful vows be made.
Beseech the King to spare this Tartar host,
For they are guiltless, all to them is lost;
I led them on, their souls with glory fired,
While mad ambition all my thoughts inspired.
In search of thee, the world before my eyes,
War was my choice, and thou the sacred prize;
With thee, my sire! in virtuous league combined,
No tyrant King should persecute mankind.
That hope is past—the storm has ceased to rave—
My ripening honours wither in the grave;
Then let no vengeance on my comrades fall,
Mine was the guilt, and mine the sorrow, all;
How often have I sought thee—oft my mind
Figured thee to my sight—o'erjoyed to find
My mother's token; disappointment came,
When thou denied thy lineage and thy name;
Oh! still o'er thee my soul impassioned hung,
Still to my father fond affection clung!
But fate, remorseless, all my hopes withstood,
And stained thy reeking hands in kindred blood."

His faltering breath protracted speech denied:
Still from his eye-lids flowed a gushing tide;
Through Rustem's soul redoubled horror ran,

Heart-rending thoughts subdued the mighty man,
And now, at last, with joy-illumined eye,
The Zábul bands their glorious Chief descry;
But when they saw his pale and haggard look,
Knew from what mournful cause he gazed and shook,
With downcast mien they moaned and wept aloud;
While Rustem thus addressed the weeping crowd
"Here ends the war! let gentle peace succeed,
Enough of death, I—I have done the deed!"
Then to his brother, groaning deep, he said—
"O what a curse upon a parent's head!
But go—and to the Tartar say—no more,
Let war between us steep the earth with gore."
Zúára flew and wildly spoke his grief,
To crafty Húmán, the Túránian Chief,
Who, with dissembled sorrow, heard him tell
The dismal tidings which he knew too well;
"And who," he said, "has caused these tears to flow?
Who, but Hujír? He might have stayed the blow,
But when Sohráb his Father's banners sought;
He still denied that here the Champion fought;
He spread the ruin, he the secret knew,
Hence should his crime receive the vengeance due!"
Zúára, frantic, breathed in Rustem's ear,
The treachery of the captive Chief, Hujír;
Whose headless trunk had weltered on the strand,
But prayers and force withheld the lifted hand.
Then to his dying son the Champion turned,
Remorse more deep within his bosom burned;
A burst of frenzy fired his throbbing brain;
He clenched his sword, but found his fury vain;
The Persian Chiefs the desperate act represt,
And tried to calm the tumult in his breast:
Thus Gúdarz spoke—"Alas! wert thou to give

Thyself a thousand wounds, and cease to live;
What would it be to him thou sorrowest o'er?
It would not save one pang—then weep no more;
For if removed by death, O say, to whom
Has ever been vouchsafed a different doom?
All are the prey of death—the crowned, the low,
And man, through life, the victim still of woe."
Then Rustem: "Fly! and to the King relate,
The pressing horrors which involve my fate;
And if the memory of my deeds e'er swayed
His mind, O supplicate his generous aid;
A sovereign balm he has whose wondrous power,
All wounds can heal, and fleeting life restore;
Swift from his tent the potent medicine bring."
—But mark the malice of the brainless King!
Hard as the flinty rock, he stern denies
The healthful draught, and gloomy thus replies:
"Can I forgive his foul and slanderous tongue?
The sharp disdain on me contemptuous flung?
Scorned 'midst my army by a shameless boy,
Who sought my throne, my sceptre to destroy!
Nothing but mischief from his heart can flow,
Is it, then, wise to cherish such a foe?
The fool who warms his enemy to life,
Only prepares for scenes of future strife."

Gúdarz, returning, told the hopeless tale—
And thinking Rustem's presence might prevail;
The Champion rose, but ere he reached the throne,
Sohráb had breathed the last expiring groan.

Now keener anguish rack'd the father's mind,
Reft of his son, a murderer of his kind;
His guilty sword distained with filial gore,

He beat his burning breast, his hair he tore;
The breathless corse before his shuddering view,
A shower of ashes o'er his head he threw;
"In my old age," he cried, "what have I done?
Why have I slain my son, my innocent son!
Why o'er his splendid dawning did I roll
The clouds of death—and plunge my burthened soul
In agony? My son! from heroes sprung;
Better these hands were from my body wrung;
And solitude and darkness, deep and drear,
Fold me from sight than hated linger here.
But when his mother hears, with horror wild,
That I have shed the life-blood of her child,
So nobly brave, so dearly loved, in vain,
How can her heart that rending shock sustain?"

    Now on a bier the Persian warriors place
The breathless Youth, and shade his pallid face;
And turning from that fatal field away,
Move towards the Champion's home in long array.
Then Rustem, sick of martial pomp and show,
Himself the spring of all this scene of woe,
Doomed to the flames the pageantry he loved,
Shield, spear, and mace, so oft in battle proved;
Now lost to all, encompassed by despair;
His bright pavilion crackling blazed in air;
The sparkling throne the ascending column fed;
In smoking fragments fell the golden bed;
The raging fire red glimmering died away,
And all the Warrior's pride in dust and ashes lay.

    Káús, the King, now joins the mournful Chief,
And tries to soothe his deep and settled grief;
For soon or late we yield our vital breath,

And all our worldly troubles end in death!
"When first I saw him, graceful in his might,
He looked far other than a Tartar knight;
Wondering I gazed—now Destiny has thrown
Him on thy sword—he fought, and he is gone;
And should even Heaven against the earth be hurled,
Or fire inwrap in crackling flames the world,
That which is past—we never can restore,
His soul has travelled to some happier shore.
Alas! no good from sorrow canst thou reap,
Then wherefore thus in gloom and misery weep?"

   But Rustem's mighty woes disdained his aid,
His heart was drowned in grief, and thus he said:
"Yes, he is gone! to me for ever lost!
O then protect his brave unguided host;
From war removed and this detested place,
Let them, unharmed, their mountain-wilds retrace;
Bid them secure my brother's will obey,
The careful guardian of their weary way,
To where the Jihún's distant waters stray."
To this the King: "My soul is sad to see
Thy hopeless grief—but, since approved by thee,
The war shall cease—though the Túránian brand
Has spread dismay and terror through the land."

   The King, appeased, no more with vengeance burned,
The Tartar legions to their homes returned;
The Persian warriors, gathering round the dead,
Grovelled in dust, and tears of sorrow shed;
Then back to loved Irán their steps the monarch led.

   But Rustem, midst his native bands, remained,
And further rites of sacrifice maintained;

A thousand horses bled at his command,
And the torn drums were scattered o'er the sand;
And now through Zábul's deep and bowery groves,
In mournful pomp the sad procession moves.
The mighty Chief on foot precedes the bier;
His Warrior-friends, in grief assembled near:
The dismal cadence rose upon the gale,
And Zál astonished heard the piercing wail;
He and his kindred joined the solemn train;
Hung round the bier and wondering viewed the slain.
"There gaze, and weep!" the sorrowing Father said,
"For there, behold my glorious offspring dead!"
The hoary Sire shrunk backward with surprise,
And tears of blood o'erflowed his aged eyes;
And now the Champion's rural palace gate
Receives the funeral group in gloomy state;
Rúdábeh loud bemoaned the Stripling's doom;
Sweet flower, all drooping in the hour of bloom,
His tender youth in distant bowers had past,
Sheltered at home he felt no withering blast;
In the soft prison of his mother's arms,
Secure from danger and the world's alarms.
O ruthless Fortune! flushed with generous pride,
He sought his sire, and thus unhappy, died.

Rustem again the sacred bier unclosed;
Again Sohráb to public view exposed;
Husbands, and wives, and warriors, old and young,
Struck with amaze, around the body hung,
With garments rent and loosely flowing hair;
Their shrieks and clamours filled the echoing air;
Frequent they cried: "Thus Sám the Champion slept!
Thus sleeps Sohráb!" Again they groaned, and wept.

Now o'er the corpse a yellow robe is spread,
The aloes bier is closed upon the dead;
And, to preserve the hapless hero's name,
Fragrant and fresh, that his unblemished fame
Might live and bloom through all succeeding days,
A mound sepulchral on the spot they raise,
Formed like a charger's hoof.

          In every ear
The story has been told—and many a tear,
Shed at the sad recital. Through Túrán,
Afrásiyáb's wide realm, and Samengán,
Deep sunk the tidings—nuptial bower, and bed,
And all that promised happiness, had fled!

But when Tahmíneh heard this tale of woe,
Think how a mother bore the mortal blow!
Distracted, wild, she sprang from place to place;
With frenzied hands deformed her beauteous face;
The musky locks her polished temples crowned.
Furious she tore, and flung upon the ground;
Starting, in agony of grief, she gazed—
Her swimming eyes to Heaven imploring raised;
And groaning cried: "Sole comfort of my life!
Doomed the sad victim of unnatural strife,
Where art thou now with dust and blood defiled?
Thou darling boy, my lost, my murdered child!
When thou wert gone—how, night and lingering day,
Did thy fond mother watch the time away;
For hope still pictured all I wished to see,
Thy father found, and thou returned to me,
Yes—thou, exulting in thy father's fame!
And yet, nor sire nor son, nor tidings, came:
How could I dream of this? ye met—but how?

That noble aspect—that ingenuous brow,
Moved not a nerve in him—ye met—to part,
Alas! the life-blood issuing from the heart
Short was the day which gave to me delight,
Soon, soon, succeeds a long and dismal night;
On whom shall now devolve my tender care?
Who, loved like thee, my bosom-sorrows share?
Whom shall I take to fill thy vacant place,
To whom extend a mother's soft embrace?
Sad fate! for one so young, so fair, so brave,
Seeking thy father thus to find a grave.
These arms no more shall fold thee to my breast,
No more with thee my soul be doubly blest;
No, drowned in blood thy lifeless body lies,
For ever torn from these desiring eyes;
Friendless, alone, beneath a foreign sky,
Thy mail thy death-clothes—and thy father, by;
Why did not I conduct thee on the way,
And point where Rustem's bright pavilion lay?
Thou hadst the tokens—why didst thou withhold
Those dear remembrances—that pledge of gold?
Hadst thou the bracelet to his view restored,
Thy precious blood had never stained his sword."

    The strong emotion choked her panting breath,
Her veins seemed withered by the cold of death:
The trembling matrons hastening round her mourned,
With piercing cries, till fluttering life returned;
Then gazing up, distraught, she wept again,
And frantic, seeing 'midst her pitying train,
The favourite steed—now more than ever dear,
The hoofs she kissed, and bathed with many a tear;
Clasping the mail Sohráb in battle wore,
With burning lips she kissed it o'er and o'er;

His martial robes she in her arms comprest,
And like an infant strained them to her breast;
The reins, and trappings, club, and spear, were brought,
The sword, and shield, with which the Stripling fought,
These she embraced with melancholy joy,
In sad remembrance of her darling boy.
And still she beat her face, and o'er them hung,
As in a trance—or to them wildly clung—
Day after day she thus indulged her grief,
Night after night, disdaining all relief;
At length worn out—from earthly anguish riven,
The mother's spirit joined her child in Heaven.

HUDUD AL ALAM
DISCOURSE ON THE COUNTRY OF KHURASAN AND ITS TOWNS

Author Unknown

Translated by V. V. Minorsky, 1982

> Although its author is still not known more than a thousand years after its publication, the tenth-century *Hudud al Alam (Boundaries of the World)*, remains a hugely important source of geographical information about the Islamic and non-Islamic world of that time. Unlike the flowery work of courtiers and bureaucrats such as Al Utbi, this is a work of much drier prose. The following extract, which describes some of the key cities, rivers and regions in Khorasan, which historically encompassed parts of today's Afghanistan, including the ancient centres of Herat, Balkh and Bamiyan, are typically clipped, less *Lonely Planet* and more *Encyclopaedia Afghanica*.

It is a country east of which is Hindustan; south of it, some of its (own) marches and some parts of the desert of Kargaskuh; west of it, the districts of Gurgan and the limits of the Ghuzz; north of it, the river Jayhun. This is a vast country with much wealth and abundant amenities. It is situated near the centre of the Inhabited Lands of the world. In it gold-mines and silver-mines are found as well as precious things such as are (extracted) from mountains. This country produces horses and its people are warlike. It is the gate of Turkestan. It produces numerous textiles, gold, silver, turquoises, and drugs. It is a country with a salubrious climate and with men strongly built and healthy. The king of Khurasan in the days of old was distinct from the king of Transoxiana but now they are one. The *mir* of Khurasan resides at Bukhara; he is from the Saman family and from Bahram Chubin's descendants. These (princes) are called Maliks of the East and have lieutenants in all Khurasan, while on the frontiers of Khurasan there are kings called "margraves."

1. Nishapur is the largest and richest town in Khurasan. It occupies an area of 1 *farsang* across and has many inhabitants. It is a resort of merchants and the seat of the army commanders. It has a citadel, a suburb, and a city. Most of its water is from the springs and has been conducted under the earth. It produces various textiles, silk, and cotton. To it belongs a special province with thirteen districts and four territories.

20. Herat, a large town with a very strong *shahristan*, a citadel, and a suburb. It has running waters. Its cathedral mosque is the most frequented in all Khurasan. The town lies at the foot of a mountain and is a very pleasant place. Many Arabs live there. It has a large river which comes from the frontier region between Ghur and Guzganan and is utilized in the districts of Herat. It produces cotton stuffs, manna, and grape-syrup.

42. Merv, a large town. In the days of old the residence of the *mir* of Khurasan was there but now he lives in Bukhara. It is a pleasant and flourishing place with a citadel built by Tahmurath; in it there are numerous castles. It was the abode of the (Sasanian) kings. In all Khurasan there is no town [better] situated. Its market is good. Their land taxes are levied on the extent of irrigation. Merv produces good cotton, root of asafoetida, *filata*-sweets, vinegar, condiments, textiles of raw silk and of *mulham* silk.

67. Balkh, a large and flourishing town which was formerly the residence of the Sasanian kings. In it are found buildings of the Sasanian kings with paintings and wonderful works, (which) have fallen into ruins. . . . (Balkh) is a resort of merchants and is very pleasant and prosperous. It is the emporium of Hindustan. There is a large river in Balkh that comes from Bamiyan and in the neighbourhood of Balkh is divided into twelve branches; it traverses the town and is altogether used for the agriculture of its districts. Balkh produces citrons and sour oranges, sugar-cane, and water-lilies. Balkh has a shahristan surrounded by a mighty wall. In its suburb there are numerous marshes.

Discourse on the Region of Khurasanian Marches

East of this region lies Hindustan; south of it, the deserts of Sind and Kerman; west of it, the borders of Herat; north of it, the borders of Gharchistan, Guzganan, and Tukharistan. Some parts of this region belong to the hot zone and some to the cold. From its mountains the Ghur-slaves are brought to Khurasan. It is a place with much cultivation. Indian articles are brought to this region.

1. Ghur, a province amid mountains and rugged country. It has a king called Ghur-shah. He draws his strength from the *mir* of Guzganan. In the days of old this province of Ghur was pagan; actually most of the people are Muslim. To them belong numerous boroughs and villages. From this province come slaves, armour, coats of mail, and good arms. The people are bad-tempered, unruly, and ignorant. They are white and swarthy.

19. Ghaznin, a town situated on the slope of a mountain, extremely pleasant. It lies in Hindustan and formerly belonged to it, but now is among the Muslim lands. It lies on the frontier between the Muslims and the infidels. It is a resort of merchants, and possesses great wealth.

20. Kabul, a borough possessing a solid fortress known for its strength. Its inhabitants are Muslims and Indians, and there are idol-temples in it. The royal power of the *raja* of Qinnauj [possibly Kannauj, on the banks of the Ganges River, capital of north India in the seventh century], is not complete until he has made a pilgrimage to those idol-temples, and here too his royal standard is fastened.

22. In Ghaznin and in the limits of the boroughs which we have enumerated, live the Khalaj Turks, who possess many sheep. They wander along climates, grazing grounds, and pasture-lands. These Khalaj Turks are also numerous in the provinces of Balkh, Tukharistan, Bust, and Guzganan. Ghaznin and the districts adjacent to it are all called Zabulistan.

RABIA BALKHI
Selection of poems

She was writing poems of love and anguish a thousand years ago. Few survive, but the woman who wrote them and who is known to have lived in the tenth century has become a legend, her serially mythologised life lit by romance and shadowed by tragedy. First the daughter, later the sister, of a king, **Rabia Balkhi** was the first known female poet to write in Persian. The most famous version of her biography tells of how she fell in love with her brother Haris's Turkish slave, a man called Bektash. The tryst came to the ears of a furious Haris, who immediately ordered the slave's execution. Rabia then slit her wrists – or was murdered by her brother. As she lay dying, she traced her last love poem on the wall in blood. She has been celebrated by generations of poets and writers ever since, from Attar of Nishapur in the twelfth century to Elizabeth Lemieux in the twenty-first. Her life story, however uncertain, continues to speak to many Afghan women, who pay their respects at Rabia's crumbling shrine in Balkh in the far north of Afghanistan.

The following four poems are translated by Dick Davis, and appear in The Mirror Of My Heart: A Thousand Years of Persian Poetry by Women *(Penguin 2021).*

My hope's that God will make you fall in love
With someone cold and callous just like you
And that you'll realize my true value when
You're twisting in the torments I've been through.

*

His love has caught me once again –
I've struggled fiercely, but in vain.
(Well, sobersides, explain to me
Just who can swim love's shoreless sea!
To reach love's goal you must accept
All you instinctively reject –
See ugliness as beauty, eat
Foul poison up and call it sweet.)
Not knowing all this would produce
Was further tightening of the noose.

*

I'm drunk with love to know my love is here tonight
And that I'm freed from sorrow and from fear tonight;
I sit beside my love, and earnestly I say,
'God, make the key to morning disappear tonight!'

*

The garden shows so many flowers, as though
Mani had painted their resplendent glow

Dawn's breezes never bore Tibetan musk,
How is the world so musky when they blow?

Are Majnun's eyes within the clouds, that they
Shed Layli's cheeks' hue on each rose below?

Like wine within an agate glass, his tears
Have filled each tulip with their crimson glow

Raise up the wine bowl, raise it generously
Since bad luck dogs deniers who say 'No'

Narcissi glow with silver and with gold
It's Kasra's crown their shining petals show

Like nuns in purple cowls the violets bloom
Do they turn into Christians as they grow?

*

The following poem is translated by Munazza Ebitkar.

Rabia:

Oh the absent and present one where are you
If you are not with me then where are you
My eyes are illuminated by you
My heart is acquainted by you
Come and invite my eyes and soul
Otherwise take a sword and end my life

Bektash:

I don't have the sight to see you
I don't have patience and rest without you
What am I going to do with you now
How can I carry this pain without you
Your hair has pierced my veil
With your face I have fallen in love
From your hair I have become under and over
Because from your hair my life has been destroyed

The following lines describe Rabia's fatal tryst with the Turkish slave Bektash:

For whichever finger that I may reach a lantern,
I shall search for you in every plain and garden

*

She awaited another evening
two hearts elated – from the encounter
when Bektash's face came into the light
twice over – Rabia's love unfolded

The following description of Rabia Balkhi appears in Ilāhī-Nāma *by the Persian Sufi poet Farid al Din Attar (Attar of Nishapur), and is translated by Munazza Ebtikar:*

The moon-faced beauty struck blood with her fingertip
With her blood she covered the walls

Many poems stemmed from her agonized heart
When no walls remained in the hamam

So, too, a few drops of blood remained
As she covered the walls with poetry

She collapsed like a fragment of a wall
Amid blood, love, fire and tears

Her sweet soul swiftly left her body with a hundred desires

INTIMATE CONVERSATIONS WITH GOD

Khwaja Abdullah Ansari
Translated by Victor Danner, 1979

Khwaja Abdullah Ansari (1006–1088) was a Sufi poet, philosopher and patron saint of the western Afghan city of Herat, a *bona fide* cultural capital. A Quranic commentator and scholar of the Hanbali school of thought, he was admired for his rhetorical and poetic skills in both Arabic and Persian, as well as for his renunciation of worldly wealth. Nicknamed 'The Pious One', he was descended from Abu Ayyub al Ansari, one of the Prophet Mohammed's closest companions, and today is remembered especially for his *Munajat Namah* (*Intimate Conversations with God*), a classic of Persian literature.

Visiting Herat in late 1933, the English traveller Robert Byron was unable to resist launching a broadside against this celebrated saint: 'Khoja Abdullah Ansari died in the year 1088 at the age of eighty-four, because some boys threw stones at him while he was at penance. One sympathises with those boys: even among saints he was a prodigious bore. He spoke in the cradle; he began to preach at fourteen; during his life he held intercourse with a thousand sheikhs, learnt a hundred thousand verses by heart (some say 1,200,000) and composed as many more. He doted on cats.'

The Song of the Dervish

O God, the *qibla*[1] of those who know is the sun of your face.
The *mihrab*[2] of all souls is the arch of your brow.
The Masjid al-Aqsa[3] of all hearts is the sanctuary of your lane.
Glance in our direction, for our gazes are upon you.

The world is an abode of affliction and trial, not a place of rest and repose.
Where is there room here for joy and gladness?
To be mindful of God in every condition is then the key to salvation.

Vexed is the seeker after this world.
Rewarded is the seeker after the next world.
Glad is the seeker after the Lord.

He who desires the world is mad.
He who desires Heaven labors under a pretext:
The goal is the Lord of the House.
Some have ambition of attaining Heaven:
Some desire the Beloved.
Happy is he whose banner reads "ALL IS HE"!

O Paradise,
I am not concerned with you: Don't be so long-winded!
O Hell,
I am not afraid of you: Don't tell me about yourself!
What is happiness?

To be concerned with loving God and to rid oneself of love for Creation.
Do you know who the traveler on the true road is?
He is one who knows what poverty is.

To be a dervish means to be a lump of sifted earth with a little water sprinkled on top.
It means to be something that neither harms the soles of the feet nor leaves a trail of dust behind.

What is poverty?
An unhypocritical exterior and a peaceful interior.

The poor has neither name nor shame.
He knows neither peace nor war.
The poor has water in the well and bread in the unseen realm.
He has neither a concern in his head nor gold in his pocket.

This rank is not attained by putting on a cloak and cap.
This felicity is attained by the striving of an enlightened heart.

If one abandons the rigor of knowledge for the delights of the black-eyed houris, the purity of his knowledge is shattered.
If a dervish seeks anything other than God Himself from God, the door to His response is closed.

What a happy abode is nothingness!

If you walk on water, you are wet.
If you fly in the air, you are a fly.
Fall in love in order to be somebody!
Fasting to endurance is a way to save on food.
Vigil and prayer is a labor for old women.
The pilgrimage is an occasion for tourism.
To distribute bread in alms is something for philanthropists:
Fall in love:
That is doing something!

Knowledge is a shoreless ocean in which the knower's soul is a signpost.

Hallaj said, "I am God" and crowned the gallows.
Abdullah said, "God" and was crowned.
What Hallaj said I too have said.
He said it aloud.
I, silently.

He who knows three things is saved from three things:
Who knows that the Creator made no mistakes at Creation is saved from caviling.
Who knows that He made no favoritism in allotting fortune is saved from jealousy.
Who knows of what he is created is saved from pride.

Look to what you do, for that is what you are worth.
True labor means neither fasting nor prayer:
True labor means defeat and needfulness.

What grief does the humble have for his daily bread?
He who conceals his affair is given no less;
He who seeks openly is given no more.
That which God has allotted neither increases one iota nor occurs one instant sooner.

Beginners have speech on their tongues.
The advanced have neither the power to speak nor the means to express.

If I am silent they will say I am mad.
If I speak they will say I am a stranger to reason.

God's favor comes unexpectedly, but only to an alert heart.

Put not your hope in people, for you will be wounded.
Put your hope in God that you may be delivered.

Strive to become a man and one who knows pain.

O God, what have you given one to whom you have not given reason?
What have you not given one to whom you have given reason?

Be intoxicated but do not cry out!
Be fulsome but do not fulminate!
Be humble and silent:
A sound jug is passed from hand to hand, but a broken one from shoulder to shoulder.
If you want salvation, become afflicted!
Seek the remaining after annihilation.
If you have, rejoice!
If you have not, seek!

---

[1] The *qibla* is the direction towards the Kaaba in Mecca to which Muslims pray.

[2] The *mihrab* is the arched niche in a mosque that indicates the qibla.

[3] The Masjid al Aqsa, which stands next to the Dome of the Rock in Jerusalem, is the third holiest site in Islam, after the Kaaba and the Prophet's Mosque in Medina. It was to Al Aqsa that the Prophet was transported during his Night Journey prior to his ascent to heaven.

ACCOUNT OF THE ALLIANCE OF THE SULTAN WITH ILEK-KHAN, AND THEIR SUBSEQUENT ESTRANGEMENT

Mohammed ibn Abd al Jabbar Utbi

Generally known as *Al Yamini*, after the moniker of Sultan Mahmud (r. 998–1030) – Yamin al Dawla, The Right Hand of the State – Al Utbi's history focuses on the two founders of the mighty but relatively short-lived Ghaznavid dynasty. At its height, the empire they established, which lasted from 977 until 1186, extended from the Oxus River to the Indus valley and the Indian Ocean. It was a particularly impressive achievement considering Sabaktagin, the empire's founder, who ruled from 977 to 997, was a former military slave of Turkic origin. Born in northern Iran in 961 and writing sometime after 1020, **Al Utbi** chronicled the earliest years of the dynasty in the fantastically florid and perfumed prose of a seasoned courtier – today we might call him a sycophant. Here he describes how the Ghaznavids regained the territories they had lost in Afghanistan and Iran to the rival Qarakhanid dynasty in Transoxiana, known to them as the Ilek Khans.

When the Sultan had cleansed the Court of Khurasan from his adversaries, and had reduced the enemies of the family of Saman to non-existence, Ilek-Khan succeeded to Mawarannahr, and obtained the princes of the family of Saman, their children and comrades. And these regions were entirely stripped of all that race and pearl-stock. And he wrote to the Sultan, and congratulated him on his inheritance of the kingdom of Khurasan, and proposed a reparation of good-will and the thread of friendship. An alliance was made between them, and motives of good inclination and attachment were established. And his discriminating nature advanced from a sincere affection to a sincere unity; and, at the time when the Sultan went to repulse the attack at Nishapur, he had sent the Imam Abu'l-Ta'ib, who was Imam of *hadith* (or of the sacred traditions) upon an embassy to Ilek-Khan, and sent (also) Tuganjuk, Prince of Sarkas, to him and expressed a desire for a noble alliance with his nobles (or noble race) and presented before his greatness, his army and his fortress, curious valuables of pieces of pure gold, with jacinths and rubies, and chains of great and small pearls, and gifts of robes and eggs of amber, and vessels of gold and silver full of perfumes of camphor, and other productions of the provinces of India, made from frankincense-bearing trees, and Damascus scimitars, and war elephants adorned with many colored trappings and jeweled bits, in describing all which gems the mind would be confused, and in specifying all which incomparable things the eyes would become turbid. And celebrated horses, with ornaments and head-trappings of gold, and various other choice and desirable things. And when the Imam Abu'l-Ta'ib arrived at the Turkish territory they exhibited much agitation and eagerness at his approach, and expressed extreme readiness to pay homage and respect to his dignity, partly on account of their honour toward His Majesty the Sultan, and partly on account of the superabundant and excelling virtues of (the envoy) in all kinds of science, he being the singular scholar of his age. He was sound in controversial tact, and in casuistical divinity, and lunar calculations. He thus attained to the object desired (i.e., to demand a daughter of Ilek-Khan for the Sultan, in marriage), caused seeking to be joined with finding, and returned, having with diligent industry fully accomplished his pilgrimage; and he presented the unequalled pearl, which, as a diver, he had sought and found in Turkestan, before the Sultan's presence, with valuable specimens of the purchased articles of Turkestan, pure gold and silver, sweet musk, high-bred horses, moon-faced slaves, well-featured girls, white falcons, packets of peacock-feathers, ermines, and tawny skins, with exquisite china vessels, and many other beautiful fabrics, so that, between the two kingdoms, an interwoven alliance and affinity became fastened, as with nails, and between them, as between artificers and officers, a partnership was established in the adjustment of benefits and union. For a long period affairs continued to be fitly ordered and duly arranged between these Courts, until, through the hateful anger of fate, the straight road of affection became damaged by ill-will, and by the interlopings of Satan the stream of the fountains of love became diminished, and the bonds of that sincere regard became untied. Some of the beauteous words of Abu'l-Ta'ib have been cited, and at the end of this chronicle several of the subject-nobles of the Sultan (who in their paths were like bright stars, and in their fixed [orbits] like constellations, each one being a star of the stars of the age, and a moon of the moons of virtue, and a column of the pillars of science) will be commemorated. And these words are from many of the niceties of the judgment and novelties of the language of Abu'l-Ta'ib: "He who offers himself before his time offers himself to the air." And this apothegm is taken from "The Words" of Abu Mansur, the divine: "Even a dog has high thoughts, and he is of the lowest extremity of baseness in whom there is a seeking for power before the times of power," etc., etc.

Account of the Passage of the Jayhun (the Amu Darya) by Ilek-Khan

The state of a sincere alliance between the Sultan and Ilek-Khan remained firm, until the creeping scorpions of ill-will, and the disturbing manoeuvrers of hatred, cut off the progress of affection, so that the flames of dispute blazed up. And Ilek watched an opportunity of withdrawal and flight, and when the standards of the Sultan were far distant he made an expedition into the frontiers of Multan, and the extent of Khurasan was destitute of the protection of the State, and the guardianship of government, and he sent Sabashitagin, who was general of his army, with an abundant force to Khurasan, and entrusted the capital, Balkh, to Jaafartagin, with a band of warriors. And Arslan-Jazib, Prince of Tus, was established at Herat, having received orders before from the Sultan, that if any new attack should occur on his weak part, and if loss should be produced on both sides, he should take up his position at Ghazna, march from Herat, and come to Ghazna. And Sabashitagin came to Herat, and sent Hasan b. Nasr to Nishapur, to enquire into the property, and to value the sources of wealth. And the majority of the nobles of Khurasan encouraged them with friendship and aid, on account of the prolongation of the days of the Sultan's absence, and the interception of intelligence, and the concealment of his footsteps, and on account of the trembling of earthquakes (confused rumours), and contracted feelings, and daily reports, and vain words. And Abu'l-'Abas Fazl b. Ahmad, in order to guard the paths and govern the provinces of the kingdom, arrived from Ghazna, as far as the frontiers of Bamiyan, with the preparation for a complete intercepting cordon. And he committed the passes of ingress and egress of that country to men of action, and a cautious corps of observation. And quick messengers ran through the whole extent of the kingdom to the Sultan with tidings of the conduct of Ilek. And the Sultan laid aside all care for other regions, and like striking lightning and a furious wind traveled that expanse over the plains and through the warriors, over the deserts, and through the tribes of people, and in a short time arrived at Ghuzni, and afforded aid to his sons of the Empire, and the nobles of His Majesty, by his horses, mules and riders, and assembled from the great spearmen a body of glorious soldiers (Verse):

> Angels upon angels, or, if they were human, such as embroidered by the needle.

And came like a raging sea to Balkh, and Jaafartagin went out from this contingency flying like a devil from exposure to the storm of ashes. But the Sultan sent Arslan-Jazib with ten thousand cavalry on his road. And Sabashitagin when he arrived at the bank of the Jayhun, and beheld that foaming sea and roaring torrent, turned aside and came to

Merv, in order to march through the desert. But the summer was hot, so that the wells were filled up, and the roads obliterated, and the path difficult to determine; therefore he began to move towards Sarkhas. But Muhsin b. Tabak, who was one of the Ghuzz chieftains, seized the road, and bestirred himself to resist him. Sabashitagin, therefore, finding no possibility of making a stand against the army of Arslan, and not even an opportunity of bathing (i.e., from the hot pursuit), was deprived of the power of proceeding, and went there from to Nasa. And as he was about to collect his baggage and march, upon occasion of one of his marches, Arslan-Jazib came down, and on account of his baggage, and the enormous weight of treasure and of goods which he had derived from the provinces of Herat, he was unable to retain those appendages, or to cope with those heroes. In order to preserve (this property) he wandered right and left until the conclusion of the affair was that he made it all the means of preserving his existence and a matter of life. Therefore he cast all this transported burden and heavy load from his back, and struck in towards Nishapur. The other army kept close after him until he halted at the frontiers of Jurjan. He threw himself amongst the cliffs and thickets of that land, and the surrounding people of Gilan struck him with the hand of slaughter and plunder, and brought to bear their killing strength upon his comrades and his troops. Several of his army fled to the safety of the protecting shadow of Shams al-Muali. He, by the route of Damistan, came as far as Nasa, and sent the remainder of his baggage to 'Ali b. Ma'mun Khorezmshah. And on the part of Ilek-Khan he entrusted him with the charge thereof, and enjoined him to preserve it, and earnestly recommended him to guard it from the impurities of treachery. And with respect to all the camp followers and the relics of the force, he dismissed them to the service of that Prince, and started for Merv, by way of the desert. The Sultan halted at Tus, for the inspection of the booty of Arslan-Jazib, and upon the arrival of intelligence that Sabashitagin came out by way of the desert, he turned on the road by which he might meet him, in order that he might perchance overtake him, and draw him into the snare of vengeance. But when the Sultan arrived he had passed to the desert. Upon this the Sultan dispatched after him 'Abdallah Tain, with an army of Arabs which was in his care; and his condition was such as Sa'id b. Hasan describes (Verse):

> I fled from a flowing rivulet and its scantiness
> Unto a superabundant water and its confused streams;
> And I was like one who eagerly rushes into a canal,
> When desiring to escape the thunder-rain

And, in the midst of a desert wherein there was no water, except Satan's saliva, and nothing brightly green except the flat of swords, they laid the sword upon his company and they took prisoners his brother, with seven hundred of his distinguished chiefs and captains. And the Sultan commanded that they should tie each one's sword below him, and place it upon his heel, and carry all to Ghazna, that all the world might take example from their misfortune and distress, and the fallaciousness of their confidence (Persian Verse):

> I have often contemplated and still no thought arrived, but
>   this good one,
> Happy he who directs himself (to serve) this Lord.
> Let him who would be at ease implore God to make his
>   burden light.
> The head of every one will be cheerful whose foot is on
>   that threshold.

Sabashitagin, with a few individuals, saved his life, and passed the Jayhun, and appeared before Ilek-Khan, who had already sent Jaafartagin, with six thousand horse, towards Balkh, in order to divert the Sultan from the pursuit of Sabashitagin. But the Sultan regarded them not, until he had concluded his immediate engagement. Then he turned his reins towards them and suddenly assaulted them, and sent the Amir Abu'l-Muzaffar Nasr, with his hunting forces and reaping troops, who held on to them until they were all expelled from the territory of Khurasan.

As for Ilek Khan he could not rest from this calamity, and dispatched a "letter of succour" to Kadir-Khan, King of China, imploring aid. And a sea of Turkish forces came like a torrent, and occupied the utmost parts of his kingdom and cities. And the army of Mawarannahr came, in a body to join them, and five thousand bridles passed the Jayhun, madly proud of the resources and strength of Kadir-Khan, of his great numbers, extreme bravery, established ability, and extensive power (Verse):

> Around him is a sea, which dashes with its billows and wears out the margin of the cliff.
> The stone from a small hill comes to them,
> It smoothes thereby the shore,
> Until it joins the fragments of the misfortune and arranges them in order.

The news of their arrival reached the Sultan, at Tukharistan: he packed up and went to Balkh, that the food of their covetousness might be cut off from those regions, and the road of provisions and pay might be closed; and the Sultan was occupied in arranging the means of war, and he collected a numerous army, of various tribes of Turks, Khalajes, and Hindus and Afghans, and the Ghuzz troops, and they met at a wide place, four farsangs from Balkh (Verse):

> The fifth of the east of the earth and the west responds,
> And their murmur reaches the ear of Gemini.
> Therein are assembled all people,
> Nor can they understand the news without an interpreter.
> Oh God, at the time of the way of sorrow thou seest it,
> And (when) the warriors and lions survive not.

Ilek then marched down with his army to battle, and for that day the young men of the army only boasted and swaggered, until the carpet of night was spread, when they separated, with the promise to fight with each other on the morrow. And the Sultan was occupied in arranging the order of battle. He assigned the centre to the Amir Nasr, brother of the Prince of Jurjan, Abu Nasr Farighuni, and Abu 'Abdallah Taini, with a body of his picked Curds and brave genii. He sent the right to the great Sahib, the Amir Altuntash, and charged Arslan Jazib with the left, and strengthened the force of the centre with five hundred elephants. And as to Ilek Khan, he, having stationed himself in the centre, had Kadir-Khan, with the army of Chin, on the right, and Jaafartagin on the left. Thus they engaged, and the earth resounded with thunder-like shouts and was in a blaze, from the terrible lightning of swords, and they sewed patches of dust upon the blue lining of the heavenly vault, and rendered the field of battle brilliant with the torches of arms and the tapers of spears, and sprinkles of blood began to rain from those lightning scimitars. And Ilek-Khan, with five hundred Turkish *ghulams* (quasi grenadiers) fought so skilfully that in the front of the army they could split a hair with their arrows, and could take a mountain from its place by the strokes of their swords. Then the sea of war was raised to a storm and the ground of the field was shaken as by an earthquake. And the Sultan, when he witnessed the mighty strength and terrible power of that body, came down to a small hill and implored the Almighty to strengthen his right hand and forgive (*his errors?*) and he placed his hand upon the end of the skirt of Heaven and trusted in God's guardianship, and asked victory from Him; and he made vows of offerings and engaged himself to give pious alms, and humbly submitted himself to God (imploring) that He would speed on victory and conquest. Then he mounted his own special elephant, and, with clear mind and sincere assurance, made a charge upon Ilek-Khan's centre; and his elephant seized the standard-bearer of Ilek-Khan and tossed him into the air, and, with weighty fury and extreme might humbled the men under his foot, and with his trunk hurled them from the back of horses, and tore them to pieces with his teeth. Upon this the chiefs of the Sultan boiled with the eagerness of opportunity and the gladness of victory, and bestirred their scimitars to strike the mass. Then came the tongue of reproach and cursing, and they compelled the troops of the Turks to leave their position, and to take the path of flight, and the Sultan's army with fury and madness cast them back to Mawarannahr, and not a trace of them remained in Khurasan. And again, these verses of Salami contain a description of the event, and a delineation of the impress of the Sultan's deeds (Verse):

"Oh sword of the religion of God thou art not pleasing to the enemy, even although thy sword like thy rectitude cuts rightly," etc.

And when the Sultan had concluded this great victory, and had allayed the heat of his anxiety, and had put an end to the series of these accidents, he determined to carry out his design of attacking Nawastah Shah (or Zab-Sais). This Prince was one of those sons of some Kings of India, unto whom the Sultan, having displayed to them the profession of Islam, had entrusted several of the provinces which he had won from the infidels, and had given the reins of the government of regions unto the hand of his fidelity and had confidence in him, and had left him deputy and viceroy in those countries. But he divested himself of the collar of religion and the robe of Islam, and put on the cloak of infidelity, and became an apostate. The Sultan twisted him from his position by one direct attack, and expelled him broken and discomforted from those limits, and a second time adorned Bahjat Malik with that kingdom, under his own sovereignty. These two great victories, and important affairs, presented a clear demonstration and a cutting proof of the exalted dignity of the Sultan, of his perfect fortunes, of the support of God, and of the aid of heavenly kindness. And thus, beneath the canopy of empire and of victory he turned his face towards Ghazna. "For those grace of God makes to believe whom He will," for God has great grace.

FARID AL DIN ATTAR

Selection of poems
Translated by Kenneth Avery and Ali Alizadeh, 2007

> Farid al Din Attar, also known as Attar of Nishapur (*c.* 1145–*c.* 1220), whom we also encountered in the section devoted to Rabia Balkhi, was a mystic Persian poet whose influence on Sufi thought and Persian poetry was both enormous and enduring. Rumi, who as a boy met the great man in his dotage, considered him one of his poetic masters, along with Sanai. Named after his profession – an *attar* is an apothecary – he doubled up as a perfumist and physician, dashing off verses in between attending to his patients and customers. He wrote beautifully about love, about saints and about man's transcendent relationship with the Divine. In later life, he chucked in his pharmacy and hit the road, travelling widely from Basra and Baghdad to Mecca and Medina, Damascus to India. He was killed by the Mongols during Genghis Khan's annihilating campaign across Central Asia.

Since there is no one to be our companion in Love
the prayer-mat is for the pious; wine-dregs and vice for us.

A place where people's souls turn and twist like polo balls
is not a place for rogues; so what's that got to do with us?

If the wine-bringers of the spirit sit with the devout
their wine is for the ascetics; lees and hangovers for us.

Cure is for the purists, consternation for the broken,
joyfulness for the do-gooders; while grief is our remembrance.

O pretender, you are not here to witness our wealth

as the Beloved extorted all that we owned within us.

Words of experience came from the messenger of truth:
O weary, as you make your way, shed your grief for us.

Attar was absorbed in sorrow along this Path.
Because he's absolutely finished, his solace is with us.

*

My heart's on fire, O wine-bringer.
O wine-bringer, where are you then? Come on!

Come on. The desire to see your face
keeps me among the flames, O wine-bringer.

A plant's survival depends on water.
I have a soul very much like that plant.

Like a dog, when my soul is nourished
it's tamed, it's a life filled with radiance.

Breath stops, life's extinct and heart burns;
nothing's left of either status or pretence.

My self changed colour to life, as if
self was copper and life alchemy.

It brought our death, and turned us from
dust into celestial antimony.

Today is our day, so pour the wine;
the wine of life into the cup of the saints.

Fill the millstone with the eyes' blood
and yourself spin, spin like the millstone.

Sacrifice yourself like Attar and chant:
This is not for me or mine.

*

I got drunk at the tavern last night;
howling, dancing, drinking the wine-dregs.

As my heart's fervour topped the flagon
the fire of my heart brought it to the boil.

The Master of the tavern heard my noise
and said: Enter, cloak-wearing boy!

I told him: Master, how do you know me?
He said: Don't speak of yourself. Be quiet.

Take up the faith of the tavern's swindlers.
Throw off your cloak and your prayer-mat.

Become a gambler, a thug, a dervish;
yell out abuse among the hoodlums.

Shed the ascetics' purity with scorn;
drink the lovers' wine-dregs with pleasure.

Tear the mask of metaphors from your eyes;
take the cotton of reproach out of your ears.

You aren't you while you're at peace with yourself.
Rip down your veil and wrangle with yourself.

The depth of your heart is an endless world.
Face the direction of that world attentively.

Buy Attar's treasure for one hundred souls.
How much would you pay for it, jewel-seller?

*

What's being in Love? Abandoning life;
relating the worlds' secrets without tongue.

Grasping Love entails escaping from self;
learning knowledge, speaking with clarity.

The mysteries of the blood-filled heart
must be spoken through a bloodied vision.

With a tongue soaked in the blood of tears
one's tales must be recounted one by one.

Like a moth at the presence of Love's flame
manifestation speaks of its concealment.

The Lover is like the butterfly who
is willing to speak of departing life.

As the lion escapes from the fire
it reports on the moth's aptitude.

Travel the Path; for how can your words
be loftier than the Seven Heavens?

If you can't travel far learn from the pen;
assuming the Path entails fluent speech.

Take action; because it's better for you
to do than talk about knowing what to do.

Give your soul to the Beloved, Attar.
Why do you keep telling us fairytales?

*

You're of our tradition if you've donned the belt of infidelity;
religion is far away from you and you're laughing at yourself.

If you haven't gone past infidelity, don't fake religion.
You can found faith if you've been razed by infidelity.

Fifty fiends lurk beneath your religious facade
if you don't assume the belt of infidelity.

Every bit of the world is an obstacle along your Path;
overcome them bit by bit if you are a clever person.

I recommend you to burn yourself like wild rue;
to the evil eye you always follow the wild rue.

Stride forth valiantly if you're the lion of the Path;
draw away and hide in a corner if you're afflicted.

O base nature, you only claim as long as you remain
unlike my soul that has risen above the world.

There's nothing in either world to compare with this truth.
You see your own worth when both worlds have ended.

Attar, you're a man of Love; be wiped out from both worlds
so that you build a bridge upon the anchor of your spirit.

SAADI

Selection of poems and stories

Another native of Shiraz, **Saadi** (1210–92) is one of the great Sufi thinkers of his age, a writer of both prose and poetry widely known and revered as 'The Wordsmith' and 'The Master'. He lost his father as a child and later studied Islamic sciences, Persian literature, history and law at the celebrated Nizamiyya University in Baghdad, the capital of the ailing Abbasid Empire – the city, nicknamed the 'Fountainhead of Scholars', was savagely destroyed by Genghis Khan's grandson Hulagu in 1258, during Saadi's lifetime. Footloose, endlessly curious and adventurous, Saadi spent much of his life on the road, travelling as a wandering dervish. Among his greatest works are *Gulistan* (*The Rose Garden*), a collection of lightly delivered, sometimes satirical, moralistic advice in prose, and *Bustan* (*The Orchard*), a compendium in verse of Sufi thinking, proverbs and practical wisdom. Alongside Attar and Hafiz, he is treasured by many Dari-speaking Afghans today. He 'raised the level of language from the soil to the stars', wrote the late Iranian critic Abd al Azim Garakani. 'For elegance and sweetness of language, choiceness and rhetoric of style, and power and range of expression, he is without rival.'

From *Bustan, The Orchard.*
Translated by A. Hart Edwards

On the reason for the writing of the book

I travelled in many regions of the globe and passed the days in the company of many men. I reaped advantages in every corner, and gleaned an ear of corn from every harvest. But I saw none like the pious and devout men of Shiraz – upon which land be the grace of God – my attachment with whom drew away my heart from Syria and Turkey.

I regretted that I should go from the garden of the world empty-handed to my friends, and reflected: "Travellers bring sugar-candy from Egypt as a present to their friends. Although I have no candy, yet have I words that are sweeter. The sugar that I bring is not that which is eaten, but what knowers of truth take away with respect."

When I built this Palace of Wealth, I furnished it with ten doors of instruction.

It was in the year 655 that this famous treasury became full of the pearls of eloquence. A quilted robe of silk, or of Chinese embroidery, must of necessity be padded with cotton; if thou obtain aught of the silk, fret not – be generous and conceal the cotton. I have heard that in the day of Hope and Fear the Merciful One will pardon the evil for the sake of the good. If thou see evil in my words, do thou likewise. If one couplet among a thousand please thee, generously withhold thy faultfinding.

Assuredly, my compositions are esteemed in Persia as the priceless musk of Khutan. Sadi brings roses to the garden with mirth. His verses are like dates encrusted with sugar – when opened, a stone is revealed inside.

*

Story of a man and a thirsty dog

In a desert a man found a dog that was dying from thirst. Using his hat as a bucket, he fetched water from a well and gave it to the helpless animal. The prophet of the time stated that God had forgiven the man his sins because of his kindly act.

Reflect, if thou be a tyrant, and make a profession of benevolence.

He who shows kindness to a dog will not do less towards the good among his fellows.

Be generous to the extent of thy power. If thou hast not dug a well in the desert, at least place a lamp in a shrine.

Charity distributed from an ox's skin that is filled with treasure counts for less than a dinar given from the wages of toil.

Every man's burden is suited to his strength – heavy to the ant is the foot of the locust.

Do good to others so that on the morrow God may not deal harshly with thee.

Be lenient with thy slave, for he may one day become a king, like a pawn that becomes a queen.

*

Subjects are as the root and the king is as the tree,
And the tree, O son, gains strength from the root.

*

Love's secret

Translated by Homa Katouzian

I tried hard to hide the secret of desire
It was not possible to stop burning on fire.
I was alert from the start not to fall in love
All reason faded seeing your face above.
Your mouth told the ears of my soul a story
And now the people's warning is all a story.
You alone can stop the riot by hiding thy face
I cannot bear to turn away my face.
Broken-hearted, if I come to dance and wine
I'd arrive on my feet, but return shoulder-high.
Come to me in peace at night
I have not slept longing for you all night.
You gave me up for nothing, yet I am determined
Not to sell a hair of yours for earth, sky and wind.
I'll describe my pain to someone who is wounded
Telling a healthy person I'd be reprimanded.
Do not say 'Sa'di give up love and passion'
It will be no use since I will not listen.
Entering a desert is better than staying put
Even if I make it not, I'll remain on foot.

From *Gulistan, The Rose Garden*.
Translated by Richard Jeffrey Newman

Story 7

The king couldn't take it anymore. On board the ship with him was a slave who'd never been to sea and whose fear of the vessel's rocking was so great that he wouldn't stop crying no matter what kindness was done for or promised to him. A philosopher who was also on board could see that the king's patience had reached its limit and offered to help the slave be quiet. The king said he would consider this a great favor, and so the wise man ordered some sailors standing nearby to throw the slave into the sea and not to pull him in until they were sure he'd swallowed several mouthfuls of the salty water. Unable to swim, certain he was going to drown, the slave thrashed about in a panic until the philosopher gave the order and the sailors pulled the man by his hair back to the boat. He clung to the stern of the ship, sputtering till he caught his breath, and then climbed onto the deck, where he sat quietly in a corner by himself.

Deeply confused by what he'd just seen, the king asked the philosopher for an explanation. "Once he got a taste of his own drowning," the sage replied, "he understood the safety provided by the boat. No one appreciates the protection he has more than one who loses it."

> You with a full belly, does barley bread
> offend your taste? Do you find my sweetheart
> ugly? Remember that in paradise
> the houris fear purgatory as hell;
> and from hell, purgatory looks like paradise.

Story 10

An Arab king who was notorious for his cruelty came on a pilgrimage to the cathedral mosque of Damascus, where he offered the following prayer, clearly seeking God's assistance in a matter of some urgency:

> "The darvish, poor, owning nothing, the man
> whose money buys him anything he wants,
> here, on this floor, enslaved, we are equals.
> Nonetheless, the man who has the most
> comes before You bearing the greater need."

When the king was done praying, he noticed me immersed in my own prayers at the head of the prophet Yahia's tomb. The monarch turned to me. "I know that God favors you darvishes because you are passionate in your worship and honest in the way you live your lives. I fear a powerful enemy, but if you add your prayers to mine, I am sure that God will protect me for your sake."

"Have mercy on the weak among your own people," I replied, "and no one will be able to defeat you."

> To break each of a poor man's ten fingers
> just because you have the strength offends God.
> Show compassion to those who fall before you,
> and others will extend their hands when you are down.
> The man who plants bad seed hallucinates
> if he expects sweet fruit at harvest time.
> Take the cotton from your ears! Give
> your people justice before justice finds you.
> All men and women are to each other
> the limbs of a single body, each of us
> created from the life God gave to Adam.
> When time's passage withers you to nothing,
> I will grieve as if I'd lost a leg;
> but you, who will not feel another's pain,
> you've lost the right to call yourself human.

In 2005, the Islamic Republic of Iran presented a carpet, handmade by the artist Mohammad Seirafian, to the United Nations in New York. Inscribed within the carpet were the following verses from Saadi's Gulistan *quoted immediately above, presented in a new English translation by Edward Eastwick on an accompanying plaque (and later repeated by the US President Barack Obama).*

All human beings are members of one frame,
Since all, at first, from the same essence came.
When time afflicts a limb with pain,
The other limbs cannot at rest remain.
If thou feel not for other's misery,
A human being is no name for thee.

*

Sweeter than these lips I have not heard anyone speak
Speak, are you sugar itself or your mouth honey?

*

No one can come between us tonight
By the dust I swear not even a particle might.
Stop the coquetry and pride; take off your headdress
Open your cummerbund and let out that cypress.

*

Whatever is produced in haste
goes easily to waste.

RUMI

Selection of poems
Translated by Coleman Barks

Born in the ancient city of Balkh in today's Afghanistan, Maulana Jalal ad Din Mohammed Balkhi (1207–73), better known to the world as **Rumi**, is one of the most famous poets on earth. His verses are just as treasured in English – he is frequently described as the most popular poet in the United States – as in their native Persian. Rumi was a Sufi saint and mystic, a Muslim scholar revered across borders for his lyrical embrace of our common humanity. In recent years his popularity in the English-speaking world has soared to the point where Brad Pitt has a (woefully translated) Rumi verse tattooed across his right bicep and Coldplay's Chris Martin claims a book of Rumi's poetry helped him get through the breakdown of his marriage to Gwyneth Paltrow. Rumi's miraculous posthumous success has been in large part down to the 'translations' of Coleman Barks, an American poet who neither reads nor writes Farsi and who has been accused of erasing Islam from Rumi's work.

Like this

If anyone asks you
how the perfect satisfaction
of all our sexual wanting
will look, lift your face
and say,

Like this.

When someone mentions the gracefulness
of the night sky, climb up on the roof
and dance and say,

Like this.

If anyone wants to know what "spirit" is,
or what "God's fragrance" means,
lean your head toward him or her.
Keep your face there close.

Like this.

When someone quotes the old poetic image
about clouds gradually uncovering the moon,
slowly loosen knot by knot the strings
of your robe.

Like this.

If anyone wonders how Jesus raised the dead,
don't try to explain the miracle.
Kiss me on the lips.

Like this. Like this.

When someone asks what it means
to "die for love," point
here.

If someone asks how tall I am, frown
and measure with your fingers the space
between the creases on your forehead.

This tall.

The soul sometimes leaves the body, then returns.
When someone doesn't believe that,
walk back into my house.

Like this.

When lovers moan,
they're telling our story.

Like this.

I am a sky where spirits live.
Stare into this deepening blue,
while the breeze says a secret.

Like this.

When someone asks what there is to do,
light the candle in his hand.

Like this.

How did Joseph's scent come to Jacob?

Huuuuu.

How did Jacob's sight return?

Huuuu.

A little wind cleans the eyes.

Like this.

When Shams comes back from Tabriz,
he'll put just his head around the edge
of the door to surprise us

Like this.

A moment of happiness

A moment of happiness,
you and I sitting on the verandah,
apparently two, but one in soul, you and I.

We feel the flowing water of life here,
you and I, with the garden's beauty
and the birds singing.
The stars will be watching us,
and we will show them
what it is to be a thin crescent moon.

You and I unselfed, will be together,
indifferent to idle speculation, you and I.

The parrots of heaven will be cracking sugar
as we laugh together, you and I.

In one form upon this earth,
and in another form in a timeless sweet land.

Only Breath

Not Christian or Jew or Muslim, not Hindu
Buddhist, Sufi, or Zen. Not any religion
or cultural system. I am not from the East
or the West, not out of the ocean or up
from the ground, not natural or ethereal, not
composed of elements at all. I do not exist,
am not an entity in this world or in the next,
did not descend from Adam and Eve or any
origin story. My place is placeless, a trace
of the traceless. Neither body or soul.
I belong to the beloved, have seen the two
worlds as one and that one call to and know,
first, last, outer, inner, only that
breath breathing human being.

The Many Wines

God has given us a dark wine so potent that,
drinking it, we leave the two worlds.

God has put into the form of hashish a power
to deliver the taster from self-consciousness.

God has made sleep so that
it erases every thought.

God made Majnun love Layla so much that
just her dog would cause confusion in him.

There are thousands of wines
that can take over our minds.

Don't think all ecstasies
are the same!

Jesus was lost in his love for God.
His donkey was drunk with barley.

Drink from the presence of saints,
not from those other jars.

Every object, every being,
is a jar full of delight.

Be a connoisseur,
and taste with caution.

Any wine will get you high.
Judge like a king, and choose the purest,

the ones unadulterated with fear,
or some urgency about "what's needed."

Drink the wine that moves you
as a camel moves when it's been untied,
and is just ambling about.

Dervish at the Door

A dervish knocked at a house
to ask for a piece of dry bread,
or moist, it didn't matter.
"This is not a bakery," said the owner.
"Might you have a bit of gristle then?"
"Does this look like a butchershop?"
"A little flour?"
"Do you hear a grinding stone?"
"Some water?"
"This is not a well."

Whatever the dervish asked for,
the man made some tired joke
and refused to give him anything.

Finally the dervish ran in the house,
lifted his robe, and squatted
as though to take a shit.

"Hey, hey!"

"Quiet, you sad man. A deserted place
is a fine spot to relieve oneself,
and since there's no living thing here,
or means of living, it needs fertilizing."

The dervish began his own list of questions and answers.

"What kind of bird are you? Not a falcon,
trained for the royal hand. Not a peacock,
painted with everyone's eyes. Not a parrot,

that talks for sugar cubes. Not a nightingale,
that sings like someone in love.

Not a hoopoe bringing messages to Solomon,
or a stork that builds on a cliffside.

What exactly do you do?
You are no known species.
You haggle and make jokes
to keep what you own for yourself.

You have forgotten the One
who doesn't care about ownership,
who doesn't try to turn a profit
from every human exchange."

Five Things to Say

The wakened lover speaks directly to the beloved:

"You are the sky my spirit circles in

The love inside of love, the resurrection-place.

Let this window be your ear.

I have lost consciousness many times

With longing for your listening silence

And your life-quickening smile.

You give attention to the smallest matters

My suspicious doubts, and to the greatest

You know my coins are counterfeit

But you accept them anyway

My impudence and my pretending!

I have five things to say, five fingers to give into your grace.

First, when I was apart from you this world did not exist nor any other.

Second, whatever I was looking for was always you.

Third, why did I ever learn to count to three?

Fourth, my cornfield is burning!

Fifth, this finger stands for Rabia[1] and this is for someone else.

Is there a difference? Are these words or tears? Is weeping speech? What shall I do, my love?"

So he speaks, and everyone around begins to cry with him, laughing crazily moaning in the spreading union of lover and beloved.

This is the true religion. All others are thrown-away bandages beside it.

This is the sema[2] of slavery and mastery of dancing together. This is not-being.

Neither words, nor any natural fact can express this.

I know these dancers day and night I sing their songs in this phenomenal cage

My soul, don't try to answer now! Find a friend, and hide.

But what can stay hidden?
Love's secret is always lifting its head
out from under the covers: "Here I am!"

---

[1] The eighth-century female mystic from Basra
[2] The deep listening of the ecstatic turning performed by Sufi whirling dervishes.

Divan-e Shams

I was dead I came alive I was tears I became smile
The kingdom of love came and I became eternally alive
I have the eye of lion I have the soul of the brave
The courage of a lion, I am Venus shining bright
You do not belong here, said he, you are not insane
I went away, went mad and put myself in chains
You are not drunk, said he, not of this cut
I went and got drunk, drowned myself in delight

THE BOOK OF SER MARCO POLO, THE VENETIAN

Marco Polo

Translated by Sir Henry Yule, 1871

Marco Polo (1254–1324) was never backward in coming forward. Like many narcissists, he habitually referred to himself in the third person. 'There was never any man, neither Christian nor Saracen nor Tartar nor pagan, who has ever explored as much of the world as did Master Marco,' he tells his readers. His 'very distinguished mind' was, in his own words, 'a wonder for all', so much so that, 'this noble youth seemed to have divine rather than human understanding'.

Boasting and bombast aside, here was a world traveller whose extraordinarily quixotic career on the Silk Road and in the service of the Mongol emperor Kublai Khan lent itself to fabulous storytelling. Fact may have been more remarkable than fiction, but that didn't stop Marco making a lot of it up. Purveyor of tall stories to the masses, he was never free from the suspicion that he was a bit of a fabulist. As one entirely plausible legend has it, children used to follow him through the streets of Venice once he had returned from his adventures, shouting, 'Messer Marco, tell us another lie!' By that point in his life, he had amassed such a fortune, most of it in priceless gems showered on him, his father Niccolò and uncle Maffeo by Kublai, that the barbs probably never hurt.

Chapter XXIX

OF THE PROVINCE OF BADASHAN

BADASHAN is a Province inhabited by people who worship Mahommet, and have a peculiar language. It forms a very great kingdom, and the royalty is hereditary. All those of the royal blood are descended from King Alexander and the daughter of King Darius, who was Lord of the vast Empire of Persia. And all these kings call themselves in the Saracen tongue Zulcarniain, which is as much as to say *Alexander;* and this out of regard for Alexander the Great.[1]

It is in this province that those fine and valuable gems the Balas Rubies are found. They are got in certain rocks among the mountains, and in the search for them the people dig great caves underground, just as is done by miners for silver. There is but one special mountain that produces them, and it is called SYGHINAN. The stones are dug on the king's account, and no one else dares dig in that mountain on pain of forfeiture of life as well as goods; nor may any one carry the stones out of the kingdom. But the king amasses them all, and sends them to other kings when he has tribute to render, or when he desires to offer a friendly present; and such only as he pleases he causes to be sold. Thus he acts in order to keep the Balas at a high value; for if he were to allow everybody to dig, they would extract so many that the world would be glutted with them, and they would cease to bear any value. Hence it is that he allows so few to be taken out, and is so strict in the matter.[2]

There is also in the same country another mountain, in which azure is found; 'tis the finest in the world, and is got in a vein like silver. There are also other mountains which contain a great amount of silver ore, so that the country is a very rich one; but it is also (it must be said) a very cold one.[3] It produces numbers of excellent horses, remarkable for their speed. They are not shod at all, although constantly used in mountainous country, and on very bad roads. [They go at a great pace even down steep descents, where other horses neither would nor could do the like. And Messer Marco was told that not long ago they possessed in that province a breed of horses from the strain of Alexander's horse Bucephalus, all of which had from their birth a particular mark on the forehead. This breed was entirely in the hands of an uncle of the king's; and in consequence of his refusing to let the king have any of them, the latter put him to death. The widow then, in spite, destroyed the whole breed, and it is now extinct.[4]]

The mountains of this country also supply Saker falcons of excellent flight, and plenty of Lanners likewise. Beasts and birds for the chase there are in great abundance. Good wheat is grown, and also barley without husk. They have no olive oil, but make oil from sesamé, and also from walnuts.[5]

[In the mountains there are vast numbers of sheep—400, 500, or 600 in a single flock, and all of them wild; and though many of them are taken, they never seem to get aught the scarcer.[6]

Those mountains are so lofty that 'tis a hard day's work, from morning till evening, to get to the top of them. On getting up, you find an extensive plain, with great abundance of grass and trees, and copious springs of pure water running down through rocks and ravines. In those brooks are found trout and many other fish of dainty kinds; and the air in those regions is so pure, and residence there so healthful, that when the men who dwell below in the towns, and in the valleys and plains, find themselves attacked by any kind of fever or other ailment that may hap, they lose no time in going to the hills; and after abiding there two or three days, they quite recover their health through the excellence of that air. And Messer Marco said he had proved this by experience: for when in those parts he had been ill for about a year, but as soon as he was advised to visit that mountain, he did so and got well at once.[7]]

In this kingdom there are many strait and perilous passes, so difficult to force that the people have no fear of invasion. Their towns and villages also are on lofty hills, and in very strong positions.[8] They are excellent archers, and much given to the chase; indeed, most of them are dependent for clothing on the skins of beasts, for stuffs are very dear among them. The great ladies, however, are arrayed in stuffs, and I will tell you the style of their dress! They all wear drawers made of cotton cloth, and into the making of these some will put 60, 80, or even 100 ells of stuff. This they do to make themselves look large in the hips, for the men of those parts think that to be a great beauty in a woman.⁹

NOTE 1.—"The population of Badakhshan Proper is composed of Tajiks, Turks, and Arabs, who are all Sunnis, following the orthodox doctrines of the Mahomedan law, and speak Persian and Turki, whilst the people of the more mountainous tracts are Tajiks of the Shiá creed, having separate provincial dialects or languages of their own, the inhabitants of the principal places combining therewith a knowledge of Persian. Thus, the Shighnáni [sometimes called Shighni] is spoken in Shignán and Roshán, the Ishkáshami in Ishkásham, the Wakhi in Wakhán, the Sanglichì in Sanglich and Zebák, and the Minjáni in Minján. All these dialects materially differ from each other." (Pand. Manphul.) It may be considered almost certain that Badakhshán Proper also had a peculiar dialect in Polo's time. Mr. Shaw speaks of the strong resemblance to Kashmírís of the Badakhshán people whom he had seen.

The Legend of the Alexandrian pedigree of the Kings of Badakhshan is spoken of by Balter, and by earlier Eastern authors. This pedigree is, or was, claimed also by the chiefs of Kaiátegín, Darwáz, Roshán, Shighnán, Wakhán, Chitrál, Gilgít, Swát, and Khapolor in Bálti. Some samples of those genealogies may be seen in that strange document called "Gardiner's Travels."

In Badakhshan Proper the story seems now to have died out. Indeed, though Wood mentions one of the modern family of Mírs as vaunting this descent, these are in fact Sáhibzádáhs of Samarkand, who were invited to the country about the middle of the 17th century, and were in no way connected with the old kings.

The traditional claims to Alexandrian descent were probably due to a genuine memory of the Graeco-Bactrian kingdom, and might have had an origin analogous to the Sultan's claim to be "Caesar of Rome"; for the real ancestry of the oldest dynasties on the Oxus was to be sought rather among the Tochari and Ephthalites than among the Greeks whom they superseded.

The cut on p. 159 presents an interesting memorial of the real relation of Bactria to Greece, as well as of the pretence of the Badakhshan princes to Grecian descent. This silver patera was sold by the family of the Mírs, when captives, to the Minister of the Uzbek chief of Kunduz, and by him to Dr. Percival Lord in 1838. It is now in the India Museum. On the bottom is punched a word or two in Pehlvi, and there is also a word incised in Syriac or Uighúr. It is curious that a pair of paterae were acquired by Dr. Lord under the circumstances stated. The other, similar in material and form, but apparently somewhat larger, is distinctly Sassanian, representing a king spearing a lion.

Zu-'l Ḳantain, "the Two-Horned," is an Arabic epithet of Alexander, with which legends have been connected, but which probably arose from the horned portraits on his coins. [Capus, l.c. p. 121, says, "Iskandr Zoulcarneïn or Alexander le Cornu, horns being the emblem of strength."—H. C.] The term appears in Chaucer (Troil, and Cress. III. 931) in the sense of non plus:—

> "I am, till Clod me letter minde send,
> At dulcamon, right at my wittes end."

And it is said to have still colloquial existence in that sense in some corners of England. This use is said to have arisen from the Arabic application of the term (*Bicorne*) to the 47th Proposition of Euclid. (Baber, 13; N. et E. XIV. 490; N. An. des V. xxvi. 296; Burnes, III. 186 seqq.; Wood, 155, 244; J. A. S. B. XXII. 300; Ayeen Akbery, II. 185; see N. and Q. 1st Series, vol. v.)

NOTE 2.—I have adopted in the text for the name of the country that one of the several forms in the G. Text which comes nearest to the correct name, viz. *Badascian*. But *Balacian* also appears both in that and in Pauthier's text. This represents *Balakhshán*, a form also sometimes used in the East. Hayton has *Balaxcen*, Clavijo *Balaxia*, the Catalan Map *Baldassia*. From the form *Balakhsh* the Balas Ruby got its name. As Ibn Batuta says: "The Mountains of Badakhshan have given their name to the Badakhshi Ruby, vulgarly called *Al Balaksh*." Albertus Magnus says the *Balagius* is the female of the Carbuncle or Ruby Proper, "and some say it is his house, and hath thereby got the name, quasi *Palatium* Carbunculi!" The Balais or Balas Ruby is, like the Spinel, a kind inferior to the real Ruby of Ava. The author of the *Masálak al Absár* says the finest Balas ever seen in the Arab countries was one presented to Malek 'Adil Ketboga, at Damascus; it was of a triangular form and weighed 50 drachms. The prices of *Balasci* in Europe in that age may be found in Pegolotti, but the needful problems are hard to solve.

> "No sapphire in Inde, no Rubie rich of price,
> There lacked than, nor Emeraud so grene,
> *Balès*, Turkès, ne thing to my device."
> (*Chaucer, 'Court of Love.'*)

> "L'altra letizia, che m'era già nota,
> Preclara cosa mi si fecc in vista,
> Qual fin *balascio* in che lo Sol percuoto."
> (*Paradiso*, ix. 67.)

Some account of the Balakhsh from Oriental sources will be found in *J. As.* sér. V. tom. xi. 109.

(*I. B.* III. 59, 394; *Alb. Mag. de Mineralibus; Pegol.* p. 307; *N. et E.* XIII. i. 246.)

["The Mohammedan authors of the Mongol period mention Badakhshan several times in connection with the political and military events of that period. Guchluk, the 'gurkhan of Karakhitai,' was slain in Badakhshan in 1218 (*d'Ohsson*, I. 272). In 1221, the Mongols invaded the country (*l.c.* I. 272). On the same page, d'Ohsson translates a short account of Badakhshan by Yakut (+ 1229), stating that this mountainous country is famed for its precious stones, and especially rubies, called *Balakhsh*." (Bretschneider, *Med. Res.* II. p. 66.)—H. C.]

The account of the royal monopoly in working the mines, etc., has continued accurate down to our own day. When Murad Beg of Kunduz conquered Badakhshan some forty years ago, in disgust at the small produce of the mines, he abandoned working them, and sold nearly all the population of the place into slavery! They continue still unworked, unless clandestinely. In 1866 the reigning Mír had one of them opened at the request of Pandit Manphul, but without much result.

The locality of the mines is on the right bank of the Oxus, in the district of Ish Káshm and on the borders of Shignan, the *Syghinan* of the text. (*P. Manph.*; *Wood*, 206; *N. Ann. des. V.* xxvi. 300.)

[The ruby mines are really in the Gháran country, which extends along both banks of the Oxus. Barshar is one of the deserted villages; the boundary between Gháren and Shignán is the Kuguz Parin (in Shighai dialect means "holes in the rock"); the Persian equivalent is "Rafak-i-Somakh." (Cf. Captain Trotter, *Forsyth's Mission*, p. 277.)—H. C.]

NOTE 3.—The mines of *Ládjwurd* (whence *l'Azur* and *Lazuli*) have been, like the Ruby mines, celebrated for ages. They lie in the Upper Valley of the Kokcha, called Korán, within the Tract called *Yamgán*, of which the popular etymology is *Hamah-Kán*, or "All-Mines," and were visited by Wood in 1838. The produce now is said to be of very inferior quality, and in quantity from 30 to 60 *poods* (36 lbs each) annually. The best quality sells at Bokhara at 30 to 60 tillas, or 12*l*. to 24*l*. the pood (*Manphúl*). Surely it is ominous when a British agent writing of Badakhshan products finds it natural to express weights in Russian poods!

The Yamgán Tract also contains mines of iron, lead, alum, salammoniac, sulphur, ochre, and copper. The last are not worked. But I do not learn of any silver mines nearer than those of Paryrfn in the Valley of Panjshir, south of the crest of the Hindu-Kúsh, much worked in the early Middle Ages. (See *Caihay*, p. 595.)

NOTE 4.—The Kataghan breed of horses from Badakhshan and Kunduz has still a high reputation. They do not often reach India, as the breed is a favourite one among the Afghan chiefs, and the horses are likely to be appropriated in transit. (*Lumsden, Mission to Kandahar*, p. 20.)

[The Kirghiz between the Yangi Hissar River and Sirikol are the only people using the horse generally in the plough, oxen being employed in the plains, and yaks in Sirikol. (Lieutenant-Colonel Gordon, p. 222, *Forsyth's Mission.*)—H. C.]

What Polo heard of the Bucephalid strain was perhaps but another form of a story told by the Chinese, many centuries earlier, when speaking of this same region. A certain cave was frequented by a wonderful stallion of supernatural origin. Hither the people yearly brought their mares, and a famous breed was derived from the foals. (*Rém. N. Mél. As.* I. 245.)

NOTE 5.—The huskless barley of the text is thus mentioned by Burnes in the vicinity of the Hindu-Kush: "They rear a barley in this elevated country which has no husk, and grows like wheat; but it is barley." It is not properly *huskless*, but when ripe it bursts the husk and remains so loosely attached as to be dislodged from it by a slight shake. It is grown abundantly in Ladak and the adjoining Hill States. Moorcroft details six varieties of it cultivated there. The kind mentioned by Marco and Burnes is probably that named by Royle *Hordeum Ægiceras*, and which has been sent to England under the name of Tartarian Wheat, though it is a genuine barley. Naked barley is mentioned by Galen as grown in Cappadocia; and Matthioli speaks of it as grown in France in his day (middle of 16th century). It is also known to the Arabs, for they have a name for it—*Sult*. [*Burnes*, III. 205; *Moore*. II. 148 *seqq.*; *Galen, de Aliment. Facult.* Lat. ed. 13; *Matthioli*, Ven. 1585, p. 420; *Eng. Cyc.*, art. Hordeum.)

Sesamé is mentioned by P. Manphul as one of the products of Badakhshan; linseed is another, which is also used for oil. Walnut-trees abound, but neither he nor Wood mention the oil. We know that walnut oil is largely manufactured in Kashmir. (*Moorcroft*, II. 148.)

[See on Saker and Lanner Falcons (*F. Sakar*, Briss.; *F. lanarius*, Schlegel) the valuable paper by Edouard Blanc, *Sur l'utilisation des Oiseaux de proie en Asie centrale* in *Rev. des Sciences natur. appliquées*, 20th June, 1895.

"Hawking is the favourite sport of Central Asian Lords," says G. Capus. (*A trouers le royaume de Tamerlan*, p. 132. Sec pp. 132-134.)

The Mirza says (*l.c.* p. 157) that the mountains of Wakhán "are only noted for producing a breed of hawks or falcons which the hardy Wâkhânis manage to catch among the cliffs. These hawks are much esteemed by the chiefs of Badakhshan, Bokhara, etc. They are celebrated for their swiftness, and known by their white colour."—H. C.]

Note 6.—These wild sheep are probably the kind called *Kachkár*, mentioned by Baber, and described by Mr. Blyth in his Monograph of Wild Sheep, under the name of *Ovis Vignei*. It is extensively diffused over all the ramifications of Hindu-Kúsh, and westward perhaps to the Persian Elburz. "It is gregarious," says Wood, "congregating in herds of *several hundreds.*" In a later chapter Polo speaks of a wild sheep apparently different and greater. (See *J. A. S. B. X.* 858 *seqq.*)

Note 7.—This pleasant passage is only in Ramusio, but it would be heresy to doubt its genuine character. Marco's recollection of the delight of convalescence in such a climate seems to lend an unusual enthusiasm and felicity to his description of the scenery. Such a region as he speaks of is probably the cool Plateau of Shewá, of which we are told as extending about 25 miles eastward from near Faizabad, and forming one of the finest pastures in Badakhshan. It contains a large lake called by the frequent name Sar-i-Kol. No European traveller in modern times (unless Mr. Gardner) has been on those glorious table-lands. Burnes says that at Kunduz both natives and foreigners spoke rapturously of the vales of Badakhshan, its rivulets, romantic scenes and glens, its fruits, flowers, and nightingales. Wood is reticent on scenery, naturally, since nearly all his journey was made in winter. When approaching Faizabad on his return from the Upper Oxus, however, he says: "On entering the beautiful lawn at the gorge of its valley I was enchanted at the quiet loveliness of the scene. Up to this time, from the day we left Talikan, we had been moving in snow; but now it had nearly vanished from the valley, and the fine sward was enamelled with crocuses, daffodils, and snowdrops." (*P. Manphul*; *Burnes*, III. 176; *Wood*, 252.)

NOTE 8.—Yet scarcely any country in the world has suffered so terribly and repeatedly from invasion. "Enduring decay probably commenced with the wars of Chinghiz, for many an instance in Eastern history shows the permanent effect of such devastations. . . . Century after century saw only progress in decay. Even to our own time the progress of depopulation and deterioration has continued." In 1759, two of the Khojas of Kashgar, escaping from the dominant Chinese, took refuge in Badakhshan; one died of his wounds, the other was treacherously slain by Sultan Shah, who then ruled the country. The holy man is said in his dying moments to have invoked curses on Badakhshan, and prayed that it might be three times depopulated; a malediction which found ample accomplishment. The misery of the country came to a climax about 1S30, when the Uzbek chief of Kunduz, Murad Beg Kataghan, swept away the bulk of the inhabitants, and set them down to die in the marshy plains of Kunduz. (*Cathay*, p. 542; *Faiz Bakhsh*, etc.)

NOTE 9.—This "bombasticall dissimulation of their garments," as the author of *Anthropometamorphosis* calls such a fashion, is on longer affected by the ladies of Badakhshan. But a friend in the Panjab observes that it still survives *there*. "There are ladies' trousers here which might almost justify Marco's very liberal estimate of the quantity of stuff required to make them;" and among the Afghan ladies, Dr. Bellew says, the silken trousers almost surpass crinoline in amplitude. It is curious to find the same characteristic attaching to female figures on coins of ancient kings of these regions, such as Agathocles and Pantaleon. (The last name is appropriate!)

Chapter XXX

OF THE PROVINCE OF PASHAI

You must know that ten days' journey to the south of Badashan there is a Province called Pashai, the people of which have a peculiar language, and are Idolaters, of a brown complexion. They are great adepts in sorceries and the diabolic arts. The men wear earrings and brooches of gold and silver set with stones and pearls. They are a pestilent people and a crafty; and they live upon flesh and rice. Their country is very hot.[1]

NOTE 1.—The name of Pashai has already occurred (sec ch. xviii.) linked with Dir, as indicating a tract, apparently of very rugged and difficult character, through which the partizan leader Nigúdar passed in making an incursion from Badakhshan towards Káshmir. The difficulty here lies in the name *Pashai*, which points to the south-west, whilst *Dir* and all other indications point to the south-east. But Pashai seems to me the reading to which all texts tend, whilst it is clearly expressed in the G. T. (*Pasciai*), and it is contrary to all my experience of the interpretation of Marco Polo to attempt to torture the name in the way which has been common with commentators professed and occasional. But dropping this name for a moment, let us see to what the other indications do point.

In the meagre statements of this and the next chapter, interposed as they are among chapters of detail unusually ample for Polo, there is nothing to lead us to suppose that the Traveller ever personally visited the countries of which these two chapters treat. I believe we have here merely an amplification of the information already sketched of the country penetrated by the Nigudarian bands whose escapade is related in chapter xviii., information which was probably derived from a Mongol source. And these countries are in my belief *both* regions famous in the legends of the Northern Buddhists, viz. Udyána and Káshmir.

Udyána lay to the north of Peshawar on the Swát River, but from the extent assigned to it by Hiuen Tsang, the name probably covered a large part of the whole hill-region south of the Hindu-Kúsh from Chitrál to the Indus, as indeed it is represented in the Map of Vivien de St. Martin (*Pèlerins Bouddhistes*, II.). It is regarded by Fahian as the most northerly Province of India, and in his time the food and clothing of the people were similar to those of Gangetic India. It was the native country of Padma Sambhava, one of the chief apostles of Lamaism, *i.e.* of Tibetan Buddhism, and a great master of enchantments. The doctrines of Sakya, as they prevailed in Udyána in old times, were probably strongly tinged with Sivaitic magic.

THE TRAVELS OF IBN BATTUTA

Ibn Battuta

Translated by Samuel Lee, 1829

> Irrepressible, indefatigable, unputdownable, **Ibn Battuta** (1304–69) was the greatest 'Traveller of Islam', a footloose Moroccan who spent twenty-nine years on the road, notching up a staggering 75,000 miles across the world – by camel, mule and horse, by junk, dhow and raft, on foot when he had to. He sired unknown numbers of children with unknown numbers of wives on several continents, dined with emperors, sultans and khans, crossed deserts, escaped from pirates, dodged the Black Death, dabbled in judicial work and lived to write his monumental tale: *The Precious Gift of Lookers into the Marvels of Cities and Wonders of Travel*. He took a dim view of the Afghans.

I next proceeded to ^{p}Kundus and Baghlān, which are villages with cultivated lands adjoining each other. In each of these is a cell for the sainted and recluse. The land is green and flourishing, and its grass never withers. In these places I remained for some time for the purpose of pasturing and refreshing my beasts.

After this I proceeded to the city of ^{q}Barwan,† in the road to which is a high mountain, covered with snow and exceedingly cold; they call it the ^{T}Hindū Kush,‡ *i. e.* Hindoo-slayer, because most of the slaves brought thither from India die on account of the intenseness of the cold. After this

---

† Perhaps the *Budaoon* of Dow (vol. i. p. 157) and the *Budaoon* of Ferishta.

‡ This Mr. Burckhardt gives in his abstract of these Travels in Nubia, p. 535, *Hindwaksh*, where he has not only disregarded the vowels given in the MSS., but has shewn that he must have been an entire stranger to the Persian language, as accurately given and translated here by our traveller.

we passed another mountain, which is called *s* Bashāi. In this mountain there is a cell inhabited by an old man, whom they call *t* Atā Evliā, that is, the Father of the Saints. It is said that he is three hundred and fifty years old. When I saw him he appeared to be about fifty years old. The people of these parts, however, very much love and revere him. I looked at his body: it was moist, and I never saw one more soft. He told me, that every hundredth year he had a new growth of hair and teeth, independently of the first, and that he was the Raja *u* Aba Rahim Ratan of India, who had been buried at *x* Multān,* in the province of Sindia. I asked him of several things; but very much doubted as to what he was, and do so still.

I next arrived at the city of Barwan. In this place I met the Turkish Emīr *y* Barantay, the largest and fattest man I had ever seen. He treated me very respectfully, and gave me some provisions. I then went on to the village of *z* El Jarkh, and thence to *a* Ghizna, the city of the warrior of the faith, and against India, the victorious Mahmūd, son of *b* Subuktagīn.† His grave is here. The place is exceedingly cold: it is ten (al. three) stages distant from *c* Kandahār. It was once a large city; but is now mostly in ruins. I then went on to *d* Kābul, which was once a large city; but is now, for the most part, in ruins. It is inhabited by a people from Persia whom they call the *e* Afghāns.‡ Their mountains are difficult of access, having narrow

---

* See a note on this place in Mr. Kosegarten, p. 27.

† An abridgment of Ferishta's reign of Mahmood will be found in Dow's *Hindostan*, vol. i. p. 52, &c.

‡ These people, according to their own statements, are descended from the house of Israel, and of the family of Saul the first Israelitish king. Ibn Shah Aālam of the tribe of Kot'h Khail, author of the Kholāsut El Ansāb, himself an Afghān, and a most sedulous enquirer, as he tells us, into their history, gravely affirms, that nothing can be more certain than that this is their origin. He then goes on to say, that they originally resided on Solomon's mount in Syria; but upon some emergency migrated to Candahār, whence many of them made their way into Hindustan, and were of considerable use in assisting Mahmūd of Ghizna, to make his first conquest in that country. He also tells us, that his ancestors, hearing in Candahār of the teaching of Mohammed, sent a deputation to him into Arabia, to inquire whether he was or not, the last Prophet mentioned in the law and the gospels; and that, upon being assured of this, the whole nation at once received the faith. If there were the least possible approximation to truth in the story of their descent, it is reasonable to suppose, that their language

passes. These are a powerful and violent people; and the greater part of them highway robbers. Their largest mountain is called the mountain of Solomon. It is said that when Solomon had ascended this mountain, and was approaching India from it, and saw that it was an oppressive country, he returned refusing to enter it. The mountain was therefore called after his name: upon this the king of the Afghāns resides.

We next left Kābul by the way of ᶻ Kirmāsh which is a narrow pass situated between two mountains, in which the Afghāns commit their robberies. We, thank God, escaped by plying them with arrows upon the heights, throughout the whole of the way.

We then passed over the Gihon into Khorāsān; and, after a journey of a day and half over a sandy desert in which there was no house, we arrived at the city of ʳ Balkh,† which now lies in ruins. It has not been rebuilt since its destruction by the cursed Jengiz Khān. The situation of its buildings is not very discernible, although its extent may be traced. It is now in ruins, and without society.

Its mosque was one of the largest and handsomest in the world. Its pillars were incomparable: three of which were destroyed by Jengiz Khān, because it had been told him, that the wealth of the mosque lay concealed under them, provided as a fund for its repairs. When, however, he had destroyed them, nothing of the kind was to be found; the rest, therefore, he left as they were.

---

would either be pure Hebrew, or a dialect very nearly approaching it: but the truth is, as far as I can learn, that nothing like this is the fact: but quite the contrary. This boasted descent is, therefore, a fable; as very probably their early attachment to the faith of Mohammed is. Some, indeed, have been credulous enough to believe this story of descent; and thence to imagine, that in them they had discovered the ten tribes of the house of Israel; which, however, is more than the Afghāns themselves imagine. That part of all the twelve tribes of Israel returned from the captivity, except such has had become real heathens, the New Testament will not allow us for a moment to doubt. I do not, therefore, see the least probability of finding them either in Candahār or elsewhere. Some part of the modern history of the Afghāns may probably be true.

† A well known city in Khorāsān, famous in history and for its wealth: between this place and Tirmidh is a distance of twelve farsangs.

The story about this treasure arose from the following circumstance. It is said, that one of the Califs of the house of Abbās was very much enraged at the inhabitants of Balkh, on account of some accident which had happened, and, on this account, sent a person to collect a heavy fine from them. Upon this occasion, the women and children of the city betook themselves to the wife of their then governor, who, out of her own money, built this mosque; and to her they made a grievous complaint. She accordingly sent to the officer, who had been commissioned to collect the fine, a robe very richly embroidered and adorned with jewels, much greater in value than the amount of the fine imposed. This, she requested might be sent to the Calif as a present from herself, to be accepted instead of the fine. The officer accordingly took the robe, and sent it to the Calif; who, when he saw it, was surprised at her liberality, and said: This woman must not be allowed to exceed myself in generosity. He then sent back the robe, and remitted the fine. When the robe was returned to her, she asked, whether a look of the Calif had fallen upon it; and being told that it had, she replied: No robe shall ever come upon me, upon which the look of any man, except my own husband, has fallen. She then ordered it to be cut up and sold; and with the price of it she built the mosque, with the cell and structure in the front of it. Still, from the price of the robe there remained a third, which she commanded to be buried under one of its pillars, in order to meet any future expenses which might be necessary for its repairs. Upon Jengiz Khān's hearing this story, he ordered these pillars to be destroyed; but, as already remarked, he found nothing.

HAFIZ
Selection of Poems

A giant of Persian poetry, **Hafiz** (c. 1325–90) has counted the most eclectic range of luminaries among his legions of foreign admirers, from Johann Wolfgang von Goethe, Friedrich Nietzsche and Johannes Brahms to Ralph Waldo Emerson, Sir Arthur Conan Doyle and Queen Victoria. While little is known of his life, he memorised the Quran at an early age, earning the title of *hafiz* – which he later chose as his nom de plume – for this distinction. A master of lyric poetry and mystical verse, he was a court poet in his home city of Shiraz before falling out of favour with the authorities later in life. His *ghazals*, lyric poems of up to fifteen couplets, are considered unparalleled in Persian poetry. His sixteenth-century successor, the poet Jami, considered them 'downright miraculous'.

Persian by birth, Hafiz enjoys a popularity and status worlds beyond that country's borders. In his original language he speaks to all Dari-speaking Afghans and was a particular favourite, among many others, of the late guerrilla commander Ahmed Shah Massoud (1953–2001). As the translator Stephen Hirtenstein has written: 'To be educated, in the eyes of a Persian or an Afghan, even today, is to have a copy of Hafiz's poems on the shelf (and know many of them by heart).'

Someone Should Start Laughing
Translated by Daniel Ladinsky

I have a thousand brilliant lies
For the question:
How are you?

I have a thousand brilliant lies
For the question:

What is God?

If you think that the Truth can be known
From words,

If you think that the Sun and the Ocean

Can pass through that tiny opening Called the mouth,

O someone should start laughing!
Someone should start wildly Laughing 'Now!

*

The Great Secret
Translated by Daniel Ladinsky

God was full of Wine last night,
So full of wine
That He let a great secret slip.
He said:

There is no man on earth
Who needs a pardon from Me –

For there is really no such thing,
No such thing
As Sin!

That Beloved has gone completely Wild – He has poured Himself into me!

I am Blissful and Drunk and Overflowing.

Dear world,
Draw life from my Sweet Body,

Dear wayfaring souls,
Come drink your fill of liquid rubies,

For God has made my heart
An Eternal Fountain!

The following poem is translated by Dick Davis.

My friend, hold back your heart from enemies,
Drink shining wine with handsome friends like these;
With art's initiates undo your collar –
Stay buttoned up with ignoramuses.

*

Last Night She Brought Me Wine, and Sat Beside my Pillow

Translated by Dick Davis

Her hair hung loose, her dress was torn, her face perspired –
She smiled and sang of love, with mischief in her eyes,
And whispering in my ear, she drunkenly inquired:

"My ancient lover, can it be that you're asleep?
The true initiate, when offered wine at night,
Would be a heretic of love if he refused
To take the draught he's given, and drink it with delight."

And as for you, you hypocrites, don't cavil at
Lovers who drain life to the lees, since we were given
This nature when the world began, and we must drink
The wine that's poured for us, whether from earth or heaven.

So take the laughing wine cup, raise it in your hand,
Caress your lover's curls, and say Hafiz has spoken;
How many vows of abstinence the world has seen
So fervently affirmed, and – like Hafiz's – broken.

Sweet Lips and Silver Ears
Translated by Dick Davis

Sweet lips and silver ears – that idol's elegance
Has snatched away my fortitude, and my good sense;

So lovely, lithe, and lively, such a fairy face,
That Turk in his cute cloak, all wiles and nonchalance –

And I'm so mad about him, so on fire for him,
I'm like a cooking cauldron's seething turbulence,

But I'll calm down when I can grab that cloak from him
And be the shirt that covers up his impudence.

And when my bones are rotting, still my soul will not
Forget his kindness to me, his benevolence.

His chest and shoulders, chest and shoulders, bore away
My faith and heart, my faith and heart – I'd no defense!

So here's your medicine, Hafiz, here's your medicine now –
Sweet lips, sweet lips, sweet lips are your deliverance!

Translated by Richard Jeffrey Newman

Call me and I will come.
From between the bars
of earth's closed cage,
a bird of heaven,
I will come.

Like rain for the earth,
bless me. Before the wind
puts my dust
beyond the reach of your hand,
touch me,
and I will come.

…

To the fragrance of your presence,
dancing I will rise,
clapping I will come to you
with a rhythm of joy.

*

Where is my Ruined Life?
Translated by Gertrude Bell

Where is my ruined life, and where the fame
Of noble deeds?
Look on my long-drawn road, and whence it came,
And where it leads!

Can drunkenness be linked to piety
And good repute?
Where is the preacher's holy monody,
Where is the lute?

From monkish cell and lying garb released,
Oh heart of mine,
Where is the Tavern fane, the Tavern priest,
Where is the wine?

Past days of meeting, let the memory
Of you be sweet!
Where are those glances fled, and where for me
Reproaches meet?

His friend's bright face warms not the enemy
When love is done–
Where is the extinguished lamp that made night day,
Where is the sun?

Balm to mine eyes the dust, my head I bow
Upon thy stair.

Where shall I go, where from thy presence? thou
Art everywhere.

Look not upon the dimple of her chin,
Danger lurks there!
Where wilt thou hide, oh trembling heart, fleeing in
Such mad haste – where?

To steadfastness and patience, friend, ask not
If Hafiz keep–
Patience and steadfastness I have forgot,
And where is sleep?

THE HISTORY OF TIMUR-BEC
KNOWN BY THE NAME OF TAMERLAIN THE GREAT, EMPEROR OF THE MOGULS AND TARTARS

Sharaf al Din Ali Yazdi

English translation published by J. Darby, 1723, based on a French translation by François Pétis de la Croix

In the fourteenth century, one man seized Central Asia, Asia Minor and much of the Middle East by the scruff of its neck and wreaked bloody havoc. His name was Timur, better known in the West as Tamerlane, and he was one of the world's greatest ever conquerors alongside Alexander the Great and Genghis Khan. From 1370 until his death in 1405 he was undefeated in battle, constantly campaigning with his Tatar hordes who won him glittering prizes from Antioch to Aleppo, Balkh to Baghdad.

His astonishing career of conquest, bloodshed and slaughter on a continental scale was closely chronicled by the fifteenth-century Persian court historian and panegyrist – today we might call him a toady – **Sharaf al Din Ali Yazdi** (d. 1454), who here describes Timur's whirlwind conquest of Afghanistan, en route to sack Delhi in 1398.

Chapter III

Timur marches against the inhabitants of Ketuer. He defeats the Siapouches, who were cloth'd in black.

Whilst Timur was encamp'd at Enderabe, the inhabitants came to cast themselves at his feet, to complain of the insults and troubles they reciev'd from the idolaters of Ketuer,[1] and from the Siapouches[2]: they represented to him that there were a great number of Musulmans, from whom the infidels exacted every year excessive sums of money, under the name of tribute and Carage; which if they fail'd to pay punctually, they kill'd their men, and made their women and children slaves.

The emperor touch'd with their complaints, and excited by zeal for the religion of which he was protector and defender, march'd immediately against these tyrants: he chose three soldiers out of every ten, and left the Mirza Charoc to command the rest of the army and the baggage at Gounandictoun,[3] where they ordinarily passed the summer. Timur decamp'd twice a day, and march'd with so much diligence, that he made two days journey in one.

He soon arrived at Perjan,[4] whence he sent Mirza Rousem, accompanied by Burhan Aglen, and other Emirs, with ten thousand men towards the left, to seek the Siapouches; and following his road, he arriv'd at Caouc,[5] where he found a demolish'd citadel, which he caus'd to be rebuilt. Many Emirs and soldiers left some of their horses at Caouc, and ascended on foot the mountain of Ketuer, where tho the sun was in Gemini, the snow lay in so great abundance, that the feet of most part of the horses, which the lords wou'd have carry'd up, fail'd 'em; yet some of 'em were spur'd on so much during the night and the forst, that they were constrained to get up: but day being come, and the snow turn'd into ice, they kept these horses under felts till evening, when they continu'd to ascend the mountain, so that at length they arriv'd at the top, and then sent for the rest of the horses. And as the infidels dwelt in narrow passages and precipices, and there was no road to get to them,

---

[1] A mountain of Bedakchan inhabited by idolaters, long.115.lat.36.

[2] An idolatrous nation cloth'd in black, inhabiting the mountains S. of the province of Bedakchan.

[3] A cool place in the mountain near Enderabe.

[4] A town in the provience of Bedakchan, two days journey from Enderabe near the Siapouches.

[5] A town at the foot of the mountain of Ketuer, long.115.lat.36.

besides what was cover'd with snow; some of the Emirs and soldiers descended by cords, while others lying on the snow, slid down to the bottom. They made a sort of raft for Timur, to which they fasten'd rings, that they might tie cords to it of one hundred and fifty cubits in length: he sat upon it, while many persons let him down from the top to the bottom of the mountain, as far as the cords wou'd reach. Others dug with pickaxes in the snow a place where he might stand firm. They who were on the top having gently descended, they let down Timur again in the machine. The place also was mark'd out where he shou'd stay next; and so on till the fifth time, when he arriv'd at the foot of the mountain. Then this monarch took a staff in his hand to rest on, and walk'd on foot a great way. These fatigues did not deter him, because of his confidence in the merit of the Gazie, which always increas'd his ardent zeal for the most difficult enterprizes. Those who work for God may rest assur'd of success. They also let down some of the emperor's horses, girding 'em about the belly and neck, with great precaution; but most of 'em thro the fault of the guides fell headlong down, so that there remain'd but two fit for service. Then Timur took horse, and all the army follow'd on foot.

The infidels of this country are strong men, and as large as the giants of the people of Aad;[6] they go all naked; their kings are nam'd Oda and Odachouh: they have a particular language,[7] which is neither Persian nor Turkish, nor Indian; and know no other than this: and if it was not for the inhabitants of the neighbouring places, who are found there by chance, and having learnt their language, serve for interpreters, no one would be able to understand 'em.

These infidels were in a citadel, at the foot of whose walls passes a great river; and on the other side of this river there was a high mountain. As they had learnt the approach of Timur twenty-four hours before his arrival, they abandon'd this post, cross'd the river, and carry'd their effects to the top of this mountain, imagining it inaccessible, especially with the intrenchments they had made there.

---

[6] Arabians in the time of Nimrod.

[7] The language of the people of Ketuer was heretofore unknown.

When the army after long fatigues arriv'd at the citadel, they found nothing there but some sheep the enemy had left, which they made themselves masters of: then having set fire to the houses, they immediately cross'd the river. The emperor order'd 'em to ascend the mountain by many narrow passages; which our soldiers did, and at the same time return'd thanks to God.

Sheik Arsan, at the head of the vanguard of the left wing,[8] attack'd the foremost of the enemies, and made himself master of a rising ground. They were also attack'd by Ali Sultan Tavachi, who came down into the place where they were encamp'd. A colonel nam'd Chamelic signaliz'd himself by many great actions; and fourteen of our bravest soldiers fell from the top of the mountain to the bottom, and were kill'd. Mobacher also behav'd himself gallantly. Mengheli Coja advanc'd at the head of his company, and gain'd the top of the mountain. Sevindgic Behader did all that cou'd be expected from the greatest valor. Cheik Ali Saliberi advanc'd as far as the ridge of the mountain with all his soldiers; he attack'd the enemy and got possession of their post. Mouffa Recmal and the Emir Hussein Courtchi behav'd themselves with the utmost resolution; and at length all the Emirs of the Hezares and Couchons attack'd the infidels on all sides in the most dangerous places. The enemy defended themselves vigorously, notwithstanding the great slaughter of their men. The fight lasted three nights with unheard-of obstinancy: but at length these unfortunate men finding themselves no longer able to make resistance, beg'd quarter with tears in their eyes. Timur sent to 'em Ac Sultan Kechi, with order to tell them that if they wou'd come to him with submission and obedience, abandon their errors, and take up a resolution to acknowledge but one God, and embrace the mahometan religion with sincerity, he wou'd not only give 'em their lives and effects, but also leave 'em to enjoy their principality as before. They had no sooner learnt this from an interpreter, than the fourth day they came to cast themselves at the feet of the emperor, conducted by Ac Sultant Kechi: they abjur'd their idolatry, and embrac'd the mahometan religion, promising to submit

---

[8] The Tartars have a vanguard to each wing, which they call Cambol.

entirely to the emperor, and obey all his commands. Timur, according to his wonted generosity, gave them clothes, and sent them away, after having encourag'd 'em by the most affectionate speeches.

Night being come, these wretches, whose hearts were more black than their garments, fell upon the regiment of Chamelic, and put all the soldiers of it to the sword, except a few, who, tho wounded and lame, escap'd their hands.

As soon as this treason was discover'd, our men flew near one hundred and fifty of 'em. All the army got up upon the mountain, and following the precept of Mahomet, who orders the women to be spar'd they put to the sword all the old and young men of these infidels, and carry'd away their women and children. At length they built towers on the top of the mountain and the end of the bridge, with the heads of these traitors, who had never bow'd their head to adore the true God. Timur order'd to be engrav'd upon marble the history of this action, which happen'd in the month of Ramadan in the year of the Hegira 800; and he added the particular Epocha which this people us'd, that their prosperity might have some knowledge of the famous valor of the ever-victorious Timur. This pillar so inscrib'd gave the greater pleasure to Timur, in that these people had never been conquer'd by any prince in the world, not even by Alexander the Great.

HABIB AL SIYAR

Khwandamir

Translated by W. M. Thackston, 1994

Khwandamir (1475/6–1535/6) was not your average historian. The Persian scholar, whose life and career spanned both Timurid and Safavid eras, had a front-row seat during a number of the landmark moments he later wrote about. He was an ambassador to the Uzbek ruler Mohammed Shaybani when this strongman took Herat in 1507 and was an eyewitness to the fall of the city to Shah Ismail I three years later as the founder of the Safavid dynasty put the finishing touches to a decade of bloody campaigning, reuniting Iran for the first time since the Arab Conquests of the seventh century and thereby ending 850 years of rule by Arab caliphs, Turkish sultans and Mongol khans. Ismail had the body of his adversary Mohammed Shaybani dismembered, his skull set into gold and fashioned into the ultimate warrior-trophy, a gem-studded drinking vessel sent to Babur as a gesture of goodwill and a reminder, if one were needed, that there was a new Muslim power to be reckoned with.

Khwandamir's universal history remains the best known of his many works. It includes a vivid retelling of the Mongol warlord Genghis Khan's sacking of Herat in 1222.

The Battle of Herat

All historians have reported that when Tolui had devastated Nishapur, he set out for Herat. After crossing the distances he camped in the Mashartu meadow and sent an envoy named Zambur to the leaders of the city with a message that the king, *cadi*, *khatib*, and famous men must come out to greet him so that they might bask in the sun of imperial favor, secure from untoward events. When Malik Shamsuddin Muhammad Jurjani, Sultan Jalaluddin's governor in Herat at that time, heard Zambur's message, he killed him in a fit of rage, saying, "May the day never dawn that I submit to infidels."

When the news of Zambur's murder spread in Tolui's camp, the Mongols swarmed out enraged and, at Tolui Khan's command, surrounded the city, killing everyone they encountered. Malik Shamsuddin Muhammad had readied himself for battle, and for seven days great valor was displayed on both sides, as many from both the Muslim and infidel camps went to heaven and hell, among them several hundred Mongols. On the eighth day Malik Shamsuddin Muhammad and a large troop were out fighting when an arrow hit him and killed him. The Heratis divided into two groups. Those who supported Sultan Jalaluddin Mänguberti and the adherents of Malik Muhammad Jurjani said, "We will not stop fighting so long as there is a breath of life left in us." The *cadis*, *ulema*, nobles, and grandees of the city, however, were inclined to make peace. Since Tolui Khan liked the sweet waters, pleasant air, pleasure parks, and gardens of the region, he did not want Herat to suffer the same devastation as other places, and so on the very day that a truce was proposed by the Heratis, he and two hundred horsemen rode up to the moat at the Firozabad Gate. He himself said, "People, know that I am Tolui Khan son of Genghis Khan. If you want your lives spared, cease fighting and come forth in obedience. Render to our representatives half of what you used to give in annual taxes to the Khwarazmshah's agents, and you will receive imperial favor." And swore a solemn oath that if they stopped resisting and opened the gates, they would be dealt with justly and equitably.

When the people of the city heard these words from the mouth of Tolui Khan, they ceased fighting and sent out Tolui Khan Amir Izzuddin Muqaddam Haravi, the chief of the weavers, with a hundred weavers, each carrying nine suits of expensive clothing. Then the nobles and grandees came out of the city to receive imperial favor. Tolui Khan killed twelve thousand men of Herat who were followers of Sultan Jalaluddin, but he did not bother any of the rest of the population. Tolui stationed Malik Abubakr as governor and Mangtai as shahna and then set out for Taligan, where his father was camped.

Malik Abubakr and Mangtai remained in Herat, providing for the citizens compassionately, and the people went about their business and agriculture with peace of mind. However, since the pen of fate had scriven the destruction of this city also, just about that time an event occurred that caused Herat to suffer the fate of the cities of Khurasan.

In this regard there are two versions found among the historians. The first, which was the choice of the chief of the learned men, Mawlana Sharafuddin Ali Yazdi, is that after Malik Abubakr and Mangtai had been ruling a short while and collecting taxes in that pleasurable spot, the news suddenly came that Sultan Jalaluddin Mänguberti had defeated Genghis Khan's forces in one of the provinces of Khurasan. Short-sighted men imagined that there would be no further fighting between Genghis Khan and the sultan and that the Mongols would flee to Turkistan. With this absurd notion, the people in all the cities of Khurasan mobbed and killed Genghis Khan's governors and agents, among them Malik Abubakr and Mangtai in Herat.

The other version, which my esteemed grandfather judged correct in his *Rawzatu's-safá*, is that while Tolui Khan was engaged in killing and pillaging the cities and fortresses of Khurasan, the Mongols, no matter how hard they tried, were unable to take the fortress of Kaliwin, which is now known as Tiratu. After Tolui Khan went to Taligan, the inhabitants of that impregnable fortress heard that the Heratis were busy preparing weapons and implements of siege and saying, "Whenever the world-conquering emperor commands us to take Tiratu, we will 'charge like mad elephants and pour forth like the River Nile,' and we will not rest until we have cast the lasso of subjugation over the parapets of that fortress." Upon hearing this, the inhabitants of Kaliwin became agitated and said to each other, "It would be better for us to cause an unresolvable strategic breach between the Mongols and the Heratis." After much thought a man named Sahib, who was unmatched for his bravery and courage, was sent into Herat with eighteen guerrillas in order to bring down Malik Abubakr and Mangtai however they could.

Dressed as tailors, Sahib and his comrades entered the city and began buying and selling in the lanes and markets. One day they spied Malik

Abubakr and Mangtai riding by the foot of the citadel and attacked and killed them with knives and daggers. The Heratis, acting upon the hemistich, "For those in love with you any excuse is sufficient," drew their swords and went berserk, killing on the spot all the governor's and *shahna*'s followers. Then they made Malik Mubarizuddin Sabzawari their governor and gave the office of *shahna* to Khwaja Fakhruddin Abdul-Rahman Ghayrani. When the news reached Genghis Khan, he flew into a rage and, addressing Tolui Khan, said, "If you had killed the people of Herat, this revolt would not have happened."

Genghis Khan dispatched Eljigidäi Noyan and eighty thousand warriors to Herat and charged them to take the city and not to leave a thing alive. Eljigidäi sped across the distances and camped on the banks of the Herat River, where he kept his men for a month in order to make preparations to take the citadel. Assistance was requested by Genghis Khan's order from some of the other cities of Khurasan where there were *darughas*, and fifty thousand additional men joined Eljigidäi's forces.

Malik Mubarizuddin and Khwaja Fakhruddin extracted promises from all, nobles, grandees, street fighters, and plebeians, that they would fight to the utmost in the coming battle and that there would be no division among the ranks as there had been the first time. After a month Eljigidäi apportioned the gates of Herat and stationed thirty thousand men all around the city, saying, "Anyone who deviates from the line of duty will be executed, and anyone who displays valor will be extremely well rewarded." Then he attacked from all four sides at once, and the Heratis, trusting in God, began their defense. For six months and seventeen days battle and bloodshed continued. In the year 619 [1222] Eljigidäi kept up battle continuously for several days, and in every assault nearly five thousand of his men were killed or wounded. However, so many stones were hurled that holes were made in the outer walls, and the towers were nearly toppled by tunnels bored beneath sawhorses. One day fity yards of the wall fell in on the sawhorses, and four hundred renowned warriors of the Tatar army were crushed to death. Three days after this event, the Heratis were driven to desperation by lack of supplies, and divisions began to appear among the ranks. On a

Friday morning during the month of Jumada II 619 [July–August 1222], Eljigidäi Noyan took Herat by force from the Khakbarsar Tower (which is now known as Khakistar) and unleashed a general massacre in which men, women, old, and young were killed. For seven days and nights the Mongols did nothing but kill, plunder, burn, and dig up. More than one million six hundred thousand Heratis were martyred.

Then Eljigidäi went to the province of Harirud, and when he reached the town of Obeh, he sent two thousand Mongols back to Herat to dispatch anyone who might have crept out of hiding. Those two thousand wretched infidels returned to Herat, gathered together nearly three thousand people, and then killed them. Aside from sixteen persons, one of whom was Mawlana Sharafuddin, the *khatib* of the village of Jighartan who had hidden in a hole in the dome of the Friday mosque, not a soul was left alive in Herat. In the history of Herat it has been related that when the city was vacated by the Mongols, one of those sixteen who had survived came out of the mosque, went to the market and sat down on the counter of a sweet shop, looking around but seeing no one. Then stroked his beard and said, "Thank God for a moment of peace and quiet."

Later another twenty-four people from the surrounding areas joined the sixteen survivors, and for fifteen years there was no one but these forty people in the entire city and surrounding countryside. They all lived next to the Friday mosque where the tomb of Sultan Ghiyasuddin is, feeding themselves for a long time on dried meat belonging to the slain. They searched through the pantries of houses and horse stables, picking up every grain of wheat and barley they saw. When they gathered a few maunds of grain, they managed to plough a small patch of earth and plant it so that the next year each one would have a handful of wheat and barley at harvest time. These forty persons made Mawlana Sharafuddin the *khatib* their leader and with difficulty kept themselves alive until such time as Ögödäi Qa'an, Genghis Khan's son, decided to rebuild Herat and sent Amir Izzuddin Muqaddam and some others to make the region flourish once again.

TAMERLANE OR TIMUR
THE GREAT AMIR
Ibn Arabshah
Translated by John Herne Sanders, 1936

To suggest the fifteenth-century Syrian chronicler **Ibn Arabshah** (1389–1450) bore ill-will towards Timur is a bit like saying Afghanistan has experienced a few disturbances in recent years. Lest anyone doubt the author's animosity towards the great conqueror, the chapter titles of Arabshah's biography remove any uncertainty: 'This Bastard Begins to Lay Waste Azerbaijan and the Kingdoms of Irak' reads one. 'How that Proud Tyrant was Broken & Borne to the House of Destruction, where he had his Constant Seat in the Lowest Pit of Hell' proclaims another. Arabshah refers to Timur throughout his narrative as 'Satan', 'demon', 'viper', 'villain', 'despot', 'deceiver' and 'wicked fool'. So much for impartiality.

Arabshah had been captured as a young boy by Timur's forces as they turned Damascus into a smoking ruin in 1401. Carted off to Samarkand as a prisoner with his mother and brothers, he learnt Persian, Turkish and Mongolian, studying under distinguished scholars and travelling widely. Later, in a curious twist of fate, he became confidential secretary to the Ottoman Sultan Mehmed I, son of Bayazid I, the man whose dazzling military career Timur had annihilated. He returned to Damascus in 1421, but never forgot the terrible scenes of rape and pillage enacted by Timur's hordes, culminating in the razing of the great Umayyad Mosque. Here he describes Timur's conquest of Herat and Sistan in 1379. The conqueror's savagery in Sistan is probably explained by this being the location where Timur as a young man on the make probably received the wounds which left him lame in both right limbs.

Chapter XV
Timur Sends a Letter to Malik Ghayatuddin, Sultan of Herat, Who Snatched Him From the Cross, and On His Account Opposed his Own Father

TIMUR then wrote a letter to the Sultan of Herat, Malik Ghayatuddin, who was really his helper, beginning it with a saying (of Mahomed), "God has written concerning every wicked soul." and praying him to submit to his sway and demanding a consignment of slaves and a contribution in proportion to his strength; adding that if he refused, he would attack his cities and destroy him.

But Malik Ghayatuddin replied: "I swear by the allies of the Prophet! You were my slave and I did good to you, and spread over you the mantle of my kindness and favour, but you have deceived and slain, destroyed unawares and given over to slaughter, acted guilefully and accomplished the crime which you have accomplished, although I rescued you from blows and the cross; but if you refuse to be a man who recognizes kindnesses, be like a dog." Then he crossed the Oxus and advanced against him, but when Ghayatuddin had not strength to meet him in open battle, his followers and townsmen at his command had assembled with their beasts around Herat and he dug round the gardens a ditch, which surrounded the wretched cowards and weaklings; but he shut himself in the fortress, thinking that in this way he would be inaccessible—because of the weakness of his counsel and the stupidity and folly, by which his mind and the condition of his state was overthrown and confounded.

I have said:

Him whose rule is not aided by fortune,
Ruin assails, though he govern well.

Timur however did not think it worth while to fight with him and make a siege, but the army surrounded him on every side, Timur holding a safe and secure position, while his enemy had exchanged open spaces for confinement. For, meantime, the nobles and commons were troubled and the cattle and beasts moved this way and that, and the town was choked with a dense mob, gentle and simple perished, disease consumed them and hunger destroyed them and wailing and murmuring arose.

Accordingly, the Sultan sent to him, seeking security, and informing him that because of him he had been brought into the greatest stress and that he had helped him previously and cared for him, and reminded him of his former kindness and the web of good service he had woven for him, and sought from him security confirmed by oath.

And Timur swore to him that he would preserve for him his ancient rights and would not shed his blood or break his skin. So he went out to him, and approaching him submitted to him; then Timur entered the city and climbed the fort and the Sultan with him, with the troops and guards of Herat surrounding him; then one of the brave men, the governor of Herat, gave a sign to the Sultan that he would slay Timur and that he was ready to sacrifice his life on his behalf and spoke to him in this wise: "I will ransom the Muslims at the risk of my life and wealth, and will kill this cripple, caring naught." But he did not consent to his intimation, and trusted to the decree of Almighty God and His will, and said: "Almighty God has supreme power over his servants and the arrow of His will cannot fail to go through them, nor can be escaped or avoided the decree, which God Almighty has made and decreed."

> When any destined thing ought to befall you, while you flee from it,
>   you will approach the nearer to it.
> Nor can this mystery of Providence fail of its issue;
> Nor can man dispute the truth of its behests.
> He who struggles with Fate, is conquered
> And he that resists Fortune is dragged along.
> Who opposes the floods of Destiny is drowned
> And he that slothfully enjoys the resorts of pleasure is choked.

Then he remembered what his father had said to him and marked its truth, but the arrow once shot could not be brought back.

Chapter XVI
How That Tyrant Visited the Venerable Zainuddin Abu Bakr of Khawaf

WHEN at length Timur came into Khorasan, he heard that in a town called Khawaf there was a man, to whom God Almighty had granted excellent gifts, a man of learning and action, born in noble station, endowed with excellent understanding, remarkable for pure virtue and wonderful holiness, ready and brilliant in daily conversation, but his deliberate speech in the assemblies excelled much more; in doctrine he was faithful, in dealing with God always true, and was called Sheikh Zainuddin Abu Bakr, who with the wings of his zeal occupied a lofty nest in the chief place in Paradise.

Timur, therefore, anxious to see him, hastened to him and his company. And when they said to the old man, "Timur comes to you desiring to see you and hoping for your blessing." the old man did not reply even a word or raise his eyes; and when Timur came to him, he dismounted from his horse and went in to him. But the old man sat occupied in his accustomed posture meditating on the carpet of adoration. But when he reached him, the old man rose, but Timur bent with his face bowed towards his own feet and the old man put his hands on his back. Timur said: "If the old man had not quickly removed his hand from my back, I should have thought it was broken; and I truly thought the sky had fallen on the earth, and that I was to be broken between the two with a mighty breaking."

Then he sat in the presence of that incomparable one ready to receive instruction and said to him courteously in conversation as though greedy to learn but not disputing: "Venerable master! Do you teach nothing to your kings concerning justice and equity and warn them not to turn to violence and tyranny?" And the old man replied to him: "We teach that in truth and for that reason we visit them; but they do not suffer themselves to be taught, and so we have appointed you Lord over them."

But as soon as he went out from the old man, his hump stood erect and he said: "I am Lord of the World by the Lord of the Kaaba! And this old man is he about whom a promise was made before to speak."

Then Timur throwing into bonds the King of Herat resolved to guard his gains, and to hold all his territories in allegiance, appointed in each a deputy, and returned to Samarkand with his booty.

But the Sultan he held prisoner in the city and forbade him to go out and entrusted him for being guarded to the citizens, to whom he joined his lions as guards, stark and staunch watchmen, because of his oath not to shed his blood and to maintain his rights; therefore he did not indeed shed his blood, but slew him in prison with hunger and thirst.

Chapter XVII

Timur Returns to Khorasan and Lays Waste the Provinces of Seistan

THEN Timur returned to Khorasan with a fixed purpose of taking revenge on Seistan, whose inhabitants went out to him asking for peace and agreement, which he granted them on condition that they should hand over their arms to him, of which they produced the whole equipment which they had, hoping in this way to escape from their extremity; and he put them on oath and ordered them to swear plainly that no further weapons of theirs were left in the city.

And as soon as they had given this guarantee, he drew the sword against them and billeted upon them all the armies of death. Then he laid the city waste, leaving in it not a tree or a wall and destroyed it utterly, no mark or trace of it remaining.

And when he went away, no one was left alive in the city; and he dealt in this manner with them only because he had first been injured by them.

An old man, skilled in the law, Zainuddin Abdul Latif, son of Mahomed, son of Abil Fatah of Kerman, a Hanifi, living at Damascus in the college of Jakmak, told me in the year 833 that those of the citizens of Seistan, who had escaped slaughter by flight, either by aid of darkness or by the special grace of God Almighty and Generous, when they had gone back to the city after the departure of Timur and wished there to hold sacred assemblies, forgot the day of assembly and did not learn it until a messenger sent to Kerman showed it to them.

HAFT AWRANG (SEVEN THRONES)
Jami

Mawlana Nur al Din Abd al Rahman, or more concisely **Jami** (1414–92), was the last great classical poet of Persia. A scholar, theologian and mystic, he was one of the Afghan city of Herat's favourite sons, the most celebrated poet of his generation. Besides his many famous works he also chronicled the turbulent rise and fall of the city he loved, describing its perpetual struggle between the forces of light and dark, war and peace, echoing the disdain men of letters have had for the hubris of rulers and the folly of empire. While rulers came and went, he wrote, 'poets live on in glory through the ages'. Dynasties pass, but literature remains.

His shrine in Herat is a mournful, windswept site, as romantic as the poetry which thrilled, inspired and saddened so many during his lifetime, so many more in the centuries that followed. When I visited it many years ago, I came across a group of teenage boys staring at the tomb, struck strangely silent by the site. The epitaph read:

> *When your face is hidden from me,*
> *Like the moon hidden on a dark night,*
> *I shed stars of tears*
> *And yet my night remains dark*
> *In spite of all those shining stars.*

Yusuf and Zulaikha
Translated by Ralph T. H. Griffith (1826–1906)

Her face was the garden of Iram, where
Roses of every hue are fair.
The dusky moles that enhanced the red
Were like Moorish boys playing in each rose-bed.
Of silver that paid no tithe, her chin
Had a well with the Water of Life therein.
If a sage in his thirst came near to drink,
He would feel the spray ere he reached the brink,
But lost were his soul if he nearer drew,
For it was a well and a whirlpool too.
Her neck was of ivory. Thither drawn,
Came with her tribute to beauty the fawn;
And the rose hung her head at the gleam of the skin
Of shoulders fairer than jasmine.
Her breasts were orbs of a light most pure,
Twin bubbles new-risen from fount Kafur,
Two young pomegranates grown on one spray,
Where bold hope never a finger might lay.
The touchstone itself was proved false when it tried
Her arms' fine silver thrice purified;
But the pearl-pure amulets fastened there
Were the hearts of the holy absorbed in prayer.

"I shall roll up the carpet of life when I see
Thy dear face again, and shall cease to be,
For self will be lost in that rapture, and all
The threads of my thought from my hand will fall;
Not me wilt thou find, for this self will have fled:
Thou wilt be my soul in mine own soul's stead.
All thought of self will be swept from my mind,
And thee, only thee, in my place shall I find;

More precious than heaven, than earth more dear,
Myself were forgotten if thou wert near."

"Mine eyes have been touched by the Truth's pure ray,
And the dream of folly has passed away.
Mine eyes thou hast opened – God bless thee for it! –
And my heart to the Soul of the soul thou hast knit.
From a fond strange love thou hast turned my feet
The Lord of all creatures to know and meet;
If I bore a tongue in each single hair,
Each and all should thy praise declare."

"By the excellent bloom of that cheek which He gave,
By that beauty which makes the whole world thy slave;
By the splendor that beams from that beautiful brow,
That bids the full moon to thy majesty bow;
By the graceful gait of that cypress, by
The delicate bow that is bent o'er thine eye;
By that arch of the temple devoted to prayer,
By each fine-woven mesh of the coils of thy hair;
By that charming narcissus, that form arrayed
In the sheen and glory of silk brocade;
By that secret thou callest a mouth, by the hair
Thou callest the waist of that body most fair;
By the musky spots on thy cheek's pure rose,
By the smile of thy lips when those buds unclose;
By my longing tears, by the sigh and groan
That rend my heart as I pine alone;
By thine absence, a mountain too heavy to bear,
By my thousand fetters of grief and care;
By the sovereign sway of my passion,
By thy carelessness whether I live or die;
Pity me, pity my lovelorn grief:
Loosen my fetters and grant relief:

An age has scorched me since over my soul
The soft sweet air of thy garden stole.
Be the balm of my wounds for a little; shed
Sweet scent on the heart where the flowers are dead.
I hunger for thee till my whole frame is weak:
O give me the food for my soul which I seek."

In his stalls had Yussuf a fairy steed,
A courser through space of no earthly breed;
Swift as the heavens, and black and white
With a thousand patches of day and night;
Now a jetty spot, now a starry blaze,
Like Time with succession of nights and days.
With his tail the heavenly Virgo's hair,
With his hoof the moon was afraid to compare.
Each foot with a golden new moon was shod,
And the stars of its nails struck the earth as he trod.
When his hoof smote sharp on the rugged flint
A planet flashed forth from the new moon's dint;
And a new moon rose in the sky when a shoe
From the galloping foot of the courser flew.
Like an arrow shot through its side in the chase,
He outstripped the game in the deadly race.
At a single bound he would spring, unpressed,
With the lightning's speed from the east to the west.

"O thou who hast broken mine honor's urn,
Thou stone of offense wheresoever I turn,
I should smite – for thy falsehood has ruined my rest –
with the stone thou art made of, the heart in my breast.
The way of misfortune too surely I trod
When I bowed down before thee and made thee my god;
When I looked up to thee with wet eyes in my woe,
I renounced all the bliss which both worlds can bestow.

From thy stony dominion my soul will I free,
And thus shatter the gem of thy power and thee."

With a hard flint stone like the Friend, as she spoke,
In a thousand pieces the image she broke.
Riven and shattered the idol fell,
And with her from that moment shall all be well.
She made her ablution, 'mid penitent sighs,
With the blood of her heart and the tears of her eyes.
She bent down her head to the dust; with a moan
She made supplication to God's pure throne:

"O God, who lovest the humble,
Thou To whom idols, their makers, their servants bow;
'Tis to the light which Thy splendor lends
To the idol's face that its worshiper bends.
Thy love the heart of the sculptor stirs,
And the idol is graven for worshipers.
They bow them down to the image, and think
That they worship Thee as before it they sink.
To myself, O Lord, I have done this wrong,
If mine eyes to an idol have turned so long.
Thou hast washed the dark stain of my sin away;
Now restore the lost blessing for which I pray.
May I feel my heart free from the brand of its woes,
And cull from the garden of Yussuf a rose."

"Where is thy youth, and thy beauty, and pride?"
"Gone, since I parted from thee!" she replied.
"Where is the light of thine eye?" said he,
"Drowned in blood-tears for the loss of thee."
"Why is that cypress-tree bowed and bent?"
"By absence from thee and my long lament."

"Where is thy pearl, and thy silver and gold,
And the diadem bright on thy head of old?"

"She who spoke of my loved one," she answered, "shed,
In the praise of thy beauty, rare pearls on my head.
In return for those jewels, a recompense meet,
I scattered my jewels and gold at her feet.
A crown of pure gold on her forehead I set,
And the dust that she trod was my coronet.
The stream of my treasure of gold ran dry;
My heart is Love's storehouse, and I am I."

"Not love thee! – ah! how much I loved
Long absent years of grief have proved.
Severe rebuke, assumed disdain,
Dwelt in my words and looks in vain:
I would not passion's victim be,
And turned from sin – but not from thee.
My love was pure, no plant of earth
From my rapt being sprung to birth:
I loved as angels might adore,
And sought, and wished, and hoped no more.
Virtue was my belov'd: and thou
Hadst virtue's impress on thy brow.
Thy weakness showed how frail is all
That erring mortals goodness call.
I thanked thee, and reproached thee not
For all the sufferings of my lot.
The God we worship was thy friend,
And led me to my destined end,
Taught the great lesson to thy heart
That vice and bliss are wide apart:
And joined us now, that we may prove
With perfect virtue, perfect love.

The beauty returned which was ruined and dead,
And her cheek gained the splendor which long had fled.
Again shone the waters which sad years had dried,
And the rose-bed of youth bloomed again in its pride.
The musk was restored and the camphor withdrawn,
And the black night followed the gray of the dawn.
The cypress rose stately and tall as of old:
The pure silver was free from all wrinkle and fold.
From each musky tress fled the traces of white:
To the black narcissus came beauty and light.

"The one sole wish of my heart," she replied,
"Is still to be near thee, to sit by thy side;
To have thee by day in my happy sight,
And to lay my cheek on thy foot at night;
To lie in the shade of the cypress and sip
The sugar that lies on thy ruby lip;
To my wounded heart this soft balm to lay;
For naught beyond this can I wish or pray.
The streams of thy love will new life bestow
On the dry thirsty field where its sweet waters flow."

Thus spoke the Angel: "To thee, O King,
From the Lord Almighty a message I bring:
Mine eyes have seen her in humble mood;
I heard her prayer when to thee she sued.
At the sight of her labors, her prayers, and sighs,
The waves of the sea of my pity rise.
Her soul from the sword of despair I free,
And here from My throne I betroth her to thee."

The following poems are taken from The Persian Mystics: Jámí, *published in 1908*

Self Dies in Love

"I shall roll up the carpet of life when I see,
Thy dear face again and shall cease to be
For self will be lost in that rapture, and all
The threads of my thought from my hand will fall;
Not me wilt thou find, for this self will have fled:
Thou wilt be my soul in mine own soul's stead.
All thought of self will be swept from my mind,
And thee only thee, in my place shall I find;
More precious than heaven, than earth more dear,
Myself were forgotten if thou wert near."

The Value of a Man

The price of a man consists not in silver and gold;
The value of a man is his power and virtue.
Many a slave has by acquiring virtue
Attained much greater power than a gentleman
And many a gentleman has for want of virtue,
Become inferior to his own slave.

Silence

No one repented for keeping a secret under seal,
But many for having revealed it.
Remain silent, because to sit quietly with a collected mind
Is better than speaking what will distract it.

ALISHER NAVOIY

Selection of Poems

Translated by Andrew Staniland with Aidakhon Bumatova

> Another native of Herat, **Alisher Navoiy** (1441–1501) was a polymath and polyglot. Poet, calligrapher, musician, sculptor, painter, politician and prolific builder, he hailed from a line of Timurid courtiers and scribes. Though, unlike Rumi, his fame barely extends beyond Central Asia, his following here is extensive to the point where he has become a national symbol in Uzbekistan, the 'Father of Uzbek literature', prized for his use of the Chaghatai language which was the foundation for modern written and spoken Uzbek. Just as he spanned different languages and cultures during his life, studying in what is today Iran and Uzbekistan, his writing continues to cross borders and find new readers with translations of his searing verses on love, life and religion.

I ached to see your beauty so,
it has addicted me to you.
The day I did, what bad luck for
me, introducing me to you.

Day after day, the more I said
I had to purge you from my heart
and memory, the more that it
habituated me to you.

I said to you, "Be true to me!"
But you tormented me and said,
"Atone for this!" I did so, my
atonement all of me to you.

You ask which peri I am mad
about. My peerless peri, it
is you, because of you this madness is demeaning me to you.

My soul, you won't hear what is wise,
as if you want one more than your
one hundred sorrows. Well, one more
is hurrying from me to you.

To wet my lips with gold, the gob-
let of Jamshid, at Khizr's spring,
oh, my wine-giver, I will give
my wealth away and me to you.

I never would have heard my song
on that sad harp of those in love,
if you had not held Navoiy
tied tightly, tying me to you.

*

That one who was to come that night,
that rose, that cypress,
that cypress, didn't come
and to my eyes that night, until
the dawn, sleep also didn't come.

Time after time, I went out in
the street and watched the way. My heart
came up into my mouth, but that
one, having teased me, didn't come.

Was it the brightness of the moon
that stopped that one from shining too?
That sky of mine was black again
that night when my moon didn't come.

Without that peri there, I cried
so crazily that to the lips
of anyone who might have mocked
me for it laughter didn't come.

Don't ask me why so many tears
came from my eyes. What came out from
them, reddened them, was blood. That night,
to my eyes, water didn't come.

No faithful friend came to my door,
if anyone like that exists,
and that one whom I wanted to
be faithful to me didn't come.

Oh, Navoiy, bring wine into
that house that is your heart. You know,
when anybody's house has had
wine in it, sorrow didn't come.

EMBASSY TO TAMERLANE 1403–1406

Ruy Gonzalez de Clavijo

Translated by Guy Le Strange, 1928

It is thanks to one of history's most auspicious shipwrecks that **Ruy Gonzalez de Clavijo** (d. 1412) was able to record the most extraordinary eyewitness account of perhaps the world's greatest conqueror. Sent as the Spanish ambassador to the court of Timur by Henry III of Castile in 1402, Clavijo had planned to meet the 'Sword of Islam' in the eastern Caucasus. So much for plans. Shipwrecked on the edge of the Bosporus, the Spaniard was forced to wait for four months in Constantinople until more favourable conditions arrived. The following spring he continued his journey to Trebizond on the north coast of modern Turkey. By this time, however, Timur had left for Samarkand, and the envoy was obliged to play catch-up, following him across his Persian dominions to the heart of Timur's empire in what is today Uzbekistan. Here at last, having travelled through Balkh in today's Afghanistan, he met the Unconquered Lord of the Seven Climes in Samarkand, 'the treasure house of his conquests'.

On Thursday the last day of July we came on from Meshed to a great city which is called Buelo [the same is Tus] and of the Khurasan province likewise. This is a most pleasant township, and it has a greater population than any other place that we had come to since leaving Sultaniyah. In this city we halted for the last hours of that day Thursday, for the authorities were engaged in getting together provisions of food for man and beast for our benefit during the next stage, since this would be to cross the desert, where there are neither inhabitants nor habitations for the space of fifty leagues. When therefore we had dined that same evening they brought us fresh horses, which we were to mount and ride crossing this desolate region, and at night-fall we set off leaving [Tus] and rode on till dawn of Friday. All that day too we rode, and also the following night and day, before we came again to any place where we found settled folk.

Chagatay herders

On the Saturday however, which was the [2nd] of August at last towards evening we came to a valley. Here much ground was under cultivation for wheat, and a river [the Tejend Ab] ran through the place, on whose banks we found numerous tents pitched where the Chagatays of Timur's Horde were out in camp. These folk were stationed here with their flocks of sheep, and herds of camels with droves of horses...

On the present occasion when we had reached the tents of the Chagatays [by the Tejend river, Mirabozar] our guide promptly made the people bring us out cooked meat with rice, and next milk and sour cream, all of which they set before us adding many melons, which in this country are in abundance and of excellent quality. These Chagatays with whom we were thus guests are a nomad folk living in tents and booths, for indeed they possess no other more permanent habitations, both summer and winter living in the open. In summer they pass to the plains beside the river, where they sow their crops of corn and cotton, and tend the melon beds: and their melons I opine are the very best and biggest that may be found in the whole world. They also raise crops of millet, a grain which forms their chief food, and which they eat boiled in sour milk. In the winter season these Chagatays migrate to lands where the climate is fairly warm. After the like fashion indeed all the host of Timur moves from camp to camp living in the open, summer and winter. But since they fear no enemy they do not need to keep together for safety and the lord Timur will proceed with his own personal horde apart, accompanied by his servants and chief nobles and courtiers, with his wives and female relatives, while the rest of the horde passes elsewhere. Thus do they all spend their lives: for these [Tartars] possess great herds, namely of camels horses and sheep, also of cattle but of cows only few.

When Timur calls his people to war all assemble and march with him, surrounded by their flocks and herds, thus carrying along their possessions with them, in company with their wives and children. These last follow the host, and in the lands which they invade their flocks, namely and particularly the sheep camels and horses, serve to ration the horde. Thus marching at the head of his people Timur has accomplished great deeds and gained many victories, for the [Tartars] are a very valiant folk, fine horsemen, very skilful at shooting with the bow, and exceeding hardy. In camp should they have victuals in plenty they eat their fill: if they have lack milk and meat without baked bread suffices them, and for a long season they can thus march with or without halting to prepare bread stuffs, living on [the meat and milk of] their flocks and herds. They suffer cold and heat and hunger and thirst more patiently than any other nation in the whole world: when food is abundant they gorge on it gluttonously, but when there is scarcity sour milk tempered with boiling water suffices them, and of this for sustenance there is never a lack. Sour milk, their special food, they prepare after the following fashion. They take and heat a great caldron full of water and before it boils they have made ready a bowl in which they have curds of sour milk, that is like cheese, which they have worked up to a paste with cold water. This is thrown into the boiling caldron, and the whole mass turns to be as sour as vinegar. Next they have kneaded very thin cakes of flour, which they bake and cut up in small pieces, afterwards throwing these into the boiling caldron. Then cooking awhile the fire is next withdrawn, and the whole mess served out into bowls. This, which is a kind of soup, without other bread or meat they eat and are satisfied, and for the most part this is their daily food and nothing more. For their cooking fires they use no wood, but only the dried dung of their herds, and it makes the fire for all purposes of roasting and boiling; and this broth of theirs which has just been described goes by the name of Ash [which in the Persian language is Soup].

Desert travel

On the [Sunday] morning following we set out [from the encampment on the Tejend river] under escort of that lord [Mirabozar] whom Timur had sent to meet us, and as we shall explain we travelled without ever halting that day and the following night and the next day throughout never passing by any settlement or village. That first [Sunday] night we slept at a great caravanserai [which was the post-house] in the desert, where they gave the horses we had brought their barley, and here we learnt that the stage from [this caravanserai] to the next resting place was twelve long leagues. Some two hours after night-fall therefore we set out again, fresh good horses being provided at the post house for our use. All through that night we rode, and the heat not abating the air was most oppressive, also nowhere on the road did we come to any water. When morning came, which was Monday, we still continued our journey, and up to the hour of none [namely three o'clock of the afternoon] went on without finding water, good or bad, for man or horse to drink. We had so ridden hard all that last night and this day that the horses were now quite tired out, and barely able to go at a walk. Also by reason of the great heat of the sun that day on the road here over the sands they came near at last to perishing of thirst. We men too were very like to have succumbed for that same want of water, had not a youth in the service of our Master in Theology had a better horse than the rest, who now made haste to ride on ahead before us. Then fortunately at last he discovered a stream where taking off his smock he dipped it in the water and returned quickly bringing the smock to us, who as many as could quenched somewhat of our thirst thereby. Most of us indeed were like to have fainted from that great heat and the lack that we suffered of water to drink; and each man rode his own way. Our escort no longer was keeping up with us, and all struggled on as best might.

At length as the sun was about to set we came to a broad valley where many tents were pitched of the Chagatay folk, and distant beyond we saw the great river which is known as the Murghab. That ride now accomplished of the night and the two days, had been of the length of at least twenty leagues of those of Castile, and here at last we came to rest and passed the night. The next morning which was Tuesday we took horse again, but only rode for about two leagues when we reached a great building like a hostel, with us, which is called here a caravanserai. This we found to be occupied by the Chagatays who are in charge of the government post-horses, and we dined and rested there that afternoon. At the hour of vespers we mounted again, fresh horses having been provided for us from the stables of this post-house, and two hours after night fall came to the great plains where we found stationed the main encampment of the Chagatays of the Horde. Here at their tents we slept that night. The following day which was Thursday we again started, resting in the afternoon at a village, but that night we passed in camp in the open beside the Murghab river. Friday the following day in the afternoon we took our rest at the tents of certain of the Chagatays here stationed, and later in the evening rode on, supplied with fresh horses of the government post, and that night slept in camp in the open.

...Sunday, on the morrow they provided us with excellent horses for the road: and that fore noon we set out again, but all that day the wind blew so violently that we were often almost unhorsed. The blast was so hot as to seem to be fire. The road lay over a sandy desert and this hot wind blew the sand over us so that we were at times blinded by it and at last began to lose our way. Time and again we found that we had gone astray from the road, and finally the lord [Mirabozar] who was escorting us had perforce to send back a man to the Chagatay encampment for one of those folk to come and guide us. Then by God's mercy we at last reached a large village called Aliabad where we rested for the afternoon waiting for the going down of the wind, and then at night-fall came on to another village named Oosh: where our horses were given their barley.

Balkh

That same night we again mounted and rode on, passing many small villages surrounded by their orchards, and by the Monday morning which was the 18th of August had come to the city of Balkh. This city is very large and it is surrounded by a broad rampart of earth which along the top measures thirty paces across. The retaining wall flanking this rampart is now breached in many places, but inside this last the city proper is enclosed by two walls, one within the other, and these protect the settlement. The area between the outer earthen rampart and the first inner wall is not occupied by any houses and no one lives here, the ground being divided up into fields where cotton is grown. In the space between the second and the innermost wall there are houses, but still this part is not very closely crowded. The innermost circle of the city however is densely populated: and unlike the other towns which we had come to in these parts, and which lay open, the two inner walls of Balkh are extremely strong and as yet well preserved. They treated us with much honour in Balkh providing us amply with provisions and excellent wine. Further we were given a horse and a robe of kincob [gold brocade].

The Oxus River (Amu Darya)

We left Balkh on the Tuesday going to our night's lodging in a village on the road. Wednesday we dined taking our afternoon rest in another township and that night slept out in the open. On Thursday the 21st of August we had come to the bank of that great river named the Ab-i-Amu [as the Persians call the Oxus] and this is one of the streams which flows down, it is said, from Paradise. It is here a league in breadth and the current is extremely strong. The river traverses a great plain and its waters are muddy. In the winter season it runs very low for at that time the current up in the mountains is hard frozen and the snows as they fall remain unmelted. But when the month of April is come the stream begins to rise, and for the next four months the flood continues to increase, after which season the water level goes back the like of what it was before. This flooding is due to the melting of the snows up in the mountains during the summer heats. During this last summer season indeed as they told us, the river had risen so high, going beyond its usual flood level, that a village that stood two thirds of a league distant from its usual bank and strand had been almost swept away by its waters, these having entered among the houses, whereby causing them to fall, much damage being wrought. The Ab i-Amu takes its rise in the mountain region [to the north] of Lesser India [or Afghanistan] flowing down through the plains of Samarqand finally passing out into the lands of Tartary, from whence the discharge of its waters is into the Caspian Sea; and thus [the Oxus] along its course is the boundary dividing the lordship of Samarqand from the lordship of Khurasan.

The lord Timur when he had completed his conquest of the land of Samarqand which lies as we have seen on the further side of the river Oxus, made up his mind to cross over that river and conquer the land of Khurasan to the south. He therefore caused a great bridge of wooden beams supported on boats to be made, whereby to cross, but as soon as he and his host had passed over he had caused the same immediately to be dismantled. Recently as we were told when he was returning home from his late campaigns, and journeying to Samarqand, for the passage of himself and his armies he had given instructions for the reestablishment of this bridge; which we who now had to pass the river were able to make use of for our passage. We were informed however that orders had already been sent by Timur a second time to dismantle the bridge even as he had done on the first occasion. And indeed we found that the bridge no longer stretched quite across to the further bank: however, beginning on the near side for a lengthy portion it stretched out over the waters, whereby our horses and sumpterbeasts could conveniently traverse, but suddenly at the end it failed [and we had to take to the ferry-boats]. It was in this great plain which here borders the Oxus that aforetime Alexander the Great fought his battle with Porus the Indian king whom he entirely defeated.

BABURNAMA

Babur

Translated by Annette Susannah Beveridge, 1912–1922

From his diminutive capital of Kabul, **Babur** 'The Tiger' (1483–1530), great-great-great-grandson of Timur, looked south for his conquests and founded the long-lived Mughal Empire that would transform the Indian subcontinent and endure until 1857. As ambitious with the pen as he was with his sword, Babur is widely loved as the author of the *Baburnama*, one of the greatest treasure troves of Muslim literature. Here is the bristling, infectious humanity of a pioneering, genre-bending warrior-poet-king, whose prose reveals a fully three-dimensional man – 'the most completely revealed individual of the sixteenth century', according to one historian. With its wine-soaked, hashish-perfumed tales of wild parties and daring military missions among the mountains, this high-spirited autobiography represents a thrilling counterpoint to the view, widespread in the West, that Islam is monolithic, austere and intolerant. The *Baburnama* is the most dazzling literary jewel, a timely and elegant reminder of the early pluralism of the Islamic world.

Description of Kabul[4]

The Kabul country is situated in the Fourth climate and in the midst of cultivated lands.[5] On the east it has the Lamghanat,[1] Parashawar (Pashawar), Hash(t)-nagar and some of the countries of Hindustan. On the west it has the mountain region in which are

---

[4] Elph. MS. fol. 97; W.-i-B. I.O. 215 f. 102*b* and 217 f. 85; Mems. p. 136. Useful books of the early 19th century, many of them referring to the *Babur-nama*, are Conolly's *Travels*, Wood's *Journey*, Elphinstone's *Caubul*, Burnes' *Cabool*, Masson's *Narrative*, Lord's and Leech's articles in JASB 1838 and in Burnes' *Reports* (India Office Library), Broadfoot's *Report* in RGS Supp. Papers vol. I.

[5] f. 1*b* where Farghana is said to be on the limit of cultivation.

Karnud (?) and Ghur, now the refuge and dwelling-places of the Hazara and Nikdiri (var. Nikudari) tribes. On the north, separated from it by the range of Hindu-kush, it has the Qunduz and Andar-ab countries. On the south, it has Farmul, Naghr (var. Naghz), Bannu and Afghanistan.[2]

(*a. Town and environs of Kabul.*)

The Kabul district itself is of small extent, has its greatest length from east to west, and is girt round by mountains. Its walled-town connects with one of these, rather a low one known as Shah-of-Kabul because at some time a (Hindu) Shah of Kabul built a residence on its summit.[3] Shah-of-Kabul begins at the Durrin narrows and ends at those of Dih-i-yaq'ub;[4] it may be 4 miles (2 *shar'i*) round; its skirt is covered with gardens fertilized from a canal which was brought along the hill-slope in the time of my paternal uncle, Aulugh Beg Mirza by his guardian, Wais Ataka.[5] The water of this canal comes to an end in a retired corner, a quarter known as Kul-kina[6] where much debauchery has gone on. About this place it sometimes used to be said, in jesting parody of Khwaja Hafiz,[1]—"Ah! the happy, thoughtless time when, with our names in ill-repute, we lived days of days at Kul-kina!"

[1] f. 131*b*. To find these *tumans* here classed with what was not part of Kabul suggest a clerical omission of "beyond" or "east of" (Lamghanat). The first syllable may be *lam*, fort. The modern form Laghman is not used in the *Babur-nama*, nor, it may be added is Paghman for Pamghan.

[2] It will be observed that Babur limits the name Afghanistan to the countries inhabited by Afghan tribesmen; they are chiefly those south of the road from Kabul to Pashawar (Erskine). *See* Vigne, p. 102, for a boundary between the Afghans and Khurasan.

[3] Al-biruni's *Indika* writes of both Turk and Hindu-shahi Kings of Kabul. *See* Raverty's *Notes* p. 62 and Stein's *Shahi Kings of Kabul*. The mountain is 7592 ft. above the sea, some 1800 ft. therefore above the town.

[4] The Kabul-river enters the Char-dih plain by the Dih-i-yaq'ub narrows, and leaves it by those of Durrin. *Cf. S.A. War*, Plan p. 288 and Plan of action at Char-asiya (Four-mills), the second shewing an off-take which may be Wais Ataka's canal. *See* Vigne, p. 163 and Raverty's *Notes* pp. 69 and 689.

[5] This, the Bala-jui (upper-canal) was a four-mill stream and in Masson's time, as now, supplied water to the gardens round Babur's tomb. Masson found in Kabul honoured descendants of Wais Ataka (ii, 240).

[6] But for a, perhaps negligible, shortening of its first vowel, this form of the name would describe the normal end of an irrigation canal, a little pool, but other forms with other meanings are open to choice, *e.g.* small hamlet (Pers. *kul*), or some compound containing Pers. *gul*, a rose, in its plain or metaphorical senses. Jarrett's *Ayin-i-akbari* writes Gul-kinah, little rose (?). Masson (ii, 236) mentions a similar pleasure-resort, Sanji-taq.

East of Shah-of-Kabul and south of the walled-town lies a large pool[2] about a 2 miles [*shar'i*] round. From the town side of the mountain three smallish springs issue, two near Kulkina; Khwaja Shamu's[3] tomb is at the head of one; Khwaja Khizr's Qadam-gah[4] at the head of another, and the third is at a place known as Khwaja Raushanai, over against Khwaja 'Abdu's-samad. On a detached rock of a spur of Shah-of-Kabul, known as 'Uqabain,[5] stands the citadel of Kabul-fort with the great walled-town at its north end, lying high in excellent air, and overlooking the large pool already mentioned, and also three meadows, namely, Siyah-sang (Black-rock), Sung-qurghan (Fort-back), and Chalak (Highwayman?),—a most beautiful outlook when the meadows are green. The north-wind does not fail Kabul in the heats; people call it the Parwan-wind;[6] it makes a delightful temperature in the windowed houses on the northern part of the citadel. In praise of the citadel of Kabul, Mulla Muhammad *Talib Mu'ammai* (the Riddler)[7] used to recite this couplet, composed on Badi'u'z-zaman Mirza's name:—

[1] The original ode, with which the parody agrees in rhyme and refrain, is in the *Diwan*, s.l. Dal (Brockhaus ed. 1854, i, 62 and lith. ed. p. 96). *See* Wilberforce Clarke's literal translation i, 286 (H.B.). A marginal note to the Haidarabad Codex gives what appears to be a variant of one of the rhymes of the parody.

[2] *aulugh kul*; some 3 m. round in Erskine's time; mapped as a swamp in *S.A. War* p. 288.

[3] A marginal note to the Hai. Codex explains this name to be an abbreviation of Khwaja Shamsu'd-din *Jan-baz* (or *Jahan-baz*; Masson, ii, 279 and iii, 93).

[4] *i.e.* the place made holy by an impress of saintly foot-steps.

[5] Two eagles or, Two poles, used for punishment. Vigne's illustration (p. 161) clearly shows the spur and the detached rock. Erskine (p. 137 n.) says that 'Uqabain seems to be the hill, known in his day as 'Ashiqan-i-'arifan, which connects with Babur Badshah. *See* Raverty's *Notes* p. 68.

[6] During most of the year this wind rushes through the Hindu-kush (Parwan)-pass; it checks the migration of the birds (f. 142), and it may be the cause of the deposit of the Running-sands (Burnes, p. 158). *Cf.* Wood, p. 124.

[7] He was Badi'u'z-zaman's *Sadr* before serving Babur; he died in 918 ah. (1512 AD.), in the battle of Kul-i-malik where 'Ubaidu'l-lah *Auzbeg* defeated Babur. He may be identical with Mir Husain the Riddler of f. 180*b*, but seems not to be Mulla Muh. *Badakhshi*, also a Riddler, because the *Habibu's-siyar* (ii, 343 and 344) gives this man a separate notice. Those interested in enigmas can find one made by Talib on the name Yahya (H.S. ii, 344). Sharafu'd-din 'Ali *Yazdi*, the author of the *Zafar-nama*, wrote a book about a novel kind of these puzzles (T.R. p. 84).

Drink wine in the castle of Kabul and send the cup round without pause;
For Kabul is mountain, is river, is city, is lowland in one.[1]

(*b. Kabul as a trading-town.*)

Just as 'Arabs call every place outside 'Arab (Arabia), 'Ajam, so Hindustanis call every place outside Hindustan, Khurasan. There are two trade-marts on the land-route between Hindustan and Khurasan; one is Kabul, the other, Qandahar. To Kabul caravans come from Kashghar,[2] Farghana, Turkistan, Samarkand, Bukhara, Balkh, Hisar and Badakhshan. To Qandahar they come from Khurasan. Kabul is an excellent trading-centre; if merchants went to Khita or to Rum,[3] they might make no higher profit. Down to Kabul every year come 7, 8, or 10,000 horses and up to it, from Hindustan, come every year caravans of 10, 15 or 20,000 heads-of-houses, bringing slaves (*barda*), white cloth, sugar-candy, refined and common sugars, and aromatic roots. Many a trader is not content with a profit of 30 or 40 on 10.[4] In Kabul can be had the products of Khurasan, Rum, 'Iraq and Chin (China); while it is Hindustan's own market.

(*c. Products and climate of Kabul.*)

In the country of Kabul, there are hot and cold districts close to one another. In one day, a man may go out of the town of Kabul to where snow never falls, or he may go, in two sidereal hours, to where it never thaws, unless when the heats are such that it cannot possibly lie.

Fruits of hot and cold climates are to be had in the districts near the town. Amongst those of the cold climate, there are had in the town the

---

[1] The original couplet is as follows:—
'*Bakhur dar arg-i Kabul mai, bagardan kasa pay dar pay,*
Kah ham koh ast, u ham darya, u ham shahr ast, u ham sahra.'
What Talib's words may be inferred to conceal is the opinion that like Badi'u'z-zaman and like the meaning of his name, Kabul is the Wonder-of-the-world. (*Cf.* M. Garçin de Tassy's *Rhétorique* [p. 165], for *ces combinaisons énigmatiques*.)
[2] All MSS. do not mention Kashghar.
[3] Khita (Cathay) is Northern China; Chin (*infra*) is China; Rum is Turkey and particularly the provinces near Trebizond (Erskine).
[4] 300% to 400% (Erskine).

grape, pomegranate, apricot, apple, quince, pear, peach, plum, *sinjid*, almond and walnut.¹ I had cuttings of the *alu-balu*² brought there and planted; they grew and have done well. Of fruits of the hot climate people bring into the town;—from the Lamghanat, the orange, citron, *amluk* (*diospyrus lotus*), and sugar-cane; this last I had had brought and planted there;³—from Nijr-au (Nijr-water), they bring the *jil-ghuza*,⁴ and, from the hill-tracts, much honey. Bee-hives are in use; it is only from towards Ghazni, that no honey comes.

The rhubarb⁵ of the Kabul district is good, its quinces and plums very good, so too its *badrang*;⁶ it grows an excellent grape, known as the water-grape.⁷ Kabul wines are heady, those of the Khwaja Khawand Sa'id hill-skirt being famous for their strength; at this time however I can only repeat the praise of others about them:—⁸

The flavour of the wine a drinker knows;
What chance have sober men to know it?

---

¹ Persian *sinjid*, Brandis, *elægnus hortensis*; Erskine (Mems. p. 138) jujube, presumably the *zizyphus jujuba* of Speede, Supplement p. 86. Turki *yangaq*, walnut, has several variants, of which the most marked is *yanghkaq*. For a good account of Kabul fruits see Masson, ii, 230.
² a kind of plum (?). It seems unlikely to be a cherry since Babur does not mention cherries as good in his old dominions, and Firminger (p. 244) makes against it as introduced from India. Steingass explains *alu-balu* by "sour-cherry, an armarylla"; if sour, is it the Morello cherry?
³ The sugar-cane was seen in abundance in Lan-po (Lamghan) by a Chinese pilgrim (Beale, p. 90); Babur's introduction of it may have been into his own garden only in Ningnahar (f. 132*b*).
⁴ i.e. the seeds of *pinus Gerardiana*.
⁵ *rawashlar*. The green leaf-stalks (*chukri*) of *ribes rheum* are taken into Kabul in mid-April from the Pamghan-hills; a week later they are followed by the blanched and tended *rawash* (Masson, ii, 7). See Gul-badan's H.N. trs. p. 188, Vigne, p. 100 and 107, Masson, ii, 230, Conolly, i, 213.
⁶ a large green fruit, shaped something like a citron; also a large sort of cucumber (Erskine).
⁷ The *sahibi*, a grape praised by Babur amongst Samarkandi fruits, grows in Kohdaman; another well-known grape of Kabul is the long stoneless *husaini*, brought by Afghan traders into Hindustan in round, flat boxes of poplar wood (Vigne, p. 172).
⁸ An allusion, presumably, to the renouncement of wine made by Babur and some of his followers in 933 AH. (1527 AD. f. 312). He may have had 'Umar *Khayyam*'s quatrain in mind, "Wine's power is known to wine-bibbers alone" (Whinfield's 2nd ed. 1901, No. 164).

Kabul is not fertile in grain, a four or five-fold return is reckoned good there; nor are its melons first-rate, but they are not altogether bad when grown from Khurasan seed.

It has a very pleasant climate; if the world has another so pleasant, it is not known. Even in the heats, one cannot sleep at night without a fur-coat.[1] Although the snow in most places lies deep in winter, the cold is not excessive; whereas in Samarkand and Tabriz, both, like Kabul, noted for their pleasant climate, the cold is extreme.

(d. Meadows of Kabul.)

There are good meadows on the four sides of Kabul. An excellent one, Sung-qurghan, is some 4 miles (2 *kuroh*) to the north-east; it has grass fit for horses and few mosquitos. To the north-west is the Chalak meadow, some 2 miles (1 *shar'i*) away, a large one but in it mosquitos greatly trouble the horses. On the west is the Durrin, in fact there are two, Tipa and Qushnadir (var. nawar),—if two are counted here, there would be five in all. Each of these is about 2 miles from the town; both are small, have grass good for horses, and no mosquitos; Kabul has no others so good. On the east is the Siyah-sang meadow with Qutluq-qadam's tomb[2] between it and the Curriers'-gate; it is not worth much because, in the heats, it swarms with mosquitos. Kamari meadow adjoins it; counting this in, the meadows of Kabul would be six, but they are always spoken of as four.

---

[1] *pustin*, usually of sheep-skin. For the wide range of temperature at Kabul in 24 hours, see Ency. Brtt. art. Afghanistan. The winters also vary much in severity (Burnes, p. 273).

[2] Index *s.n.* As he fought at Kanwaha, he will have been buried after March 1527 AD.; this entry therefore will have been made later. The Curriers'-gate is the later Lahor-gate (Masson, ii, 259).

[3] For lists of the Hindu-kush passes *see* Leech's Report VII; Yule's *Introductory Essay to Wood's Journey* 2nd ed.; PRGS 1879, Markham's art. p. 121.

The highest *cols* on the passes here enumerated by Babur are,—Khawak 11,640 ft.—Tul. height not known,—Parandi 15,984 ft.—Baj-gah (Toll-place) 12,000 ft.—Walian (Saints) 15,100 ft.—Chahar-dar (Four-doors) 18,900 ft. and Shibr-tu 9800 ft. In considering the labour of their ascent and descent, the general high level, north and south of them, should be borne in mind; *e.g.* Charikar (Char-yak-kar) stands 5200 ft. and Kabul itself at 5780 ft. above the sea.

(e. *Mountain-passes into Kabul.*)

The country of Kabul is a fastness hard for a foreign foe to make his way into.

The Hindu-kush mountains, which separate Kabul from Balkh, Qunduz and Badakhshan, are crossed by seven roads.[3] Three of these lead out of Panjhir (Panj-sher), *viz.* Khawak, the upper-most, Tul, the next lower, and Bazarak.[1] Of the passes on them, the one on the Tul road is the best, but the road itself is rather the longest whence, seemingly, it is called Tul. Bazarak is the most direct; like Tul, it leads over into Sir-i-ab; as it passes through Parandi, local people call its main pass, the Parandi. Another road leads up through Parwan; it has seven minor passes, known as Haft-bacha (Seven-younglings), between Parwan and its main pass (Baj-gah). It is joined at its main pass by two roads from Andar-ab, which go on to Parwan by it. This is a road full of difficulties. Out of Ghur-bund, again, three roads lead over. The one next to Parwan, known as the Yangi-yul pass (New-road), goes through Wa(lian) to Khinjan; next above this is the Qibchaq road, crossing to where the water of Andar-ab meets the Surkh-ab (Qizil-su); this also is an excellent road; and the third leads over the Shibr-tu pass;[2] those crossing by this in the heats take their way by Bamian and Saighan, but those crossing by it in winter, go on by Ab-dara (Water-valley).[3] Shibr-tu excepted, all the Hindu-kush roads are closed for four or five months in winter.[4] After crossing Shibr-tu people go on through Ab-dara. In the heats, when the waters come down in flood, these roads have the same rule as in winter,

---

[1] *i.e.* the hollow, long, and small-bazar roads respectively. Panjhir is explained by Hindus to be Panj-sher, the five lion-sons of Pandu (Masson, iii, 168).

[2] Shibr is a Hazara district between the head of the Ghur-bund valley and Bamian. It does not seem to be correct to omit the *tu* from the name of the pass. Persian *tu*, turn, twist (syn. *pich*) occurs in other names of local passes; to read it here as a *turn* agrees with what is said of Shibr-tu pass as not crossing but turning the Hindu-kush (Cunningham). Lord uses the same wording about the Haji-ghat (var. -kak etc.) traverse of the same spur, which "turns the extremity of the Hindu-kush". See Cunningham's *Ancient Geography*, i, 25; Lord's *Ghur-bund* (JASB 1838 p. 528), Masson, iii, 169 and Leech's *Report* VII.

[3] Perhaps through Jalmish into Saighan.

[4] *i.e.* they are closed.

because no road through a valley-bottom is passable when the waters are high. If any-one thinks to cross the Hindu-kush at that time, over the mountains instead of through a valley-bottom, his journey is hard indeed. The time to cross is during the three or four autumn months when the snow is less and the waters are low. Whether on the mountains or in the valley-bottoms, Kafir highwaymen are not few.

The road from Kabul into Khurasan passes through Qandahar; it is quite level, without a pass.

Four roads lead into Kabul from the Hindustan side; one by rather a low pass through the Khaibar mountains, another by way of Bangash, another by way of Naghr (var. Naghz),[1] and another through Farmul;[2] the passes being low also in the three last-named. These roads are all reached from three ferries over the Sind. Those who take the Nil-ab[3] ferry, come on through the Lamghanat.[4] In winter, however, people ford the Sind-water (at Haru) above its junction with the Kabul-water,[5] and

---

[1] It was unknown in Mr. Erskine's day (Mems. p. 140). Several of the routes in Raverty's *Notes* (p. 92 etc.) allow it to be located as on the Iri-ab, near to or identical with Baghzan, 35 *kurohs* (70 m.) s.s.e. of Kabul.

[2] Farmul, about the situation of which Mr. Erskine was in doubt, is now marked in maps, Urghun being its principal village.

[3] 15 miles below Atak (Erskine). Mr. Erskine notes that he found no warrant, previous to Abu'l-fazl's, for calling the Indus the Nil-ab, and that to find one would solve an ancient geographical difficulty. This difficulty, my husband suggests, was Alexander's supposition that the Indus was the Nile. In books grouping round the *Babur-nama*, the name Nil-ab is not applied to the Indus, but to the ferry-station on that river, said to owe its name to a spring of azure water on its eastern side. (*Cf.* Afzal Khan *Khattak*, R.'s *Notes* p. 447.)

I find the name Nil-ab applied to the Kabul-river:—1. to its Arghandi affluent (Cunningham, p. 17, Map); 2. through its boatman class, the Nil-abis of Lalpura, Jalalabad and Kunar (G. of I. 1907, art. Kabul); 3. inferentially to it as a tributary of the Indus (D'Herbélot); 4. to it near its confluence with the grey, silt-laden Indus, as blue by contrast (Sayyid Ghulam-i-muhammad, R.'s *Notes* p. 34). (For Nil-ab (Naulibis?) in Ghur-bund *see* Cunningham, p. 32 and Masson, iii, 169.)

[4] By one of two routes perhaps,—either by the Khaibar-Ningnahar—Jagdalik road, or along the north bank of the Kabul-river, through Goshta to the crossing where, in 1879, the 10th Hussars met with disaster. *See S.A. War*, Map 2 and p. 63; Leech's *Reports* II and IV (Fords of the Indus); and R.'s *Notes* p. 44.

[5] Haru, Leech's Harroon, apparently, 10 m. above Atak. The text might be read to mean that both rivers were forded near their confluence but, finding no warrant for supposing the Kabul-river fordable below Jalalabad, I have guided the translation accordingly; this may be wrong and may conceal a change in the river.

ford this also. In most of my expeditions into Hindustan, I crossed those fords, but this last time (932 AH.—1525 AD.), when I came, defeated SI. Ibrahim and conquered the country, I crossed by boat at Nil-ab. Except at the one place mentioned above, the Sind-water can be crossed only by boat. Those again, who cross at Din-kot[6] go on through Bangash. Those crossing at Chaupara, if they take the Farmul road, go on to Ghazni, or, if they go by the Dasht, go on to Qandahar.[7]

(*f. Inhabitants of Kabul.*)

There are many differing tribes in the Kabul country; in its dales and plains are Turks and clansmen[1] and 'Arabs; in its town and in many villages, Sarts; out in the districts and also in villages are the Pashai, Paraji, Tajik, Birki and Afghan tribes. In the western mountains are the Hazara and Nikdiri tribes, some of whom speak the Mughuli tongue. In the north-eastern mountains are the places of the Kafirs, such as Kitur (Gawar?) and Gibrik. To the south are the places of the Afghan tribes.

Eleven or twelve tongues are spoken in Kabul,—'Arabi, Persian, Turki, Mughuli, Hindi, Afghani, Pashai, Paraji, Gibri, Birki and Lamghani. If there be another country with so many differing tribes and such a diversity of tongues, it is not known.

(*e. Sub-divisions of the Kabul country.*)

The [Kabul] country has fourteen *tumans*.[2]

Bajaur, Sawad and Hash-nagar may at one time have been dependencies of Kabul, but they now have no resemblance to cultivated countries

---

[6] known also as Dhan-kot and as Mu'azzam-nagar (*Ma'asiru'l-'umra* i, 249 and A.N. trs. H.B. index *s.n.* Dhan-kot). It was on the east bank of the Indus, probably near modern Kala-bagh, and was washed away not before 956 ah. (1549 ad. H. Beveridge).

[7] Chaupara seems, from f. 148*b*, to be the Chapari of Survey Map 1889. Babur's *Dasht* is modern Daman.

[1] *aimaq*, used usually of Mughuls, I think. It may be noted that Lieutenant Leech compiled a vocabulary of the tongue of the Mughul Aimaq in Qandahar and Harat (JASB [Journal of the Asiatic Society of Bengal] 1838, p. 785).

[2] The *Ayin-i-akbari* account of Kabul both uses and supplements the *Babur-nama*.

(*wilayat*), some lying desolate because of the Afghans, others being now subject to them.

In the east of the country of Kabul is the Lamghanat, 5 *tumans* and 2 *buluks* of cultivated lands.³ The largest of these is Ningnahar, sometimes written Nagarahar in the histories.⁴ Its *darogha*'s residence is in Adinapur,⁵ some 13 *yighach* east of Kabul by a very bad and tiresome road, going in three or four places over small hill-passes, and in three or four others, through narrows.¹ So long as there was no cultivation along it, the Khirilchi and other Afghan thieves used to make it their beat, but it has become safe² since I had it peopled at Qara-tu,³ below Quruq-sai. The hot and cold climates are separated on this road by the pass of Badam-chashma (Almond-spring); on its Kabul side snow falls, none at Quruq-sai, towards the Lamghanat.⁴ After descending this pass, another world comes into view, other trees, other plants (or grasses), other animals, and other manners and customs of men. Ningnahar is nine torrents (*tuquz-rud*).⁵ It grows good crops of rice and corn,

---

³ *viz.* 'Ali-shang, Alangar and Mandrawar (the Lamghanat proper), Ningnahar (with its *buluk*, Kama), Kunar-with-Nur-gal, (and the two *buluks* of Nur-valley and Chaghan-sarai).

⁴ See Appendix E, *On Nagarahara*.

⁵ The name Adinapur is held to be descended from ancient Udyanapura (Garden-town); its ancestral form however was applied to Nagarahara, apparently, in the Baran-Surkh-rud *du-ab*, and not to Babur's *darogha*'s seat. The Surkh-rud's deltaic mouth was a land of gardens; when Masson visited Adinapur he went from Bala-bagh (High-garden); this appears to stand where Babur locates his Bagh-i-wafa, but he was shown a garden he took to be this one of Babur's, a mile higher up the Surkh-rud. A later ruler made the Char-bagh of maps. It may be mentioned that Bala-bagh has become in some maps Rozabad (Garden-town). See Masson, i, 182 and iii, 186; R.'s *Notes*; and Wilson's *Ariana Antiqua*, Masson's art.

¹ One of these *tangi* is now a literary asset in Mr. Kipling's *My Lord the Elephant*. Babur's 13 y. represent some 82 miles; on f. 137*b* the Kabul-Ghazni road of 14 y. represents some 85; in each case the *yighach* works out at over six miles. Sayyid Ghulam i-muhammad traces this route minutely (R.'s *Notes* pp. 57, 59).

² Masson was shewn "Chaghatai casdes", attributed to Babur (iii, 174).

³ Dark-turn, perhaps, as in Shibr tu, Jal tu, *etc.* (f. 130*b* and note to Shibr-tu).

⁴ f. 145 where the change is described in identical words, as seen south of the Jagdalik-pass. The Badam-chashma pass appears to be a traverse of the eastern rampart of the Tizin-valley.

⁵ Appendix E, *On Nagarahara*.

excellent and abundant oranges, citrons and pomegranates. In 914 AH. (1508–9 AD.) I laid out the Four-gardens, known as the Bagh-i-wafa (Garden-of-fidelity), on a rising-ground, facing south and having the Surkh-rud between it and Fort Adinapur.[6] There oranges, citrons and pomegranates grow in abundance. The year I defeated Pahar Khan and took Lahor and Dipalpur,[7] I had plantains (bananas) brought and planted there; they did very well. The year before I had had sugar-cane planted there; it also did well; some of it was sent to Bukhara and Badakhshan.[8] The garden lies high, has running-water close at hand, and a mild winter climate. In the middle of it, a one-mill stream flows constantly past the little hill on which are the four garden-plots. In the south-west part of it there is a reservoir, 10 by 10,[9] round which are orange-trees and a few pomegranates, the whole encircled by a trefoil-meadow. This is the best part of the garden, a most beautiful sight when the oranges take colour. Truly that garden is admirably situated!

The Safed-koh runs along the south of Ningnahar, dividing it from Bangash; no riding-road crosses it; nine torrents (*tuquz-rud*) issue from it.[1] It is called Safed-koh[2] because its snow never lessens; none falls in the lower parts of its valleys, a half-day's journey from the snow-line. Many places along it have an excellent climate; its waters are cold and need no ice.

The Surkh-rud flows along the south of Adinapur. The fort stands on a height having a straight fall to the river of some 130 ft. (40 50 *qari*)

---

[6] No record exists of the actual laying-out of the garden; the work may have been put in hand during the Mahmand expedition of 914 AH. (f. 216); the name given to it suggests a gathering there of loyalists when the stress was over of the bad Mughul rebellion of that year (f. 216*b* where the narrative breaks off abruptly in 914 ah. and is followed by a gap down to 925 AH.—1519 AD.).

[7] No annals of 930 AH. are known to exist; from Safar 926 AH. to 932 AH. (Jan. 1520-Nov. 1525 AD.) there is a lacuna. Accounts of the expedition are given by Khafi Khan, i, 47 and Firishta, lith. ed. p. 202.

[8] Presumably to his son, Humayun, then governor in Badakhshan; Bukhara also was under Babur's rule.

[9] here, *qari*, yards. The dimensions 10 by 10, are those enjoined for places of ablution.

[1] Presumably those of the *tuquz rud*, *supra*. *Cf*. Appendix E, *On Nagarahara*.

[2] White mountain; Pushtu, Spin-ghur (or ghar).

and isolated from the mountain behind it on the north; it is very strongly placed. That mountain runs between Ningnahar and Lamghan;[3] on its head snow falls when it snows in Kabul, so Lamghanis know when it has snowed in the town.

In going from Kabul into the Lamghanat,[4] if people come by Quruq-sai, one road goes on through the Diri-pass, crosses the Baran-water at Bulan, and so on into the Lamghanat,—another goes through Qara-tu, below Quruq-sai, crosses the Baran-water at Aulugh-nur (Great-rock?), and goes into Lamghan by the pass of Bad-i-pich.[5] If however people come by Nijr-au, they traverse Badr-au (Tag-au), and Qara-nakariq (?), and go on on through the pass of Bad-i-pich.

Although Ningnahar is one of the five *tumans* of the Lamghan *tuman* the name Lamghanat applies strictly only to the three (mentioned below).

One of the three is the 'Ali-shang *tuman*, to the north of which are fastness-mountains, connecting with Hindu-kush and inhabited by Kafirs only. What of Kafiristan lies nearest to 'Ali-shang, is Mil out of which its torrent issues. The tomb of Lord Lam,[1] father of his Reverence the prophet Nuh (Noah), is in this *tuman*. In some histories he is called Lamak and

---

[3] *i.e.* the Lamghanat proper. The range is variously named; in (Persian) Siyah-koh (Black-mountain), which like Turki Qara-tagh may mean non-snowy; by Tajiks, Bagh-i-ataka (Foster-father's garden); by Afghans, Kanda-ghur, and by Lamghanis Koh-i-bulan,—Kanda and Bulan both being ferry-stations below it (Masson, iii, 189; also the Times Nov. 20th 1912 for a cognate illustration of diverse naming).

[4] A comment made here by Mr. Erskine on changes of name is still appropriate, but some seeming changes may well be due to varied selection of land-marks. Of the three routes next described in the text, one crosses as for Mandrawar; the second, as for 'Ali-shang, a little below the outfall of the Tizin-water; the third may take off from the route, between Kabul and Tag au, marked in Col. Tanner's map (PRGS 1881 p. 180). *Cf.* R's Route 11; and for Aulugh-nur, Appendix F, *On the name Nur*.

[5] The name of this pass has several variants. Its second component, whatever its form, is usually taken to mean *pass*, but to read it here as pass would be redundant, since Babur writes "pass (*kutal*) of Bad-i-pich". Pich occurs as a place name both east (Pich) and west (Pichghan) of the *kutal*, but what would suit the bitter and even fatal winds of the pass would be to read the name as Whirling-wind (*bad i-pich*). Another explanation suggests itself from finding a considerable number of pass names such as Shibr-tu, Jal-tu, Qara-tu, in which *tu* is a synonym of *pich*, turn, twist; thus Bad i pich may be the local form of Bad-tu, Windy turn.

[1] See Masson, iii, 197 and 289. Both in Pashai and Lamghani, *lam* means fort.

Lamakan. Some people are observed often to change *kaf* for *ghain* (k for gh); it would seem to be on this account that the country is called Lamghan.

The second is Alangar. The part of Kafiristan nearest to it is Gawar (Kawar), out of which its torrent issues (the Gau or Kau). This torrent joins that of 'Ali-shang and flows with it into the Baran-water, below Mandrawar, which is the third *tuman* of the Lamghanat.

Of the two *buluks* of Lamghan one is the Nur-valley.[2] This is a place (*yir*) without a second;[3] its fort is on a beak (*tumshuq*) of rock in the mouth of the valley, and has a torrent on each side; its rice is grown on steep terraces, and it can be traversed by one road only.[4] It has the orange, citron and other fruits of hot climates in abundance, a few dates even. Trees cover the banks of both the torrents below the fort; many are *amluk*, the fruit of which some Turks call *qara-yimish*;[5] here they are many, but none has been seen elsewhere. The valley grows grapes also, all trained on trees.[6] Its wines are those of Lamghan that have reputation. Two sorts of grapes are grown, the *arah-tashi* and the *suhan-tashi*;[1] the first are yellowish, the second, full-red of fine colour. The first make the more cheering wine, but it must be said that neither wine equals its reputation for cheer. High up in one of its glens, apes (*maimun*) are found, none below. Those people (*i.e.* Nuris) used to keep swine but they have given it up in our time.[2]

---

[2] See Appendix F, *On the name Dara-i-nur*.

[3] *ghair mukarrar*. Babur may allude to the remarkable change men have wrought in the valley-bottom (Appendix F, for Col. Tanner's account of the valley).

[4] f. 154.

[5] *diospyrus lotus*, the European date-plum, supposed to be one of the fruits eaten by the Lotophagi. It is purple, has bloom and is of the size of a pigeon's egg or a cherry. See Watts' *Economic Products of India*; Brandis' *Forest Trees*, Illustrations; and Speede's *Indian Hand-book*.

[6] As in Lombardy, perhaps; in Luhugur vines are clipped into standards; in most other places in Afghanistan they are planted in deep trenches and allowed to run over the intervening ridges or over wooden framework. In the narrow Khulm-valley they are trained up poplars so as to secure them the maximum of sun. See Wood's *Report* VI p. 27; Bellew's *Afghanistan* p. 175 and *Mems.* p. 142 note.

[1] Appendix G, *On the names of two Nuri wines*.

[2] This practice Babur viewed with disgust, the hog being an impure animal according to Muhammadan Law (Erskine).

Another *tuman* of Lamghan is Kunar-with-Nur-gal. It lies somewhat out-of-the-way, remote from the Lamghanat, with its borders in amongst the Kafir lands; on these accounts its people give in tribute rather little of what they have. The Chaghan-sarai water enters it from the north-east, passes on into the *buluk* of Kama, there joins the Baran-water and with that flows east.

Mir Sayyid 'Ali *Hamadani*,[3]—God's mercy on him!—coming here as he journeyed, died 2 miles (1 *shar'i*) above Kunar. His disciples carried his body to Khutlan. A shrine was erected at the honoured place of his death, of which I made the circuit when I came and took Chaghan-sarai in 924 AH.[4]

The orange, citron and coriander[5] abound in this *tuman*. Strong wines are brought down into it from Kafiristan.

A strange thing is told there, one seeming impossible, but one told to us again and again. All through the hill-country above Multa-kundi, *viz.* in Kunar, Nur-gal, Bajaur, Sawad and

> (*Author's note to Multa-kundi.*) As Multa-kundi is known the lower part of the tuman of Kunar-with-Nur-gal; what is below (i.e. on the river) belongs to the valley of Nur and to Atar.[6]

---

[3] The *Khazinatu'l-asfiya* (ii, 293) explains how it came about that this saint, one honoured in Kashmir, was buried in Khutlan. He died in Hazara (Pakli) and there the Pakli Sultan wished to have him buried, but his disciples, for some unspecified reason, wished to bury him in Khutlan. In order to decide the matter they invited the Sultan to remove the bier with the corpse upon it. It could not be stirred from its place. When, however a single one of the disciples tried to move it, he alone was able to lift it, and to bear it away on his head. Hence the burial in Khudan. The death occurred in 786 AH. (1384 AD.). A point of interest in this legend is that, like the one to follow, concerning dead women, it shews belief in the living activities of the dead.

[4] The MSS. vary between 920 and 925 AH.—neither date seems correct. As the annals of 925 AH. begin in Muharram, with Babur to the east of Bajaur, we surmise that the Chaghan-sarai affair may have occurred on his way thither, and at the end of 924 AH.

[5] *karanj, coriandrum sativum*.

[6] some 20–24 m. north of Jalalabad. The name Multa-kundi may refer to the Ram-kundi range, or mean Lower district, or mean Below Kundi. *See* Biddulph's *Khowari Dialect s.n.* under; R.'s *Notes* p. 108 and *Dict. s.n. kund*; Masson, i, 209.

thereabouts, it is commonly said that when a woman dies and has been laid on a bier, she, if she has not been an ill-doer, gives the bearers such a shake when they lift the bier by its four sides, that against their will and hindrance, her corpse falls to the ground; but, if she has done ill, no movement occurs. This was heard not only from Kunaris but, again and again, in Bajaur, Sawad and the whole hill-tract. Haidar-'ali *Bajauri*,—a sultan who governed Bajaur well,—when his mother died, did not weep, or betake himself to lamentation, or put on black, but said, "Go! lay her on the bier! if she move not, I will have her burned."[1] They laid her on the bier; the desired movement followed; when he heard that this was so, he put on black and betook himself to lamentation.

Another *buluk* is Chaghan-sarai,[2] a single village with little land, in the mouth of Kafiristan; its people, though Musalman, mix with the Kafirs and, consequently, follow their customs.[3] A great torrent (the Kunar) comes down to it from the north-east from behind Bajaur, and a smaller one, called Pich, comes down out of Kafiristan. Strong yellowish wines are had there, not in any way resembling those of the Nur-valley, however. The village has no grapes or vineyards of its own; its wines are all brought from up the Kafiristan-water and from Pich-i-kafiristani.

The Pich Kafirs came to help the villagers when I took the place. Wine is so commonly used there that every Kafir has his leathern wine-bag (*khig*) at his neck, and drinks wine instead of water.[4]

---

[1] *i.e.* treat her corpse as that of an infidel (Erskine).
[2] It would suit the position of this village if its name were found to link to the Turki verb *chiqmaq*, to go out, because it lies in the mouth of a defile (Dahanah-i-koh, Mountain-mouth) through which the road for Kafiristan goes out past the village. A not-infrequent explanation of the name to mean White-house, Aq-sarai, may well be questioned. *Chaghan*, white, is Mughuli and it would be less probable for a Mughuli than for a Turki name to establish itself. Another explanation may lie in the tribe name Chugani. The two forms *chaghan* and *chaghar* may well be due to the common local interchange in speech of *n* with *r*. (For Dahanah-i-koh *see* [some] maps and Raverty's Bajaur routes.)
[3] Nimchas, presumably,—half-bred in custom, perhaps in blood—; and not improbably, converted Kafirs. It is useful to remember that Kafiristan was once bounded, west and south, by the Baran-water.
[4] Kafir wine is mostly poor, thin and, even so, usually diluted with water. When kept two or three years, however, it becomes clear and sometimes strong. Sir G. S. Robertson never saw a Kafir drunk (*Kafirs of the Hindu-kush*, p. 591).

Kama, again, though not a separate district but dependent on Ningnahar, is also called a *buluk*.[1]

Nijr-au[2] is another *tuman*. It lies north of Kabul, in the Kohistan, with mountains behind it inhabited solely by Kafirs; it is a quite sequestered place. It grows grapes and fruits in abundance. Its people make much wine but, they boil it. They fatten many fowls in winter, are wine-bibbers, do not pray, have no scruples and are Kafir-like.[3]

In the Nijr-au mountains is an abundance of *archa, jilghuza, bilut* and *khanjak*.[4] The first-named three do not grow above Nigr-au but they grow lower, and are amongst the trees of Hindustan. *Jilghuza*-wood is all the lamp the people have; it burns like a candle and is very remarkable. The flying-squirrel[5] is found in these mountains, an animal larger than a bat and having a curtain (*parda*), like a bat's wing, between its arms and legs. People often brought one in; it is said to fly, downward from one tree to another, as far as a *giz* flies;[6] I myself have never seen one fly. Once we put one to a tree; it clambered up directly and got away, but, when people went after it, it spread its wings and came down, without hurt, as if it had flown. Another of the curiosities of the Nijr-au mountains is the *lukha* (var. *luja*) bird, called also *bu-qalamun* (chameleon) because, between head and tail, it has four or five changing colours, resplendent like a pigeon's throat.[7] It is about as large as the *kabg-i-dari* and seems to

---

[1] Kama might have classed better under Ningnahar of which it was a dependency.

[2] *i.e.* water-of-Nijr; so too, Badr-au and Tag-au. Nijr-au has seven-valleys (JASB 1838 p. 329 and Burnes' *Report* X). Sayyid Ghulam-i-muhammad mentions that Babur established a frontier-post between Nijr-au and Kafiristan which in his own day was still maintained. He was an envoy of Warren Hastings to Timur Shah *Sadozi* (R.'s *Notes* p. 36 and p. 142).

[3] *Kafirwash*; they were Kafirs converted to Muhammadanism.

[4] *Archa*, if not inclusive, meaning conifer, may represent *juniperus excelsa*, this being the common local conifer. The other trees of the list are *pinus Gerardiana* (Brandis, p. 690), *quercus bilut*, the holm-oak, and *pistacia mutica* or *khanjak*, a tree yielding mastic.

[5] *ruba-i-parran, pteromys inornatus*, the large, red flying-squirrel (Blanford's *Fauna of British India, Mammalia*, p. 363).

[6] The *giz* is a short-flight arrow used for shooting small birds etc. Descending flights of squirrels have been ascertained as 60 yards, one, a record, of 80 (Blanford).

[7] Apparently *tetrogallus himalayensis*, the Himalayan snow-cock (Blanford, iv, 143). Burnes (*Cabool* p. 163) describes the *kabg-i-dari* as the *rara avis* of the Kabul

be the *kabg-i-dari* of Hindustan.¹ People tell this wonderful thing about it:—When the birds, at the on-set of winter, descend to the hill-skirts, if they come over a vineyard, they can fly no further and are taken.² There is a kind of rat in Nijr-au, known as the musk-rat, which smells of musk; I however have never seen it.³

Panjhir (Panj-sher) is another *tuman*; it lies close to Kafiristan, along the Panjhir road, and is the thoroughfare of Kafir highway-men who also, being so near, take tax of it. They have gone through it, killing a mass of persons, and doing very evil deeds, since I came this last time and conquered Hindustan (932 AH.–1526 AD.).⁴

Another is the *tuman* of Ghur-bund. In those countries they call a *kutal* (*koh?*) a *bund*;⁵ they go towards Ghur by this pass (*kutal*); apparently it is for this reason that they have called (the *tuman?*) Ghur-bund. The Hazara hold the heads of its valleys.⁶ It has few villages and

Kohistan, somewhat less than a turkey, and of the *chikor* (partridge) species. It was procured for him first in Ghur-bund, but, when snow has fallen, it could be had nearer Kabul. Babur's *bu-qalamun* may have come into his vocabulary, either as a survival direct from Greek occupation of Kabul and Panj-ab, or through Arabic writings. PRGS 1879 p. 251, Kaye's art. and JASB 1838 p. 863, Hodgson's art.

¹ Bartavelle's *Greek-partridge*, *tetrao-* or *perdrix-rufus* [f. 279 and Mems. p. 320 n.].
² A similar story is told of some fields near Whitby:—"These wild geese, which in winter fly in great flocks to the lakes and rivers unfrozen in the southern parts, to the great amazement of every one, fall suddenly down upon the ground when they are in flight over certain neighbouring fields thereabouts; a relation I should not have made, if I had not received it from several credible men." *See Notes to Marmion* p. xlvi (Erskine); Scott's *Poems*, Black's ed. 1880, vii, 104.
³ Are we to infer from this that the musk-rat (*Crocidura cærulea*, Lydekker, p. 626) was not so common in Hindustan in the age of Babur as it has now become? He was not a careless observer (Erskine).
⁴ Index *s.n. Babur-nama*, date of composition; also f. 131.
⁵ In the absence of examples of *bund* to mean *kutal*, and the presence "in those countries" of many in which *bund* means *koh*, it looks as though a clerical error had here written *kutal* for *koh*. But on the other hand, the wording of the next passage shows just the confusion an author's unrevised draft might shew if a place were, as this is, both a *tuman* and a *kutal* (*i.e.* a steady rise to a traverse). My impression is that the name Ghur-bund applies to the embanking spur at the head of the valley-*tuman*, across which roads lead to Ghuri and Ghur (PRGS 1879, Maps; Leech's Report VII; and Wood's VI).
⁶ So too when, because of them, Leech and Lord turned back, *re infectâ*.

little revenue can be raised from it. There are said to be mines of silver and lapis lazuli in its mountains.

Again, there are the villages on the skirts of the (Hindu-kush) mountains,[7] with Mita-kacha and Parwan at their head, and Dur-nama[1] at their foot, 12 or 13 in all. They are fruit-bearing villages, and they grow cheering wines, those of Khwaja Khawand Sa'id being reputed the strongest roundabouts. The villages all lie on the foot-hills; some pay taxes but not all are taxable because they lie so far back in the mountains.

Between the foot-hills and the Baran-water are two detached stretches of level land, one known as *Kurrat-taziyan*,[2] the other as *Dasht-i-shaikh* (Shaikh's-plain). As the green grass of the millet[3] grows well there, they are the resort of Turks and (Mughul) clans (*aimaq*).

Tulips of many colours cover these foot-hills; I once counted them up; it came out at 32 or 33 different sorts. We named one the Rose-scented, because its perfume was a little like that of the red rose; it grows by itself on Shaikh's-plain, here and nowhere else. The Hundred-leaved tulip is another; this grows, also by itself, at the outlet of the Ghur-bund narrows, on the hill-skirt below Parwan. A low hill known as Khwaja-i-reg-rawan (Khwaja-of-the-running-sand), divides the afore-named two

---

[7] It will be noticed that these villages are not classed in any *tuman*; they include places "rich without parallel" in agricultural products, and level lands on which towns have risen and fallen, one being Alexandria ad Caucasum. They cannot have been part of the unremunerative Ghur bund *tuman*; from their place of mention in Babur's list of *tumans*, they may have been part of the Kabul *tuman* (f. 178), as was Koh-daman (Burnes' *Cabool* p. 154; Haughton's *Charikar* p. 73; and Cunningham's *Ancient History*, i, 18).

[1] Dur-namai, seen from afar (Masson, iii, 152) is not marked on the Survey Maps; Masson, Vigne and Haughton locate it. Babur's "head" and "foot" here indicate status and not location.

[2] Mems. p. 146 and *Méms*. i, 297, Arabs' encampment and *Cellule des Arabes*. Perhaps the name may refer to uses of the level land and good pasture by horse *qafilas*, since *Kurra* is written with *tash did* in the Haidarabad Codex, as in *kurra-taz*, a horse breaker. Or the *taziyan* may be the fruit of a legend, commonly told, that the saint of the neighbouring Running-sands was an Arabian.

[3] Presumably this is the grass of the millet, the growth before the ear, on which grazing is allowed (Elphinstone, i, 400; Burnes, p. 237).

pieces of level land; it has, from top to foot, a strip of sand from which people say the sound of nagarets and tambours issues in the heats.[4]

Again, there are the villages depending on Kabul itself. South-west from the town are great snow mountains[5] where snow falls on snow, and where few may be the years when, falling, it does not light on last year's snow. It is fetched, 12 miles may-be, from these mountains, to cool the drinking water when ice-houses in Kabul are empty. Like the Bamian mountains, these are fastnesses. Out of them issue the Harmand (Halmand), Sind, Dughaba of Qunduz, and Balkh-ab,[1] so that in a single day, a man might drink of the water of each of these four rivers.

It is on the skirt of one of these ranges (Pamghan) that most of the villages dependent on Kabul lie.[2] Masses of grapes ripen in their vineyards and they grow every sort of fruit in abundance. No-one of them equals Istalif or Astarghach; these must be the two which Aulugh Beg Mirza used to call his Khurasan and Samarkand. Pamghan is another of the best, not ranking in fruit and grapes with those two others, but beyond comparison with them in climate. The Pamghan mountains are a snowy range. Few villages match Istalif, with vineyards and fine orchards on both sides of its great torrent, with waters needing no ice, cold and, mostly, pure. Of its Great garden Aulugh Beg Mirza had taken forcible possession; I took it over, after paying its price to the owners. There is a pleasant halting-place outside it, under great planes, green, shady and beautiful. A one-mill stream, having trees on both banks, flows constantly through the middle of the garden; formerly its course was zig-zag and irregular; I had it made straight and orderly; so the place

---

[4] Wood, p. 115; Masson, iii, 167; Burnes, p. 157 and JASB 1838 p. 324 with illustration; Vigne, pp. 219, 223; Lord, JASB 1838 p. 537; *Cathay and the way thither*, Hakluyt Society vol. I. p. xx, para. 49; *History of Musical Sands*, C. Carus Wilson.

[5] *West* might be more exact, since some of the group are a little north, others a little south of the latitude of Kabul.

[1] Affluents and not true sources in some cases (Col. Holdich's *Gates of India, s.n.* Koh-i baba; and PRGS 1879, maps pp. 80 and 160).

[2] The Pamghan range. These are the villages every traveller celebrates. Masson's and Vigne's illustrations depict them well.

became very beautiful. Between the village and the valley-bottom, from 4 to 6 miles down the slope, is a spring, known as Khwaja Sih-yaran (Three-friends), round which three sorts of tree grow. A group of planes gives pleasant shade above it; holm-oak (*quercus bilut*) grows in masses on the slope at its sides, these two oaklands (*bilutistan*) excepted, no holm-oak grows in the mountains of western Kabul, and the Judas-tree (*arghwan*)[3] is much cultivated in front of it, that is towards the level ground,—cultivated there and nowhere else. People say the three different sorts of tree were a gift made by three saints,[4] whence its name. I ordered that the spring should be enclosed in mortared stone-work, 10 by 10, and that a symmetrical, right-angled platform should be built on each of its sides, so as to overlook the whole field of Judas-trees. If, the world over, there is a place to match this when the *arghwans* are in full bloom, I do not know it. The yellow *arghwan* grows plentifully there also, the red and the yellow flowering at the same time.[1]

In order to bring water to a large round seat which I had built on the hillside and planted round with willows, I had a channel dug across the slope from a half-mill stream, constantly flowing in a valley to the south-west of Sih-yaran. It became a very good halting-place. I had a vineyard planted on the hill above the seat. The date of cutting this channel was found in *jui-khush* (kindly channel).[2]

Another of the *tumans* of Kabul is Luhugur (mod. Logar). Its one large village is Chirkh from which were his Reverence Maulana Ya'qub and

---

[3] *Cercis siliquastrum*, the Judas tree. Even in 1842 it was sparingly found near Kabul, adorning a few tombs, one Babur's own. It had been brought from Sih-yaran where, as also at Charikar, (Char-yak-kar) it was still abundant and still a gorgeous sight. It is there a tree, as at Kew, and not a bush, as in most English gardens (Masson, ii, 9; Elphinstone, i, 194; and for the tree near Harat, f. 191 n. to Safar).

[4] Khwaja Maudud of Chisht, Khwaja Khawand Sa'id and the Khwaja of the Running-sands (Elph. MS. f. 104*b*, marginal note).

[1] The yellow flowered plant is not *cercis siliquastrum* but one called *mahaka* (?) in Persian, a shrubby plant with pea like blossoms, common in the plains of Persia, Biluchistan and Kabul (Masson, iii, 9 and Vigne, p. 216).

[2] The numerical value of these words gives 925 (Erskine). F. 246*b et seq.* for the expedition.

Mulla-zada 'Usman.[3] Khwaja Ahmad and Khwaja Yunas were from Sajawand, another of its villages. Chirkh has many gardens, but there are none in any other village of Luhugur. Its people are Aughan-shal, a term common in Kabul, seeming to be a mispronouncement of Aughan-sha'ar.[4]

Again, there is the *wilayat*, or, as some say, *tuman* of Ghazni, said to have been[5] the capital of Sabuk-tigin, Sl. Mahmud and their descendants. Many write it Ghaznin. It is said also to have been the seat of government of Shihabu'd-din *Ghuri*,[6] styled Mu'izzu'd-din in the *Tabaqat-i-nasiri* and also some of the histories of Hind.

Ghazni has little cultivated land. Its torrent, a four-mill or five-mill stream may-be, makes the town habitable and fertilizes four or five villages; three or four others are cultivated from under-ground water-courses (*karez*). Ghazni grapes are better than those of Kabul; its melons are more abundant; its apples are very good, and are carried to Hindustan. Agriculture is very laborious in Ghazni because, whatever the quality of the soil, it must be newly top-dressed every year, it gives a better return, however, than Kabul. Ghazni grows madder; the entire crop goes to Hindustan and yields excellent profit to the growers. In the open-country of Ghazni dwell Hazara and Afghans. Compared with Kabul, it is always a cheap place. Its people hold to the Hanafi faith, are good, orthodox Musalmans, many keep a three months' fast,[1] and their wives and children live modestly secluded.

One of the eminent men of Ghazni was Mulla 'Abdu'r-rahman, a learned man and always a learner (*dars*), a most orthodox, pious and virtuous person; he left this world the same year as Nasir Mirza (921 AH.–1515 AD.).

---

[3] f. 178. I.O.MS. No. 724, Haft-iqlim f. 135 (Ethé, p. 402); Rieu, pp. 21a, 1058b.

[4] of Afghan habit. The same term is applied (f. 139b) to the Zurmutis; it may be explained in both places by Babur's statement that Zurmutis grow corn, but do not cultivate gardens or orchards.

[5] *aikan dur*. Sabuk-tigin, d. 387 AH.–997 AD., was the father of Sl. Mahmud *Ghaznawi*, d. 421 AH.–1030 AD.

[6] d. 602 AH.–1206 AD.

[1] Some Musalmans fast through the months of Rajab, Sha'ban and Ramzan; Muhammadans fast only by day; the night is often given to feasting (Erskine).

Sl. Mahmud's tomb is in the suburb called Rauza,[2] from which the best grapes come; there also are the tombs of his descendants, Sl. Mas'ud and Sl. Ibrahim. Ghazni has many blessed tombs. The year[3] I took Kabul and Ghazni, over-ran Kohat, the plain of Bannu and lands of the Afghans, and went on to Ghazni by way of Duki (Dugi) and Ab-istada, people told me there was a tomb, in a village of Ghazni, which moved when a benediction on the Prophet was pronounced over it. We went to see it. In the end I discovered that the movement was a trick, presumably of the servants at the tomb, who had put a sort of platform above it which moved when pushed, so that, to those on it, the tomb seemed to move, just as the shore does to those passing in a boat. I ordered the scaffold destroyed and a dome built over the tomb; also I forbad the servants, with threats, ever to bring about the movement again.

Ghazni is a very humble place; strange indeed it is that rulers in whose hands were Hindustan and Khurasanat,[1] should have chosen it for their capital. In the Sultan's (Mahmud's) time there may have been three or four dams in the country; one he made, some three *yighach* (18 m. ?) up the Ghazni-water to the north; it was about 40–50 *qari* (yards) high and some 300 long; through it the stored waters were let out as required.[2] It was destroyed by 'Alau'u'd-din *Jahan-soz Ghuri* when he conquered the country (550 AH.–1152 AD.), burned and ruined the tombs of several descendants of Sl. Mahmud, sacked and burned the town, in short, left undone no tittle of murder and rapine. Since that time, the Sultan's dam has lain in ruins, but, through God's favour, there is hope that it may become of use again, by means of the money which was sent, in Khwaja Kalan's hand, in the year Hindustan was conquered (932 AH.–1526 AD.).[3] The Sakhandam is another, 2 or 3 *yighach* (12–18 m.), maybe, on the

---

[2] The Garden; the tombs of more eminent Musalmans are generally in gardens (Erskine). *See* Vigne's illustrations, pp. 133, 266.

[3] *i.e.* the year now in writing. The account of the expedition, Babur's first into Hindustan, begins on f. 145.

[1] *i.e.* the countries groupable as Khurasan.
[2] For picture and account of the dam, *see* Vigne, pp. 138, 202.
[3] f. 295b.

east of the town; it has long been in ruins, indeed is past repair. There is a dam in working order at Sar-i-dih (Village-head).

In books it is written that there is in Ghazni a spring such that, if dirt and foul matter be thrown into it, a tempest gets up instantly, with a blizzard of rain and wind. It has been seen said also in one of the histories that Sabuk-tigin, when besieged by the Rai (Jai-pal) of Hind, ordered dirt and foulness to be thrown into the spring, by this aroused, in an instant, a tempest with blizzard of rain and snow, and, by this device, drove off his foe.[4] Though we made many enquiries, no intimation of the spring's existence was given us.

In these countries Ghazni and Khwarizm are noted for cold, in the same way that Sultania and Tabriz are in the two 'Iraqs and Azarbaijan.

Zurmut is another *tuman*, some 12–13 *yighach* south of Kabul and 7 8 south-east of Ghazni.[1] Its *darogha*'s head-quarters are in Girdiz; there most houses are three or four storeys high. It does not want for strength, and gave Nasir Mirza trouble when it went into hostility to him. Its people are Aughan-shal; they grow corn but have neither vineyards nor orchards. The tomb of Shaikh Muhammad *Musalman* is at a spring, high on the skirt of a mountain, known as Barakistan, in the south of the *tuman*.

Farmul is another *tuman*,[2] a humble place, growing not bad apples which are carried into Hindustan. Of Farmul were the Shaikh-zadas, descendants of Shaikh Muhammad *Musalman*, who were so much in favour during the Afghan period in Hindustan.

Bangash is another *tuman*.[3] All round about it are Afghan highwaymen, such as the Khugiani, Khirilchi, Turi and Landar. Lying out-of-the-way, as it does, its people do not pay taxes willingly. There has been no time to

---

[4] The legend is told in numerous books with varying location of the spring. One narrator, Zakariya *Qazwini*, reverses the parts, making Jai pal employ the ruse; hence Leyden's note (Mems. p. 150; E. and D.'s *History of India* ii, 20, 182 and iv, 162; for historical information, R.'s *Notes* p. 320). The date of the events is shortly after 378 ah. 988 ad.

[1] R.'s *Notes s.n.* Zurmut.

[2] The question of the origin of the Farmuli has been written of by several writers; perhaps they were Turks of Persia, Turks and Tajiks.

[3] This completes the list of the 14 *tumans* of Kabul, *viz*. Ningnahar, 'Ali-shang, Alangar, Mandrawar, Kunar-with-Nur-gal, Nijr-au, Panjhir, Ghur-bund, Koh-daman (with Kohistan?), Luhugur (of the Kabul *tuman*), Ghazni, Zurmut, Farmul and Bangash.

bring it to obedience; greater tasks have fallen to me,—the conquests of Qandahar, Balkh, Badakhshan and Hindustan! But, God willing! when I get the chance, I most assuredly will take order with those Bangash thieves.

One of the *buluks* of Kabul is Ala-sai,[4] 4 to 6 miles (2–3 *shar'i*) east of Nijr-au. The direct road into it from Nijr-au leads, at a place called Kura, through the quite small pass which in that locality separates the hot and cold climates. Through this pass the birds migrate at the change of the seasons, and at those times many are taken by the people of Pichghan, one of the dependencies of Nijr-au, in the following manner:—From distance to distance near the mouth of the pass, they make hiding-places for the bird-catchers. They fasten one corner of a net five or six yards away, and weight the lower side to the ground with stones. Along the other side of the net, for half its width, they fasten a stick some 3 to 4 yards long. The hidden bird-catcher holds this stick and by it, when the birds approach, lifts up the net to its full height. The birds then go into the net of themselves. Sometimes so many are taken by this contrivance that there is not time to cut their throats.[1]

Though the Ala-sai pomegranates are not first-rate, they have local reputation because none are better there-abouts; they are carried into Hindustan. Grapes also do not grow badly, and the wines of Ala-sai are better and stronger than those of Nijr-au.

Badr-au (Tag-au) is another *buluk*; it runs with Ala-sai, grows no fruit, and for cultivators has corn-growing Kafirs.[2]

(f. Tribesmen of Kabul.)

Just as Turks and (Mughul) clans (*aimaq*) dwell in the open country of Khurasan and Samarkand, so in Kabul do the Hazara and Afghans. Of

---

[4] Between Nijr-au and Tag-au (Masson, iii, 165). Mr. Erskine notes that Babur reckoned it in the hot climate but that the change of climate takes place further east, between 'Ali-shang and Auzbin (*i.e.* the valley next eastwards from Tag-au).

[1] *bughuzlarigha fursat bulmas*; *i.e.* to kill them in the lawful manner, while pronouncing the *Bi'smi'llah*.

[2] This completes the *buluks* of Kabul *viz*. Badr-au (Tag-au), Nur-valley, Chaghan-sarai, Kama and Ala-sai.

the Hazara, the most widely-scattered are the Sultan-mas'udi Hazara, of Afghans, the Mahmand.

(g. *Revenue of Kabul.*)

The revenues of Kabul, whether from the cultivated lands or from tolls (*tamgha*) or from dwellers in the open country, amount to 8 *laks* of *shahrukhis*.[3]

(h. *The mountain-tracts of Kabul.*)

The mountains to the eastward of the cultivated land of Kabul are of two kinds as also are those to its westward. Where the mountains of Andar-ab, Khwast,[4] and the Badakh-shanat have conifers (*archa*), many springs and gentle slopes, those of eastern Kabul have grass (*aut*), grass like a beautiful floor, on hill, slope and dale. For the most part it is *buta-kah* grass (*aut*), very suitable for horses. In the Andijan country they talk of *buta-kah*, but why they do so was not known (to me?); in Kabul it was heard-say to be because the grass comes up in tufts (*buta, buta*).[1] The alps of these mountains are like those of Hisar, Khutlan, Farghana, Samarkand and Mughulistan, all these being alike in mountain and alp, though the alps of Farghana and Mughulistan are beyond comparison with the rest.

From all these the mountains of Nijr-au, the Lamghanat and Sawad differ in having masses of cypresses,[2] holm-oak, olive and mastic (*khanjak*); their grass also is different, it is dense, it is tall, it is good neither for horse nor sheep. Although these mountains are not so high as those already described, indeed they look to be low, none-the-less,

---

[3] The *rupi* being equal to 2½ *shahrukhis*, the *shahrukhi* may be taken at 10*d*. thus making the total revenue only £33,333 6s. 8*d*. See *Ayin-i-akbari* ii, 169 (Erskine).

[4] *sic* in all B.N. MSS. Most maps print Khost. Muh. Salih says of Khwast, "Who sees it, would call it a Hell" (Vambéry, p. 361).

[1] Babur's statement about this fodder is not easy to translate; he must have seen grass grow in tufts, and must have known the Persian word *buta* (bush). Perhaps *kah* should be read to mean plant, not grass. Would Wood's *bootr* fit in, a small furze bush, very plentiful near Bamian? (Wood's Report VI, p. 23; and for region al grasses, Aitchison's *Botany of the Afghan Delimitation Commission*, p. 122.)

[2] *nazu*, perhaps *cupressus torulosa* (Brandis, p. 693).

they are strongholds; what to the eye is even slope, really is hard rock on which it is impossible to ride. Many of the beasts and birds of Hindustan are found amongst them, such as the parrot, *mina*, peacock and *luja* (*lukha*), the ape, *nil-gau* and hog-deer (*kuta-pai*);[3] some found there are not found even in Hindustan.

The mountains to the west of Kabul are also all of one sort, those of the Zindan-valley, the Suf-valley, Garzawan and Gharjistan (Gharchastan).[4] Their meadows are mostly in the dales; they have not the same sweep of grass on slope and top as some of those described have; nor have they masses of trees; they have, however, grass suiting horses. On their flat tops, where all the crops are grown, there is ground where a horse can gallop. They have masses of *kiyik*.[5] Their valley-bottoms are strongholds, mostly precipitous and inaccessible from above. It is remarkable that, whereas other mountains have their fastnesses in their high places, these have theirs below.

Of one sort again are the mountains of Ghur, Karnud (var. Kuzud) and Hazara; their meadows are in their dales; their trees are few, not even the *archa* being there;[6] their grass is fit for horses and for the masses of sheep they keep. They differ from those last described in this, their strong places are not below.

The mountains (south-east of Kabul) of Khwaja Isma'il, Dasht, Dugi (Duki)[1] and Afghanistan are all alike; all low, scant of vegetation, short of water, treeless, ugly and good-for-nothing. Their people take after them, just as has been said, *Ting bulma-ghuncha tush bulmas*.[2] Likely enough the world has few mountains so useless and disgusting.

---

[3] f. 276.

[4] A laborious geographical note of Mr. Erskine's is here regretfully left behind, as now needless (Mems. p. 152).

[5] Here, mainly wild-sheep and wild goats, including *mar khwar*.

[6] Perhaps, no conifers; perhaps none of those of the contrasted hill-tract.

[1] While here *dasht* (plain) represents the eastern skirt of the Mehtar Sulaiman range, *duki* or *dugi* (desert) seems to stand for the hill tracts on the west of it, and not, as on f. 152, for the place there specified.

[2] Mems. p. 152, "A narrow place is large to the narrow-minded"; *Méms.* i, 311, "Ce qui n'est pas trop large, ne reste pas vide." Literally, "So long as heights are not equal, there is no vis-a-vis," or, if *tang* be read for *ting*, "No dawn, no noon," *i.e.* no effect without a cause.

(h. Fire-wood of Kabul.)

The snow-fall being so heavy in Kabul, it is fortunate that excellent fire-wood is had near by. Given one day to fetch it, wood can be had of the *khanjak* (mastic), *bilut* (holm-oak), *badamcha* (small-almond) and *qarqand*.[3] Of these *khanjak* wood is the best; it burns with flame and nice smell, makes plenty of hot ashes and does well even if sappy. Holm-oak is also first-rate fire-wood, blazing less than mastic but, like it, making a hot fire with plenty of hot ashes, and nice smell. It has the peculiarity in burning that when its leafy branches are set alight, they fire up with amazing sound, blazing and crackling from bottom to top. It is good fun to burn it. The wood of the small-almond is the most plentiful and commonly-used, but it does not make a lasting fire. The *qarqand* is quite a low shrub, thorny, and burning sappy or dry; it is the fuel of the Ghazni people.

(i. Fauna of Kabul.)

The cultivated lands of Kabul lie between mountains which are like great dams[4] to the flat valley-bottoms in which most villages and peopled places are. On these mountains *kiyik* and *ahu*[1] are scarce. Across them, between its summer and winter quarters, the dun sheep,[2] the *arqarghalcha*, have their regular track,[3] to which braves go out with

---

[3] I have not lighted on this name in botanical books or explained by dictionaries. Perhaps it is a Cis-oxanian name for the *sax-aol* of Transoxania. As its uses are enumerated by some travellers, it might be *Haloxylon ammodendron*, *ta-ghaz* etc. and *sax-aol* (Aitchison, p. 102).

[4] f. 135b note to Ghur-bund. *See also*, Additional Notes, p. 798.

[1] I understand that wild goats, wild-sheep and deer (*ahu*) were not localized, but that the dun sheep migrated through. Antelope (*ahu*) was scarce in Elphinstone's time.

[2] *qizil kiyik* which, taken with its alternative name, *arqarghalcha*, allows it to be the dun sheep of Wood's *Journey* p. 241. From its second name it may be *Ovis amnon* (Raos), or *O. argali*.

[3] *tusqawal*, var. *tutqawal*, *tusaqawal* and *tushqawal*, a word which has given trouble to scribes and translators. As a sporting-term it is equivalent to *shikar i-nihilam*; in one or other of its forms I find it explained as *Weg hüter*, *Fahnen hüter*, *Zahl meister*, *Schlucht*, *Gefahrlicher-weg* and *Schmaler weg*. It recurs in the B.N. on f. 197b l. 5 and l. 6 and there might mean either a narrow road or a *Weg-hüter*. If its Turki root be *tus*, the act of stopping, all the above meanings can follow, but there may be two separate roots, the second, *tush*, the act of descent (JRAS 1900 p. 137, H. Beveridge's art. *On the word nihilam*).

dogs and birds[4] to take them. Towards Khurd-kabul and the Surkh-rud there is wild-ass, but there are no white *kiyik* at all; Ghazni has both and in few other places are white *kiyik* found in such good condition.[5]

In the heats the fowling-grounds of Kabul are crowded. The birds take their way along the Baran-water. For why? It is because the river has mountains along it, east and west, and a great Hindu-kush pass in a line with it, by which the birds must cross since there is no other near.[6] They cannot cross when the north wind blows, or if there is even a little cloud on Hindu-kush; at such times they alight on the level lands of the Baran-water and are taken in great numbers by the local people. Towards the end of winter, dense flocks of mallards (*aurduq*) reach the banks of the Baran in very good condition. Follow these the cranes and herons,[7] great birds, in large flocks and countless numbers.

(*j. Bird-catching.*)

Along the Baran people take masses of cranes (*turna*) with the cord; masses of *auqar*, *qarqara* and *qutan* also.[8] This method of bird-catching is unique. They twist a cord as long as the arrow's[1] flight, tie the arrow at one end and a *bildurga*[2] at the other, and wind it up, from the arrow-end, on a piece of wood, span-long and wrist-thick, right up to

---

[4] *qushlik, aitlik*. Elphinstone writes (i, 191) of the excellent greyhounds and hawking birds of the region; here the bird may be the *charkh*, which works with the dogs, fastening on the head of the game (Von Schwarz, p. 117, for the same use of eagles).

[5] An antelope resembling the usual one of Hindustan is common south of Ghazni (Vigne, p. 110); what is not found may be some classes of wild sheep, frequent further north, at higher elevation, and in places more familiar to Babur.

[6] The Parwan or Hindu kush pass, concerning the winds of which *see* f. 128.

[7] *tuma u qarqara*; the second of which is the Hindi *bugla*, heron, *egret ardea gazet ta*, the furnisher of the aigrette of commerce.

[8] The *auqar* is *ardea cinerea*, the grey heron; the *qarqara* is *ardea gazetta*, the egret. *Qutan* is explained in the Elph. Codex (f. 110) by *khawasil*, goldfinch, but the context con cems large birds; Scully (Shaw's Voc) has *qodan*, water-hen, which suits better.

[1] *giz*, the short flight arrow.

[2] a small, round headed nail with which a whip-handle is decorated (Vambéry). Such a stud would keep the cord from slipping through the fingers and would not check the arrow-release.

the *bildurga*. They then pull out the piece of wood, leaving just the hole it was in. The *bildurga* being held fast in the hand, the arrow is shot off[3] towards the coming flock. If the cord twist round a neck or wing, it brings the bird down. On the Baran everyone takes birds in this way; it is difficult; it must be done on rainy nights, because on such nights the birds do not alight, but fly continually and fly low till dawn, in fear of ravening beasts of prey. Through the night the flowing river is their road, its moving water showing through the dark; then it is, while they come and go, up and down the river, that the cord is shot. One night I shot it; it broke in drawing in; both bird and cord were brought in to me next day. By this device Baran people catch the many herons from which they take the turban-aigrettes sent from Kabul for sale in Khurasan.

Of bird-catchers there is also the band of slave-fowlers, two or three hundred households, whom some descendant of Timur Beg made migrate from near Multan to the Baran.[4] Bird-catching is their trade; they dig tanks, set decoy-birds[5] on them, put a net over the middle, and in this way take all sorts of birds. Not fowlers only catch birds, but every dweller on the Baran does it, whether by shooting the cord, setting the springe, or in various other ways.

(*k. Fishing.*)

The fish of the Baran migrate at the same seasons as birds. At those times many are netted, and many are taken on wattles (*chigh*) fixed in

---

[3] It has been understood (Mems. p. 158 and *Méms.* i, 313) that the arrow was flung by hand but if this were so, something heavier than the *giz* would carry the cord better, since it certainly would be difficult to direct a missile so light as an arrow without the added energy of the bow. The arrow itself will often have found its billet in the closely-flying flock; the cord would retrieve the bird. The verb used in the text is *aitmaq*, the one common to express the discharge of arrows *etc*.

[4] For Timurids who may have immigrated the fowlers *see* Raverty's *Notes* p. 579 and his Appendix p. 22.

[5] *milwah*; this has been read by all earlier translators, and also by the Persian annotator of the Elph. Codex, to mean *shakh*, bough. For decoy ducks *see* Bellew's *Notes on Afghanistan* p. 404.

the water. In autumn when the plant known as *wild-ass-tail*¹ has come to maturity, flowered and seeded, people take 10–20 loads (of seed?) and 20–30 of green branches (*guk-shibak*) to some head of water, break it up small and cast it in. Then going into the water, they can at once pick up drugged fish. At some convenient place lower down, in a hole below a fall, they will have fixed before-hand a wattle of finger-thick willow-withes, making it firm by piling stones on its sides. The water goes rushing and dashing through the wattle, but leaves on it any fish that may have come floating down. This way of catching fish is practised in Gul-bahar, Parwan and Istalif.

Fish are had in winter in the Lamghanat by this curious device: People dig a pit to the depth of a house, in the bed of a stream, below a fall, line it with stones like a cooking-place, and build up stones round it above, leaving one opening only, under water. Except by this one opening, the fish have no inlet or outlet, but the water finds its way through the stones. This makes a sort of fish-pond from which, when wanted in winter, fish can be taken, 30–40 together. Except at the opening, left where convenient, the sides of the fish-pond are made fast with rice-straw, kept in place by stones. A piece of wicker-work is pulled into the said opening by its edges, gathered together, and into this a second piece, (a tube,) is inserted, fitting it at the mouth but reaching half-way into it only.² The fish go through the smaller piece into the larger one, out from which they cannot get. The second narrows towards its inner mouth, its pointed ends being drawn so close that the fish, once entered, cannot turn, but must go on, one by one, into the larger piece.

---

¹ *qulan quyirughi*. Amongst the many plants used to drug fish I have not found this one mentioned. *Khar zahra* and *khar-faq* approach it in verbal meaning; the first describes colocynth, the second, wild me. See Watts' *Economic Products of India* iii, 366 and Bellew's *Notes* pp. 182, 471 and 478.

² Much trouble would have been spared to himself and his translators, if Babur had known a lobster-pot.

³ The fish, it is to be inferred, came down the fall into the pond.

¹ Burnes and Vigne describe a fall 20 miles from Kabul, at "Tangi Gharoi", [below where the Tag au joins the Baran-water,] to which in their day, Kabulis went out for the amusement of catching fish as they try to leap up the fall. Were these migrants seeking upper waters or were they captives in a fish-pond?

Out of that they cannot return because of the pointed ends of the inner, narrow mouth. The wicker-work fixed and the rice-straw making the pond fast, whatever fish are inside can be taken out;[3] any also which, trying to escape may have gone into the wicker-work, are taken in it, because they have no way out. This method of catching fish we have seen nowhere else.[1]

(*March 5th*) Next morning when the Court rose, we rode out for an excursion, entered a boat and there drank '*araq*.[1] The people of the party were Khwaja Dost-khawand, Khusrau, Mirim, Mirza Quli, Muhammadi, Ahmadi, Gadai, Na'man, Langar Khan, Rauh-dam,[2] Qasim-i-'ali the opium-eater (*tariyaki*), Yusuf-i-'ali and Tingri-quli. Towards the head of the boat there was a *talar*[3] on the flat top of which I sat with a few people, a few others fitting below. There was a sitting-place also at the tail of the boat; there Muhammadi, Gadai and Na'man sat. '*Araq* was drunk till the Other Prayer when, disgusted by its bad flavour, by consent of those at the head of the boat, *ma'jun* was preferred.

Those at the other end, knowing nothing about our *ma'jun* drank '*araq* right through. At the Bed-time Prayer we rode from the boat and got into camp late. Thinking I had been drinking '*araq* Muhammadi and Gadai had said to one another, "Let's do befitting service," lifted a pitcher of '*araq* up to one another in turn on their horses, and came in saying with wonderful joviality and heartiness and speaking together, "Through this dark night have we come carrying this pitcher in turns!" Later on when they knew that the party was (now) meant to be otherwise and the hilarity to differ, that is to say, that [there would be that] of the *ma'jun* band and that of the drinkers, they were much disturbed because

---

[3] The fish, it is to be inferred, came down the fall into the pond.

[1] Burnes and Vigne describe a fall 20 miles from Kabul, at "Tangi Gharoi", [below where the Tag au joins the Baran-water,] to which in their day, Kabulis went out for the amusement of catching fish as they try to leap up the fall. Were these migrants seeking upper waters or were they captives in a fish-pond?

[1] Here this will be the fermented juice of rice or of the date-palm.
[2] *Rauh* is sometimes the name of a musical note.
[3] a platform, with or without a chamber above it, and supported on four posts.

never does a *ma'jun* party go well with a drinking-party. Said I, "Don't upset the party! Let those who wish to drink *'araq*, drink *'araq*; let those who wish to eat *ma'jun*, eat *ma'jun*. Let no-one on either side make talk or allusion to the other." Some drank *'araq*, some ate *ma'jun*, and for a time the party went on quite politely. Baba Jan the *qabuz*-player had not been of our party (in the boat); we invited him when we reached the tents. He asked to drink *'araq*. We invited Tardi Muhammad *Qibchaq* also and made him a comrade of the drinkers. A *ma'jun* party never goes well with an *'araq* or a wine-party; the drinkers began to make wild talk and chatter from all sides, mostly in allusion to *ma'jun* and *ma'junis*. Baba Jan even, when drunk, said many wild things. The drinkers soon made Tardi Khan mad-drunk, by giving him one full bowl after another. Try as we did to keep things straight, nothing went well; there was much disgusting uproar; the party became intolerable and was broken up.

(*March 7th*) On Monday the 5th of the month, the country of Bhira was given to Hindu Beg.

(*March 8th*) On Tuesday the Chin-ab country was bestowed on Husain *Aikrak*(?) and leave was given to him and the Chin-ab people to set out. At this time Sayyid 'Ali Khan's son Minuchihr Khan, having let us know (his intention), came and waited on me. He had started from Hindustan by the upper road, had met in with Tatar Khan *Kakar*;[1] Tatar Khan had not let him pass on, but had kept him, made him a son-in-law by giving him his own daughter, and had detained him for some time.

(*o. The Kakars.*)

In amongst the mountains of Nil-ab and Bhira which connect with those of Kashmir, there are, besides the Jud and Janjuha tribes, many Jats, Gujurs, and others akin to them, seated in villages everywhere on every rising-ground. These are governed by headmen of the Kakar tribes, a headship like that over the Jud and Janjuha. At this time (925 ah.) the headmen of the people of those hill-skirts were Tatar *Kakar* and Hati *Kakar*, two descendants of one forefather; being paternal-uncles' sons.[1]

[1] so-written in the MSS. *Cf.* Raverty's *Notes* and G. of I.

[1] Anglicé, cousins on the father's side.

Torrent-beds and ravines are their strongholds. Tatar's place, named Parhala,[2] is a good deal below the snow-mountains; Hati's country connects with the mountains and also he had made Babu Khan's fief Kalanjar,[3] look towards himself. Tatar *Kakar* had seen Daulat Khan (*Yusuf-khail*) and looked to him with complete obedience. Hati had not seen Daulat Khan; his attitude towards him was bad and turbulent. At the word of the Hindustan begs and in agreement with them, Tatar had so posted himself as to blockade Hati from a distance. Just when we were in Bhira, Hati moved on pretext of hunting, fell unexpectedly on Tatar, killed him, and took his country, his wives and his having (*bulghani*).[4]

(*p. Babur's journey resumed.*)

Having ridden out at the Mid-day Prayer for an excursion, we got on a boat and 'araq was drunk. The people of the party were Dost Beg, Mirza Quli, Ahmadi, Gadai, Muhammad 'Ali *Jang-jang*, 'Asas,[5] and Aughan-birdi *Mughul*. The musicians were Rauh-dam, Baba Jan, Qasim-i-'ali, Yusuf-i-'ali, Tingri-quli, Abu'l-qasim, Ramzan *Luli*. We drank in the boat till the Bed-time Prayer; then getting off it, full of drink, we mounted, took torches in our hands, and went to camp from the river's bank, leaning over from our horses on this side, leaning over from that, at one loose-rein gallop! Very drunk I must have been for, when they told me next day that we had galloped loose-rein into camp, carrying torches, I could not recall it in the very least. After reaching my quarters, I vomited a good deal.

(*k. The Mirzas entertain Babur in Heri.*)

A few days after Muzaffar Mirza had settled down in the White-garden, he invited me to his quarters; Khadija Begim was also there, and

---

[2] The G. of I. describes it.
[3] Elph. MS. f. 183*b*, *mansub*; Hai. MS. and 2nd W.-i-B. *bisut*.
[4] The 1st Pers. trs. (I.O. 215 f. 188*b*) and Kehr's MS. [Ilminsky p. 293] attribute Hati's last-recorded acts to Babur himself. The two mistaken sources err together elsewhere. M. de Courteille corrects the defect (ii, 67).
[5] night-guard. He is the old servant to whom Babur sent a giant *ashrafi* of the spoils of India (Gul-badan's H.N. *s.n.*).

with me went Jahangir Mirza. When we had eaten a meal in the Begim's presence,[1] Muzaffar Mirza took me to where there was a wine-party, in the Tarab-khana (Joy-house) built by Babur Mirza, a sweet little abode, a smallish, two-storeyed house in the middle of a smallish garden. Great pains have been taken with its upper storey; this has a retreat (*hujra*) in each of its four corners, the space between each two retreats being like a *shah-nishin*;[2] in between these retreats and *shah-nishins* is one large room on all sides of which are pictures which, although Babur Mirza built the house, were commanded by Abu-sa'id Mirza and depict his own wars and encounters.

Two divans had been set in the north *shah-nishin*, facing each other, and with their sides turned to the north. On one Muzaffar Mirza and I sat, on the other Sl. Mas'ud Mirza[3] and Jahangir Mirza. We being guests, Muzaffar Mirza gave me place above himself. The social cups were filled, the cup-bearers ordered to carry them to the guests; the guests drank down the mere wine as if it were water-of-life; when it mounted to their heads, the party waxed warm.

They thought to make me also drink and to draw me into their own circle. Though up till then I had not committed the sin of wine-drinking[4] and known the cheering sensation of comfortable drunkenness, I was inclined to drink wine and my heart was drawn to cross that stream (*wada*). I had had no inclination for wine in my childhood; I knew nothing of its cheer and pleasure. If, as sometimes, my father pressed wine on me, I excused myself; I did not commit the sin. After he died, Khwaja Qazi's right guidance kept me guiltless; as at that time I abstained from forbidden viands, what room was there for the sin of wine? Later on when, with the young man's lusts and at the prompting of sensual passion, desire for wine arose, there was no-one to press it on me, no-one

---

[1] A suspicion that Khadija put poison in Jahangir's wine may refer to this occasion (T.R. p. 199).
[2] These are *jharokha-i-darsan*, windows or balconies from which a ruler shews himself to the people.
[3] Mas'ud was then blind.
[4] Babur first drank wine not earlier than 917 ah. (f. 49 and note), therefore when nearing 30.

indeed aware of my leaning towards it; so that, inclined for it though my heart was, it was difficult of myself to do such a thing, one thitherto undone. It crossed my mind now, when the Mirzas were so pressing and when too we were in a town so refined as Heri, "Where should I drink if not here? here where all the chattels and utensils of luxury and comfort are gathered and in use." So saying to myself, I resolved to drink wine; I determined to cross that stream; but it occurred to me that as I had not taken wine in Badi'u'z-zaman Mirza's house or from his hand, who was to me as an elder brother, things might find way into his mind if I took wine in his younger brother's house and from his hand. Having so said to myself, I mentioned my doubt and difficulty. Said they, "Both the excuse and the obstacle are reasonable," pressed me no more to drink then but settled that when I was in company with both Mirzas, I should drink under the insistence of both.

Copy of a Letter to Humayun[2]

"The first matter, after saying, 'Salutation' to Humayun whom I am longing to see, is this:

Exact particulars of the state of affairs on that side and on this[3] have been made known by the letters and dutiful representations brought on Monday the 10th of the first Rabi' by Beg-gina and Bian Shaikh.

    (*Turki*)   Thank God! a son is born to thee!
                   A son to thee, to me a heart-enslaver (*dil-bandi*).

May the Most High ever allot to thee and to me tidings as joyful! So may it be, O Lord of the two worlds!"

---

[2] The copies of Babur's Turki letter to Humayun and the later one to Khwaja Kalan (f. 359) are in some MSS. of the Persian text translated only (I.O. 215 f. 214); in others appear in Turki only (I.O. 217 f. 240); in others appear in Turki and Persian (B.M. Add. 26,000 and I.O. 2989); while in Muh. Shirazi's lith. ed. they are omitted altogether (p. 228).

[3] Trans- and Cis-Hindukush. Payanda-hasan (in one of his useful glosses to the 1st Pers. trs.) amplifies here by "Khurasan, Ma wara'u'n-nahr and Kabul".

"Thou sayest thou hast called him Al-aman; God bless and prosper this! Thou writest it so thyself (*i.e.* Al-aman), but hast over-looked that common people mostly say *alama* or *ailaman*.[1] Besides that, this *Al* is rare in names.[2] May God bless and prosper him in name and person; may He grant us to keep Al-aman (peace) for many years and many decades of years![3] May He now order our affairs by His own mercy and favour; not in many decades comes such a chance as this!"[4]

"Again:—On Tuesday the 11th of the month (*Nov. 23rd*) came the false rumour that the Balkhis had invited and were fetching Qurban[5] into Balkh."

"Again: Kamran and the Kabul begs have orders to join thee; this done, move on Hisar, Samarkand, Heri or to whatever side favours fortune. Mayst thou, by God's grace, crush foes and take lands to the joy of friends and the down-casting of adversaries! Thank God! now is your time to risk life and slash swords.[6] Neglect not the work chance has brought; slothful life in retirement befits not sovereign rule:

(Persian) He grips the world who hastens;
          Empire yokes not with delay;
          All else, confronting marriage, stops,
          Save only sovereignty.[7]

---

[1] The words Babur gives as mispronunciations are somewhat uncertain in sense; manifestly both are of ill-omen:—Al-aman itself [of which the *alama* of the Hai. MS. and Ilminsky may be an abbreviation,] is the cry of the vanquished, "Quarter! mercy!"; *Ailaman* and also *alaman* can represent a Turkman raider.

[2] Presumably amongst Timurids.

[3] Perhaps Babur here makes a placatory little joke.

[4] *i.e.* that offered by Tahmasp's rout of the Auzbegs at Jam.

[5] He was an adherent of Babur. *Cf.* f. 353.

[6] The plural "your" will include Humayun and Kamran. Neither had yet shewn himself the heritor of his father's personal dash and valour; they had lacked the stress which shaped his heroism.

[7] My husband has traced these lines to Nizami's *Khusrau* and *Shirin*. [They occur on f. 256b in his MS. of 317 folios.] Babur may have quoted from memory, since his version varies. The lines need their context to be understood; they are part of Shirin's address to Khusrau when she refuses to marry him because at the time he is fighting for his sovereign position; and they say, in effect, that while all other work stops for marriage (*kadkhudai*), kingly rule does not.

If through God's grace, the Balkh and Hisar countries be won and held, put men of thine in Hisar, Kamran's men in Balkh. Should Samarkand also be won, there make thy seat. Hisar, God willing, I shall make a crown-domain. Should Kamran regard Balkh as small, represent the matter to me; please God! I will make its defects good at once out of those other countries."

"Again: As thou knowest, the rule has always been that when thou hadst six parts, Kamran had five; this having been constant, make no change."

"Again: Live well with thy younger brother. Elders must bear the burden![1] I have the hope that thou, for thy part, wilt keep on good terms with him; he, who has grown up an active and excellent youth, should not fail, for his part, in loyal duty to thee."[2]

"Again: Words from thee are somewhat few; no person has come from thee for two or three years past; the man I sent to thee (Beg Muhammad ta'alluqchi) came back in something over a year; is this not so?"

"Again: As for the 'retirement', 'retirement', spoken of in thy letters, retirement is a fault for sovereignty; as the honoured (Sa'di) says:[3]

(*Persian*) *If thy foot be fettered, choose to be resigned;*
If thou ride alone, take thou thine own head.

No bondage equals that of sovereignty; retirement matches not with rule."

---

[1] *Aulughlar kutarimlik kirak*, 2nd Pers. trs. *buzurgan bardasht mi baid kardand*. This dictum may be a quotation. I have translated it to agree with Babur's reference to the ages of the brothers, but *aulughlar* expresses greatness of position as well as seniority in age, and the dictum may be taken as a Turki version of "*Noblesse oblige*", and may also mean "The great must be magnanimous". (*Cf.* de C.'s Dict *s.n. kutarimlik*.) [It may be said of the verb *bardashtan* used in the Pers. trs., that Abu'l-fazl, perhaps translating *kutarimlik* reported to him, puts it into Babur's mouth when, after praying to take Humayun's illness upon himself, he cried with conviction, "I have borne it away" (A.N. trs. H.B. i, 276).]

[2] If Babur had foreseen that his hard-won rule in Hindustan was to be given to the winds of one son's frivolities and the other's disloyalty, his words of scant content with what the Hindustan of his desires had brought him, would have expressed a yet keener pain (*Rampur Diwan* E.D.R.'s ed. p. 15 l. 5 fr. ft.).

[3] *Boston*, cap. *Advice of Noshirwan to Hurmuz* (H.B.).

"Again: Thou hast written me a letter, as I ordered thee to do; but why not have read it over? If thou hadst thought of reading it, thou couldst not have done it, and, unable thyself to read it, wouldst certainly have made alteration in it. Though by taking trouble it can be read, it is very puzzling, and who ever saw an enigma in prose?[4] Thy spelling, though not bad, is not quite correct; thou writest *iltafāt* with *[?]ā* (*iltafā[?]*) and *qūlinj* with *yā* (*qīlinj?*).[5] Although thy letter can be read if every sort of pains be taken, yet it cannot be quite understood because of that obscure wording of thine. Thy remissness in letter-writing seems to be due to the thing which makes thee obscure, that is to say, to elaboration. In future write without elaboration; use plain, clear words. So will thy trouble and thy reader's be less."

"Again: Thou art now to go on a great business;[1] take counsel with prudent and experienced begs, and act as they say. If thou seek to pleasure me, give up sitting alone and avoiding society. Summon thy younger brother and the begs twice daily to thy presence, not leaving their coming to choice; be the business what it may, take counsel and settle every word and act in agreement with those well-wishers."

"Again: Khwaja Kalan has long had with me the house-friend's intimacy; have thou as much and even more with him. If, God willing, the work becomes less in those parts, so that thou wilt not need Kamran, let him leave disciplined men in Balkh and come to my presence."

"Again: Seeing that there have been such victories, and such conquests, since Kabul has been held, I take it to be well-omened; I have made it a crown-domain; let no one of you covet it."

"Again: Thou hast done well (*yakhshi qilib sin*); thou hast won the heart of Sl. Wais;[2] get him to thy presence; act by his counsel, for he knows business."

---

[4] A little joke at the expense of the mystifying letter.

[5] For *ya*, Mr. Erskine writes *be*. What the mistake was is an open question; I have guessed an exchange of ī for ū, because such an exchange is not infrequent amongst Turki long vowels.

[1] That of reconquering Timurid lands.

[2] of *Kulab*; he was the father of Haram Begim, one of Gul badan's personages.

"Until there is a good muster of the army, do not move out."

"Bian Shaikh is well-apprised of word-of-mouth matters, and will inform thee of them. These things said, I salute thee and am longing to see thee."

The above was written on Thursday the 13th of the first Rabi' (*Nov. 26th*). To the same purport and with my own hand, I wrote also to Kamran and Khwaja Kalan, and sent off the letters (by Bian Shaikh).

Copy of a Letter to Khwaja Kalan

"After saying 'Salutation to Khwaja Kalan', the first matter is that Shamsu'd-din Muhammad has reached Etawa, and that the particulars about Kabul are known."

"Boundless and infinite is my desire to go to those parts.[5] Matters are coming to some sort of settlement in Hindustan; there is hope, through the Most High, that the work here will soon be arranged. This work brought to order, God willing! my start will be made at once."

"How should a person forget the pleasant things of those countries, especially one who has repented and vowed to sin no more? How should he banish from his mind the permitted flavours of melons and grapes? Taking this opportunity,[6] a melon was brought to me; to cut and eat it affected me strangely; I was all tears!"

"The unsettled state[1] of Kabul had already been written of to me. After thinking matters over, my choice fell on this:—How should a country hold together and be strong (*marbut u mazbut*), if it have seven or eight Governors? Under this aspect of the affair, I have summoned my elder sister (Khan-zada) and my wives to Hindustan, have made Kabul and its

---

[5] Kabul and Tramontana.

[6] Presumably that of Shamsu'd-din Muhammad's mission. One of Babur's couplets expresses longing for the fruits, and also for the "running waters", of lands other than Hindustan, with conceits recalling those of his English contemporaries in verse, as indeed do several others of his short poems (*Rampur Diwan* Plate xvii A.).

[1] Hai. MS. *na marbutlighi*; so too the 2nd Pers. trs. but the 1st writes *wairani u karabi* which suits the matter of defence.

neighbouring countries a crown-domain, and have written in this sense to both Humayun and Kamran. Let a capable person take those letters to the Mirzas. As you may know already, I had written earlier to them with the same purport. About the safe-guarding and prosperity of the country, there will now be no excuse, and not a word to say. Henceforth, if the town-wall[2] be not solid or subjects not thriving, if provisions be not in store or the Treasury not full, it will all be laid on the back of the inefficiency of the Pillar-of-the State."[3]

"The things that must be done are specified below; for some of them orders have gone already, one of these being, 'Let treasure accumulate.' The things which must be done are these:—First, the repair of the fort; again:—the provision of stores; again:—the daily allowance and lodging[4] of envoys going backwards and forwards;[5] again:—let money, taken legally from revenue,[6] be spent for building the Congregational Mosque; again:—the repairs of the Karwan-sara (Caravan-sarai) and the Hot-baths; again:—the completion of the unfinished building made of burnt-brick which Ustad Hasan 'Ali was constructing in the citadel. Let this work be ordered after taking counsel with Ustad Sl. Muhammad; if a design exist, drawn earlier by Ustad Hasan 'Ali, let Ustad Sl. Muhammad finish the building precisely according to it; if not, let him do so, after making a gracious and harmonious design, and in such a way that its floor shall be level with that of the Audience-hall; again:—the Khwurd-Kabul dam which is to hold up the But-khak-water at its exit from the Khwurd-Kabul narrows; again:—the repair of the Ghazni dam;[1] again:—the

---

[2] *qurghan*, walled-town; from the *mazbut* following, the defences are meant.
[3] viz. Governor Khwaja Kalan, on whose want of dominance his sovereign makes good-natured reflection.
[4] *'alufa u qutial*; cf. 364b.
[5] Following *ailchi* (envoys) there is in the Hai. MS. and in I.O. 217 a doubtful word, *bumla, yumla*; I.O. 215 (which contains a Persian trs. of the letter) is obscure, Ilminsky changes the wording slightly; Erskine has a free translation. Perhaps it is *yaumi*, daily, misplaced (*see* above).
[6] Perhaps, endow the Mosque so as to leave no right of property in its revenues to their donor, here Babur. *Cf.* Hughes' *Dict. of Islam* s.nn. *shari'*, *masjid* and *waqf*.

[1] f. 139. Khwaja Kalan himself had taken from Hindustan the money for repairing this dam.

Avenue-garden in which water is short and for which a one-mill stream must be diverted;[2] again:—I had water brought from Tutum-dara to rising ground south-west of Khwaja Basta, there made a reservoir and planted young trees. The place got the name of Belvedere,[3] because it faces the ford and gives a first-rate view. The best of young trees must be planted there, lawns arranged, and borders set with sweet-herbs and with flowers of beautiful colour and scent; again:—Sayyid Qasim has been named to reinforce thee; again:—do not neglect the condition of matchlockmen and of Ustad Muhammad Amin the armourer;[4] again:—directly this letter arrives, thou must get my elder sister (Khan-zada Begim) and my wives right out of Kabul, and escort them to Nil-ab. However averse they may still be, they most certainly must start within a week of the arrival of this letter. For why? Both because the armies which have gone from Hindustan to escort them are suffering hardship in a cramped place (*tar yirda*), and also because they[5] are ruining the country."

"Again:—I made it clear in a letter written to 'Abdu'l-lah (*'asas*), that there had been very great confusion in my mind (*dúghdugha*), to counterbalance being in the oasis (*wadi*) of penitence. This quatrain was somewhat dissuading (*mani'*):—[6]

Through renouncement of wine bewildered am I;
How to work know I not, so distracted am I;
While others repent and make vow to abstain,
I have vowed to abstain, and repentant am I.

---

[2] *sapqun alip*; the 2nd Pers. trs. as if from *satqun alip*, *kharida*, purchasing.
[3] *nazar-gah*, perhaps, theatre, as showing the play enacted at the ford. Cf. ff. 137, 330. Tutun-dara will be Masson's Tutam-dara. Erskine locates Tutun-dara some 8 *kos* (16 m.) n.w. of Hupian (Upian). Masson shews that it was a charming place (*Journeys in Biluchistan, Afghanistan and the Panj-ab*, vol. iii, cap. vi and vii).
[4] *jibachi*. Babur's injunction seems to refer to the maintaining of the corps and the manufacture of armour rather than to care for the individual men involved.
[5] Either the armies in Nil-ab, or the women in the Kabul-country (f. 375).
[6] Perhaps what Babur means is, that both what he had said to 'Abdu'l-lah and what the quatrain expresses, are dissuasive from repentance. Erskine writes (*Mems.* p. 403) but without textual warrant, "I had resolution enough to persevere"; de Courteille (*Mems.* ii, 390), "*Voici un quatrain qui exprime au juste les difficultés de ma position.*"

A witticism of Banai's came back to my mind:—One day when he had been joking in 'Ali-sher Beg's presence, who must have been wearing a jacket with buttons,[1] 'Ali-sher Beg said, 'Thou makest charming jokes; but for the buttons, I would give thee the jacket; they are the hindrance (mani').' Said Banai, 'What hindrance are buttons? It is button-holes (*madagi*) that hinder.'[2] Let responsibility for this story lie on the teller! hold me excused for it; for God's sake do not be offended by it.[3] Again: that quatrain was made before last year, and in truth the longing and craving for a wine-party has been infinite and endless for two years past, so much so that sometimes the craving for wine brought me to the verge of tears. Thank God! this year that trouble has passed from my mind, perhaps by virtue of the blessing and sustainment of versifying the translation.[4] Do thou also renounce wine! If had with equal associates and boon-companions, wine and company are pleasant things; but with whom canst thou now associate? with whom drink wine? If thy boon-companions are Sher-i-ahmad and Haidar-quli, it should not be hard for thee to forswear wine. So much said, I salute thee and long to see thee."[5]

---

[1] The surface retort seems connected with the jacket, perhaps with a request for the gift of it.

[2] Clearly what recalled this joke of Banai's long-silent, caustic tongue was that its point lay ostensibly in a baffled wish—in 'Ali-sher's professed desire to be generous and a professed impediment, which linked in thought with Babur's desire for wine, baffled by his abjuration. So much Banai's smart verbal retort shows, but beneath this is the *double entendre* which cuts at the Beg as miserly and as physically impotent, a defect which gave point to another jeer at his expense, one chronicled by Sam Mirza and translated in Hammer-Purgstall's *Geschichte von schönen Redekünste Persiens*, art. CLV. (*Cf.*f. 179–80.)—The word *madagi* is used metaphorically for a button-hole; like *na-mardi*, it carries secondary meanings, miserliness, impotence, *etc.* (*Cf.* Wollaston's *English-Persian Dictionary s.n.* button hole, where only we have found *madagi* with this sense.)

[3] The 1st Pers. trs. expresses "all these jokes", thus including with the double-meanings of *madagi*, the jests of the quatrain.

[4] The 1st Pers. trs. fills out Babur's allusive phrase here with "of the *Walidiyyah*". His wording allows the inference that what he versified was a prose Turki translation of a probably Arabic original.

[5] Erskine comments here on the non translation into Persian of Babur's letters. Many MSS., however, contain a translation (f. 348, p. 624, n. 2 and E's n. f. 377*b*).

(*j. Kabul gained.*)

From that camp we marched to the Aq-sarai meadow of the Qarabagh and there dismounted. Khusrau Shah's people were well practised in oppression and violence; they tyrannized over one after another till at last I had up one of Sayyidim 'Ali's good braves to my Gate[1] and there beaten for forcibly taking a jar of oil. There and then he just died under the blows; his example kept the rest down.

We took counsel in that camp whether or not to go at once against Kabul. Sayyid Yusuf and some others thought that, as winter was near, our first move should be into Lamghan, from which place action could be taken as advantage offered. Baqi Beg and some others saw it good to move on Kabul at once; this plan was adopted; we marched forward and dismounted in Aba-quruq.

My mother and the belongings left behind in Kahmard rejoined us at Aba-quruq. They had been in great danger, the particulars of which are these: Sherim Taghai had gone to set Khusrau Shah on his way for Khurasan, and this done, was to fetch the families from Kahmard. When he reached Dahanah, he found he was not his own master, Khusrau Shah went on with him into Kahmard, where was his sister's son, Ahmad-i-qasim. These two took up an altogether wrong position towards the families in Kahmard. Hereupon a number of Baqi Beg's Mughuls, who were with the families, arranged secretly with Sherim Taghai to lay hands on Khusrau Shah and Ahmad-i-qasim. The two heard of it, fled along the Kahmard-valley on the Ajar side[2] and made for Khurasan. To bring this about was really what Sherim Taghai and the Mughuls wanted. Set free from their fear of Khusrau Shah by his flight, those in charge of the families got them out of Ajar, but when they reached Kahmard, the Saqanchi (var. Asiqanchi) tribe blocked the road, like an enemy, and plundered the families of most of Baqi Beg's men.[3] They made prisoner Qul-i-bayazid's little son, Tizak; he came into Kabul three or four years later. The plundered and unhappy families crossed by the Qibchaq-pass, as we had done, and they rejoined us in Aba-quruq.

[1] *i.e.* where justice was administered, at this time, outside Babur's tent.
[2] They would pass Ajar and make for the main road over the Dandan shikan Pass.
[3] The clansmen may have obeyed Ahmad's orders in thus holding up the families.

Leaving that camp we went, with one night's halt, to the Chalak-meadow, and there dismounted. After counsel taken, it was decided to lay siege to Kabul, and we marched forward. With what men of the centre there were, I dismounted between Haidar *Taqis*[1] garden and the tomb of Qul-i-bayazid, the Taster (*bakawal*);[2] Jahangir Mirza, with the men of the right, dismounted in my great Four-gardens (*Char-bagh*), Nasir Mirza, with the left, in the meadow of Qutluq-qadam's tomb. People of ours went repeatedly to confer with Muqim; they sometimes brought excuses back, sometimes words making for agreement. His tactics were the sequel of his dispatch, directly after Sherak's defeat, of a courier to his father and elder brother (in Qandahar); he made delays because he was hoping in them.

One day our centre, right, and left were ordered to put on their mail and their horses' mail, to go close to the town, and to display their equipment so as to strike terror on those within. Jahangir Mirza and the right went straight forward by the Kucha-bagh;[3] I, with the centre, because there was water, went along the side of Qutluq-qadam's tomb to a mound facing the rising-ground;[4] the van collected above Qutluq-qadam's bridge, at that time, however, there was no bridge. When the braves, showing themselves off, galloped close up to the Curriers'-gate,[5] a few who had come out through it fled in again without making any stand. A crowd of Kabulis who had come out to see the sight raised a great dust when they ran away from the high slope of the glacis of the citadel (*i.e.* Bala-hisar). A number of pits had been dug up the rise between the bridge and the gate, and hidden under sticks and rubbish; Sl. Quli *Chunaq* and several others were thrown as they galloped over them. A few braves of the right exchanged sword-cuts with those who came out of the town, in amongst the lanes and gardens, but as there was no order to engage, having done so much, they retired.

[1] The name may be from Turki *taq*, a horse shoe, but I.O. 215 f. 102 writes Persian *naqib*, the servant who announces arriving guests.
[2] Here, as immediately below, when mentioning the Char-bagh and the tomb of Qutluq-qadam, Babur uses names acquired by the places at a subsequent date. In 910 ah. the Taster was alive; the Char-bagh was bought by Babur in 911 ah., and Qutluq-qadam fought at Kanwaha in 933 ah.
[3] The Kucha-bagh is still a garden about 4 miles from Kabul on the north west and divided from it by a low hill-pass. There is still a bridge on the way (Erskine).
[4] Presumably that on which the Bala-hisar stood, the glacis of a few lines further.
[5] *Cf*. f. 130.

Those in the fort becoming much perturbed, Muqim made offer through the begs, to submit and surrender the town. Baqi Beg his mediator, he came and waited on me, when all fear was chased from his mind by our entire kindness and favour. It was settled that next day he should march out with retainers and following, goods and effects, and should make the town over to us. Having in mind the good practice Khusrau Shah's retainers had had in indiscipline and longhandedness, we appointed Jahangir Mirza and Nasir Mirza with the great and household begs, to escort Muqim's family out of Kabul[1] and to bring out Muqim himself with his various dependants, goods and effects. Camping-ground was assigned to him at Tipa.[2] When the Mirzas and the Begs went at dawn to the Gate, they saw much mobbing and tumult of the common people, so they sent me a man to say, "Unless you come yourself, there will be no holding these people in." In the end I got to horse, had two or three persons shot, two or three cut in pieces, and so stamped the rising down. Muqim and his belongings then got out, safe and sound, and they betook themselves to Tipa.

It was in the last ten days of the Second Rabi' (Oct. 1504 ad.)[3] that without a fight, without an effort, by Almighty God's bounty and mercy, I obtained and made subject to me Kabul and Ghazni and their dependent districts.

---

[1] One of Muqim's wives was a Timurid, Babur's first-cousin, the daughter of Aulugh Beg *Kabuli*; another was Bibi Zarif Khatun, the mother of that Mah chuchuq, whose anger at her marriage to Babur's faithful Qasim Kukuldash has filled some pages of history (Gulbadan's H.N. *s.n.* Mah-chuchuq and Erskine's B. and H. i, 348).

[2] Some 9m. north of Kabul on the road to Aq sarai.

[3] The Hai. MS. (only) writes First Rabi but the Second better suits the near approach of winter.

'KABUL'

Saib Tabrizi

Translated by Dr Josephine Barry Davis

In the late nineteenth century, Sir Mortimer Durand, the British ambassador to Tehran, presented the Shah with a petition from the Omar Khayyam Club in London requesting the monarch's help with the restoration of the celebrated poet's tomb. The Shah burst into laughter. 'Why all this fuss about poor Omar? Don't you know that Persia has a hundred poets much greater than Omar, and who bothers about their tombs?' It is unlikely he would have said the same thing about **Saib Tabrizi** (c. 1592–1676), a master of the *ghazal*, a form of Arabic and Persian poetry defined by rhyming couplets. His poetry was in such demand that he was received into the court of Shah Jahan in India and later granted the title 'King of Poets' by the Persian Shah Abbas II.

Many of the poems in this anthology speak of human anguish and heartbreak, the sorrows and tragedies brought about by war and the fragile position of women in Afghan society. Not so Saib Tabrizi's poem Kabul, which celebrates the beauty of this bustling, mountain-girdled, flower-filled city in heart-lifting verse. Readers who have their wits about them may spot the 'thousand splendid suns' within Kabul's walls, a line which Khaled Hosseini later pinched as the title for his eponymous bestselling novel.

Kabul

Ah! How beautiful is Kabul encircled by her arid mountains
And Rose, of the trails of thorns she envies
Her gusts of powdered soil, slightly sting my eyes
But I love her, for knowing and loving are born of this same dust

My song exalts her dazzling tulips
And at the beauty of her trees, I blush
How sparkling the water flows from Pul-i-Bastaan!
May Allah protect such beauty from the evil eye of man!

Khizr chose the path to Kabul in order to reach Paradise
For her mountains brought him close to the delights of heaven
From the fort with sprawling wall, A Dragon of protection
Each stone is there more precious than the treasure of Shayagan

Every street of Kabul is enthralling to the eye
Through the bazaars, caravans of Egypt pass
One could not count the moons that shimmer on her roofs
And the thousand splendid suns that hide behind her walls

Her laughter of mornings has the gaiety of flowers
Her nights of darkness, the reflections of lustrous hair
Her melodious nightingales, with passion sing their songs
Ardent tunes, as leaves enflamed, cascading from their throats

And I, I sing in the gardens of Jahanara, of Sharbara
And even the trumpets of heaven envy their green pastures

'THE EMPEROR BABUR'

E. M. Forster

Babur had no shortage of literary fans. Mountstuart Elphinstone, the nineteenth-century Scottish statesman and onetime Governor of Bombay, who toiled for seven years on an English translation of the *Baburnama*, praised its writer as 'natural, lively, affectionate, simple, retaining on the throne all the best feelings and affections of common life'. Babur's diary makes him the Islamic world's answer to Benvenuto Cellini.

Among Babur's many admirers the writer **E. M. Forster** (1879–1970) may appear one of the least obvious. A gay Englishman, conscientious objector and member of the Bloomsbury Group might not seem the likeliest bedfellow for the imperialist warrior Babur at first glance, but this would be to miss the intellectual connection. Babur had an artistic sensibility. He loved and wrote poetry, was introspective, self-aware and self-critical. He was witty and amusing, never pompous on the page. And besides, there was the interest in India, however different it may have been, that linked both men.

Forster included his 1921 essay on the emperor Babur in his collection *Abinger Harvest* (1936). No wonder Forster found him so fascinating. We all do. Babur's diary alone makes him of profound interest to writers and historians. Forster likened the *Baburnama* to a 'mountain stream' with 'sentences that jostle against one another like live people in a crowd'. He might have extended the analogy and added sparkling and effervescent to its many qualities.

At the time that Machiavelli was collecting materials for *The Prince*, a robber boy, sorely in need of advice, was scuttling over the highlands of Central Asia. His problem had already engaged the attention and sympathy of the Florentine; there were too many kings about, and not enough kingdoms. Tamurlane and Gengis Khan (the boy was descended from both) had produced between them so numerous a progeny that a frightful congestion of royalties had resulted along the upper waters of the Jaxartes and the Oxus, and in Afghanistan. One could scarcely travel two miles without being held up by an Emperor. The boy had inherited Ferghana, a scrubby domain at the extreme north of the fashionable world; thinking Samarkand a suitable addition, he conquered it from an uncle when he was thirteen. Then Ferghana revolted, and while trying to subdue it he lost Samarkand, too, and was left with nothing at all. His affairs grew worse; steal as he might, others stole quicker, and at eighteen his mother made him marry—a tedious episode. He thought of escaping to China, so hopeless was the block of uncles, and cousins, and aunts; poisoned coffee and the fire-pencil thinned them out, but only for a moment; up they sprang; again he conquered, lost, conquered and lost for ever Ferghana and Samarkand. Not until he was twenty-one, and had taken to drink, did the true direction of his destiny appear; moving southward, he annexed Kabul. Here the horizon expanded: the waters flow southward again from Kabul, out of the Asian continent into the Indian; he followed them, he took Delhi, he founded the Moghul Empire, and then, not to spoil the perfect outline of his life, he died. Had Machiavelli ever heard of Babur? Probably not. But if the news had come through, how he would have delighted in a career that was not only successful, but artistic! And if Babur had ever heard of Machiavelli, how gladly he would have summoned him and shown him a thing or two! Yes—a thing or two not dreamt of in that philosophy, things of the earth mostly, but Machiavelli didn't know about them, all the same.

These sanguine and successful conquerors generally have defects that would make them intolerable as companions. They are unobservant of all that does not assist them towards glory, and, consequently, vague and pompous about their past; they are so busy; when they have any charm, it is that of our Henry V—the schoolboy unpacking a hamper that doesn't belong to him. But what a happiness to have known Babur! He had all that one seeks in a friend. His energy and ambition were touched with sensitiveness; he could act, feel, observe, and remember; though not critical of his senses, he was aware of their workings, thus fulfilling the whole nature of man. His admirers—and he has many—have called him naïf, because they think it somewhat silly of an emperor to love poetry and swimming for their own sake, and to record many years afterwards that the first time a raft struck, a china cup, a spoon, and a cymbal fell into the water, whereas the second time the raft struck, a nobleman fell in, just as he was cutting up a melon. Charming and quaint (they say), but no more: not realizing that Babur knew what he was about, and that his vitality was so great that all he had experienced rang and glowed, irrespective of its value to historians. It is the temptation of a cultivated man to arrange his experiences, so that they lose their outlines; he, skilled in two languages and all the arts of his day, shunned that false logic, and the sentences in his Memoirs jostle against one another like live people in a crowd:

> 'Zulnun Arghun distinguished himself among all the other young warriors in the presence of Sultan Abusaid Mirza by the use of the scimitar, and afterwards, on every occasion on which he went into action, he acquitted himself with distinction. His courage is unimpeached, but certainly he was rather deficient in understanding. . . . He was a pious and orthodox believer, never neglected saying the appointed prayers, and frequently repeated the supererogatory ones. He was madly fond of chess; if a person played at it with one hand he played at it with his two hands. He played without art, just as his fancy suggested. He was the slave of avarice and meanness.'

No one of the above sentences accommodates its neighbour. The paragraph is a series of shocks, and this is characteristic of Babur's method, and due to the honesty of his mind. But it is not a naïf paragraph. He desires to describe Zulnun Arghun, and does so with all possible clearness. Similarly, when he is autobiographical. No softening:

> 'When, from the force of youthful imagination and constitutional impulse, I got a desire for wine, I had nobody about my person to invite me to gratify my wishes; nay, there was not one who suspected my secret longing for it. Though I had the appetite, therefore, it was

difficult for me, unsolicited as I was, to indulge such unlawful desires. It now came into my head that as they urged me so much, and as, besides, I had come into a refined city like Heri, in which every means of heightening pleasure and gaiety was possessed in perfection, in which all the incentives and apparatus of enjoyment were combined with an invitation to indulgence, if I did not seize the present moment I never could expect such another. I therefore resolved to drink wine.'

Here is neither bragging nor remorse; just the recording of conflicting emotions and of the action that finally resulted. On a subsequent page he does feel remorse. On still a subsequent he drinks himself senseless. Fresh, yet mature, the *Memoirs* leave an ambiguous and exquisite impression behind. We are admitted into the writer's inmost confidence, yet that confidence is not, as in most cases, an enervating chamber; it is a mountain stream, arched by the skies of early manhood. And since to his honesty, and energy, and sensitiveness, Babur added a warm heart, since he desired empire chiefly that he might advance his friends, the reader may discover a companion uncommon among the dead and amongst kings. Alexander the Great resembles him a little, but Alexander is mystic and grandiose, whereas there are neither chasms nor fences in Babur, nothing that need hinder the modern man if he cares to come.

Nevertheless ... old books are troublesome to read, and it is right to indicate the difficulty of this one.

Those awful Oriental names! They welter from start to finish. Sometimes twenty new ones occur on a page and never recur. Among humans there are not only the Turki descendants of Tamurlane and the Moghul descendants of Gengis Khan, all royal, and mostly in motion; long lists of their nobles are given also. Geography is equally trying; as Babur scuttles over the earth a mist of streams, and villages, and mountains arises, from the Jaxartes, in the centre of Asia, to the Nerbudda, in the centre of India. Was this where the man with the melon fell over-board? Or is it the raft where half of us took spirits and the rest *bhang*, and quarrelled in consequence? We can't be sure. Is that an elephant? If so, we must have left Afghanistan. No: we must be in

Ferghana again; it's a yak. We never know where we were last, though Agra stands out as the curtain falls, and behind it, as a tomb against the skyline, Kabul. Lists of flowers, fruits, handwritings, headdresses.... We who are not scholars may grow tired.

The original manuscript of the *Memoirs* was in Turki, and this brings us to our concluding point, that Babur belongs to the middle of Asia, and does not interpret the mind of India, though he founded a great dynasty there. His description of Hindustan is unfavourable, and has often been quoted with gusto by Anglo-Indians. 'The people,' he complains, 'are not handsome, have no idea of the charms of friendly society, of frankly mixing together, or of familiar intercourse ... no good fruits, no ice or cold water, no good food or bread in their bazaars, no baths or colleges, no candles, no torches, not a candlestick.' Witty and unphilosophic, definite and luxuriant as a Persian miniature, he had small patience with a race which has never found either moral or æsthetic excellence by focussing upon details. He had loved details all his life. Consequently, his great new empire, with its various species of parrots, concerning which he failed to get reliable information, and its myriads of merging gods, was sometimes a nightmare, and he left orders that he was to be buried at Kabul. Nothing in his life was Indian, except, possibly, the leaving of it. Then, indeed, at the supreme moment, a strange ghost visits him, a highly unexpected symptom occurs—renunciation. Humayun, his son, lay sick at Agra, and was not expected to recover. Babur, apprised that some sacrifice was necessary, decided (who told him?) that it must be self-sacrifice. He walked ceremonially three times round the bed, then cried, 'I have borne it away.' From that moment strength ebbed from him into his son, a mystic transfusion of the life-force was accomplished, and the five senses that had felt and discriminated so much blended together, diminished, ceased to exist, like the smoke from the burning ghats that disappears into the sky. Not thus had he faced death in the past. Read what he felt when he was nineteen, and his enemies closed round the upland garden in Ferghana. Then he was rebellious and afraid. But at fifty, by the banks of the sacred Jumna, he no longer desired to continue, discovering, perhaps, that the so-called Supreme Moment is, after all, not supreme, but an additional detail, like a cup that falls into the water, or a game of chess played with both hands, or the plumage of a bird, or the face of a friend.

[1921]

THE MAN BEHIND THE MOSQUE

Amitav Ghosh

As if any further evidence were needed of Babur's sheer readability and enduring relevance, here comes the Indian writer and superstar **Amitav Ghosh** (1956–) with a 7,000-word tribute to the founder of the Mughal Empire. Ghosh is one of India's best-known and most successful novelists, a serial prizewinner across continents. Among his most notable works, his Ibis trilogy (*Sea of Poppies*, *River of Smoke*, *Flood of Fire*, published between 2008 and 2015) tells the story of the East India Company's nineteenth-century opium trade between India and China. In 2018 Ghosh won the Jnanpith Award, India's oldest and most prestigious literary honour, for his 'outstanding contribution to literature'. Ghosh's interaction with both Babur and the Baburnama is captivating. Look out for his retelling of the extraordinary story of Babur's death in 1530. He considers Babur 'both a Caesar and a Cervantes' and the *Baburnama* 'one of the true marvels of the medieval world'. Hear, hear!

In December 1992, the 16th century mosque built by the Mogul Emperor Babur was demolished by Hindu fanatics, reminding us that India, which would like to be a secular state, has always been a religious battleground. It was the most publicised victory for the new wave of Hindu fundamentalism, and history made way for myths old and new. Here's a fresh look at Babur – poet, warrior and founder of the Mogul dynasty – beyond the mundane realm of praise and blame. The Baburnama, the autobiography of India's first Mogul emperor, Zahiruddin Mohammad Babur (1483–1530), is one of the true marvels of the medieval world. It belongs with that tiny handful of the world's literary works that can accurately be described as unique: that is without precedent and without imitators. In the western tradition the military memoir has a pedigree that goes back to Xenophon and Julius Caesar. Babur had no such precedents available: indeed, as Wheeler M. Thackston, The Baburnama's most recent translator, notes: "Babur's memoirs are the first – and until relatively recent times, the only – true autobiography in Islamic literature." In other words, in setting out to write an autobiography, Babur did something that very few writers have ever done. He invented a form out of whole cloth: his true literary peers, in this sense, are such epochal figures as Lady Murasaki and Cervantes. Yet Babur was also the founder of a great empire: in other words he was both a Caesar and a Cervantes. What made him pen this immense book (382 folio pages in the original Turkish) and how on earth did he find the time? Between the moment when he gained his first kingdom at the age of 12 and his death 35 years later, there seems scarcely to have been a quiet day in Babur's life. His first kingdom was the only one he didn't have to risk his life for: he inherited it from his father, a scion of a dynasty that was far richer in aspiring rulers than in thrones. Babur took a matter-of-fact view of his father: "He was short in stature, had a round beard and a fleshy face, and was fat... He used to drink a lot. Later in life he held drinking parties once or twice a week.

He was fun to be with in a gathering and was good at reciting poetry for his companions. He grew rather fond of *ma'jun* (a narcotic) and under its influence would lose his head. He was of a scrappy temperament and had many scars and brands to show for it." Although scarcely a model parent, Babur's father, Umar-Shaykh Mirza, was the very soul of docility compared to the rest of his family. More or less the first thought that occurred to Babur on hearing of his father's death was to flee to the mountains so that "at least I would not fall captive... to one of my uncles." Of one of his uncles Babur writes: "He never missed the five daily prayers, even when he was drinking... He was a good drinker. Once he started drinking, he drank continually for twenty or thirty days, but when he stopped he did not drink again for the same amount of time." Of another: "He was addicted to vice and debauchery. He drank wine continually. He kept a lot of catamites, and in his realm wherever there was a comely, beardless youth, he did everything he could to turn him into a catamite." Predictably, Babur's uncles and cousins attacked his territories soon after he had acceded to the throne. Not to be outdone, Babur counter-attacked. At the age of 13 he led an army to Samarkand, to join a clutch of cousins and second-cousins who were taking advantage of another relative's absence to lay siege to the fabled city. After a siege of seven months Babur succeeded in having himself crowned the ruler of Samarkand. He was to rule the city for no more than a hundred days but in many ways this was the defining moment of Babur's life. He was to besiege, conquer and lose Samarkand many times over before he was finally and decisively driven southward. But up to the end of his life, even when he had conquered a realm far vaster, richer and more promising than those that had been taken from him, he still pined for his lost city: for Babur Samarkand was the epitome of civilisation, the centre of the world's urbanity and the fountainhead of all culture.

He won a sizeable chunk of India, the land whose riches had triggered Europe's Age of Exploration. But to the end of his life all he really wanted was Samarkand. Babur's link with Samarkand was, in the first instance, familial. His ancestor Timur Lang (Tamerlane 1336–1405) had made Samarkand the capital of a vast empire and built it into a great centre of art and literature. For Babur, as for his innumerable Timurid uncles and cousins, to rule Samarkand was to claim succession to their glorious ancestor, the guarantor of their own titles to rule. The idea of conquering empires was a part of Babur's family heritage: he traced his descent not just to Timur Lang, but also to Genghis Khan (1167–1227). The story of his kingdom-seeking adolescence and youth has its genesis ultimately in that epochal churning of peoples and cultures that was set in motion by Genghis Khan in the 13th century. Genghis Khan's descendants evidently inherited his remarkable cultural and social adaptability. In the course of his life, the old man had become increasingly Sinicised and seems to have had little empathy for the cultures and traditions of western Asia: certainly the Muslims and Christians of those regions never encountered a more determined enemy. Yet within a generation or two Genghis Khan's descendants took on the cultural and religious (if not linguistic) colourings of the regions they ruled. One of his grandsons, Kubilai Khan, became emperor of China and a cornerstone of the Confucian order, while another became the Sultan of Persia and a devout and fervent Muslim. Babur traced his lineage to Genghis Khan's second son, Chagatay. When the worlds that Genghis Khan had conquered came to be divided amongst his progeny Chagatay inherited Central Asia, a region in which Islam was the principal religion and Persian the language of cultural prestige. Chagatay's inheritance soon fragmented into a number of warring principalities, but he bequeathed his name not just to a realm but also to a lineage and a language – eastern Turkish, the tongue whose greatest literary exponent Babur was to become. Central Asia was again briefly re-united by Timur Lang, an extra-dynastic usurper who nonetheless thought it politic to lay claim to the legacy of the Great Khan by marrying a Genghisid princess. His descendants, however, fought each other with the usual courtly relish of medieval princelings. By the time of Babur's birth the valleys and steppes of central Asia teemed with Timurid princes in search of realms to rule. It was a time, as E. M. Forster observed, when "one could scarcely travel two miles without being held up by an Emperor". Such was the magic of the Timurid pedigree that nobody who owned it ever seems to have forfeited the right to a throne. From the age of 12 onward Babur (like his innumerable cousins and uncles) took it for granted that he was born to rule. Ruling was in a sense a job, a calling, the only thing he knew how to do and could conceive of doing.

Even at times when he possessed little more than his horse and the clothes on his back, he and the members of his tiny entourage took it for granted that a kingdom would somehow transpire, if not in this district then perhaps the next. It was thus, half-reluctantly, that Babur came to be pushed into eastern Afghanistan and eventually northern India. These were not realms of his choice, but they were better than the prospect of unpensioned retirement. The instrument of Babur's misery in his early kingdom-seeking years was a chief called Shaybani ('Wormwood') Khan (1451–1510), an Uzbek and a hereditary enemy. The wheel that Genghis Khan had put in motion had now come full circle: just as his armies had displaced other Turco-Mongol groups, pushing them further and further to the south and the west, so now Babur and his cousins found themselves facing a people who had decided to create their own moment of destiny. With the methodical precision of a cherry-picker, Shaybani Khan picked Babur and his fellow Timurids off, one by one, driving them steadily before him. "For nearly 140 years the capital Samarkand had been in our family," writes Babur. "Then came the Uzbeks, the foreign foe from God knows where, and took over." Babur was too close to the events to notice, of course, but there were some marvelous symmetries to these centuries-long processes of displacement in Central Asia; these patterns of encroachment and migration, of the sudden ascendancy of a nation or a dynasty, of the meteoric rise and decline of glittering cities like Bukhara and Samarkand, Ghazni and Herat. Some of these symmetries even seeped into Babur's own life. In much the same way as Shaybani Khan the Uzbek was harrying Babur, Genghis Khan had once pursued a young warrior-poet, one whose life was perhaps even more colourful than Babur's. The name of the Great Khan's prey was Jalal al-din, and he was the heir presumptive of the great kingdom of Khwarizm, centred in the region between the Caspian and the Aral seas. Genghis Khan had a special grudge against the king of Khwarizm and after seizing the kingdom, in 1220, he sent a detachment of his swiftest riders to hunt down its ruling family. In what must count as one of the most amazing escapes in history, the 14-year-old Jalal al-din rode without a break for 40 days, circling through the deserts, steppes and mountains of Iran and Afghanistan, managing somehow to stay ahead of the great Mongol general, Jebe – known even among his fast-riding peoples as 'The Arrow'. Genghis Khan finally hunted Jalal al-din to a place from which no escape seemed possible: a gorge above the upper Indus. But here again Jalal-al din succeeded in evading the Khan: he spurred his horse over the cliff and into the river, more than a hundred feet below. Legend has it that after calling off the chase, Genghis Khan summoned his entourage and pointed to the young prince swimming in the torrent below. "There," said Genghis Khan, who knew about these things, "goes a brave man." He would have said no less for his own descendant: Babur was nothing if not brave.

On one occasion in The Baburnama, he takes on a hundred men more or less single-handed. "Sultan-Ahmad Tambal was standing, maintaining his position with around a hundred men... shouting, 'Strike! Strike!'... At that point three men were left with me... I shot an arrow I had in my thumb ring... When I had another arrow on the string, I went forward. The other three remained behind." There are times when he glimpses the end of the road. Led into a trap by an old retainer, he writes: "Suddenly I felt odd. There is nothing worse in the world than fear for one's life... I felt I could endure no more. I rose and went to a corner of the orchard. I thought to myself that whether one lived to a hundred or a thousand in the end one had to die... I readied myself for death." Minutes later, help arrives. Often he is in despair. His nineteenth year proves to be a hard one: "During this period in Tashkent I endured much hardship and misery. I had no realm – and no hope of any realm – to rule. Most of my liege men had departed. The few who were left were too wretched to move about with me... Finally I had had all I could take of homelessness and alienation. 'With such difficulties,' I said to myself, 'it would be better to go off on my own so long as I am alive, and with such deprivation and wretchedness it would be better for me to go off to wherever my feet will carry me, even to the ends of the earth.'" But in the end, stoically, he resigns himself to the difficult business of finding a realm: "When one has pretensions to rule and a desire for conquest, one cannot sit back and just watch if events don't go right once or twice." Eventually his perseverance paid off. In 1504, "at the beginning of my twenty-third year (when) I first put a razor to my face", moving ever southward, staying one step ahead of the Uzbeks, he stumbles upon the kingdom of Kabul and decides to seize it for himself. His new realm was full of surprises: 'Eleven or twelve dialects are spoken in Kabul Province: Arabic, Persian, Turkish, Mongolian, Hindi... It is not known if there are so many different peoples and languages in any other province'. Slowly, inevitably, his attention is drawn to the vast subcontinent on the far side of the mountains. He observes speculatively: "Four roads lead (to Kabul) from Hindusthan". But his principal ambitions are still directed towards the north and Samarkand. He even succeeds in taking the city of his dreams, only to find himself expelled from it once again shortly afterwards. With his northern options closed, he turns to the south. Through all his adventures, Babur kept writing, mainly poetry. Even while fleeing from the Uzbeks, he found time to carve a verse on a rock beside a spring. "Like us many have spoken over this spring, but they were gone in the twinkling of an eye,/We conquered the world with bravery and might, but we did not take it with us to the grave." It is a commentary on our times, that to us it seems if not odd, then certainly unexpected that a warrior and statesman should devote his attention to intricate questions of scansion and metrics.

But Babur came from a long line of literary rulers: some of the greatest works of Persian literature were composed in the court of his great-grandfather, Timur Lang. But his ancestors' literary ambitions usually stopped at connoisseurship, patronage and upon occasion, the composing of a divan – the collection of poems that was expected of every man of good breeding. Babur did indeed compose collections of poems, but he was the only man of his lines to embark on a work of extended prose. He did it moreover, not in the literary language of his court, Persian, but in the domestic demotic of his family, Chagatay Turkish. To read The Baburnama is constantly to ask oneself what could possibly have prompted a man in Babur's position to write his memoirs. Historically, autobiography was not a form that flourished in Asia, certainly not in Central Asia, where Babur's roots lay. As for the Indian subcontinent, I know of only one autobiography written there before the 19th century: a brief account of the life of a merchant. The closest Babur comes to explaining his motives is this: "I have simply written the truth. I do not intend by what I have written to compliment myself: I have simply set down exactly what happened. Since I have made it a point in this history to write the truth of every matter and to set down no more than the reality of every event, as a consequence I have reported every good and evil I have seen of father and brother and set down the actuality of every fault and virtue of relative and stranger. May the reader excuse me; may the listener take me not to task." But he may have come closer to the truth in his first poem, a ghazal, written at the age of 18: "Other than my own soul I never found a faithful friend/ Other than my own heart I never found a confidant." It was possibly a sense of loneliness – or rather apartness – that compelled Babur to set down these reflections on his life; it was probably the intimacy of that endeavor that led him to choose Turkish – his domestic language – rather than the courtly Persian that was generally used in his circle. Whatever the reason, the result was a memoir that was anything but a judicious chronicle of affairs of state. Written centuries before the discovery of the Self, The Baburnama is still, astonishingly, a narrative of self-discovery. Its tone is disarmingly open and trusting, and in self-revelation it yields nothing to the confessional memoir of the 1990s. Babur does not, for instance, neglect to record the sexual hesitancies of his first marriage ("since it was my first marriage I was bashful, I went to her only once every 10, 15 or 20 days"); he writes lyrically about an adolescent infatuation with a boy ("before this experience I had never felt a desire for anyone, nor did I listen to talk of love and affection or speak of such things"). His estimations of his relatives and contemporaries are so frank and unguarded as to suggest that he did not expect his memoirs to be widely circulated.

Babur writes no less trenchantly about women than men: as friends or adversaries they were evidently a formidable force in his life. The women of The Baburnama are strong-willed and independent, and they declare their own agency without hesitation, in matters political and personal. We see him going into the women's quarters to ask advice at critical moments; we read about the delinquency of a widowed aunt who gives away her son's kingdom to none other than the dreaded Uzbek, Shaybani Khan, in the hope of winning his love ("in her lust to get a husband, that wretched, feebleminded woman brought destruction on her son"); and about the sorry end of yet another aunt who was so domineering that her husband dared not "go to any of his other wives"; we hear of powerful princes being swiftly dispatched by ambitious concubines; we even learn of women who take the initiative in courting Babur. The Muslim fundamentalists of contemporary Afghanistan would do well to read The Baburnama: they would find that the past they want to return to is not quite what they imagine it to be. Babur is at his most self-revelatory in his description of his drinking life. Although he came from a hard-drinking line, Babur was 29 before he touched his first drink: "In my childhood I had no desire for wine, for I was unaware of the enjoyment of it. Occasionally my father had offered me some, but I had made excuses. After my father's death I was abstinent... Later, with the desires of young manhood and the promptings of the carnal soul, when I had an inclination for wine, nobody offered – no one even knew that I was interested." Then, at a party in the city of Herat, in south-western Afghanistan, his nobles arranged a party for him and offered him wine. "It crossed my mind," writes Babur, "that since they were making such proposals, and here we had come to a fabulous city like Herat, where all the implements of pleasure and revelry were present, and all the devices of entertainment and enjoyment were close at hand, if I didn't drink now, when would I? Deliberating thus with myself, I resolved to make the leap." This was the beginning of a decades-long love affair with wine: Babur seems to have dedicated much of his time in Afghanistan to the pursuit of wine and *ma'jun*. So much for Afghan fundamentalism. Babur provides us with meticulous descriptions of the parties of his Kabul years. "At midday we rode off on an excursion, got on a boat, and drank spirits... We drank on the boat until late that night, left the boat roaring drunk, and got on our horses. I took a torch in my hand and, reeling to one side and then the other, let the horse gallop free-reined along the riverbank all the way to the camp. I must have been really drunk. The next morning they told me that I had come galloping into camp holding a torch. I didn't remember a thing, except that when I got to my tent I vomited a lot." And so things went, until he led his fifth and final expedition into India. In 1527, shortly before a decisive battle, Babur made a spectacular gesture: he took a public oath of temperance. The cellars in his camp were emptied into the sand and he personally broke his sumptuous gold and silver wineglasses and goblets and distributed the pieces to the poor. A few weeks later he led his army into battle at Khanua, against a massive force assembled by Rana Sangram Singh, the most powerful Rajput ruler in North India. Babur prevailed. Babur did not find temperance easy, even though he consoled himself liberally with *ma'jun*. "Everybody regrets drinking and then takes the oath," he wrote,

"But I have taken the oath and now regret it." But Babur was true to his word: he never drank again. In the course of the two decades he spent in Kabul, Babur led four expeditions into India. His fifth and final campaign was launched in October 1525. It had a characteristically light-hearted beginning: "We mostly drank and had morning draughts on drinking days". Between marches Babur and his nobles wrote poetry, collected obscene jokes, and gave chase to the occasional rhinoceros.

Delhi was then in the control of the Lodi Sultans, a dynasty of Afghan Muslim rulers who did a great deal to enrich the architectural heritage of the city that was to become India's capital. Despite internal dissensions the Lodis managed to field an army of 100,000 men and 1,000 elephants against Babur's paltry force of 12,000. The armies met on April 20, 1526, at the historic battlefield of Panipat a few miles north of Delhi. Despite the odds, Babur routed the Lodi Sultan and took possession of Delhi. With the defeat of Rana Sangram Singh's Rajput coalition the following year, Babur secured his hold on northern India. There were skirmishes and minor battles to be fought but for the most part, Babur was content to occupy himself in distributing the spoils to his followers and retainers and in making detailed observations of his new kingdom. With his usual curiosity, he made extensive inquiries about the natural history of northern India, and on the beliefs and customs of its inhabitants. It is clear from his notes that he found much that did not please him: the climate was too hot, its fruit unfamiliar, its peoples bafflingly unlike any he had ever known. But then Babur was never very easy to please, especially where people were concerned: his was a tribal world, and his loyalties and pride were largely invested in his kinsmen and lineage. For Afghans, Shias, Uzbeks, Indians and others who fell outside that circle he reserved an overarching and curiously unprejudiced dislike. A strain of deep melancholy runs through the last pages of the The Baburnama, as though Babur had come to realise that ruling his new kingdom would entail permanent exile from the landscapes of his childhood. "Our concern for going thence (to Kabul) is limitless and overwhelming," he wrote to a friend, the year before his death. "How can one forget the pleasures of that country? Especially when abstaining from drinking, how can one forget a licit pleasure like melons and grapes? Recently a melon was brought and as I cut it and ate it I was oddly affected. I wept the whole time I was eating it." His Indian victories seem to have left Babur with the feeling that his life's work was over: homesickness, nostalgia and abstinence evidently combined to rob him of his will to live. Of the many stories told of Babur none is more wonderful than that of his death. In 1530 Humayun, Babur's beloved eldest son and heir-apparent, was stricken by a fever. He was brought immediately to Babur's court at Agra, but despite the best efforts of the royal physicians, his condition steadily worsened. Driven to despair, Babur consulted a man of religion who told him that the remedy "was to give in alms the most valuable thing one had and to seek cure from God." Babur is said to have replied thus: "I am the most valuable thing that Humayun possesses; than me he has no better thing; I shall make myself a sacrifice for him. May God the Creator accept it." Greatly distressed, Babur's courtiers and friends tried to explain that the sage had meant that he should give away money, or gold or a piece of property: Humayun possessed a priceless diamond, they said, which could be sold and the proceeds given to the poor... Babur would not hear of it. "What value has worldly wealth?" Babur is quoted to have said. "And how can it be a redemption for Humayun? I myself shall be his sacrifice." He walked three times around Humayun's bed, praying: "O God! If a life may be exchanged for a life, I who am Babur, I give my life and my being for a Humayun." A few minutes later, he cried: "We have borne it away, we have borne it away." And sure enough, from that moment Babur began to sicken, while Humayun grew slowly well. Babur died near Agra on December 21, 1530. He left orders for his body to be buried in Kabul. As a writer, intellectual and soldier Babur stood very far above the men of his time: as a ruler, on the other hand, his ideas never extended beyond those he had absorbed from his cousins and uncles in his kingdom-seeking days in the steppes.

The model of governance he brought to his Indian empire was essentially that which he had learnt in his early youth, where the business of ruling entailed little more than knocking a rival off his perch and taking his place. He had little interest in creating instruments of government and as a result he left behind a throne that stood on very weak supports. Nine years after his death, his son Humayun was driven out of India by Sher Shah Suri, a soldier of extraordinary talent and vision. Born in the eastern province of Bihar, into a relatively humble Muslim family, Sher Shah created a bureaucratic and administrative machine of extraordinary complexity. He was to rule in Delhi for only five years, but on his death in 1545 he left behind a sound administrative infrastructure. Ten years later Humayun invaded northern India and conquered Delhi once again from Sher Shah's unworthy heirs. It was probably fortunate for the Mogul dynasty that Humayun didn't linger long on his throne. He died within a few months of entering Delhi, stumbling down a steep staircase, while under the influence. It fell to Babur's grandson Akbar, then a boy of 13, to take the throne. Akbar (1542-1605) proved to be one of the greatest rulers in the history of the Indian subcontinent. He had a profound understanding of Indian institutions of kingship and particularly of the concept of the 'universal ruler'. He proved adept at incorporating the many different religious, linguistic and dynastic traditions of his empire into the culture of his court. He even synthesised various Muslim and Hindu traditions into a religion of his own devising – the Din-i-Ilahi: a creed that was, not unpredictably, centred on himself. Although the new religion never quite caught on, Akbar still enjoyed an exceptionally long reign. He ruled for almost half a century and the aura of legitimacy he left behind was to sustain Mogul rule for generations afterwards. History, notoriously, is not about the past. In recent years, extremist Hindus in India have succeeded in creating a fire-storm of political controversy by exhuming aspects of Mogul history.

In 1992, in a matter of hours, a well-organised Hindu mob tore down a 16th century mosque in the city of Ayodhya, creating one of the most serious crises in the history of the Indian Republic. Named after the first Mogul, the mosque was known as the Babri Masjid: it was the Hindu zealots' contention that the mosque stood upon the site of a Hindu temple dedicated to Lord Ram, the divine hero of the Ramayana epic. A political (and archaeological) controversy over the site still rages, with politicians, academics and experts weighing in on both sides. The text of The Baburnama leaves no doubt that its writer was a devout Muslim. Babur took great pride for example, in the title of 'Ghazi' – 'Slayer of Infidels' – which he assumed after the battle of Khanua. In his autobiography Babur repeatedly announces his intention of destroying Hindu temples and images. These declarations were clearly intended, in part, to garner support among local Indian Muslims. So far as actually building mosques and demolishing temples is concerned, Babur's declarations were almost certainly greatly in excess of his real intentions. However, had he indeed erected mosques on the sites of temples (and there is no clear evidence that he did) he would have done no more than Hindu rulers had themselves done, centuries earlier. Archaeological evidence indicates that many important Hindu temples are built upon earlier Buddhist sites: the great Krishna temple of Mathura, for example, stands on what was probably a Buddhist monastery. Yet, despite Babur's protestations of religious zeal, it is clear from the pages of his autobiography that he was no bigot. Hindus evidently frequented his court and many entered his service. The Sikhs – who were to become dedicated adversaries of the Mogul state in the 17th century – have long cherished a story, preserved in their scriptural tradition, about an encounter between Babur and the founder of their faith, Guru Nanak. In the process of sacking a town in the Punjab, Babur's soldiers are said to have imprisoned Guru Nanak and one of his disciples.

Learning of a miracle performed by the Guru, Babur visited him in prison. Such was the presence of the Guru that Babur is said to have fallen at his feet, with the cry: "On the face of this *faqir* one sees God himself." In any event, it is beyond dispute that Babur's descendants presided over a virtually unprecedented efflorescence in Hindu religious activity. Hinduism as we know it today – especially the Hinduism of north India – was essentially shaped under Mogul rule, often with the active participation and support of the rulers and their officials and feudatories. The Ramcharitmanas, for example, the version of the Ramayana that was to be canonised as the central text of north Indian devotional practice, was composed in Akbar's reign by the great saint-poet Tulsidas. The early years of Mogul rule also coincided with a great renaissance in the theology of Krishna. It was in this period that Rupa Goswami and other disciples of Chaitanya Mahaprabhu rediscovered and mapped out the sacred geography of the Krishna legend. Brajbhumi – the region that is most sacred to Krishna bhakti – lies between Agra and Delhi, the two principal centres of Mogul power in the 16th century. The road connecting these two imperial cities runs right past the sacred sites of Braj. It is self-evident that if the Moguls had wished to persecute Vaishnavites they could easily have done so. But far from suppressing the burgeoning activity in this area, Akbar and his nobles actively supported it. The Hindu generals and officials of his court built several of the most important temples in this area, with Akbar's encouragement. Akbar was personally responsible for sustaining some of these temples: he granted land and revenue in perpetuity to no less than 35 of them. Hinduism would scarcely be recognisable today if Vaishnavism had been actively suppressed in the 16th century: other devotional forms may have taken its place, but we cannot know what those would have been. It is a simple fact that contemporary Hinduism as a living practice would not be what it is if it were not for the devotional practices initiated under Mogul rule. The sad irony of the assault on the Babri mosque is that the Hindu fanatics who attacked it destroyed a symbol of the very accommodations that made their own beliefs possible. W. M. Thackston's translation of The Baburnama is splendidly illustrated with reproductions of photographs and paintings from the collections of the Freer and Arthur M. Sackler galleries in Washington. This is the third English translation of The Baburnama, after Erskine's 1826 version, and the famous Annette Beveridge edition, published between 1912 and 1921. For all her literary talents, Annette Beveridge was not a professional scholar and W. M. Thackston, who is Professor of Near Eastern Languages at Harvard, does not mince his words in criticising her translation: "(it) reads like a student's effort – all the words have been looked up in the dictionary and put together".

Clearly Dr Thackston is something of a Babur himself, to tilt so blithely at a work that earned the admiration of no less a writer than

E.M. Forster. Having myself first encountered The Baburnama in the Beveridge translation, as a schoolboy, I was initially outraged at his easy dismissal of his predecessor. But on comparing key passages, I found that Dr Thackston had on the whole fulfilled his promise of a more "fluent, idiomatic and colloquial" rendition: too much so if anything. A sentence that Mrs Beveridge renders as "Stay here while I look along the Gava road", becomes in Dr Thackston's translation: "You stay here... I'll go check out the Gava road". But then, I know of no rule that says that Babur must sound more like an Edwardian gentleman than a Massachusetts mallrat. In his useful and informative introduction Dr Thackston informs us that "Mogul" is a misnomer for the dynasty that Babur founded. Babur and his descendants identified themselves as 'Gurkani' (sons-in-law), the Timurids being in-laws of the line of Genghis Khan. To Babur the word 'Mogul' denoted various "quasi-Buddhistic, quasi-shamanistic" groups and tribes in the remoter parts of central Asia. His loathing of Moguls surpassed even his detestation of Uzbeks, Shias, Afghans and assorted infidels. "Havoc and destruction," writes Babur, "have always emanated from the Mogul nation. Up to the present date they have rebelled against me five times – not from any particular impropriety on my part, for they have often done the same with their own khans." It is probably too late to entertain objections to the Mogul title, no matter how well founded. Are we likely ever to speak of Steven Spielberg or Subhash Ghai as movie Gurkanis? I don't think so. The British had a particular affection for Babur in whom they imagined themselves to have discovered a precursor for their hard-drinking, free-living imperialist pioneers. Colonial historiography actively promoted a view of the Raj as a successor state to an earlier imperial regime, also established by "foreign conquerors".

This last especially was a recurrent theme in the British discourse on the Moguls [I was recently reminded by Agha Ashraf Ali, the Kashmiri educationist and scholar, that Vincent Smith's life of Akbar begins with the line: "Akbar was a foreigner..."]. In the British view the Mogul period was iconic of India itself: a period of unequalled magnificence, the defining moment of Indian history. Given the general effectiveness of

British historical propaganda these views had an enormous impact and continued to be in general circulation until well after Independence. It is only in the last 10 to 15 years that alternative views have begun to gain currency. Thus, for the better part of a century official histories, both British and Indian, contrived to make the Mogul period a paradigm of Indian statehood. The governments of post-Independence India and Pakistan, like the British colonial regime before them, strove to appropriate aspects of Mogul symbolism (it is surely no coincidence that to this day, India's Prime Ministers deliver their annual Independence Day speeches from the ramparts of Shah Jahan's Red Fort in Delhi). The Moguls have not been well-served by this disproportionate official attention, at home and abroad. Having been credited with the most important artistic and political achievements of "medieval India", they now tend also to attract more than their share of the blame for the perceived failures of that time. It is in the nature of symbols of official grandeur that they sometimes become the focus of frustrations that ought properly to be directed elsewhere: this was quite possibly one of the elements that contributed to the escalation of the Babri Mosque controversy. The Moguls are today in the unenviable position of having to carry the blame for several subsequent appropriations of their reputation. Is it really surprising that so much anger has come to be focused on official historical paradigms of the Indian state, especially those that stress grandeur, monumentality and territorial expansion to the exclusion of all else?

These readings of Indian history choose to glorify everything that contemporary Indians are justly suspicious of: grand imperial states, entrenched bureaucracies, centralism, dynastic rule... There is little here that could appeal to people of democratic or secular inclination – and it is a sad irony that it is exactly such people who now find themselves compelled to swallow this bitter pill. The attempt to combat the quasi-fascistic ideology of the RSS and other Hindu revivalist organisations by defending the 'secularism' of the Moguls, is to my mind ultimately self-defeating, although undoubtedly well-meant: we would do better to restore the balance by paying closer attention to the many competing local traditions – Hindu, Muslim, Adivasi, Christian, Jain, Buddhist and so on – that make up the history of the living constellation of India. South Asian history has an enormous wealth of traditions that are anarchic, millenarian, ecstatic, egalitarian and syncretistic: why then should we allow our view of the past to be pegged to a certain kind of hieratic statism?

The fact is that the Mogul period is no more iconic of India than any other moment in the subcontinent's history. To treat it as such is to do it a profound disservice, in the sense that it is to burden it with more than its fair share of the discontents of the present. The simple truth is that in its most brilliant period the Mogul empire had barely a toehold in the Deccan peninsula. Through much of this period the kingdom of Vijaynagar far outshone its northern rival. The later Moguls tried hard to extend their domains but their southern border tended to snap like a rubber band every time they took a finger off its edge. Aurangzeb, the last of the six great Moguls, effectively doomed the empire by over-extending it in the south. In the long view, the Mogul period was really nothing more than a lucky time-out, a magnificent hallucination whose end had been conceived even before it was born. For the truth is that while Babur was fighting his epic battles in the Indo-Gangetic plain, the future of the subcontinent was being decided in a series of much smaller engagements on the west coast. For the Indian subcontinent as a whole the decisive military engagement of the 16th century was not Babur's victory at Panipat (as I was taught in school and college) but rather the naval battle of Diu, fought in 1509, when a Portuguese fleet attacked and defeated the combined naval forces of the Muslim ruler of Gujarat, the Hindu king of Calicut and the Sultan of Egypt. After Diu the control of the Indian Ocean passed decisively into European hands, never to be recovered. On the occasion of this victory Dom Francisco de Almeida, the Portuguese viceroy, pointed to the moral of his victory: "As long as you may be powerful at sea you will hold India as yours; and if you do not possess this power, little will avail you a fortress on shore." He could not have been more prescient. The task of tending the "fortress on shore" fell to the Moguls and a sorry hash they made of it.

Astonishingly for a man of such intelligence and curiosity, Babur either had no knowledge of the Portuguese presence in western India or else thought it beneath notice. He never so much as mentions the Portuguese, even though, by the time he was seated on the throne of Delhi, they had already founded Goa. He remained to the end a child of the steppes: having never seen the sea, he could scarcely be expected to possess an appreciation of naval power. Babur's descendants had the advantage of him: they extended their domains all the way to both coasts. Yet they too, to a degree that is quite baffling, in retrospect, had their gaze turned resolutely inland – so much so that their emissaries to Persia generally took the difficult and dangerous overland route rather than much easier sea-going one. It is hard to imagine a greater handicap for a dynasty that would be called upon to defend its realm in an age of maritime power. For me the saddest aspect of Babur's brief Indian sojourn is that he died without setting eyes on the most splendid sight the subcontinent could have offered him: the open ocean. What would he have made of it, this endlessly questing, insatiably curious man of the steppes? We can only wonder.

AN ACCOUNT OF THE KINGDOM OF CAUBUL

Mountstuart Elphinstone

When Kabul fell to the Taliban in the summer of 2021, the British woke up to another nightmare of their own making. How could a nation which had already gone through three Afghan Wars, including the abject humiliation of the retreat from Kabul in 1842, return to lose another? Politicians and journalists scurried back to the history books, incredulous historians rushed out screeds of why-oh-why comment pieces and the world looked on aghast.

One name which cropped up again and again was **Mountstuart Elphinstone** (1779–1859), the Scottish diplomat, East India Company administrator, statesman and first British historian of Afghanistan. Published in 1815, his *Account of the Kingdom of Caubul* grew out of his appointment as the first British envoy to the Court of Kabul in 1808, charged with securing a treaty with Shah Shuja, the self-declared Afghan king, to counter Napoleon's anticipated designs on India. That mission came to nothing with Shah Shuja's removal from the throne by his brother (years later he would reappear to take up his fateful role in the First Anglo-Afghan War of 1839–42). Reading Elphinstone today brings to mind E. M. Forster's words, not about Babur but the British: 'we are perfide Albion, the island of hypocrites, the people who have built up an Empire with a Bible in one hand, a pistol in the other, and financial concessions in both pockets'.

In a nutshell it is an imperialist's handbook. It aims for the comprehensive, covering geography, history, customs and traditions, tribal divisions, an extract from a surveyor, a detailed map and illustrations of Afghans of different ethnicities. No wonder that the British relied on it for decades to follow, while blithely ignoring its author's advice. As Elphinstone warned ahead of the disastrous First Anglo-Afghan War, taking Kandahar would be straightforward, but installing Shah Shuja as king 'in poor, cold, strong, and remote country, among a turbulent people like the Afghans... seems to me to be hopeless... The Afghans were neutral... they will now be disaffected and glad to join any invader to drive you out.' How right he was.

BOOK II.

GENERAL ACCOUNT OF THE INHABITANTS OF AFGHAUNISTAUN.

Chapter I

Introduction, Origin, and Early History of the Afghauns.

THE description, which I have attempted, of the country of the Afghauns, has been rendered difficult by the great variety of the regions to be described, and by the diversity even of contiguous tracts. No less a diversity will be discovered in the people who inhabit it; and, amidst the contrasts that are apparent, in the government, manners, dress, and habits of the different tribes, I find it difficult to select those great features, which all possess in common, and which give a marked national character to the whole of the Afghauns. This difficulty is increased by the fact, that those qualities which distinguish them from all their neighbours, are by no means the same, which, without reference to such a comparison, would appear to Europeans to predominate in their character. The freedom which forms their grand distinction among the nations of the East, might seem to an Englishman a mixture of anarchy and arbitrary power; and the manly virtues, that raise them above their neighbours, might sink in his estimation almost to the level of the opposite defects. It may, therefore, assist in appreciating their situation and character to figure the aspects they would present to a traveller from England, and to one from India.

If a man could be transported from England to the Afghaun country, without passing through the dominions of Turkey, Persia, or Tartary, he would be amazed at the wide and unfrequented deserts, and the mountains, covered with perennial snow. Even in the cultivated part of the country, he would discover a wild assemblage of hills and wastes, unmarked by enclosures, not embellished by trees, and destitute of navigable canals, public roads, and all the great and elaborate productions of human industry and refinement. He would find the towns few, and far distant from each other; and, he would look in vain for inns or other conveniencies, which a traveller would meet with in the wildest parts of Great Britain. Yet, he would sometimes be delighted with the fertility and populousness of particular plains and valleys, where he would see the productions of Europe, mingled in profusion with those of the torrid zone; and, the land, laboured with an industry and a judgment no where surpassed. He would see the inhabitants, following their flocks in tents, or assembled in villages, to which the terraced roofs and mud walls give an appearance entirely new. He would be struck at first with their high, and even harsh features, their sun-burned countenances, their long beards, their loose garments, and their shaggy mantles of skins. When he entered into the society, he would notice the absence of regular courts of justice, and of every thing like an organized police. He would be surprised at the fluctuation and instability of the civil institutions. He would find it difficult to comprehend how a nation could subsist in such disorder; and would pity those, who were compelled to pass their days in such a scene, and whose minds were trained by their unhappy situation to fraud and violence, to rapine, deceit, and revenge. Yet, he would scarce fail to admire their martial and lofty spirit, their hospitality, and their bold and simple manners, equally removed from the suppleness of a citizen, and the awkward rusticity of a clown; and, he would, probably, before long discover, among so many qualities that excited his disgust, the rudiments of many virtues.

But, an English traveller from India, would view them with a more favourable eye. He would be pleased with the cold climate, elevated by the wild and novel scenery, and delighted by meeting many of the productions of his native land. He would first be struck with the thinness of the fixed population, and then with the appearance of the people; not fluttering in white muslins, while half their bodies are naked, but soberly and decently attired in dark coloured woollen clothes; and wrapt up in brown mantles, or in large sheep-skin cloaks. He would admire their strong and active forms, their fair complexions and European features; their industry, and enterprise; the hospitality, sobriety, and contempt of pleasure, which appear in all their habits; and, above all, the independence and energy of their character. In India, he would have left a country where every movement originates in the government or its agents, and where the people absolutely go for nothing; and, he would find himself among a nation where the controul of the government is scarcely felt, and where every man appears to pursue his own inclinations, undirected and unrestrained. Amidst the stormy independence of this mode of life, he would regret the ease and security in which the state of India, and even the indolence and timidity of its inhabitants, enable most parts of that country to repose. He would meet with many productions of art and nature that do not exist in India; but, in general, he would find the arts of life less advanced, and many of the luxuries of Hindostan unknown. On the whole, his impression of his new acquaintances would be favourable; although he would feel, that without having lost the ruggedness of a barbarous nation, they were tainted with the vices common to all Asiatics. Yet, he would reckon them virtuous, compared with the people to whom he had been accustomed; would be inclined to regard them with interest and kindness; and could scarcely deny them a portion of his esteem.

Such would be the impressions made on an European, and an Indian traveller, by their ordinary intercourse with the Afghauns. When they began to investigate their political constitution, both would be alike perplexed with its apparent inconsistencies and contradictions, and with the union which it exhibits of turbulent independence and gross oppression. But, the former would, perhaps, be most struck with the despotic pretensions of the general government; and, the latter, with the democratic licence, which prevails in the government of the tribes.

TRAVELS INTO BOKHARA

Alexander Burnes

Alexander Burnes (1805–41) was a dashing, multilingual adventurer, explorer and servant of the British Empire at the height of the Great Game, the competition between Russia and Great Britain for influence in Central and South Asia. His views of Afghans as childish and idle were typical of the nineteenth-century, empire-seeking British. *Travels into Bokhara* is the rollicking account of his exploration up the Indus River to Lahore, Kabul and Bukhara in the years immediately before the First Anglo-Afghan War. During that conflict Burnes served as the British political officer for Kabul. On 1 November 1841 he congratulated his outgoing boss, Sir William Hay Macnaghten, on the prevailing peace of the country. A day later, Burnes was hacked to death by a mob, his severed head mounted on a pike in the market square for all to see. By 23 December, the remnants of Macnaghten's mutilated and headless corpse were hung up in the bazaar of Char Uhouk. All that was left to unfold was the calamitous British retreat from Kabul, which began on 6 January 1842 and resulted in one of the worst military disasters in British history.

Introduction to the chief of Cabool

Our first object, after arrival, was to be introduced to the chief of Cabool, Sidar Dost Mahommed Khan. The Nawab intimated our wishes, and we were very politely invited to dine with the governor on the evening of the 4th of May. Dr. Gerard was unable to attend from sickness; but Mr. Wolff and myself were conducted, in the evening, to the Bala Hissar, or Palace of the Kings, where the governor received us most courteously. He rose on our entrance, saluted in the Persian fashion, and then desired us to be seated on a velvet carpet near himself. He assured us that we were welcome to his country; and, though he had seen few of us, he respected our nation and character. To this I replied as civilly as I could, praising the equity of his government, and the protection which he extended to the traveller and the merchant. When we sat down, we found our party consist of six or eight native gentlemen, and three sons of the chief. We occupied a small but neat apartment, which had no other furniture than the carpet. The conversation of the evening was varied, and embraced such a number of topics, that I find it difficult to detail them; such was the knowledge, intelligence, and curiosity that the chief displayed. He was anxious to know the state of Europe, the number of kings, the terms on which they lived with one another; and, since it appeared that their territories were adjacent, how they existed without destroying each other. I named the different nations, sketched out their relative power, and informed him, that our advancement in civilisation did no more exempt us from war and quarrels than his own country; that we viewed each other's acts with jealousy, and endeavoured to maintain a balance of power, to prevent one king from overturning another. Of this, however, there were, I added, various instances in European history; and the chief himself had heard of Napoleon. He next requested me to inform him of the revenues of England; how they were collected; how the laws were enacted; and what were the productions of the soil. He perfectly comprehended our constitution from a brief explanation; and said there was nothing wonderful in our universal success, since the only revenue which we drew from the people was to defray the debts and expenses of the state. "Your wealth, then," added he, "must come from India." I assured him that the revenues of that country were spent in it; that the sole benefits derived from its possession consisted in its being an outlet to our commerce; and that the only wealth sent to the mother country consisted of a few hundred thousand pounds, and the fortunes taken away by the servants of the government. I never met an Asiatic who credited this fact before. Dost Mahommed Khan observed, that "this satisfactorily accounts for the subjection of India. You have left much of its wealth to the native princes; you have not had to encounter their despair, and you are just in your courts." He enquired into the state of the Mahommedan principalities in India, and as to the exact power of Runjeet Sing, for sparing whose country he gave us no credit. He wished to know if we had any designs upon Cabool. He had heard from some Russian merchants of the manner of recruiting the armies by conscription in that country, and wished to know if it were general in Europe. He had also heard of their foundling hospitals, and required an explanation of their utility and advantage. He begged I would inform him about China; if its people were warlike, and if their country could be invaded from India; if its soil were productive, and its climate salubrious; and why the inhabitants differed so much from those of other countries. The mention of Chinese manufactures led to a notice of those in England; he enquired about our machinery and steam engines, and then expressed his wonder at the cheapness of our goods. He asked about the curiosities which I had seen, and which of the cities in Hindostan I had most admired. I replied, Delhi. He then questioned me if I had seen the rhinoceros, and if the Indian animals differed from those of Cabool. He had heard of our music, and was desirous of knowing if it surpassed that of Cabool. From these matters he turned to those which concerned myself; asked why I had left India, and the reasons for changing my dress. I informed him that I had a great desire to see foreign countries, and I now purposed travelling towards Europe by Bokhara; and that I had changed my dress to prevent my being pointed at in this land; but that I had no desire to conceal from him and the chiefs of every country I entered, that I was an Englishman, and that my entire adoption of the habits of the people had added to my comfort. The chief replied in very kind terms, applauded the design, and the propriety of changing our dress.

*

Tomb of the Emperor Baber

I lost no time in making excursions near Cabool, and chose the earliest opportunity to visit the tomb of the Emperor Baber, which is about a mile from the city, and situated in the sweetest spot of the neighbourhood. The good Nawab was my conductor in the pilgrimage. I have a profound respect for the memory of Baber, which had been increased by a late perusal of his most interesting Commentaries. He had directed his body to be interred in this place, to him the choicest in his wide dominions. These are his own words regarding Cabool:—"The climate is extremely delightful, and there is no such place in the known world."—"Drink wine in the citadel of Cabool, and send round the cup without stopping: for it is at once a mountain, a sea, a town, and a desert."

The grave is marked by two erect slabs of white marble, and, as is usual, the last words of the inscription give the date of the Emperor's death. The device in the present instance seems to me happy: "When in heaven, Roozvan asked the date of his death. I told him that heaven is the eternal abode of Baber Badshah." He died in the year 1530. Near the Emperor, many of his wives and children have been interred; and the garden, which is small, has been once surrounded by a wall of marble. A running and clear stream yet waters the fragrant flowers of this cemetery, which is the great holiday resort of the people of Cabool. In front of the grave, there is a small but chaste mosque of marble; and an inscription upon it sets forth that it was built in the year 1640, by order of the Emperor Shah Jehan, after defeating Mahommed Nuzur Khan in Balkh, and Budukhshan, "that poor Mahommedans might here offer up their prayers." It is pleasing to see the tomb of so great a man as Baber honoured by his posterity.

Prospect from Baber's tomb

There is a noble prospect from the hill which overlooks Baber's tomb, and a summer house has been erected upon it by Shah Zuman, from which it may be admired. The Nawab and myself climbed up to it, and seated ourselves. If my reader can imagine a plain, about twenty miles in circumference, laid out with gardens and fields in pleasing irregularity, intersected by three rivulets, which wind through it by a serpentine course, and wash innumerable little forts and villages, he will have before him one of the meadows of Cabool. To the north lie the hills of Pughman, covered half way down with snow, and separated from the eye by a sheet of the richest verdure. On the other side, the mountains, which are bleak and rocky, mark the hunting preserves of the kings; and the gardens of this city, so celebrated for fruit, lie beneath, the water being conducted to them with great ingenuity. I do not wonder at the hearts of the people being captivated with the landscape, and of Baber's admiration; for, in his own words, "its verdure and flowers render Cabool, in spring, a heaven."

Intercourse with the people

Our intercourse with the people was on a much better footing at Cabool than in Peshawur, for we were no longer in the house of a chief, and not troubled by too many visitors. The Nawab occupied one side of a large mansion, and left the other part to us. He, however, rallied round him many good sort of people, with whom we became acquainted; he brought them over in person, and we passed to and fro between each other's apartments during the whole day. The habits which we had adopted, now gave us many advantages in our communications with the people. We sat along with them on the same carpet, ate with them, and freely mingled in their society. The Afghans are a sober, simple, steady people. They always interrogated me closely regarding Europe, the nations of which they divide into twelve "*koollahs*," or crowns, literally hats. It was delightful to see the curiosity of even the oldest men. The greatest evil of Mahommedanism consists in its keeping those who profess it within a certain circle of civilisation. Their manners do not appear ever to alter. They have learning, but it is of another age, and anything like philosophy in their history is unknown. The language of the Afghans is Persian, but it is not the smooth and elegant tongue of Iran. Pooshtoo is the dialect of the common people, but some of the higher classes cannot even speak it. The Afghans are a nation of children; in their quarrels they fight, and become friends without any ceremony. They cannot conceal their feelings from one another, and a person with any discrimination may at all times pierce their designs. If they themselves are to be believed, their ruling vice is envy, which besets even the nearest and dearest relations. No people are more incapable of managing an intrigue. I was particularly struck with their idleness; they seem to sit, listlessly for the whole day, staring at each other; how they live it would be difficult to discover, yet they dress well, and are healthy and happy. I imbibed a very favourable impression of their national character.

Cabool; its bazars

Cabool is a most bustling and populous city. Such is the noise in the afternoon, that in the streets one cannot make an attendant hear. The great bazar, or "Chouchut," is an elegant arcade, nearly 600 feet long, and about 30 broad: it is divided into four equal parts. Its roof is painted; and over the shops are the houses of some of the citizens. The plan is judicious; but it has been left unfinished; and the fountains and cisterns, that formed a part of it, lie neglected. Still there are few such bazars in the East; and one wonders at the silks, cloths, and goods, which are arrayed under its piazzas. In the evening it presents a very interesting sight: each shop is lighted up by a lamp suspended in front, which gives the city an appearance of being illuminated. The number of shops for the sale of dried fruits is remarkable, and their arrangement tasteful. In May, one may purchase the grapes, pears, apples, quinces, and even the melons of the by-gone season, then ten months old. There are poulterers' shops, at which snipes, ducks, partridges, and plovers, with other game, may be purchased. The shops of the shoemakers and hardware retailers are also arranged with singular neatness. Every trade has its separate bazar, and all of them seem busy. There are booksellers and venders of paper, much of which is Russian, and of a blue colour. The month of May is the season of the "falodeh" which is a white jelly strained from wheat, and drunk with sherbet and snow. The people are very fond of it, and the shop-keepers in all parts of the town seem constantly at work with their customers. A pillar of snow stands on one side of them, and a fountain plays near it, which gives these places a cool and clean appearance. Around the bakers' shops crowds of people may be seen, waiting for their bread. I observed that they baked it by plastering it to the sides of the oven. Cabool is famed for its *kabobs*, or cooked meats, which are in great request: few cook at home. "Rhuwash" was the dainty of the May season in Cabool. It is merely blanched rhubarb, which is reared under a careful protection from the sun, and grows up rankly under the hills in the neighbourhood. Its flavour is delicious. "Shabash rhuwash! Bravo rhuwash!" is the cry in the streets; and every one buys it. In the most crowded parts of the city there are story-tellers amusing the idlers, or dervises proclaiming the glories and deeds of the Prophets. If a baker makes his appearance before these worthies, they demand a cake in the name of some prophet; and, to judge by the number who follow their occupation, it must be a profitable one. There are no wheeled carriages in Cabool: the streets are not very narrow; they are kept in a good state during dry weather, and are intersected by small covered aqueducts of clean water, which is a great convenience to the people. We passed along them without observation, and even without an attendant. To me, the appearance of the people was more novel than the bazars. They sauntered about, dressed in sheep-skin cloaks, and seemed huge from the quantity of clothes they wore. All the children have chubby red cheeks, which I at first took for an artificial colour, till I found it to be the gay bloom of youth. The older people seem to lose it. Cabool is a compactly built city, but its houses have no pretension to elegance. They are constructed of sun-dried bricks and wood, and few of them are more than two stories high. It is thickly peopled, and has a population of about sixty thousand souls. The river of Cabool passes through the city; and tradition says that it has three times carried it away, or inundated it. In rain, there is not a dirtier place than Cabool.

Traditions of Cabool

It is in the mouth of every one, that Cabool is a very ancient city; they call it 6000 years old. It formed once, with Ghuzni, the tributary cities of Bameean. Strange has been the reverse of circumstances;—Ghuzni, under Mahmood, in the eleventh century, became a great capital; and Cabool is now the metropolis both over it and Bameean. It is said that Cabool was formerly named Zabool, from a kaffir, or infidel king, who founded it; hence the name of Zaboolistan. Some authors have stated, that the remains of the tomb of Cabool, or Cain, the son of Adam, are pointed out in the city; but the people have no such traditions. It is, however, a popular belief, that when the devil was cast out of heaven, he fell in Cabool. In Cabool itself there are not exactly traditions of Alexander, but both Herat and Lahore are said to have been founded by slaves of that conqueror, whom they call a prophet. Their names were Heri (the old name of Herat) and Lahore. Candahar is said to be an older city than either of these.

Coins

While at Cabool, I made every attempt to procure coins, but without success, excepting a Cufic coin of Bokhara, which was 843 years old. Among the rarities brought to the Cabool mint, I heard of a coin of the shape and size of a sparrow's egg,—a whimsical model. Triangular and square coins are common: the latter belong to the age of Acbar.

*

Gardens of Cabool

Since our departure, we had been travelling in a perpetual spring. The trees were blossoming as we left Lahore, in February; and we found them full blown in March, at Peshawur. We had now the same joyous state of the season in Cabool, and arrived at an opportune time to see it. This state of the spring will give a good idea of the relative height of the different places, and of the progress of their seasons. Cabool is more than 6000 feet above the level of the sea. I passed some delightful days in its beautiful gardens. One evening I visited a very fine one, in company with the Nawab, about six miles from the city. They are well kept and laid out; the fruit trees are planted at regular distances; and most of the gardens rise with the acclivity of the ground in plateaus, or shelves, over one another. The ground was covered with the fallen blossom, which had drifted into the corners, like so much snow. The Nawab and myself seated ourselves under a pear-tree of Samarcand, the most celebrated kind in the country, and admired the prospect. Great was the variety and number of fruit trees. There were peaches, plums, apricots, pears, apples, quinces, cherries, walnuts, mulberries, pomegranates, and vines, all growing in one garden. There were also nightingales, blackbirds, thrushes, and doves, to raise their notes, and chattering magpies, on almost every tree, which were not without their attraction, as reminding me of England. I was highly pleased with the nightingale; and, on our return home, the Nawab sent me one in a cage, which sang throughout the night. It is called the "Boolbool i huzar dastan," or, the nightingale of a thousand tales; and it really seemed to imitate the song of every bird. The cage was surrounded by cloth; and it became so noisy a companion, that I was obliged to send it away before I could sleep. This bird is a native of Budukhshan. The finest garden about Cabool is that called the King's garden, laid out by Timour Shah, which lies north of the town, and is about half a mile square. The road which leads to it is about three miles long, and formed the royal race-ground. There is a spacious octagon summer-house in the centre, with walks that run up from each of its sides, shaded with fruit trees, having a very pretty effect. A marble seat in front shows where the kings of Cabool sat in their prosperity, among

> — "the pears
> And sunniest apples that Cabool,
> In all its thousand gardens, bears."

The people are passionately fond of sauntering about these gardens, and may be seen flocking to them every evening. The climate of Cabool is most genial. At mid-day the sun is hotter than in England; but the nights and evenings are cool, and only in August do the people find it necessary to sleep on their balconies. There is no rainy season, but constant showers fall as in England. The snow lasts for five months in winter. During May, the thermometer stood at 64° in the hottest time of the day; and there was generally a wind from the north, cooled by the snow that covers the mountains. It must usually blow from that quarter, since all the trees of Cabool bend to the south.

Fruits and wines of Cabool
Cabool is particularly celebrated for its fruit, which is exported in great abundance to India. Its vines are so plentiful, that the grapes are given,

for three months of the year, to cattle. There are ten different kinds of these: the best grow on frame-works; for those which are allowed to creep on the ground are inferior. They are pruned in the beginning of May. The wine of Cabool has a flavour not unlike Madeira; and it cannot be doubted, that a very superior description might be produced in this country with a little care. The people of Cabool convert the grape into more uses than in most other countries. They use its juice in roasting meat; and, during meals, have grape powder as a pickle. This is procured by pounding the grapes before they get ripe, after drying them. It looks like Cayenne pepper, and has a pleasant acid taste. They also dry many of them as raisins, and use much grape syrup. A pound of grapes sells for a halfpenny. I have already mentioned the "rhuwash," or rhubarb of Cabool: it grows spontaneously under the snowy hills of Pughman; and Cabool has a great celebrity from producing it. The natives believe it exceedingly wholesome, and use it both raw, and cooked as vegetables. They tell an anecdote of some Indian doctors, who practised for a short time at Cabool, and waited for the fruit season, when the people would probably be unhealthy. Seeing this rhubarb in May and June, these members of the faculty abruptly left the country, pronouncing it a specific for the catalogue of Cabool diseases. This, at all events, proves it to be considered a healthy article of food. When the rhubarb is brought to market, the stalks are about a foot long, and the leaves are just budding. They are red; the stalk is white: when it first appears above ground, it has a sweet taste like milk, and will not bear carriage. As it grows older, it gets strong, stones being piled round to protect it from the sun. The root of the plant is not used as medicine. There are no date trees in Cabool, though they are to be found both east and west of it—at Candahar and Peshawur. There the people are ignorant of the art of extracting an intoxicating juice from them, as in India. Peshawur is celebrated for its pears; Ghuzni for its plums, which are sold in India under the name of the plum of Bokhara; Candahar for its figs, and Cabool for its mulberries; but almost every description, particularly stone fruits, thrive in Cabool. Fruit is more plentiful than bread, and is considered one of the necessaries of human life. There are no less than fourteen different ways of preserving the apricot of Cabool: it is dried with and without the stone; the kernel is sometimes left, or an almond is substituted in its stead; it is also formed into cakes, and folded up like paper. It is the most delicious of the dried fruits.

Bala Hissar, or palace prison of the princes

Among the public buildings in Cabool, the Bala Hissar, or citadel, claims the first importance; but not from its strength. Cabool is enclosed to the south and west by high rocky hills; and at the eastern extremity of these the Bala Hissar is situated, which commands the city. It stands on a neck of land, and may have an elevation of about 150 feet from the meadows of the surrounding country. There is another fort under it, also called the Bala Hissar, which is occupied by the governor and his guards. The citadel is uninhabited by the present chief; but his brother built a palace in it called the "Koollah i Firingee," or the Europeans' Hat, which is the highest building. Dost Mahommed Khan captured the Bala Hissar, by blowing up one of its towers: it is a poor, irregular, and dilapidated fortification, and could never withstand an escalade. The upper fort is small, but that below contains about five thousand people. The King's palace stands in it. The Bala Hissar was built by different princes of the house of Timour, from Baber downwards. Aurungzebe prepared extensive vaults under it, to deposit his treasure; and which may yet be seen. While it formed the palace of the kings of Cabool, it was also the prison of the younger branches of the royal family, in which they were confined for life. They tell a story, that, when set free from their prison, after murdering their keeper, they looked with astonishment at seeing water flow—so close had been the confinement in their walled abode. It is difficult to say, whether these unfortunate men were not happier than in their present state, which is that of abject poverty. Many of the sons of Timour Shah came in absolute hunger to solicit alms from us. I advised them to make a petition to the chief for some permanent relief, but they said that they had no mercy to expect from the Barukzye family, now in power, who thirsted after their blood.

Difference between Asiatic and European manners

The difference between Eastern manners, and those of Europe, is nowhere more discernible than in their manner of saying good things. An European enjoys an anecdote; but he would be very much surprised to be called on in a company to tell one for its amusement. In the East, there are professional anecdote makers; in the West, we are content with a bon-mot as it flows in the course of conversation. Both may be traced to the government: for, in the East, though there is much familiarity, there is little social intercourse; and, in Europe, good manners teach us to consider every one at the same board on an equality.

Tomb of Timour Shah

I was conducted to the tomb of Timour Shah, which stands outside the city, and is a brick building of an octagon shape, rising to the height of 50 feet. The interior of it is about 40 feet square, and the architecture resembles that of Delhi. The building is unfinished. A lamp was formerly lighted on this sepulchre; but the sense of this king's favours, like that of many others, has faded. Timour Shah made Cabool his capital, and here is his tomb. His father is interred at Candahar, which is the native country of the Dooranees.

Alchymy and minerals

I moved about everywhere during the day, and had the pleasure of many sociable evenings with our host the Nawab, whom I found, like many of his countrymen, in search of the philosopher's stone. Such an opportunity as our arrival seemed to promise him a rich harvest. I soon undeceived him, and laughed at the crucibles and recipes, which he produced. I explained to him, that chemistry had succeeded alchymy, as astronomy had followed astrology; but as I had to detail the exact nature of these sciences, my asseverations of being no alchymist had little effect. He therefore applied himself to the doctor, from whom he requested recipes for the manufacture of calomel and quinine plasters and liniments; which it was no easy matter to furnish. He could not credit that the arts of giving and manufacturing medicines were distinct; and set us down as very ignorant or very obstinate. He would not receive the prepared medicines, as they would be of no use to him after we had left. We found this feeling generally prevalent; and woe be to the doctor in these parts who gives medicines which he cannot make. We kept the Nawab in good humour, though we would not believe that he could convert iron into silver. We heard from him the position of many metallic veins in the country. He produced among other curiosities some asbestos, here called cotton-stone (sung i poomba), found near Julalabad. The good man declared that he must have some of our knowledge in return for what he told so freely.

Freemasonry

I informed him that I belonged to a sect called Freemasons, and gave some account of the craft, into which he requested to be admitted without delay. But, as the number of brethren must be equal to that of the Pleiades, we put it off to a convenient opportunity. He confidently believed that he had at last got scent of magic in its purest dye; and had it been in my power, I would have willingly initiated him. He made me promise to send some flower-seeds of our country, which he wished to see in Cabool; and I faithfully forwarded them. I cut the plates out of Mr. Elphinstone's History of Cabool, and presented them to the Nawab at a large party; and not only is the costume exact, but in some of the figures, to their great delight, they discovered likenesses. Pictures are forbidden among the Soonee Mahommedans; but in the present instance they proved very acceptable. Among the Nawab's friends we met a man 114 years old, who had served with Nadir Shah. He had been upwards of eighty years in Cabool, and seen the Dooranee dynasty founded and pass away. This venerable person walked up stairs to our rooms.

Afghans. Jewish origin

From the crowd of people we constantly met at the house of our host, I was resolved on gathering some information on the much disputed point of the Afghans being Jews. They brought me all their histories, but I had no time to examine them, and wished for oral information. The Afghans call themselves, "Bin i Israeel," or children of Israel; but consider the term of "Yahoodee," or Jew, to be one of reproach.

Their traditions

They say that Nebuchadnezzar, after the overthrow of the temple of Jerusalem, transplanted them to the town of Ghore, near Bameean; and that they are called Afghans, from their chief Afghana, who was a son of the uncle of Asof (the vizier of Solomon), who was the son of Berkia. The genealogy of this person is traced from a collateral branch, on account of the obscurity of his own parent, which is by no means uncommon in the East. They say that they lived as Jews, till Khaleed (called by the title of Caliph) summoned them, in the first century of Mahommedanism, to assist in the wars with the Infidels. For their services on that occasion, Kyse, their leader, got the title of Abdoolrusheed, which means the Son of the mighty. He was also told to consider himself the "butan" (an Arabic word), or *mast* of his tribe, on which its prosperity would hinge and by which the vessel of their state was to be governed. Since that time, the Afghans are sometimes called *Putan*, by which name they are familiarly known in India. I never before heard this explanation of the term. After the campaign with Khaleed, the Afghans returned to their native country, and were governed by a king of the line of Kyanee, or Cyrus, till the eleventh century, when they were subdued by Mahmood of Ghuzni. A race of kings sprung from Ghore, subverted the house of Ghuzni, and conquered India. As is well known, this dynasty was divided, at the death of its founder, into the divisions east and west of the Indus; a state of things which lasted till the posterity of Timourlane reduced both to a new yoke.

Opinions regarding these traditions

Having precisely stated the traditions and history of the Afghans, I can see no good reason for discrediting them, though there be some anachronisms, and the dates do not exactly correspond with those of the Old Testament. In the histories of Greece and Rome we find similar corruptions, as well as in the later works of the Arab and Mahommedan writers. The Afghans look like Jews; they say they are descended from Jews; and the younger brother marries the widow of the elder, according to the law of Moses. The Afghans entertain strong prejudices against the Jewish nation; which would at least show that they had no desire to claim, without a just cause, a descent from them. Since some of the tribes of Israel came to the East, why should we not admit that the Afghans are their descendants, converted to Mahommedanism? I am aware that I am differing from a high authority; but I trust that I have made it appear on reasonable grounds.

JOURNAL OF THE DISASTERS IN AFGHANISTAN, 1841–42

Florentia Sale

A redoubtable woman nicknamed 'the Grenadier in Petticoats' for her travels with the British army alongside her officer husband Brigadier-General Robert Henry Sale, **Florentia Sale** (1790–1853) was an eyewitness to the devastating 1842 retreat from Kabul in which 690 British soldiers, 2,840 Indian soldiers and 12,000 followers were killed or, in a few cases, such as that of Florentia Sale, taken prisoner. The significant number of Afghan casualties, largely Ghilzai tribesmen, remains unknown.

Wounded in the initial fighting and shot in the wrist, Sale was kept a prisoner for nine months, during which time she kept her memorable diary detailing the hardships suffered, battles witnessed and Afghans encountered. When it was published in London in 1843, by which time she and her fellow prisoners had been released following the payment of a bribe to their Afghan jailer, it electrified the British public, who considered her a heroine.

THE CAPTIVITY

We must now return to the General and his party. At daybreak on the 13th the Sirdar had again changed his mind; and instead of following up the troops, he decided to move to the position they had vacated, and remain there during the day; and should the ladies and officers left at Khoord Cabul arrive in the evening, that all should start the next morning over the mountains to the valley of Lughman, north of Jellalabad. At 8 a. m., they mounted their horses; and with the Sirdar and his party rode down the pass, which bore fearful evidence to the last night's struggle. They passed some 200 dead bodies, many of them Europeans; the whole naked, and covered with large gaping wounds. As the day advanced, several poor wretches of Hindostanees (camp followers, who had escaped the massacre of the night before) made their appearance from behind rocks and within caves, where they had taken shelter from the murderous knives of the Affghans and the inclemency of the climate. They had been stripped of all they possessed; and few could crawl more than a few yards, being frostbitten in the feet. Here Johnson found two of his servants: the one had his hands and feet frostbitten, and had a fearful sword cut across one hand, and a musket ball in his stomach; the other had his right arm completely cut through the bone. Both were utterly destitute of covering, and had not tasted food for five days.

This suffices for a sample of the sufferings of the survivors.

About four o'clock Sultan Jan (a cousin of the Sirdar) arrived with the ladies and gentlemen; also Lieut. Melville of the 54th, and Mr. Magrath, surgeon of the 37th, both of whom had been wounded between Khoord Cabul and Tézeen. A large party of cavalry accompanied Sultan Jan, both Affghan and our irregular horse, who had deserted, as before mentioned.

14*th*.—We marched twenty-four miles to Kutz-i-Mahommed Ali Khan: started at about 9 a.m.; the Sirdar with Gen. Elphinstone; Brig. Shelton, and Capt. Johnson bringing up the rear.

We travelled over a dreadfully rough road: some of the ascents and descents were fearful to look at, and at first sight appeared to be impracticable. The whole road was a continuation of rocks and stones, over which the camels had great difficulty in making their way; and particularly in the ascent of the Adrak-Budrak pass, where I found it requisite to hold tight on by the mane, lest the saddle and I should slip off together.

Had we travelled under happier auspices, I should probably have been foolish enough to have expressed fear, not having even a saces to assist me. Still I could not but admire the romantic tortuous defile we passed through, being the bed of a mountain torrent, which we exchanged for the terrific pass I have mentioned, and which was rendered doubly fearful by constant stoppages from those in front, which appeared to take place at the most difficult spots.

At the commencement of the defile, and for some considerable distance, we passed 200 or 300 of our miserable Hindostanees, who had escaped up the unfrequented road from the massacre of the 12th. They were all naked, and more or less frostbitten: wounded, and starving, they had set fire to the bushes and grass, and huddled all together to impart warmth to each other. Subsequently we heard that scarcely any of these poor wretches escaped from the defile; and that driven to the extreme of hunger they had sustained life by feeding on their dead comrades.

The wind blew bitterly cold at our bivouac; for the inhabitants of the fort refused to take us in; stating that we were Kaffirs. We therefore rolled ourselves up as warm as we could; and with our saddles for pillows braved the elements. Gen. Elphinstone, Brig. Shelton, and Johnson considered themselves happy when one of the Affghans told them to accompany him into a wretched cowshed, which was filled with dense smoke from a blazing fire in the centre of the hut. These officers and Mr. Melville were shortly after invited by Mahommed Akbar Khan to dine with him and his party in the fort. The reception room was not much better than that they had left: they had, however, a capital dinner, some cups of tea, and luxurious rest at night; the room having been well heated by a blazing fire with plenty of smoke, with no outlet for either heat or smoke, except through the door and a small circular hole in the roof.

15th January.—A bitterly cold wind blowing, we started at 7 a. m.; crossed two branches of the Punjshir river, which was not only deep, but exceedingly rapid. The chiefs gave us every assistance. Mahommed Akbar Khan carried Mrs. Waller over behind him on his own horse. One rode by me to keep my horse's head well up the stream. The Affghans made great exertions to save both men and animals struggling in the water; but in spite of all their endeavours five unfortunates lost their lives. We passed over many ascents and declivities; and at about 3 p.m. arrrived at Tighree, a fortified town in the rich valley of Lughman; having travelled twenty miles over a most barren country, without a blade of grass or drop of water until we approached Tighree. Our route lay along a tract of country considerably higher than Lughman, with scarcely a footpath visible the whole way. The road was good for any kind of carriage. We passed over the Plain of Methusaleh; and saw at a short distance the Kubber-i-Lamech, a celebrated place of pilgrimage, about two miles from Tighree and twenty-five from Jellalabad.

The Sirdar desired the General, the Brigadier, and Johnson to take up their quarters with him, whilst the ladies and the other gentlemen were located in another fort.

A great number of Hindu Bunneahs reside at Tighree. We went to the fort of Gholab Moyenoodeen, who took Mrs. Sturt and myself to the apartments of his mother and wife. Of course we could not understand much that they said; but they evidently made much of us, pitied our condition, told us to ask them for any thing we required, and before parting they gave us a lump of goor filled with pistaches, a sweetmeat they are themselves fond of.

16*th*.—Halted. They tell us we are here only thirty miles from Jellalabad. It being Sunday, we read prayers from a Bible and Prayer Book that were picked up on the field at Bhoodkhak. The service was scarcely finished when a clannish row commenced. Some tribes from a neighbouring fort who had a blood feud with the chiefs with us came against the fort: a few juzails were fired; there was great talking and noise; and then it was all over.

17*th*.—Early in the morning we were ordered to prepare to go higher up the valley. Thus all hopes (faint as they were) of going to Jellalabad were annihilated; and we plainly saw that, whatever might be said, we were virtually prisoners, until such time as Sale shall evacuate Jellalabad, or the Dost be permitted by our government to return to this country.

We had a little hail this morning; and shortly after, at about nine o'clock, we started, and travelled along the valley, which was a continuation of forts, until we arrived at Buddeeabad (about eight or nine miles): it is situated almost at the top of the valley, and close to the first range of hills towards Kaffiristan.

Six rooms, forming two sides of an inner square or citadel, are appropriated to us; and a tykhana to the soldiers. This fort is the largest in the valley, and is quite new; it belongs to Mahommed Shah Khan: it has a deep ditch and a fausse-braye all round. The walls of mud are not very thick, and are built up with planks in tiers on the inside. The buildings we occupy are those intended for the chief and his favourite wife; those for three other wives are in the outer court, and have not yet been roofed in. We number 9 ladies, 20 gentlemen, and 14 children. In the tykhana are 17 European soldiers, 2 European women, and 1 child (Mrs. Wade, Mrs. Burnes, and little Stoker).

Mahommed Akbar Khan, to our horror, has informed us that only one man of our force has succeeded in reaching Jellalabad (Dr. Brydon of the Shah's force: he was wounded in two places). Thus is verified what we were told before leaving Cabul; "that Mahommed Akbar would annihilate the whole army, except one man, who should reach Jellalabad to tell the tale."

Dost Mahommed Khan (the brother of Mahommed Shah Khan) is to have charge of us. Our parties were divided into the different rooms. Lady Macnaghten, Capt. and Mrs. Anderson and 2 children, Capt. and Mrs. Boyd and 2 children, Mrs. Mainwaring and 1 child, with Lieut. and Mrs. Eyre and 1 child, and a European girl, Hester Macdonald, were in one room; that adjoining was appropriated for their servants and baggage. Capt. Mackenzie and his Madras Christian servant Jacob, Mr. and Mrs. Ryley and 2 children, and Mr. Fallon, a writer in Capt. Johnson's office, occupied another. Mrs. Trevor and her 7 children and European servant, Mrs. Smith, Lieut. and Mrs. Waller and child, Mrs. Sturt, Mr. Mein, and I had another. In two others all the rest of the gentlemen were crammed.

It did not take us much time to arrange our property; consisting of one mattress and resai between us, and no clothes except those we had on, and in which we left Cabul.

Mahommed Akbar Khan, Sultan Jan, and Ghoolam Moyen-oo-deen visited us. The Sirdar assured me we were none of us prisoners; requested that we would make ourselves as comfortable as circumstances would admit of; and told us that as soon as the roads were safe we should be safely escorted to Jellalabad. He further informed me that I might write to Sale; and that any letters I sent to him he would forward. Of this permission I gladly took advantage to write a few guarded lines to say that we were well and safe.

19th.—We luxuriated in dressing, although we had no clothes but those on our backs; but we enjoyed washing our faces very much, having had but one opportunity of doing so before, since we left Cabul. It was rather a painful process, as the cold and glare of the sun on the snow had three times peeled my face, from which the skin came off in strips.

We had a grand breakfast, dhall and radishes; the latter large hot ones that had gone to seed, the former is a common pulse eaten by the natives: but any change was good, as we find our chupatties made of the coarse ottah anything but nice. Ottah is what in England is called pollard; and has to be twice sifted ere it becomes flour. The chupatties are cakes formed of this ottah mixed with water, and dried by standing by the fire set up on edge. Eating these cakes of dough is a capital recipe to obtain the heartburn. We parch rice and barley, and make from them a substitute for coffee. Two sheep (alias lambs) are killed daily; and a regular portion of rice and ottah given for all. The Affghans cook; and well may we exclaim with Goldsmith, "God sends meat, but the devil sends cooks," for we only get some greasy skin and bones served out as they are cooked, boiled in the same pot with the rice, all in a lump. Capt. Lawrence divides it; and portions our food as justly as he can. The chupatty is at once the plate and bread: few possess other dinner-table implements than their fingers. The rice even is rendered nauseous by having quantities of rancid ghee poured over it, such as in India we should have disdained to use for our lamps.

21st.—The weather cleared up at noon. Major Pottinger is said to have received information that Zeman Shah Khan and all the Dooranees have surrendered to Shah Shoojah; and that his Majesty was at the bottom of the whole affair to turn us out of Affghanistan.

22nd.—I heard from Sale, dated the 19th. Our force can hold out at Jellalabad for six months. It is calculated that Col. Wylde must be at Jellalabad to-day with 5000 men. Gen. Pollock is coming with an army across the Punjab.

We hear that Mahommed Akbar has been offered the Sirdar-i-sirdaranee; but has refused it. He is said to be gone, or going, to the Khyber.

23rd, Sunday.—After prayers Mahommed Akbar Khan and Sultan

Jan paid us a visit: the latter took charge of a letter from me for Sale. He told me that Abdool Guffoor Khan says that Sale is quite well.

They say that Shah Shoojah demanded Conolly and three other hostages to be given up to him to put them to death; but Zeman Shah Khan refused.

24*th*.—A day or two ago the Sirdar sent some chintz to be divided amongst us. A second quantity was to-day given out; and we are working hard that we may enjoy the luxury of getting on a clean suit of clothes. There are very few of us that are not covered with crawlers; and, although my daughter and I have as yet escaped, we are in fear and trembling.

It is now said that the General gave Anderson's horse permission to go over to the enemy: a circumstance that does not at all agree with his conduct on the day following our taking protection; when he wished for Anderson's return lest the men should desert.

Dost Mahommed Khan took Mrs. Trevor's boys and some of the gentlemen out walking in the sugar-cane fields near the fort, which they enjoyed very much.

25*th*.—The Sirdar sent eight pieces of long cloth to be divided amongst us. I fancy he is generous at little cost; and that it is all a part of the plunder of our camp. He is said to have received letters from the Khyber stating that our force has been defeated there; two guns taken, and some treasure: and that Mackeson is shut up in Ali Musjid with 300 men.

26*th*.—As soon as the Bukhraeed is over, Shah Shoojah is to send 4000 men, and all the guns we left in Cabul, against Jellalabad. A Mussulman force is also now at Balabagh.

Mahommed Akbar Khan has had a private conference with Major Pottinger; of which no account has transpired. We had two shocks of earthquake at night.

27*th*.—A report that Sale has made another sally, and has taken a number of prisoners. I heard from him to-day: he has sent me my chest of drawers, with clothes, &c.: they were all permitted to come to me unexamined. I had also an opportunity of writing to him by Abdool

Guffoor Khan, who brought them to me. I was rejoiced to see any one I had known before; and especially one who was well inclined towards the English, though nominally on the side of Akbar.

4th.—The irregular cavalry have had their horses and everything taken away from them; and have been turned adrift. I wrote to Sale, but my note did not go.

5th.—My note to Sale was sent to-day. I got another from him dated the 29th, and replied to it.

9th.—We hear that all our horses are to be taken away; as also our servants. Rain to-day, as if the clouds wept for our misfortunes.

10th.—I received boxes from Sale, with many useful things; and also books, which are a great treat to us. I wrote to him, but fear my letter will not reach him, as all notes that came for us were kept back by the Sirdar; who is very angry, having detected a private cossid between Capt. Macgregor and Major Pottinger: if we behave ill again, the Sirdar says, woe will betide us. Abdool Guffoor again came to see us; and I had again the comfort to hear that Sale was well. We had rain to-day. Major Griffith arrived, with Mr. Blewitt.

Major Griffith tells me, that on the morning of the 13th, at daylight, the miserable remains of the force, reduced to about 100 Europeans of all ranks, including 20 officers, worn out with fatigue and hunger, and encumbered with very many wounded, some on horseback and some on foot, were, when within four miles of the bridge of Gundamuk, surrounded by a considerable number of the enemy both horse and foot. They had only thirty-five muskets and but little ammunition remaining; finding it impossible to proceed further, a position was taken up on a hill to the left of the road; and a parley opened with the enemy by means of waving a white cloth. This produced a cessation of the firing; and brought four or five men up to ascertain the cause. It was unanimously agreed that he (Major Griffith), as senior officer of the party, should go to the chief, and endeavour to make some terms for the peaceful march of the party to Jellalabad. He accordingly went, accompanied by Mr. Blewitt as interpreter, escorted by one or two of the enemy. On reaching the chief, they were hurried off without his giving them the opportunity of making any proposal. The last sight Major Griffith had of the party he had left, they appeared to be engaged in hostilities with the Affghans, whose numbers had gradually increased. He afterwards understood that the waving of a loonghee is considered by them as an act of unconditional surrender; and as our party would not give up their arms, the Affghans resorted to force; but were driven off the hill for the time. The few natives who had accompanied us so far did not go up the hill; but kept the road, and were seen to be plundered by the enemy. This he was afterwards told by Capt. Souter; who was brought to the village of Tootoo some hours after Major Griffith was taken there. This village was between two and three miles to the right of the scene of action. The same evening Major Griffith and Mr. Blewitt were taken to the Khan's fort, four or five miles further on the hills; where they found three or four European soldiers, who had escaped from the slaughter, wounded and taken prisoners. Some days after five more Europeans were brought in, who had proceeded in advance of our party. Major Griffith opened a communication with Jellalabad; and was in great hopes of effecting the release of the prisoners on ransom: but, owing to the jealousy and suspicion of the Khan Ghobam Jan Uzbezee, in whose power they were, nothing could be arranged. At last, after twenty days' confinement, he allowed one of their party, Serg.-Major Lisson, 37th N. T., to proceed to Jellalabad, and endeavour to explain matters. The party in all consisted of ten: two of these died, and Capt. Souter was left wounded at Tootoo.

The man who accompanied the Sergeant-Major returned the third day, and told them all was right. He was understood to have received 500 rupees as the ransom of the Sergeant-Major, who remained at Jellalabad. The party had strong hopes of liberation: but unfortunately the Sirdar, Mahommed Akbar Khan, heard of their being prisoners and sent to demand them. After some hesitation it was agreed to; and they were marched off to Charbagh to the Sirdar, and from thence to Buddeeabad.

Major Griffith was severely wounded in the right arm on the 8th of January, just at the entrance of the Khoord Cabul pass; and, from want of dressing, the wound had become very painful the day he was taken prisoner.

TRAVELS IN THE PUNJAB, AFGHANISTAN AND TURKISTAN

Mohan Lal

The nineteenth century witnessed no shortage of foreign, often British, travellers to Afghanistan. Many returned to write their obligatory travel books. Few offered the sort of cross-cultural perspective that **Mohan Lal** (1812–77), an Indian diplomat, traveller and author, provided in this vim-filled account of his adventures in Central Asia. In 1831, Lal met a kindred spirit in Alexander Burnes, whose retinue he joined on a British government mission to gather political and military intelligence in Central Asia. That experience led to Lal's appointment as political assistant to Burnes in Kabul during the First Anglo-Afghan War, a conflict which he, unlike Burnes, survived. He was one of the key masterminds of the British intelligence networks in Afghanistan.

May 1. — At two o'clock in the morning, we departed towards Kabul, a distance of twenty-five miles. On approaching the city, the climate assumed a refreshing coolness, and we only required to be our own masters, to enjoy the ever-varying scenes which were opened before us; but our heartless conductor pursued his way, and we were obliged to follow him through rain, sunshine, and darkness. Having kept moving for twenty-four hours together, we arrived at Kabul.

We travelled at night, and could see nothing of the country; but the very perceptible ascent of the roads, and the increasing cold, assured me that we had attained a very considerable elevation. I was impatient to feast my eyes upon the beauties of the place, which is considered the garden of India. I often sighed for daylight to put to sleep the stars, that I might actually behold what I had long only dreamt of, and vaguely imaged to my mind; but when daylight came, it made me blush, for nothing was visible but a desert of hard and naked rocks, which denied even to the snow a place of rest. The city was indicated by a dark haze, as if it had no connection with the uniform sterility around; and after such a dismal approach, I had little hopes of being gratified in entering it. It is no wonder that the kings of Kabul left their dreary territories, to plunder the rich plains of India.

We crossed the river on a bridge, which was in some parts overflowed. On our left, the road was generally a broad causeway, running for two miles in a straight line, till it terminated in a view of a noble building called Balahisar, which was formerly the residence of the king, and now Dost Mohammed Khan, the governor of Kabul, occupies that celebrated place. We were welcomed by our host, Nawab Jabbar Khan, who gave us a very fine house to reside in.

May 2 to 5. Kabul. — We remained at Kabul to see the curiosities and antiquities, which shall be described hereafter.

The day after our arrival, on the 2nd of May, we were delighted by meeting a fellow-traveller, who had overcome the difficulties of the road from Bokhara, after encountering many misfortunes. Mr. Wolff is a zealous missionary, wandering like the apostles of old over foreign countries, for the sake of enlightening the various nations of the earth; but with what success he did not mention. His sole object is to discover the lineal descent of the Jews, and in Afghanistan he had a fertile field for research, as the people themselves trace their genealogy to the tribes of Israel; but in so interesting a tract of country Mr. Wolff did not stop sufficiently long, and after the disasters he met with, it is not to be wondered at if he was anxious to quit so inhospitable a region. Amongst his adventures, he related having been made a slave; but fortunately for him he was not considered of much value, and got released. He next came into the hands of robbers, who took away all his money, and even the clothes from his back. Lastly, he was deprived of his horse by the deep snow of the Hindu Kush, and was compelled to walk naked into Kabul, like the *faqirs* of India. All these details were not very consolatory to us, who were to tread in his footsteps; but there is an attraction even in the idea of danger, that makes its actual sufferings shrink into insignificance, on such a journey as this.

Mr. Wolff was very kind to me, especially when I told him that my religion consisted in the worship of one sole Supreme Being. He seemed pleased to hear of the Delhi Institution, and asked if there were others educated like myself. He thought that sacred instruction should be inculcated as well as knowledge, but it is questionable whether this would not defeat the object of the academy. He promised to become a patron, and, with the assistance of Lord W. Bentinck, to improve the instruction. If he visits Delhi, I take the liberty to commend him to the kindness and favour of the college committee and my friends in India.

May 6. — An evening ride led me through the Balahisar to the residence of the present ruler. It is partly commanded by the southern hills, and partly by the western, besides being separately walled. The northern and eastern walls are defensible. It contains twelve large brass guns, regularly made. On my return, I bent my course through the Shor Bazar, which was roofed with very large rafters and mats. The shops, having numerous fine things, looked very beautiful.

May 7. — Early in the morning I proceeded to try the bath, accompanied by Dr. Gerard. The water was very fine and clear. There are neither flies nor any other insects to be found either in the outer or inner room, where rich men are generally allowed to bathe. The skylights overlook the Kabul River. It was built in the time of Vazir Fatah Khan, and adjoins the edifice of that nobleman.

At evening we set out to see the garden of the Shah, or the Bagh Shah, which is planted on the northern side of the city, in a beautiful spot. A stream of water, running from the river, passes the entrance of the garden. The road, or *khayaban*, was very clean and straight, like that of India. Its runs from the gate of the city, and ends in a view of a high hill, eight miles distant.

Poplar trees, which are not found in India (but are in England, as Dr. Gerard told me), adorn the surrounding walls of the garden. There are thousands of trees of many different kinds of fruit, for which the city is celebrated. Above me were the clear and blue skies; on each side were masses of snow, which tempered by their cold aspect the glow of the sun.

The appearance of Kabul is not remarkable; and its grey walls of mud ill correspond with the scene which opens upon the traveller on entering the city. But how shall I describe the bazar or *charsu*, so full of people, all strangers, not only in face, in dress, and in their dialects, but in all their customs; while every article of trade or of manufacture is equally dissimilar from that of Hindustan! The whole scene is entirely new, and one wonders that in so short a space there should be such a singular contrast. I thought of Delhi, with its palaces, its tall menarets, its splendid architecture, and its showy people, the flowing robes and brilliant ornaments, the braids and bracelets, the rose-odours, the bright eyes, and raven hair, and in the dance, "the many twinkling feet, so small and sylph-like." I looked in vain for the scenes of my youth, their true and false enjoyments; but they were gone!

The shops displayed a profusion of those fruits which I used to esteem costly luxuries. The parts of the bazar which are arched over exceed anything the imagination can picture. The shops rise over each other, in steps glittering in tinsel splendour, till, from the effect of elevation, the whole fades into a confused and twinkling mass, like stars shining through clouds, and the people themselves, not so big as beetles, seem as if of the pigmy race. These bazars were made by Ali Mardan Khan, to whose liberality and magnificent works his posterity is indebted for many fine and noble edifices which adorn India and other parts of Asia.

Next to the bazar, or I should say preceding it in importance, is Dost Mohammed Khan, the ruler of Kabul, who deserves particular notice, not only as a ruler, but as a man. I might be able to delineate him in Persian, but I am not sufficiently qualified in the English language to do his character justice, therefore I must comprise my description of him in a few words. His tall stature and haughty countenance, with his proud tone of speech and plain dress, indicate his high rank and sovereign power. He trusts none but himself, and is surrounded by numerous enemies, both of his own family and court.

If we judge the conduct of Dost Mohammed Khan as an encourager of commerce and a politician, we must allow him considerable praise, though he is not a character in whom one could place the confidence either of permanent friendship or political alliance. He has killed many chiefs of the country, and deprived many of the priesthood of their estates, after having sworn seven times by the holy soul of Mohammed, and even upon the Koran, which he afterwards said were the leaves of a common book. I am not quite sure whether the necessity of the times or his natural ambition excited him to the murders he has committed. He is very desirous to make himself the sole monarch of Afghanistan, but is in want of money. He seems not to be friendly towards the British Government; and I dare say he will side with that power which appears the strongest in the field. He has many wives, and also many sons, three of whom are the rulers of different places. He is very cautious not to give them much power, for fear of their turning against him. When he drove Sultan Mohammed Khan Sardar out of Kabul, he possessed himself of one of his dearest (intended) wives, which has heightened the animosity between the two brothers.

May 8 to 17. — I had the pleasure of talking with Mr. Wolff, who came into my room, and told me to listen to the Bible, and be converted to Christianity, which is the best religion in the world. My answer pleased the reverend gentleman very much. He added the following most singular speech: — That in the city of Bokhara he had an interview with Jesus Christ, who informed him that the pleasant valley of Kashmir will be the New Jerusalem after a few years. I copied his narrative, which he sent to Lady Georgiana, in Malta. He gave me a certificate, and promised to recommend me to his relation, Lady W. Bentinck, in Calcutta.

The inhabitants of Kabul are Sunis, Shias, and Hindus. The Shias live separately in a walled street called Chandaul. They believe the Panjtan, and always quarrel with the Sunis, the followers of Charyar; but the Shias, by their unanimity, generally gain the honours of the field. Nadir Shah brought a few Qizal Bash from Persia, and colonized them in Kabul, where they increased to 5,000. Their dress and custom of living are more decent than those of the Sunis or Afghans, who occupy the major part of the country. The people do not possess good features, and are fond of pleasure. They drink clandestinely, and rove about. The females, both of high and low family, desert the path of virtue and pursue bad principles. The proverbial saying which follows, and prevails among the inhabitants, confirms my explanation regarding the sex: — "The flour of Peshawer is not without a mixture of barley, and the women of Kabul are not without lovers."

The people and the merchants of the city generally speak Persian; but in the country, a very harsh Pashto continues to be spoken. The Hindus are nearly two thousand in number, and many of them are the first inhabitants of Kabul. They have large families, and are allowed all the privileges of their religion. They are known by their robes, and by their painted foreheads. Their shops are spread over all the streets and bazars, while their Mohammedan neighbours, though they are prejudiced against them, treat them very tolerantly.

At noon we paid a visit to the tomb of the emperor Babar, which is worthy of description. Having passed through the street of Javan Sher, or Shias, we followed the right bank of the Maidan River, which flows close by the city walls. We came now to a small village, where we refreshed ourselves with dry fruits of the past year. Again, we entered an old ruined gate, which led us through a beautiful square, shaded with fruit-trees of different kinds, and washed by numerous crystal canals. The green flower-beds, and the pleasant wind, along with the music of beautiful birds, quite surprised me, and I stood without motion, meditating whether I was dreaming of paradise, or had come into an unknown region. In the meantime, my eyes suddenly opened, and my sleepy heart, tired of the view of the barren rocks, awoke and said to me, "No doubt the emperor Babar was judicious in choosing this spot for his grave." We ascended four or five steps, and saw on our left hand a magnificent mosque, built entirely of beautiful marble. The breadth of the room (my companion measured it) was eight paces, and the length twenty. There were four open arches in the building. The marble was very fine, white, and clear; our faces were reflected in it. The expense of building the mosque was forty thousand rupees, and it was completed in the space of two years by Shah Jahan, after the conquest of Balk and Badakhshan.

Having climbed a few paces more, we came to a rising ground, which abounds with numerous tombs, made of marble, equal in size, and similar in shape, to each other. There was no difference between the tomb of the emperor and the tombs of his royal family, except in the inscription of the name of the buried.

The mausoleum of the emperor is not much raised above the surface of the earth; a few pieces of broken but fine marble cover the tomb, and at the head stands a small menar, called a "Lauh," which contains verses, beautifully cut, signifying the date of the emperor's death.

We are highly indebted to the English translation of "Babar's Memoirs," which gives us valuable intelligence of the whole country of Kabul. After a long description of the mountain, the emperor mentions that the famous pass of Hindu Kush is so high, and the wind is so strong, that the birds, being unable to fly, are obliged to creep over the top. They are often caught by the people, who kill and roast them for dinner. This is said by Dr. Gerard to be probably owing to the thinness of the air at that great elevation.

The original name of Kabul, described by the Persian authors, was Bakhtar, and is what we call the ancient Bactria. In the reign of the Chaghatah sovereign, it was called the division or *parganah* of the city of Bagram, which is now Peshawer. Tradition says that, in former days, the whole country of Kabul contained nothing but a vast forest.

Farhad or Kohkan, the famous lover of Shirin, a beautiful queen in Persia, happened to come to Bactria, and cut through a large hill, from whence a spring of clear water issued. On this he placed a colony of a few Persians, who invited over a great many foreigners to occupy their new found country. There is a long story about the paramour above described. After the country was inhabited and improved by science and art, the king Zabul, an infidel, possessed himself of Bakhtar. When Zabul died, the initial letter of his name, which is Z, in Persian, was changed for that of K and the city is since known by the name of Kabul.

Trade has enriched the city of Kabul beyond any other capital in Afghanistan. The caravan of Lohanis, which consists of between six hundred and seven hundred camels, furnishes it once a year with English and Indian goods. They come through Multan and Ghaznin, where they are not ill-treated. Great part of their merchandise is conveyed to Bokhara, which furnishes the merchants in return with fine silk, and also with a good breed of beautiful horses. These fine animals, purchased in Kabul, are sold in India at a price, quadruple their original cost, surpassing the expectations of their first Uzbeg masters. A great number go back with the Lohanis, who also take numerous loads of fruit for sale in that country. The *qafilah* returns in the month of October.

In the garden of the Shah, I happened to meet a respectable Lohani merchant, who fell into discourse with me; and when I was talking with him upon the subject of traffic, he said that if the British Government would make some arrangement with Ranjit Singh not to put heavy duties upon goods, and pay a small sum of money to the Khaibaris west of the Indus, to allow the caravan to pass safe through their valley, they would make an immense fortune by exporting English goods to Afghanistan, &c. by the road of Lodiana, which may be better frequented than that of Multan. In Shah Shujah's reign, the road of Khaibar was traversed without any danger.

The town duty of Peshawer and Kabul was heavier than it is now. The above king gave the chiefs of Khaibar a salary of 60,000 rupees a year, and held them responsible for the loss of every traveller.

When the merchant added, that the copper, steel, iron, and lace of Russia supplied the whole of Afghanistan through the distant deserts of Tartary, I was quite amazed to find that India, being so near Kabul, allows foreign articles to appear in the market. The blue paper of Russia is used throughout the whole Afghan states. The English manufactures and other articles are sent from Kabul to Peshawer, where they are very dear. With the imitation brocade of Russia, the rich men make saddles for their horses, and cover the floors of their houses. Bagu, a Shikarpuri merchant, told me that English goods, worth 300,000 rupees, are yearly sold in Kabul, and those of Russia to the value of 200,000.

The whole revenue of the country of Kabul, some say, amounts to 24,00,000 rupees, and others, to 25,00,000; but it is certain that the city itself owes much to the intercourse of trade.

Kabul is famous for its pleasant spring, during which time the whole region is refreshed with different and beautifully-coloured flowers. It is remarkable for flowers, as the following Persian verse declares: —

"The flowers of Kabul and the wine of Sheeraz have charming colours; the curling locks of the Persians and the delicate waist of the Indians have an attractive character."

The winter is severe here for three months. From the 1st of December snow falls very heavily till the beginning of March, and continues more or less till April. The roads to Bokhara and Candahar are blocked up till the arrival of spring. They are very seldom opened on account of the cold. The inhabitants buy up all the provisions for the winter season, and many never come out of their lodgings till the forty days of extreme cold are passed. They wear postins made of goat skins, and sit always round a fire, which is put under a kind of chair covered with a blanket, to prevent its being extinguished by the cold.

On account of the above-mentioned circumstances, the people find great difficulty in sustaining existence.

RETURN OF A KING

William Dalrymple

> Britain's leading travel writer and historian **William Dalrymple** (1965–) broke important new ground with this landmark history of the First Anglo-Afghan War, published in 2013. Until then, all too many Western histories of Afghanistan had been written from exclusively Western sources. This riveting account, packed with new material in Russian, Urdu and Persian, together with eight contemporary accounts of the conflict in Persian, broke the mould with a galloping narrative of this first, and sadly not the last, military encounter between the Afghans and the British.

The same morning that Pollock's sepoys were storming their way up the Khyber, Shah Shuja finally gave up on his British allies. Having heard nothing from MacGregor in reply to his last and most desperate note, the Shah decided he now had no option but to leave the shelter of his fortress and head off to Jalalabad.

He had spent a sleepless night 'restlessly walking up and down, calling on God, and constantly asking the eunuch servants what time of the night it was'. He then performed his ablutions, said goodbye to his wives and packed a small travelling pouch with the pick of his remaining reserves of diamonds, rubies and emeralds. 'At the first glimmer of true dawn, His Majesty prayed the two prostrations of the customary prayer in his private apartments in the fort, intending to pray the remaining obligatory two prostrations at the Siyah Sang camp. He mounted his palanquin and urged the porters to move quickly so as not to be late for the main prayer in camp. His Majesty was accompanied by only a minimal escort of personal servants.'

The previous day, 4 April, Shuja had left the Bala Hisar for the first time since the outbreak of the rebellion on 2 November. He rode out to his tent at the Siyah Sang, and there he held a review of the troops and a public audience for the Kabul nobles. It was at this audience that he formally announced his departure for Jalalabad and appointed his favourite son, Prince Shahpur, as governor of Kabul during his absence. Nasrullah, the eldest son of Aminullah Khan Logari, was appointed Shahpur's acting chief minister. According to Mirza 'Ata, the Shah brought with him '200,000 Rupees in cash and several bolts of double shawl cloth with which to honour the Kabul chiefs, each according to his rank and merit. He especially favoured Naib Aminullah Khan Logari who had become his closest confidant. Shuja then mounted his palanquin with his son and returned to spend a last night with his harem in the Bala Hisar Fort.'

Unbeknown to Shuja, however, this action of publicly honouring Aminullah Khan had been interpreted as a deliberate insult to his other principal ally, Nawab Zaman Khan Barakzai. He and Naib Aminullah Khan were now barely on speaking terms, and the public demonstration of the Shah's closeness to Aminullah at the Siyah Sang durbar had caused huge offence in the camp of the Nawab, who was from by far the grander lineage. 'Zaman Khan was a great lord with many fighters in his retinue,' wrote Mirza 'Ata,

> while Aminullah Khan Logari had recently merely been one of his attendants. At the durbar Nawab Zaman Khan and others close to Amir Dost Mohammad Khan had received no cloaks of honour from the King and indeed were quite passed over in the gaze of royal favour. This change in fortune did not sit well with the Nawab. Had the King seen fit to bestow his favours more equitably, the hidden discord might have been healed rather than enflamed. But the Nawab and his followers were seething with rage and pique at the King's taking no notice of them.

Most upset of all was Shuja' al-Daula, Zaman Khan's eldest son, 'who ... had received his name from his godfather [Shah Shuja's] own lips' and at whose birth the Shah had been present.

> Shuja' al-Daula, whose name means bravery or valour, a name which influenced his character, complained thus to his father: 'That Aminullah

Khan Logari was a mere servant of ours. He and those other minor chiefs with no solid base in society, they have now received all the King's favours, all the honourable appointments. Meanwhile we have been passed over, all our services to the crown and sacrifices for the cause forgotten: we look on dry-lipped, receiving no sign of gratitude, while the others get all the praise. I'm going to kill him if ever I am able to do so!' In spite of his father remonstrating that now was not the moment and that it was the time to concentrate on fighting the English, the boy took no notice and planned to ambush the King as he came from the fort to the army camping ground in the morning. Before dawn, he hid with 15 gunmen until the royal cavalry escort approached.

As Shah Shuja's party headed down the corkscrewing road from the Bala Hisar, the Nawab's son appeared and hailed his godfather's palanquin. The carriers paused and put down the palanquin. The Shah peered out of the curtains, and at that moment the waiting gunmen opened fire. The bloodied figure of Shuja stumbled out and tried to limp away across the fields. The assassins were already making off from the scene of the crime when one of them spotted the Shah and shouted to his employer to finish the job properly. 'So Shuja' al-Daula gave chase and pounced on the prostrate monarch, stabbing him pitilessly with his sword, shouting "Give me that cloak of honour now!" He stripped the dead King of his jewels and golden arm-band, belt and sword – all worth some one million Rupees. The King's gentle body, bred to rest on soft cushions of fine wool and velvet, was now dragged by the feet on rough stony ground and dumped in a ditch.'

'That blameless monarch', commented Herati,

> was martyred between two prayers, all the while repeating the holy names of God in his dawn litany, while the foul murderers earned only eternal damnation! Shahnawaz, one of His Majesty's attendants, tried to resist and wounded two of the assassins, but then seeing that the place was empty and abandoned, and that the travelling case of jewels was unattended, grabbed it and rushed towards the fort. He hid it in a crack

in an old wall, intending to retrieve it at a later stage and sell the contents. But his actions were observed and so it was that the jewels fell into the hands of the murderer of Shah Shuja and his father Nawab Zaman Khan.

Alas for that monarch, who once walked the avenues of the royal gardens but never picked the flowers of his hopes and ambitions! Instead he remained lying in blood and dust, unburied in the open plain. He died on the 23rd of the month of Safar, fixing his permanent abode in the kingdom of heaven. 'For we belong to God and to Him we return!'

Prince Shahpur hastened at once to the Bala Hisar fort to protect the royal women and children. The body of his father was left to lie where it fell for twenty-four hours, while the Sadozais barred the gates of the fort and gathered together, with the old blind Zaman Shah taking charge, as they tried to work out a strategy to save their position and seek revenge on the murderers. 'Meanwhile the Barakzais shouted out their gleeful congratulations, and Mir Haji promptly returned from his pretended jihad with his battle standards announcing, "We've sent the greater Lord [Shah Shuja] to join the lesser Lord [Macnaghten]." All were congratulating each other, saying "Now we've uprooted these infidel foreigners from our country!"'

Only one man saw it as his duty to attend to the corpse of the murdered Shah. Shuja's faithful water carrier, Mehtar Jan Khan Ishaqzai, who had followed Shuja into exile in Ludhiana, returned to the corpse late that night and remained next to it, guarding it from mutilation. The following morning he and another old retainer of the Shah's, 'Azim Gol Khan, the 'Arz-begi, helped prepare the corpse for burial. Working alone, the two men dug a shallow grave inside a ruined mosque near the place of the murder. This they covered with earth, and placed the King's palanquin on top. They also raised a small cairn of stones to mark the place of the murder.

Later that summer, the stones and the bloodstained palanquin were still lying where the two loyal retainers had left them.

SALE'S BRIGADE IN AFGHANISTAN
Reverend George Gleig

George Gleig (1796–1888) was a Scottish soldier, army chaplain and military writer. A veteran of Wellington's army who had fought in both Europe and the United States, he resumed his studies at Oxford University in 1816, took holy orders in 1820 and picked up his pen to write about his experiences on the battlefield. *Sale's Brigade in Afghanistan* (1846) took its name from Brigadier-General Robert Henry Sale, whose wife Florentia wrote her famous Afghan memoir. Gleig is best known today for some of the final lines from this book which make an excoriating summary of the First Anglo-Afghan War.

Chapter XXIII
EVACUATION OF AFGHANISTAN

WHILE Sale with his gallant followers conducted back their liberated friends in triumph, an expedition was fitted out by the commander-in-chief at Cabul; and sent to disperse a band of rebels which had gathered under the banner of a Kohistan chief, and established itself at Istaliff. Of the extreme beauty of that place, and of the surrounding country, I took occasion to speak while describing the movements of the force which headed back Dost Mohammed from Purandurrah. Standing upon the side of a mountain, which is overhung with gardens and orchards in terraces, Istaliff, both for the salubrity of its climate and the exquisite loveliness of its scenery, is without a rival in Central Asia; and being surrounded by walls, with towers here and there, so planted as to be very difficult of approach, it offers to the soldier a military position of no ordinary strength. There a considerable body of

Afghans had drawn together; and a holy war being by Akbar's directions proclaimed, they gave out, from day to day, that they should presently advance upon Cabul, destroy the unbelievers, and liberate the place. They were anticipated in this generous purpose by the march of General MacCaskill and a division of the army towards their strong-hold. A smart affair ensued, which ended, as all such were accustomed to do, in the total defeat of the enemy; and the town being entered sword in hand, it was given up to plunder. No lives were, however, taken after resistance ceased. A large number of women and children were, indeed, secured, and placed under guard, only that they might be sent back, without ransom, as soon as the fighting ceased, to their friends; but they were treated throughout with marked tenderness, neither insult nor injury being offered to them. It cannot be said, however, that much mercy was shown to the property of the people. Istaliff was the capital of a district which had rendered itself conspicuous during the troubles of 1841 for the cruel and treacherous conduct of its chiefs and people to their European visitors. Here were cut off, while dwelling at peace in the midst of them, Lieutenant Rattray and Captain Codrington, both in the Company's service; and here, also, Major Pottinger sustained much suffering, his followers being slain, and himself escaping, covered with wounds, as if by a miracle. These things were not forgotten by the troops who forced an entrance that day into Istaliff; and it was this remembrance which urged them to the perpetration of a work of vengeance, which must continue to be felt as long as the present generation shall last: for they did not leave a house standing. Fire consumed both castle and cottage; and gardens, vineyards, orchards, &c., were all cut down. Had there been at hand sufficient means of transport, the victors would have returned to Cabul encumbered with spoil. As it was, they cast into the flames every article, no matter how costly, which was too cumbersome to be conveyed about the persons of the men.

Having thus re-established the prestige of British invincibility (for General Nott had marched in triumph from the side of Candahar, winning back Ghuznee, and overthrowing with great slaughter every armed body which ventured to face him), General Pollock made ready, in agreement with the orders under which he acted, to return to the British provinces. A son of Shah Shujah, Futteh Jung by name, had hoisted his standard over the Balla Hissar, and proclaimed himself king. Few men of any note rallied under it; and the weak young man was given distinctly to understand that he need not look to the Feringhees for the support which his own countrymen withheld from him. At the same time the Balla Hissar was freely given up to him; and because he besought that it might be spared, the General neither broke down the walls nor suffered a torch to be applied to the wood-work. But every gun that was found in the place he caused to be destroyed; and blew up as many of his own battering-train as he found that he was without strength of cattle to drag through the passes. Having settled these points, General Pollock gave directions for inflicting upon the guilty capital the punishment which it deserved. With natural vanity Akbar Khan had built a mosque to commemorate the destruction of Elphinstone's force, to which he gave the name of the Feringhee Mosque, and which his flatterers affected to regard as one of the wonders of the world. It was levelled with the ground; and then followed the blowing up of the bazaars, the burning of chiefs' houses, the destruction of the city gates, and, last of all, a conflagration which spread everywhere till the waters of the river stayed it. That the work of plunder could be wholly stopped, amid the confusion attendant on such proceedings, was not to be expected. In spite of guards, camp-followers and soldiers made their way into the burning town, and loaded themselves with articles, scarcely one of which they were able, after the march began, to carry beyond the encampment. And here and there accidents occurred, of which it speaks well in praise of the discipline of the force that they were not multiplied fifty-fold.

The work of destruction began upon the 7th of October. It continued all that day and the next, and throughout both nights; and, indeed, till the mountains of the Bootkak shut it from them, the soldiers of Sale's brigade saw the whole face of the sky red with the flames which they had contributed to raise. But Sale's brigade did not linger long near the ruins of the Afghan capital; for on the 12th of October the army began its march towards the provinces. It moved by divisions, the first, to which the garrison of Jellalabad was attached, leading. It threaded the passes, not altogether unopposed, yet without sustaining any serious inconvenience; and having abandoned and destroyed a few heavy guns, which, for lack of draft animals, could not be carried forward, came in, in due time, to Jellalabad. That city shared the fate of Cabul and Ghuznee: it was razed to the ground; and the sick being moved forward, and the detachments gathered in which had heretofore protected them and maintained posts of halt for the main body, the whole proceeded through the Khyber and the Punjaub to the Sutlej.

So ended a war begun for no wise purpose, carried on with a strange mixture of rashness and timidity, and brought to a close, after suffering and disaster, without much of glory attaching either to the government which directed, or the great body of the troops which waged it. One portion of the army of the Indus did, indeed, win for itself a fame which shall be deathless. The garrison of Jellalabad well earned the epithet which the Governor-General, by his proclamation, bestowed upon it. But as soon as we avert our eyes from the heroic deeds of that handful of men, there is not much in the military history of those times on which we shall care to rest them. Doubtless, the massacre of the Koord Cabul was avenged. By the destruction of their chief towns, and the devastation of their villages and orchards, the Afghans were taught that England is powerful to punish as well as to protect. And in all the encounters with the armed men who resisted them, our soldiers proved themselves to be both dauntless and enduring. But not one benefit, either political or military, has England acquired by the war. Indeed, our evacuation of the country resembled almost as much the retreat of an army defeated as the march of a body of conquerors, seeing that to the last our flanks and rear were attacked, and that such baggage as we did save, we saved by dint of hard fighting. Nevertheless, the gates of Somnauth were carried back to the land whence Nadir had removed them; and British India proclaimed, what the whole world good-naturedly allowed, that we had redeemed our honour, and were once more victorious.

NARRATIVE OF EVENTS IN AFGHANISTAN

General Frederick Roberts,
Despatch from the Government of India, 1880

Small in stature – hence the affectionate 'Bobs' nickname – Field Marshal **Frederick Sleigh Roberts**, 1st Earl Roberts (1832–1914), was one of the military giants of his generation at a time of peak British Empire. After fighting for the East India Company Army as an officer during the Indian Rebellion of 1857, a campaign for which he was awarded the Victoria Cross for gallantry, he served as a British army officer first in Abyssinia then in Afghanistan, where he achieved considerable fame in Britain. He rose to become the last Commander-in-Chief of the Forces, before the position was abolished in 1904. His correspondence from Afghanistan, above all this famous warning from 1880 in the immediate aftermath of the Second Anglo-Afghan War – inevitably unheeded – remains as relevant today as it was more than 140 years ago.

"The Afghanistan of today is very different from the Afghanistan which existed at the time that the Treaty of Gandamak was made. Ruled by a strong Amir, possessed of a large standing army, and equipped with a numerous artillery and vast munitions of war, Afghanistan was a power which it became absolutely necessary for India to have access to and some control over. Kabul, the seat of government, had become a huge arsenal and barrack, and it was inexpedient that her ruler should be permitted to hold direct communication with Russia, receiving a Russian whilst declining a British envoy, and neglecting offers of friendly intercourse with India.

"Afghanistan is but a wreck of her former self, and, though no doubt still capable of strong combinations and powerful for mischief, she no longer exists as a military power, and has practically ceased to be a menace to India.

"The occupation of Kabul in October 1879 revealed to us much valuable information concerning the offensive power which the Amir possessed in his army, his well stocked arsenal, and his skilful artisans. With such means at his disposal for good or evil, it is easy to foresee what serious complications might at any time have arisen were he assisted by Russia either with men, money, or officers.

"This unmasking of the Amir's considerable warlike preparations, hitherto carefully concealed from us, is surely in itself a sufficient justification of the line of action taken by the Indian Government when it declared war against Afghanistan in 1878. Moreover, these revelations prove the wisdom of that portion of the Gandamak Treaty which insisted on the rectification of our own frontier and the location of British troops in the Khyber and Kuram. So long as Afghanistan continued to be a formidable and ill-disposed neighbour, it was all important that we should be within striking distance of the capital.

"Were the Afghan nation in the same condition now it was a year or even less ago, no one, thoroughly conversant with the policy of the North-West frontier of India, would hesitate to recommend that either the Kuram, or Khyber or both routes should be held in such strength as would admit of a considerable force being moved rapidly on Kabul. But, as I have stated above, these conditions are quite altered, and it is open to consideration whether there is any real necessity for us now to incur the expense and responsibility of occupying with troops either the Kuram or Khyber line."

After stating the military considerations which led him to the conclusion that any offensive operations necessary hereafter to be undertaken against Russian could most advantageously be carried out from the side of Kandahar, Sir F Roberts continued: –

"My own opinion, which I offer with considerable diffidence, is that the Kuram line should be given up altogether, and that the responsibilities which we ought to incur on the Khyber route should be limited to such as would ensure the execution and integrity of any guarantees we have given to the rules of Lalpura and Kunar.

"Viewing Kabul in the altered and powerless condition in which we shall leave it, with a ruler quite unable to cause us trouble or even anxiety in India, and knowing (as we now do) with what ease and quickness we can again at any time make ourselves masters of Kabul by either of the two roads under consideration, I can see no reason why regular troops should be kept either in Kuram or the Khyber.

"We are now also fully aware of the extraordinary difficulties which Russia would have to encounter were she at any time to advance upon India via Kabul, and to how great an extent we could injure and harass her by raising the tribes along the line of communications which it would be necessary for her to maintain, or by taking the initiative from our advanced yet secure based at Kandahar. The longer and more difficult the line of communication is, the more numerous and greater the obstacles which Russian would have to overcome, and, so far from shortening one mile of the road, I would let the web of difficulties extend to the very mouth of the Khyber Pass.

"On political grounds it would probably be necessary for us to have control of the Khyber, or perhaps as far as Lundi Kotal, Pesh Bolak, or any other selected place. To secure this I would make use of Hazara or Afridi levies, but I would strongly deprecate the employment of any regular troops beyond Peshawur."

In explanation of the change in his former opinions on these questions, General Roberts observed: –

"I would ask His Excellency the Viceroy and Governor General to bear in mind that no one has been a more zealous supporter of the present policy, and that no one has more strongly advocated an unsparing reduction of the military power of Afghanistan, than I have. The objects of this policy have, I consider, been most thoroughly attained. Nearly a year's residence at Kabul has convinced me of the truth of this, and manifested how completely Afghanistan has ceased to be a cause of danger to our Indian empire.

"The state of affairs which brough the Treaty of Gandamak has completely changed. In place of our being obliged to occupy the advanced strategic positions secured to us by that treaty, and which the safety of our Indian empire forced us to hold as long as Kabul was the centre of a great political and military power, we can now afford to withdraw our troops within our original frontier. We have nothing to fear from Afghanistan, and the best thing to do is to leave it as much as possible to itself.

"It may not be very flattering to our amour propre, but I feel sure I am right when I say that the less the Afghans see of us, the less they will dislike us.

"Should Russian in future years attempt to conquer Afghanistan, or invade India through it, we should have a better chance of attaching the Afghans to our interests if we avoid all interference with them in the meantime.

"The military occupation of Kandahar is, as I have before stated, of vital importance; even there we should make our presence but little felt, merely controlling the foreign policy of the ruler of that province."

CHARLES MASSON OF AFGHANISTAN
EXPLORER, ARCHAEOLOGIST, NUMISMATIST AND INTELLIGENCE AGENT

Gordon Whitteridge

Afghan Wars aside, Charles Masson (alias of James Lewis, 1800–53) was one of the more remarkable foreign figures involved with Afghanistan in the nineteenth century. He combined many roles: soldier, explorer, reporter, spy and numismatist-cum-archaeologist. After deserting from the East India Company artillery and changing his name to Charles Masson in 1827, he pursued his own path, first joining an unlikely expedition by the American Josiah Harlan to overthrow Dost Mohammed Khan, the Afghan ruler in Kabul. Later, after deserting Harlan, he travelled across Afghanistan on foot, having been blackmailed into spying for the British in return for an official pardon for desertion in 1835. He started excavations of Buddhist sites around Kabul and Jalalabad in the early 1830s and by the time of his return to England in 1842 had amassed a collection of 47,000 coins – the Masson Project at the British Museum, which aims to publish his extensive collection, is ongoing. Masson did not endear himself to his British colleagues for correctly predicting disaster for any British invasion.

In the 1930s, a French archaeological expedition found graffiti in one of the caves above the 55-metre Buddha in Bamiyan (tragically destroyed by the Taliban in 2001). It read:

If any fool this high samooch [cave] explore,
Know that Charles Masson has been here before.

Gordon Whitteridge (1908–95), the author of this enthralling study of Masson, was a British diplomat who served as ambassador to Afghanistan from 1965 to 1968.

Chapter VIII

MASSON'S ARCHAEOLOGICAL AND NUMISMATIC DEBUT

All passes, Art alone
Enduring stays to us;
The Bust outlasts the throne –
The Coin, Tiberius.

H. A. Dobson *Ars Victrix*

The weather in January and February, 1833 of which Masson gives a vivid account, continued exceptionally severe, and spring was slow in coming. By May, however, he was able to extend his excursions beyond the city limits and to start examining certain remains which had previously caught his attention. But he had to proceed with great caution lest he arouse animosity or cupidity in various quarters. The following passage gives a good idea of the difficulties which were to persist throughout his archaeological labours; of his methods and finds; and of the successful use he made then and later of his wide acquaintance among Afghans of all classes. 'Having now resided a year without interruption, and in perfect security in the country, I was emboldened to essay whether objections would be made to the examination of some of the numerous artificial mounds on the skirts of the hills. I was unable to direct my attention to the massive topes, where considerable expense was required; still, the inferior indications of the olden times might repay the labour bestowed upon them, and by testing the feeling which my excavations created I might smooth the way for the time when I should be in a condition to undertake the superior monuments. Without asking permission of anyone, I commenced an operation upon a mound at the skirt of the hill Koh Takht Shah . . . Below, or east of it, was a castle and garden, belonging to Akhund Iddaitulah. I had become acquainted with his sons, who interested themselves to forward my researches . . .

In the course of four or five days we discovered, nearly at one of the angles of the mound, a tak, or arched recess, ornamentally carved, and supported by two slender pillars. In it we found the remains of several earthen images; the heads of the two larger ones only were sufficiently entire to bear removal. They were evidently of female figures, and of very regular and handsome features.** Affected by moisture, which had naturally in the course of centuries completely pervaded the mound, and everything of mere earth contained within it, we could yet from slight traces ascertain that the figures had been originally covered with layers of white and red paint, and that over the latter had been placed a surface of gold leaf. The hair of the heads, tastefully arranged in curls, had been painted with an azure colour. The recess also had been embellished with gold leaf and lapis lazuli tints. Accompanying the figures were a variety of toys, precisely such as the Hindus make at the present day and in no better taste, representing horses, sheep, cows etc. of cement.'

The more important discovery remained. At the base of the recess were hewn stones, and on their removal he found jammed in between them Nagari writings on birch bark which had suffered badly from the all-penetrating damp. He next uncovered a suite of small apartments. In one of them, he found several images lying horizontally, one of them eight or ten feet in length. They were all of pure earth, and had been covered with gold leaf. His Moslem companions amused themselves by trying to scrape it off, but with limited success as the images were so saturated. In another apartment also decorated with mouldings, and painted with white, red and azure colours, he found three earthen lamps, an iron nail and one or two fragments of iron.

His researches became the subject of conversation in the capital and the son of Akhund Iddaitulah having sold the gold leaf he scraped from the images to a goldsmith for less than a rupee, Masson's friends begged him to desist from such labours in future. They urged that the country was bad, as were the people, and that he would probably get

---

** No doubt heads of Buddha which are often effeminate in appearance in Gandhara sculpture.

into trouble. He pointed out that little notice would be taken of him so long as broken idols were the sole fruits of his endeavours. Mahomed Akbar Khan,* son of Dost Mahomed Khan, hearing of his discoveries, sent for him and wished to see them. He was enraptured with the two 'female' heads, and lamented that the ideal beauties of the sculptor could not be realised in nature. An acquaintanceship grew up between Masson and the young sirdar who would frequently send for him. He became a pretty constant visitor at Mohamed Akbar Khan's tea-table and obtained from him an order, addressed to the various headmen and chiefs of the Kohistan and Ghorband, to assist him in any researches he might undertake in those districts, of which the sirdar was the governor. Masson was both gratified and surprised at the good sense shown by the young sirdar as to the nature and object of his researches.

His relations with the sirdar allayed the misgivings of his friends, and encouraged him to continue his researches without fear. He was, he says, always of the opinion that no umbrage would be taken, and felt assured that if he acted openly and fairly he would be fairly dealt with. Nothing further of consequence was extracted from the mound; but when Dr Gerard arrived in Kabul at the end of that year, Masson pointed out the spot to him as one likely to yield a desirable find to carry with him to India. From it he obtained the marble sculptured slab forwarded to the Asiatic Society of Bengal, an account of which, written by his secretary and companion, Mohan Lal, appeared in the Journal of the Society for September 1834.

Masson was fortunate in his choice of site to make his archaeological debut, not only as regards the quality of his finds, but also in the confidence it gave him. He was fortunate too, in gaining the interest and protection of Mahomed Akbar Khan. It was not always to be so, and he had to be circumspect whenever he attacked a site in an unfamiliar district. He now started to examine the neighbourhood of Charikar in a series of trips on foot. His intention was to make a preliminary study

---

* He murdered Sir W. McNaghten in 1841 and gave undertakings of safe conduct to the British force which led to the notorious retreat, but did not, or perhaps in the circumstances could not, implement them.

of the local conditions and the antiquities in the area. For a stranger, travelling without tent or servants, it was difficult to obtain a lodging for the night, unless the mosque could be regarded as quarters; to pass the night in the open was neither safe nor seemly. He succeeded in forming acquaintances at all the stage villages on the several roads between Kabul and Charikar and was certain whenever he dropped in on any of them to be received with civility. In the course of these trips he visited the picturesque township of Istalif, nowadays a favourite tourist attraction,* which he lovingly describes. He also examined the stupa at Dara which he hoped to excavate and of which he drew a sketch.

But he was looking for something much more important. Alexander the Great founded several cities in the Afghan area, one of which, Alexandria ad Caucasum, was believed to be located in the Kohistan north of Kabul and close to the Hindu Kush. Masson thought that the village of Begram and its great plain might well prove to be the site. He had previously reached the edge of the plain and had heard strange stories of the innumerable coins and other relics found on the soil but had been unable to procure a specimen, all to whom he applied, whether Hindu or Moslem, denying they had any such things in their possession. A friendly headman provided him with an escort of half a dozen horsemen to enable him to traverse and survey the plain, which was dangerous owing to the marauders infesting it.

At Killa Bolend at the beginning of the Begram plain there were seven considerable Hindu traders, but no coins were forthcoming. At another village he heard fresh tales of Begram and the treasures found there. His curiosity was so intensely excited that he determined to revisit it taking along Mir Afzil, the headman's son, who had friends in the vicinity. Mir Afzil produced Baloch Khan, a 'fine honest young man, who brought me a present of melons and grapes. This was the commencement of an acquaintance which continued as long as I remained at Kabul; and Baloch Khan greatly assisted me in my subsequent researches, as I could

---

* Or was, prior to the invasion by the Soviet Union at Christmas 1979, since when it has been heavily bombed.

always when needed call upon him and his armed followers to attend me in my excursions, and to protect the people I sent. He now exerted himself to procure coins; and at last an old defaced one was produced by a Mahomedan, for which I gave two pais, which induced the appearance of others, until the Hindus ventured to bring forth their bags of old monies, from which I selected such as suited my purpose. I had the satisfaction to obtain in this manner some eighty coins of types which led me to anticipate bright results from the future'. The fears and scruples of the owners having been overcome, he remained some time at Killa Bolend, securing their confidence. They had been anxious lest Masson should employ forced labourers to scour the plain in search of antique relics and had therefore determined to conceal from him, if possible, the existence of such objects. He took care to ascertain how and by whom these coins were found. The clue to them once discovered, the collection became an easy matter although it subsequently proved that a long time was necessary before he became fully master of the plain.

His interest in finding and deciphering coins was now fully aroused: 'The discovery of so interesting a locality as that of Begram imposed upon me new, agreeable, and I should hope not unprofitable employment. I availed myself of every opportunity to visit it, as well with the view to secure the rich memorials of past ages it yielded, as to acquire a knowledge of the adjacent country. Before the commencement of winter, when the plain, covered with snow is of course closed to research, I had accumulated one thousand eight hundred and sixty-five copper coins, besides a few silver ones, many rings, signets and other relics. The next year, 1834, the collection which fell into my hands amounted to one thousand nine hundred copper coins, besides other relics. In 1835 it increased to nearly two thousand five hundred copper coins, and in 1836 it augmented to thirteen thousand four hundred and seventy copper coins. In 1837, when I had the plain well under control and was enabled constantly to locate my people upon it, I obtained sixty thousand copper coins, a result at which I was well pleased, having at an early period of my researches conjectured that so many as thirty thousand coins might annually be procured. The whole of the coins and other antiquities, from Begram, with several thousands of other coins brought to light in various parts of Afghanistan, have been forwarded to the Honourable the East India Company...

Masson's own verdict on his numismatic finds runs: 'It may be superfluous to dwell upon the importance of the Begram collections; independently of the revelation of unknown kings and dynasties, they impart great positive knowledge, and open a wide field for speculation and inquiry on the very material subjects of the languages and religions prevailing in Central Asia during the dark period of its history... Besides coins, Begram has yielded very large numbers of engraved seals, some of them with inscriptions, figures of men and animals, particularly of birds, cylinders, and parallelogramic amulets with sculptured sides, rings and a multitude of other trinkets and miscellaneous articles, generally of brass and copper; many of which are curious and deserve description'. To this modest claim may be appended Professor Wilson's appreciation: '... in addition to new coins of Greek princes already known, he found those of several whose names are not mentioned in history as Antialkidas, Lysias, Agathocles, Archebias (sic), Pantaleon and Hermaeus. He also found the coins of the king whose titles only are specified as the Great King of Kings, the Preserver, and of others whose names assuming a Greek form indisputably denote barbaric or Indo-Scythic princes:- Undapherres [Gondopheres], Azes, Azilises, Kadphises, and Kanerkes [Kanishka]. Mr Masson described the most remarkable of them and furnished linear delineations of them, which were engraved in the Journal and which, although not pretending to merit as works of art, were satisfactory confirmations of the correctness of his descriptions and decypherings. The first great step in the series of Bactrian numismatic discovery was thus accomplished, and the great object of later investigations has been to complete and extend the structure of which such broad foundations were laid'.

'THE YOUNG BRITISH SOLDIER' and 'FORD O' KABUL RIVER'

Rudyard Kipling

Many writers have left powerful images of Afghanistan and the wars which have been fought here during the past two centuries, perhaps none more so – for British readers at least – than **Rudyard Kipling** (1865–1936). His famous poem 'The Young British Soldier' contains no end of excellent advice for fresh-faced soldiers arriving in India about how to conduct themselves on and off the battlefield. One of the first *Barrack-Room Ballads*, it was published in 1890, shortly after Kipling had returned to England, and a decade after the Second Anglo-Afghan War, which still simmered in the popular memory. If you are wounded and left on the battlefield, Kipling writes, there's only one thing for it: blow your brains out before the women come out to carve you up, 'An' go to your Gawd like a soldier'.

The Young British Soldier

WHEN the 'arf-made recruity goes out to the East
'E acts like a babe an' 'e drinks like a beast,
An' 'e wonders because 'e is frequent deceased
Ere 'e's fit for to serve as a soldier.
Serve, serve, serve as a soldier,
Serve, serve, serve as a soldier,
Serve, serve, serve as a soldier,
So-oldier of the Queen!
Now all you recruities what's drafted to-day,
You shut up your rag-box an' 'ark to my lay,

An' I'll sing you a soldier as far as I may:
A soldier what's fit for a soldier.
Fit, fit, fit for a soldier . . .

First mind you steer clear o' the grog-sellers' huts,
For they sell you Fixed Bay'nets that rots out your guts –
Ay, drink that 'ud eat the live steel from your butts –
An' it's bad for the young British soldier.
Bad, bad, bad for the soldier . . .
When the cholera comes - as it will past a doubt –
Keep out of the wet and don't go on the shout,
For the sickness gets in as the liquor dies out,
An' it crumples the young British soldier.
Crum-, crum-, crumples the soldier . . .
But the worst o' your foes is the sun over'ead:
You must wear your 'elmet for all that is said:
If 'e finds you uncovered 'e'll knock you down dead,
An' you'll die like a fool of a soldier.
Fool, fool, fool of a soldier . . .
If you're cast for fatigue by a sergeant unkind,
Don't grouse like a woman nor crack on nor blind;
Be handy and civil, and then you will find
That it's beer for the young British soldier.
Beer, beer, beer for the soldier . . .
Now, if you must marry, take care she is old –
A troop-sergeant's widow's the nicest I'm told,
For beauty won't help if your rations is cold,
Nor love ain't enough for a soldier.
'Nough, 'nough, 'nough for a soldier . . .
If the wife should go wrong with a comrade, be loath
To shoot when you catch 'em - you'll swing, on my oath! –
Make 'im take 'er and keep 'er: that's Hell for them both,

An' you're shut o' the curse of a soldier.
Curse, curse, curse of a soldier . . .
When first under fire an' you're wishful to duck,
Don't look nor take 'eed at the man that is struck,
Be thankful you're livin', and trust to your luck
And march to your front like a soldier.
Front, front, front like a soldier . . .
When 'arf of your bullets fly wide in the ditch,
Don't call your Martini a cross-eyed old bitch;
She's human as you are - you treat her as sich,
An' she'll fight for the young British soldier.
Fight, fight, fight for the soldier . . .
When shakin' their bustles like ladies so fine,
The guns o' the enemy wheel into line,
Shoot low at the limbers an' don't mind the shine,
For noise never startles the soldier.
Start-, start-, startles the soldier . . .
If your officer's dead and the sergeants look white,
Remember it's ruin to run from a fight:
So take open order, lie down, and sit tight,
And wait for supports like a soldier.
Wait, wait, wait like a soldier . . .
When you're wounded and left on Afghanistan's plains,
And the women come out to cut up what remains,
Jest roll to your rifle and blow out your brains
An' go to your Gawd like a soldier.
Go, go, go like a soldier,
Go, go, go like a soldier,
Go, go, go like a soldier,
So-oldier of the Queen!

Ford o' Kabul River

Kabul town's by Kabul river –
Blow the bugle, draw the sword –
There I lef' my mate for ever,
Wet an' drippin' by the ford.
Ford, ford, ford o' Kabul river,
Ford o' Kabul river in the dark!
There's the river up and brimmin',
An' there's 'arf a squadron swimmin'
'Cross the ford o' Kabul river in the dark.

Kabul town's a blasted place –
Blow the bugle, draw the sword –
'Strewth I sha'n't forget 'is face
Wet an' drippin' by the ford!
Ford, ford, ford o' Kabul river,
Ford o' Kabul river in the dark!
Keep the crossing-stakes beside you,
An' they will surely guide you
'Cross the ford o' Kabul river in the dark.

Kabul town is sun and dust –
Blow the bugle, draw the sword –
I'd ha' sooner drownded fust
'Stead of 'im beside the ford.
Ford, ford, ford o' Kabul river,
Ford o' Kabul river in the dark!
You can 'ear the 'orses threshin',
You can 'ear the men a-splashin',
'Cross the ford o' Kabul river in the dark.

Kabul town was ours to take –
Blow the bugle, draw the sword –
I'd ha' left it for 'is sake –

'Im that left me by the ford.
Ford, ford, ford o' Kabul river,
Ford o' Kabul river in the dark!
It's none so bloomin' dry there;
Ain't you never comin' nigh there,
'Cross the ford o' Kabul river in the dark?

Kabul town'll go to hell –
Blow the bugle, draw the sword –
'Fore I see him 'live an' well –
'Im the best beside the ford.
Ford, ford, ford o' Kabul river,
Ford o' Kabul river in the dark!
Gawd 'elp 'em if they blunder,
For their boots'll pull 'em under,
By the ford o' Kabul river in the dark.

Turn your 'orse from Kabul town –
Blow the bugle, draw the sword –
'Im an' 'arf my troop is down,
Down an' drownded by the ford.
Ford, ford, ford o' Kabul river,
Ford o' Kabul river in the dark!
There's the river low an' fallin',
But it ain't no use o' callin'
'Cross the ford o' Kabul river in the dark.

'TORTURES AND METHODS OF EXECUTION'
IN *UNDER THE ABSOLUTE AMIR*
Frank Martin

By now it should have become apparent that Afghanistan is no place for shrinking violets. For all its spectacular natural beauty and the legendary hospitality of its people, it is a hard and often violent place. For eight years **Frank Martin** had a front-row seat as engineer-in-chief to Amir Abdur Rahman Khan (r. 1880–1901) and later the Amir's son and successor, Habibullah (r. 1901–19). Abdur Rahman was certainly no mouse. He deftly managed to avoid invasion or occupation by either the British or Russians and was no less successful dealing with internal challenges, suppressing around forty rebellions and consigning his enemies, both real and imagined, to often appalling deaths, without counting the untold thousands slaughtered by his army and those who died from starvation and disease. Frank Martin met the Amir regularly in the course of his duties and recounted many of his conversations in *Under the Absolute Amir*. Published in 1907, it offers a very European perspective on a man who, for all his cruelty, has been described as a military genius.

Chapter X

TORTURES AND METHODS OF EXECUTION

Amir's iron rule—Hanging by hair and skinning alive—Beating to death with sticks—Cutting men in pieces—Throwing down mountain-side—Starving to death in cages—Boiling woman to soup and man drinking it before execution—Punishment by exposure and starvation—Scaffold scenes—Burying alive—Throwing into soap boilers—Cutting off hands—Blinding—Tying to bent trees and disrupting—Blowing from guns—Hanging, etc.

THE Amir once told me, when speaking of the unruly character of the people, and the difficulty of making them, by the example of others who were punished, become peaceful and law-abiding, that he had ordered over a hundred thousand to be executed since the beginning of his reign, and that there were still others who thought they could set his laws at defiance. The Amir ruled his people with an iron hand, and, considering their character, such is necessary, if order is to be maintained. I was one day in durbar at the Bagh-i-bala palace, and one of the soldiers committed some offence, and was ordered to be brought in by the Amir, who inquired into the circumstances, and then instructed one of his officers to take the man down the hill adjoining the palace, and cut his throat there. This was done, and two little slave boys, who went with the executioners to see the *tamasha*, came back with white faces and trembling limbs. It was the first time they had seen such a sight, but those who were attached to the Amir's court, were not long in his service before becoming used to happenings of this sort.

Although the Amir punished many small offences with death, he was not always enraged when one man killed another, unless the murdered person happened to be one whom he knew and liked, then his anger was ungovernable, and the murderer was generally ordered death in some particularly horrible manner. One of the slave boys, of whom the Amir was very fond, and had raised to a position of influence and power, and who consequently became arrogant and overbearing in manner to others, and so gained for himself a good many enemies, was shot by a soldier one evening while riding across the square in Sherpur cantonment. When the soldier was brought before the Amir, the latter, suspecting that he could have had no enmity against the slave boy, questioned him as to who instigated him to commit this deed, and the soldier refused to answer. This further enraged the Amir, and he gave orders that the man was to be tied to the bough of a tree by his hair in the palace garden, and so many square inches of skin taken off his body daily until he confessed.

The man died on the third day without confessing anything to incriminate another, but the name of one of the generals was mentioned freely by the people as the instigator of the crime, in revenge for the slave boy insulting him in the Amir's presence shortly before.

Another case showing the severity of the Amir towards the relatives of those who escaped his vengeance was that of an old man brought before him, whose son had run away from the country. The old man's son, with two or three others, had been concerned in, or accused of, swindling the treasury, and knowing what was being said against them, and the fate in store should they be convicted, they determined on escaping to India. The Kotwal, however, got wind of their intention, and came on the night proposed for escape with some twenty of his men, and posted them outside the gate, where some horses belonging to those in the house were standing ready saddled. The son, and those with him, discovering that the Kotwal and his men were lying in wait for them, determined on cutting through them, so, suddenly opening the door, they rushed out armed with swords and revolvers. The Kotwal was not noted for personal courage, and the Kotwali sepoys generally are seldom courageous, perhaps through being of mixed races, and they gave way after one or two of their men had been cut down, and then the young fellows made a dash to the horses, and cutting down those who held them, mounted and got away, and were not heard of again. The father, who was left in the house, was seized by the Kotwal and taken to the Amir, where, not knowing whether his son had escaped or not, he begged the Amir to forgive him, urging that he was guiltless of the crime of which others had accused him, and offered his own life if his son's might be spared, saying the Amir might kill him himself where he stood. The Amir, enraged at the young men escaping his vengeance, seized his stick and struck the old man down with it, and then ordered others there to go on beating him; and in the Amir's presence the old man was thrashed until he was dead, and his body was afterwards exhibited on a *charpai* (bedstead) in the bazar for two days, as a warning to others. The Amir invariably punished the nearest relatives of those who ran away to escape punishment, and knowing this, many a man returned and gave himself up in order that his relatives might go free.

Beating with sticks is a common punishment, so many blows being given on the man's back as he lies spreadeagled on the ground, two soldiers, one on either side, administering the blows, while others hold the man down, and sometimes the Amir orders the blows of such a number that the man shall die under the punishment. A master carpenter, who did not get on with the work ordered in a new part of the palace, was given a hundred and fifty blows with sticks, and died the day after, but the sticks used are at times so heavy that the bones of the back are broken and the flesh mortifies, so that a lesser number of blows will sometimes cause death.

The present Amir had fifteen Kotwali sepoys beaten for neglect of duty, in not reporting the transgressions of their superior officer, until eight of them died under the blows, and the others were unable to move for weeks after, and being kept in prison received no medical treatment to alleviate their sufferings. On a later occasion, when one of his attendants had committed some mischief, with the object of getting the blame put on another fellow-servant, and was detected, the Amir, who was at the time on the temporary roof covering the new palace in the Arak garden, had the man brought before him, and there beaten with sticks until partly insensible, then the man was hauled to the edge of the roof and thence thrown to the ground, after which he was dragged by a rope fastened to his legs from where he lay to the Kotwali, but life was extinct on arrival, though he was still living after being thrown from the roof.

The present Amir is very scrupulous about all things surrounding him being kept clean and tidy, not only in the house and garden, but the roads leading to the palace must be kept swept and clean too. He was one day passing out of one of the smaller gates in the wall of the Arak garden, and noticed that the ground round the gateway was unswept; so, stopping there, he sent for the man whose duty it was to sweep the place. A woman came in reply, and said that she was the man's wife, and her husband was too ill with fever to get up, and she had been so busy attending him that she had found no time to sweep the place herself, and also she was, as he could see, heavy with child. The Amir replied that he would relieve her of her burden, and ordered the woman fifty strokes with sticks on the abdomen. The woman was accordingly laid on her back, on the ground, and beaten, and died almost immediately afterwards.

The late Amir was very savage in punishing those who falsely reported his death. When the cholera epidemic broke out in 1900, the Amir went to live at Paghman, which is situated at the foot of the Hindu Kush, while the epidemic was raging, for the Amir and all his family greatly fear cholera, and run away at once from the affected area. Towards the close of the epidemic, two men came in to Kabul from Paghman, and gave out in the bazars that the Amir was dead of the disease; and when the Amir returned to the city a few days after, he had these men caught and brought before him, and said the wish was certainly father to the report which they had spread; so he ordered them to be cut in pieces, and their remains to be exhibited in the bazars as a warning to others. On another occasion when he had again been reported dead, he ordered the man who spread the report to be taken to the top of the Asman Heights, and there, on a part overlooking the river which is very precipitous, be put into a barrel and rolled down the mountain-side to the valley below. A similar case, but more brutally executed, was that of an old man, a moullah, who had given out that the Amir was not a true Mussulman, and was ordered to be thrown down the mountain from the same point. When thrown over the cliff, by the Kotwali sepoys, his clothes caught on a jutting rock, which suspended him, and prevented further fall, and the sepoys, releasing the clothes, took the man back and threw him over again, this time successfully.

The Amir, after the style of the Mikado of dramatic fame, always tried to let the punishment fit the crime, although his punishments were sometimes such as to make one think that he greatly exaggerated the crime. For instance, a man who stole the food of some poor children, leaving them nothing, was put in a cage, in the bazar, and there starved; but to make the punishment fit his crime more closely, bread and water were brought to him two or three times each day, and placed just out of his reach, and this was continued until the man died of starvation.

In another case, a man and a woman, who loved not wisely but too well, both being married people, determined on running away together, hoping thereby to secure their future happiness in each other's society, but in their endeavour to reach India, where they intended living together, they were caught and brought back. The Amir, in ordering their punishment, said that, as the man was so fond of the woman, he should have her as completely as was possible. So the woman was thrown alive into a huge cauldron of boiling water, and boiled down to soup, and a basin of this soup was given to the man, who was forced to drink it, and after drinking it he was hanged. In this case the Amir's object was to punish, not only in this life, but in the next, for a cannibal cannot enjoy the delights of Paradise as depicted in the Koran.

'THE BOUNDARIES OF AFGHANISTAN AND THE DURAND MISSION'
IN *THE LIFE OF ABDUR RAHMAN: AMIR OF AFGHANISTAN* (Vol. 2)

Amir Abdur Rahman

Translated by Mir Munshi Sultan Mahomed Khan

By and large Western readers on Afghanistan read Western sources. Those who do not read Pashto, Dari or Uzbek, which will be most of us, therefore gain a very Western perspective on the country and its history, people, conflicts and so on. Which makes the autobiography of one of Afghanistan's most important rulers essential reading. **Amir Abdur Rahman Khan** (r. 1880–1901) had many claims to fame. He united the country after years of war, negotiated its borders with Britain, launched a whirlwind of modernisation and along the way notched up mind-boggling numbers of executions – 100,000 by one account. In light of all the many eggs which were broken to make his national omelette, his nickname 'The Iron Amir' seems understated. Not so the preface of the second volume, which was probably ghost-written by Sultan Mohammed Khan, who claims 'since the time of the great Mogul Emperors – Timur, Babur, and Akbar, etc. no Muslim sovereign has written his autobiography in such an explicit, interesting, and lucid manner as the Amir has done...' Reading this extract on Great Power machinations, it is difficult not to feel some sympathy for the Afghan sovereign. 'My country is like a poor goat on whom the lion and the bear have both fixed their eyes,' he writes of the ever encroaching British and Russians, 'and without the protection and help of the Almighty Deliverer the victim cannot escape very long.'

Chapter VI

THE BOUNDARIES OF AFGHANISTAN AND THE DURAND MISSION

THE readers of my book will by this time have formed an idea of the way in which I had made a kingdom of Afghanistan, which before had been divided into so many independent States ruled over by separate chiefs; and how I had extended my dominions, which, at the time of my accession, were no more than the city of Kabul and Jellalabad, together with a few other places. They will have learned how I took possession of the Kandahar and Herat provinces in 1881, and those of Roshan and Shignan in 1883 (though the last-named was under dispute up to 1893, when it was officially settled by the Durand Mission). In the same year I appointed my own governor, named Ghafar Khan Kirgiz as governor of Wakhan, instead of Ali Merdan, the native chief of Wakhan. This was a hill state to the south of Shignan; on the south of Wakhan lies Chitral. My readers have also seen how I extended my dominions by occupying Maimana in 1885; Hazarajat in 1893, and Kafiristan in 1895; though I had to subdue the last-named after the Durand Mission, by which it was decided to belong to my Government.

At the same time when I was occupied in breaking down the feudal system of Afghanistan and moulding the country into a strong consolidated kingdom, I was not unaware nor neglectful of the necessity of defining my boundaries with the neighbouring countries. I well knew that it was necessary to mark out the boundary lines between my dominions and those of my neighbours, for the safety and protection of my kingdom, and for the purpose of putting a check on their advances, and getting rid of misunderstandings and disputes.

I know that it has become a custom in this century for great Powers to absorb small countries; and to carry out their desires of annexing the weak countries they adopt various modes and schemes. For instance, the first is by the partition of the weak nations, by which every one of the strong usurpers takes his share, and the justice given to the weak nations by these strong Powers reminds me of the story of a poor man, whose watch had been taken by a robber. He went to one of the chiefs of the robbers, who called himself a magistrate. But this magistrate said: "I cannot get your watch back, but what are you going to give me for my share?" The poor man cried hard for justice, saying that he did not come to give more, but to get back what had been already taken from him. The answer was: "There is no reason that you should give your watch to a weaker person than myself, and I not have my share?" He thereupon demanded the chain as his share. The man went to a higher judge, who took the man's ring in the same manner. Where-upon the poor man thought that if he went to the Lord Chief-Justice there would be no jewellery left at all, and his share would only be his turban and clothes, leaving him without a stitch of clothing to cover him. He therefore went home, contented with half justice. I believe that if the readers of my book will compare the story of this justice with the case of China, they will find that I am not very far wrong. The second mode is this: That the great Powers enter into underhand intrigues and understandings with each other, which they call statesmanship and policy, and agree with each other that "if you take such-and-such a country, and I take such-and-such, we will not interfere with each other."

The third mode of their taking these countries is this: That at a time when they are defining their boundaries with another Government, certain countries or provinces on which they have cast their eye they leave undecided; these they call neutral; and they say to the neighbouring Power: "Now this must be left independent; neither must you interfere nor we interfere." By these pretences of calling such countries or provinces neutral, they cancel the claims of the neighbouring weak Governments to these provinces, which either wholly or in part belong to them. This being done, they begin to play their game in this so-called neutral country in such a manner that they give to the chief of the neutral territory an old worn-out riding horse, some old uniforms, and so many guns or revolvers, saying to him: "We will be friends with each other, and our friendship will be sufficient to save you from the attacks or aggression of your neighbour; and you are to be our friend and independent ally." The poor fellow thinks that there is no harm in being friends, so long as they acknowledge his independence; and that, on the contrary, it is to his advantage that they should take the responsibility of his protection against foreign aggressors. But very soon after, they easily find some excuse to accuse this neutral chief of having broken his promise of faithful friendship; or sometimes they persuade his own subjects to appeal for justice against his cruelties to these illustrious judges. And after listening to one or other pretence like this, they take possession of his country. If the neighbouring Power says that this is against the treaty, and they must leave this territory neutral, they answer: "Ah, yes! it was left neutral at the time, but the ruler himself made a subsequent treaty with us, by which he placed himself and his country under our protection and our sphere of influence. This bars you from having any right to interfere in the affairs of the country which has been so many years considered under our influence and included in our sphere of Government, therefore you have no right to interfere with our belongings!" And there the matter ends.

'SKIN OF THE DONKEY, TEETH OF THE DOG'

Sir Henry Mortimer Durand

For many Afghans the name Durand is synonymous with the country's disputed international border with Pakistan – the 1,660-mile Durand Line – recognised by every country in the world apart from Afghanistan, where it remains a controversy that rankles to this day.

On 6 November, 1907, **Sir Henry Mortimer Durand** (1850–1924), a former foreign secretary of India, rose to address the members of the Central Asian Society in London. His talk offered a quintessentially British, and at times affectionate, portrait of Amir Abdur Rahman, the Afghan sovereign, and the sensitive border negotiations Durand had conducted with him in 1893, precipitated by a Russian demand that the Afghans should withdraw from some districts they then occupied north of the Amu Darya, or Oxus, River, in breach of a previous agreement. It was Abdur Rahman's misfortune that he found himself caught in the middle of the Great Game between Britain and Russia. If the 'Iron Amir' left a deep and lasting impression on Durand, it is surely no exaggeration to suggest that the Durand Line, in many Afghan eyes, represents a baleful colonial legacy, the source of ongoing contention with Pakistan and a regular igniter of Pashtun nationalism.

A key problem with the Durand Line is that 85 per cent of it runs along rivers and other physical features, rather than ethnic boundaries. It thereby divides a large Pashtun population into two, assigning one to Afghanistan and the other to Pakistan.

THE AMIR ABDUR RAHMAN KHAN

BY

THE RIGHT HON. SIR H. MORTIMER DURAND, G.C.M.G., ETC.

Delivered November 6, 1907

On October 2 we marched into Kabul, and the Amir gave us a magnificent reception. Troops were under arms in all directions. Some miles out, at the Logar Bridge, we found awaiting us the Amir's carriage and a large escort of his household cavalry. As we drove into the city a salute of twenty-one guns was fired, and the bands played 'God save the Queen'. Every possible civility was shown in the way of inquiries and good wishes, and we were given as quarters a fine house on a mound near the western foot of the Kabul range. The climate was ideal, not a cloud in the sky.

Here, in our pleasant quarters in the Chardeh Valley, we remained for six weeks, until the 15th of November.

My first interview with Abdur Rahman himself was on the 5th of October. We drove over to the garden in which the Amir was living, and were received inside it by the Shahgassi, a tall, fine-looking Afghan, very carefully dressed, and bearing a gold wand of office. By the side of the path were drawn up a number of Hotchkiss and Gardner guns, made in the Amir's workshops. The present Amir, then a smooth-faced, pleasant-spoken young man, was standing outside the Amir's house, wearing a red coat and broad G.C.S.I. ribbon. Inside the Durbar room stood the Amir, leaning on his stick.

I was much struck with the change which eight years had effected in him. He looked well—better than in 1885—though thinner. He seemed more contented and easy in mind. The look of power was still there, but the Abdur Rahman of 1893 was a quiet, gentlemanly man, with a much softer and more refined voice and manner. He seemed to suffer much from gout, and walked with difficulty, leaning on a stick. He shook hands with each of us in turn. Nothing could have been kinder and more cordial than his manner to us all. He held my hand for a long time, saying more than once that I was an old friend, and that now I had been sent to Kabul all would go well.

The real business began a day or two later, and, on the whole, it would have been hard to find a more satisfactory person to deal with than Abdur Rahman. He did all the negotiating himself, sitting at the end of a long table in a room of his garden-house in the Chardeh Valley. This room was almost a veranda, for the outer wall was pierced by five large windows, which were always open. In spite of the cloudless sky, it was often very cold. We sat on his right, looking out across the garden to the blue Pagman range; his own staff, including the Englishman Pyne, sat on his left. The discussion went on in Persian, the Amir objecting to an interpreter on the ground that interpreters only confused business, and were no good. He never consulted any of his people; as in 1885, he did everything himself, personally discussing each point involved to the minutest detail. At times he would take a sheet of foolscap and a box of coloured chalks and dash off, in his swift, imperious way, a rough sketch map of some country we were discussing. Sometimes he would begin our sittings, which lasted from about eleven till four, by relating experiences in his life, and telling us anecdotes. He was an excellent raconteur, with a fund of ready humour and much natural eloquence, and long as our sittings were, I thoroughly enjoyed many of them. From beginning to end they were interesting, and enlivened by much 'chaff' and laughter.

The Amir's sense of humour was keen. He had a way of making a joke and looking at you with eyes and mouth open, to see if you had caught it, and then going into a roar of laughter, which was very infectious. His changes of mood were rapid. He would suddenly stop laughing and look down on the ground with a deep sigh, remaining silent for a minute or more; after which he would, perhaps, break into a dignified and pathetic lament over the fallen fortunes of his country, or the sorrows and humiliation of a life of exile.

At times he was very touching. There was something which went to one's heart about the man, standing there between England and Russia, playing his lone hand. Like all men who have got accustomed to unlimited power, he was impatient of opposition, and his temper was quick; but it was easy to bring him round, and he was soon laughing again.

Often blunt, and occasionally ignorant as to details, he was consistently courteous and pleasant. What was best of all, he thoroughly knew his own mind, and once he had accepted a thing, he never went back from his word. One felt one was dealing with a man of business, and a man one could trust, I have had some thirty years' experience now in dealing with diplomatists, Eastern and Western, and I can confidently say that among them all the most satisfactory negotiator I ever had to do with was the Afghan Amir.

Of course, as I have said, the negotiations, like all negotiations, had their ups and downs, and at times it seemed as if we had come to a hopeless impasse. But the primary object of the mission was attained with no great difficulty or delay. Abdur Rahman hated retiring from any position he had taken up, but he was too shrewd and sensible not to see that by occupying the districts north of the Oxus the Afghans had put themselves in the wrong, and, like all really strong men, he was not afraid of admitting a mistake. After a week of discussion he agreed to withdraw from Roshan and Shignan, and then turned to the question of his frontier towards the east. Far from showing unwillingness to discuss the matters connected with this frontier, he pressed me to take them up, and, indeed, wished to consider them before taking up the Oxus question at all. They were, of course, rather complicated, and it took us a long time to thresh them all out. Abdur Rahman, though he knew his frontier country well, knew it from personal visits or hearsay, not from the study of maps; consequently, he was at times at fault regarding the position of places. It was no use producing a map, for he would say, 'That is no use. It is all wrong. I *know*. I have been to those places. Your maps are guess-work.' Chageb, for example, a name which often came up, was, according to him, quite wrongly placed in our survey map, which made it twice as far from the Helmund as it ought to be.

'Whenever you are dealing with one of my alleged encroachments, it is made very big on the map. When you are dealing with one of your own, I notice, it is quite a tiny little thing.' It was no good arguing the point, so I could only shake my head and laugh, and try to put the matter in a different way. Then at times he would stand on some point of dignity. Once I said to him: 'After all, Amir Sahib, if there is so little population and wealth in the country you describe, what good will it do you?' His answer was one word. He turned upon me slowly with a very steady look into my eyes, and said: 'Nam,' (name, honour). On such points he was inflexible.

So the negotiations went on for some weeks, and in the end all was settled to the satisfaction of both sides. When they were over the Amir held a great Durbar in his citadel, to which we were invited, together with some 400 Afghan notables. Abdur Rahman made a long speech, summing up the course of the negotiations, expressing his great pleasure at the results, and exhorting his people to remain henceforward true to the British alliance. The assembly replied by presenting to him an address on the part of the tribes and people of Afghanistan, approving of all he had done. The Amir read out this address, dwelling upon his position as the chosen representative of the Afghan nation.

The Amir asked me to address the assembly also, and declined to let me do it through an interpreter. 'You do not speak Persian perfectly,' he said with characteristic frankness, 'but they will understand you better than an interpreter. If you are at a loss for a word I will help you.' The ordeal proved less formidable than I had expected.

In the course of his speech Abdur Rahman disclosed for the information of his people, and incidentally for the information of the Indian newspapers and the world in general, the true objects of the mission, which had till then been kept secret. But this did no particular harm.

On the 15th of November we said good-bye to the Amir. There had been a smart shock of earthquake, and he had been sleeping in a felt kibitka in his garden. He was most cordial in his messages to various people in England, and most friendly to us. I said good-bye with real regret. I never saw him again.

Our march down was uneventful, and the only thing which struck me was the increased freedom accorded to us and the extreme friendliness of the people, which was unmistakable. All along the road they crowded about us, bringing presents of fruit and flowers and showing every sign of goodwill, and the escort no longer kept them at arm's-length. Word had come from the Amir that for the future the English and Afghans were friends, and they seemed really anxious to prove that they heartily accepted the situation.

I have seen it stated more than once since that time that the agreement at which Abdur Rahman arrived about his frontier towards India was forced upon him against his will. Nothing can be farther from the truth. The settlement was, as I have said, entered upon at his own pressing request, and the conclusion was accepted of his own free-will, with the fullest expressions of satisfaction and pleasure. It was his wish to obtain a definite frontier all round his country, and it is not the least of the many benefits conferred on Afghanistan by his far-sighted statesmanship.

It has also been stated that the arrangement was a dangerous step in advance on our part, the embodiment of a reckless, forward policy. That also is wholly untrue. The arrangement merely embodied the principle asserted over and over again by successive Governments in India and in England—the principle that for the peace and security of our own border we must be free to deal direct with the various independent tribes from Chitral to Baluchistan, and could not recognize any claim on the part of the Afghan Amirs to suzerainty over them. Abdur Rahman had the good sense and the strength of character to accept that principle, and to undertake that he would leave the tribes alone for the future. This is a plain question of fact, and the fact can be proved beyond the possibility of denial from the contents of many Blue books. There was nothing new in the arrangement, except that for the first time the principle was definitely and formally accepted by an Amir who was strong enough and wise enough to prefer peace and goodwill with us to the maintenance of shadowy and dangerous pretensions.

Before closing this paper I will mention one or two further points about Abdur Rahman unconnected with the frontier negotiations.

The foundation of all things is physical courage, and Abdur Rahman possessed it to a degree which made him a marked man even among the Afghans—an exceptionally brave people. He showed it on innumerable occasions. I will refer to one which I have often heard cited. He was seated in a chair watching a regiment march past when a man dropped back from the rear rank of a company, and, taking deliberate aim, fired at him from a distance of a few yards. The bullet grazed his coat, and killed a man behind him. It is said by the Afghans that Abdur Rahman never took the slightest notice, not even raising his hand from the arm of his chair.

Abdur Rahman preferred to be addressed simply as 'Amir Sahib,' not by any lofty Oriental title. He prided himself on being the fighting chief of a fighting people, and despised all hyperbole. His dress and Court were very simple. He was essentially a personal ruler, with much thought for business and little for form. I was much struck by his patriotism. He was very proud of his country, and really anxious to carry the Afghans with him in all he did. He was a despotic ruler, no doubt, and cared little for individual opinion. I should have been sorry for any man who ventured to differ from him. But he was not, I think, insincere in putting forward Afghan sentiment as a force to be considered. He watched it carefully, and often deferred to it.

His great desire as regards military matters was for money and big guns for the defence of his northern frontier. He wanted no advice or other help from us. Breech-loading rifles and Hotchkiss guns he could manufacture or buy. He had a curious belief in the usefulness of forty-pounders. With them and money he thought he could organize his country for defence much better than we could. A European adventurer once brought him a large telescope for sale, and told him it would show him the whole geography of the moon. His answer, as repeated to me was, 'Oh, blow the moon! What is the use of the moon to me? Can't you make a gun of the thing?'

He disbelieved in trying to turn his Afghans into a standing army on Sher Ali's pattern. For the defence of their country against a foreign enemy he believed in their national methods of tribal warfare, supplemented by modern weapons. He had some regular regiments, but even these were mostly territorial, consisting of men of one tribe or district. They were quartered in parts of the country at a distance from their homes, but this was for reasons of internal policy.

Throughout his reign Abdur Rahman was occupied in strengthening his rule over all parts of the country, and it must be admitted that he had great success. Tribe after tribe which had maintained some sort of independence was reduced to order, and scattered in colonies all over the country. Many nests of freebooters were extirpated, some of them very formidable strongholds. One large band, for example, holding a mountain fastness near Jellalabad, harried the country for years, and was only reduced after twenty-six days' continuous fighting by a force of 12,000 men. Roads were cleared in all directions, and safely held. Altogether Abdur Rahman established a very firm grip on his turbulent kingdom.

As an instance, I may mention that on our return march from Kabul we spent two days on bullock-skins floating down the Kabul River. At one point where a river passes through a gorge in the mountains, we found ourselves carried by a rapid close under a rocky cliff. Among the rocks above us, within the few yards we saw some Momund tribesmen armed with jezails. One of our rafts carried some Afghan soldiers, who called to the Momunds to put their arms down on the ground. This was done at once, though the escort could not possibly have got at them.

Wherever we went cultivation was increasing, and the people seemed prosperous and contented.

In matters of trade Abdur Rahman was, to our views, not enlightened or liberal. He said his people were so poor and ignorant that he was obliged to manage their trade himself. He created numerous monopolies, and acted in defiance of recognized commercial principles. It must be added that he showed remarkable interest in developing on his own account certain branches of industry. The workshops he erected in Kabul were a striking feature. In them he manufactured everything necessary for the armament and equipment of his army. Guns, rifles, ammunition, saddlery, all were of excellent quality. The mint turned out coins of accurate weight and good finish. The coins of former Afghan

Amirs had been chunks of silver chopped off a rough bar, and flattened and stamped by hand with one blow on a rickety anvil. Soap, candles, brandy, and other things were also manufactured in considerable quantities. The machinery, including heavy steam-engines and a massive steam-hammer, had all been brought from India over difficult mountain passes, and most of it in pieces not too heavy for a camel to carry.

There was one thing for which Abdur Rahman was often and severely criticized—the terrible nature of his punishments; and it must be admitted that he did at times inflict upon his subjects punishments which to the European mind appeared to be cruel and barbarous. The Government of India felt strongly about this, and let its feelings be known. But Abdur Rahman cannot be judged by European standards. His punishments were, after all, no worse than those inflicted to the present day in other Oriental countries. He had to deal with a very turbulent population, and his argument was that he must make examples or he would have disorder all over the country. The Afghans, the Ban-i-Israel, were fierce and fickle, like the people from whom they claim descent. He was merciless, but he said, and I believe with perfect truth, that he took no pleasure in cruelty. In the latter part of his reign barbarous punishments on a large scale were much less frequent than when he was stamping out disloyalty and rebellion.

Taking him altogether, Abdur Rahman was a very striking figure, and did very remarkable work. It was his personal character and reputation among the Afghans which really brought him to the throne of Kabul. When he came to it he found his country disorganized by war, and split up into fragments, with several other claimants in the field, and the tribes completely out of control. Gradually, with some little help from us, but chiefly by his own courage and capacity, he reunited Afghanistan and established his rule over every part of it. When he died he left to his son a comparatively well-ordered and prosperous kingdom, with definite frontiers and a fixed policy. To that inheritance the new Amir succeeded in peace. Long may he and his heirs continue to enjoy it!

Of course, Abdur Rahman had his faults and his limitations. He was not modest or self-denying or pitiful. But he was brave, and able, and resolute as few men are. His shrewdness and power of work and sense of humour were unfailing. In essentials he was faithful to his engagements. He was proud of his country and jealous of its independence and honour. To those whom he liked he was generous and affectionate. Of all the men with whom I have had to deal he was unquestionably the strongest. If he had been born under a luckier star, in an age which allowed free scope for the display of his high qualities, he would, I believe, have achieved a great renown. Fate set bounds to his ambition, and now, after life's fitful fever, he sleeps well. But to my eyes at least he will always stand out as a great ruler and a great man.

THE ROAD TO OXIANA
Robert Byron

Had he been writing today, there seems little doubt that the English traveller, art critic and historian **Robert Byron** (1905–41) would have been swiftly cancelled. However appreciative he may have been of the crowning glories of Islamic architecture – 'If the outside is lyrical, the inside is Augustan,' he wrote of Isfahan's Sheikh Lutfullah Mosque, comparing its richness to Versailles, the porcelain rooms at Schönbrunn, the Doge's Palace or St Peter's, while acknowledging that each one fell short – his trenchant caricatures of foreigners would surely have landed him in very hot water. And yet *The Road to Oxiana* (1937), the diary of his ten-month travels across the Middle East, Afghanistan and India in 1933–34, remains sublime. His writing about Herat, and its Timurid golden age, is a microcosm of his Oxiana: beautifully paced, stylistically sophisticated, hilarious and erudite, a tour de force of travel writing encompassing everyone from Babur to Gibbon, Timur to Macaulay, and a handful of comic cameos besides.

Herat (3,000 ft), 21 November

Noel got visas and brought me here; or rather, I brought him. Having driven the whole way from London, he was glad to give the wheel to someone else. He left this afternoon by the southern road to Kandahar.

But for the staff of the Russian Consulate, who lead the life of prisoners, I am the only European in the place, and am on my best behaviour; the public stare demands it. There is company at the hotel in three Parsi Indians, who are riding round the world on bicycles and have come from Mazar-i-Sherif by the new road opened this summer. They met various Russians on the way, who had escaped over the Oxus and were proceeding under escort to Chinese Turkestan by the Wakhan-Pamir road. One of these was a journalist, who gave them a letter describing his sufferings. His boots were already in holes, but he was intending to walk to Pekin.

Herat has its own Secretary for Foreign Affairs, who is known as the Mudir-i-Kharija and says that if I can find transport, I may proceed to Turkestan. I also had audience of the Governor, Abdul Rahmin Khan, a handsome old fellow wearing a tall black astrakhan hat and grey Hindenburg moustaches. He too gives me leave to go where I want, and will furnish me with letters to the authorities en route.

*

Later I called on the Muntazim-i-Telegraph, who speaks English.

'Where is Amanullah Khan?' he asked suddenly, glancing out of the window to see that no one was about.

'In Rome, I suppose.'

'Is he coming back?'

'You ought to know better than I do.'

'I know nothing.'

'His brother, Inyatullah, is in Teheran now.'

The Muntazim sat up. 'When did he arrive?'

'He lives there.'

'What does he do?'

'Plays golf. He plays so badly that the foreign diplomats avoid him. But as soon as they knew King Nadir Khan had been assassinated, they all telephoned inviting him to play.'

The Muntazim shook his head over this sinister information. 'What is golf?' he asked.

A gentleman from the Municipality called this evening to know if I was comfortable. I admitted I should be comfortable if the windows of my room had glass in them. The hotel is managed by Seyid Mahmud, an Afridi by the look of him, who used to work in a hotel at Karachi. He showed me his visitors' book, from which I saw that Graf von Bassewitz, the German consul in Calcutta, stayed here in August on his way back from leave. This is the first I have heard of him since 1929.

Herat, 22 November

Herat stands in a long cultivated plain stretching east and west, being three miles equidistant from the Hari river on the south and the last spurs of the Paropamisus mountains on the north. There are two towns. The old is a maze of narrow twisting streets enclosed by square ramparts, and bisected diagonally by the tunnel of the main bazaar, which is two miles long; on the north stands the Citadel, an imposing medieval fortress built on a mound, whence it dominates the surrounding plain. Opposite this lies the New Town, which consists of one broad street leading northward from the bazaar entrance, and a similar street intersecting it at right-angles. These streets are lined with open fronted shops. Above them towers the second storey of the hotel, situated among the coppersmiths, whose clang between dawn and sunset deters the guests from sloth. Further on at the crossroads, is the ticket office for lorries, where passengers assemble daily among bales of merchandise and vats of Russian petrol in wooden crates.

Engrossed by the contrast with Persia, I return the people's stare. The appearance of the ordinary Persian, addressed by Marjoribanks' sumptuary laws, is a slur on human dignity; impossible, one thinks, for this swarm of seedy mongrels to be really the race that have endeared themselves to countless travellers with their manners, gardens, horsemanship, and love of literature. How the Afghans may endear themselves remains to be seen. Their clothes and their walk are credential enough to begin with. A few, the officials, wear European suits, surmounted by a dashing lambskin hat. The townsmen too sport an occasional waistcoat in the Victorian style, or the high-collared frock-coat of the Indian Mussulman. But these importations, when accompanied by a turban as big as a heap of bedclothes, a cloak of parti-coloured blanket, and loose white peg-top trousers reaching down to gold-embroidered shoes of gondola shape, have an exotic gaiety, like an Indian shawl at the Opera. This is the southern fashion, favoured by the Afghans proper. The Tajiks, or Persian element, prefer the quilted gown of Turkestan. Turcomans wear high black boots, long red coats, and busbies of silky black goats' curls. The most singular costume is that of the neighbouring highlanders, who sail through the streets in surtouts of stiff white serge, dangling false sleeves, almost wings, that stretch to the back of the knee and are pierced in patterns like a stencil. Now and then a calico beehive with a window at the top flits across the scene. This is a woman.

Hawk-eyed and eagle-beaked, the swarthy loose-knit men swing through the dark bazaar with a devil-may-care self-confidence. They carry rifles to go shopping as Londoners carry umbrellas. Such ferocity is partly histrionic. The rifles may not go off. The physique is not so impressive in the close-fitting uniform of the soldiers. Even the glare of the eyes is often due to make-up. But it is a tradition; in a country where the law runs uncertainly, the mere appearance of force is half the battle of ordinary business. It may be an inconvenient tradition, from the point of view of government. But at least it has preserved the people's poise and their belief in themselves. They expect the European to conform to their standards, instead of themselves to his, a fact which came home to me this morning when I tried to buy some arak; there is not a drop of alcohol to be had in the whole town. Here at last is Asia without an inferiority complex. Amanullah, the story goes, boasted to Marjoribanks that he would westernize Afghanistan faster than Marjoribanks could westernize Persia. This was the end of Amanullah, and may like pronouncements long be the end of his successors.

On approaching Herat, the road from Persia keeps close under the mountains till it meets the road from Kushk, when it turns downhill towards the town. We arrived in a dark but starlit night. This kind of night is always mysterious; in an unknown country, after a sight of the wild frontier guards, it produced an excitement such as I have seldom felt. Suddenly the road entered a grove of giant chimneys, whose black outlines regrouped themselves against the stars as we passed. For a second, I was dumbfounded—expecting anything on earth, but not a factory; until, dwarfed by these vast trunks, appeared the silhouette of a broken dome, curiously ribbed, like a melon. There is only one dome in the world like that, I thought, that anyone knows of: the Tomb of Tamerlane at Samarcand. The chimneys therefore must be minarets. I went to bed like a child on Christmas Eve, scarcely able to wait for the morning.

Morning comes. Stepping out on to a roof adjoining the hotel, I see seven sky-blue pillars rise out of the bare fields against the delicate heather-coloured mountains. Down each the dawn casts a highlight of pale gold. In their midst shines a blue melon-dome with the top bitten off. Their beauty is more than scenic, depending on light or landscape. On closer view, every tile, every flower, every petal of mosaic contributes its genius to the whole. Even in ruin, such architecture tells of a golden age. Has history forgotten it?

Not quite. The miniatures of Herat in the fifteenth century are famous, both for themselves and as the source of Persian and Mogul painting afterwards. But the life and the men that produced them, and these buildings as well, hold no great place in the world's memory.

The reason is that Herat lies in Afghanistan; while Samarcand, the capital of Timur, but not of the Timurids, has a railway to it. Afghanistan, till literally the other day, has been inaccessible. Samarcand, for the last fifty years, has attracted scholars, painters, and photographers. Thus the setting of the Timurid Renascence is conceived as Samarcand and Transoxiana, while its proper capital, Herat, remains but a name and a ghost. Now the position is reversed. The Russians have closed Turkestan. The Afghans have opened their country. And the opportunity arrives to redress the balance. Strolling up the road towards the minarets, I feel as one might feel who has lighted on the lost books of Livy or an unknown Botticelli. It is impossible, I suppose, to communicate such a feeling. The Timurids are too remote for most people to romance over them. But such is the reward of my journey to me.

All the same, these Oriental Medici were an extraordinary race. With the exception of Shah Rukh, Timur's son, and of Babur who conquered India, they sacrificed public security to private ambitions; each remained, in politics, what Timur himself had been, a free-booter in search of a kingdom. Timur, in founding an empire by this impulse, had delivered Oxiana from the nomads and brought the Turks of Central Asia within the orbit of Persian civilization. His descendants, by the same impulse, undid this work and destroyed themselves. They recognized no law of succession. They murdered their cousins, and boast among them one parricide. One after another they drank themselves to death. Yet if pleasure was the object of their lives, these princes believed the arts to be the highest form of pleasure, and their subjects followed their example; so that to be a gentleman was to be, if not an artist oneself, at least a devotee of the arts. When the famous minister Ali Shir Nevai records of Shah Rukh, that though he did not write poetry, he often quoted it, there is an accent of surprise on the first part of the statement. Their taste was inventive. They sent to China for new ideas in painting. Not content with classical Persian, they wrote in Turki as well, a more forcible medium of expression, such as Dante, not content with Latin, found in Italian. Among the gifts of the age was an instinct for biographical detail. Though its chronology is insupportable, a tedious record of intrigue and civil war, the actors are flesh and blood. Their characters correspond with our own acquaintance. We know very often, from portraits, how they looked, dressed, and sat. And the monuments they built have a similar impress. There is a personal idiosyncrasy about them which tells of that rare phenomenon in Mohammadan history, an age of humanism.

Judged by European standards, it was humanism within limits. The Timurid Renascence, like ours, took place in the fifteenth century, owed its course to the patronage of princes, and preceded the emergence of nationalist states. But in one respect the two movements differed. While the European was largely a reaction against faith in favour of reason, the Timurid coincided with a new consolidation of the power of faith. The Turks of Central Asia had already lost contact with Chinese materialism; and it was Timur who led them to the acceptance of Islam, not merely as a religion, for that was already accomplished, but as a basis of social institutions. Turks, in any case, are not much given to intellectual speculation. Timur's descendants, in diverting the flow of Persian culture to their own enjoyment, were concerned with the pleasures of this world, not of the next. The purpose of life they left to the saints and theologians, whom they endowed in life and commemorated in death. But the practice of it, inside the Muhammadan framework, they conducted according to their own common sense, without prejudice or sentiment except in favour of a rational intelligence.

The quality of mind thus fostered is preserved in the Memoirs of Babur, which were written in Turki at the beginning of the sixteenth century and have been twice translated into English. They show a man as concerned with day-to-day amenities, conversation, clothes, faces, parties, music, houses, and gardens, as with the loss of a princedom in Oxiana and the acquisition of an empire in India; as interested in the natural world as the political, and so remarking such facts as the distance swum by Indian frogs; and as honest about himself as others, so that in this picture of himself—so real that even in translation one can almost hear him speak—he has left a picture of his whole line. Born in the sixth generation after Timur, it was not until the end of his life that he conquered India and became the first Mogul. Even that was only second best, after he had spent thirty years trying to re-establish himself in Oxiana. But as a man of taste he did what he could to make life possible in so odious a country, and his comments on it show the standards he aspired to. He thought the Indians ugly, their conversation a bore, their fruit tasteless, and their animals ill-bred; 'in handicraft and work there is no form or symmetry, method or quality... for their buildings they study neither elegance nor climate, appearance nor regularity'. He denounced their habits as Macaulay denounced their learning, or as Gibbon denounced the Byzantines, by the light of a classical tradition. And since that tradition, after the Uzbeg conquest of Oxiana and Herat, was extinguished elsewhere, he set about implanting it anew. He and his successors changed the face of India. They gave it a lingua franca, a new school of painting and a new architecture. They revived again that theory of Indian unity which was to become the basis of British rule. Their last emperor died in exile at Rangoon in 1862, to make way for Queen Victoria. And the posterity of Timur survives to this day, in poverty and pride, among the labyrinths of Delhi.

To return to my hotel in the coppersmiths' bazaar, where Babur, in Mrs Beveridge's translation, occupies the table and I am in my fleabag on the floor. Herat lies midway between the two halves of Timur's empire, Persia and Oxiana; and of the two roads that join them, it commands the easier, the one that I shall take; for the other, via Merv, is desert and waterless. Geographically, therefore, it was more suited to be capital than Samarcand; and on Timur's death, in 1405, Shah Rukh made it so. Politically, culturally, and commercially it became the metropolis of middle Asia. Embassies came to it from Cairo, Constantinople, and Pekin; Bretschneider in *Mediaeval Researches from Eastern Asiatic Sources* gives the Chinese descriptions of it. After the twenty years' confusion that followed Shah Rukh's death in 1447, it was taken by Hussein Baikara, a descendant of Timur's son Omar Sheikh. And he gave it peace for another forty years. This was the summer of the Renascence, when Mirkhond and Khondemir were writing their histories, Jami was singing, Bihzad painting, and Ali Shir Nevai was the champion of literary Turki. It was the Herat of this epoch, when the Uzbegs were on the march and Samarcand had already fallen, that Babur saw as a young man. 'The whole habitable world,' he recalls afterwards, 'had not such a town as Herat had become under Sultan Hussein Mirza... Khorasan, and Herat above all, was filled with learned and matchless men. Whatever work a man took up, he aimed and aspired to bring it to perfection.'

Babur was here for three weeks in the autumn of 1506. He may have had the same sort of weather: crisp, sunny days growing shorter and colder. Every day he rode out sight seeing. This morning I followed him and looked at the buildings he looked at. There is not much left. Seven minarets and a broken mausoleum are all my portrait of the age. But their history supplies the rest, and for this I must turn to later writers, soldiers and archaeologists. Two in particular have guided my curiosity here.

There was a long interval before they came; for the light of the Timurid Renascence went out in 1507, when Herat fell to the Uzbegs. Babur, seeing that it would, had removed himself, and vents his annoyance by recording how Shaibani, their leader, was so puffed up of his own culture that he presumed to correct Bihzad's drawing. Three years later it was taken by Shah Ismail and joined to his new Persia. The shadows deepen. A last flicker of the old splendour greets the arrival of Humayun, Babur's son, on his way from India to visit Shah Tahmasp at Isfahan in 1544. Three hundred years later, the curtain lifts on the fragments of Nadir Shah's empire and the military travellers of the nineteenth century.

Several British officers visited Herat in the early part of that century. One of them, Eldred Pottinger, organized the town's defences against a Persian army in 1838 and has become the hero of a novel by Maud Diver; not a bad one either, if you like the Flora Annie Steel school of fiction. Another was Burnes, later assassinated in Kabul, whose Indian secretary, Mohun Lal, published a notice of the monuments in the *Journal of the Bengal Asiatic Society* for 1834. There was also Ferrier, a French soldier of fortune, who in 1845 made two attempts to reach Kabul in disguise and was eventually turned back. He too sits on my table, though the weight of the book has hardly been worth the confusion. Then, in the middle of the century came two scholars, the Hungarian Vambéry and the Russian Khanikov. The authenticity of Vambéry's journey to Bokhara has often been doubted; certainly his description of Herat contains nothing he could not have gleaned from such officers as Conolly and Abbott. Khanikov is almost equally disappointing. Though he was in Herat a whole winter, his account in the *Journal Asiatique* of 1860 contains only a few inscriptions and a plan.

In 1885 the military come to the rescue after all. Russian troops were massing on the north-west frontier of Afghanistan, and the Government of India could not stop them because neither it nor the Afghans knew where the frontier was. A joint Commission was arranged between the two powers to settle it, whose historians, on the English side, were two brothers, A. C. and C. E. Yate. Travelling through what was then almost unknown country, they reported on everything with soldierly precision, and the latter devotes a chapter to the antiquities of Herat as if they were a new field gun—though he was by no means insensible to their beauty. He is the first of my two main guides, and I have transferred him from the table to my lap.

The second is also a soldier, if the word can be applied to a man who tries to make a war single-handed. In the autumn of 1914 a small body of Germans assembled in Constantinople on their way to make trouble for the British in Asia. Some stayed in Persia, among whom was Christopher's hero Wassmuss. Some went on to Afghanistan, and how well the latter succeeded was proved by Amanullah's attack on India in 1919, a year too late. Among these was Herr Oskar von Niedermayer.

In 1924 his photographs of the country were published as a picture book. To this Professor Ernst Diez contributed a preface, in which, by collating Niedermayer's photographs with historical and travellers' references, he identifies and dates most of the buildings here. Diez is an old acquaintance; I started out from Teheran with his *Churasanische Baudenkmäler*, a gigantic quarto whose weight probably broke the Morris's axle. Niedermayer I did not know. By good luck I found his book in the Consulate at Meshed, when I called to leave the other Diez behind, lest it should expose Noel's Rolls to a like fate.

Enough of this for the moment. The local doctor has called.

A friendly Punjabi, in the Afghan medical service. He came for news and to practise his English. I told him of my interview with the Governor, remarking that it was pleasant to escape from Persian suspicions into this freer atmosphere.

'You make large mistake, sir, when you think there are no suspicions here. It is all suspicions. I tell you, sir, Persia cannot compare with Afghanistan in this respect. At the present time, twenty foreigners reside in this town, Indians and Russians. About one hundred and twenty agents are employed to watch them. You suppose they do not watch you? Downstairs they watch you now. I see them. They see me. They watch me all the time. They will report immediately that I have ascended to your room. Also the Russians watch you, I expect. Undoubtedly they are curious for your movements here. They are in everything here. I tell you for certain they control the post office. In the beginning of this year I wrote a letter to a relative in England, in which by chance I referred to the Russian railway at Kushk and the distance from here. Yes, it is only eighty miles away. The next time I visited the Russian Consulate, professionally of course, they said to me straight out: "Why do you give away this kind of informations? You have no business." They were not pretending to hide that they had read my letter. So I have not written any letters since then at all.

'It is bad time to be here, sir, in Afghanistan. There will be trouble now King Nadir Shah is murdered. In one month there will be trouble. Or perhaps in the spring, when the tribes can move better in the mountains.

But I think in one month. Do what you want here, sir, quickly. See what you want. Then clear out, double time. I go on leave now. When I can arrange lorry, I and my family go. We go to Kandahar, and then to my home in Lahore. This is a bad country, sir. I hope I will not return ever.'

Herat, 23 November

Keeping my two guides in my head, I walked up the northern of the four New Town roads in the direction of a gigantic mound, about 600 yards long, which appears to be artificial and must resemble, from all accounts, the mounds in the neighbourhood of Balkh. Hence one can climb up on to another wall, an outwork of the town's defences, and survey the lie of the Musalla. This is the popular name for the whole of the seven minarets and the mausoleum. But actually they were part of separate buildings built at different times, some in the reign of Shah Rukh, one in that of Hussein Baikara.

*

All the minarets are between 100 and 130 feet high. They lean at various angles; their tops are broken, their bases twisted and eaten away. The furthest distance between them, stretching from west-south-west to east-northeast is about a quarter of a mile. The two on the west are fatter than the others, but like the four on the east have one balcony each. The middle one, which stands by itself, has two balconies. The mausoleum lies between the two on the west, but to the north of them. It is only half their height, but from a distance seems less.

This array of blue towers rising haphazard from a patchwork of brown fields and yellow orchards has a most unnatural look. The monarchs of Islam in early days had a habit of putting up isolated minarets, singly or in pairs: witness the Kutb at Delhi and the base of its fellow. But this did not extend till the fifteenth century, and never to such a number as seven. However, it can be seen from the insides of these minarets, where the tilework stops short some forty feet from the ground, that they were originally joined by walls or arches and must have formed part of a series of mosques or colleges. What has happened to these buildings? Things on this scale may fall down, but they leave some ruin. They don't vanish of their own accord without trace or clue, as these have done.

It is a miserable story. Even Yate, who saw it happen, betrays an unsoldierly sigh. Ferrier thought these buildings, ruined as they then were, the finest in Asia. The other travellers concur in their extraordinary beauty, the radiance of their mosaic and the magnificence of their gilt inscriptions. Conolly, if I remember right, speaks of thirty minarets. In fact, allowing for the difference between English prose and Persian, his description is not unlike Khondemir's of the buildings in their prime.

In the seventies and eighties Herat was incessantly on English lips. It even crops up in Queen Victoria's letters. If the Russians took it, as they were expected to do, the low-lying Kandahar road would be theirs for a railway to the Indian border. In 1885 the Panjdeh incident occurred. Though St Petersburg had already agreed to the joint Boundary Commission, Russian troops attacked the Afghans south-east of Mery and drove them back. An advance on Herat was expected any day, and the Emir Abdurrahman sent orders that the town was to be placed in a state of defence. The Russians would approach from the north. All buildings, therefore, that might give them cover on this side of the town must be demolished. For years officers of the Indian Army had been advising on such measures. I suspect this particular order was on British inspiration; though proof must wait till the archives of Delhi and the War Office give up their dead. In any case the most glorious productions of Mohammedan architecture in the fifteenth century, having survived the barbarism of four centuries, were now razed to the ground under the eyes, and with the approval, of the English Commissioners. Nine minarets and the mausoleum escaped.

Even this epitaph of an epitaph is insecure. Two minarets have already disappeared since Niedermayer was here. They fell during an earthquake in 1931, which also destroyed a second domed mausoleum photographed by him. I saw the site of it yesterday, near the fork of the roads to Kushk and the Persian frontier: a mound of rubble. Unless repairs are done and foundations strengthened, the other monuments will soon be rubble too.

However, there is enough left, and enough information, to show how the buildings stood up to 1885.

The minarets that fell down the year before last were a pair to the two fat ones on the west. Together, the four marked the corners of a mosque. This was the real Musalla. According to an inscription on one of the minarets, which Niedermayer photographed and which must have perished in the earthquake, it was built, at her private expense, by Gohar Shad Begum, the wife of Shah Rukh, son of Timur, between the years 1417 and 1437. The architect, in all probability, was Kavamad-Din of Shiraz, who served Shah Rukh in that capacity during the greater part of his reign, and is mentioned by the historian Daulat Shah as one of the four great lights of his court.

Diez, who knows the subject as well as anyone, and is not the slave of his journey's emotions like me, says these minarets are adorned with such 'fabulous richness and subtle taste' ('märchenhafter Pracht and subtilem Geschmack') that no others in Islam can equal them. He speaks from photographs only. But no photograph, nor any description, can convey their colour of grape-blue with an azure bloom, or the intricate convolutions that make it so deep and luminous. On the bases, whose eight sides are supported by white marble panels carved with a baroque Kufic, yellow, white, olive green and rusty red mingled with the two blues in a maze of flowers, arabesques and texts as fine as the pattern on a teacup. The shafts above are covered with small diamond-shaped lozenges filled with flowers, but still mainly grape-blue. Each of these is bordered with white faience in relief, so that the upper part of each minaret seems to be wrapped in a glittering net.

In point of decoration minarets are generally the least elaborate parts of a building. If the mosaic on the rest of the Musalla surpassed or even equalled what survives today, there was never such a mosque before or since.

Yet I don't know. Gohar Shad built another mosque, inside the shrine at Meshed. This mosque is still intact. I must see it somehow if I come back this way.

Looked at in detail, the decoration of the mausoleum is inferior to that of the two minarets. The drum of the dome is encircled with tall panels filled with hexagons of lilac mosaic combined with triangles of raised stucco. The dome itself is turquoise, and the ribs, like those of Timur's mausoleum at Samarcand, are scattered with black and white diamonds. Each rib is three-quarters in the round and as fat as a 64-foot organ-pipe. The walls below are bare, but for a few glazed bricks and a peculiar three-windowed bay that reminds one of a villa in Clapham. But the quality of these separate elements, if sometimes coarse, is transcended by the goodness of their proportions and the solidity of the whole idea. Few architectural devices can equal a ribbed dome for blind, monumental ostentation.

This too seems to have been the work of Gohar Shad. Babur speaks of her three buildings: her mosque, which is the Musalla; her Madrassa or college; and her mausoleum. And Khondemir states several times that the mausoleum was inside the college. She was certainly buried in the mausoleum; Yate noted the inscription on her tombstone. He also noted those on five others, all of Timurid princes. Twenty-five years earlier Khanikov had noted nine altogether. Now there are only three, of a matt black stone, shaped like oblong boxes and carved with flower designs. One is smaller than the others.

Next, on the east of the mausoleum, stands the solitary minaret with two balconies. The origin of this baffles me. Its ornament of blue lozenges, jewelled with flowers but separated by plain brickwork, is not to be compared with that of the Musalla minarets. Perhaps it was part of Gohar Shad's college. A college would naturally be more sober than a mosque. Babur speaks as if college, mosque, and mausoleum were all close together.

I feel some curiosity about Gohar Shad, not on account of her piety in endowing religious foundations, but as a woman of artistic instinct. Either she had that instinct, or she knew how to employ people who had it. This shows character. And besides this, she was rich. Taste, character, and riches mean power, and powerful women, apart from charmers, are not common in Mohammedan history.

Four minarets remain, near the bridge over a winding canal. They too are girt with a white network; though their blue is brighter than that of the Musalla minarets, so that from close at hand it seems as if one saw the sky through a net of shining hair and as if it had been planted, suddenly, with flowers. These mark the corners of the College of Hussein Baikara, who ruled Herat from 1469 to 1506. His grandfather's tombstone, of the same type as those in the mausoleum but known as the Stone of the Seven Pens from its more profuse carving, lies close by and is still revered as a popular shrine.

The lyrical and less stately beauty of these minarets reflects the reign that produced it. Unlike Gohar Shad, Hussein Baikara is more than a name. His body at least is familiar. Bihzad drew it. Babur described it, and his amusements as well. He had slant eyes, a white beard, and a slender waist. He dressed in red and green. Ordinarily he wore a small lambskin cap. But on feast-days he would 'sometimes set up a threefold turban, wound broad and badly, and stick a heron's plume in it and so go to prayers'. This was the least he could do; for towards the end of his life he was so crippled with rheumatism that he could not perform the prayers properly. Like small people, he enjoyed flying pigeons, and matching fighting cocks and fighting rams. He was also a poet, but published his verses anonymously. To meet he was cheerful, and pleasant, but immoderate in temper and loud-spoken. In love, orthodox and unorthodox, he was insatiable. He had innumerable concubines and children who destroyed the peace of the state and his old age. As a result 'what happened with his sons, the soldiers and the town was that everyone pursued vice and pleasure to excess'.

Babur was not a puritan. But the parties in Herat obliged him to get drunk. And in explaining how this happened, for the first time in his life, he reveals the effect of such an atmosphere on a young man's equilibrium. Nevertheless, looking back to Herat when he himself had become great, he still writes with deference, as one who has seen a great age, and having learned how to live, has seen it vanish—like Talleyrand. The humanism of that age was the model of his life. His achievement in history was to replant it, and leave descendants to cherish it, amid the drab heats and uncouth multitudes of Hindustan.

The Mudir-i-Kharija tells me a lorry is leaving for Andkhoi in four days' time. This will mean finding another from there to Mazar-i-Sherif. He adds that the road from Turkestan to Kabul is excellent, and that the post-lorries are still running.

The Imperial Bank of Persia in Meshed gave me rupee drafts on its branch in Bombay to use in Afghanistan. This morning I went to change one with the Shirkat Asharmi, the newly established State Trading Company. No one in the office could read the draft or even its figures. But they took my word for its being worth 100 rupees, and after discovering, apparently by telepathy, the current rate of exchange in Kandahar, counted out 672 silver coins each the size of a shilling. These I took away in two sacks, plodding through the bazaar crowds like a millionaire in a cartoon.

*

Teheran, 17 January

I called on Shir Ahmad, the Afghan ambassador yesterday, to tell him about my journey. Wrapped in a dressing-gown of iridescent velvet, stroking his egg-cosy beard, he looked more tigerish than ever.

RB: If Your Excellency gives me permission, I shall go back to Afghanistan in the spring.

Shir Ahmad: You will go back? (Roaring) OF COURSE you will go back.

RB: And Sykes hopes to accompany me.

Shir Ahmad: Hope? He need not hope. (Roaring) OF COURSE he will accompany you. I will give him visa.

RB: I liked the Afghans because they speak loud and speak the truth. They are not full of intrigues.

Shir Ahmad (leering): Ha, ha, you are wrong. They have many intrigues, many, many. You are not clever, you have not seen them.

RB (crestfallen): At all events, Your Excellency, your people were hospitable to me. If I write anything about Afghanistan, I shall show it to you first.

Shir Ahmad: WHY?

RB: In case it should offend you.

Shir Ahmad: There is no need, no need, I will not see it. I do not wish. If you write kindly, we are pleased that a friend praise us. If you write not-kindly, we are pleased that friend give advice. You shall write what you think, you are honest man.

RB: Your Excellency is too good.

Shir Ahmad: I am good, ha, ha. All Afghans good peoples. They have good lives, no wines, no other men's wives. They believe God and religion. All Afghans good peoples, all fiddles.

RB: Fiddles?

Shir Ahmad: Fiddles, no? Is it French? Faithfuls, yes?

RB: Very different from the Persians.

Shir Ahmad: Not different. Not different. Persians also fiddles.

A SHORT WALK IN THE HINDU KUSH

Eric Newby

> Much travel writing ages very badly. Some is timeless. First published in 1958, this classic account of a hapless mountaineering expedition in Afghanistan by **Eric Newby** (1919–2006) is still very, very funny. In the following decades Newby became one of Britain's best-loved travel writers, his reputation cemented by this breakthrough book. His unlikely travels up the Panjshir Valley with the strait-laced British diplomat Hugh Carless take the reader back to an age of almost prelapsarian innocence in Afghanistan. Two decades later the valley would become the heart of the Afghan resistance to the Soviets, under the leadership of the guerrilla leader Ahmad Shah Massoud.

We were accompanied up the Chamir Valley by a Tajik to whom some strange mutation had given pink eyes and a blond moustache. With this Albino, the *Thanador* (literally the Keeper of Nothingness) of the Nawak Pass, the keeper of the Pass retained at a salary of 500 Afghanis a year to oversee it, we never got on good terms. He came at his own request, 'to protect us from brigands' as he put it. How he was to do this unarmed without recourse to bribery was not clear.

His name was Abdullah, *The Slave of God* (it was unseemly, as he backfired like an early motor-car all the way up the valley). Shir Muhammad and Badar Khan ragged him unmercifully at the frequent halts he insisted on making at the nomad encampments to eat *mast*, for he was a greedy man.

'Look at his face.'

'Look at his hair.'

'Look at his eyebrows.' He had no eyebrows.
'Like a bastard German.'
'O, Abdullah, who was your father?'
And so on.

Abdul Ghiyas took little part in these pleasantries. He was in his element. Down by the river the Pathan women, beautiful savage-looking creatures, were washing clothes. Now as Hugh had predicted he vanished into the tents on one pretext or another, ostensibly to gather information, having first warned the laundresses to veil themselves.

The Chamar was a wide glen, more colourful than the Darra Samir, with grass of many different shades of green and full of tall hollyhocks in flower. The nomad tents were everywhere and there were sheep high on the mountains. At seven we rested at a small hamlet of bothies, Dal Liazi. Behind us, above Parian, we could see the way to the Nawak Pass with Orsaqao, the big brown mountain which it crossed, with a serpent of snow wriggling across it.

It was an interrupted journey. At the instigation of Abdullah we had stopped at seven, at eight we stopped again and this time everyone disappeared into the tents for half an hour, leaving Hugh and myself outside with the horses, fuming and sizzling in the heat. But when he wanted to stop at nine, even Abdul Ghiyas protested.

'O thou German,' said the drivers.
'My mother was a Kafir.'
'Ha!'

Like small boys at prep school, they mocked him. From now on he sulked.

As we climbed, the country became more and more wild, the tents of the Chanzai Pathans, in which the drivers had been assuaging themselves, less frequent. From the rocks on either side marmots whistled at us officiously like ginger-headed referees. Here the horses stopped continuously to eat wormwood, *artemisia absinthium*, a root for which they had a morbid craving.

After five hours on the road we came to the mouth of a great cloud-filled glen stretching to the west.

'East glacier,' said Hugh, 'we're nearly there. Pity about the cloud.'

As we stood there peering, it began to lift. Soon we could see most of the north face of the mountain as far as the rock wall, and the summit, a snow-covered cone with what seemed a possible route along the ridge to it. Our spirits rose. 'If we can only get to the ridge we can make it,' we said.

With the cloud breaking up and lifting fast, the whole mountain seemed on fire; the cloud swirled like smoke about the lower slopes and drove over the ridge clinging to the pinnacles. From out of the glen came a chill wind and the rumble of falling rock. It was like a battlefield stripped of corpses by Valkyries. In spite of the heat of the valley we shivered.

'If the south face is no good we can always come back and try here,' said Hugh. As always he seemed unconscious of the effect he created by such a remark.

Ahead of us in the main valley a waterfall tumbled down over a landslide of rocks; climbing up beside it we rounded the easternmost bastion of the mountain and entered the upper valley of the Chamar.

We felt like dwarfs. On our right the whole southern aspect of Mir Samir revealed itself: the east ridge like a high garden wall topped with broken glass; the snow-covered summit; the glaciers receding far up under the base of the mountain in the summer heat; and below them the *moraines*, wildernesses of rock pouring down to the first pasture, with the river running through it, a wide shallow stream fed by innumerable rivulets. To the east the mountains rose straight up to a level 17,000 feet, then, rising and falling like a great dipper, encircled by the head of the valley, forming the final wall of the south-west glacier where we had made our unsuccessful effort among the ice toadstools on the other side two days before.

'On the other side of that,' said Hugh, pointing to the sheer wall with patches of snow on it to the east, 'is Nuristan.' It was a lonely place; the last nomad tents were far down the valley in the meadow below the waterfall. Here there was only one solitary *aylaq*, a wall of stones built against an overhanging rock and roofed over with turf, the property of the headman of Shahr i Boland, a Tajik village we had passed in Parian on the way to the Chamar. The shepherd was the headman's son. As we came, more dead than alive with our tongues lolling, to the camping place on a stretch of turf hemmed in by square boulders, he appeared with a bowl of *mast*, wearing long robes and a skull cap, the image of Alec Guinness disguised as a Cardinal.

It was midday. The light was blinding. To escape it we crawled into clefts in the rocks and lay there in shadow, each at a different level, in our own little boxes, like a chest of drawers.

As soon as he had eaten, the *Thanador* of the Nawak Pass went off without a word to anyone.

'What's wrong with him?'

'He's in a huff because they kept calling him a German.'

'Well, it is rather insulting. I wouldn't like it myself.'

'But he was such a bore.'

All through the afternoon we rested, moving from rock to rock to escape the sun as it spied us out. Hugh read *The Hound of the Baskervilles*; I studied a grammar of the Kafir language. Apart from the pamphlets on mountaineering, this was the only serious book the expedition possessed. (Put to other uses our library was disappearing at an alarming rate.) Both of us had already read all John Buchan, who in the circumstances in which we found ourselves had been found wanting, the mock-modesty of his heroes becoming only too apparent, the temptation to transport them in the imagination to the Hindu Kush too great to resist. Remarks something like 'Though I say it who shouldn't, I'm a pretty good mountaineer, but this was the hardest graft I ever remember,' cut very little ice with people in our position about to embark on a similar venture with no qualifications at all.

Notes on the Bashgali (Kafir) Language, by Colonel J. Davidson of the Indian Staff Corps, Calcutta, 1901, had been assembled by the author after a two-year sojourn in Chitral with the assistance of two Kafirs of the Bashgali tribe and consisted of a grammar of the language and a collection of sentences. I had not shown this book to Hugh. He had been pretty scathing about my attempts to learn Persian, no easy matter in my thirty-sixth year, confronted by Tajiks who at any rate had their own ideas on how it should be spoken.

I had schemed to memorize a number of expressions in the Kafir language and surprise Hugh when we met up with the people, but, in the midst of all our other preoccupations, the book had been lost in one of the innumerable sacks; now with Nuristan just over the mountain, it was discovered in the bottom of the rice sack, where it had been ever since I had visited the market in Kabul.

Reading the 1,744 sentences with their English equivalents, I began to form a disturbing impression of the waking life of the Bashgali Kafirs.

'*Shtal latta wos ba padre u prett tu nashtonti mrlosh*. Do you know what that is?'

It was too late to surprise Hugh with a sudden knowledge of the language. 'What?'

'In Bashgali it's "If you have had diarrhoea many days you will surely die."'

'That's not much use,' he said. He wanted to get on with Conan Doyle.

'What about this then? *Bilugh ao na pi bilosh*. It means, "Don't drink much water; otherwise you won't be able to travel."'

'I want to get on with my book.'

Wishing that Hyde-Clark had been there to share my felicity I continued to mouth phrases aloud until Hugh moved away to another rock, unable to concentrate. Some of the opening gambits the Bashgalis allowed themselves in the conversation game were quite shattering. *Ini ash ptul p'mich e manchi mrisht waria'm*. 'I saw a corpse in a field this morning', and *Tu chi se biss gur biti?* 'How long have you had a goitre?', or even *Ia juk noi bazisna prelom*. 'My girl is a bride.'

Even the most casual remarks let drop by this remarkable people had the impact of a sledgehammer. *Tu tott baglo piltia*. 'Thy father fell into the river.' *I non angur ai; tu ta duts angur ai*. 'I have nine fingers; you have ten.' *Or manchi aiyo; buri aish kutt*. 'A dwarf has come to ask for food.' And *Ia chitt bitto tu jarlom*, 'I have an intention to kill you', to which the reply came pat, *Tu bilugh le biwida manchi assish*, 'You are a very kind-hearted man.'

Their country seemed a place where the elements had an almost supernatural fury: *Dum allangiti atsiti i sundi basna bra*. 'A gust of wind came and took away all my clothes', and where nature was implacable and cruel: *Zhi mare badist ta wo ayo kakkok damiti gwa.* 'A lammergeier came down from the sky and took off my cock.' Perhaps it was such misfortunes that had made the inhabitants so petulant: *Tu biluk wari walal manchi assish.* 'You are a very jabbering man.' *Tu kai duga ia ushpe pa vich: tu ia oren vichiba o tu jarlam.* 'Why are you pushing me? If you push me I will do for you.'

A race difficult to ingratiate oneself with by small talk: *To'st kazhir krui p'pti ta chuk zhi prots asht?* 'How many black spots are there on your white dog's back?' was the friendly inquiry to which came the chilling reply: *Ia krui brobar adr rang azza: shtring na ass.* 'He is a yellow dog all over, and not spotted.'

Perhaps the best part was the appendix which referred to other books dealing with the Kafir languages. One passage extracted from a book by a Russian savant, a M. Terentief, gave a translation of what he said was the Lord's Prayer in the language of the Bolors or Siah-Posh Kafirs:

Babo vetu osezulvini. Malipatve egobunkvele
egamalako Ubukumkani bako mabuphike. Intando
yako mayenzibe. Emkhlya beni, nyengokuba isenziva egulvini. Sipe
namglya nye ukutiye kvetu kvemikhla igemikhla. Usikcolele izono
zetu,
nyengokuba nati siksolela abo basonaio tina. Unga
singekisi ekulingveli zusisindise enkokhlakalveni,
ngokuba bubobako ubukumkhani namandkhla
nobungkvalisa, kude kude igunapakade. Amene.

'It does not agree with the Waigal or Bashgal dialect as recorded in any book which I have seen,' the Colonel wrote rather plaintively. 'There are no diacritical marks.' But later in a supplementary appendix he was able to add a dry footnote to the effect that since writing the above a copy of the translation had been submitted by Dr Grierson, the distinguished editor of the Linguistic Survey of India, to Professor Khun of Munich who pronounced that it was an incorrect copy of the version of the Lord's Prayer in the language of the Amazulla Kaffirs of South Africa.

LAND OF THE HIGH FLAGS
A TRAVEL MEMOIR OF AFGHANISTAN

Rosanne Klass

Born in Iowa, **Rosanne Klass** (1929–2015) was one of the first Western women to teach in Afghanistan in the 1950s, an experience which led to the publication in 1964 of *Land of the High Flags*. Her first book about the country was a moving and sensitively written account of her experiences living, working and travelling in Afghanistan and represented a first step towards becoming a respected authority on its politics and culture. In the 1980s, alarmed by the Soviet invasion of Afghanistan, she joined Freedom House, the American democracy and human rights organisation, and became the director of its Afghanistan Information Center. There she wrote extensively about the war, supported the *mujahideen* resistance to the Soviets, and edited and co-authored *Afghanistan: The Great Game Revisited* (1987), an important reference on the Soviet occupation. Here she writes about the preternaturally beautiful Bamian Valley, northwest of Kabul, once a world-illuminating centre of Buddhism. Tragically, the colossal Buddhas of Bamian which she eulogises in this passage no longer proclaim 'the glory of the faith', as they had for almost 1,500 years, because the Taliban destroyed them in 2001.

At the stroke of noon the midday gun boomed out over the city and men everywhere made their way to the mosques or knelt in quiet corners to pray, oblivious of passers-by. On the streets the mullahs appeared in their severely handsome garb of black and white, the color of script or of print, of The Word itself made plain. In the crowded bazaars when one saw a Sikh or Hindu merchant, he was isolated by his bright turban in a land where man, beast and earth share the same somber hues—ochre, gray, umber—the colors of clothing, of walls, of turbans and camels and mountainsides. Wherever one looked, whenever one looked, there was a constant awareness, constantly renewed, that this was a land of faith and that the faith was Islam. It seemed an inevitable conjunction: the austere land and the austere faith. The hand of God was severe, but He was close: He was raised upon no altar, for His hand lay on every man's shoulder.

Islam has ruled here for almost nine hundred years. It was hard to realize that the Buddha had held this land in his uplifted palm for nearly as long, or longer.

Much of Afghanistan's history before the coming of Islam is like a landscape wrapped in mist, in which one can discern scattered rocks of knowledge solid enough to stand on, linked by unsteady bridges of theory and speculation. No one knows just how much history lies buried in Afghan soil: the archaeologists dig, and with each spadeful of earth the story as it has been known is transformed. In 1952, for example, rumors got around in Kabul that a French expedition had made an important find. The archaeologists themselves, cornered over a drink at the French Club, smiled deprecatingly and noted that every time you dug up an old pot there was always someone who was sure that it was filled with gold. As it turned out, they had indeed struck a veritable Klondike at Surkh Kotal: the ruins of the Kushan court of the first or second century. They were merely hugging their secret to themselves until they could get it safely into print in the academic journals, where scholars fire deadly footnotes at one another over the bodies of wounded and dying theories. There the implications of that discovery are still being argued today, and they will shape the histories written from now on.

So discovery follows discovery. This land has been more than the funnel through which the world poured into India and the valve through which India released its own creations, although it has certainly been these things. But Afghanistan has in itself repeatedly been a creative center from earliest times until relatively recently—Zoroaster taught here, and Avicenna—and it has besides transformed the cultures it has received, sending its own influence out along the historic routes of trade and civilization in every direction. Lapis lazuli from the Afghan hills was counted among the treasures of the Pharaohs before the time of Moses, and ideas travel in the same pack with precious stones.

There is much more to know than the fragments available so far, but a great many of the secrets of history in this land have yet to be wrenched from the silent grasp of time. Yet not everything is thus buried. Bamian is not buried.

One of the visible rocks in the historic landscape of Afghanistan is Alexander's passage. In 330 B.C. he swept across the land like a wind and soon, like the wind, was gone, leaving little of visible permanence behind him. But in his wake, what is today one country was left in two, with the great central mountain ranges dividing them. In northern Afghanistan, Macedonian officers had remained to establish a satrapy in Bactria; but with Alexander dead, the Bactrian kingdom centered around the Oxus plains gradually slipped its Greek moorings and established ties with a new power which had risen to the south of it, the great empire of Gandhara.

Gandhara stretched from the southern slopes of the Hindu Kush across the plains of the Ganges to the Bay of Bengal, binding together all of northern India; and in India the rising tide of Buddhism was already threatening to overwhelm the ancient Hindu faith. Ashoka, the greatest emperor of Gandhara, was converted, and by 250 B.C. he had proclaimed Buddhism as the faith of the empire. For the next eight hundred years it held sway over the lands of the Hindu Kush both north and south. Indeed, as Hinduism in India recovered its strength and drove Buddhism out of the land of its birth, Afghanistan, at the core of Gandhara, became the great Buddhist heartland.

Under Ashoka and his successors and then under the converted Kushan kings who ruled the empire in the early centuries of our own era, missionaries went forth from Gandhara to spread the teachings of the Buddha across Central Asia into China, Korea, Japan. Pilgrims poured in to visit the great shrines and schools and monasteries here.

The landscape—Afghanistan was green then, lavishly blanketed with forests—was dotted with stupas, brilliantly painted and rich with sculpture. There are parts of the country where even today a farmer can hardly plow his fields without turning up some bit of statuary from that vanished past.

If Alexander's actual mark on the land was debatable, he had certainly left a memory and an influence. He had reminded the worlds of east and west of the channels between them, and those channels were kept open and enlarged: the Kushans are said to have had intimate ties with imperial Rome. Thus in Gandhara the two worlds met at the very moment when Buddhism was searching for artistic forms into which it could pour its symbolic content; and the techniques of Greco-Roman art stood ready to hand. Together, mingling the serenity of the Buddha with the grace of Apollo, they created a new art of exquisite beauty.

In the heart of this heartland of a vigorous faith full of creative vitality, the valley of Bamian lay high among the mountains, a graceful pause between the exhausting heights of the Hindu Kush and the Koh-i-Baba ranges; and Bamian became perhaps the greatest monastic and artistic center of all. Some even think that it was here that Buddhism emerged in its dominant sophisticated form.

It stood on the ancient Silk Route which led to Balkh, where the northern and southern branches of that great artery met. As the caravans wound their way through the mountains, they paused at Bamian to gather strength between the rigors of the passes on either side. Men of every land mingled there before they moved on across Sinkiang to the Celestial Kingdom, which guarded the eastern edge of the world, or to Malabar in the south, or across the deserts of Persia and Syria to Tyre and later Byzantium, gateways to the Roman world of the West. Those were the fringes then, and this was the center. The valley had its citizens devoted to the traveler's mundane needs, and to commerce. The rubies of Badakhshan and the silver of Panjsher must often have changed hands here, with a portion of the profit going, perhaps, to the glorification of the faith—and of the Valley. For while the royal cities of Gandhara were elsewhere, Bamian was great in the faith.

The valley was scarcely twenty miles long and perhaps a mile wide, guarded by royal fortress-cities at either end, and filled with thousands of the devout from every nation. Along the pink sandstone cliffs edging the valley a vast honeycomb of monastic chambers was carved into the mountainside itself. From here saffron-robed monks and pilgrims, merchants and artists came and went in every direction, outward to China, north to the Gobi, down into India, departing, returning, teaching, learning, mixing and mingling all that they carried with them and gathered along the way, as bees make their busy way across wide fields and return to pour their gathered nectar into the common honey of the hive; and then go forth again to cross-pollinate as they pass, to fertilize, to create a new flowering.

Here without a doubt the faith of the Enlightened One stood triumphant. Who could question its permanence when, among the hundreds of cells cut into the valley wall, the monks had carved two colossal standing figures of the Buddha as Lord of the World—one nearly one hundred and seventy-five feet tall, the other a little smaller; covered with gold leaf and brilliantly painted—which must surely proclaim the glory of the faith forever.

In the fifth century one Fa-Hsien came the long road from China, and found ten thousand monks in Bamian. The valley was at the height of its splendor: the monasteries were flourishing, the great Buddhas towered magnificent in their vaulted niches, surrounded with splendid frescos, and the face of the cliff into which they were carved was studded as well with smaller niches holding lesser figures of the Buddhist pantheon, behind which lay the honeycomb of rooms, elaborately plastered and painted and busy with life and thought.

A century later the White Huns smashed their way across the land. They left the monasteries in ruins, the survivors of their butchery broken. When in 632 another pilgrim made the long trip across the Gobi and down through Turkestan, he found Bamian in decay—its people devout, but its monks few and its life feeble. The two great Buddhas still stood: he noted in his journal that the golden surface and precious ornaments dazzled him from afar. But the monasteries and stupas were ruined, overgrown with weeds. The great age of Bamian was over, and with it the great age of Gandhara art.

Buddhism lingered in the land for another five or six hundred years, shattered, struggling for survival among other faiths—renascent Hinduism, Mithraic cults, Zoroastrianism, the first Muslim footholds in Afghanistan, and other sects obscured and long forgotten—until in the tenth and eleventh centuries Islam became dominant and bit by bit the others dwindled away. At last Genghis Khan came to the valley and murdered it, and the story was ended.

One day during a midsummer holiday we set out with Shaban and the Kayeums to visit Bamian and, beyond it, the lakes of Band-i-Amir in the Hazarajat. Shaban had as usual arranged for a car, and had indicated his own readiness for roughing it by adding a pith helmet to his customary brown business suit: thus outfitted, he looked extremely uncomfortable with himself. We drove along the now familiar road through the Koh-i-daman valley, past Istalif to Charikar; but this time we turned west into the gorge of the Ghorband River, which leads to the Shibar Pass and Bamian. The road lay along the bottom of a deep slot carved by the river between sheer cliffs. The stream tumbled away from us and narrowed as we climbed toward its headwaters.

Early in the afternoon we reached the town of Chardeh, whose houses clung to the slopes at the widest point of the valley. Karim, a young teacher, lived in Chardeh; he was at home visiting his family, and he had asked us to stop as we passed through. Parking the car in the midst of the bazaar, we found a loitering boy and sent him off to locate Karim, who came to guide us on foot up through a maze of narrow alleys, just wide enough for a panniered donkey to squeeze between the high mud walls on either side. The door he opened to us was one of many similar battered, unprepossessing wooden gates in the otherwise blank walls. We stepped through a dim passageway and found ourselves on a vine-covered veranda overlooking a garden which fell away in terraces down the mountainside. The upper terraces were bedded with strawberries and flowers; roses scented the air. Below there were orchards, where a few sheep and skittish goats browsed under the trees. Along one side of the garden a brook tumbled in its channel from terrace to terrace, turning tiny water wheels as it went.

Two young boys were already busy spreading cushions and pillows in a corner of the veranda. Karim's brother and uncle were waiting, and by the time we were all introduced and settled among the cushions, children began bringing trays of food: fruit, almonds, and pistachios, roasted sweet corn, and pots of rich sweetened milk, flavored with cardamom and rosewater. Other children appeared with brass ewers and basins; we washed; ewers, basins, and children vanished again. We sat back comfortably, talking and laughing and sipping our hot milk, while the dust and ache of hours on the road slipped away from us like an unwanted skin shed by a happy snake. Meanwhile, a constant stream of children sidled in and out, apparently drawn from every corner of the neighborhood, looking for excuses to take a peek at the company. They refilled our cups or suggested that we needed more fruit; they added cushions, removed cushions, and rearranged cushions; they looked hopefully for flies to be shooed away; and when they ran out of ideas they just gathered shyly inside the hallway peering out, content as long as no one seemed to notice them but bursting into giggles and running away if any of the guests was so inconsiderate as to smile at them directly.

We stayed too long and were urged to stay longer, but by late afternoon we knew we must go or give up hope of reaching Bamian that night. So out into the dusty world we went again, and drove on through the narrow throat of the gorge.

Along its red sandstone walls, fantastical stripings of dull crimson, orange, purple, ochre, and russet dipped and writhed across the cliffs, telling in the florid palette of their stratification a geological story far older than the ancient country and its ancient peoples. The red light of sunset struck the rocks aglow with a strange wild burst of bloody color. Then the canyon ended as abruptly as a tunnel, and in the evening dusk we wound our way over the Shibar Pass and on toward Bamian.

A few miles before we reached the mouth of the valley we emerged from another defile and stopped to rest at the foot of a mountain. An overgrown footpath wound upward: in the fading light we could just make out on the cliffs above us the crumbling turrets and desolate walls of Shahr-i-Golgola, the City of Clamor and Lamentation.

When Genghis Khan led his army into Bamian in 1221, the fortress cities refused to yield and fought for their lives. In the midst of battle a luckless arrow struck down and killed the Great Khan's favorite grandson, and in his fury Genghis proclaimed that this valley would be known forever as the Valley of Sorrow, that the city would be known forever as the City of Sorrow. His orders went out: no looting in Bamian, and no taking of prisoners. When the valley fell, everything was to be destroyed and no living thing left to live. And so it was. Every man, woman, and child was put to the sword; every dog, every cat, every sheep, goat, bird; the trees were cut down, the barley slashed to the root. No living thing was left to live where the grandson of Genghis Khan had died. Such was his revenge, more complete even than his destruction of Herat—for at Herat, if a million and more were killed, forty are said to have survived. In Bamian: no one and nothing.

For more than a hundred years his curse lay upon the abandoned valley, and the city was known, as he had proclaimed, as Maobaligh: the Accursed City, the City of Sorrow. When men took up life in the valley again, they built little farming villages among the neat fields. The ramparts of the destroyed cities remain forever empty under the spell of their terrible fate; and it has come to be said that in the night their broken towers echo again with ghostly sounds of murder and the lamentation of the doomed.

Darkness fell before we entered Bamian itself and drew up at the hotel, which was set on top a low hill directly across the valley from the Buddhist ruins. The lobby was filled with an ebullient crowd of German engineers and their families on their way back to Sarobi from a camping expedition at Band-i-Amir. They assured us that we would find Band-i-Amir delightful: it was beautiful, and there was wonderful fishing. You just exploded a few fish bombs and scooped up all the trout you could eat. In fact, they would have stayed longer but the lakes were so full of fish that their bombs had killed thousands, and the stench had driven them away. By the time we got there, they assured us, the smell would undoubtedly be gone. They offered us their left-over fish bombs, which we declined, and then went off to their sleeping bags in the main dining room, where they were thriftily camping en masse.

The manager screened off a corner and set dinner for us. We ate hastily by the light of a kerosene lamp, speeded by our own weariness and the gentle snores and murmurs that emerged from the darkness around us. Then we went directly to our rooms to sleep, planning an early start for the next day.

When I had blown out the lamp and was about to go to bed, I stopped, and went to the window. I found that it looked straight across the valley to the sculptured cliff. The moon was high, and by its pale light I saw for the first time those two great figures, tiny from afar, standing like rods of silver in the dark shadow of their niches. For a long time I stood looking; and, touched with moonlight, they calmly and steadily seemed to return my gaze.

In the morning we stood halfway up the cliff, at the foot of the greater colossus, looking up, up—beyond the gigantic legs, the togalike robe, the shattered arms, to a blind face far overhead: ephemeral Lilliputians in awe before an eternal Gulliver. The gold leaf which once covered the figure had long since disappeared, the colors had weathered away. Of the brilliant frescoes which had decorated the stucco surface of the niche, there were now only faded remnants high up in the arched dome. The statues themselves had been literally defaced: much of the faces, the uplifted hands, and great pieces of the trunk and legs were blasted away over the centuries by zealous Muslim sharpshooters bent on the holy work of idol-breaking: it is singular that so much of what man has created in the name of the glory of God has so often and everywhere been despoiled in the name of the glory of God. On the great face so far above us only the mouth and chin remained, the full lips curved in a serene enigmatic smile.

We had come from the lesser Buddha a mile or more away, past the cliff pocked with empty niches and entrances to the hundreds of chambers within. A few yards from where we stood, a door in the wall led into a half-ruined staircase which wound upward through the cliff to the top of the statue, where a doorway opened out onto the huge head. A schoolboy from a nearby village offered to guide us, and we started up the long, ill-lit climb.

Part way up, a window looked out into the niche: before us were the shoulders of the statue, and on the walls above we could glimpse bits of fresco. Further on, a crevasse gaped across the passage where the weakened face of the cliff had started to split away. The walls had been propped and the passageway strengthened with timbers, but the only way to go on was to leap the crevasse. I must have made some sort of sound, because Joan turned to look at me and said, "You're green. Sit down." I took this advice abruptly; apparently my knees were trembling. Shaban, who had been climbing without any visible enthusiasm, promptly said, "You should stay here. I'll stay to keep you company. Let them go on." But I managed to get across the chasm at last, and we all continued upward. The corridor leveled out, and we found ourselves at the doorway overlooking the head of the statue, more than big enough for half a dozen people to sit on.

On the walls and vaulted ceiling overhead, the faded colors of the old frescoes swirled in fragments of sinuous gesture. The arch itself framed the view before us like a Byzantine panel: below a crescent of blue sky the valley was unrolled like a green silk carpet at the feet of the Buddha. Birds caroled in the poplar groves far below and miles away. It seemed as though we looked out with the eyes of the great stone Buddha itself, and saw a vision of peace.

The road to Band-i-Amir led westward for another fifty miles or so into the central massif of the Hazarajat, across an empty landscape of tawny, barren mountains—rock-strewn, utterly lifeless, weathered and worn into an ocean of stone waves. Only the faint track of the road marked the vast tangle of mountain desert. There was not a spring, not a trickle of water, not a drop of it; not a withered shrub or a clump of tough mountain grass to say that life had ever been sustained here. Only mile after mile of mountain lying defenseless under a merciless sun. The heaving landscape was like the bony structure of the earth itself made visible under a thin, taut shell of rock.

Then suddenly in the heart of a barren valley there was a chain of brilliant blue lakes, sparkling and glittering and dancing in the sunlight like a bracelet of sapphires thrown into a clay bowl: Band-i-Amir.

They were incredible. They could not be real, but they were: intensely blue, lapis blue, cerulean, sapphire, aquamarine, rising one above the other, each spilling into the next with a crystal fan of waterfalls which glistened over the rocks in a multitude of streams. Where the lowest lakes spilled over into the valley, there were faint streaks of dull moss-green for a little distance until the desert blotted up the water. Other than that, nothing: absolute desert wrapped around brilliant jewels of blue: no stream flowing into them, none flowing out. A handful of lakes in the middle of a desert ten or eleven thousand feet high—just simply, fantastically there.

At some places barren brown cliffs fell away straight down to the blue waters, and on down into their bottomless depths; at others, there were low craterlike mineral formations which held the lakes above the valley floor as a setting holds a gem. Around these shallower sides, the edges of the lakes were rimmed with the green of water plants, while farther in and under the surface there was a shimmer of frosty white where minerals had crystallized like white lace coral.

There were a few poor huts along the shore, one of them a crude little mosque, and a few men stood casting for fish: Hazaras, the Mongol people who give the area its name. They are said to be descended from soldiers of Genghis Khan who settled here and they have a well-earned reputation as fighting men, but on their high plateau now they are impoverished farmers, and in the cities they do menial work.

We drew up near the fishermen. Seen close, the lakes seemed even more unbelievable than when they were seen from a distance. The water was transparent as glass. Except for the white mineral formations, there was no shelf at the shoreline: the walls of the lake dropped vertically down, and through the crystal-clear water one could see pale silvery fish gliding past far below. Then the waters darkened into deep and deeper blue, and hid whatever lay in their depths. The water was icy: we had hoped to swim, but when Abdul plunged in among the rushes at the shallows, he had not gone three yards when he turned back and climbed out blue-lipped, numb, and shivering.

There was absolutely no visible source for the waters, or for the fish that swam in them. I suppose they must be fed by springs, very deep, but if the source is known, all I was ever able to learn of it was what the fishermen told me:

Although most Afghans are members of the Sunni sect, which dominates Islam, most Hazaras are Shi'ites, who particularly revere Ali, the Fourth Caliph, over whose presumed tomb the Blue Mosque rises in Mazar-i-Sharif. When Ali visited Afghanistan, oh, hundreds and hundreds of years ago (the fishermen said), he came this way, across the Hazarajat, and through this very valley; and in his great footsteps the lakes miraculously sprang forth as testimony to his holiness.

The fishermen were casting for trout with a long weighted line which they wrapped around one hand, whirling the weighted end above their heads and flinging it out with a quick twisting movement of the wrist. The fishing was not as good as it had been, they said, for the foreigners' bombs had killed so many fish and frightened off the rest. Still, they caught enough to give us some, and shared their barley bread, too. We offered the fruit and eggs we had brought from the hotel, they made a fire, and with the fish and the dry barley cakes, we all had lunch together.

We left Band-i-Amir before nightfall and returned to the green valley, its pink walls, its lonely colossi. In Bamian I thought again of Pompeii, where it is possible to imagine that life might at any moment take up again just as it left off: where one would not be at all surprised to turn a corner and bump into a Roman matron on her way to market. In Pompeii, life seems suspended.

Bamian is dead. Nothing waits in its empty halls. In Bamian, death blew out all the lamps, and they were never lit again; silence descended, and it was never broken. One thinks: from the hand of God, many survived; here, at the hand of man, none.

Yet this valley is serene. It is, I think, the most peaceful place I have ever known. Its tranquillity floods the soul.

At the foot of the sculptured cliffs the houses turn windowless backs to the great statues. The people of the valley know them not, and look elsewhere now. But still the blind Buddhas look out across their valley, towering, faintly golden in the sunlight and pale beneath the moon, silent before the unassuming grace of fields and running brooks as once they were silent before the unspeakable: forever blind, forever seeing; forever silent, forever an echoing voice.

THE LIGHT GARDEN OF THE ANGEL KING

Peter Levi

Peter Levi (1931–2000) was many things. The son of a Jewish merchant who had converted to Catholicism, he was a sometime Jesuit priest, poet, professor, archaeologist, travel writer, translator, biographer, critic, indefatigable collector of people, claret fanatic and impoverished bon vivant. Entranced by Oscar Wilde's writings as a boy, he inherited the Irishman's love of classical Greek language and culture, a passion elegiacally expressed in *The Hill of Kronos*, one of his trio of travel books. A restless free spirit, he cast off his Ignatian straitjacket and exchanged priestly celibacy for a rapturous marriage to Cyril Connolly's widow Deirdre. He was the author of more than sixty books and from 1984 to 1989 was professor of poetry at Oxford. Published in 1972, *The Light Garden of the Angel King* told the sparkling story of an unlikely expedition with Bruce Chatwin to unearth the classical heritage of Afghanistan from Greek conquerors to Buddhist monks. It was, the travel writer Jan Morris reckoned, 'a beautiful book, a poetic evocation and worthy of a place beside *Eothen* and Robert Byron's *Road to Oxiana*'.

Chapter 13

Ay Khanoum* stands on the east back of the Kokcha, just at the point where it flows into the Oxus.† It is the site of a Greek city founded soon after Alexander the Great reduced the easternmost province of the Persian Empire and left it as a Greek province held down by Macedonian garrisons.

It is extremely likely that Ay Khanoum was originally a city called Alexandria on the Oxus, founded in the name of Alexander himself. If that is true, it was probably founded in the twenties of the third century B.C., when Alexander was about twenty-eight years old, and within five or six years of his death. But it now looks almost certain that Ay Khanoum was a Persian city before it was Greek. Some of the stone elements in the great Hellenistic palace of the ruler were older stones re-used, and among the foundations of the palace is an undisputed bell-shaped Persian column-base. The site of the city is defensive. It stands on the only unfordable stretch of the Oxus for miles in both directions, opposite a short range of steep rough hills on the Russian bank, although this is not the ideal spot to guard either the crossing of the Kokcha or the road from east to west along the south bank of the Oxus.

The Greek city is protected by a gigantic mound on the south which once must have been the acropolis, the Kokcha washes it on the west and the Oxus on the north; the lower town is penned in by this mound and the two rivers, on a long, almost triangular, swathe of ground between the acropolis and the Oxus, with the top of the triangle closed by a powerful wall. To put the first question first, what was the military or mercantile importance of this site for the Persians? It must have been

---

* The place name means The Moon Woman. The official reports on the excavations at Ay Khanoum are to be found in *Comptes Rendus de l'Academie des Inscriptions*, annually from 1965.

† The local name of the Oxus is the *Amu Darya*. Along most of its length the Oxus is the border that divides Russia from Afghanistan. This is not at all a heavily defended frontier, but both sides are very sensitive about allowing foreigners anywhere near it, hence my difficulty in reaching Ay Khanoum.

close to the furthest eastern extent of Persian penetration, it was in shelter from the nomads north of the Oxus, the 'princes of felts and furs' as the Chinese called them, the townless forest-living and cave-living herdsmen of Ptolemy, whose pressure from the north-east on the Persian Empire was already known to Herodotos. It was not on any trade route the Persians are likely to have used to India, but it faced the way down from the Kokcha, the source of lapis lazuli and balas rubies, the entrance to the Wakan corridor and the pass that led to China, and it was the effective presence of Persia in the grazing-grounds of the upper Oxus. It is hard to believe it was not a 'royal fortress' to control the frontier like the Persian fort on the Indus which separated the Opiai from the Indoi and was refounded as Opian Alexandria. What Alexander occupied was not virgin territory or an untamed barbarous world, but the eastern Persian Empire, including of course its frontier fortresses.

I went north in a hired Land-Rover so battered that it wore holes in my trousers. The mountain crests were powdered with freshly fallen snow and in the winter clarity you could see the site of Kapisa, which I had failed to reach so many times, quite clearly. In the mountains the shadows were more definite than the trees, and the sunlight was so bright it seemed to be dying like a leaf when it turns colour. Near the top of the pass a soft barrage of clouds hung on the mountainside with the taller peaks showing naked above it. Soldiers stood shivering over their spades and picks. The cloud was a dense, snowy vapour leaning on the crest of the mountain from the north side and hardly overflowing to the south, so halfway through the long ill-lit concrete bunker of the Salang tunnel we ran into freezing fog. The windscreen froze faster than it could be cleaned, and the world outside the tunnel was almost as obscure as inside it, dark grey fog, grey ice and snow on the road, and glimpses of glittering white snow and ice whenever the fog lifted. I saw an eremurus crystallized in ice, and as the clouds lifted or we passed below them a herd of goats moved down the hillside with snow and ice in their fleeces. The driver and I were both shivering, and when we drove through the avenue of catalpas at Baghlan an hour or two later, it was still cool. Swallows and mynahs were in big flocks, and by the river south of the last gorge before Kunduz I saw fifty or a hundred horses grazing together and a whole village of black tents.

In Kunduz I went to see Tawab. A general election was nearing its climax. There are fifteen days of voting, and on the first day at one at least of the Kabul voting stations only four people voted. Parliamentary government was a new idea in Afghanistan, and the king still appointed the ministers without reference to election, although members of the royal family had in 1964 been debarred from holding these positions, perhaps because a cousin as prime minister rather weakens than strengthens the king's position. There were no parties in the European sense. I saw villagers being led to vote at Ghazni in a procession with drums and flutes, and in several places I met lorry-loads of voters travelling with ancient flute-players on the roof of the driver's cab. The Nashir family headquarters was as busy as the stock exchange. Four hundred voters had to be fed at midday and another four hundred in the evening. A count had been announced at Chardara, where a cousin of Tawab's got in, but there were five more days of elections. When the results came through, word was passed outside and four or five guns went off in the air. A powerful-looking, tense group of lieutenants came out of the room where the wireless was, followed by Tawab's preoccupied uncles, and finally Mr Nashir himself, looking cool and businesslike and remarkably young, and wearing a brown European suit and a bow-tie. More rifle shots went off further away. Tawab had been pressed into service and was longing for it all to be over; so was the driver who took me to the Spinzar hotel – he said it was his hundredth errand that day and his jeep was overheated.

The next morning I insisted on setting off extremely early; we drove north through the dark on the asphalt road towards the Russian frontier where I waved a paper at a sleepy soldier, and we turned off into the desert some way north of the Archi bridge. Dawn broke slowly and coldly in the desert. The sun came up brilliant over a sand-dune exactly ahead of us. Before and after dawn long caravans of camels passed us going west, otherwise there was nothing. Most of the birds were hawks and when we stopped for breakfast after sunrise the silence was absolute. We were following a broad tangle of droving tracks between the dunes, which brought us out to a small fertile oasis and a village called Dasht-i Archi.* A dozen donkeys were drinking side by side under a bridge, and a villager was leading an ape along the track like a dog on a lead.

In another hour we were among semi-desert hills in an even more purely central Asian landscape of very bright yellow stubble and toasted thistles, the tents and herds of nomads, and children who waved and jumped and shouted at the sight of a car. Driving on through sun and silence and resigned to another several hours' travelling we came suddenly down to Hodjigar, a village with trees and a watersplash where more than half the men we saw were riding horses. I noticed with some horror the fearful condition of the track I might easily have taken from Taliqan. As we came out of the village into the Kokcha plain I could see Russia; the mountainous hills a few miles away to the north were the hills that marked the course of the Oxus opposite Ay Khanoum.

We bucketed along for a mile or so over the plain to the lowest Kokcha bridge. Beside this bridge is one of the new stations for sheep-dipping, a proof if any were needed that this is one of the routes that the nomads use to move their animals in and out of the summer grazing-grounds. It is impossible to say whether there was always a bridge here. It may be possible to ford the river with camels or horses, but I should not like to have to do it with donkeys† or a flock of sheep, unless perhaps in winter when the snow freezes and the rivers are low. In the plain east of the Kokcha, nomads were encamped in their black tents. I noticed several mysterious bumps; one of them was the ruins of a long canal, which seems to be connected with the Ay Khanoum mound. It is not certain when this canal was dug or whether it was simply for irrigation.

* This name seems to mean Archi desert, but *dasht* can also mean a desert grazing-ground. The Archi is a little river that runs into the Kunduz river between Kunduz and the Oxus.
† Herodotos in fact remarks that the Scythians have no donkeys or mules (4, 28) and this might be relevant.

Canals did exist in Russian Turkestan as early as the first half of the third millennium B.C., and with just the same measurements as canals that are still in use today, and the Ay Khanoum canal has been explored but not yet excavated.

At the end of the plain we came to a sleepy village called Dasht-i Qala, where a single dusty hoopoe flittered through a melancholy graveyard. I was taken to the chief of police, a fat man in civilian robes bargaining lazily in the bazaar. He knew nothing about me and went away to telephone. Meanwhile I found the liveliest and strongest frescoed room I had ever seen; its whole wallspace was covered in big red painted flowers, red and blue architectural drawings and geometric decorations, wheels and running spirals, and some of the motifs were not unlike the chip-carved designs on wooden architecture that we saw at Ishtiwi and Kamdesh. The village market square seemed to alter while I waited for the policeman from an almost laughable tranquillity to an atmosphere of tensity and dust. I begged a mug of hot water and shaved to keep my spirits up. He came wandering back, poking at the vegetables, and it was all right. We were given a policeman to guide us finally to the hamlet of Ay Khanoum, on the banks of the Kokcha below the south bastion of the great mound, and up the track through the barricade of the ruined walls to the excavation. The track enters the city through the space in the walls where its gateway once stood.

The general history of any site can only be the last result of a long excavation and it looks as if Professor Bernard will be at work for many seasons to come. This is the only Greek city in central Asia ever to have been scientifically excavated; it holds the answers to old questions and the beginnings of new ones. Its central building is an ambitious Hellenistic palace of the Seleucid period with some important Persian features and possibly an earlier Persian building underneath it; another smaller house near the Kokcha at the western extremity of the city has the same ground plan, which seems to be Persian since it occurs also at Persepolis but never in the west. The palace has an open outer courtyard with long colonnades, but the central courts of the palace buildings are roofed rooms with a huge roofspan, surrounded by corridors giving on to smaller rooms. The reason for this roofed grandeur may possibly be a magnificent style of living; but it is more likely to be coolness in summer and warmth in winter; one should remember the climate. As an engineering feat it depended on fine timber, very likely deodars.

Some reconstruction, for example in the temple now being excavated which dominated the city from below the acropolis, took place in the Greek period. The whole city seems to have been destroyed by fire, but it was later occupied by squatters whose origin is hard to place. Later again the bricks and stones were pillaged and the surviving pillars felled like trees probably for the bronze bindings of their bases, so that bases survived like tree-stumps and capitals like broken fruit or the fragments of branches. The hero-shrine outside the palace gates, which is older than the layout of the palace, was broken open by tunnelling; and three of its four tombs were looted. In modern times a few huts stood on the abandoned ground, and the Uzbeks used it for encampments; it was also used for *buzkashi*. The mound of the acropolis, which is not unlike Aliabad, is about two hundred feet high and the abundant fragments of pottery include some Islamic wares; it is easy enough to trace its defences, but trial trenches in selected spots have not yet revealed anything of interest.

At the time of my visit the most interesting building was the temple. It was a square building not exactly oriented, probably because of the lie of the land and in order for it to face the acropolis. Its outer walls had originally a series of recessed squared niches like window-frames, each niche recessed in a series of three diminishing rectangles one inside the other; this is an Achaemenid Persian style but when the temple was reconstructed these smart and elaborate walls were cloaked in massive claybrick. The base of the Achaemenid walls was a pair of very tall rounded steps like the shapes of old-fashioned jellymoulds. These walls were painted white but not stuccoed. The inside was T-shaped, with the entry at the base of the T and an outer room in the upright with two subsidiary store-rooms or sacristies beside it. The mudbrick of this outer room was strengthened by vertical beams and some traces of burnt stucco have been found there. The right-hand sacristy was full of scraps of ivory and small carbonized fragments of wooden ornamental mouldings and Professor Bernard himself has recovered a carbonized wooden Ionic capital here almost complete.* The cult statue stood on a bench-like platform in the inner shrine; one of its marble feet has been recovered; it was the sandalled foot of a male figure that must have stood some ten or perhaps fifteen feet high. Maybe only its white parts were marble, but the workmanship is rich and the design crisp. Its ornamentation includes a thunderbolt, which suggests Zeus or a king identified with Zeus. My own guess is that this monstrous work of art represents the rebuilding of the temple with a new and atavistic dedication. I find it hard not to connect the original dedication with the goddess on a silver-gilt plaque found in the left-hand sacristy hidden under storage jars on the second day of the 1969 excavation. The goddess is Kybele.

The plaque is a repoussé disc of silver about a foot across, with the figures gilded. The workmanship is extremely fine. The head of a young Greek sun-god with thirteen rays sprouting from behind his head, a crescent moon and a sixteen-point star of rays look down on a mountain landscape indicated by rocky ground. A chariot drawn by two soberly prancing lions, and driven by a girl in Greek dress facing forwards, is carrying a robed woman with a chimney-pot head-dress (she is wearing a *polos*) and more flowing robes, who faces you. She is the goddess Kybele. Behind the chariot walks a priest in a Persian hat and a long tunic holding an umbrella above Kybele's head. This honorific shade is sketchy and the priest when I saw the plaque was a little indistinct. The chariot moves to the right across level rocky ground towards an altar which is purely Persian. It consists of six steep steps like separate blocks of diminishing size, with a straight front towards the lions. A priest in a long tunic and girdle and a conical hat has mounted to the third step, his waist is level with the top and he makes an offering in or on a small vessel which is like a seventh step of the altar. He is facing the goddess.

* It was the Asian and Indian type of Ionic capital, with a deep dip and a pronounced curl, something like a pair of ram's horns. It is from this kind of capital that Swat and Nuristan wooden capitals ultimately derive.

A mixture of religions can seldom have been so clearly expressed in a mixture of styles at such a high level of art. Kybele was the Persian mother-goddess adopted by the Greeks in Asia Minor; she was easily identified with Rhea, mother of Zeus, and with the vague Mother of the gods, whose cult in Athens was very ancient. But Kybele was not publicly worshipped in any city in mainland Greece until the time of the Roman Empire; her worship in Greece began as a private religious cult imported by foreigners. Still, she was of all Asian goddesses probably the only one the Greeks in Asia knew already in the early third century B.C. It is at least not impossible that she had a cult at Ay Khanoum before the Greeks arrived, but this silver-gilt disk is a perfect fusion of Greek and Persian elements in a Greek setting. It is even possible the goddess may be not Kybele, but Artemis Nanaia, an offshoot of Ishtar: without written evidence it is impossible to know. Artemis Nanaia is sometimes identified with Anahita the goddess of the Oxus.

Whatever else we know of the religious and the public life of Ay Khanoum is Greek. There was a typical Hellenistic palaestra near the river, which has yielded a grave and ageing head of Herakles. The hero-shrine was two or three times rebuilt; it was a small chapel with two brick graves and two sarcophagi, with a pair of columns at the entrance to the outer room; the mound it stands on is perhaps the grave of the founder of the city. The most interesting of the few Ay Khanoum inscriptions stood outside the chapel, which it refers to as 'the sacred enclosure of Kineas'. Kineas seems to be a man and not a god, and the graves in his shrine suggest a dynastic cult. It is hard to see what except founding the city could make a man otherwise unknown to history so important here. If Ay Khanoum was really Alexandria on the Oxus, it is probable that Kineas founded it in Alexander's name, just as the Egyptian Alexandria was founded, but this is a problem we shall never solve without written evidence.

The inscription, which is written in verse, in lettering of before 250 B.C., records that Klearchos copied out the precepts of the famous men of ancient times, which he saw at Delphi, and has inscribed them here, in the sacred enclosure of Kineas. The stone tablet with the Delphic inscriptions has perished; only one maxim survives on the same stone as the first inscription. There is a third inscription encouraging people to the various virtues proper to the different ages of human life. To preserve this peculiarly Greek wisdom cut in stone in so remote a spot must have been a conscious and purposeful act. Can it posssibly have been Klearchos, the pupil of Aristotle, who was responsible?

Ay Khanoum was a rich city, and today it is a heady site. From the mound you can see the shining pebbly Kokcha where it runs into the Oxus. The Kokcha is much deeper and stronger and faster than it looked from a distance; it ruffles the Oxus where they join with a noise and glitter like the tide. In the evening I swam in it; it splits into three streams between pebble banks for a few yards, and I was told I could cross the first and swim in the second, but if I entered the third I would probably be shot by a Russian sentry. There was no Russian sentry for several miles and both sides of the river are undefended.

Since I had only two days I walked indefatigably around the monuments through a golden crop of vicious Greek thistles; the city was about the size of Sounion or Delphi, with a disproportionately big palace. The pink and grey Russian cliffs rise to about four hundred feet, the Oxus is a hundred and fifty yards across and licks its stones noisily, but there are traces of ramparts facing the river. The main city walls facing the plain have a deep fosse and a series of towers thirty or forty feet high constructed entirely with small mudbricks; the substructure of the walls is a mixture of pebbles and clay. The exact shapes of these walls as of everything else stood out most clearly in the earliest sun of the day.

Upstream but plainly visible from Ay Khanoum stands another site, right on the edge of the Oxus opposite some fertile woody land. It seems to consist of a large round tower-like mound on a flatter base. It is said to be Kushan but there seems no particular reason for believing this, and in fact the site has never been properly investigated. To make things worse the same pottery occurs almost everywhere, and some of the ancient types can be exactly matched from the modern kiln which was found on the site of the palaestra. A mass of interesting pottery is coming out of the house by the Kokcha, including some quite fine and thin fragments of black glazed cups, but the classification of all the pottery of Ay Khanoum is going to be a long and intricate task.

The luxury of the palace is hard to describe. Its floors were tiled and its weight-carrying walls were massive mudbrick; no art has come out of it except its architecture; the spiny nodding leaves of stone acanthus. There were traces of old rose on its upper mouldings like the deep rose pink of the walls in the house by the Kokcha. These decorations were exactly worked, and the Corinthian column-bases were not only elaborately designed but also perfectly regular. Admittedly the surface skin of the column drums was less fine than marble would be, but there were traces of white plaster on them which alters the picture. The stone seems to be local and the Russians claim to have found the precise quarry it came from about thirty miles upstream. If this is right it has the implication that Greek influence must have reached at least that distance to the north-east. The road from the main gate travels north-east; I traced it for some way over the plain, and near where it must have reached the first barrier of hills I could see drovers' tracks; it would be an important contribution if someone could tell us where it went.

At night there was a sand of stars, in the morning before dawn a schoolmaster's bell. I was asking myself so many questions of detail that I almost forgot where I was. *Vedeva Troia in cenere e caverne.* A continual plume of dust blew from the excavations. Swallows skimmed and little green bee-eaters uttered their strange cries. I admit to hoping it was called Alexandria; it would be a good place to be remembered by.

As we drove back through the desert it was full of birds: vultures, bee-eaters, hawks of various sizes, a buzzard and one splendid hoopoe. The journey seemed swifter than before, and now that it was light I could see the mounds north of Kunduz; they seemed less surprising than they would have done three months ago. We reached Kunduz in a yellow haze of sunset and cattle-dust and I remember that there was a smell of bread and smoke and melons. Wazir Mohammed was sad. The theatre company had quarrelled and broken up, and he told me he had decided to leave Afghanistan. His first idea was to go to consult with Charlie Chaplin about the state of the theatre all over the world, and then to become an actor in another society and another language. He asked if I had heard any classical Afghan music. Then he sat down cross-legged in Tawab's house and someone brought him a portable harmonium with an oversweet tone. He played and sang a long lament for dead kings. It was a desert of warbles and groans. After two hours he finished and Tawab nodded. There was nothing more that any of us could say.

Next day I went to Kabul, then to England, and unloaded my pebbles on to my desk.

AN HISTORICAL GUIDE TO AFGHANISTAN

Nancy Hatch Dupree

The American writer, Afghan scholar and conservationist **Nancy Hatch Dupree** (1927–2017) was a life-enhancing force of nature. She first travelled to Kabul in the 1960s as a diplomat's wife, then left her husband after falling in love with both Afghanistan and Louis Dupree, the anthropologist and director of the American Archaeological Mission to Afghanistan. She lived for nearly five decades in Kabul, long after Louis's death in 1989, writing about Afghanistan in a series of books which became standard references at a time when travel for foreign visitors was hardly straightforward. In later years she became a fierce and sharp-witted champion of Afghan culture and its people, seeing off generations of Communists, Islamist fundamentalists, warlords and foreign invaders. She became director of the Afghanistan Center at Kabul University, a pivotal role in securing the national heritage through the collection, preservation and archiving of historical documents. She was so well connected, according to *The Economist*, that a young, pre-al-Qaeda Osama bin Laden requested her assistance to secure permits to dig tunnels in Kabul. While Afghans knew her fondly as the 'Grandmother of Afghanistan', she described herself as an ancient monument.

A generous and big-hearted figure, Hatch Dupree encouraged writers and scholars with an interest in Afghanistan across the generations. Several months before she died in her ninetieth year, she guided me towards elusive sources for sixteenth-century Kabul in a flurry of jaunty, high-spirited and enormously helpful correspondence. RIP Nancy Hatch Dupree.

Chapter 26

BALKH

From Balkh to:	Distance	Time
Mazar-i-Sharif	18 km; 11 mi.	15 min.
Shibarghan	113 km; 71 mi.	1½ hrs.
Population:	10,000	
Altitudes:	Mazar-i-Sharif	377 m; 1237 ft.
	Balkh	*357 m; 1171* ft.
	Aqcha	296 m; 971 ft.
	Shibarghan	330 m; 1083 ft.
Hotel:	Hotel Balkh: Good; meals on request.	
Petrol:	In town on Central Square.	

BALKH, today a growing town in Balkh Province, is a town of prodigious antiquity where Zoroaster preached sometime between 1000 and 600 B.C. Licentious rites celebrated at the shrine to Anahita, Goddess of the Oxus, attracted thousands during the 5th century B.C.; Alexander the Great chose it for his base from 329–327 B.C., and in the early centuries A.D., under the Kushans, when Buddhism was practiced throughout Afghanistan, many holy Buddhist temples flourished in Balkh. For several hundreds of years scores of Buddhist pilgrims flocked to worship at the feet of "a figure of Buddha, lustrous with noted gems" as it was described by Hsuan-tsang, the Chinese pilgrim-traveller-chronicler who passed through in the 7th century A.D., just before the arrival of a new religion from the west, Islam.

The Arabs, the bearers of Islam, called Balkh the Mother of Towns, so impressed were they with its importance and its magnificence. By the 9th century two score Friday Mosques stood within the city which was paramount among the cities ruled by the Samanid Dynasty (873–999) from their capital at Bokhara. During this period of cultural revitalization Balkh was the home of some of the more famous names in early Persian literature, including the beautiful star-crossed Rabi'a

Balkhi, first woman of the Islamic period to compose poems in Persian.

Embellished by the Ghaznavids and the Seljuks, who claimed it in 1040, Balkh continued as an intellectual and spiritual mecca. Mawlana Jalaluddin Balkhi, known in the west as Rumi, was born in Balkh in 1207, son of a renowned Sufi teacher. Perhaps the most eminent Sufi poet of all time, Jalaluddin Balkhi's *Mathnawi* is considered by many to be the greatest poem ever written in the Persian language.

Balkh's glorious history closed in 1220 when 10,000 mounted men following Genghis Khan rode through and left it utterly devastated. The Great Khan's grandson stopped by for a little lion hunting in 1256, but Hulagu pitched his tents of gold cloth secured by solid gold pegs on the plain, for the desolation was so complete that even one hundred years later (1333) Ibn Battuta found the entire area "in ruins."

Balkh did, nevertheless, lie on an important trade route and eventually it won recovery under the enlightened rule of Shah Rukh and his Queen, Gawhar Shad, of Herat. After their deaths Bokhara and Kabul fought for control of the north. Ahmad Shah Durrani (1747–1772) finally established the frontier on the Amu Darya in 1768 and Balkh became the seat of successive Governors-General of Afghan Turkestan trying valiantly to impose their rule on independent-minded Uzbak chieftains. Chronically rampant malaria and distressingly frequent outbreaks of cholera made their task difficult. In the end, Balkh was abandoned for Mazar-i-Sharif in 1866, after which it languished, a mean and forgotten village, until modernization schemes launched in the 1930s and 1940s ushered in a new era of prosperity.

Midway between Mazar-i-Sharif and Balkh (markers 434/435; 5 min. from Mazar), the road passes through the ruins of **Takht-i-Pul**. This was once an elite suburb of Balkh built by Amir Afzal Khan in 1855 while he governed Afghan Turkestan for his father, Amir Dost Mohammad. Escaping from the pestilential climate of Balkh, the court built spacious two-storey houses in Takht-i-Pul surrounded by flowering gardens and orchards. From the upper stories they enjoyed a view of the mountains and the fresh breezes which blew from them. Amir Abdur Rahman (1880–1901), Afzal Khan's son, maintained the capital at Mazar and Takht-i-Pul became a strong, fortified cantonment enthusiastically described by the Amir's British physician, Dr. Grey, when he inspected the hospital here in 1889. A jumble of ruined houses behind a protective wall on the north, massive walls cut by the modern road, and the dome of a mosque are all that survive today. The interior of the mosque is richly decorated with floral panels painted in bright reds and blues, with touches of green. Stalactite niches and plaster panels sculptured with arabesques, foliated scrolls and rosettes add to the complexity of its decor. The plain mud-plastered dome rises from plowed fields today, giving no hint of its inner splendor.

SIGHT-SEEING

(1) SHRINE OF KHWAJA ABU NASR PARSA

Situated in the center of Balkh's Central Park, this shrine was built in memory of a distinguished theologian who taught at the college in Herat established by Firuza Begam, mother of Sultan Husain Baiqara. The Timurid ladies of Herat vied with the men in their patronage of the arts and learning. Khwaja Parsa later settled in Balkh and died here in 1460. Built in the late Timurid style, its blue dome, fluted and resting on stalactite corbels 25 m; 80 ft. above the ground, sits above a colorfully tiled octagonal base. The portal is flanked by magnificent corkscrew pillars. Preservation of the badly deteriorated façade and dome was initiated in June 1974, with the assistance of the Archaeological Survey of India.

(2) MADRASSA (COLLEGE) OF SAYID SUBHAN QULI KHAN

Built in the 17th century by a great scholar of Balkh, this magnificent fragment of what was a huge academic establishment be-speaks the renaissance of Balkh during the Timurid and Uzbak periods. The interior of the arch is elaborately embellished with decorative architectural motifs popular in Herat during the height of the Timurid period.

(3) TOMB OF RABI'A BALKHI

The tomb of this tragic poetess lies to the south of the Parsa Shrine. Here she spent her last fainting moments writing a poem with blood that trickled slowly from wrists slashed by an irate brother. Poems to a slave lover had brought her here to die and the dungeon which became her tomb was discovered in 1964. Scholars may look askance at the newly designated shrine, questioning its authenticity, but young girls come to ask the poetess for inspiration in solving their own romantic problems. As they leave, they tie a strip of cloth to the bars through which one views the underground tomb, to remind her of their quest. The poetry of Rabi'a Balkhi continues to live in the hearts of Afghanistan's young lovers.

(4) BALA HISSAR

The massive ruins of ancient Balkh lie to the north of the Central Park. Here one may pick up bits and pieces of glazed pottery from the Timurid period, and before, including pieces of Chinese pottery, for great caravans laden with the luxuries of the world, stopped here.

The crumbling walls encircling the fort area were built for the most part in the Timurid period upon earlier foundations which may go back to the Kushan period in the early centuries A.D. The great knot of ruins to the east was the Arg or Citadel.

Several teams of archaeologists from France (DAFA: 1924–25, under the direction of M. Alfred Foucher; 1947–48 and 1955–56, under the direction of M. Daniel Schlumberger) and the United States (R. Young, 1953) have dug at Balkh looking for the more ancient city. No conclusive evidence has yet been discovered, however, and some scholars think the really ancient city must have been at another spot. The search continues.

(5) THE SOUTHERN WALLS

Early Balkh expanded to the south from the Bala Hissar area, then continued to grow to the east, and then west, the whole surrounded by massive walls with stout towers which are very well preserved on the south. The new approach to Balkh from the paved road runs straight through these walls which are particularly photogenic in the early morning light.

(6) TOP-I-RUSTAM AND TAKHT-I-RUSTAM

Two mounds standing by the south shoulder of the paved road at the turnoff to the town of Balkh are all that remain of the sumptuous monastery and stupa described by the Chinese pilgrim Hsuan-tsang in 630 A.D. A 61 m; 200 ft. high stupa sat atop the easternmost mound, today called Top-i-Rustam. The mound to the west of the unpaved road which separates these two mounds, today called Takht-i-Rustam, was crowned by a convent housing several sacred relics of the Buddha: his washing basin covered with gold and precious gems, a tooth, and his broom with jewel-encrusted handle. The figure of the Buddha in the monastery was "lustrous with noted gems, and the hall in which it stands is also adorned with precious substances of rare value. This is the reason why it has often been robbed by chieftains of neighbouring countries, covetous of gain." (Hsuan-tsang) The process continues, for today the villagers take bricks from these mounds for their own building, and earth for their fields. They have long been abandoned, for even by the time Hsuan-tsang visited Balkh, Buddhism was slowly dying out. The city still had over a hundred Buddhist monasteries but the pious pilgrim has this to say about the monks in attendance: "so irregular are they in morning and night in their duties, that it is hard to tell saints from sinners."

(7) MASJID-I-HAJI PIYADA (MASJID-I-NO GUMBAD)

This exquisitely ornamented mosque is the earliest Islamic monument yet identified in Afghanistan. Built during the early years of the 9th century A.D. when the first local Islamic dynasties were asserting their independence from the harsh rule of Arabic governors, it coupled outside influences with local ingenuity. As such it continued a tradition mentioned throughout this history, from the Achaemenid (Delbarjin Tepe, northwest of Balkh), Graeco-Bactrian (Ai Khanoum), and Kushano-Sasanian (Balkh), periods. Few datable examples of mosque architecture exist anywhere in the world from this early period. Only a handful featuring an architectural plan with nine domes (No Gumbad) are scattered throughout the former Arab Empire, from Balkh to Cairo to Toledo in Spain, dating from the 9th to the 12th centuries A.D.

The mosque is not large, being only 10 m; 33 ft. square. It was originally covered by nine domes but the domes have fallen and the floor is now buried under more than a meter of rubble which also encases the lower half of the columns which supported the domes. On the north corner, however, the present ground level is a little lower permitting one to note that the columns stand on bases above which there is a wide band of decorated stucco narrower in diameter than either the shaft or the base. The northeast façade with an arcade of three arches was the original entrance but it is now blocked by later constructions.

The elegantly carved stucco decoration is the wonder and the beauty of this mosque. The capitals of the columns and the arches which span them exhibit an infinite variety of geometric and abstract floral designs: vine-scrolls twist around grape-leaves forming circles and semicircles, squares, rectangles, and polygons within borders of pearls, hatchings, mazes and meanders. On the capitals pairs of palmettes frame trefoil lotus blossoms and plump pomegranates sprout at their base.

Sasanian styles and traditions suggest themselves and the most striking comparisons may be made with the carved stucco decoration at Samarra, the short-lived capital of the Abbasid Caliphate north of Baghdad. Samarra flourished from 836 A.D. to 890 A.D., the period to which scholars have assigned the construction of this mosque. Time has taken its toll at Samarra and it is difficult to fully determine architectural styles. Here at the Masjid-i-Haji Piyada the form and elegance of style and decoration are remarkably preserved, though nature's wear is yearly more visible.

A modest shrine of modern construction is attached to the north wall. Local belief holds that here lies Ka'b, an early 7th century resident of

Balkh who converted from Judaism to Islam. In the open courtyard in front of the shrine there are a number of tombstones, many elaborately carved, dating from the 11th through the 17th centuries A.D.

THE HAZARAS OF AFGHANISTAN
AN HISTORICAL, CULTURAL, ECONOMIC AND POLITICAL STUDY

S. A. Mousavi

Afghanistan is a tapestry of peoples and tribes. Although one of the largest ethnic groups in the country, alongside the Pashtuns, Tajiks and Uzbeks, the Persian-speaking, Shia Muslim Hazaras have often been marginalised and persecuted by politically more powerful forces. In recent times the Taliban in particular have perpetrated atrocities against the Hazaras.

The Hazaras' origins, like so many questions in Afghanistan, are hotly contested. Some scholars, citing Quintus Curtius Rufus, the Roman historian of Alexander the Great's campaigns in Afghanistan, claim the Hazaras are the original inhabitants of today's Afghanistan. Others, pointing to recent genetic studies, argue for Turkic and Mongol origins. One of the most common – and historically evocative – suggestions is that the Hazaras are the descendants of Genghis Khan's conquering Mongol hordes. Given the movements across Asia by untold numbers of men, women and children over untold numbers of centuries, complete precision is perhaps neither possible nor desirable.

Educated at the Universities of East Anglia and Oxford, **Sayed Askar Mousavi** (1956–), an Afghan Hazara writer, novelist and editor, has made a powerful contribution to Afghanistan studies with this important study, first published in 1998.

Political Leadership

Political leadership in its modern form is a very new phenomenon in Hazara society, going back only to the period after 1978. Political organization and parties too, by implication, are new phenomena. In many ways it is this newness which makes the study of political leadership in Hazara society particularly interesting.

As mentioned before, the 1980s were a period of transition from traditional leadership to modern forms of leadership. Although very dependant on the religious leadership, secular leaders have played their part in recent Hazara politics too, in particular in the military, organizational, and cultural dimensions. But it was in the early 1990s that the Hazara political leadership made its mark and its presence felt nationally, in coming together to form *Hizb-e Wahdat*, under the leadership of Abdul Ali Mazari. Under his leadership *Hizb-e Wahdat* became the strongest political party representing Afghanistan's Hazara and Shi'a population.

Born in 1946 in a poor farming Hazara family in the Nanwayee village in Charkent, in Mazar-e Sharif Province, Abdul Ali Mazari left for Najaf and Qom to complete his religious studies after completing his primary education in his home province. In Qom he came across and developed the progressive convictions which took him back to Charkent in 1978 to lead the first ever rebellion against the PDPA government in Afghanistan, and kept him fighting for justice until the end of his rather short life. Mazari was the first political leader to speak up for and on behalf of a unified Hazara and Shi'a political party, putting their case to the UN and the international community. He achieved an unprecedented degree of popularity among the Hazara and Shi'a community, which called him *babah* (father). After his death his body was carried by the people all the way from Ghazni to Bamiyan on foot.

Mazari's most significant achievement was in bringing together in his person and in a modern organization all three strands of leadership: ethnic, religious and political. After many years of struggle against suspicion and mistrust, Mazari succeeded to bring together the many sections, forces and classes within Hazara and Shi'a society, and to represent a unified people nationally, regionally and internationally. Thus, it can be said, that the process started by Mir Yazdan Baksh 150 years ago to unite the Hazara and Shi'a community under a unified leadership was realized 150 years later by Mazari. Indeed, many similarities exist between Mir Yazdan Baksh and Mazari. Both men believed passionately in the need for unity in the Hazara and Shi'a population; both lived in times of active struggle between the Tajiks, Uzbeks, Pashtuns and Hazaras. While Mir Yazdan Baksh witnessed the first war against the British, Mazari lived through the war of resistance against the Soviets. Even their deaths bore uncanny resemblance. Mir Yazdan Baksh too was betrayed: he had been invited by Haji Khan Kakar, who had sworn on the Quran to keep his word. Once at Haji Khan's camp though Mir Yazdan Bakhsh was captured and later killed in the most brutal manner. His death marked the end of any hope for Hazara unity for 150 years, and the start of bitter Hazara-Pashtun enmity. Mazari too had signed an agreement with the Taliban leadership soon after their emergence on the political scene in Afghanistan in 1993, but a few days later was captured and met a similar brutal fate to Mir Yazdan Bakhsh. His death in the spring of 1995 also marked the end of a fateful phase in Hazara political development and history.

9.2 Resistance of West Kabul: 1992–95

West Kabul consists of areas of the city to the west of the Shir-Darwaza, Asmayee, Kafir and Afshar mountains, which split Kabul down the middle into two main areas to the northeast and the southwest. Although the Hazaras had come to inhabit most parts of Kabul by 1992, having originally settled in the Chindawol and Moradkhani areas to the north of the city, West Kabul housed by far the largest concentration of the city's Shi'as and Hazaras. According to some estimates, the Hazaras made up one half of Kabul's entire population at the time of Najibullah's downfall (around 3 million), the largest concentration of Hazaras anywhere in the country. For this reason, in the aftermath of seizure of power by the

Mujahideen, more than half of Kabul was in the hands of the Hazaras.

At this stage, *Hizb-e Wahdat* leadership was not yet based in Kabul, although active party cells had been present in the city for some time. Once in Kabul, *Hizb-e Wahdat* found itself unwillingly involved in consecutive battles against the forces of the Interim Government, to safeguard its control over its sections of the city and to protect West Kabul's Hazara and Shi'a civilian population. Between May 1992 and March 1995, West Kabul was the scene of twenty-seven battles in all, making this part of Kabul the country's main battle field.

The combination of the right social conditions, political party and a unified leadership brought about for the Hazaras once again in 1992 the possibility of standing up to the regime in Kabul for their ethnic and religious rights on the one hand, and for their share in the nation's decision-making process, on the other hand. The reason behind *Hizb-e Wahdat*'s opposition to the Mujahideen Interim Government was that it had been excluded from it. The Interim Government plan had been drawn up in Peshawar by the Mujahideen groups based there and led by Sayyaf. Not only had *Hizb-e Wahdat* not been present in the decision-making process, the plan had completely ignored the fate of the Shi'a and Hazara population, in effect denying their very existence in Afghanistan. The battles were thus between the various factions of the Interim Government on the one hand, and *Hizb-e Wahdat* on the other. Thus, West Kabul's inhabitants found themselves bombarded aerially from all directions, and engaged in ground battles also from different directions. The struggle put up by the *Hizb-e Wahdat* and its forces for the defence of the rights of the Hazara and Shi'a community came to be known as the 'resistance of West Kabul'.

This resistance, which began in May 1992 and ended in defeat in March 1995, marked a turning point in the contemporary history of Afghanistan in general, and in the fate of Afghanistan's Shi'a and Hazara populations in particular. By resiliently defending and holding on to its positions for the intervening three years, *Hizb-e Wahdat* brought the struggle of the Hazaras to the attention of regional and international powers. Furthermore, despite their defeat in Kabul, they had become one of faction-ridden Afghanistan's four main political forces.

The resistance of West Kabul shared similarities with the 1890s uprisings. In both cases, Sunni-Shi'a conflicts were used as a means of oppressing the Hazaras; and in both cases the Hazaras were eventually defeated. However, the two movements were essentially different from one another. The resistance of West Kabul differed from the 1890s uprisings in its location, its timing, its method of action, and its clarity of demands and objectives. The 1890s uprisings had taken place throughout Hazarajat. Furthermore, they had been disorganized and random, lacked unified leadership, political or military organization, and contact with the outside; with changing demands. The 1890s uprisings had been basically a rural rebellion against the ruling Pashtun regime. The resistance of West Kabul, on the other hand, was centred in the country's capital, enjoyed a unified leadership backed by an organized political party; had extensive contact with the outside world, where it had effective representation, and had specific short-term and long-term objectives and demands. In short, the resistance of West Kabul, which began exactly one century after the end of the 1890s uprisings, was an organized urban resistance movement, and this time in opposition to a Tajik-dominated regime.

The Afshar massacre

One of the civil war's most horrific moments occurred on 11 February 1993, in the Afshar district of West Kabul, where hundreds of its Hazara residents were massacred by government forces, under the direct order of President Rabbani and his chief commander, Massoud. The Afshar district lies at the foot of the Afshar mountains and covers a wide area in West Kabul. The district is also the site of Kabul Polytechnic and the Institute of Social Sciences, chosen by the *Hizb-e Wahdat* leadership as its headquarters upon its arrival in the city, because of its perceived shielded position between the Kafir and Afshar mountains. At one o'clock on the morning of 11 February, while the inhabitants of Afshar lay asleep in their beds, the Institute of Social Sciences was attacked from three sides: from the west by Sayyaf's *Ittehad-e Islami* forces, and from the north and south, by Rabbani's forces, helped by traitors from within the Party, who had already been bought off. Faced with such an offensive, *Hizb-e Wahdat* retreated from its positions in the district. Following this withdrawal, forces loyal to Sayyaf and Ahmad Shah Massoud raided the area. For the next twenty-four hours they killed, raped, set fire to homes, and took young boys and girls as captives. By the time the news was broadcast in Kabul and internationally the following day, some 700 people were estimated to have been killed or to have disappeared. One year later, when parts of the district were retaken by *Hizb-e Wahdat* forces, several mass graves were unearthed containing a further fifty-eight bodies.

The massacre was condemned by regional neighbours and international human rights organizations. However, its perpetrators were never caught or brought to justice. Although, Rabbani's government did condemn the massacre as one of his government's 'mistakes', the tragedy was blamed on his soldiers, who like soldiers everywhere are never held responsible for such war crimes. Today, Afshar remains a ghost district, its surviving inhabitants having fled in the aftermath of the massacre. Its legacy, however, remains very much in the hearts and minds of the Shi'a and Hazara population, further fuelling ethno-religious conflict.

The massacre had a further outcome. It brought together in alliance *Hizb-e Wahdat* and the Pashtun *Hizb-e Islami*, against their common enemy, the ruling Tajiks. The Hazaras found themselves faced with a totally new socio-political set of dynamics, calling for a revised socio-political analysis of Hazara-Pastun relations. Up until this point, the Hazaras had considered the Pashtuns their foremost oppressors. In the aftermath of the Afshar massacre Hazara relations changed with both their historical enemy, the Pashtuns, and with the other ethnic groups, such as the Tajiks. The result was a new four-party alliance between *Hizb-e Wahdat*, Hekmatyar's *Hizb-e Islami*, Dostom's *Jonbesh-e Melli-Islami*, and Mujaddidi's *Jabha-ye Nijat-e Melli*. In other words, the Hazaras, Pashtuns and Uzbeks were allied against the Tajiks. The alliance came to be known as the *Shura-ye 'Ali-ye Hamahangi* and remained effective until mid-1996.

The fall of West Kabul (March 1995)

The little known group, the Taliban, which swept through much of Afghanistan's southern and eastern provinces, following its liberation of a Pakistani trade convoy on its way through Afghanistan to Central Asia in 1994, reached the outskirts of Kabul in February 1995. Here, they temporarily halted their offensive in consideration for the month of Ramadan, during which fighting is forbidden; although in reality they were preparing for their offensive on Kabul. Given their proximity to the centre of power, and their rapid advance through the country, the various political parties, including *Hizb-e Wahdat*, set about negotiating with the Taliban. By the end of Ramadan, some sort of agreement was apparently reached between the Taliban and *Hizb-e Wahdat*, wherein the two agreed not to fight one another, so that the latter could concentrate its strength in its defensive against government forces.

Consequently, following their successful defensive, on 6 March, against the forces of Massoud who had launched one of their heaviest offensives against *Hizb-e Wahdat*, the Party allowed Taliban forces inside its frontlines in West Kabul. However, once there, the Taliban proceeded to disarm *Hizb-e Wahdat* fighters, while at the same time, proving unable to defend their newly occupied positions against the government offensive and withdrawing. Within hours, government soldiers broke through *Hizb-e Wahdat* frontlines and entered West Kabul, for the first time since the Mujahideen had entered the city. West Kabul fell, ending three years of brave resistance by the Hazaras and Shi'as. In their withdrawal from West Kabul, the Taliban took with them the leader of *Hizb-e Wahdat*, Mazari, and seven of his trusted entourage, who were all found murdered within days of their departure from Kabul.

The fall of West Kabul, followed by the capture and murder of the leader of *Hizb-e Wahdat*, in effect brought to a rapid end a significant phase in the active presence and struggle of the Hazaras and Shi'as in Afghanistan. The emergence of the Taliban, backed by foreign powers, totally redefined political boundaries and developments in Afghanistan. The first force undermined by the Taliban was the *Hizb-e Islami*, followed by *Hizb-e Wahdat*, and a year later in late 1996, the coalition government of Kabul led by the *Jam'iyat-e Islami*. By the end of 1996 the Taliban were the most powerful military and political force in Afghanistan.

9.3 Phase two (1995–97)

The fall of West Kabul and the lost opportunity it represented had a deep effect on Hazara society. But, surprisingly, this proved both positive and negative. Although the fall represented another bitter defeat for the Hazaras, reminiscent of their defeat a century ago, the existence of a unified political party and leadership this time around enabled the Hazaras to reorganize themselves quickly. The costly experiences gained has left Hazara society more aware and unified than ever before, both inside Afghanistan and abroad.

Following their withdrawal from Kabul, *Hizb-e Wahdat* faced, in 1995, a year of reconstruction and reorganization. The first step in this direction was the election to leadership of the Party's number two man and spokesman under Mazari, Abdul Karim Khalili. With the loss of control over West Kabul, the party moved its headquarters to Hazarajat and reassembled in Bamiyan. The following year, 1996, saw the formation of the *Shura-ye 'Ali-ye Difa'*, the alliance between *Hizb-e Wahdat*, *Jonbesh* and their enemy of the previous four years, *Jam'iyat*, against the Pakistani-backed Pashtun *Taliban*. After the capture of Kabul by *Taliban* from *Jam'iyat* in late 1996, *Hizb-e Wahdat* was once again faced with the options of either allying itself with or opposing the *Taliban*, as it had done in early 1995. Given the tragic outcome of that previous alliance, *Hizb-e Wahdat* opted this time to join the formation of the new anti-Taliban *Shura-ye 'Ali-ye Difa'*, under the leadership of Abdul Rashid Dostom, leader. Since then the Hazarajat and *Hizb-e Wahdat* have on the whole entered a period of relative stabilization. Thus, phase two is a continuation of the stabilization of Hazara society begun in phase one, without the military dimension. The outcome of this period depends very much on developments in Kabul. If events favour the *Shura-ye Difa'*, there is room for hope for the future of peace and stability in Hazarajat. However, if the *Taliban* succeed, Hazarajat will once again fall into turmoil, with the anti-Pashtun sentiments of the Hazaras renewed, especially following the murder of their first and only leader, Mazari, by the *Taliban*.

FAḌĀ'IL-I BALKH, or THE MERITS OF BALKH

Shaikh al Islam Abu Bakr Abdullah al Waiz

Translated by Arezou Azad and Edmund Herzig

With a history stretching back several thousand years, the Silk Road city of Balkh is one of the most ancient in Afghanistan. It was built on the northern plain between the towering Hindu Kush mountains and the Amu Darya River, the Oxus of antiquity. Persian legend suggests it was founded by Keyumars, the first king in the world. The elusive Zoroaster may have preached here sometime around 600 BCE, when it became an important centre of the Zoroastrian religion. As Bactra, it was the seat of the Bactrian Empire from the fourth century BCE, 'land of a thousand golden cities' – and was used by Alexander as his military base in 329–327 BCE.

Under the Kushans in the early centuries CE, it was a thriving Buddhist community and over the centuries passed between Persians, Arabs and Turkic rulers. For eighth-century Arabs, who brought Muslim mosques to add to the Buddhist temples, it was simply Umm al Bilad, the Mother of Cities. Then, in 1220, the curtain came down abruptly, and with spectacular violence, on Balkh's illustrious history. The Mongol conqueror Genghis Khan dispatched 100,000 horsemen to sack the city, a task they performed so thoroughly that both Marco Polo in 1275 and Ibn Battuta in 1333 described the city as in ruins. Although Timur chose to be crowned imperial ruler of Chaghatai here in 1370, Balkh's days of glory were over.

Compiled by **Shaikh al Islam Abu Bakr Abdullah al Waiz** in 1214, on the cusp of the carnage about to be inflicted by Genghis, *The Merits of Balkh* is the oldest surviving history of the city.

Part two
ON THE SPECIAL QUALITIES (*SHAMĀ'IL-HĀ*) [OF BALKH] THAT ARE PERCEPTIBLE TO THE SENSES

The Shaykh al-Islām Wāʿiẓ says that recollecting Balkh's blessings is obligatory for the people of Balkh. The blessings that are characteristic of this city are visible and clear, and it is not necessary to explain them at length. This is because there are two kinds of blessings: [P-23a] the religious and the worldly.

The first religious blessing that is characteristic of this city is that it was built in the time of Islam,[257] and that its people were firm and solid in [their belief in] Islam. It is for this reason that they called this place "the dome of Islam." Thus, it was said in the introduction to this book that the city of Balkh was in ruins until the eve of Islam and was rebuilt in the Islamic period in the time of Asad b. ʿAbd Allāh al-Qasrī. This means that most of the quarters had Arabic names.

The first house[258] and quarter coming from the Naw Bahār gate is the House of Ḥarb b. ʿIrwān al-Saʿīd,[259] after whom the Ḥarb Mosque is named. Today they call it the Spindlemakers' Quarter. The second quarter is the House of Muhallab b. Rāshid, which they call the Chequewriters' Quarter. The third is the House of Farāwaja. The fourth is the House of the Euphrates. The fifth is the House of Sugarmakers.[260] The sixth is the House of Muqātil b. Sulaymān, and today they call it the Nawand Quarter. The seventh is the House of ʿAbd al-ʿAzīz Maqbarī. The eighth is the House

---

[257] The author explicitly recognizes that there was a city at Balkh before Islam, but because it was in ruins he discounts it, and considers the Islamic era city to be a purely Muslim foundation.

[258] Here and elsewhere in this section, *dār* (q.v.) is used in the sense of a residence or mansion.

[259] It is not clear who Ḥarb b. ʿIrwān al-Saʿīd is. Ḥabībī offers no comment (al-Wāʿiẓ 1971: 43).

[260] Read *sukkarī*. On sugar-making in the medieval Islamic world, see Waines 1997.

of Muqātil Maqbarī. The ninth is the House of Muhallab,[261] the tenth the House of Abū Fāṭima,[262] and the eleventh the House of Ijtihād. All these [names] are proof that [the quarters] were built in the Islamic period.

The second blessing is that all the people [of Balkh] were Muslims, and it was devoid of people who came from other lands, such as Jews, Christians, Zoroastrians, *dhimmīs*, and so on.[263] There was no one from outside the community of the true [monotheistic] religion.[264] This good fortune and blessing sufficed [for this city], because no one in this place was an idolator or a polytheist.[265]

The third blessing is that other than the doctrine of the Sunnis, there was no bad doctrine or innovation.[266] Even though the people of Balkh were gentle, warm, generous, and patient, they were severe and uncompromising on matters of religious doctrine.

The fourth blessing is that on all occasions they maintained the proper reliance and trust in their Creator, and in all important matters they sought recourse in none other than God. They limited their freedom of choice and bridled their desires according to the decree of God. Therefore, the omnipotent God with His abundant grace took care of their important affairs.

The fifth blessing is their hospitality to and care for strangers, which has turned them into an example for all the corners of the world.

---

[261] This quarter is probably named after the famous al-Muhallab b. Abī Ṣufra (d. 82/702 or 83/703), since we have already learned that the second quarter was named after Muhallab b. Rāshid (q.v.), the only other Muhallab mentioned in the text.

[262] Perhaps Abū Fāṭima al-Azdī, an intimate supporter of the *murji'a* revolt under al-Ḥārith b. Surayj. Madelung 1988: 17.

[263] See "*dhimma*." This text differentiates Christians, Jews, and Zoroastrians from the *dhimmīs*, which suggests that the latter term may refer to Buddhists or followers of local cults.

[264] In this context, we have understood *millat-i ḥanafī* in the broad sense of the followers of right religion, but it could also be a more explicit reference to followers of the Ḥanafī *madhhab*, which was affirmedly strong in Balkh. This distinction might have been lost on our author and his readers.

[265] Read *mālik al-mulūk* (Persan-115); *mālik al-milk* (all other manuscripts). See "*butparast*" and "*shirk*".

[266] The phrasing is clumsy, but the author's intention is clear: there was only good Sunni doctrine in Balkh and no bad, heterodox doctrine.

The sixth blessing consists of their companionship, friendship, and charity for the poor and weak, their love of righteous people, the education of their ulama, and their praiseworthy manners and agreeable actions, which are [all] amongst their likeable features. Their nobles and common people, for the most part, were learned and strong in their religious beliefs. And they taught all things to the common people in Persian so that all could benefit from [Islamic] knowledge.

The seventh blessing is that they were humble, gentle, beneficent, and generous, and they never remained in the hands of an oppressor or tyrant [for long], because when they turned to the most exalted and almighty God, He took care of their important matters.

The eighth blessing is that they worked miracles[267] with their discourses and sweet allusions, and with their Arabic compositions, metaphors, subtleties, and intricacies. And they knew all the sciences well.

Another special aspect of this city is that it is more ancient than all the other cities, and its fame and renown has reached all corners and regions of the world. [Balkh] is famous in Turkistān and all the lands around it, and from India all the way to the very remotest lands. Even in Byzantium (Rūm) all of the history books of that land and the comings and goings of [their] merchants speak of [Balkh]. And the favour [bestowed upon Balkh by] Muslim kings and the legitimately designated caliphs needs no elaboration.

But in the non-Arab lands during pre-Islamic times, it was the sanctuary and temple of the Magians. It is attributed to Ibn Shawdhab that the devil has his home in Khurāsān, and they call it "the Naw Bahār of Balkh," and every year, he dons a white garb and makes a pilgrimage to that house. Previously[268] it was the sanctuary of the Magians and the temple of worship of the non-Arab lands. They also relate from Ibn Shawdhab that when the new solar year began, the great and noble ones of Ṭukhāristān,[269] India, and Turkistān and the lands of Iraq, Syria, and

---

[267] *Yad-i bayḍā* literally refers to the miracle of light that emanated from the hand of Moses.
[268] P has *az īn qabīl* ("of this ilk"), but all the other manuscripts have *az īn qabl*.
[269] Corrected from the nonsensical "Ṭakhīristān" (Persan-115).

Greater Syria would come to this city and celebrate for seven days at the Naw Bahār site.

When the time of the rule of the Prophet [Muḥammad] arrived, Balkh was conquered at the hands of Saʿīd b. ʿUthmān in the time of Muʿāwiya. It is attributed to Layth [b.] Saʿīd[270] that the conquest of Balkh occurred at the hands of Ḥajjāj b. Yūsuf[271] in the year 91/709–10, and that this is another reason for this city's fame.

Another point is that this city is located between two frontiers[272] and is their gatehouse. It is a major frontier and gateway: on one side, it is the frontier and gateway to India, and on the other side, it is the gateway to Turkistān. And there is a barrier between India and Balkh.[273] The land of the Turks consists of two great river valleys: those of the Jaxartes and the Oxus. Moreover, this city is such a meeting place for [different] peoples and a gathering-place for caravans that nobody can show its like in any other city, except in Mecca during the *hajj* pilgrimage season.

Furthermore, processions of caravans would arrive each year, one after the other, from India. Traders would bring fine aromatic roots and fragrances such as aloe wood, camphor, and the like; delicious sweet things, such as sugar and sugar-candy; a multitude of precious goods of unlimited value; pretty slave girls and white slave boys from Turkistān;[274] Tamghājī silver coins;[275] Farghāna silk; round precious stones; and many jewels that require no further explanation. Another point is that this land is full of resources. Near it are deposits of pure and fine silver and gold, some coming from the mountains and others from the rivers. The rubies of Badakhshān are on one side [of Balkh] and are world-famous. The mountains of Balkh have a limitless supply of copper, sulphur, lead, salt, and timber.

[270] See "al-Maqbarī."
[271] See "Ḥajjāj b. Yūsuf al-Thaqafī."
[272] *Thaghr*, gap; breach; opening; term used for points of entry between the *dār al-Islām* and the *dār al-ḥarb* beyond it.
[273] Possibly a reference to the Hindu Kush mountain range.
[274] On the countries of the Jaxartes "where the chief industry of the merchants was the slave trade," see Le Strange 1930: 487.
[275] Read *sawm-hā-yi tamghājī*. Tamghāj is a title used by the Qarākhānid rulers, and it refers to their claim to be rulers of China (Tu. Tabghach > Tamghāj). Fedorov 2003: 262.

Another point is that the prosperity of this city was such that God Almighty, without human intervention, enabled delightful and pleasant waters to flow smoothly in surface streams. In this it is unlike the cities of Khurāsān and other places where great industry and toil is expended on digging underground channels and building dams and dykes. In some places they labour hard to bring running water to the surface.[276] The water of this city flows out from sweet [freshwater] springs and pure stones and runs down to the desert lands of Balkh.

Furthermore, this water has all the elements considered essential by the sages. First, it has a strong current, its source is far away, and the pathway of the water runs through pure places. It is not contaminated by sulphur, alum, or salt, and it does not flow through putrid places.

Another proof of the purity of this soil is that it accepts any tree or plant that you plant, and they bear fruit quickly. For example, if you plant a branch or a cutting of an apple tree without any root, it will take and quickly grow strong. The soil only very rarely hosts venomous animals, such as the snakes and vipers of Egypt and Sīstān, the black scorpions of the cities of Nisībīs [Mesopotamia], the yellow scorpions of Ahwāz, or the mosquitoes of the riverbanks. Another special aspect of this city is the healthy air, which wards off leprosy and the plague.

Another feature is the magnitude of the city, the multitude of its people, and the extent of their beneficial interactions, good living, and comforts. These are all proof of the abundance of blessings and contentment of the people [of Balkh]. Moreover, the benefits derived from the multitude of flourishing villages, famous rivers, and abundant agricultural produce from Ṭukhāristān and the Bāmiyān Valley are innumerable. In most of [its villages[277]] there is a Friday mosque and a bazaar, as well as a *muftī*, a teacher, and a proper judge. And there are good fruits in every district of Balkh and throughout the surrounding area.

---

[276] The city was, and still is, watered by the Balkhāb River.
[277] Persan-115 reads *dar bīshtar-i qarā-yi way*. All other manuscripts read *dar dīh-hāyi* way.

This place [Balkh] is special also for its great, deep valley, known as the Oxus.[278] On one side [of the Balkh oasis] are high mountains that surround the city's margins and in whose environs there are many castles and forts. The city delights in the abundance of water, trees, beautifully decorated buildings[279], sown fields, and alluring greenery that brighten the eye. Whatever you see from top to bottom in the city is for the comfort and livelihood of the people. The kinds of merits that have been mentioned, as well as those found in these mountains, are watered without human intervention. Amongst the many mountain resources there are one hundred thousand trees bearing fruit and fragrant plants which smell like a perfume store. On the other side [of the Balkh oasis] there are boats plying the Oxus, loaded with countless goods. People at all levels of society – whether soldiers or craftspeople or others – lived their lives without hardship. The kings ensured that salary payments were made in full every year to the garrison that defended the frontier, and they never subjected anyone to tyranny or oppression. The farmers of this province made large returns and sold at good prices to the boat people. The craftspeople made good earnings because of the multitude of people, all depending on one another. Furthermore, merchants would come from all directions and bring many goods, and there was a lot of buying and selling, and they made large profits.

All the people were busy with construction, and they raised tall and strong buildings, such as mosques, madrasas, hospices, and so on. The people who had expertise in the field [of construction] reaped exceptionally high profits. The poor who lacked in disposition, skill, or ability worked as water carriers or wood carriers and subsisted in that way. And the poor and destitute were never neglected and they never suffered from hunger, because the people of this city were known to be charitable and to give alms.

---

[278] The term *wādī* here refers to the entire Balkh oasis and plain.

[279] The reference to beautifully decorated buildings seems out of place in this passage, and the Persian is sufficiently vague that it is possible this phrase refers to something more in keeping with the context – the pleasing layout of the water-courses, fields and gardens, perhaps.

And if the people of this city faced a threat, they sought refuge in [one of] three places. If the threat was military, the people gathered in the mountains, and the army of the city defended it from the Oxus side. And if, *God forbid*, famine struck, large provisions of goods would be brought from Ṭukhāristān, Kūhistān, and Transoxania. And if the city's air deteriorated, and became putrid, the people would go to the towns and villages that had cool breezes.

Moreover, all the kings and sultans of pre-Islamic and Islamic times resided here and made [Balkh] the seat of their government. The inhabitants of this city were all able-bodied, eloquent, generous, liberal, clever, learned, and courageous. They were loved by the ulama, the legal scholars, the shaykhs, and the great people.[280] Their [character] was a compound of focus of mind, sharpness, ingenuity in all occupations, good nature, and rapid penetration of obscure discourse.

The famous kings called this place "the blessed city".[281] In times of trouble, *God forbid*, the evil was warded off by the blessings emanating from the spirits of the pure [people] who are buried in this holy ground. Then, in the time of Nīzak Ṭarkhān, *the almighty and blessed God* gave strength to the Muslims so that [Nīzak] was killed at the hands of Qutayba.[282]

Then [there was] Ṭalḥa's[283] injustice and sudden death, and the arrival of Yaʿqūb Layth,[284] ʿAmr Layth,[285] and other unjust people who intended to [attack the city]. *The almighty and blessed God* destroyed them in the shortest time. And most people have come to the opinion that there is a reason these attacks were repelled and the evildoers broken. Some suggest that the city was charmed. I[286] have been watching since 570/1174–75, and in [the past] forty years, more than twenty rulers of

---

[280] Read *mashāyikh wa kubarā*.
[281] *Kawra*, var. *kūra*, city; *kawra* was one of the ancient divisions of the Sasanian lands.
[282] See "Qutayba b. Muslim."
[283] See "Ṭalḥa b. Ṭāhir."
[284] This is Yaʿqūb b. al-Layth al-Ṣaffār. See "Ṣaffārids."
[285] This is ʿAmr b. al-Layth al-Ṣaffār. See "Ṣaffārids."

this city have perished on account of [their] tyranny and corruption. Shaykh al-Islām Wāʿiẓ says, "Since 570/1174–75, I have observed and counted more than twenty-six rulers of this city. In the course of these forty years I have seen repentant, righteous, oppressive, and wicked kings and princes: all of them perished. The tyrants and the oppressors, the minions and the tax collectors – God Almighty extirpated them all."

Shaykh al-Islām [al-Wāʿiẓ] says, "I heard from trustworty informants that in recent times there was a tyrant named S.(t).ūd B.k,[287] who besieged the city. He pitched camp at the city's gate with a large army near the place of prayer. He stuck a spear in the ground and said: 'I call on the people of this city to give me riches that reach up to the [tip of this spear] so that I give protection to their households, women, and children.' The people of the city were powerless. The next day, that tyrant headed for the city. When the people of the city saw what was happening, they all appealed to *the almighty God* and recited: **Thee do we worship, and Thine aid do we seek.**[288] All cried out at the same time. When the tyrant arrived at the city gate, he was seized by colic and expired instantly."

Moreover, the number of ulama and legal scholars in Balkh is high, the taxes are low,[289] and oppressors are removed. The city is situated in a spot that has a pleasant climate and where cool winds blow from the North, and from the other direction, the mountains of Transoxania,

---

[286] The authorial "I" here is presumably al-Wāʿiẓ al-Balkhī, the Arabic author, looking back from 610/1214, the year of the composition of the Arabic text, forty years later.

[287] Ḥabībī (al-Wāʿiẓ 1971: 53, n. 6) offers "Sūd Bek/Buk." The Turkish "tigin" is a princely title, and the text may be referring to his name only. The author's reference to "recent times" does not speak in favour of this theory, but it is difficult to assess what qualifies as "recent."

[288] Read *iyyāka na 'budu wa-iyyāka nastaʿīn*. Q: 1: V.

[289] See "*kharāj*."

[290] *Mushk*, Ar. *misk*, the gland secretion of the male musk deer. Al-Masʿūdī and other authors after him report that the "musk gazelle" lives in a region extending from Tibet to China, but that Tibetan musk is of a higher quality. As an ingredient of perfumes, musk was a highly prized commodity in the medieval period, and was traded to the Islamic world along routes through the Pamirs and Badakhshān, passing through Balkh and other cities.

comes a gentle breeze that has a lovely smell of musk pods,[290] the aroma of which touches the soul of the inhabitants of this place. The city had four gates, and as you entered through each gate there was a bazaar with a variety of goods, and all of the quarters had access to a bazaar.[291]

Anyone who wants to study fully the merits, excellences, heritage, and great people of this city should turn to the book *Manāqib-i Balkh*,[292] which Malik al-Islām Abū Zayd [al-] Balkhī collected and compiled.[293] One of the most trustworthy learned men and greatest ulama has said that there is no other compilation or book composition that exhibits such soundness of division, such excellent organization, such precise information, and such complete explanations.

The story is long. There is no end in sight to the merits of the city of Balkh[294] and the excellent qualities of its people. *May God make us grateful for His blessings, and may we articulate our gratitude and be patient in our trials and tribulations. May He also make us content with our fate. God is most forgiving and most compassionate.*

Shaykh al-Islām Ṣafī al-Dīn [Wāʿiẓ] says: "The shaykh of all shaykhs Yaḥyā b. Muʿādh Rāzī[295] composed the following poem in honour of Balkh and its people:

> We departed early in the morning from the people of Balkh,
>> Upon Balkh, and upon those in it, let there be peace!
> We stayed for some time in Balkh in luxurious pleasure,[296]
>> For they are generous people.
> If ever you want to stay with people,
>> Then in Balkh you will have a pleasant stay.

---

[291] This indicates that the four gates still stood at the time of writing.
[292] i.e. "The virtues of Balkh."
[293] See "Abū Zayd Aḥmad b. Sahl al-Balkhī."
[294] Read *turbat-i Balkh*, lit. "shrine of Balkh." The implication is that Balkh is a sanctuary of the saints and is, therefore, a place of worship and pilgrimage.
[295] See "Yaḥyā b. Muʿādh al-Rāzī."
[296] *Fī al-surūri* is a mistake for *fī surūrin*, correct in al-Thaʿālibī's *Laṭāʾif al-maʿārif*.

THE HIDDEN WAR
A RUSSIAN JOURNALIST'S ACCOUNT OF THE SOVIET WAR IN AFGHANISTAN

Artyom Borovik

In 1979, it was the Russians' turn to invade Afghanistan. For a decade the mighty Soviet Union tried to preach the Communist gospel with its arsenal of puppet politicians, tanks, bombers, helicopter gunships and hundreds of thousands of fresh-faced, ever-hungry, habitually abused conscripts. It found few adherents among the Afghans, whose *mujahideen* fighters, supported by the West, mounted an extraordinarily fierce and ultimately successful resistance. By 1989 they had forced the exhausted Russians to the exit in an undignified end to another foreign invasion.

Artyom Borovik (1960–2000), a pioneer of Russian investigative journalism, was an eyewitness to the Soviet occupation, joining Russian forces there in 1988 and winning a medal for 'valour in battle'. Published in 1989, *The Hidden War* has been likened to Michael Herr's seminal *Dispatches*, a darkly gripping and unflinching account of 'Russia's Vietnam'.

Two days later the battalion was up at dawn.
Our armored carriers lined up along the road as the last of the darkness was melting away.

Ushakov came out onto the road and looked the battalion over. Eleven vehicles – almost a whole company – were missing. Six had left earlier with the commander of the regiment. The rest he'd passed on to the greens.

A red flag flapped on the antenna of the second armored carrier from Mokasiy's company. It resembled the wing of a *podranok* [a Russian bird].

"Stick the flag up your butt, soldier!" Ushakov shouted angrily. "This isn't a parade. Better take all the rubbish off the car. If something happens, you won't be able to turn your gun."

The soldier wanted to answer, but the commander of the company quickly warned him to keep his mouth shut.

A political deputy from another battalion attempted to intervene. "I'm counting this as—" he began, but Ushakov abruptly interrupted him.

"Why don't you count to a hundred," Ushakov said. "I'm going to act the way I see fit."

The company commander backed Ushakov up. "Instead of the flag, we'll stick the political deputy's head on the car with bows in his hair," he said. "The journalists in Termez will piss in their pants."

Klimov's mortar battery had gotten held up on its way out of the post; a broken-down armored carrier blocked the exit. Adliukov had been unsuccessfully poking around in the engine for two hours.

Ushakov ran around the paralyzed vehicle, muttering and cursing as he went. "Stupid pups. You wouldn't listen to the battalion commander, who's been around. Didn't I tell you to check the cars the night before?"

But the armored carrier couldn't be started. So they dumped two buckets of diesel fuel on it and used a rocket gun to set it on fire. A single flare went up in the air with a blaze.

The metal joints of the battalion cracked in unison, and it slowly started to climb up the mountain.

The engines roared madly and filled the air with exhaust fumes. Then the treads began to turn, tossing back dirty wads of snow with each forward lunge.

Soon the column disappeared behind a mountain. Two kilometers below, the Second Airborne Battalion was climbing toward the Salang Tunnel.

The third platoon was accompanied by APC #427. A bunch of soldiers were huddled together, clinging to its tower. Andrei Lanshenkov, Sergei Protapenko, and Igor Liakhovich sat in the back. They all wore bulletproof jackets.

That evening, a little after seven o'clock, the battalion stopped at the Forty-second Post, near the *kishlak* of Kalatak. This was the place where

Major Urasov had died, and where he had been so harshly avenged by Colonel Antonenko.

The black of the night spread through the sky like ink on a blotter.

The commander of the battalion ordered the marking lights of all the cars to be turned off.

"Another twenty-four hours and we'll be at the border," Liakhovich said. "It's hard to believe."

"If the troops don't get jammed up at the pass," Lanshenkov replied, "we will."

"God willing," Protapenko added.

Liakhovich had served in the sapper company, where he'd been nicknamed "Sapper." He was later transferred to Senior Lieutenant Ovchinikova's special intelligence platoon, but the nickname stuck with him.

Sapper had arrived at the Fortieth Post in December of the past year. His job was to sweep for mines, thus ensuring that blockades could be set up safely.

During the entire year the platoon hadn't suffered any casualties.

It was getting colder by the minute. The driver started the engine, and soon the soldiers were inhaling hot exhaust.

In a few minutes the entire battalion was roaring, but no one moved.

The technical deputy's Ural refused to start. He opened the hood and checked the starter.

Major Dubovsky came up to APC #427 and grabbed a crescent wrench, but the driver needed a tetrahedral wrench.

"I need a number seventeen," the driver said.

Suddenly a GAZIK pulled up to the Ural. The commander of the division stuck his head out the window.

"Hey, you son of an inferior nation," he shouted through a loudspeaker. "What are you doing? Don't switch the gears. Start the car up and let's go."

The driver probably didn't understand him. He didn't respond and continued fussing with the engine. The GAZIK sped away.

At regular intervals a compressor kicked air into the tires of the armored carrier.

The commander of the company and the major returned with the right wrench and gave it to the driver. Then they climbed back into the APC to get warm. One by one, eight lights appeared inside. The soldiers were smoking, warming their bluish lips and fingers with cigarette smoke.

"Nice," Sapper said to Lanshenkov as he took a deep puff.

He was going to say something else, but suddenly a spray of submachine-gun fire cut across the road. The red dotted lines of tracers pierced the darkness.

The shots came from the post, which had just been handed over to the greens.

The armored carrier up ahead fired a warning round into the sky. The rest were silent. Apparently the commander of the battalion had decided not to get involved in the shooting.

Lanshenkov heard Sapper wheezing something into his ear. Turning toward him, he saw Sapper helplessly sucking air into his mouth.

"What?" Lanshenkov asked. "What?"

Sapper remained sitting in the same position. Then his head fell back; he was looking at the sky.

"Sapper!" Lanshenkov shouted. "What's wrong?"

Sapper didn't answer.

The company commander ran up to the APC. Shaking Sapper on the shoulder, he yelled to the driver: "Turn your lights on! Where did he get hit?"

Sapper was carefully lowered from the vehicle and placed on the ground, where he was enveloped in a yellow circle of electric light. A little red stream of blood trickled its way over the ice toward the curb.

"A neck wound," the company commander said, getting up from his knees. "The bullet went right through and came out the back of his head. Damn it!"

An ensign squatted next to Sapper, feeling his left wrist.

"He still has a pulse," he said.

Two soldiers cut off the sleeve of Sapper's *bushlat*. The medical supervisor injected Promedol into his gray arm, which was already growing cold. He made a tourniquet, waited for the vein to swell, and inserted an IV.

"There it goes," Lanshenkov said.

The company commander radioed the battalion commander and yelled into the mike: "I've got a three hundred or a twenty-one. Do you read me?"

"Take him to the Forty-sixth," came the reply.

There was a first-aid station at the post.

Sapper was put on the APC. The driver started the vehicle. With a sudden jerk, it began to move up the mountain.

"Put in a second IV!" the company commander shouted.

The medical supervisor put it in, but the liquid wouldn't flow. It was frozen.

"Fuck!" the company commander cursed. He took someone's *bushlat* and used it to cover Sapper, who was lying on the silvery surface of the APC's sharklike snout, looking up at the stars.

The crescent moon resembled a lifeboat in the sky.

"Fuck!" the company commander cursed again. A grimace twisted his face.

We reached the Forty-sixth Post. Sapper was wrapped in a blanket and carried to the doctor. The doctor fussed over him for about five minutes, listening to his pulse and examining his wound.

Finally the doctor opened the door and came outside. "That's it," he said. "The bullet went through his vertebrae. There's damage to the base of the skull, a hemorrhage of the brain. That's it."

They carried Sapper into the fresh air and put him back on the APC.

The moonlit sky illuminated Sapper's face.

His skin had come to look like waxed paper. Blood still streamed from his nose and ears. The reflection of the night sky was in his eyes, just as it had been twenty minutes ago.

"Shut his eyes and cover his face," somebody said.

Sapper's body was wrapped in a blanket and placed on the stretcher.

Five minutes later the blanket was covered with snow.

The soldiers gathered around the APC.

In the eyes of one was the question "Sapper, why you?"

In the eyes of another, "Good-bye."

In the eyes of a third, "Better you than me."

In the eyes of a fourth, "If I'm not lucky, we'll meet soon."

In the eyes of a fifth, "Fuck!"

In the eyes of the company commander, tears.

Not a single one of them wished to become the *last Soviet soldier to be killed in Afghanistan.*

So Sapper had taken it upon himself, saving the several thousand Soviet soldiers who still remained.

He'd also put the period at the end of the war.

BOYS IN ZINC

Svetlana Alexievich

It sounds like a zingy title for a book. *Boys in Zinc*. In fact it is anything but. While the Soviet government pumped out the sort of war propaganda – or bilge – that American and British political and military leaders would unwittingly echo from 2001, thousands of dead Russian soldiers were being sent back to the Motherland in zinc coffins whose seals were unable to prevent the stink of decomposing human flesh, 'a bit rank, like wild sheep'. In **Svetlana Alexievich** (1948–), an uncompromising Belarusian writer and investigative journalist, the Soviet invasion of Afghanistan found its perfect chronicler. *Boys in Zinc* is a brilliant and brutal oral history of the war through the voices of those most directly affected, from privates on the front line to press officers, doctors, nurses, wives, brothers and sisters and mothers. Alexievich pulls no punches. A nurse sees 'a roasted man... something shrivelled up, covered in a yellow crust. No screaming, just a growling from under the crust.' This is reportage that hits you in the face, punch after punch of unimaginable pain and horror, shame and outrage.

First published in 1991, as the Soviet Union was imploding, *Boys in Zinc* caused a sensation. After receiving death threats, Alexievich was forced into hiding. In 2015 she was awarded the Nobel Prize in Literature 'for her polyphonic writings, a monument to suffering and courage in her time'.

I'm afraid to start telling you about it. Those shadows will pounce on me again...

Every day... Every day out there I used to tell myself: 'I'm a fool, a fool. Why did I do it?' Especially at night I used to get thoughts like that, when I wasn't working. But during the day they were different: how can I help everyone? The wounds are terrible... I was staggered: what were bullets like this for? Who invented them? Could a human being really have invented them? The entry hole is small, but inside... the intestines, the liver, the spleen – it's all chopped up and ripped apart. It's not enough to kill and injure, they have to make a man suffer all that torment. They always called out 'Mama!' when it hurt. That was the only word I heard...

I wanted to get away from Leningrad, maybe just for a year or two, but get away. My child died, then my husband died. There was nothing to keep me in that city. On the contrary, everything reminded me, it was driving me away. This is the place where I met him for the first time... This is the place where we kissed for the first time... I had my baby in this maternity home...

The chief physician summoned me. 'Will you go to Afghanistan?'

'Yes, I'll go.' I needed to see that others were worse off than me. And I saw it.

The war, we were told, was a just one. We were helping the Afghan people put an end to feudalism and build a bright socialist society. The fact that our boys were being killed was glossed over somehow. What we understood was that there were a lot of infectious diseases: malaria, typhoid fever, hepatitis. 1980... The beginning... We flew to Kabul. The old English stables had been allocated for the hospital. There was nothing. One syringe for everyone... The officers drank the medical spirit and we had to treat the wounds with petrol. The wounds healed poorly. But the sun helped. Bright sunlight kills microbes. I saw my first wounded men in underwear and boots. Without pyjamas. It was quite a while before pyjamas appeared. Or slippers. Or blankets. One boy... I remember that boy: his body bent in all directions, as if there were no bones. His legs were floppy, like string. They took about twenty pieces of shrapnel out of him.

All through March we dumped the amputated arms and legs right there, beside the wards. The dead bodies... they lay in a separate ward. Half-naked with their eyes gouged out; one with a star carved into the stomach. I'd seen things like that before in films about the Civil War. There weren't any zinc coffins yet; they still hadn't laid in any stocks of them.

Soon we started thinking a little bit, wondering who we were. The command wasn't pleased by our doubts. There still weren't any slippers or pyjamas, but they were already hanging up the slogans, calls to action and posters that had been brought in. And against the background of those slogans – the thin, sad faces of our boys. They stuck in my mind forever. Twice a week there was political instruction. All the time they taught us: 'It's a sacred duty, the border must be locked down.' The most unpleasant thing in the army is informing on people, the order to inform about every tiny little thing. To rat on every wounded man, every patient. It was called 'knowing the mood'. The army had to be healthy. It was required to rat on everybody: you mustn't pity them. But we did pity them. Pity was what held everything together…

We went there to save, to help, to love. That's what we went for… After some time went by, I caught myself thinking that I hated everything. I hated this soft, light sand that burned like fire. I hated these mountains. I hated these stunted *kishlaks*, from which they can shoot at any moment. I hated the occasional Afghan, carrying a basket of melons or standing beside his house. Who could tell where he had been last night and what he was doing? They killed an officer I knew, who had been treated in the hospital recently. They slaughtered two wards of soldiers. In another place the water was poisoned. Someone picked up a beautiful cigarette lighter and it exploded in his hand. These were our boys who were being killed. Our own boys. You have to understand that… Have you ever seen a roasted man? You haven't. No face, no eyes, no body. Something shrivelled up, covered in a yellow crust. No screaming, just a growling from under the crust.

Hate helped people to live out there. They survived by hating. And a sense of guilt? That didn't appear there, but here, after I looked at things from the outside. There it had all seemed like justice. Here I was horrified to remember a little girl lying in the dust with no arms and no legs. Like a broken doll. After our bombardment… And we were astonished that they didn't like us. They were treated in our hospital: when I gave a woman medicine she didn't look up at me, she never smiled. It was actually insulting. I felt insulted there, but not here. Here

I'm a normal human being and all my feelings have come back to me.

I have a good profession – saving people – and it saved me too. I can try to make excuses: we were needed there. We didn't save everyone we could have saved – that's the most terrible thing. I could have saved someone, but we didn't have the right medicine. I could have saved someone, but he was brought in too late. (Who were in the combat medical squads? Poorly trained soldiers, who had only learned how to apply bandages.) I could have saved someone, but I couldn't wake up the drunken surgeon. I could have saved someone… We couldn't even write the truth in the death notifications. They were blown up by mines. Often all that was left of a man was half a bucket of flesh… And we wrote: 'Killed in a road accident', 'Fell over a cliff', 'Food poisoning'. When there were already thousands of them, then we were allowed to tell the relatives the truth. I got used to dead bodies. But the fact that they were so young, so endearing, like little children – it was impossible to come to terms with that.

They brought in a wounded man. I happened to be on duty. He opened his eyes and looked at me.

'That's it then,' he said. And he died.

They searched for a man for three days in the mountains. They found him. They brought him in. He was raving: 'Doctor! Doctor!' He saw a white coat and thought: 'I'm saved!' But his injury was fatal. It was only there that I learned what it means to be wounded in the cranium… I have my own graveyard in my head, my own portrait gallery. With black frames.

Even in death they weren't equal. For some reason the ones who were killed in action were pitied more. The ones who died later in hospital were pitied less. Sometimes they screamed out as they died… They screamed so terribly! I remember a major who died in intensive care. His wife had come to see him. He died in front of her eyes. And she started screaming. Like an animal. I wanted to close all the doors, so that no one would hear. Because soldiers were dying nearby. Boys. And there was no one to weep for them. They were dying alone. She was out of place among us…

'Mama! Mama!'

'I'm here, son,' I used to say, deceiving them.

We became their mothers and sisters. And we always wanted to justify that trust.

The soldiers would bring in a wounded man, hand him over and not leave. 'Girls, we don't want anything. Can we just sit with you for a while?'

But here, at home… They have their own mothers, sisters and wives. They don't need us here. Out there they trusted us with things about themselves that they wouldn't tell anyone in this life. Those conditions put a man under a spotlight. If he was a coward it soon became clear that he was a coward. If he was an informer then it was immediately obvious that he was an informer. If he was a womanizer then everyone knew he was a womanizer. I'm not sure anyone would admit it here, but there I heard more than one man say that you could get to like killing, that killing was a pleasure. It's a powerful feeling. A warrant officer I knew who was going back to the Soviet Union didn't even try to conceal it: 'How am I going to live now, when I've got the urge to kill?' It's probably another kind of passion: they used to talk about it quite openly. The boys used to tell us with real enthusiasm about how they burned a *kishlak* and flattened everything. They must be insane, surely? How many of them have come back like that… Killing a man means nothing to them… Once we were visited by a major; he had come from somewhere near Kandahar. In the evening we had to say goodbye to him, and he locked himself in an empty room and shot himself. They say that he was drunk, I don't know. It's hard. It was hard to live through a single day there. A boy on sentry duty shot himself after three hours in the sun. A home-loving boy, he couldn't bear it. There were a lot who were insane. At first they used to lie in the general wards, then they were accommodated separately. They started trying to escape: they were frightened by the barred windows. They felt better together with all the others. I remember one especially.

'Sit down. I'll sing you a discharge song.' He sang and sang until he fell asleep.

When he woke up, he used to call out: 'Home! Home! To mama. It's too hot for me here…' He was always asking to go home.

Lots of them smoked. Hashish, marijuana, whatever they could get hold of. They explained to me that it makes you strong, free from everything. In the first place, from your body. As if you're walking on tiptoe. You feel a lightness in every cell. You can feel every muscle. You want to fly! It's as if you are flying! An irrepressible joy. Everything pleases you: you laugh at the merest trifle. You hear better. You see better. You can distinguish more smells, more sounds. In that state it's easier to kill – you're anaesthetized. There's no pity. It's easy to die – the fear goes away. You feel as if you're wearing a bulletproof vest, you're armoured. I could understand what they said. Twice I… I smoked it myself twice. In both cases when I couldn't take any more, psychologically or physically. I was working in the infectious diseases ward. There were supposed to be thirty beds, but there were three hundred men lying there. Typhoid fever, malaria. They were issued sheets and a blanket, and they lay on their own greatcoats, on the bare ground. In their underpants, with their heads shaved. And the lice poured down off them… Body lice… Head lice… I'd never even imagined so many lice… And in the *kishlak* nearby the Afghans strolled about in our hospital pyjamas, with our sheets on their heads instead of turbans. I don't blame them for it. No… Most of the time I don't blame them. Our boys died for three roubles a month – our soldiers received eight hard currency checks a month. Three roubles… They were fed maggoty meat and fish that had turned rusty-looking. All of us had scurvy and all my front teeth fell out. They used to sell blankets and buy hash. Or something sweet. Trinkets… There were such bright little shops there, and so many attractive things in those shops. Back home in the Union there wasn't any of that, they'd never seen it before. And they used to sell guns and cartridges, only to be killed by those same automatic rifles and cartridges. They bought chocolate with them… Pies…

After everything out there I saw my country with different eyes. My pupils even changed: they got wider. It was frightening to come back here. Strange, somehow. As if all my skin had been ripped off. I kept crying all the time. I couldn't bear to see anyone except people who had been there. I could have spent all day and all night with them. Other people's conversations seemed like some kind of idle nonsense, silly nonsense. It went on like that for six months. But now I swear myself when I'm standing in the queue for meat. I try to live a normal life, the way I did 'before'. But I can't do it. I've become indifferent to myself and my own life. Life's over, there's not going to be any more. And for men the experience is even more agonizing. A woman can cling onto her children, but men have nothing to cling onto. They come back, fall in love and have children, but even so Afghanistan comes before everything else. I myself would like to figure out why it's like that. What was it all for? Why does it affect me so much? Back there everything was driven inside, and now it has come creeping out here.

They should be pitied. All of them who were there should be pitied. I'm a grown adult – I was thirty then – and look how it shattered me. But they were little children; they didn't understand anything. They were taken out of their homes and guns were put in their hands. They were told: 'You're going on a sacred mission. The Homeland won't forget you.' Now people turn their eyes away from them and try to forget the war. It's over! And the first ones to do that are the ones who sent us there. Even we talk about the war less and less often when we meet. Nobody loves that war. Although to this day I still cry when they play the Afghan national anthem. I learned to love all Afghan music. It's like a narcotic.

Not long ago I met a soldier in a bus. He was one of our patients. He'd lost his right arm. I remembered him well, another Leningrader.

'Perhaps I could help you in some way, Seryozha?'

But he just replied angrily: 'You go to hell!'

I know he'll find me and ask me to forgive him. But who will ask him to forgive them? And ask everyone who was there, everyone who was broken and mutilated, to forgive them? I'm not talking just about the cripples. What kind of loathing for your own people does it take to send them to something like that! It's not just every war that I hate now, I even hate little boys' fights. And don't tell me that the war is over. A hot, dusty breath of summer wind, a bright glint on a circle of stagnant water, the acrid odour of dry flowers... It's like a blow to the temple.

It will pursue us all our lives.

A nurse

AN UNEXPECTED LIGHT
TRAVELS IN AFGHANISTAN
Jason Elliot

> Published on the cusp of 9/11, as the Taliban closed in on Kabul and Afghanistan started its slow slide into two ruinous decades of war, *An Unexpected Light* was a stunning debut by the English writer **Jason Elliot** (1965–) and a tour de force of travel writing. Winner of the 2000 Thomas Cook Travel Book Award, it interweaves two separate visits to Afghanistan, the first as an impressionable young guest of the *mujahideen* during the Soviet occupation, the second, a decade later, as the more mature observer of the Taliban's tightening grip across the country.

Shortly before I left, I was invited with half a dozen friends, together with two visiting European journalists, to an informal dinner with some government officials. Our defence ministry liaison, Amrullah, was there, Hāroun and his wife and brother, and three of Massoud's closest advisers.

We did not mistake our hosts for saints; by means of such events they kept themselves abreast of their guests' opinions, and found generally sympathetic ears for their own; but they were courteous to a fault and it was hard not to be touched by the fact that they had taken time off from running their government, and a war, to treat us to a generous meal.

While the various guests were arriving, a printed document in English on a table caught my eye. It was the report of a foreign development agency which had recently made a two-week visit to the country 'to assess Afghanistan's current and projected aid needs and priorities in the light of predicted future political and security scenarios and recommend a forward strategy...'

The words swam in front of my eyes. 'The review methodology adopted a common framework of explicit assessment criteria and semi-structured interviews with key informants ...' I wondered if the Afghan sitting next to me knew that his country displayed 'relative social mobility, extreme political fluidity, and organisational diversity that characterise both the micro- and macro-levels', and felt a pang of sympathy for the men endeavouring to rebuild their government.

The conversation was friendly. But there was a note of frustration when it came to the recent news of America's 'covert' intention to destabilise the regime in neighbouring Iran. America: it was an old and tender theme. Afghans still felt abandoned by their former ally, whom they had supposed would return after the defeat of the Soviets and help rebuild their ruined country. News that Washington had now agreed to sponsor the undermining of a neighbouring government came as a kind of cynical confirmation.

'We see the American logic,' said a thoughtful voice, 'and we see the logic of Iran. We don't support either. But the American action is deeply offensive. It's as if we told the Americans how to live!'

The assembled men were not politically naive but the old vision of America as a benevolent and freedom-loving nation was dying a stubborn death in Afghanistan. Behind this disbelieving tone was, in part, a feeling of having been shunned in their hour of need. Even the government's former adversaries in Russia and Iran had agreed to recognise and support the effort from Kabul to resist the Taliban's advance. But the Americans had held back, and their reluctance to recognise the government officially was a source of bitter disappointment. Washington had also refrained from expressing disapproval of the Taliban; an American congressman had even spoken up publicly strongly in their favour, suggesting they were the sole candidates for leadership of the country.

'Positive support by America could have been so good for regional security,' said someone else. 'It needn't have come to this.'

The note of the conversation was not so much hostile as sad. After the meal we sat around the fire; occasionally the windows would rattle as the thump of artillery sounded from far away. We sipped tea. It was a difficult evening if your favourite topics weren't religion or politics.

For a few minutes I talked privately with one of Massoud's closest advisers. He spoke fluent and thoughtful English. Sometimes his walkie-talkie would crackle into life and he would issue a few instructions and return it to the table in front of us.

He had come recently from a meeting with state department officials in the north of the country, to discuss terms by which the Americans would agree to recognise the government officially. The results had been deeply disappointing, the terms impossible to meet. One was the return of the former king, Zaher Shah, from his thirty-year exile in Italy. It had worked in Cambodia, the Americans said, and it could work in Afghanistan.

He gave an exasperated sigh, as if nothing could be less relevant to the country: what had the king done for them in the last thirty years?

Was he still hoping it was possible, I asked, to build the necessary bridges, in spite of everything?

'Yes,' he said, 'we deal with realities. We want to be a part of the world. But we don't know what we've done to deserve this. If it's for some reason we don't know, we want to look at that. But if it's because we're too independent for them – well, we're proud of that.'

Then half to himself, he said:

'Why have we had to go through this, I wonder? Sometimes I even wish that the Taliban could take over the whole of Afghanistan – just for a day – to show the Americans how bad it could get.'

It was already bad. I could think of only one positive aspect to things. All the failed efforts of Afghanistan's would-be rulers – of which the Taliban appeared to be the crowning proof – were evidence that the country was beyond the domination of a single authority. There would, eventually, be compromise. The conflict could no longer be restricted to a local affair, but was part of a violent synthesis in which a greater than ever portion of humanity was implicated. At such moments it seemed just possible that the catastrophes of recent years were the result of something even more implacable than war itself – an organic, supracultural, and ultimately unitive force; not slouching, as in the poem, towards its Bethlehem, but stampeding like an elephant through a jungle, uprooting obstacles violently and drawing together in its wake new strands of culture like stitches over a wound: perhaps, after all, the country was not dying, but healing.

*

Often during those final days, as things turned ever worse from the visible point of view, I was prone to spontaneous moments of burgeoning joy. Even the sight of the crippled and wounded, or news of some particularly tragic event, no longer had the power to bring down that oppressive mantle of grief under which I'd earlier taken shelter. The opposite, in fact: terrible as such things were, they had the capacity to uplift. Something had changed.

For much of the journey I had found myself looking towards positive moments to redeem the difficult ones, and struggled with consolatory explanations for painful events. But the one was a troublesome see-saw of feeling, and the other self-defeating. I had noticed this tendency from the very outset of the journey: this instinctive longing to shunt painful experience towards some form of expression, to clothe it quickly with some kind of action in the feelings or intellect. I had earlier set myself a personal challenge: was it possible to enlarge the space in oneself where the raw material of experience might sit awhile, before being decanted in the usual way? To fashion some intermediary vessel in which to bear the raw impressions of life, like freshly pressed grapes with all their husks and ugly stalks? I was not sure what the outcome might be; a sort of stretching, a deepening of one's ability to stand up to life and absorb it as it happens.

But I now found out that the change had begun to happen of its own accord. Contradictory moments, and the extremes of feeling they evoked, had grown less antithetical, and the distance between them was mysteriously reduced. Now the poles from which they sprang were no longer irreconcilable, but intertwined like the serpents of a caduceus. Something had definitely changed; I was infected not with the sense of despair I'd so often felt at the beginning of the journey, but with a strange hopefulness.

*

The following day I checked the flight list, and found my name on it. The Red Cross bus was leaving for the airport the next afternoon. I stripped down my belongings, made gifts of my warm clothes, and hurriedly bought some small presents with my remaining cash. The world was deflating with horrible swiftness and I wanted to get away as quickly as possible.

The wily Sultan caught me at the door as I left.

'I have left you something inside,' I said.

His eyes narrowed. 'Dollars or pounds?'

*

I watched the mountains sink back into the land as we flew southeast. Half an hour later the little plane had broken from the embrace of light, and began descending.

In the morning I woke up in a capacious bedroom between crisp sheets, uncertain whether I'd dreamed what had gone before or whether I had awoken into a dream. I was in Pakistan. The Red Cross fleet mechanic, a kind-hearted Frenchman, had put me up for the night at his home. I had a vague memory of dinner the previous evening at the American club and, among the foreign guests, a vision of pale faces as sad as those of old men lingering outside betting offices.

Outside it was sunny and humid; the air smelled of exotic plants and dust and diesel fumes: Peshawar again. The sky was heavy and hazy and for the first time since the beginning of the journey, it was warm. I slung my coat over my shoulder and walked for a while alongside the railway tracks, where more than a decade before I had met my first Afghan refugees, and trespassed with such longing on their world.

It felt like spring. Beyond the tracks spread some scattered houses among fields where the vegetation was lush and green and a man was leading a sleek calf along a path. Someone was watering bright bougainvillea in his garden and the water sparkled as it fountained into the dust.

A few colourfully dressed children were playing nearby. It was utterly peaceful. I felt a kind of welling up and, a little further on, sat down by the tracks, and began to weep.

THE PLACES IN BETWEEN

Rory Stewart

Like so many of the writers represented in this book, **Rory Stewart** (1973–) is a man of many parts. Soldier, travel writer, explorer, politician and academic, this restless and talented character first came to the public's eye in 2004 with the publication of his first book, *The Places in Between*, the story of a courageous journey on foot across Afghanistan from Herat to Kabul. Shot at by humans, attacked by wolves, Stewart depended for company on his toothless mastiff, the improbably named Babur – how the Muslim founder of the Mughal Empire would react to sharing his name with a dog is a moot point. *The Places In Between* won the Royal Society of Literature's Ondaatje Prize in 2005, has been translated into nine languages and launched Stewart's career with impressive fanfare.

The New Civil Service

I watched two men enter the lobby of the Hotel Mowafaq.

Most Afghans seemed to glide up the centre of the lobby staircase with their shawls trailing behind them like Venetian cloaks. But these men wore western jackets, walked quietly and stayed close to the banister. I felt a hand on my shoulder. It was the hotel manager.

'Follow them.' He had never spoken to me before.

'I'm sorry, no,' I said. 'I am busy.'

'Now. They are from the government.'

I followed him to a room on a floor which I didn't know existed and he told me to take off my shoes and enter alone in my socks. The two men were seated on a heavy black-wood sofa, beside an aluminium spittoon. They were still wearing their shoes. I smiled. They did not. There were lace curtains across the windows and there was no electricity in the city, so it was dark in the room.

'*Chi kar mikonid?*' What are you doing? asked the man in the black suit and collarless Iranian shirt. I expected him to stand in the normal way, shake hands and wish me peace. He remained seated.

'*Salaam aleikum,*' Peace be with you, I said and sat down.

'*Waleikum a-salaam. Chi kar mikonid?*' he repeated quietly, leaning back and running his fat manicured hand along the purple velveteen arm of the sofa. His bouffant hair and goatee beard were neatly trimmed. I felt conscious of not having shaved in eight weeks.

'I have explained what I am doing many times to His Excellency, Yuzufi, in the Foreign Ministry,' I said. 'I was told to meet him again now. I am late.'

A pulse was beating strongly in my neck. I knew it would be visible. I tried to breathe more slowly. Neither of us spoke. After a little while, I looked away.

The thinner man drew out a small new radio, said something into it and straightened his stiff jacket over his traditional shirt. I didn't need to see the shoulder holster. I had already guessed that they were members of the Security Service. They did not care what I said or what I thought of them. They had watched people through hidden cameras in bedrooms, in torture cells and on execution grounds. They knew that, however I presented myself, I could be reduced. But why had they decided to question me? In the silence, I heard a car reversing in the courtyard and then the first slow notes of the call to prayer.

'Let's go,' said the man in the black suit. He told me to walk in front. On the stairs, I passed a waiter to whom I had spoken. He turned away. I was led to a small Japanese car, parked on the dirt forecourt. The paintwork of the car was new and it had been washed recently. They told me to sit in the back. There was nothing in the pockets or on the floor of the car. It looked as though it had just come from the factory. Without saying anything, they turned on to the main boulevard.

It was January 2002. The American-led coalition was ending its bombardment of the Tora Bora complex; Usama Bin Laden and Mullah Muhammad Omar had apparently escaped; operations in Gardez were beginning. The new government, which had taken over from the Taliban, had been in place for two weeks. The laws banning television and female education had been dropped. Political prisoners had been released, refugees were returning home. Some women were coming out without veils. The UN and the US military were running the basic infrastructure and food supplies. There was no frontier guard and I had entered the country without a visa. The Afghan government seemed to me hardly to exist. Yet these men were apparently already well established.

The car turned into the Foreign Ministry, and the gate guards saluted and stood back. As I walked up the stairs, I felt that I was walking unnaturally quickly and that the men had noticed this. A secretary showed us straight into Mr Yuzufi's office without knocking. For a moment Yuzufi stared at us and did not move from his desk, then he stood, straightened his baggy pinstriped jacket, and showed the others to the most senior position in the room. The two men walked slowly down the linoleum floor. They looked at the furniture, which Yuzufi had managed to assemble since he had inherited an empty office: the splintered desk, the four mismatched filing cabinets in different olive greens and the stove, which made the room smell strongly of petrol.

The week I had known Yuzufi comprised half his career in the Foreign Ministry. A fortnight earlier he had been in Pakistan. The day before he had given me tea and a boiled sweet, told me he admired my journey, laughed at a photograph of my father in his kilt and discussed Persian poetry. This time he did not greet me but instead sat in a chair facing me and asked, 'What has happened?'

Before I could reply the man with the goatee cut in, 'What is this foreigner doing here?'

'These men are from the Security Service,' said Yuzufi.

I nodded. I noticed that Yuzufi had clasped his hands together and that his hands, like mine, were trembling slightly.

'I will translate to make sure you understand what they are asking,' continued Yuzufi. 'Tell them your intentions. Exactly as you told me.'

I looked into the eyes of the man on my left. 'I am planning to walk across Afghanistan. From Herat to Kabul. On foot.' I was not breathing enough to complete my phrases.

I was surprised they didn't interrupt. 'I am following in the footsteps of Babur, the first emperor of Mughal India. I want to get away from the roads. Journalists, aid workers and tourists mostly travel by car but I …'

'There are no tourists,' said the man in the stiff jacket, who had not yet spoken. 'You are the first tourist in Afghanistan. It is midwinter: there are three metres of snow on the high passes, there are wolves and this is a war. You will die, I can guarantee. Do you want to die?'

'Thank you very much for your advice. I note those three points.' I guessed from his tone that such advice was intended as an order. 'But I have spoken to the Cabinet,' I said, misrepresenting a brief meeting with the young secretary to the Minister of Social Welfare. 'I must do this journey.'

'Do it in a year's time,' said the man in the black suit.

He had taken from Yuzufi the tattered evidence of my walk across South Asia and was examining it: the clipping from the newspaper in western Nepal, 'Mr Stewart is a pilgrim for peace'; the letter from the Conservator, Second Circle, Forestry Department, Himachal Pradesh, India: 'Mr Stewart, a Scot, is interested in the environment'; from a District Officer in the Punjab and a Secretary of the Interior in a Himalayan state and a Chief Engineer of the Pakistan Department of Irrigation requesting 'All Executive Engineers (XENs) on the Lower Bari Doab to assist Mr Stewart, who will be undertaking a journey on foot to research the history of the canal system'.

'I have explained this,' I added, 'to His Excellency the Emir's son, the Minister of Social Welfare, when he also gave me a letter of introduction.'

'From His Excellency Mir Wais?'

'Here.' I handed over the sheet of headed paper which I had received from the Minister's secretary. 'Mr Stewart is a medieval antiquary interested in the anthropology of Herat'.

'But it is not signed.'

'Mr Yuzufi lost the signed copy.'

Yuzufi, who was staring at the ground, nodded slightly.

The two men talked together for a few minutes. I did not try to follow what they were saying. I noticed, however, that they were using Iranian not Afghan Persian words in their conversation. That and their clothes and their manner made me think they had spent a great deal of time with the Iranian intelligence services. I had been questioned by the Iranians, who seemed to suspect me of being a spy. I did not want to be questioned by them again.

The man in the stiff jacket said, 'We will allow him to walk to Chaghcharan. But our gunmen will accompany him all the way.' Chaghcharan was halfway between Herat and Kabul and about a fortnight into my journey.

The villagers with whom I was hoping to stay would be terrified by a secret police escort. This was presumably the point. But why were they letting me do the journey at all rather than expelling me? I wondered if they were looking for money. 'Thank you so much for your concern for my security,' I said, 'but I am quite happy to take the risk. I have walked alone across the other Asian countries without any problems.'

'You will take the escort,' said Yuzufi, interrupting for the first time, 'that is non-negotiable.'

'But I have introductions to the local commanders. I will be much safer with them than with Heratis.'

'You will go with our men,' he repeated.

'I cannot afford to pay for an escort. I have no money.'

'We were not expecting any money,' said the man in the stiff jacket.

'This is non-negotiable,' repeated Yuzufi. His broad knee was now jigging up and down. 'If you refuse this you will be expelled from the country. They want to know how many of their gunmen you are taking.'

'If it is compulsory, one.'

'Two ... with weapons,' said the man in the dark suit, 'and you will leave tomorrow.'

The two men stood up and left the room. They said goodbye to Yuzufi but not to me.

TALIBAN
THE POWER OF MILITANT ISLAM IN AFGHANISTAN AND BEYOND

Ahmed Rashid

This was the book rushed onto every policymaker's desk around the world from the end of 2001. Published with uncanny and impeccable timing in October 2001, a month after al-Qaeda's 9/11 attacks on the United States, *Taliban* lifted the veil on the horror show underway in Afghanistan. Part James Bond film, part Islamist nightmare, it charted the rise of the Taliban from its earliest beginnings to its incubation of al-Qaeda terrorists and the rise of Osama bin Laden, via sectarian and religious conflict, tribal tensions, a rampant narcotics trade, meddling neighbours and poisonous politics.

For **Ahmed Rashid** (1948–), then the *Daily Telegraph*'s relatively dormant Central Asian correspondent, it was a masterful, accessible and life-changing book which thrust him onto the world stage as an expert on the hitherto unknown Taliban.

KANDAHAR 1994: THE ORIGINS OF THE TALIBAN

The Taliban Governor of Kandahar, Mullah Mohammed Hassan Rehmani, has a disconcerting habit of pushing the table in front of him with his one good leg. By the time any conversation with him is over, the wooden table has been pushed round and round his chair a dozen times. Hassan's nervous twitch is perhaps a psychological need to feel that he still has a leg or perhaps he is just exercising, keeping his one good leg on the move at all times.

Hassan's second limb is a wooden peg-leg, in the style of Long John Silver, the pirate in Robert Louis Stevenson's *Treasure Island*. It's an old wooden stump. The varnish rubbed off long ago, scratches cover its length and bits of wood have been gouged out —no doubt by the difficulties of negotiating the rocky terrain outside his office. Hassan, one of the oldest Taliban leaders at over 40 and one of the few who actually fought Soviet troops, was a founder member of the Taliban and is considered to be number two in the movement to his old friend Mullah Omar.

Hassan lost his leg in 1989 on the Kandahar front, just before Soviet troops began their withdrawal from Afghanistan. Despite the availability of new artificial limbs now being fitted to the country's millions of amputees by international aid agencies, Hassan says he prefers his peg-leg. He also lost a finger tip, the result of another wound caused by shrapnel. The Taliban leadership can boast to be the most disabled in the world today and visitors do not know how to react, whether to laugh or to cry. Mullah Omar lost his right eye in 1989 when a rocket exploded close by. The Justice Minister Nuruddin Turabi and the former Foreign Minister Mohammed Ghaus are also one-eyed. The Mayor of Kabul, Abdul Majid, has one leg and two fingers missing. Other leaders, even military commanders, have similar disabilities.

The Taliban's wounds are a constant reminder of 20 years of war, which has killed over 1.5 million people and devastated the country. The Soviet Union poured some US$5 billion a year into Afghanistan to subdue the Mujaheddin or a total of US$45 billion —and they lost. The US committed some four to five billion dollars between 1980 and 1992 in aid to the Mujaheddin. US funds were matched by Saudi Arabia and together with support from other European and Islamic countries, the Mujaheddin received a total of over US$10 billion. Most of this aid was in the form of lethal modern weaponry given to a simple agricultural people who used it with devastating results.

The war wounds of the Taliban leaders also reflect the bloody and brutal style of war that took place in and around Kandahar in the 1980s. The Durrani Pashtuns who inhabit the south and Kandahar received far less aid through the CIA and Western aid pipeline which armed, financed and provided logistics such as medical facilities to the Mujaheddin, as compared to the Ghilzai Pashtuns in the east of the country and around Kabul. The aid was distributed by Pakistan's Interservices Intelligence (ISI), who tended to treat Kandahar as a backwater and the Durranis with suspicion. As a consequence the nearest medical facilities for a wounded Kandahari Mujaheddin was a bone-shaking two-day camel ride to Quetta across the border in Pakistan. Even today first-aid amongst the Taliban is rare, doctors are all too few and surgeons on the front line non-existent. Virtually the only medical practitioners in the country are the hospitals of the International Committee of the Red Cross (ICRC).

By chance I was in Kandahar in December 1979 and watched the first Soviet tanks roll in. Teenage Soviet soldiers had driven for two days from the Soviet Republic of Turkmenistan in Central Asia to Herat and then on to Kandahar along a metalled highway that the Soviets had themselves built in the 1960s. Many of the soldiers were of Central Asian origin. They got out of their tanks, dusted off their uniforms and ambled across to the nearest stall for a cup of sugarless green tea—a staple part of the diet in both Afghanistan and Central Asia. The Afghans in the bazaar just stood and stared. On 27 December Soviet Spetsnatz or Special Forces had stormed the palace of President Hafizullah Amin in Kabul, killed him, occupied Kabul and appointed Babrak Karmal as President.

When the resistance began around Kandahar it was based on the tribal network of the Durranis. In Kandahar the struggle against the Soviets was a tribal jihad led by clan chiefs and *ulema* (senior religious scholars) rather than an ideological jihad led by Islamicists. In Peshawar there were seven Mujaheddin parties which were recognised by Pakistan and received a share of aid from the CIA pipeline. Significantly none of the seven parties were led by Durrani Pashtuns. In Kandahar all seven parties had a following, but the most popular parties in the south were those based on tribal ties such as the Harakat-e-Inquilab Islami (Movement of the Islamic Revolution) led by Maulvi Mohammed Nabi Mohammedi and another Hizb-e-Islami (Party of Islam) led by Maulvi Younis Khalis. Before the war both leaders were well known in the Pashtun belt and ran their own *madrassas* or religious schools.

For commanders in the south party loyalty depended on which

Peshawar leader would provide money and arms. Mullah Omar joined Khalis's Hizb-e-Islami while Mullah Hassan joined Harakat. 'I knew Omar extremely well but we were fighting on different fronts and in different groups but sometimes we fought together,' said Hassan. Also popular was the National Islamic Front led by Pir Sayed Ahmad Gailani, who advocated the return of the Durrani ex-King Zahir Shah to lead the Afghan resistance—a move that was strongly opposed by Pakistan and the USA. The ex-King was living in Rome and continued to be a popular figure amongst the Kandaharis, who hoped that his return would reassert the leadership role of the Durrani tribes.

The contradictions within the Pashtun Mujaheddin leadership were to weaken the Pashtuns as the war progressed. The *ulema* valued the historical ideals of early Islamic history and rarely challenged traditional Afghan tribal structures like the Jirga. They were also much more accommodating towards the ethnic minorities. The Islamicists denigrated the tribal structure and pursued a radical political ideology in order to bring about an Islamic revolution in Afghanistan. They were exclusivists which made the minorities suspicious of them.

Thus Harakat had no coherent party structure and was just a loose alliance between commanders and tribal chiefs, many of whom had just a rudimentary *madrassa* education. On the other hand Gulbuddin Hikmetyar's Hizb-e-Islami built a secretive, highly centralized, political organization whose cadres were drawn from educated urban Pashtuns. Prior to the war the Islamicists barely had a base in Afghan society, but with money and arms from the CIA pipeline and support from Pakistan, they built one and wielded tremendous clout. The traditionalists and the Islamicists fought each other mercilessly so that by 1994, the traditional leadership in Kandahar had virtually been eliminated, leaving the field free for the new wave of even more extreme Islamicists—the Taliban.

The battle for Kandahar was also determined by its own particular history. Kandahar is Afghanistan's second largest city with a 1979 pre-war population of about 250,000 and twice that today. The old city has been inhabited since 500 BC, but just 35 miles away lies Mundigak, a Bronze-Age village settled around 3,000 BC, which was once part of the Indus Valley civilization. Kandaharis have always been great traders as the city was located at the intersection of ancient trade routes—eastwards across the Bolan Pass to Sind, the Arabian Sea and India and westwards to Herat and Iran. The city was the main crossing point for trade, arts and crafts between Iran and India and the city's numerous bazaars have been famous for centuries.

The new city has changed little from that laid out in grand proportions in 1761 by Ahmad Shah Durrani, the founder of the Durrani dynasty. The fact that the Durranis from Kandahar were to create the Afghan state and rule it for 300 years gave the Kandaharis a special status amongst the Pashtuns. As a concession to their home base, Kabul's kings absolved the Kandaharis from providing manpower for the army. Ahmad Shah's mausoleum dominates the central bazaar and thousands of Afghans still come here to pray and pay their respects to the founder of the nation.

Next to his tomb is the shrine of the Cloak of the Prophet Mohammed—one of the holiest places of worship in Afghanistan. The Cloak has been shown only on rare occasions such as when King Amanullah tried to rally the tribes in 1929 and when a cholera epidemic hit the city in 1935. But in 1996 in order to legitimise his role as leader and one ordained by God to lead the Afghan people, Mullah Omar took out the cloak and showed it to a large crowd of Taliban who then named him Amir-ul Momineen or Leader of the Faithful.

However, Kandahar's fame across the region rests on its fruit orchards. Kandahar is an oasis town set in the desert and the summer heat is devastating, but around the city are lush, green fields and shady orchards producing grapes, melons, mulberries, figs, peaches and pomegranates which were famous throughout India and Iran. Kandahar's pomegranates decorated Persian manuscripts written one thousand years ago and were served at the table of the British Governor General of India in Delhi during the last century. The city's truck transporters, who were to give major financial support to the Taliban in their drive to conquer the country, began their trade in the last century when they carried Kandahar's fruit as far as Delhi and Calcutta.

The orchards were watered by a complex and well-maintained

irrigation system until the war, when both the Soviets and the Mujaheddin so heavily mined the fields that the rural population fled to Pakistan and the orchards were abandoned. Kandahar remains one of the most heavily mined cities in the world. In an otherwise flat landscape, the orchards and water channels provided cover for the Mujaheddin who quickly took control of the countryside, isolating the Soviet garrison in the city. The Soviets retaliated by cutting down thousands of trees and smashing the irrigation system. When the refugees were to return to their devastated orchards after 1990, they were to grow opium poppies for a livelihood, creating a major source of income for the Taliban.

With the Soviet withdrawal in 1989 there followed a long struggle against the regime of President Najibullah until he was overthrown in 1992 and the Mujaheddin captured Kabul. Much of Afghanistan's subsequent civil war was to be determined by the fact that Kabul fell, not to the well-armed and bickering Pashtun parties based in Peshawar, but to the better organized and more united Tajik forces of Burhanuddin Rabbani and his military commander Ahmad Shah Masud and to the Uzbek forces from the north under General Rashid Dostum. It was a devastating psychological blow because for the first time in 300 years the Pashtuns had lost control of the capital. An internal civil war began almost immediately as Hikmetyar attempted to rally the Pashtuns and laid siege to Kabul, shelling it mercilessly.

Afghanistan was in a state of virtual disintegration just before the Taliban emerged at the end of 1994. The country was divided into warlord fiefdoms and all the warlords had fought, switched sides and fought again in a bewildering array of alliances, betrayals and bloodshed. The predominantly Tajik government of President Burhanuddin Rabbani controlled Kabul, its environs and the north-east of the country, while three provinces in the west centring on Herat were controlled by Ismael Khan. In the east on the Pakistan border three Pashtun provinces were under the independent control of a council or Shura (Council) of Mujaheddin commanders based in Jalalabad. A small region to the south and east of Kabul was controlled by Gulbuddin Hikmetyar. In the north the Uzbek warlord General Rashid Dostum held sway over six provinces and in January 1994 he had abandoned his alliance with the Rabbani government and joined with Hikmetyar to attack Kabul. In central Afghanistan the Hazaras controlled the province of Bamiyan. Southern Afghanistan and Kandahar were divided up amongst dozens of petty ex-Mujaheddin warlords and bandits who plundered the population at will. With the tribal structure and the economy in tatters, no consensus on a Pashtun leadership and Pakistan's unwillingness to provide military aid to the Durranis as they did to Hikmetyar, the Pashtuns in the south were at war with each other.

International aid agencies were fearful of even working in Kandahar as the city itself was divided by warring groups. Their leaders sold off everything to Pakistani traders to make money, stripping down telephone wires and poles, cutting trees, selling off factories, machinery and even road rollers to scrap merchants. The warlords seized homes and farms, threw out their occupants and handed them over to their supporters. The commanders abused the population at will, kidnapping young girls and boys for their sexual pleasure, robbing merchants in the bazaars and fighting and brawling in the streets. Instead of refugees returning from Pakistan, a fresh wave of refugees began to leave Kandahar for Quetta.

For the powerful mafia of truck transporters based in Quetta and Kandahar, it was an intolerable situation for business. In 1993 I travelled the short 130 miles by road from Quetta to Kandahar and we were stopped by at least 20 different groups, who had put chains across the road and demanded a toll for free passage. The transport mafia who were trying to open up routes to smuggle goods between Quetta and Iran and the newly independent state of Turkmenistan, found it impossible to do business.

For those Mujaheddin who had fought the Najibullah regime and had then gone home or to continue their studies at *madrassas* in Quetta and Kandahar, the situation was particularly galling. 'We all knew each other—Mullahs Omar, Ghaus, Mohammed Rabbani (no relation to President Rabbani) and myself—because we were all originally from Urozgan province and had fought together,' said Mulla Hassan. 'I moved back and forth from Quetta and attended *madrassas* there, but whenever we got together we would discuss the terrible plight of our people living under these bandits. We were people of the same opinions and we got on with each other very well, so it was easy to come to a decision to do something,' he added.

Mullah Mohammed Ghaus, the one-eyed Foreign Minister of the Taliban said much the same. 'We would sit for a long time to discuss how to change the terrible situation. Before we started we had only vague ideas what to do and we thought we would fail, but we believed we were working with Allah as His pupils. We have got so far because Allah has helped us,' said Ghaus.

Other groups of Mujaheddin in the south were also discussing the same problems. 'Many people were searching for a solution. I was from Kalat in Zabul province (85 miles north of Kandahar) and had joined a *madrassa*, but the situation was so bad that we were distracted from our studies and with a group of friends we spent all our time discussing what we should do and what needed to be done,' said Mullah Mohammed Abbas, who was to become the Minister of Public Health in Kabul. 'The old Mujaheddin leadership had utterly failed to bring peace. So I went with a group of friends to Herat to attend the Shura called by Ismael Khan, but it failed to come up with a solution and things were getting worse. So we came to Kandahar to talk with Mullah Omar and joined him,' Abbas added.

After much discussion these divergent but deeply concerned groups chalked out an agenda which still remains the Taliban's declared aims —restore peace, disarm the population, enforce Sharia law and defend the integrity and Islamic character of Afghanistan. As most of them were part-time or full-time students at *madrassas*, the name they chose for themselves was natural. A *talib* is an Islamic student, one who seeks knowledge compared to the mullah who is one who gives knowledge. By choosing such a name the Taliban (plural of *Talib*) distanced themselves from the party politics of the Mujaheddin and signalled that they were a movement for cleansing society rather than a party trying to grab power.

All those who gathered around Omar were the children of the jihad but deeply disillusioned with the factionalism and criminal activities of the once idealised Mujaheddin leadership. They saw themselves as the cleansers and purifiers of a guerrilla war gone astray, a social system gone wrong and an Islamic way of life that had been compromised by corruption and excess. Many of them had been born in Pakistani refugee camps, educated in Pakistani *madrassas* and had learnt their fighting skills from Mujaheddin parties based in Pakistan. As such the younger Taliban barely knew their own country or history, but from their *madrassas* they learnt about the ideal Islamic society created by the Prophet Mohammed 1,400 years ago and this is what they wanted to emulate.

Some Taliban say Omar was chosen as their leader not for his political or military ability, but for his piety and his unswerving belief in Islam. Others say he was chosen by God. 'We selected Mullah Omar to lead this movement. He was the first amongst equals and we gave him the power to lead us and he has given us the power and authority to deal with people's problems,' said Mullah Hassan. Omar himself gave a simple explanation to Pakistani journalist Rahimullah Yousufzai. 'We took up arms to achieve the aims of the Afghan jihad and save our people from further suffering at the hands of the so-called Mujaheddin. We had complete faith in God Almighty. We never forgot that. He can bless us with victory or plunge us into defeat,' said Omar.

No leader in the world today is surrounded by as much secrecy and mystery as Mullah Mohammed Omar. Aged 39, he has never been photographed or met with Western diplomats and journalists. His first meeting with a UN diplomat was in October 1998, four years after the Taliban emerged, when he met with the UN Special Representative for Afghanistan Lakhdar Brahimi, because the Taliban were faced with a possibly devastating attack by Iran. Omar lives in Kandahar and has visited the capital Kabul twice and only then very briefly. Putting together the bare facts of his life has become a full-time job for most Afghans and foreign diplomats.

Omar was born sometime around 1959 in Nodeh village near Kandahar to a family of poor, landless peasants who were members of the Hotak tribe, the Ghilzai branch of Pashtuns. The Hotaki chief Mir Wais, had captured Isfahan in Iran in 1721 and established the first Ghilzai Afghan empire in Iran only to be quickly replaced by Ahmad

Shah Durrani. Omar's tribal and social status was non-existent and notables from Kandahar say they had never heard of his family. During the 1980s jihad his family moved to Tarinkot in Urozgan province—one of the most backward and inaccessible regions of the country where Soviet troops rarely penetrated. His father died while he was a young man and the task of fending for his mother and extended family fell upon him.

Looking for a job, he moved to Singesar village in the Mewand district of Kandahar province, where he became the village mullah and opened a small *madrassa*. His own studies in *madrassas* in Kandahar were interrupted twice, first by the Soviet invasion and then by the creation of the Taliban. Omar joined Khalis's Hizb-e-Islami and fought under commander Nek Mohammed against the Najibullah regime between 1989 and 1992. He was wounded four times, once in the right eye which is now permanently blinded.

Despite the success of the Taliban, Singesar is still like any other Pashtun village. Mud-brick homes plastered with more mud and straw are built behind high compound walls—a traditional defensive feature of Pashtun homes. Narrow, dusty alleyways, which turn into mud baths when it rains, connect village homes. Omar's *madrassa* is still functioning —a small mud hut with a dirt floor and mattresses strewn across it for the boys to sleep on. Omar has three wives, who continue living in the village and are heavily veiled. While his first and third wives are from Urozgan, his teenage second wife Guljana, whom he married in 1995, is from Singesar. He has a total of five children who are studying in his *madrassa*.

A tall, well-built man with a long, black beard and a black turban, Omar has a dry sense of humour and a sarcastic wit. He remains extremely shy of outsiders, particularly foreigners, but he is accessible to the Taliban. When the movement started he would offer his Friday prayers at the main mosque in Kandahar and mix with the people, but subsequently he has become much more of a recluse, rarely venturing outside Kandahar's administrative mansion where he lives. He now visits his village infrequently and when he does he is always accompanied by dozens of bodyguards in a convoy of deluxe Japanese jeepsters with darkened windows.

Omar speaks very little in Shura meetings, listening to other points of view. His shyness makes him a poor public speaker and despite the mythology that now surrounds him, he has little charismatic appeal. All day he conducts business from a small office in the mansion. At first he used to sit on the cement floor alongside visiting Taliban, but he now sits on a bed while others sit on the floor—a move that emphasises his status as leader. He has several secretaries who take notes from his conversations with commanders, ordinary soldiers, *ulema* and plaintiffs and there is always the crackle of wireless sets as commanders around the country communicate with him.

Business consists of lengthy debate and discussions which end with the issuing of 'chits' or scraps of paper on which are written instructions allowing commanders to make an attack, ordering a Taliban governor to help out a plaintiff or a message to UN mediators. Formal communications to foreign embassies in Islamabad were frequently dictated by Pakistani advisers.

In the early days of the movement I collected numerous chits written on cigarette boxes or wrapping paper, allowing me to travel from city to city. Now more regular paper pads are used. Beside Omar is a tin trunk from which he dishes out wads of Afghani notes to commanders and plaintiffs in need. As success came, another tin trunk was added —this one containing US dollars. These tin trunks are the treasury of the Taliban movement.

In important meetings, Mullah Wakil Ahmad, Omar's trusted confidant and official spokesman is usually beside him. Wakil, a young *madrassa* student from the Kakar tribe who studied under Omar, started out as his companion, driver, food taster, translator and note-taker. He quickly progressed to higher things such as communicating with visiting foreign diplomats and aid agency officials, travelling to meet Taliban commanders and meeting with Pakistani officials. As Omar's spokesman he is the Taliban's main contact with the foreign press as well as its chastiser, when he feels that journalists have criticized the

Taliban too harshly. Wakil acts as Omar's ears and eyes and is also his doorkeeper. No important Afghan can reach Omar without first going through Wakil.

There is now an entire factory of myths and stories to explain how Omar mobilized a small group of Taliban against the rapacious Kandahar warlords. The most credible story, told repeatedly, is that in the spring of 1994 Singesar neighbours came to tell him that a commander had abducted two teenage girls, their heads had been shaved and they had been taken to a military camp and repeatedly raped. Omar enlisted some 30 *Talibs* who had only 16 rifles between them and attacked the base, freeing the girls and hanging the commander from the barrel of a tank. They captured quantities of arms and ammunition. 'We were fighting against Muslims who had gone wrong. How could we remain quiet when we could see crimes being committed against women and the poor?' Omar said later.

A few months later two commanders confronted each other in Kandahar, in a dispute over a young boy whom both men wanted to sodomise. In the fight that followed civilians were killed. Omar's group freed the boy and public appeals started coming in for the Taliban to help out in other local disputes. Omar had emerged as a Robin Hood figure, helping the poor against the rapacious commanders. His prestige grew because he asked for no reward or credit from those he helped, only demanding that they follow him to set up a just Islamic system.

At the same time Omar's emissaries were gauging the mood of other commanders. His colleagues visited Herat to meet with Ismael Khan and in September Mulla Mohammed Rabbani, a founding member of the Taliban, visited Kabul and held talks with President Rabbani. The isolated Kabul government wished to support any new Pashtun force that would oppose Hikmetyar, who was still shelling Kabul, and Rabbani promised to help the Taliban with funds if they opposed Hikmetyar.

However the Taliban's closest links were with Pakistan where many of them had grown up and studied in *madrassas* run by the mercurial Maulana Fazlur Rehman and his Jamiat-e-*Ulema* Islam (JUI), a fundamentalist party which had considerable support amongst the Pashtuns in Baluchistan and the North West Frontier Province (NWFP).

More significantly Maulana Rehman was now a political ally of Prime Minister Benazir Bhutto and he had access to the government, the army and the ISI to whom he described this newly emerging force.

Pakistan's Afghan policy was in the doldrums. After the collapse of the Soviet Union in 1991, successive Pakistani governments were desperately keen to open up direct land routes for trade with the Central Asian Republics (CARs). The major hindrance was the continuing civil war in Afghanistan, through which any route passed. Pakistan's policy-makers were thus faced with a strategic dilemma. Either Pakistan could carry on backing Hikmetyar in a bid to bring a Pashtun group to power in Kabul which would be Pakistan-friendly, or it could change direction and urge for a power-sharing agreement between all the Afghan factions at whatever the price for the Pashtuns, so that a stable government could open the roads to Central Asia.

The Pakistani military was convinced that other ethnic groups would not do their bidding and continued to back Hikmetyar. Some 20 per cent of the Pakistan army was made up of Pakistani Pashtuns and the pro-Pashtun and Islamic fundamentalist lobby within the ISI and the military remained determined to achieve a Pashtun victory in Afghanistan. However, by 1994 Hikmetyar had clearly failed, losing ground militarily while his extremism divided the Pashtuns, the majority of whom loathed him. Pakistan was getting tired of backing a loser and was looking around for other potential Pashtun proxies.

When Benazir Bhutto was elected as Prime Minister in 1993, she was keen to open a route to Central Asia. The shortest route was from Peshawar to Kabul, across the Hindu Kush mountains to Mazar-e-Sharif and then to Tirmez and Tashkent in Uzbekistan, but this route was closed due to the fighting around Kabul. A new proposal emerged, backed strongly by the frustrated Pakistani transport and smuggling mafia, the JUI and Pashtun military and political officials. Instead of the northern route the way could be cleared from Quetta to Kandahar, Herat and on to Ashkhabad, the capital of Turkmenistan. There was no fighting in the south, only dozens of commanders who would have to be adequately bribed before they agreed to open the chains.

In September 1994 Pakistani surveyors and ISI officers discreetly travelled the road from Chaman on the Pakistani border to Herat, to survey the road. The Pashtun-born Interior Minister Naseerullah Babar also visited Chaman that month. The Kandahar warlords viewed the plan with mistrust, suspecting the Pakistanis were about to try and intervene militarily to crush them. One commander, Amir Lalai, issued a blunt warning to Babar. 'Pakistan is offering to reconstruct our roads, but I do not think that by fixing our roads peace would automatically follow. As long as neighbouring countries continue to interfere in our internal affairs, we should not expect peace,' said Lalai.

Nevertheless, the Pakistanis began to negotiate with the Kandahar warlords and Ismael Khan in Herat to allow traffic through to Turkmenistan. On 20 October 1994, Babar took a party of six Western ambassadors to Kandahar and Herat, without even informing the Kabul government. The delegation included senior officials from the departments of Railways, Highways, Telephones and Electricity. Babar said he wanted to raise US$300 million from international agencies to rebuild the highway from Quetta to Herat. On 28 October, Bhutto met with Ismael Khan and General Rashid Dostum in Ashkhabad and urged them to agree to open a southern route, where trucks would pay just a couple of tolls on the way and their security would be guaranteed.

However, before that meeting a major event had shaken the Kandahar warlords. On 12 October 1994 some 200 Taliban from Kandahar and Pakistani *madrassas* arrived at the small Afghan border post of Spin Baldak on the Pakistan-Afghanistan border just opposite Chaman. The grimy grease pit in the middle of the desert was an important trucking and fuelling stop for the transport mafia and was held by Hikmetyar's men. Here Afghan trucks picked up goods from Pakistani trucks, which were not allowed to cross into Afghanistan and fuel was smuggled in from Pakistan to feed the warlords' armies. For the transport mafia, control of the town was critical. They had already donated several hundred thousand Pakistani Rupees to Mullah Omar and promised a monthly stipend to the Taliban, if they would clear the roads of chains and bandits and guarantee the security for truck traffic.

The Taliban force divided into three groups and attacked Hikmetyar's garrison. After a short, sharp battle they fled, losing seven dead and several wounded. The Taliban lost only one man. Pakistan then helped the Taliban by allowing them to capture a large arms dump outside Spin Baldak that had been guarded by Hikmetyar's men. This dump had been moved across the border from Pakistan into Afghanistan in 1990, when the terms of the Geneva Accords obliged Islamabad not to hold weapons for Afghans on Pakistani territory. At the dump the Taliban seized some 18,000 kalashnikovs, dozens of artillery pieces, large quantities of ammunition and many vehicles.

The capture of Spin Baldak worried the Kandahar warlords and they denounced Pakistan for backing the Taliban, but they continued bickering amongst themselves rather than uniting to meet the new threat. Babar was now getting impatient and he ordered a 30 truck test-convoy to travel to Ashkhabad with a load of medicines. 'I told Babar we should wait two months because we had no agreements with the Kandahar commanders, but Babar insisted on pushing the convoy through. The commanders suspected that the convoy was carrying arms for a future Pakistani force,' a Pakistani official based in Kandahar later told me.

On 29 October 1994, the convoy drawn from the army's National Logistics Cell (NLC), which had been set up in the 1980s by the ISI to funnel US arms to the Mujaheddin, left Quetta with 80 Pakistani ex-army drivers. Colonel Imam, the ISI's most prominent field officer operating in the south and Pakistan's Consul General in Herat, was also on board. Along with him were two young Taliban commanders, Mullahs Borjan and Turabi. (Both were later to lead the Taliban's first assault on Kabul where Mullah Borjan was to meet his death.) Twelve miles outside Kandahar, at Takht-e-Pul near the perimeter of Kandahar airport, the convoy was held up by a group of commanders, Amir Lalai, Mansur Achakzai, who controlled the airport, and Ustad Halim. The convoy was ordered to park in a nearby village at the foot of low-lying mountains. When I walked the area a few months later the remains of camp fires and discarded rations were still evident.

The commanders demanded money, a share of the goods and that Pakistan stop supporting the Taliban. As the commanders negotiated with Colonel Imam, Islamabad imposed a news blackout for three days on the convoy hijack. 'We were worried that Mansur would put arms aboard the convoy and then blame Pakistan. So we considered all the military options to rescue the convoy, such as a raid by the Special Services Group (Pakistan army commandos) or a parachute drop. These options were considered too dangerous so we then asked the Taliban to free the convoy,' said a Pakistani official. On 3 November 1994, the Taliban moved in to attack those holding the convoy. The commanders, thinking this was a raid by the Pakistani army, fled. Mansur was chased into the desert by the Taliban, captured and shot dead with ten of his bodyguards. His body was hung from a tank barrel for all to see.

That same evening, the Taliban moved on Kandahar where, after two days of sporadic fighting they routed the commanders' forces. Mullah Naquib, the most prominent commander inside the city who commanded 2,500 men, did not resist. Some of his aides later claimed that Naquib had taken a substantial bribe from the ISI to surrender, with the promise that he would retain his command. The Taliban enlisted his men and retired the Mullah to his village outside Kandahar. The Taliban captured dozens of tanks, armoured cars, military vehicles, weapons and most significantly at the airport six Mig-21 fighters and six transport helicopters—left-overs from the Soviet occupation.

In just a couple of weeks this unknown force had captured the second largest city in Afghanistan with the loss of just a dozen men. In Islamabad no foreign diplomat or analyst doubted that they had received considerable support from Pakistan. The fall of Kandahar was celebrated by the Pakistan government and the JUI. Babar took credit for the Taliban's success, telling journalists privately that the Taliban were 'our boys'. Yet the Taliban demonstrated their independence from Pakistan, indicating that they were nobody's puppet. On 16 November 1994 Mullah Ghaus said that Pakistan should not bypass the Taliban in sending convoys in the future and should not cut deals with individual warlords. He also said the Taliban would not allow goods bound for

Afghanistan to be carried by Pakistani trucks—a key demand of the transport mafia.

The Taliban cleared the chains from the roads, set up a one-toll system for trucks entering Afghanistan at Spin Baldak and patrolled the highway from Pakistan. The transport mafia was ecstatic and in December the first Pakistani convoy of 50 trucks carrying raw cotton from Turkmenistan arrived in Quetta, after paying the Taliban 200,000 rupees (US$5,000) in tolls. Meanwhile thousands of young Afghan Pashtuns studying in Baluchistan and the NWFP rushed to Kandahar to join the Taliban. They were soon followed by Pakistani volunteers from JUI *madrassas*, who were inspired by the new Islamic movement in Afghanistan. By December 1994, some 12,000 Afghan and Pakistani students had joined the Taliban in Kandahar.

As international and domestic pressure mounted on Pakistan to explain its position, Bhutto made the first formal denial of any Pakistani backing of the Taliban in February 1995. 'We have no favourites in Afghanistan and we do not interfere in Afghanistan,' she said while visiting Manila. Later she said Pakistan could not stop new recruits from crossing the border to join the Taliban. 'I cannot fight Mr [President Burhanuddin] Rabbani's war for him. If Afghans want to cross the border, I do not stop them. I can stop them from re-entering but most of them have families here,' she said.

The Taliban immediately implemented the strictest interpretation of Sharia law ever seen in the Muslim world. They closed down girls' schools and banned women from working outside the home, smashed TV sets, forbade a whole array of sports and recreational activities and ordered all males to grow long beards. In the next three months the Taliban were to take control of 12 of Afghanistan's 31 provinces, opening the roads to traffic and disarming the population. As the Taliban marched north to Kabul, local warlords either fled or, waving white flags, surrendered to them. Mullah Omar and his army of students were on the march across Afghanistan.

THE SEWING CIRCLES OF HERAT

Christina Lamb

> If any foreign correspondent has a knack of being in the right place at the right time and bringing back the biggest story, especially when it comes to Afghanistan, it is surely **Christina Lamb** (1965–), doyenne of war journalists, who has an enviable track record of reporting in the country. *The Sewing Circles of Herat* takes its title from the courageous group of young women who met covertly with their professors to discuss literature at a time when girls' education was outlawed. Lamb's narrative manages somehow to be both horrifying and uplifting, a remarkable blend of outrage, compassion and hope. A torturer recalls how he used to beat his victims with logs soaked in water 'like a knife cutting through meat until the room ran with their blood or their spines snapped'. Juxtaposed against these spectacularly vile criminals is the poignant story of the brave few who resisted them.

The hotel was on the corner of two wide treelined avenues, Blood-bank Street and Cinema Street. I chose to explore the latter, though the cinema had been demolished by the Taliban. A crowd of beggar women and children quickly collected in my wake, tugging at my clothes. Looking for a place to escape, I ducked into a gateway just along from the hotel. A path led to a white colonial-style building with a sign saying in English and Persian *Literary Circle of Herat*.

I stared at it, intrigued. First settled five thousand years ago, Herat has always been regarded as the cradle of Afghan civilisation, so renowned as a centre of culture and learning that one of its leading patrons of arts in the fifteenth century, Ali Sher Nawa'i (See page 171), claimed, 'here in Herat one cannot stretch out a leg without poking a poet in the ass'. Babur, the first Moghul Emperor, descended from Tamerlane on his father's side (and Genghis Khan on his mother's), visited his cousins in Herat in 1506, only a year before it fell to the Uzbeks. In his memoir *The Baburnama*,* a sort of personal odyssey which tells of what he calls his 'throneless years' wandering Central Asia in search of a kingdom, having lost his own tiny Ferghana, he wrote of the city being 'filled with learned and matchless men'.

Herat's golden era was under Queen Gowhar Shad, wife of Tamerlane's youngest son, Shah Rukh. The name of Herat's most important queen is almost unknown in the West but she used her power as wife of a ruler whose empire stretched from Turkey to China to find and promote the best architects to carry out such grand projects as the ruined *musalla*. She also sponsored painters, calligraphers and poets, usually in the romantic language of Persian even though the Timurids themselves were Turkish-speaking. One of her protégés was Abdur Rahman Jami (See page 163), widely considered the greatest-ever Persian poet with his prolific outpouring of *ghazals* and couplets. Her court artist Bihzad is regarded as the master of Persian miniatures for his intricate depictions of hunting scenes and chivalrous encounters between tall princes and reclining maidens in intense colours such as deep lapis blue made from powdered jewels. One of the first miniaturists to sign his paintings, he headed the Herat Academy from 1468 to 1506 and became so famous that many miniaturists tried to emulate his style, signing their work 'Worthy of Bihzad', though Babur was characteristically frank, writing, 'he painted extremely delicately but he made the faces of beardless people badly by drawing the double chin too big'.

Over the years the city had been sacked so many times that it was hard to imagine any of this artistic spirit had survived. The door of the Literary Circle was open and I walked in, unsure what I would find. The building seemed to rumble in protest as overhead planes flew low,

---

* Written in Chagatai Turkish, the language of the Timurids, rather than Persian, the lingua franca of Central Asia at that time, it became a sort of handbook for Moghul rulers and was widely copied, but the original version was last seen during the reign of Emperor Shah Jahan.

American bombers heading south to Kandahar where the Taliban were threatening to fight to the last after Mullah Omar had announced that he had had another dream that he would stay in power. The rooms were bare and deserted but I noticed a pair of scuffed black sandals outside a door on the left. Inside a man in a black polo neck who looked like a young Robert de Niro was sitting at a desk moodily staring into space. He introduced himself as Ahmed Said Haghighi, the society's president, and invited me to sit down.

I asked him how the Circle had survived the onslaught on culture of the Taliban years and he smiled wearily. 'It was not just those years,' he said. 'Here in Herat we've been fighting a war on culture for hundreds of years. Ever since the death of Queen Gowhar Shad you could say.'

'How old is the Literary Circle then?'

'It was founded in 1920 by the poets of the city to make known the rich culture and heritage of Herat. We used to have literary evenings when people would come and read their works but we've always been opposed by governments. Many times the doors of this place have been shut down. The Communists locked up many intellectuals and when the Russians came in 1980 they wanted to turn this into an institute of propaganda so many of our members fled to Iran. But the Taliban was the worst time. First they tried to turn us into a propaganda voice, then they came and padlocked the door and publicly whipped our members so we were forced to become an underground movement, meeting in members' houses to secretly read stories and poems.'

On the shelves were piles of stapled papers that looked like a monthly journal. 'Yes, we call it the Eighth Orang, it means throne in English, after a poem called *Haft Awrang**, the *Seven Thrones* written by Jami, the most famous poet of Herat, during the most turbulent years of the Timurid Empire. We thought if he could write such a work at that time then why shouldn't we in our difficult time.'

I was surprised that they had been able to get it past the head of censorship. 'The Taliban were stupid,' he replied. 'They didn't realise

---

* This is also the Persian name for the constellation Ursa Major.

what we were writing. We used symbolic language as in any totalitarian state to convey our messages. Some writers used devices such as the discourse of birds and animals.'

He fell silent and I wondered if I should leave. There was not even a paraffin heater in the room and in the sub-zero temperature my feet felt like blocks of ice, but then he started speaking again without looking at me.

'In other cities, where there had been fighting between factions and lots of crime and insecurity, when the Taliban came they were greeted with relief. But we had not had those problems. So to us they were simply a bunch of illiterate religious fanatics who did not speak our language and had come to make life difficult for us. Barbarians who hung people from electricity poles and crossroads. One day I counted eighteen people hanging. Can you imagine seeing that?

'It was particularly hard for our female members. They closed the girls' schools and banned women from the university, initially saying this was temporary while they worked things out. But then they captured Kabul and started turning girls' schools into mosques, banned our language and stopped paying women teachers, so we knew. For a while we waited, hoping they would be defeated but when it became clear that they were going to retain control of Herat we sat around discussing what we could do to stop the culture of our city dying and to help our girls. There was only one thing we could think of.'

'What was that?' I asked. Haghighi studied me for a moment as if trying to make his mind up about something. I shifted in my seat and found myself pulling forward my scarf which was always slipping off my hair, already feeling uncomfortable to be stared at so openly in a land where men usually do anything to avoid a woman's gaze. He pushed his chair back from the table and got up.

'Come with me.'

His brusque tone brooked no possibility of asking where we were going and I found myself following meekly as he walked quickly along the road back past the hotel, across the Flower traffic island with the laughing traffic policeman, past Aziz barber's shop which was busy with men shaving off their beards, and down a small mud-walled alleyway.

Some way along by a doorway on the left was a blue sign. *Golden Needle, Ladies' Sewing Classes, Mondays, Wednesdays, Saturdays.*

'This is what we did,' he said. I stared uncomprehendingly. 'The one activity which women could do and involved lots of coming and going was making clothes,' he explained. The innocuous plaque masked an underground network of writers and poets, who had become the focus of resistance in this ancient city, risking their lives for literature and to educate women.

Three times a week for the previous five years, young women, faces and bodies disguised by their Taliban-enforced uniforms of washed-out blue burqas and flat shoes, would knock at the yellow wrought-iron door. In their handbags, concealed under scissors, cottons, sequins and pieces of material, were notebooks and pens. Had the authorities investigated they would have discovered that the dressmaking students never made any clothes. The house belonged to Mohammed Nasir Rahiyab, a forty-seven-year-old literature professor from Herat University, and, once inside, the women would pull off their burqas, sit on cushions around a blackboard and listen to him teach forbidden subjects such as literary criticism, aesthetics and Persian poetry as well as be introduced to foreign classics by Shakespeare, James Joyce and Nabokov.

Mr Haghighi banged on the door and it was opened by a small boy who showed us into a long windowless room with cushions on the floor, a board at one end, an oil painting of a man at a desk, and some glass wall-cases containing a few books including a Persian-English dictionary, some volumes of Persian poetry, and a book in English on Poisoning. Professor Rahiyab came and sat down with us beneath his own portrait, and a flask of green tea and a dish of pistachios were brought even though it was Ramadan. 'I don't go to the mosque,' he explained with a shrug. He was a shy soft-spoken man who only became passionate when talking about his beloved Russian writers and he showed me his bust of Pushkin, which he used to keep hidden, only taking it out for the classes.

While lessons were underway his children would be sent to play in the alleyway outside. If a Talib or any stranger approached, one of the children would slip in to warn him and he would then escape into his study with his books while his place running the class was quickly taken by his wife holding up a half-finished garment which they always kept ready.

Only once were they almost exposed when the professor's daughter was ill in bed and his son had run to buy bread so there was no one to raise the alarm when a black turbaned Talib rapped at the door. 'Suddenly he was in the courtyard outside. I just got out of the room in time and my wife ran in and the girls hid their books under the cushions. I realised that I had not cleaned the board or hidden Pushkin. I sat in the other room, drinking tea, my hand shaking so much my cup was rattling. Fortunately the Taliban were such ignorant people they did not know what they were seeing.'

In a society where even teaching one's own daughter to read was a crime, the Sewing Circle was a venture that could easily have ended in more bodies swinging above Gul Crossroads and I asked the professor why he had taken such a risk.

'If the authorities had known that we were not only teaching women but teaching them high levels of literature we would have been killed,' he replied. 'But a lot of fighters sacrificed their lives over the years for the freedom of this city. Shouldn't a person of letters make that sacrifice too?

'We were poor in everyday life,' he added. 'Why should we be poor in culture too? If we had not done what we did to keep up the literary spirit of the city, the depth of our tragedy would have been even greater.'

To lessen suspicion, Professor Rahiyab never openly criticised the regime and carried on quietly teaching his male students at the university, even though the Taliban had decimated his syllabus, forcing him to replace most of his literature classes with lectures on Islamic culture and Shariat and insisting the only books he use were those which he said were 'brought from the mosque'. Literary Theory was reduced from ten hours to two hours a week, European Literature scrapped altogether, and Islamic Culture increased from four hours to fourteen hours. 'I had an extremely long beard,' he added, rubbing his close-shaven chin with a wry smile.

Inspired by the *Golden Needle*, hundreds of similar courses were held all over the city, mostly in central places where there were lots of comings and goings so a few more would not draw too much attention.

Some of the Literary Circle's writers even disguised themselves in burqas to go to women's houses to teach. A Unicef official later told me that an estimated 29,000 girls and women in Herat province received some form of secret education while the city was under Taliban control.

'A society needs poets and storytellers to reflect its pain – and joy,' said Professor Rahiyab as we got up to leave. 'A society without literature is a society that is not rich and does not have a strong core. If there wasn't so much illiteracy and lack of culture in Afghanistan then terrorism would never have found its cradle here.'

THE KITE RUNNER
Khaled Hosseini

No Afghan writer of recent times has enjoyed the spectacular international success of **Khaled Hosseini** (1965–). Read a few pages of *The Kite Runner*, his first novel, and it's not difficult to see why. Set across several generations and encompassing some of Afghanistan's most tumultuous times, it is a lacerating story of human friendship and betrayal, guilt and redemption. In the US, where it sold more than 10 million copies (38 million worldwide), the book proved highly controversial among Afghan-Americans, many of whom objected to its sexually explicit content and the laying bare of ethnic faultlines – a Pashtun rapes a Hazara boy in one of the book's defining moments – and attempted to have it removed from libraries. Hosseini was unfazed. 'They never say I am speaking about things that are untrue. Their beef is, "Why do you have to talk about these things and embarrass us? Don't you love your country?"' Like so many Afghan writers forced out of the country by war, Hosseini now lives outside Afghanistan in the US.

When we were children, Hassan and I used to climb the poplar trees in the driveway of my father's house and annoy our neighbors by reflecting sunlight into their homes with a shard of mirror. We would sit across from each other on a pair of high branches, our naked feet dangling, our trouser pockets filled with dried mulberries and walnuts. We took turns with the mirror as we ate mulberries, pelted each other with them, giggling, laughing. I can still see Hassan up on that tree, sunlight flickering through the leaves on his almost perfectly round face, a face like a Chinese doll chiseled from hardwood: his flat, broad nose and slanting, narrow eyes like bamboo leaves, eyes that looked, depending on the light, gold, green, even sapphire. I can still see his tiny low-set ears and that pointed stub of a chin, a meaty appendage that looked like it was added as a mere afterthought. And the cleft lip, just left of midline, where the Chinese doll maker's instrument may have slipped, or perhaps he had simply grown tired and careless.

Sometimes, up in those trees, I talked Hassan into firing walnuts with his slingshot at the neighbor's one-eyed German shepherd. Hassan never wanted to, but if I asked, *really* asked, he wouldn't deny me. Hassan never denied me anything. And he was deadly with his slingshot. Hassan's father, Ali, used to catch us and get mad, or as mad as someone as gentle as Ali could ever get. He would wag his finger and wave us down from the tree. He would take the mirror and tell us what his mother had told him, that the devil shone mirrors too, shone them to distract Muslims during prayer. "And he laughs while he does it," he always added, scowling at his son.

"Yes, Father," Hassan would mumble, looking down at his feet. But he never told on me. Never told that the mirror, like shooting walnuts at the neighbor's dog, was always my idea.

The poplar trees lined the redbrick driveway, which led to a pair of wrought-iron gates. They in turn opened into an extension of the driveway into my father's estate. The house sat on the left side of the brick path, the backyard at the end of it.

Everyone agreed that my father, my Baba, had built the most beautiful house in the Wazir Akbar Khan district, a new and affluent neighborhood in the northern part of Kabul. Some thought it was the prettiest house in all of Kabul. A broad entryway flanked by rosebushes led to the sprawling house of marble floors and wide windows. Intricate mosaic tiles, handpicked by Baba in Isfahan, covered the floors of the four bathrooms. Gold-stitched tapestries, which Baba had bought in Calcutta, lined the walls; a crystal chandelier hung from the vaulted ceiling.

Upstairs was my bedroom, Baba's room, and his study, also known as "the smoking room," which perpetually smelled of tobacco and cinnamon. Baba and his friends reclined on black leather chairs there after Ali had served dinner. They stuffed their pipes – except Baba always called it "fattening the pipe" – and discussed their favorite three topics: politics, business, soccer. Sometimes I asked Baba if I could sit with them, but Baba would stand in the doorway. "Go on, now," he'd say. "This is grown-ups' time. Why don't you go read one of those books of yours?" He'd close the door, leave me to wonder why it was *always* grown-ups' time with him. I'd sit by the door, knees drawn to my chest. Sometimes I sat there for an hour, sometimes two, listening to their laughter, their chatter.

The living room downstairs had a curved wall with custom-built cabinets. Inside sat framed family pictures: an old, grainy photo of my grandfather and King Nadir Shah taken in 1931, two years before the king's assassination; they are standing over a dead deer, dressed in knee-high boots, rifles slung over their shoulders. There was a picture of my parents' wedding night, Baba dashing in his black suit and my mother a smiling young princess in white. Here was Baba and his best friend and business partner, Rahim Khan, standing outside our house, neither one smiling – I am a baby in that photograph and Baba is holding me, looking tired and grim. I'm in his arms, but it's Rahim Khan's pinky my fingers are curled around.

The curved wall led into the dining room, at the center of which was a mahogany table that could easily sit thirty guests – and, given my father's taste for extravagant parties, it did just that almost every week. On the other end of the dining room was a tall marble fireplace, always lit by the orange glow of a fire in the wintertime.

A large sliding glass door opened into a semicircular terrace that overlooked two acres of backyard and rows of cherry trees. Baba and Ali had planted a small vegetable garden along the eastern wall: tomatoes, mint, peppers, and a row of corn that never really took. Hassan and I used to call it "the Wall of Ailing Corn."

On the south end of the garden, in the shadows of a loquat tree, was the servants' home, a modest little mud hut where Hassan lived with his father.

It was there, in that little shack, that Hassan was born in the winter of 1964, just one year after my mother died giving birth to me.

In the eighteen years that I lived in that house, I stepped into Hassan and Ali's quarters only a handful of times. When the sun dropped low behind the hills and we were done playing for the day, Hassan and I parted ways. I went past the rosebushes to Baba's mansion, Hassan to the mud shack where he had been born, where he'd lived his entire life. I remember it was spare, clean, dimly lit by a pair of kerosene lamps. There were two mattresses on opposite sides of the room, a worn Herati rug with frayed edges in between, a three-legged stool, and a wooden table in the corner where Hassan did his drawings. The walls stood bare, save for a single tapestry with sewn-in beads forming the words *Allah-u-akbar*. Baba had bought it for Ali on one of his trips to Mashad.

It was in that small shack that Hassan's mother, Sanaubar, gave birth to him one cold winter day in 1964. While my mother hemorrhaged to death during childbirth, Hassan lost his less than a week after he was born. Lost her to a fate most Afghans considered far worse than death: She ran off with a clan of traveling singers and dancers.

Hassan never talked about his mother, as if she'd never existed. I always wondered if he dreamed about her, about what she looked like, where she was. I wondered if he longed to meet her. Did he ache for her, the way I ached for the mother I had never met? One day, we were walking from my father's house to Cinema Zainab for a new Iranian movie, taking the shortcut through the military barracks near Istiqlal Middle School – Baba had forbidden us to take that shortcut, but he was in Pakistan with Rahim Khan at the time. We hopped the fence that surrounded the barracks, skipped over a little creek, and broke into the open dirt field where old, abandoned tanks collected dust. A group of soldiers huddled in the shade of one of those tanks, smoking cigarettes and playing cards. One of them saw us, elbowed the guy next to him, and called Hassan.

"Hey, you!" he said. "I know you."

We had never seen him before. He was a squatty man with a shaved head and black stubble on his face. The way he grinned at us, leered, scared me. "Just keep walking," I muttered to Hassan.

"You! The Hazara! Look at me when I'm talking to you!" the soldier barked. He handed his cigarette to the guy next to him, made a circle with the thumb and index finger of one hand. Poked the middle finger of his other hand through the circle. Poked it in and out. In and out. "I knew your mother, did you know that? I knew her real good. I took her from behind by that creek over there."

The soldiers laughed. One of them made a squealing sound. I told Hassan to keep walking, keep walking.

"What a tight little sugary cunt she had!" the soldier was saying, shaking hands with the others, grinning. Later, in the dark, after the movie had started, I heard Hassan next to me, croaking. Tears were sliding down his cheeks. I reached across my seat, slung my arm around him, pulled him close. He rested his head on my shoulder. "He took you for someone else," I whispered. "He took you for someone else."

I'm told no one was really surprised when Sanaubar eloped. People *had* raised their eyebrows when Ali, a man who had memorized the Koran, married Sanaubar, a woman nineteen years younger, a beautiful but notoriously unscrupulous woman who lived up to her dishonorable reputation. Like Ali, she was a Shi'a Muslim and an ethnic Hazara. She was also his first cousin and therefore a natural choice for a spouse. But beyond those similarities, Ali and Sanaubar had little in common, least of all their respective appearances. While Sanaubar's brilliant green eyes and impish face had, rumor has it, tempted countless men into sin, Ali had a congenital paralysis of his lower facial muscles, a condition that rendered him unable to smile and left him perpetually grim-faced. It was an odd thing to see the stone-faced Ali happy, or sad, because only his slanted brown eyes glinted with a smile or welled with sorrow. People say that eyes are windows to the soul. Never was that more true than with Ali, who could only reveal himself through his eyes.

I have heard that Sanaubar's suggestive stride and oscillating hips sent men to reveries of infidelity. But polio had left Ali with a twisted, atrophied right leg that was sallow skin over bone with little in between except a paper-thin layer of muscle. I remember one day, when I was eight, Ali was taking me to the bazaar to buy some *naan*. I was walking behind him, humming, trying to imitate his walk. I watched him swing his scraggy leg in a sweeping arc, watched his whole body tilt impossibly to the right every time he planted that foot. It seemed a minor miracle he didn't tip over with each step. When I tried it, I almost fell into the gutter. That got me giggling. Ali turned around, caught me aping him. He didn't say anything. Not then, not ever. He just kept walking.

Ali's face and his walk frightened some of the younger children in the neighborhood. But the real trouble was with the older kids. They chased him on the street, and mocked him when he hobbled by. Some had taken to calling him *Babalu*, or Boogeyman. "Hey, Babalu, who did you eat today?" they barked to a chorus of laughter. "Who did you eat, you flat-nosed Babalu?"

They called him "flat-nosed" because of Ali and Hassan's characteristic Hazara Mongoloid features. For years, that was all I knew about the Hazaras, that they were Mogul descendants, and that they looked a little like Chinese people. School textbooks barely mentioned them and referred to their ancestry only in passing. Then one day, I was in Baba's study, looking through his stuff, when I found one of my mother's old history books. It was written by an Iranian named Khorami. I blew the dust off it, sneaked it into bed with me that night, and was stunned to find an entire chapter on Hazara history. An entire chapter dedicated to Hassan's people! In it, I read that my people, the Pashtuns, had persecuted and oppressed the Hazaras. It said the Hazaras had tried to rise against the Pashtuns in the nineteenth century, but the Pashtuns had "quelled them with unspeakable violence." The book said that my people had killed the Hazaras, driven them from their lands, burned their homes, and sold their women. The book said part of the reason Pashtuns had oppressed the Hazaras was that Pashtuns were Sunni Muslims, while Hazaras were Shi'a. The book said a lot of things I didn't know, things my teachers hadn't mentioned. Things Baba hadn't mentioned either. It also said some things I *did* know, like that people called Hazaras *mice-eating, flat-nosed, load-carrying donkeys*. I had heard some of the kids in the neighborhood yell those names to Hassan.

The following week, after class, I showed the book to my teacher and pointed to the chapter on the Hazaras. He skimmed through a couple of pages, snickered, handed the book back. "That's the one thing Shi'a people do well," he said, picking up his papers, "passing themselves as martyrs." He wrinkled his nose when he said the word Shi'a, like it was some kind of disease.

But despite sharing ethnic heritage and family blood, Sanaubar joined the neighborhood kids in taunting Ali. I have heard that she made no secret of her disdain for his appearance.

"This is a husband?" she would sneer. "I have seen old donkeys better suited to be a husband."

In the end, most people suspected the marriage had been an arrangement of sorts between Ali and his uncle, Sanaubar's father. They said Ali had married his cousin to help restore some honor to his uncle's blemished name, even though Ali, who had been orphaned at the age of five, had no worldly possessions or inheritance to speak of.

Ali never retaliated against any of his tormentors, I suppose partly because he could never catch them with that twisted leg dragging behind him. But mostly because Ali was immune to the insults of his assailants; he had found his joy, his antidote, the moment Sanaubar had given birth to Hassan. It had been a simple enough affair. No obstetricians, no anesthesiologists, no fancy monitoring devices. Just Sanaubar lying on a stained, naked mattress with Ali and a midwife helping her. She hadn't needed much help at all, because, even in birth, Hassan was true to his nature: he was incapable of hurting anyone. A few grunts, a couple of pushes, and out came Hassan. Out he came smiling.

As confided to a neighbor's servant by the garrulous midwife, who had then in turn told anyone who would listen, Sanaubar had taken one glance at the baby in Ali's arms, seen the cleft lip, and barked a bitter laughter.

"There," she had said. "Now you have your own idiot child to do all your smiling for you!" She had refused to even hold Hassan, and just five days later, she was gone.

Baba hired the same nursing woman who had fed me to nurse Hassan. Ali told us she was a blue-eyed Hazara woman from Bamiyan, the city of the giant Buddha statues. "What a sweet singing voice she had," he used to say to us.

What did she sing, Hassan and I always asked, though we already knew – Ali had told us countless times. We just wanted to hear Ali sing.

He'd clear his throat and begin:

On a high mountain I stood,
And cried the name of Ali, Lion of God.
O Ali, Lion of God, King of Men,
Bring joy to our sorrowful hearts.

Then he would remind us that there was a brotherhood between people who had fed from the same breast, a kinship that not even time could break.

Hassan and I fed from the same breasts. We took our first steps on the same lawn in the same yard. And, under the same roof, we spoke our first words.

Mine was *Baba*.

His was *Amir*. My name.

Looking back on it now, I think the foundation for what happened in the winter of 1975 – and all that followed – was already laid in those first words.

THE BOOKSELLER OF KABUL

Åsne Seierstad

Sent to Afghanistan to cover the fall of the Taliban in late 2001, the Norwegian journalist and writer **Åsne Seierstad** (1970–) chances upon Shah Muhammad Rais (alias Sultan Khan) in his bookshop and with the war correspondent's instincts for a good story immediately senses 'a history book on two feet'. She gets herself invited into the Khans' home and stays several months, exploiting the advantage conferred upon Western women in a Muslim society of being treated both as a woman – with privileged access to the family's wives and daughters – and an honorary man. She moves easily between these two often polarised worlds, recording everything she encounters and offering glimpses into all aspects of Afghan life, from the planning of arranged marriages and furtive courtships which may result in death, to women bathing in the hammam and undersexed men setting off on a pilgrimage to the northern city of Mazar-i-Sharif. The tension between the clashing worldviews of a Scandinavian liberal feminist on the one hand and a patriarchal Afghan paterfamilias on the other makes this an electrifying read.

Published in 2002, *The Bookseller of Kabul* was a controversial international bestseller. In an unexpected postscript in 2007, Shah Muhammad, who objected strongly to the way he and his family had been portrayed, published his riposte in *Once Upon a Time There Was a Bookseller in Kabul*. Rais's second wife Suraia meanwhile sued for defamation and in 2010 a court in Oslo found Seierstad guilty of defamation and 'negligent journalistic practices', ordering her to pay damages. In a later appeal, however, Seierstad was cleared of invading the privacy of the Rais family.

When Sultan Khan thought the time had come to find himself a new wife, no one wanted to help him. First he approached his mother.

"You will have to make do with the one you have," she said.

Then he went to his eldest sister. "I'm fond of your first wife," she said. His other sisters replied in the same vein.

"It's shaming for Sharifa," said his aunt.

Sultan needed help. A suitor cannot himself ask for a girl's hand. It is an Afghan custom that one of the women of the family convey the proposal and give the girl the once-over to assure herself that she is capable, well brought up, and suitable wife material. But none of Sultan's close female relations wanted to have anything to do with this offer of marriage.

Sultan had picked out three young girls he thought might fit the bill. They were all healthy and good-looking, and of his own tribe. In Sultan's family it was rare to marry outside the clan; it was considered prudent and safe to marry relatives, preferably cousins.

Sultan's first candidate was sixteen-year-old Sonya. Her eyes were dark and almond-shaped and her hair shining black. She was shapely, voluptuous, and it was said of her that she was a good worker. Her family was poor and they were reasonably closely related. Her mother's grandmother and Sultan's mother's grandmother were sisters.

While Sultan ruminated over how to ask for the hand of the chosen one without the help of family women, his first wife was blissfully ignorant that a mere chit of a girl, born the same year she and Sultan were married, was Sultan's constant preoccupation. Sharifa was getting old. Like Sultan, she was a few years over fifty. She had borne him three sons and a daughter. The time had come for a man of Sultan's standing to find a new wife.

"Do it yourself," his brother said finally.

After some thought, Sultan realized that this was his only solution, and early one morning he made his way to the house of the sixteen-year-old. Her parents greeted him with open arms. Sultan was considered a generous man and a visit from him was always welcome. Sonya's mother boiled water and made tea. They reclined on flat cushions in the mud cottage and exchanged pleasantries until Sultan thought the time had come to make his proposal.

"A friend of mine would like to marry Sonya," he told the parents.

It was not the first time someone had asked for their daughter's hand. She was beautiful and diligent, but they thought she was still a bit young. Sonya's father was no longer able to work. During a brawl a knife had severed some of the nerves in his back. His beautiful daughter could be used as a bargaining chip in the marriage stakes, and he and his wife were always expecting the next bid to be even higher.

"He is rich," said Sultan. "He's in the same business as I am. He is well educated and has three sons. But his wife is starting to grow old."

"What's the state of his teeth?" the parents asked immediately, alluding to the friend's age.

"About like mine," said Sultan. "You be the judge."

Old, the parents thought. But that was not necessarily a disadvantage. The older the man, the higher the price for their daughter. A bride's price is calculated according to age, beauty, and skill and according to the status of the family.

When Sultan Khan had delivered his message, the parents said, as could be expected, "She is too young."

Anything else would be to sell short to this rich, unknown suitor whom Sultan recommended so warmly. It would not do to appear too eager. But they knew Sultan would return; Sonya was young and beautiful.

He returned the next day and repeated the proposal. The same conversation, the same answers. But this time he got to meet Sonya, whom he had not seen since she was a young girl.

She kissed his hand, in the custom of showing respect for an elder relative, and he blessed the top of her head with a kiss. Sonya was aware of the charged atmosphere and flinched under Uncle Sultan's searching look.

"I have found you a rich man, what do you think of that?" he asked. Sonya looked down at the floor. A young girl has no right to have an opinion about a suitor.

Sultan returned the third day, and this time he made known the suitor's proposition: a ring, a necklace, earrings, and bracelet, all in red gold; as many clothes as she wanted; 600 pounds of rice, 300 pounds of cooking oil, a cow, a few sheep, and 15 million afghani, approximately $500.

Sonya's father was more than satisfied with the price and asked to meet this mysterious man who was prepared to pay so much for his daughter. According to Sultan, he even belonged to their tribe, in spite of their not being able to place him or remember that they had ever met him.

"Tomorrow," said Sultan, "I will show you a picture of him."

The next day, fortified by a sweetener, Sultan's aunt agreed to reveal to Sonya's parents the identity of the suitor. She took a photograph with her – a picture of Sultan Khan himself – and with it the uncompromising message that they had no more than an hour to make up their minds. If the answer was yes, he would be very grateful, and if it was no, there would be no bad blood between them. What he wanted to avoid at all costs was everlasting bargaining about maybe, maybe not.

The parents agreed within the hour. They were keen on Sultan Khan, his money, and his position. Sonya sat in the attic and waited. When the mystery surrounding the suitor had been solved and the parents had decided to accept, her father's brother came up to the attic. "Uncle Sultan is your wooer," he said. "Do you consent?"

Not a sound escaped Sonya's lips. With tearful eyes and bowed head, she hid behind her long shawl.

"Your parents have accepted the suitor," her uncle said. "Now is your only chance to express an opinion."

She was petrified, paralyzed by fear. She did not want the man but she knew she had to obey her parents. As Sultan's wife, her standing in Afghan society would go up considerably. The bride money would solve many of her family's problems. The money would help her parents buy good wives for their sons.

Sonya held her tongue, and with that her fate was sealed. To say nothing means to give one's consent. The agreement was drawn up, the date fixed.

Sultan went home to inform his family of the news. His wife, Sharifa, his mother, and his sisters were seated around a dish of rice and spinach. Sharifa thought he was joking and laughed and cracked some jokes in return. His mother too laughed at Sultan's joke. She could not believe that he had entered into a proposal of marriage without her blessing. The sisters were dumbfounded.

No one believed him, not until he showed them the kerchief and sweetmeats the parents of a bride give the suitor as proof of the engagement.

Sharifa cried for twenty days. "What have I done? What a disgrace. Why are you dissatisfied with me?"

Sultan told her to pull herself together. No one in the family backed him up, not even his own sons. Nevertheless, no one dared speak out against him – he always got his own way.

Sharifa was inconsolable. What really rankled was the fact that the man had picked an illiterate, someone who had not even completed nursery school. She, Sharifa, was a qualified Persian language teacher. "What has she got that I haven't got?" she sobbed.

Sultan rose above his wife's tears.

No one wanted to attend the engagement party. But Sharifa had to bite the bullet and dress up for the celebrations.

"I want everyone to see that you agree and support me. In the future we will all be living under the same roof and you must show that Sonya is welcome," he demanded. Sharifa had always humored her husband, and now too, in this worst circumstance, giving him to someone else, she knuckled under. He even demanded that Sharifa should put the rings on his and Sonya's fingers.

Twenty days after the proposal of marriage the solemn engagement ritual took place. Sharifa pulled herself together and put on a brave face. Her female relatives did their best to unsettle her. "How awful for you," they said. "How badly he has treated you. You must be suffering."

The wedding took place two months after the engagement, on the day of the Muslim New Year's Eve. This time Sharifa refused to attend.

"I can't," she told her husband.

The female family members backed her up. No one bought new dresses or applied the normal amount of makeup required at wedding ceremonies. They wore simple coiffures and stiff smiles – in deference to the superannuated wife who would no longer share Sultan Khan's bed. It was now reserved for the young, terrified bride – but they would all be under the same roof, until death did them part.

'MUTTON STEW WITH THE LION OF THE PANJSHIR'

Justin Marozzi

In the winter of 1996, I was on my way to a new job as the *FT*'s stringer in the Philippines, the lowliest rank of foreign correspondent. The meagre monthly salary, too little to live on by itself, was supplemented by modest 'lineage' payments. If you didn't get stories published, in other words, you didn't eat. I made the journey to Manila via a busman's holiday in Afghanistan, hoping to interview Ahmad Shah Massoud, who was then leading the fight against the Taliban from his mountain headquarters in Jebel Seraj. A quarter of a century later it remains my favourite interview.

As those Russian soldiers who fought him in Afghanistan during the 1980s will tell you, Commander Ahmed Shah Massoud is an extremely difficult man to hunt down – let alone have lunch with. These are testing times for Afghanistan's most celebrated guerrilla commander and ousted defence minister, now leading the fight against the Taliban Islamic militia which took Kabul in September and now controls two-thirds of the country. With the first heavy snowfalls of winter upon him, Massoud is under pressure to retake the capital or reach a settlement.

After four days, a high-speed car chase and fruitless attempts to corner him in blizzards and sub-zero temperatures, Massoud finally consents to a press conference at his military headquarters in Jebel Seraj, a windswept town high in the Hindu Kush mountains 40 miles north of Kabul. Lunch *à deux* seems an unlikely prospect.

Jebel Seraj is heavy with Massoud's forces, a grisly Aladdin's cave littered with the paraphernalia of war. Tanks rumble through the muddy streets, past armoured personnel carriers, rocket launchers, artillery guns and shivering soldiers armed with Kalashnikovs. Amid this noisy military orchestra, four-wheel drive Toyotas with tinted windows ferry its conductor, Massoud, to and fro at breakneck speed.

"The Lion of Panjshir" is the sobriquet that he earned after his exploits against the Russian invaders in the Panjshir valley. Fearing that lunch with the FT may not be top of agenda on retiring for the day, I ask him if he is feeling hungry. The interpreter looks long and hard at me, a stony expression indicating this is not the sort of question one asks the great man.

After some cajoling, he sheepishly translates my crude hint and, after conferring with his leader, an aide announces in polished French that if I would like to have lunch with the commander, I would be most welcome.

Massoud motions me courteously into a private dining room – harshly lit and empty save for a small table, a set of chairs and a sink. This is one of the few Kalashnikov-free zones in town. Other than an uninspiring still life, the white walls are bare. There is no carpet on the concrete floor.

The Chitrali cap, sported at a rather rakish angle, sits atop a handsome face lined with two decades of warfare. At 42, Massoud is already beyond the average life expectancy of Afghan men and admits his best years are behind him. The eyes are deep, dark and in earnest as he looks back with pride to his leading role in harrying the Soviets out of Afghanistan in 1989, 10 years after their invasion.

A matching woollen waistcoat worn over an army sweater, khaki fatigues and black boots – he is rumoured to have a penchant for the custom-made Russian paratrooper variety – completes the ensemble of the mountain warrior. There is an unmistakable whiff of power and authority about him, but for a man who has done little else but wage war since 1973 he is remarkably gentle and softly spoken. A quiet dignity underpins his massive presense.

"I am sorry lunch is going to be very basic," he says in mellifluous Dari [Afghan Farsi], waving a large hand over the table on which two bowls of mutton, potato, onion and tomato stew, served with heaps of nan bread. "If I had known you were coming a little earlier, I would have had something special prepared."

The counter-revolutionary career took off at the age of 19, he tells me, in the wake of the coup which overthrew King Mohammed Zahir Shah, installed a pro-communist regime, and declared Afghanistan a republic. He abandoned an engineering degree at Kabul University, then home to the conflicting movements of Islamic nationalism and communism.

Formal education ended there but Massoud remained a voracious reader. After Kabul's recent fall, he relocated his home to Panjshir, taking with him his 3,000 volumes of literature. In the little spare time war affords him, he enjoys reading the 14th-century spiritual Iranian poet Hafiz.

We face each other across a cheap plastic table cover. I ask him his favourite food and the interpreter looks startled again. Massoud is used to reporting his latest military advance but admits, almost shyly, to finding "personal questions the most difficult to answer." The interpreter suggests milk as Massoud's preferred tipple, realises this is insufficient as an answer, and then remarks with an air of finality, "Commander Massoud likes whatever he eats."

Subject closed. Massoud is here to talk Afghanistan and not milkshakes.

It is something he does with ease and charm and an animation which stems from an intense religious faith and a profound love of Afghanistan, notwithstanding the fact that he has done much to destroy the country himself. The Russians left Kabul virtually unscathed. Today, after more than four years of factional fighting between Massoud and rival Mujahideen, much of the capital lies in rubble.

I suggest Afghanistan is doomed always to fall victim to its deep ethnic fault-lines. The current war pits Tajik Massoud – in coalition with Uzbek warlord General Dostam – against the Pashtun Taliban. He shakes his head and moves both elbows on to the table, citing a host of examples to prove that these division are not fixed; Uzbeks fight Tajiks, Pashtuns embrace Tajiks and so on.

"This is only one part of the problem," he observes. Afghanistan's war, he says, has always been the creation of foreign powers, with Pakistan the master villain. "It has been very difficult to get rid of the Russians and then deal with Pakistan," he says, stroking his beard sadly.

"Pakistan created the Taliban."

Returning to his own background, his mood lightens and the face creases into a smile while he informs me that at 25 he could look back on two *coups d'état* and a failed provincial rebellion.

"I had a Sten gun and 20 men with me in the Panjshir. We robbed a bank and told everyone there had been a coup in Kabul. But there was nothing in the newspapers or radio to confirm it and people soon discovered nothing had happened." He was now a wanted man but the episode is recounted as though it were merely a boyish prank, the sort of thing Just William might have got up to on a lazy half holiday.

My mutton is getting cold, I tackle it dutifully, expecting the worst, but am pleasantly surprised by a tender and spicy concoction. The robust potatoes are a tasty relief after the monotony of bread and kebabs and we both tuck into second helpings. After earlier experiences, I avoid the glass of water which sits temptingly at my elbow. The unfortunate interpreter, who looks ravenous, is unable to grab even a mouthful, forever struggling to keep up with Massoud, who is hugely engaging but rarely concise.

Mutton removed, we turn our attention to a plate of grapes which have seen better days. Discussing his immediate military plans, he stops chewing and vigorously disputes the idea that he and his forces are on the back foot against the advancing Taliban. He borrows my pen, makes a hasty sketch of Afghanistan and the positions of the opposing sides, and details an extension of the front line into the Taliban's weakest spots. I feel it is best not to argue.

A pot of tea arrives with a bowl of toffees, walnuts and almonds. As lunch draws to a close, I ask him whether there are any plans to retire from the battlefield and perhaps write a book. He laughs at first but then the gravitas of the man of war returns. "I have never fought for happiness, nor have I fought for power. I don't want to continue fighting one more day but while I am alive I will do everything to defend my country."

He makes another graceful apology for our simple repast, slips quietly out of the room, and disappears, swallowed up by the entourage of waiting generals.

'A LETTER TO THE PEOPLE OF THE UNITED STATES OF AMERICA'

Ahmad Shah Massoud

One of the world's most famous and charismatic guerrilla leaders, **Ahmad Shah Massoud** (1953–2001) was the face of the Afghan resistance to the Soviet occupation from 1979 to 1989, a heroic role which earned him the affectionate nickname 'Lion of the Panjshir'. An ethnic Tajik from the Panjshir Valley of northern Afghanistan, he was a handsome, poetry-loving man frequently photographed with his trademark *pakol* perched on his head at a rakish angle. He became defence minister in the 1990s and later led the military opposition to the Taliban until his assassination on the eve of al-Qaeda's 9/11 attacks.

Massoud's 1998 message to the American people is a stirring call to arms against the Taliban, a piercing *J'accuse* levelled at the Pakistani state and a resonating reaffirmation of his quest 'to preserve our freedom, independence, right to self-determination and dignity'. It makes for poignant reading in the light of his assassination on 9 September 2001 by al-Qaeda terrorists disguised as television journalists. By removing Massoud from the battlefield, al-Qaeda had successfully eliminated the 'West's Best Friend in Afghanistan'.

I send this message to you today on behalf of the freedom and peace-loving people of Afghanistan, the Mujahedeen freedom fighters who resisted and defeated Soviet communism, the men and women who are still resisting oppression and foreign hegemony, and in the name of more than one and a half million Afghan martyrs who sacrificed their lives to uphold some of the same values and ideals shared by most Americans and Afghans alike. This is a crucial and unique moment in the history of Afghanistan and the world, a time when Afghanistan has crossed yet another threshold and is entering a new stage of struggle and resistance for its survival as a free nation and independent state.

I have spent the past 20 years, most of my youth and adult life, alongside my compatriots, at the service of the Afghan nation, fighting an uphill battle to preserve our freedom, independence, right to self-determination and dignity. Afghans fought for God and country, sometime alone, at other times with the support of the international community. Against all odds, we, meaning the free world and Afghans, halted and checkmated Soviet expansionism a decade ago. But the embattled people of my country did not savor the fruits of victory. Instead they were thrust in a whirlwind of foreign intrigue, deception, great-gamesmanship and internal strife. Our country and our noble people were brutalized, the victims of misplaced greed, hegemonic designs and ignorance. We Afghans erred too. Our shortcomings were as a result of political innocence, inexperience, vulnerability, victimization, bickering and inflated egos. But by no means does this justify what some of our so-called Cold War allies did to undermine this just victory and unleash their diabolical plans to destroy and subjugate Afghanistan.

Today, the world clearly sees and feels the results of such misguided and evil deeds. South-Central Asia is in turmoil, some countries on the brink of war. Illegal drug production, terrorist activities and planning are on the rise. Ethnic and religiously-motivated mass murders and forced displacements are taking place, and the most basic human and women's rights are shamelessly violated. The country has gradually been occupied by fanatics, extremists, terrorists, mercenaries, drug Mafias and professional murderers. One faction, the Taliban, which by no means rightly represents Islam, Afghanistan or our centuries-old cultural heritage, has with direct foreign assistance exacerbated this explosive situation. They are unyielding and unwilling to talk or reach a compromise with any other Afghan side.

Unfortunately, this dark accomplishment could not have materialized without the direct support and involvement of influential governmental and non-governmental circles in Pakistan. Aside from receiving military logistics, fuel and arms from Pakistan, our intelligence reports indicate that more than 28,000 Pakistani citizens, including paramilitary personnel and military advisers are part of the Taliban occupation forces in various parts of Afghanistan. We currently hold more than 500 Pakistani citizens including military personnel in our POW camps. Three major concerns – namely terrorism, drugs and human rights – originate from Taliban-held areas but are instigated from Pakistan, thus forming the inter-connecting angles of an evil triangle. For many Afghans, regardless of ethnicity or religion, Afghanistan, for the second time in one decade, is once again an occupied country.

Let me correct a few fallacies that are propagated by Taliban backers and their lobbies around the world. This situation over the short and long-run, even in case of total control by the Taliban, will not be to anyone's interest. It will not result in stability, peace and prosperity in the region. The people of Afghanistan will not accept such a repressive regime. Regional countries will never feel secure and safe. Resistance will not end in Afghanistan, but will take on a new national dimension, encompassing all Afghan ethnic and social strata.

The goal is clear. Afghans want to regain their right to self-determination through a democratic or traditional mechanism acceptable to our people. No one group, faction or individual has the right to dictate or impose its will by force or proxy on others. But first, the obstacles have to be overcome, the war has to end, just peace established and a transitional administration set up to move us toward a representative government.

We are willing to move toward this noble goal. We consider this as part of our duty to defend humanity against the scourge of intolerance, violence and fanaticism. But the international community and the democracies of the world should not waste any valuable time, and instead play their critical role to assist in any way possible the valiant people of Afghanistan overcome the obstacles that exist on the path to freedom, peace, stability and prosperity.

Effective pressure should be exerted on those countries who stand against the aspirations of the people of Afghanistan. I urge you to engage in constructive and substantive discussions with our representatives and all Afghans who can and want to be part of a broad consensus for peace and freedom for Afghanistan.

With all due respect and my best wishes for the government and people of the United States,

Ahmad Shah Massoud

POETRY OF THE TALIBAN

Alex Strick van Linschoten and
Felix Kuehn (Editors)

Ever since they first emerged out of the chaos of the Afghan civil war in the mid-1990s, the Taliban have been well known for their martial abilities. Their literary talents have received rather less attention. Who knew, for instance, that the fighters contained so many poets in their ranks? Outside Afghanistan, and before this book was published in 2012, hardly anybody would be my guess. And yet here they are in all their glory, over two hundred of them, bursting into verse in a reminder that this is a culture in which poetry is an everyday and deeply cherished phenomenon. There are the lovelorn, the romantic poets writing mournfully about unrequited love, then there are the nationalist sons of Afghanistan sworn to removing the infidel invader, the religiously inclined defenders of the faith, those who revel in the thrill of battle and those who deplore the violence which has done so much to disfigure Afghanistan and its society. It is easy to stereotype the Taliban, although rather more difficult after reading this remarkable and thought-provoking book.

Alex Strick van Linschoten is a former researcher who read Arabic and Farsi at London's School of Oriental and African Studies and worked in Afghanistan from 2006. **Felix Kuehn** is a researcher and writer who has written about the Taliban insurgency and the history of Afghanistan. Van Linschoten and Kuehn collaborated on *An Enemy We Created*, a study of the Afghan Taliban and their relationship to al-Qaeda.

I am an Afghan Mujahed

Gun in my hand and dagger under my arm, I am going to battle;
I am an Afghan *mujahed*, I am an Afghan *mujahed*.
I may be a victim for my homeland a hundred times;
I am an Afghan *mujahed*, I am an Afghan *mujahed*.
I have my religion; I have my faith and the law of the holy *Qur'an*;
I am an Afghan *mujahed*, I am an Afghan *mujahed*.
Anyone who looks the wrong way at me will find himself lost for ever,
Look, I am a known champion in history,
I am an Afghan *mujahed*, I am an Afghan *mujahed*.
We have the proper *shari'a* and believe in it at all times,
Shari'a is my light and I am light of heart in its light,
I am an Afghan *mujahed*, I am an Afghan *mujahed*.
We want a free life, we want stability for every place,
Because I love truth and will never tolerate injustice:
I am an Afghan *mujahed*, I am an Afghan *mujahed*.
We hate the war, but we are fighting in the war.
If war is imposed on us, then I am the man of the field,
I am an Afghan *mujahed*, I am an Afghan *mujahed*.
Oh cruel coloniser! Take it from me, Qatin,
I avenge the people, I am committed to my promise:
I am an Afghan *mujahed*, I am an Afghan *mujahed*.

Qatin
October 28, 2008

Trenches

Hot, hot trenches are full of joy;
Attacks on the enemy are full of joy.
Guns in our hands and magazine belts over my shoulders;
Grenades on my chest are full of joy.
The enemy can't resist when he sees them;
Black hair and stiff moustaches are full of joy.
He who fights in the field is manly;
Houses full of black-haired women are full of joy.
We become eager two times after hearing it:
The clang, clang and rockets are full of joy.
Leave the lips and spring, O poet!
Poems full of feeling are full of joy.
Jawad, I say, on the true path of *jihad*,
All kinds of troubles are full of joy.

Jawad
May 21, 2008

Afghanistan is the home of Afghans

Afghanistan is the home of Afghans;
It is the home of the brave and courageous.
Foreigners won't be able to weaken it by force;
This is the home of Mirwais' sons.
These people defeated Brydon's armies;
This is the home of Macnaghten's murderers.
They gave an embarrassing defeat to the Russians;
Gromov admits that this is the home of victors.
Tribes and clans are found here;
This is the home of the Hazaras and Turkmen.
Tajiks, Uzbeks, Pashtuns and Baluch;
This the home of devoted Afghans as well.
These mountains are ours and we belong to these mounts;
This is the home of the eagles.
Jackals can't hold out here;
This is the home of *Allah's* great lions.
Ahmad Shah's sword did not cool down yet;
This is the home of the followers of the right religion.
These are the sons of Ghouri and Ghaznawi;
This is the home of those heroes.
Great Jamaluddin Afghan;
This is the home of his followers.
These people give their heads for their religion;
This is the home of Islam's servants.
The invading forces will eventually leave;
This is the home of strong heroes.

Dardmand
August 26, 2008

I live in flames

I live in thorns like a flower;
Like the butterfly, I live in flames.
If anyone asks you about me,
I am an Afghan living in the valleys.
I don't like anybody else's palaces;
I am the son of Afghans; I live in a tent.
When I see the country's wounds,
I start screaming and sigh.
I will always care about my country;
What happened to Afghans? I live in thought.
The enemy came and became our boss today,
My country was destroyed; I live in ruins.
My country cries aloud here,
That's why I live in grief once again.
Is there anyone who will wash away my tears?
I am Kabul, living in red flames.
Light has left my homeland,
I am falling in every direction; I live in the dark.
I am Watanyar, in mourning for my country,
I am awake each night until dawn.

Abdul Basir Watanyar
June 20, 2008

Afghans bring me to tears

The cruelties of the entire world bring me to tears;
Aside from my rival and the bearer of news, my beloved also makes me cry.
He rolls around in the soil with his bare head and feet,
These orphans of our country bring me to tears.
Autumn has made the flowers of the garden fall and wilt,
The nightingale's cries in the garden bring me to tears.
Pretty like parrots dispersed and wandering around,
Afghans wandering in other countries bring me to tears.
The *kuffar* don't permit me to be happy in my own country,
Ready with swords in hand, the cruel ones bring me to tears.
When I recall Malalai being injured, I feel regret,
But for now, they don't permit me; my own wishes bring me to tears.
I imagine any other country is beautiful like a flower,
Kabul smells of gunpowder, it brings me to tears.

Hayatullah Khaksar
December 4, 2007

DANCING IN THE MOSQUE
AN AFGHAN MOTHER'S LETTERS TO HER SON

Homeira Qaderi

All too often the voices of Afghan women go unheard. Some would argue that one of the reasons for Afghanistan's terrible and enduring tragedies has been the exclusion of Afghan women from the public sphere. In recent years, however, a growing number of women writers have been published, in Afghan languages and in English. Inevitably some of these writings have been from exile as the country continues to export so many of its people fleeing strife. **Homeira Qaderi** (1980–), a writer, activist and professor of Persian literature, quickly fell foul of the Taliban regime while still a teenager, receiving death threats after secretly home-schooling girls and boys and publishing a short story. Forced into exile in Iran, she became director of a cultural society for Afghan writers there.

Published in 2020, *Dancing in the Mosque* is Qaderi's seventh book, a blazing memoir of a woman's life in a profoundly conservative, patriarchal society.

Bread and Bullets

Afghanistan is the land of invisible bullets and the land of a death foretold, the land of doomed destinies, and the land of dejected and disgruntled youth, waiting forever for dreams that will never come true. This is how *Madar*, my mother, Ansari, and *Nanah-jan*, my grandmother, Firozah, described my homeland to me when I was barely four years old. In their eyes, Afghanistan was divided between the Russian occupiers and their communist government allies on the one side and the mujahideen on the other. But for me, Afghanistan was divided between the street in front of our house where I played during cease-fires, and the dangerous world beyond our walls when war returned and kept me stuck inside.

I was a bright, playful child, too young and energetic to understand fear, whether of invisible bullets buzzing through the air or of Russian tanks rumbling in the street outside our house. Inside those walls, there was a courtyard filled with apple and mulberry trees, and red and green grapes growing on the vine. We were three generations living there: *Baba-jan* and *Nanah-jan*, their four daughters, my aunts Kurbra, Hajar, Zahra, and Azizah, my uncles Naseer and Basheer, *Agha* and *Madar*, plus my baby brother, Mushtaq, and me.

Nanah-jan always said, "A girl should have fear in her eyes."

I spent a lot of time in front of the hallway mirror, examining my eyes to discover where the fear was hiding.

Aunt Zahra told me, "A girl's fear is right on her eyelids."

I would turn my eyelids inside out, hoping to detect the shape or color of fear.

Madar often said, "The night this girl was born, we were surrounded by fire. It felt like the city was giving birth. Before Homeira heard her own cries, she heard other people's screams. No wonder she isn't afraid of anything."

Zahra was seventeen when she was struck by one of those invisible bullets while she was trying to pull me out of the grapevine and carry me to safety in the basement. My poor aunt fell down on her face. I could hear her gasping for breath. Blood was pouring out of her eyes. I stopped searching for the kittens and tried to find the invisible bullet in her eye, the place where a girl's fear is hidden.

I can't remember a time when my homeland was not at war. My childhood began with jet-fighter attacks, bombs falling from the sky, and me trying to count invisible bullets. War and hunger, those are my earliest memories. I remember *Madar* trying to breast-feed my brother, even after he was past the age of two, because there was no food left to eat. Mushtaq chewed and bit my mother's breast. I heard *Madar*'s quiet whimpering when she knew she had no milk left.

During each attack I watched *Nanah-jan* tie her hijab tighter so that she wouldn't die without her veil and be thrown into hell in the hereafter. Even though she was illiterate, she often pretended to read the Holy Qur'an as she would run her index finger over the written lines of the scripture. She wanted to die a Muslim, holding the Holy Book close to her chest. And when I heard *Baba-jan* reading *Surah Yaseen*, the chapter on God's sovereignty, the Day of Judgment, and a warning to nonbelievers, I knew that another bombing attack was coming.

My childhood world was within the bounds of a small window, low in the wall of our house, and a mother who was always trying to keep me away from that window. She knew bullets could pierce glass. She tried her best to keep me surrounded by four solid cement walls. My mother was like a spider trying to safeguard me within her web. But I was a wild, stubborn baby spider. I kept tearing her web apart to escape. I never tired of the struggle to get outside. I was always looking for a chance to sneak into our walled garden. I wanted to be the first to discover the new bullet holes in the walls. I wanted to be the first one to touch the damaged trees and the burnt timber. To be the first to find the kittens hiding under our grapevine. Finding those invisible bullets was my most secret wish. I asked my mother, "Where do all these invisible bullets come from?"

"Homeira," she said, smoothing my hair, "we cannot see where they come from and we never see where they will go until they strike a tree or a wall or, God forbid, a person."

But there were good days, too. I remember sneaking out of the house with Azizah on a day when there was no shooting. I remember the bright sunshine and the flow of a gentle wind of the season. I sat with my back against the sun-warmed wall of our house, playing in the dust and watching people passing by. I was totally unaware of the Russian tanks approaching on the nearby streets.

During cease-fires, I had the habit of going to the smoldering rubble of the bombed houses to see the new ruins and how the gardens had been laid to waste. I wanted to see the crumbling walls, the broken windows, the smashed closets, and the shattered china.

Once, in one of the houses that had been destroyed three or four days earlier, I saw a Russian soldier with his pants down; he was pressing his hand on the mouth of a neighbor's daughter. From behind the wall I laughed at the Russian soldier's bare bottom. He heard my laughter. He quickly got up, put one hand between his legs, and with his other hand he slapped me on my face until it burned. Then he spat in front of me. The girl used that moment to get up, put on her head scarf, and run away through the ruins.

Later I would laughingly tell everyone this story about how red the Russian soldier's buttocks were. Upon hearing my account of the event, Uncle Basheer punched the wall with his fists in anger. *Baba-jan* didn't laugh at the story. He just wiped his tears.

In those days, Herat was a very strange mixture of heaven and hell. Sometimes, when the city was at peace, you could hear the returning birds chirping in trees. Sometimes, I could hear sweet musical notes as our neighbor's son, Shuaib, sat on the wall playing a reed flute. I would dance to his music on our terrace, but *Nanah-jan* feared that melody, believing that the sound of the flute foretold early death. And soon, indeed, Shuaib died in a fire that consumed his house.

Nanah-jan once said, "I wish we were all birds, so we could fly out of this place."

Almost every morning there was a long row of olive-green Russian tanks on the street in front of the hospital near our house, their engines idling under the tall pine trees that lined the road in a cacophony of noise. They would disappear in the haze of dusk. I asked my grandfather, "*Baba-jan*, tell me, where do the tanks come from every morning and where do they go every night?"

Baba-jan looked and whispered under his breath, "They come from hell and they go back to hell."

I told Azizah that we should follow behind the Russian tanks so we could discover the path to hell.

"It's too far away, Homeira," she said emphatically. "We would get very tired."

I told her she was afraid of the Russian tanks.

When *Nanah-jan* no longer had nuts in her pockets, she could no longer bribe Azizah and me to stay in the house. As soon as the city lapsed into silence, we would escape into the street when *Madar* and *Nanah-jan* weren't looking. Once, a soldier gave me a tin of canned food. Because we were always hungry, I brought it home. *Nanah-jan* was horrified, shouting, "*Haram! Haram!* These cans are filled with frogs," she said. "That's what the red soldiers eat."

When Azizah and I heard this, we ran into the backyard and threw up.

A few frogs lived in the small stream in our garden, jumping around during the day and croaking their special songs in the evening. On the nights when there was silence, my heart broke for those poor little frogs. I knew the Russians had eaten them. I cried for them under my blanket.

During the cease-fires, our entertainment was collecting pinecones or running among the tanks, playing hide-and-seek with the boys. When the boys hid and I couldn't find them, the Russian soldiers sitting on the tank turrets would point to the boys' hiding spots. I remember that whenever I found a boy, the soldiers would clap and shout, their faces growing red with their laughter. Then I understood why we called the Soviet Army the "Red Army."

One day, when it was my turn to hide, one of those red soldiers beckoned me over, a big smile on his round face. He bent down from the top of the tank, reaching his arms toward me. I held my arms up to him. He took my hands and pulled me up into the tank, scraping my shoulder against its hot iron side. My shoulder hurt, but I forgot the pain as soon as I looked around. I stared in amazement at the hundreds of buttons and blinking lights. It was stuffy inside and very hot. Another soldier was sitting on a metal seat. When he caught sight of me, he leaned toward me and said something to the first soldier, who answered quickly. They both started laughing. Then the seated man put his face against a round object.

I crawled over and began to touch some buttons beside him.

Looking at me over his shoulder, he said, "*Nyet. Na, na.*"

I pointed at the tube. He leaned back in his seat and motioned for me to stand in front of him. I put my eye against the end of the tube. Inside I saw a small, round city. When the soldier turned a knob, the city became smaller. He turned the knob more, and the city inside became tiny and far away. I got scared and pulled my eye away. I looked around. We were all still the same size inside the tank. The soldier laughed and turned the knob again. He gestured with his chin, asking me to look into the tube again. The city came closer. The trees got bigger. The size of people standing and crying in front of the hospital grew larger. I saw Azizah, who was still looking for me. Her face was big enough in the tube to see the fear in her eyes. I saw girls in flowery dresses collecting pinecones. The boys had lost the game; they couldn't find me.

I was five when I saw my city from inside the viewfinder of a Russian tank, my small city, my big city, the city that was very far from me and yet very close to me again. The soldier gave me chocolate. I looked at him and felt ashamed.

On one of those days, one of those tanks fired at our neighborhood and left half of our street in ruins. Another hit our grapevine. We then went to the basement and were living there for a while. We covered the floor with two large rugs and brought down blankets and slept there at night.

I played for hours with a doll that *Nanah-jan* had made for me. I asked *Nanah-jan*, "Can you make another dress for my doll so she becomes happy again?"

Nanah-jan promised that she would, as soon as she found some nice fabric.

So I was overjoyed when the tailor shop down the street took a direct hit. As soon as the jets disappeared from the sky, I ran outside and searched the ruins for some beautiful cloth for my doll. Rummaging through the debris, I found a few nice pieces that were only a little dusty.

I ran home and showed them to *Nanah-jan*. I was so excited about getting a new dress made for my doll that I forgot to tell her I saw a hand moving in the rubble. My grandmother looked at the fabric and her eyes widened. "Take it back! This is *haram*!"

"These aren't frogs!" I said.

I never gave them back to the moving hand. I hid them under the grapevine.

During the war, there was no flour, so *Nanah-jan* couldn't bake bread anymore, not even the usual two small cakes for Azizah and me. It got even worse later when the roads to Herat were all blocked by the fighting and we didn't even have potatoes to eat.

Nanah-jan said that the mujahideen were starving as well.

"They can eat frogs," I said. "Or those big Russian chocolates with honey inside."

"Homeira," a startled *Nanah-jan* said. "How do you know what's inside Russian chocolate?"

In an attempt to survive the Russian onslaught, people had learned how to pretend to be sympathetic to Russians by hoisting red banners on their front doors or roofs. Aunt Hajar hung a bright red cloth from the clothesline in the yard, so when the Russian jets were spinning above they would see our household as being sympathetic to them and wouldn't bomb us. My grandmother, who considered any sympathy with the communists a sin, cursed her, saying we would all die as *kaffirs*, nonbelievers, and end up in hell. "We are not communists! Take down that red cloth from the clothesline," she said.

"Does being a Muslim or a *kaffir* depend on a red cloth? She considers the hoisting of the red cloth an act of blasphemy and doesn't understand these murderous Russians. Does she really think God is that unmerciful?" Hajar said. "I just don't want to be killed."

At night, it was the mujahideen's turn. They did a house-to-house search for communists and collaborators, climbing walls and jumping into gardens and courtyards. Aunt Hajar hung a green cloth from the clothesline. I teased her, saying, "Should I tell the mujahideen that you hang a red cloth out in the daytime?"

"Homeira! I will tell them you ate Russian chocolate," she said.

I became frightened and ran to my grandmother. "Tell Aunt Hajar not to scare me, *Nanah-jan*."

My aunt laughed and stuck out her tongue.

Uncle Naseer was a mujahid, a resister of the Russian invasion. Mujahideen were labeled rebels by the government, but people liked them and supported them and called them "the defenders of the faith."

They fought the Russians and suffered a lot, but they were eventually able to expel the invading Soviet forces from Afghanistan. That's when they were also considered the defenders of the homeland.

Uncle Naseer came and went like a ghost, jumping into our yard after dark and hiding on the roof with his Kalashnikov. I'd hear his footsteps overhead and then hear him land in the yard.

Every night my grandfather took a mattress, a pillow, and blankets up to the roof. He always looked worried when my uncle was nearby. "Where did Uncle go, *Baba-jan*?" "*Hush*, child; he's gone to count the stars."

"Where does he sleep, *Baba-jan*?"

"Uncle Naseer's house is on the moon, Homeira."

"Can one sleep better on the moon, *Baba-jan*?"

Baba-jan sighed. "Yes, Homeira, but you must wake up before the moon sets or it will swallow you."

Every night I watched the moon, worried that if Uncle Naseer overslept, the moon would swallow him.

That very night, agents of KhAD, the State Intelligence Agency, stormed into our house looking for Uncle Naseer. Terrified, I pointed to the roof and said, "Stars! Stars!"

My dear Siawash,

I am sure that someday when you learn that your mother has been alive all these years, you will be angry. You will ask yourself, "How could a mother just walk away and leave her child behind?" It was never my wish.

I wish that neither of us belonged to a society that victimizes mothering and motherhood. I hope that by the time you grow up, this attitude will have changed or disappeared. I, my mother, my mother's mother, and my mother's mother's mother have all spent our lives hoping for that change. Please don't think that my yearning for you and even for your father has left me completely. Not so ... but I have learned to pay a price for my ambitions. I don't regret the sacrifices I have made, for I know that through this suffering I am, I hope, making a difference for other women, the ones who will come after me.

Trust me and believe in the history that I'm trying to make. Try not to be angry at me for this separation. Instead believe in yourself, for it is you and I together who must create a new Afghanistan. I look forward to the day when the two of us will live in a society of equals. Even from the darkness of this dungeon, I look forward to the day when a blue sky will unfurl its bright and beautiful horizons. Nobody is going to give us this blue sky for free. We must take it by and for ourselves.

SEARCHING FOR SALEEM
AN AFGHAN WOMAN'S ODYSSEY
Farookha Gauhari

In *Searching for Saleem*, **Farookha Gauhari** reminds us that the tragedies of Afghanistan are multiple and go back generations. They go way back in time beyond the fall of Kabul to the Taliban V2.0 in 2021, the beginning of the US-led war in 2001, the inter-*mujahideen* fighting and collapse of the government to Taliban V1.0 in 1996 and the Soviet invasion and decade of occupation from 1979 to 1989.

The daughter of a teacher, Gauhari was the first woman in Afghanistan to take a Master's degree and the first Afghan to win a Fulbright Scholarship. This heart-wrenching memoir tells the story of her quest to find out what happened to her missing husband in the aftermath of the communist coup of 1978. Gauhari thrusts us into the dark world of totalitarian rule, abrupt disappearances, summary executions, unanswered questions and the harrowing decision to leave the country with her three children.

Do not ask me why I have postponed writing down my memoirs for so long. At first I was not able to write them all. Whenever I sat down to write, thousands of teardrops would fall and the paper would disappear behind the shadows of my mind. Even though more than fifteen years have gone by, it still hurts whenever I remember my past.

Today, however, I feel obligated to write. I am writing now because I owe it to myself, to my husband, to my beloved country, Afghanistan, and to my friends and others who have gone through their own silent and hideous inner battles caused by wars, executions, and simple human ignorance. This battle within me took such a toll that it cut years off my life; I used to constantly fall to my knees and only by sheer willpower could I stand upright, holding onto that last vestige of pride and dignity. Only with great pain was I able to conceal my grief. I was perpetually afraid of losing my job, my mind, but above all the unity of my family.

My story is that of Saleem, the man I married. He came into my life on a spring day and was taken away from me on another spring day. I used to love springtime for giving new life to the world. Now spring makes me melancholy, because it has taken life away from my world. I feel such emptiness and loneliness that nothing can fill the holes in my soul and psyche. Saleem committed himself to his family until the last moments he spent with us. He always made me feel tall, proud, and confident whenever I was among others. He gave his love unendingly not only to us but to all of his friends and acquaintances as well.

My story is about my unrelenting, desperate, and unsuccessful search for my husband after the April 1978 coup. How deeply I wish that someone in this world could show me the place where he rests eternally. Today, on Memorial Days and similar occasions, I find myself in nearby cemeteries looking for a forgotten grave to put flowers on. There I sit for hours; I pray for its occupant and for my husband, who asked me once to pray for him at his grave.

My story is about a family who lived in Afghanistan, a family with deep love for their homeland, in many ways an ordinary family. It is about parents, brothers, and sisters who always gave me moral support. Whenever I felt lonely, they were there for me. Because of me they left their homeland under the worst conditions.

My story is about my mother, who still cannot adjust to life in the United States, who feels that we have trapped her in a cage by bringing her here, even though she is surrounded by her family and many good and friendly neighbors.

My story is about my children, my relatives, and my friends, who surround me and give me the assurance and confidence I still need. Finally, my story is about my husband and those I love whose whereabouts are unknown to me, of those with whom I can no longer communicate, but for whom I continue to pray.

My life story is not a heroic one. It is merely one of the many similar stories that happen every day around us in this hard world. Given the same circumstances and situations, most people would have acted similarly to me, making me far from unique.

I kept a diary, but it is not complete by any means. Whenever I had a bad day, I was too tired to write in the evening and hated to remember the events. Also, I was afraid to write down how I felt about things, because what if the diary had been discovered by the government's agents? The government agents were known to search houses at any time of day or night. Thus, my entire family and friends would have been put in jeopardy. Whenever my day's search yielded something positive, like someone saying that my husband was alive, I would sit down and take the time and risk of recording the events. In all such notes I was always very careful not to say anything against the government officials; on the contrary, I often praised them. For example, if there was shooting in the city, I would add, after briefly describing the episode, "I don't know why these WESTERN AGENTS do not let us live in peace, in spite of all our government's efforts to keep us happy!" I hoped that if my notes were discovered, the added statement would keep my family safe and secure.

If the following story touches you, do not be overly concerned about me, because I am only one survivor among many. I wish I had the power to shout loudly and clearly enough for all the world to hear: PLEASE STOP THE WARS! I have learned that in war there are no winners. In every war many are badly hurt – mothers, children, friends. Let me tell you that one can cope with natural calamity and deaths, but it is nearly impossible to contend with the unnatural upheaval which is the result of human greed and struggle for power.

My book is a cry against wars and executions. It strongly pleads for peace and justice – justice for those Afghans who have lost a member of their family in this miscalculated, senseless war. Peace be upon all those Soviet mothers and wives who opposed the invasion of a neighboring country, Afghanistan; were caught in this turmoil unwillingly; and have lost their loved ones. They were told that these soldiers were in Afghanistan on a friendly mission!

If I could, I would wipe away forever the tears and sorrow of all those brave Afghan women and their children who have suffered more in this war than anyone else though we hardly hear from them. They have lost their only breadwinners and are struggling hard for survival. No amount of money can buy their happiness and all the Gorbies, Bushes, Castros, and Thatchers of the world can never bring back the joy that has been taken away.

A question always comes to mind: Did Afghanistan spell the doom of the Soviet empire? Maybe not, but it certainly played a major role in the USSR's fall. The Russian leaders who were enemies of yesterday are our friends today. Let's not forget the crimes that were done by them and their puppets in Afghanistan; the flame that was ignited in this war will burn the country and the region for generations to come.

My book is already past due. There are reasons for the delay. First, it took me years to overcome my grief. Second, it was hard to decide whether it was worth the sacrifice of my family's privacy, and I had to struggle with the dilemma of whether or not my story would jeopardize my friends' safety back home. And many times I relinquished writing because of the thought "Who cares? It's my personal life."

Today I am convinced that if my writings are able to get the message across to five readers and stop a single man's death somewhere in the world, it will have been well worth my efforts, sacrifice, and the inherent risks as well. I sincerely hope, too, that my book will be an inspiration to all those educated Afghan women living around the world to record their side of the story and the disasters caused by this terrible war. Let the world know what a beautiful, proud culture and people we have, so that Afghanistan will no longer be considered an exotic and mysterious land to outsiders.

PROVERBS
Edward Zellem

Few military personnel deployed to Afghanistan can have used their time as fruitfully as **Captain Edward Zellem,** a now retired US Navy captain. A new Dari speaker, he spent much of his eighteen months in the country as part of the American 'surge' in 2010 collecting and using Afghan proverbs, partly as a way to improve his language skills. A decade later and his books of proverbs have been published in fifteen languages and scooped up armfuls of awards.

Proverbs in any language reveal an awful lot about a country and its people and Zellem's collections are no different. 'Dress well, eat well, life is short,' goes one, a reminder that Afghans like to enjoy the moment, rarely knowing when the next good times will return. As for the person who is 'Joking about everything, even Grandfather's beard', be warned, he or she is playing with fire.

Proverbs in Dari
From Zarbul Marsalha: 151 Afghan Dari Proverbs

A fast donkey is better than a slow horse

Seek knowledge from cradle to grave

Good language is the comfort of life, bad language is the enemy of life

A hundred strikes by a goldsmith, one strike by a blacksmith

Dress well, eat well, life is short

Joking about everything, even Grandfather's beard

Mother shakes the cradle with one hand, and shakes the world with the other hand

Black carpet cannot become white by washing

A sword wound will heal, but not a wound from words

Another's carpet is until midnight

Beauty without charm, soup without onion

From one hand comes no sound

Your mouth cannot become sweet by saying "Halwa"

Old sandals in the desert are a blessing

Good to good, punishment to bad

If the bald man was really a doctor, he would have cured his own head

Forty darweysh can sleep on one carpet, but two kings cannot fit in one land

Jesus to his religion, Moses to his

Proverbs in Pashto
From Mataluna: 151 Afghan Pashto Proverbs

The labor of one's own hand is beautiful.

A mother rocks the cradle with one hand, and the world with the other hand.

There is a reason why one thing is cheap, and another is expensive.

Too much of anything is poisonous.

Although a cow is black, her milk is white.

A friend makes you cry, an enemy makes you laugh.

Even if the flour-mill is your father's, you still have to wait your turn.

Better to let your enemy kill the snake.

Use a sword against a shield, and a bold front against words.

The work gets done by doing it.

Spit once spat does not return to the mouth.

Wisdom can be learned from those who don't have it.

An idler's brain is the devil's workshop.

A rich wife will make you a slave.

You cannot clap with one hand.

Carpentry is not monkey's business.

A stone will never be soft and an enemy never a friend.

Better killed by a sword than defiled by an enemy.

HERAT
PEARL OF KHORASAN
Charles Gammell

Charles Gammell is a former British diplomat and historian of Iran and Afghanistan. He has written widely on Herat, worked in Afghanistan for the International Committee of the Red Cross (where he interpreted in both Dari and Pashto) and advised UNESCO on cultural and historical projects. Drawing on Persian, Pashto and British sources, *Herat: Pearl of Khorasan* is a beautifully written love letter to the city through its many triumphs and tragedies, from the devastation wrought by Genghis Khan in 1221 and the poetry-filled glories of the Timurid era to the turbulence of today.

Herat in an Age of High Art, Imperial Favour and Low Politics, 1381–1510

In 1404 Timur's empire was secure; Herat was a pliant and conquered vassal. Timurid forces had sacked Delhi in 1398, and in the autumn of 1400 these troops pushed further into Arab territories, crushing the Mamluk Sultans, taking major cities one by one: Aleppo, Hama, Baalbek and Damascus. In the summer of 1402, Timur's armies pushed north and defeated the Ottoman ruler, Bayezid I (r.1389–1402). At this point, Timur's empire stretched from Egypt to the borders of China, and in a nod to the global ambitions of his hero, Chingiz Khan, Timur then launched a campaign into China. This was to be his last, however. Timur succumbed to a fever after an energetic drinking bout on 18 February 1405 in the town of Otrar, where Khorasan's fate had been sealed in 1218.

Some mourned Timur's passing: others did not. The unity provided by his leadership of such a vast empire was gone in an instant, resulting in furious internecine conflict. Khorasan and Central Asia had fought bitter wars for the scraps of Chingiz Khan's legacy in the thirteenth century; Herat now feared that history would repeat itself. On hearing of Timur's death, Herat's then governor, Shah Rukh, a son of Timur, made preparations to safeguard the province and city. He raised money and ordered the armies of Badghis to Herat. He sent emissaries to Samarqand in pursuit of intelligence. Herat's ramparts were restored to the 'apogee of their height', and the moats were sunk to the 'very nadir of depth'. With Herat's fortifications more secure and its treasure gathered in the citadel, Shah Rukh set out for Samarqand to stake his claim to the Timurid throne.

In Samarqand, Timur had been succeeded by his grandson, the young prince and noted romantic, Khalil Sultan (r.1405–7). Khalil Sultan presided over a brief rule of rare profligacy. A chronicler noted how Khalil Sultan 'threw open the treasury that Amir Timur had amassed throughout his reign from the taxes on Iran and Turan and, like the April rain, nay the mines of Badakhshan and the sea of Oman, scattered silver and pearls over soldiers and civilians'. On account of this liberality, and his deep infatuation with the courtesan Shad Malek Agha, Khalil Sultan's rule and his liberty were cut short by a rebellious coup. Meanwhile, Shah Rukh was marching his army from Herat, and owing to the chaos unfolding in Samarqand he faced little in the way of stiff resistance. He conquered with relative ease, and with all the major claimants to the imperial throne dead or in chains, Shah Rukh became the ruler of a fractured Timurid empire. Shah Rukh resolved to govern his newly won lands not from Samarqand, where his son assumed the role of governor, but from Herat, the 'dome of Islam'.

Shah Rukh's decision to move his capital south represented a desire to appeal to an Islamic heritage which would burnish his religious credentials in the eyes of those over whom and through whom he would rule. He wished to cloak himself in a blanket of Sunni orthodoxy and to do away with the Mongol heritage that had so defined Timur's imperial ambitions. Timur's tombstone in Samarqand carries an inscription which directly links his ancestry to Alanqoa, a mythical Mongol queen whose offspring were said to include Chingiz Khan himself, and Timur married his sons to Chingizid princesses (NB this tombstone was erected in the

1430s by Prince Baysanghur). Timur's empire had seen a continuation of legal traditions in the name of the Mongol *yasa* (Mongol law code which is said to have originated with Chingiz Khan and was codified under Mongke Khan). This uneasy balance he had struck between Islamic and Mongol traditions would be reversed by Shah Rukh's conscious move towards a more Islamic self-image.

For Shah Rukh the old steppe notions of legitimacy seemed to be of little use as he built his imperial edifice on self-consciously Islamic foundations, but still the tension between the urban and the nomadic, the shamanistic and the Islamic persisted through artistic expression and the actions of the Timurid military elites residing in Herat. In many ways this tension defines Shah Rukh's rule over Herat, for whilst he is portrayed as the 'Emperor of Islam', and not the hybrid amalgam of Mongol and Muslim preferred by other Mongol or Timurid rulers, hints at the survival of Mongol practices can be found up until the Timurid dynasty's fall. Shah Rukh quickly restored the *sharia* as the legal code of his empire, dispensing with the Mongol *yasa*, so beloved of Timur, and his coinage, minted in Herat and exhibiting the phrase *Khallada Allahu khilafatahu* (May God perpetuate his caliphate), are evidence of intentions to create an Islamic imperial capital at Herat. Shah Rukh's very first actions in Herat on assuming imperial power were to build religious institutions through which he could promulgate and codify his Sunni religious credentials. Indeed, such was Shah Rukh's Islamic piety that Herat's chroniclers portrayed him as a saint, describing how miracles occurred around him. Herat's fame as a city of Sufi shrines, a valley lined with the dust of the saints, and its upstanding Sunni orthodoxy – and yet the distinctly fluid boundaries between Sunni and Sufi, Shia and Alid – meant that it was the perfect place on which to construct Shah Rukh's imperial edifice.

Yet Shah Rukh could never totally discard his Mongol ancestry, or the language and imagery of earlier histories. Indeed, one chronicler observed that such was the strength of Mongol traditions amongst Herat's Timurid elites that were Shah Rukh to have outlawed Mongol law, his followers would 'flee like asses to the gate'. A genealogy commissioned in Herat during Shah Rukh's rule, the *Muizz al-ansab* (The Glorifier of Genealogies), is an extension of a work begun under Chingiz Khan. In this work, the Timurid line is traced directly back to Chingiz Khan and beyond, showing how Herat played host to a broader struggle for identity between Timurid nobles who embraced their past and those who rejected it in favour of Islamic legitimation. Perhaps it was a sop to some Timurid aristocrats who felt that Shah Rukh was in danger of forgetting his history? From this we get the distinct image that all is not as it appears in Timurid Herat, subtly undermining the glorious Islamic edifice its rulers created for the city.

In regional political terms, the greatest challenge facing Shah Rukh came in the form of the Qara Qoyunlu tribe (Black Sheep), described by one historian as 'the great unresolved problem of the Timurid empire'. The Qara Qoyunlu were a Shia Turcoman tribe who exercised control over present-day Azerbaijan, northern Persia and Iraq-e Arab. The Qara Qoyunlu had earlier taken Baghdad from the Jalayirid dynasty, and had subdued territories from the Caucasus to Qazvin. In battle they had killed Miranshah, Herat's erstwhile governor and one-time destroyer. Although the campaigns outside Herat were frequent and costly and Shah Rukh's control of his fragmentary empire was tenuous, he could be assured of Herat's internal stability and was more or less confident of his control over it. One Timurid chronicler wrote how Herat's peasantry enjoyed peace and prosperity that 'have never been known in any other epoch from the time of Adam until today'. Shah Rukh could thus present himself as the very ideal of a just Islamic ruler who provided peace in his territories, allowing life to function, Islam to flourish and his lands to prosper. Peace is also good for the historian, for aside from providing a welcome break from an endless cycle of siege and conflict, it affords us the luxury to look at Herat in a more or less thematic fashion, albeit within the framework of a dynasty of roughly two parts: the stability and prosperity of Shah Rukh's reign, and then – with a messy interlude – the bright lights of Husain Bayqara's Herat.

With his authority secured, Shah Rukh could turn his attention to creating a capital worthy of the great Timurid name, and a city to rival the ostentation and scale of ambition of Timur's Samarqand. It was thus in 1410 that a great Timurid building boom began, given impetus by access to imperial coffers and taking its lead from the Kartid city of the previous century. In the same year, Shah Rukh ordered the construction of his own *madrasa* and *khaneqah* within Herat's city walls, to the east of the citadel, in an area on which the Kartids had themselves built. Timur had embodied the tension between sedentary and nomadic. He was a man who spent vast sums making Samarqand a city of breathtaking scale and beauty, yet who also roundly chastised a fellow steppe warrior for fortifying the city of Balkh and thus violating nomadic traditions. For Shah Rukh, however, it seemed there was no such tension. His architectural additions to Herat were a clear affirmation of his assimilation to Persianate urban life and his desire to leave behind the ways of the steppe. His early endeavours were designed to consolidate Herat and to establish power; this was the building of the utilitarian spaces – mosque, *madrasa*, defences and bazaars – as if Shah Rukh were somehow preparing Herat for the explosion of culture and brilliance that Husain Bayqara would later unleash on Herat. This was Shah Rukh, the conservative pious ruler bringing order to spaces which had seen so much chaos. Timurid power and wealth met Herat's religious repute and cultural sophistication: mutually assured seduction.

In these endeavours Shah Rukh was assisted by his wife, the most extraordinary woman to have graced Herat, Queen Gawhar Shad. Gawhar Shad means 'joyous jewel' in Persian, and her contributions to Herat and Mashhad – mosques, colleges, gardens and so much more – were on a scale to rival any of the region's great medieval patrons. Gawhar Shad was a daughter of a Chagataid noble, and as a patron of art and architecture ranks alongside the most cultured Medici or stylish Renaissance pontiff. Were her talents to have ended simply at architectural magnificence, she would still deserve a place in history, but she was also a political operator of great skill and ruthlessness, qualities which sit uneasily with her exquisite taste for beautiful floral motifs on sky-high minarets. Her great patronage was largely directed towards monumental structures, most notably the *Masjed-e Gawhar Shad* (Gawhar Shad Mosque) which now abuts the shrine to Imam Reza, the eighth Shia Imam, in the Khorasanian city of Mashhad. Her greatest gift to Herat was the Gawhar Shad *madrasa* and her own mausoleum, whose crumbling remains can be found to the north of the Old City walls. She was aided in her great building projects by a native of Shiraz, Qawam al-Din Shirazi, the most brilliant of a number of Shirazi architects of the period. Shirazi was responsible for some of the most significant additions to a glittering Timurid skyline in Herat. Now they are all but gone, ruined by centuries of conflict.

The remains of these buildings, their scale so characteristic of a bombastic Timurid architectural style, give tantalising glimpses of the ambition, expertise and thinking of Timurid Herat. Gawhar Shad's *mosalla* (this term refers to a large complex of religious buildings, often situated outside city walls and centred upon an *idgah*, a large space used for Ramadan prayers in particular) acted as a place where those from the surrounding districts came to pay their respects to God. Yet it seems that paying homage to the munificence and charity of Herat's ruling elite surely was not far from the minds of those who commissioned and designed these edifices; it was not just God who was to be worshipped in Timurid Herat. Gawhar Shad's famous structure was framed by an entrance portal of over 80 feet in height; four minarets of real beauty and scale sat in the corners of the inner courtyard. A visitor to the city in the late nineteenth century made the following observations:

> The main building consists of a lofty dome some 75 feet in diameter, with a smaller dome behind it, and any number of rooms and buildings around it. The entrance to this dome is through a lofty archway on the east, some 80 feet in height, the face of which is entirely covered with tile-work and huge inscriptions in gilt; while above the archway is a lot of curious little rooms and passages, the use of which I cannot tell. To the east of this arch is a large courtyard some 80 yards square, surrounded with corridors and rooms several storeys in height – all covered with tile-work. The main entrance of all is on the eastern side of this court, through another huge archway, also some 80 feet in height, but though the inside of the arch is all lined with tiles, or rather mosaic-work in regular patterns, the outside is bare, and looks as if it had never been finished. Four minarets, some 120 feet in height, form the four corners of the building: a good deal of

the tile-work has been worn off by the weather... but when they were new, they must have been marvelously handsome.

This courtyard played host to large numbers of worshippers who came into Herat for the feasts marking special dates in the Islamic calendar. Gawhar Shad's *madrasa* was a monumental vehicle for the propagation of Timurid legitimacy, combining the Persian and Islamic with the Timurid obsession with powerful and sizeable architectural features. It was a space to impress Herat's visiting imperial dignitaries, but also a place in which to educate Herat's next generation of scholars and clerics.

The mausoleum itself – in which Baysanghur and Gawhar Shad, among others, are buried, their tombs still visible today – resembles the Gur-e Amir in Samarqand, the resting place of Timur, in that 'the ribbed bulbous dome is supported on a high drum which rises from the cubical structure with no visible transitional zone'. As the English travel writer Robert Byron remarked, with his customary wit, 'Few architectural devices can equal a ribbed dome for blind, monumental ostentation.' The monumental ostentation Byron remarked on is sadly no longer in evidence and the cupola is scarred with shoddy repairs, weather damage and the odd bullet hole. To the east of Gawhar Shad's crumbling mausoleum, and within the confines of this once great complex, is one minaret. It leans precariously, saved from falling by cabling. It is now home to pigeons. The stump of another minaret stands at the south-west corner of the garden, kept company by an equally destroyed Soviet tank. Today, the use of the area as a garden for picnics has saved it from total ruin, and there is a nice resonance that this garden abutting Gawhar Shad's mausoleum is known today as the *bagh-e zananeh*, the ladies' garden, for it is reserved for women and small children on Fridays.

The architecture of Herat at this time was of a scale and precision that would have astounded everyone who saw it: imperial envoys, tradesmen, poets and the everyday Herati passing by. For size and grandeur, it was revolutionary; for its veneration of the ruling house and Timur, it was unsurpassed. Even today the mausoleum, or what remains of it, and the leaning minaret to its east make a mockery of the tacky architecture – Pakistani-style 'palaces' – that has begun to engulf Herat's Old City; the solidity and elegance of the Timurid architecture will outlast the hastily and poorly built high-rises that make up Herat's present-day shiny urban skyline.

During 2014, I had the great privilege to work with UNESCO on conservation projects relating to Gawhar Shad's mausoleum. I spent many afternoons inspecting the tiles and discussing glazings with European architects and ceramicists and talking with Herat's own craftsmen on the buildings that UNESCO hoped to conserve and restore. The quality of the glaze on the Timurid tiles and the precision of the motifs astound the world's leading experts on architecture, ceramics and tile glazing. The same level of accuracy and consistency, the tile-works on the ribbed dome, the *muqaranas* (the stalactite features which visually support the ribbed dome of the cupola) and the *kufic* (Quranic verses) band which encircles the drum, still partially visible, might never be reproduced in Herat. Herat's depleted stock of ceramicists and glazers can do little but shrug at the beauty and complexity of their ancestors' craftsmanship. Yet they continue to work, inheritors of a tradition in the Friday Mosque, chipping away, glazing and always aiming to reach the heights of achievement of the fifteenth century. Experienced and renowned Italian ceramicists with whom I worked could not believe the consistency of glaze and colour, made even more extraordinary for the fact that it has withstood the passage of time and conflict. Herat's 120-day hot summer winds, blowing through the city year after year, have also worn away the exposed sides of remaining minarets and Gawhar Shad's mausoleum. These staggeringly beautiful faience patterns of flower and geometry that one can still see on the minarets and parts of the drum surrounding Gawhar Shad's mausoleum are a distinctively 'Timurid' architectural feature. To have held them in my hands was humbling and exhilarating at the same time.

While our UNESCO team worked on the dome, I used the mausoleum as an 'office', setting up a laptop each morning on a rickety table, with Gawhar Shad and Husain Bayqara's tombs visible over the top of my screen. The temptation to label it 'surreal' was to be avoided at all times;

everything and nothing in Herat is surreal. The beautiful deep reds and heavenly blues of the colouring of the inside of the mausoleum and the interwoven meshed stalactite arches reaching upwards to support the ribbed dome create a sense of space and even motion which is truly captivating; it is a space in which it is a pleasure to exist. The walls and arches are now faded, blues and reds no longer as brilliant, but the glories of the architecture and its intentions still strike anyone who enters. In the fifteenth century the mausoleum held no official Islamic function (and its veneration of a non-religious figure is not without its controversies amongst Herat's conservative religious elites), yet it is a space in which the sacred is palpable and calm is everywhere. In a poignant reminder of the decline of this all but destroyed seat of learning, this monument to one of Herat's greatest patrons of the art and the sciences, at the back of the mausoleum currently stand three book cabinets in which are kept a bizarre assortment of obscure English textbooks (on, variously, computer programming and maths), Persian poetry and books on Afghan politics. There is a computer, long broken, that sits as some sort of a trophy behind the desk. We would eat our lunch next to the tombstones.

A popular story relating to Gawhar Shad and the *madrasa* she founded is told today in Herat, although owing to its scandalous nature, it currently gets a poorer reception than it might have done in the fifteenth century. When Gawhar Shad went to inspect her college upon its completion, she arrived at the building on what might well have been a glorious summer's afternoon, along with over 200 ladies in waiting. The young men studying in the school had all been sent away for fear of any impropriety should they come into contact with the ladies of the royal court. Yet one young student had remained behind, having fallen asleep in an alcove of the college. He woke to see a 'ruby lipped lady'. Desire overwhelmed both the student and the lady in waiting and their lustful tryst was betrayed when the young lady returned to the royal inspection as her clothes were askew and her face flushed. Gawhar Shad, in her infinite wisdom and compassion, decided to bless this happening, not condemn it. Every one of her 200 ladies in waiting was married off to a young seminary to whom she gave a salary, a bed and clothes. Husband and wife could meet once a week, but the students were required to continue their studies. Whether Gawhar Shad really did this to 'arrest the progress of adultery', or not, we shall never know, but it speaks of real humanity and no little common sense. It is little wonder that Heratis still sang ballads in praise of Gawhar Shad and her wondrous works well into the early twentieth century, and today she is a hero for Herat's young girls. One Indian visitor to the city in the early nineteenth century was so moved by tales of her genius and artistic patronage that he described her as 'the most incomparable woman in the world'.

NIGHT LETTERS
GULBUDDIN HEKMATYAR AND THE AFGHAN ISLAMISTS WHO CHANGED THE WORLD

Chris Sands and Fazelminallah Qazizai

In 1969 Richard Nixon became President of the United States, Neil Armstrong became the first person to walk on the moon and an Afghan student called Gulbuddin Hekmatyar (1949–) founded an Islamist organisation which vowed to end American and Soviet influence in Afghanistan.

Meticulously researched and written with the page-turning pace of a thriller, *Night Letters* charts the hair-raising career of Hekmatyar, committed jihadist, two-time prime minister and one of the most notorious figures in Afghanistan. In 1975, he founded Hizb-e Islami and by the late 1980s was attracting tens of thousands of followers drawn to his vision of an Islamist utopia on Earth, exporting jihad from Kashmir to Jerusalem.

In 2017, as the merry-go-round of Afghan politics revolved again, Hekmatyar returned to government in his first public appearance in Kabul in twenty years, his critics deploring the resurgence of the 'Butcher of Kabul' who has been accused of multiple acts of terrorism, war crimes and atrocities.

Chris Sands is a British journalist who has reported from Afghanistan since 2005. **Fazelminallah Qazizai** is an Afghan journalist with a degree in Islamic Law from Kabul University.

As the sun set on a chill January day in northern Tehran, Gulbuddin Hekmatyar waited. Shadows from the Alborz mountain range played across the third floor room, covering him half in darkness. The years of living in exile, forgotten and humiliated, were about to end. His moment had come. Four months had passed since a band of fanatics crashed planes into the Twin Towers and the Pentagon, shattering the myth that America ruled unchallenged over the post-Cold War world. A conflict between the forces of militant Islam and the US now raged in his homeland, Afghanistan, just as he had always predicted it would. In the spreading tumult he sensed the chance for his resurrection.

Less than a decade earlier Hekmatyar had been the most formidable Islamist insurgent on earth, on the brink of seizing Kabul after leading the mujahideen to victory over the Soviet Union. Back then, he intended to make the Afghan capital the centre of a messianic empire that would ignite revolutions from Kashmir to Jerusalem. His greatest wish, however, was to wage war against America, and he had planned to mobilise his army of tens of thousands of radical Muslims for a confrontation that would reshape the international order. But in 1992, with Kabul about to fall into his grasp, rival Afghan militant groups counter-attacked and the city descended into violent chaos. Hekmatyar was defeated and fled to Iran.

As the years dragged on, the torpor of exile took its toll; his beard turned grey and his eyesight began to fail. Although the embers of his youthful zeal still burned, at the age of fifty-three he feared he had become yesterday's man. Then came 9/11 and his imagination was sparked back into life. Within weeks of the attacks on New York and Washington the US had invaded Afghanistan, looking for revenge. The conflict galvanised Hekmatyar. Suddenly, he felt relevant again.

As American air strikes pounded villages and local warlords drove the Taliban from power, Hekmatyar sprung into action as Al-Qaeda's fixer. Paid by Kuwaiti and Emirati middle-men, in the autumn and winter of 2001 he used his unrivalled contacts in the region's militant and criminal underground to smuggle Osama bin Laden's lieutenants out of Afghanistan, outflanking US Special Forces and the CIA. Hekmatyar provided the fugitives with shelter, setting them up in safe houses in Iran as he embarked on the first stage of his comeback; he was determined to become a revolutionary in word and deed once more. Senior military and intelligence officials in the Iranian government monitored the operation and quietly smoothed its progress, content to let him move into position. They knew they could keep him as a wild card they could play against the US later, if the need arose.

Saif al-Adel, a brilliant Egyptian military strategist who served as Al-Qaeda's security chief, was among those to benefit from Hekmatyar's aid. He would soon turn Al-Qaeda from a tight knit organisation into a decentralised movement that thrived on multiple fronts, lighting the fuse for 'a war everywhere in the world.' Abu Musab al-Zarqawi, the future godfather of ISIS, would lead the way in this murderous campaign. Badly bruised and with broken ribs as a result of a US air strike on the southern Afghan city of Kandahar, Zarqawi was hell-bent on revenge when Hekmatyar sheltered him at an orchard on the outskirts of Tehran. The Jordanian was not yet a member of Al-Qaeda and his arrogant demeanour alienated many of his fellow militants, but Hekmatyar was happy to help him and would come to admire his toughness, courage and independence.

Zarqawi and Adel both sensed that America had been lulled into a false sense of superiority by the swiftness of its post-9/11 victory in Afghanistan, and they were convinced Iraq was next in its sights. Hekmatyar had visited Baghdad in the year 2000 on a clandestine fact-finding mission and he concurred. He had his own reasons for wanting to drag the Americans into a wider conflict, and that winter he worked together with Al-Qaeda and its affiliates to make it happen. While Adel and Zarqawi strategised at separate locations inside Iran, Hekmatyar looked on with pride. It would soon be time for stage two of his comeback—a return to Afghanistan.

*

In the fading light that first week of January, Hekmatyar was waiting for a group of visitors he planned to use as unwitting messengers for his cause. They arrived at his villa in Niavaran, a plush suburb 7.5 miles north of central Tehran, just after 5pm. Hekmatyar rose to his feet and descended the stairs, a black turban wound tightly on his head, thick-lensed glasses balanced on his aquiline nose. There was a regal authority to his bearing and a certain grace to his movements; he had not been fattened by the trappings of wealth or slowed by infirmity. When he reached the ground floor, Hekmatyar greeted the three men who had come to see him with his customary limp handshake and a thin smile. Out of politeness they called him 'Engineer Sahib,' an honorific reflecting the subject he had studied at university in the late 1960s. Hekmatyar invited his visitors to join him in the evening *Maghrib* prayer. They filed into line behind him, letting him lead the ritual as he began to recite verses from the Qur'an. The pitch of his voice perfectly captured the hypnotic cadence of the words. When he finished a few minutes later he led them back up the stairs, this time settling on the second floor, where he liked to entertain guests.

The three men were former mujahideen who had served in Hekmatyar's militant group, Hizb-e Islami (the Islamic Party), during the resistance to the 1979–1989 Soviet occupation of Afghanistan. Now civil society activists who had turned their backs on soldiering, they were in Tehran to attend a UN conference on the reconstruction of their battered country. One of the men was from Helmand, in Afghanistan's southwest, and specialised in helping refugees; another was a writer and journalist from Badakhshan in the northeast; the third was an NGO worker from Panjshir, near Kabul.

In contrast to Hekmatyar, the visitors had welcomed the 7 October 2001 American invasion as a necessary evil, believing it was the only way to bring lasting peace to their homeland. Now they wanted to know their former emir's intentions. They had no idea he was already aiding and abetting Al-Qaeda. As the guests sipped tea, Hekmatyar launched into an eloquent denunciation of the Americans. His words were delivered with the subtle malevolence typical of his past status as one of Afghanistan's great orators. At his peak, Hekmatyar's confidence and charisma had been electric and, with his spirits now revived, that old magnetism was returning. This time, however, he was preaching to a sceptical audience. As the evening wore on, the relief worker from Helmand grew agitated and complained that Afghans were tired of bloodshed. Hekmatyar laughed. 'I am old and you also seem old but jihad is not the job of old people, it is the task of the young,' he said. The relief worker continued to protest; he reminded Hekmatyar that when the mujahideen fought the Russians they received help from governments throughout the world, including the US. Now the international community overwhelmingly backed American military action. 'The Qur'an says that if you are a Muslim you must do jihad,' Hekmatyar replied, confident that political and military realities would eventually bend to God's will. 'When the Afghan youth start to fight the Americans and the puppet government, people inside and outside Afghanistan will support them,' he said. This was the message Hekmatyar wanted his guests to convey to the world: he was still the same mixture of firebrand cleric and guerrilla leader who believed in an endless jihad without frontiers. If he was to die fighting, at least he would die a martyr.

After two hours of debate, the guests prepared to leave, convinced Hekmatyar did not understand the insurmountable odds he faced. The relief worker from Helmand could not resist delivering a warning. 'Be careful,' he remarked, only half joking. 'If you think like this the Americans might count you as a member of Al-Qaeda.' Hekmatyar brushed the comment aside, but knew he would not be able to conceal his secret links with the Arab extremists forever. In fact, the CIA had already been alerted to his partnership with Al-Qaeda, and the US State Department was increasingly confident that Tehran would transfer him to the custody of the Afghan interim government and ultimately to American control. If his final chance at redemption was not to slip through his hands, he had to move.

*

Across town, the atmosphere at the UN conference was optimistic for very different reasons. While Hekmatyar was busy stoking the global conflict he had spent his life working towards, the seventy delegates at the international summit believed Afghanistan to be on the cusp of a bright new dawn. The Taliban had been forced out from every major city in the country and it seemed only a matter of time before

Osama bin Laden and his militants were captured—or, more likely, killed. The Afghan interim government was planning for a long and prosperous future. Sayed Mustafa Kazimi, Kabul's genial new minister of commerce, charmed the conference with his intelligence and wit, but his easy-going disposition belied the scale of the challenge facing him and his colleagues. More than twenty years of conflict had obliterated Afghanistan's infrastructure and traumatised the national psyche: roads were unpaved and agricultural fields were laced with landmines; the public health system was in ruins and most of the population was illiterate. Even if peace prevailed and prosperity could be assured it would take decades for the country to recover. Hekmatyar knew this gave him an advantage over his adversaries. With several Al-Qaeda operatives under his protection, and his own network of radical loyalists reactivated, he was primed to exploit the vast problems the US and its allies would inevitably encounter trying to rebuild such a desperately shattered land. He was also convinced that Afghans were, at their core, hostile to foreign occupation. Those who had been seduced by the West's money and power had forgotten the most important lesson of their country's history: in the end, invading armies are always vanquished.

On 11 January, three days after the UN summit finished, the US sent its first prisoners to Guantanamo Bay, blindfolded, shackled and dressed in orange jumpsuits. Hekmatyar took this as confirmation that America was not just engaged in another foreign war but had embarked upon a religious crusade like the Christian forces of old. Always fastidious, he became obsessed with the minutiae of the prison flights. One particular detail stood out to him: the thought that the captives had been left to defecate into bags, on the long journey from Afghanistan to Cuba, was an indignity he regarded as the worst kind of torture imaginable for pious Muslims.

Hekmatyar was under no illusions about his relationship with Tehran. He was dispensable to the Iranians and, in the right circumstances, he knew they would not think twice about giving him up. On his arrival in 1997, Tehran had granted him diplomatic status not out of sympathy for his plight or support for his cause, but in the knowledge that he might one day serve as a useful bargaining chip in its own conflict with the US. Hekmatyar accepted the offer of refuge out of reluctant pragmatism; he simply had nowhere else to go. He was a Sunni extremist who had long viewed most Shia, including Iran's rulers, with suspicion. All that united him with Tehran was their mutual hostility towards the US and their shared hatred of the Taliban regime, which Iran regarded as a threat to its sovereignty and which Hekmatyar blamed for his defeat in the Afghan civil war. Hekmatyar viewed the wild-looking mullahs in the Taliban as little more than uneducated hicks who had usurped his rightful place as national leader, aided by traitorous mujahideen rivals. He despised their lack of ambition and parochial, insular approach to Islam. While they wanted only to rule Afghanistan, he wanted to spread his radical vision across the world. The Taliban's leadership had hosted Al-Qaeda not because of a strong affinity with bin Laden's internationalist agenda, but out of a sense of duty laid down by ancient Afghan tribal codes. In contrast, Hekmatyar viewed Al-Qaeda as the ideological offspring of his party, Hizb-e Islami.

By early 2002 the alliance of convenience between him and Tehran had reached breaking point. The Taliban had scattered and Iran's priority was to end its diplomatic and economic isolation by improving its relations with the West. Several officials in the reformist government of Mohammed Khatami were ready to give Hekmatyar up to facilitate this thaw. Even the hardliners in the Iranian intelligence establishment who had helped Hekmatyar shelter his Al-Qaeda proteges were prepared to hand him to the Americans. Just as a deal was about to be reached, however, US President George W. Bush used his State of the Union Address on 29 January 2002 to condemn Iran as part of an 'axis of evil' that included Iraq and North Korea. Furious at the insult and fearing it was already on Washington's hit list precisely for harbouring men like Hekmatyar, Tehran decided to let him return to the battlefield to face the Americans.

In early February, a senior official from Iran's intelligence ministry travelled to Niavaran, carrying an urgent message. The moderates in the government were about to end their formal connection with Hekmatyar and revoke his diplomatic status, he said. The next step would be his expulsion—albeit on Tehran's, rather than Washington's, terms. He asked Hekmatyar if he was serious about starting an insurgency against American troops in Afghanistan. 'You do know they have Apaches?' he said, in reference to the formidable helicopter gunships which were a symbol of US firepower. 'The Russians also had helicopters,' replied Hekmatyar. The Iranian placed his hand on a Qur'an lying on a table in front of them and took an oath of loyalty. 'If you are really doing jihad, we are ready to help,' he declared.

*

Little more than a week later, on a Monday afternoon in mid-February, an official representing Iran's Ministry of Foreign Affairs made much the same journey as the mysterious intelligence agent before him, but, as promised, carried a far more abrasive message. Arriving at the villa, he found Hekmatyar waiting with his secretary. Accompanied by several colleagues, the official issued the Hizb-e Islami leader with a formal warning: leave the country by Wednesday or be deported, by order of 'the highest authorities.' Hekmatyar sought to buy some time by pointing out that the Iranians were holding his diplomatic passport, having recently taken it for renewal, and insisted he would have already left if the travel documents had been in his possession. Embarrassed, the official apologised and, changing to a more respectful tone, extended the deadline by a few hours. Hekmatyar would, he said, still have to leave Iran by Wednesday afternoon.

As soon as the delegation left, Hekmatyar instructed his staff to prepare a car for his escape. A lifetime of intrigue and double dealing had given him a well honed instinct for conspiracy, and he was convinced that elements of Iran's political establishment were preparing to sell him out to Washington. Hekmatyar was determined to leave in a manner, and at a time, of his choosing. His family lived with him in the spacious villa but his two wives and nine children were out that day—only his mother was home. Following the late afternoon *'Asr* prayer he walked upstairs to bid her farewell and began to make the final preparations for the difficult journey ahead. The first step was to disguise his appearance: reluctant to trim his facial hair, he used curlers and a flat iron to restyle his beard; he put on a wooly hat and stuck two white plasters across his nose and cheeks, in the shape of a large cross, as if he had suffered an injury to his face. That evening his driver, Majeed Yarizada, was waiting to take him away in a black Toyota Land Cruiser. Just before leaving, Hekmatyar gave clear instructions to his secretary not to tell anyone about his impending escape. 'Say nothing to anyone for three days,' he told him, writing it down to emphasise the point.

The original plan was to drive into central Tehran and catch a bus to Zahedan, a bleak desert town near the tip of a triangle where south-east Iran meets Afghanistan and Pakistan. It would have been a bone-jarring, twenty-two-hour ride, but as they headed to the bus station an aide came up with a better alternative. Rather than travel by road, he decided they should catch a plane, convinced that no one in airport security would cross-check their credentials for a domestic flight. Airlines flew regularly to Zahedan, so the driver dropped Hekmatyar, the aide and a third Hizb-e Islami member at Tehran's Mehrabad International Airport, where they waited anxiously. Hekmatyar had a habit of carrying two pistols with him in Iran and he was accustomed to passing security checks with the weapons barely concealed, confident his diplomatic status would protect him from being searched. But he was now travelling incognito and on a second ordinary Afghan passport. It hadn't occurred to him that this time he should leave the weapons behind. As he walked through a metal detector at the airport, the alarm sounded. With their cover about to be blown, his quick-thinking aide casually remarked that Hekmatyar must have loose change or keys in his pockets. The guards shrugged and let them go.

Back at the villa, Hekmatyar's driver told the secretary about the decision to catch a plane rather than a bus and asked him to phone Hizb-e Islami's office in Zahedan to say some party members would soon be arriving. The secretary made the call and, in case the phone was tapped, purposely withheld the fact that it was Hekmatyar on the aircraft. After a two hour flight the three fugitives arrived in Zahedan. A colleague, Malim Ghulam Sarwar, was waiting at the local airport and took them to his house, where everyone except Hekmatyar started to relax. Sarwar was an ethnic Tajik who spoke with the thick accent of an Afghan from the western province of Herat. Stern and punctilious, he was also loyal to a fault and had played a minor role in helping some of the Al-Qaeda fighters settle in Iran earlier that winter.

With its flat, featureless landscape, stifling heat and air of lingering menace, Zahedan resembled a tough frontier town from an old Hollywood western. Once known by the name *Dozda,* the Farsi word for 'thieves,' it was more popular with bootleggers and drug traffickers than tourists or government officials, who were wary of the large and often hostile Sunni community. Bandits roamed a nearby mountain range and even the locals didn't venture out much after dark. Hekmatyar had no desire to stay there any longer than necessary and he told his men to make sure that come sunrise he was not praying in Iran. He wanted to return as soon as possible to the one place he knew he would be safe: eastern Afghanistan. There, he would move the last pieces of his plan into position and suck the Americans deeper into the war. Just as he had done as a young man, he would change the world.

THE LOOMING TOWER
AL-QAEDA'S ROAD TO 9/11

Lawrence Wright

In the wake of the 9/11 attacks on America, many trees were lost to satisfy the publishing feeding frenzy which followed. Few, if any of these books, provided the colour and depth of analysis on the central figures in al-Qaeda and their operations in Afghanistan as *The Looming Tower*. Published in 2006, it was an instant *New York Times* bestseller and the deserved winner of numerous awards, including a Pulitzer Prize for non-fiction. It provided a sweeping narrative, taking readers from Sayyid Qutb, the Egyptian firebrand cleric who provided some of the most important ideological underpinnings of radical Islam in the twentieth century, to Osama bin Laden and his twin roles as jihadist, first against the Soviets in Afghanistan, later as the head of the most notorious terrorist organisation on Earth.

Lawrence Wright (1947–), a staff writer at the *New Yorker* magazine, is an American writer and journalist.

BREAD AND WATER

MULLAH OMAR SENT a delegation to Tora Bora to greet bin Laden and learn more about him. Bin Laden's declaration of war and the subsequent international media storm had shocked and divided the Taliban. Some of them pointed out that they had not invited bin Laden to Afghanistan in the first place and were not obliged to protect a man who was endangering their relations with other countries. The Taliban had no quarrel at the time with the United States, which was nominally encouraging their stabilizing influence on the country. Moreover, bin Laden's attacks on the Saudi royal family were a direct violation of a pledge Mullah Omar had made to Prince Turki to keep his guest under control.

On the other hand, the Taliban were hopeful that bin Laden could help rebuild Afghanistan's ravaged infrastructure and provide jobs to revivify the dead economy. They flattered him, saying that they considered themselves like the supporters of the Prophet when he took refuge in Medina. They emphasized that so long as he refrained from attacking their sponsor, Saudi Arabia, or speaking to the press, he would be welcome to remain under their protection. In return, bin Laden endorsed their rule unconditionally, although he immediately broke their trust.

In March 1997, a television crew for CNN was driven into the frigid mountains above Jalalabad to a blanket-lined mud hut to meet with Osama bin Laden. Since arriving in Afghanistan, the exiled Saudi had already spoken with reporters from the London-based newspapers the *Independent* and *Al-Quds al-Arabi,* but this was the first television interview he had ever granted. Peter Bergen, the producer, observed that bin Laden seemed to be ill. He walked into the room using a cane and coughed softly throughout the interview.

It is possible that, until now, bin Laden had not killed an American or anyone else except on the field of battle. The actions in Aden, Somalia, Riyadh, and Dhahran may have been inspired by his words, but it has never been demonstrated that he commanded the terrorists who carried them out. Although Ramzi Yousef had trained in an al-Qaeda camp, bin Laden was not connected to the 1993 World Trade Center bombing. Bin Laden told the London-based Palestinian editor Abdel Bari Atwan that al-Qaeda was responsible for the ambush of American forces in Mogadishu in 1993, the National Guard Training Center bombing in Riyadh in 1995, and the Khobar Towers bombing in 1996, but there is no evidence to substantiate these claims. He was certainly surrounded by men, like Zawahiri, who had plenty of blood on their hands, and he supported their actions in Egypt. He was, as the CIA characterized him at the time, a terrorist financier, albeit a financier without much money. Declaring war on America, however, proved to be a dazzling advertisement for himself and his cause—and irresistible for a man whose fortunes had been so badly trampled upon. Of course, his Taliban hosts forbade such publicity, but once bin Laden had gotten hold of the world's attention, he would allow nothing to pull it out of his grasp.

Peter Arnett, the CNN reporter, began by asking bin Laden to state his criticism of the Saudi royal family. Bin Laden said that they were subservient to the United States, "and this, based on the ruling of Sharia, casts the regime outside the religious community." In other words, he was declaring *takfir* against the royal family, saying that they were no longer to be considered Muslims and therefore could be killed.

Arnett then asked, what kind of society he would create if the Islamic movement were to take over Saudi Arabia. Bin Laden's exact response was this: "We are confident, with the permission of God, praise and glory be to Him, that Muslims will be victorious in the Arabian Peninsula and that God's religion, praise and glory be to Him, will prevail in this peninsula. It is a great pride and a big hope that the revelation unto Mohammed, peace be upon him, will be resorted to for ruling. When we used to follow Mohammed's revelation, peace be upon him, we were in great happiness and in great dignity, to God belongs the credit and praise."

What is notable about this response, filled as usual with ritualistic locutions, is the complete absence of any real political plan, beyond imposing Sharia, which of course was already in effect in Saudi Arabia. The happiness and dignity that bin Laden invoked lay on the other side of history from the concepts of nationhood and the state. The radical Islamist movement has never had a clear idea of governing, or even much interest in it, as the Taliban would conclusively demonstrate. Purification was the goal; and whenever purity is paramount, terror is close at hand.

Bin Laden cited American support for Israel as the first cause of his declaration of war, followed by the presence of American troops in Arabia. He added that American civilians must also leave the Islamic holy land because he could not guarantee their safety.

In the most revealing exchange, Arnett asked whether, if the United States complied with bin Laden's demands to leave Arabia, he would call off his jihad. "The reaction came as a result of the aggressive U.S. policy toward the entire Muslim world, not just the Arabian Peninsula," bin Laden said. Therefore, the United States has to withdraw from any kind of intervention against Muslims "in the whole world." Bin Laden was already speaking as the representative of the Islamic nation, a caliph-in-waiting. "The U.S. today has set a double standard, calling whoever goes against its injustice a terrorist," he complained. "It wants to occupy our countries, steal our resources, impose on us agents to rule us . . . and wants us to agree to all these. If we refuse to do so, it will say, 'You are terrorists.'"

THIS TIME MULLAH OMAR sent a helicopter to Jalalabad and summoned bin Laden to Kandahar. It wasn't clear whether bin Laden would prove to be an ally or a rival. In either case, Omar couldn't afford to leave him in Jalalabad, on the opposite side of the country, in an area that the Taliban only marginally controlled. The talkative Saudi obviously had to be restrained or expelled.

The two men met at the Kandahar airport. Omar told bin Laden that the Taliban intelligence service claimed to have uncovered a plot by some tribal mercenaries to kidnap him; whether or not the story was true, it provided the excuse for Mullah Omar to order bin Laden to evacuate his people from Jalalabad and relocate to Kandahar, where the Taliban could keep an eye on him. Omar personally extended his protection to bin Laden, but he said that the interviews must come to a stop. Bin Laden said he had already decided to freeze his media campaign.

Three days later, bin Laden flew all of his family members and supporters to Kandahar, and he followed by car. Once again his entire movement had been uprooted; once again discouraged followers drifted away. Omar gave bin Laden and al-Qaeda the choice of occupying a housing complex built for the workers of the electric company, which had all the necessary utilities, or an abandoned agricultural compound called Tarnak Farms, which had none, not even running water. Bin Laden chose the dilapidated farm. "We want a simple life," he said.

Behind the ten-foot walls of the compound were about eighty mud-brick or concrete structures, including dormitories, a small mosque, storage facilities, and a crumbling six-story office building. Bin Laden's three wives were all crowded into a walled compound where they lived, according to one of bin Laden's bodyguards, "in perfect harmony." Outside the walls, the Taliban stationed two T-55 Soviet tanks.

As always, bin Laden drew strength from privation and seemed oblivious to the toll such circumstances took on others. When a Yemeni jihadi, Abu Jandal, went to his chief complaining that there was nothing for the men to eat, bin Laden replied, "My son Jandal, we have not yet reached a condition like that of the Prophet's companions, who placed stones against their middles and tightened them around their waists. The Messenger of Allah used two stones!"

"Those men were strong in faith and God wished to test them," Abu Jandal protested. "We, on the other hand, have sinned, and God would not test us."

Bin Laden laughed.

Meals were often little more than stale bread and well water. Bin Laden would dip the hard bread in the water and say, "May God be praised. We are eating, but there are millions of others who wish that they could have something like this to eat." There was little money to buy provisions. One of the Arabs came to bin Laden asking for funds for an emergency trip abroad; bin Laden went into the house, collected all the cash he could find, and emerged with about $100. Realizing that bin Laden was emptying the treasury, Abu Jandal complained, "Why did you not leave a part of that money for us? Those who are staying here are more deserving than those who are leaving." Bin Laden replied, "Do not worry. Our livelihood will come to us." But for the next five days, there was nothing to eat in the camp except the green pomegranates that grew around bin Laden's house. "We ate raw pomegranates with bread, three times a day," Abu Jandal recalled.

THE LEDGER
ACCOUNTING FOR FAILURE IN AFGHANISTAN

David Kilcullen and Greg Mills

The blame game started early in the summer of 2021, intensified by pictures of the West's ignominious and world-stunning scuttle from Kabul. While *The Ledger* (2021) doesn't go in for that kind of discourse, it does provide an insider's withering analysis of why a large, well-funded military force was ultimately and comprehensively defeated by the Taliban. In one of many damning moments, Mills reveals how, as the Taliban were poised to take the Afghan capital, the technocrat president Ashraf Ghani was more focused on administrative detail, academic minutiae and development theory than responding to the crisis directly. Ultimately he proved more interested in his own survival than in staying to resist the Taliban, and fled his capital leaving his government and people to face the storm without him.

David Kilcullen (1967–), a former Australian soldier and expert on guerrilla warfare, has written extensively about, and advised the US government on, counterinsurgency. **Greg Mills** (1962–), director of the Brenthurst Foundation, an African development think tank, is a South African writer with an expertise in state failure. Both men have spent years working in Afghanistan.

Conclusion

THE LEDGER—LESSONS FROM FAILURE IN AFGHANISTAN

'One by one we're going to find [Al-Qaeda and the Taliban] and piece by piece we'll tear their terrorist network apart.'

President George W. Bush

'They believe in a universe of divine justice where the human race is guilty of sin, but they also believe in a secular justice where human beings are presumed innocent. You can't have both.'

Viet Thanh Nguyen

The images of panicked Afghans camped out at Hamid Karzai International Airport are now ingrained in our collective consciences. The pathetic bundles of bloodied clothing left behind after a suicide bomber took the lives of another 200 Afghans and 13 American military personnel outside the airport, days before the 31 August withdrawal deadline, tell their story of foreboding and the collapse of hope.

More than 124,000 Afghans would eventually be evacuated, a remarkable effort under the chaotic circumstances, and given the egregiously botched planning of the evacuation mission. As thousands of veterans and private networks of concerned individuals strove to extract vulnerable Afghans, working around the clock, others—several of them in the White House—apparently had a different agenda. They were listing excuses as to why some would inevitably be left behind, and how the fight was being taken to the perpetrators of the airport bombing. Others, on cable news or in political opposition parties, began seeking, instantly and inevitably, to make domestic political capital from the debacle.

*

One of the least attractive aspects of the Afghanistan post-mortem has been the victim blamegame. US politicians, from the president down, along with military and diplomatic 'leaders', have been some of the most contemptible in this regard, making repeated attempts to shift responsibility to the Afghans for everything that went wrong: soldiers who couldn't be trained to fight, politicians who were on the take, and leaders who were incompetent and egocentric to a fault.

Yet the one thing Afghans can do without any Western training is to fight, when they believe in their cause: the Taliban did, and so did many SOF (Special Operations Forces) units and a large portion of the regular Afghan army, right up until the moment when their political leaders left them nothing to fight for. The Kabul government was indeed corrupt, like many governments in many parts of the world, but not uniquely so. There is thus plenty of blame to go around.

In our view, ten key factors explain why the international mission failed to bring stability and modernity to Afghanistan.

The West's Best Wasn't Good Enough. The lives of some 10,000 international troops, contractors and NGO workers and an estimated 200,000 Afghan civilians and military forces were insufficient to turn the tide against a highly motivated Taliban. This should not obscure the failure to insist from the outset that this was a long-term strategic undertaking involving far more than the toppling of the Taliban as the host of Al-Qaeda, and far more than mere counter-terrorism.

The usual excuse is that the United States became distracted by Iraq. This is perfectly true, but it does not explain why Afghanistan still could not be stabilised even when greater resources became available. As explained in Chapter 4, the tendency to transfer techniques from Iraq to Afghanistan and the mistaken notion—engendered by the unique circumstances of the Iraq surge and the Sunni awakening—that a magic set of COIN techniques could bring swift victory, were part of the problem. The fact that Western political leaders lacked a strategy, or the patience necessary to execute a longer war, or the moral fortitude to persuade their people that this was necessary, were other issues.

There Was No Single Campaign Plan. The plan evolved by iteration, subject to changes in personalities—of ambassadors, commanders and politicians. It also varied from nation to nation, from sector to sector across the reconstruction effort, and from province to province. The war was striking for the eclipse of strategy by operational art as it morphed from regime change to nation-building, counter-terrorism to counter-insurgency to security force assistance, with measures of success constantly reverse-engineered from a convenient subset of facts on the ground.

By operating this way, the West became little more than another localised warlord, albeit a large and powerful—if transient—one, to be managed, fought against, allied with, exploited to settle scores with local (and hence more important) enemies, and even co-operated with, both for resources and in the realisation that it would eventually leave.

The Absence of Political Leadership. Whatever the military failures, and these were legion, those of politicians, diplomats and aid agencies were spectacular by their relative invisibility. The past twenty years have been about the failure of politics: internationally, regionally, and internally, among Afghans. In particular, little energy was put into making regional peace until too late in the day, or for that matter, into peace with the Taliban in Afghanistan itself. If war is the result of a failure of politics, then politics is the only real means to end the fighting.

Solutions were Driven by Fear and a Misguided Search for Institutional Relevance. Not only did the West dramatically overestimate its own influence and agency, but the bureaucratic powerhouses of NATO, the UN, the Special Representative structure, the World Bank, the International Monetary Fund, donor conferences and a plethora of other US-dominated global institutions exacerbated this dynamic, supercharging the international actors' detachment, jargon and militarisation of their own self-interest. The chosen metrics suited the mission until that mission no longer suited the prevalent politics of its only real enabler, Washington.

Geography Trumped Goodwill. Not only did the Taliban prove to be a formidable and resourceful foe, they also received critical financial and material support from outside. Most of the neighbourhood had reason to resent and ultimately reject the Western presence. Pakistan's perception of the West's role was, from the outset, shaped by what Islamabad saw as a US betrayal after the Soviet withdrawal in 1989, leaving it with a civil war on its borders and four million Afghan refugees within them. Thereafter the US retreated, only to return, rebranding itself as an ally but issuing periodic menacing threats ('you are with us, or you are with the terrorists') after 9/11.

Afghanistan again became a casualty of greater strategic interests, including the complex relationship between the West and Pakistan, complicated by the Pakistan-India relationship, and, overall, Islamic sentiment towards a Western presence. Iran and the Central Asian countries initially wanted an end to instability and to maintain their own spheres of interest in Afghanistan; this changed as the West became mired in the struggle and the direction of US-Iran and US-Russia relations continued to sour.

The strategic sophistication of the final, 2021 Taliban offensive, designed to pressure Kabul by closing off access to its northern trading 'ports' into the 'Stans and forcing dependence on its southern routes via Pakistan, perfectly illustrates the pattern and extent of regional influences.

A Failure of Development Assistance. With a few exceptions, the measures of effectiveness for aid agencies became centred on the volume of expenditure rather than the outcomes achieved, fuelling massive corruption, fraud, waste and abuse. Since the vast majority of jobs in developing countries are in the private sector, there is a need to work out exactly what this sector requires to succeed.

Afghanistan showed that aid programmes are, by and large, antithetical to economic development since they are often led by those who apparently neither understand nor particularly like business. The traditional route of an entrepreneur with a good idea—borrowing money and starting a business—was lost in the flood of easy money, where entrepreneurial talent was diverted from creating new enterprises to cynically tapping the more than $100 billion in soft donor money that flowed to Afghanistan.

The Weakness of Multilateralism. The United Nations was effectively marginalised by the coalition that formed after 9/11. For the first time in its history, NATO invoked Article 5 of the Atlantic Treaty, which considers an attack against one ally as an attack on all. After the Bonn Conference, endorsed by UN Security Council Resolution 1383, installing Hamid Karzai as interim head of government, the UN had very limited impact at least at a strategic level. It should be asked whether things might have been worse without the UN, no matter the number of committed individuals within its ranks? Or did its presence contribute to the integration of security, developmental and political concerns as the United Nations Assistance Mission in Afghanistan's (UNAMA) mandate implies? Overall, the record of multilateral success in Afghanistan is dire, though the internal assessment process will likely white-wash any failings. The same was true for the World Bank, despite the early positive impact of its National Solidarity Program—later the Citizen's Charter. At the end of the day, however, against the backdrop of the US-led 'Big War', these programmes amounted to little more than a sideshow.

The Poverty of Local Ownership. As the guerrilla adviser T.E. Lawrence famously put it, 'Better the Arabs do it tolerably than you do it perfectly.' Not for nothing was Afghanistan's history defined by its handling of foreign invaders and occupiers. At the same time, these local solutions have to be more attractive than those offered by the insurgents. Ultimately, too often the West wanted its Afghan partners to succeed more than they did themselves, and so at every turn stepped in to help them, like snowplough parents anxiously clearing every obstacle from the path of their children and then wondering why they remained dependent and lacking in resilience.

This paternalism—and the resulting reluctance to wait for real, organic solutions to develop on their own—meant that too many actors and projects spent too much time chasing too many short-term projects with too much donor money. The West overwhelmed and undermined already fragile institutions in the search for quick fixes over longer-term capacity development.

A Failure to Understand why Things did and didn't Happen. Everyone was to blame for the failures in Afghanistan, but the West bears a huge responsibility, in large part for failing to understand the nature of Afghanistan and its region, and arrogantly assuming its own ways were best. Military assets matter, but so does the will to fight, usually built on a strong connection to society and a willingness to defend values. Local ownership of the problem and the solution is crucial. At the same time, locals should not trust the rhetoric and commitment of outside actors: they need to plan and act towards an international exit from the start.

A Failure of Moral Character. In 2002, then-Senator Joe Biden said, on returning from a trip to Afghanistan, that the failure to establish a solid national government could create a 'lawless safe haven for anti-American terrorists', adding that 'security is the basic issue in Afghanistan. Whatever it takes, we should do it. History will judge us harshly if we allow the hope of a liberated Afghanistan to evaporate because we failed to stay the course.' Biden's own words are an appropriate judgment on his character.

As the Americans showed in Vietnam, the British in Aden, the Egyptians in Palestine, and the Soviets in Afghanistan, insurgents can lose every battle yet still win the war if they can keep going and hold enough support from the population. What happened in Afghanistan in 2021 was not a defeat, but something between a betrayal and a moral collapse.

Politicians such as President Biden, no less than other coalition heads of government, would do well to remember Winston Churchill's observation in the darkest hour of the Second World War: nations that go down fighting rise again; those that surrender tamely are lost forever. Nobody—with the exception of some of our Afghan colleagues, or of those in the veterans' networks who were, months later, still working night and day to help Afghan partners—went down fighting. The moral stench of this betrayal will cling to them forever, and so it should.

MY LIFE WITH THE TALIBAN

Abdul Salaam Zaeef

> For many people outside Afghanistan – and no shortage of Afghans, too – the Taliban are terrorists. The other side of the coin, and a view shared by many Afghans, is that they are proud, nationalist fighters who successfully rid the country of foreign invaders, just as the *mujahideen* of the 1980s forced the Soviets out. In the West we tend to hear much of the first view and little of the second. Which is why this autobiography by **Abdul Salaam Zaeef** (1968–), a gripping counter-narrative by the onetime *mujahid*, founding member of the Taliban, later government minister and Guantanamo inmate, is nothing less than required reading.

In 1992, I returned to Afghanistan and became the *Imam* of the mosque of the late *Hajji* Khushkiar Aka in a tiny village inhabited by no more than ten or fifteen people located on the way to Panjwayi district centre. I felt calm and for once life passed easily, allowing me to keep busy with my studies. I avoided the city altogether and never went anywhere near the various checkpoints and known hangouts of local criminals and gangs. Whenever I needed anything I would ask a member of my congregation to bring it for me. I spent little time with my friends from the *jihad* period, just meeting them occasionally when they happened to pass through the village.

Many of the people who went to the city would come back with tales of anarchy and chaos, and often I heard artillery fire in the distance. The stories made me feel uneasy; I remembered the *jihad* and the sacrifices we had made. It seemed that it had been for nothing, but I still remained patient and gave the same advice to my congregation.

Two old friends came to visit me at the mosque. Abdul Qudus and Neda Mohammad were both *mujahedeen* and we had fought side-by-side during the *jihad*. They stayed for dinner and we talked till late at night. Abdul Qudus, who was later martyred in northern Kabul, said that life had become unbearable. Stealing and looting were unavoidable. Homosexuality and adultery were everywhere. People acted without any thought of morality. "What shall we do, *Mullah Saheb*?" he asked. "We have lost our way."

This was not the first time old friends and people from the village had come to me. For months I had heard them telling me how helpless they felt with no one to turn to, no court or police who would help them. I myself felt helpless as I listened to them, and it affected me deeply. I spent a lot of my time wondering whether it was my religious duty to act, if this was still part of my *jihad* to fight against Afghans who were squeezing the life out of their own people for the sake of money and power.

My friends were young; they were part of a new generation that spoke easily about the intolerable situation but who did not think of the consequences of taking action. I told them to be patient, to wait. God is great, I told them, and things might still change. But the two young men, Abdul Qudus and Neda Mohammad, said they could not just sit around and wait.

In Pashmol near their home, Commander Saleh operated a checkpoint on the Kandahar–Kabul highway. He and his men were not just harassing people and robbing them of their money but had been raping women as well. They planned to ambush him at the Arghandab river. Saleh had become engaged to a girl in Sperwan and travelled every day to her across the river. They wanted to make their move at the river and kill him there. At least then the people will be rid of him, they said.

They had put together a serious plan and I heard them out, but I could not agree with it. All over Afghanistan people faced the same situation; the entire province of Kandahar was crawling with rogue commanders and bandits lingering along the roads and cities. Just killing one of them would make no difference, I said. I turned to my friends and scrutinized their plans.

"So let's suppose you kill Saleh," I said. "Don't you think there are other people already waiting to take his place and continue what he is doing? And when Saleh's tribe learns that you have killed him, do you think anyone in Kandahar will protect you from their thirst for revenge, or even to get you in front of a *shari'a* court?"

They had no answers to my questions and sat silent for a while before they replied. "So what should we do then? What should be done *Mullah Saheb*?"

"The things that should be done are out of our hands now," I said. "Of course the things that we do are our duty and responsibility, but we should leave it to God. We don't know anything at the moment. Things could get better, they could get worse."

We were still discussing the situation when Abdul Mohammad came into the room. He was a young man and a member of my congregation. He had just returned from the city and I invited him to join us for a cup of tea. I asked him about the situation in the city.

Abdul Mohammad looked surprised. "*Hajji Mullah Saheb*," he said. "Why are you asking about the situation in the city? Just a few minutes ago we were nearly killed right here on the road!" I asked him what had happened, if there had been a car crash.

"No! There were bandits on the road," he explained. "They came with a motorbike and stopped our car. One of the men pointed his gun at us, while the other told us to hand over our watches and money."

Abdul Mohammad continued his story. He had confronted the armed men and shouted at them. "What are you doing, robbing people in broad daylight while our country is falling apart!" They told him to shut up.

Instead of handing over his money, though, he was quick to act and attacked one of the men. They were wrestling in the middle of the street and Abdul Mohammad called on the other passengers to attack the other bandit, but they did not move.

The second man raised his Kalashnikov. He wanted to shoot Abdul Mohammad but he couldn't get a clear shot while the two grappled with each other. He could not shoot him without risking his friend's life. He stepped back and shouted, "If you don't let him go I will kill you all." The other passengers in the car were afraid and asked him to let the man go. Abdul Mohammad released him and the bandits escaped on the motorbike.

Everyone became animated when they heard the story. They were already talking about tracking down the men and going to their houses. I stayed silent until Abdul Mohammad had left. Then I spoke.

"First, we need more men, a force big enough to be able to hold its own ground and defend itself. We need enough men to stand up to other groups of bandits and robbers, a group that cannot just defend itself, but also other people's rights. We need the support of the people and we need to find a solution together with the people. We should not only focus on our own problems."

I continued. "I think we need to consult our friends. We need to learn more about their opinions and learn from their points of view to find a way that combines all our opinions, and can lead to success." They both agreed with me, but said that we needed to put the plan into action as soon as possible.

*

We started to meet other *mujahedeen* and *Taliban* from the time of the Soviet *jihad*. After a few days we decided to hold a meeting in Pashmol. Thirty-three people came to the mosque to attend the meeting which was chaired by *Mullah* Abdul Rauf Akhund.

The discussions lasted for several hours before we reached a plan of action: we would seek the support of other *mujahedeen* and *Taliban* and together with them we would clear the streets of the rogue commanders and checkpoints. We decided to send out three groups. The first group would talk to those religious *mujahedeen* who were playing no part in the looting and robberies, and who were pious and virtuous men.

A second group was to meet with the *Taliban* and other virtuous people to gain their support, or at least to gain their assurance that they would not stand against us. The third group would go and meet with the *Ulema'*, would consult with them and gain their support. In particular we sought the approval of *Mawlawi Sayyed* Mohammad Pasanai *Saheb*, the respected and well-known judge whom we hoped would issue a *fatwa* to give our movement legal backing.

After all the groups had carried out their tasks another meeting would be convened in Pashmol in which each would present their findings. A month went by before this second meeting took place. The report of the first group was encouraging and it seemed that many *mujahedeen* would lend their support to our plan. The second group, however, came back with only negative responses. The *Taliban* and their commanders had not only said that they would not cooperate, but some had even opposed them. The reply given by *Mawlawi* Pasanai *Saheb* was positive, but he did not agree with all parts of our plan.

We decided that we would stick with the broad outline regardless of his criticisms, though. The meeting continued and the issue of leadership was raised.

People were discussing what kind of person should be selected to lead our group. Most of the people in the room suggested that I should be selected as temporary leader, but I did not think that I was the right person. I suggested that the older commanders, even those who weren't themselves looting, did not support us, and that they would be the first to stand against us. We should, I argued, find a leader who is not a prominent figure, who doesn't have any standing as a commander and thus does not have any political relations from the past with any of the known commanders. According to these criteria I thought I wasn't the right man for the leadership post. We decided to postpone the selection of a leader and would spend some time searching for such a figure.

Groups were sent out to meet with known commanders like *Mawlawi* Abdul Samad, *Mullah* Mohammad Omar Akhund, *Mullah* Obaidullah Akhund and others in Helmand such as Abdul Ghaffar Akhundzada, Chief *Mullah* Abdul Wahed and *Mawlawi* Atta Mohammad.

I was part of the group deputed to meet with *Mullah* Mohammad Omar Akhund and *Mullah* Obaidullah Akhund because I had suggested them for their abilities and leadership qualities. The late *Mullah* Sattar, *Mullah* Neda Mohammad and I went to Sangisar to the house of *Mullah* Mohammad Omar Akhund.

Mullah Mohammad Omar's wife had just given birth to a son, and he was holding the traditional recitation of the *Qur'an* when we arrived. Others had been invited to his house for his ceremony; the *Imams* of the mosque and all his friends had gathered there. We joined them and also recited a section from the *Qur'an*. The final prayer was uttered and food was prepared. After dinner most guests left. We went to a separate room with *Mullah Saheb* and told him about our previous meetings in Pashmol and about the plan. We told him that he had been proposed as a leader who could implement our plan. He took a few moments to think after we had spoken, and then said nothing more for some time. This was one of *Mullah* Mohammad Omar's common habits, and he never changed this. He would listen to everybody with focus and respect for as long as they needed to talk, and would never seek to cut them off. After he had listened, he then would answer with ordered, coherent thoughts. Finally he said that he agreed with our plan and that something needed to be done. "But, I cannot accept the leadership position," he said. Turning his face to *Mullah* Abdul Sattar and myself, he asked, "Why did you not accept it?" We explained the reasons why we were unable to lead the group, but still he seemed to have his doubts. He argued that it would be a dangerous mission, and asked us what guarantees he could have that everyone wouldn't just abandon him if things became tough. We assured him that all those involved were true *Taliban* and *mujahedeen*.

After this short discussion he told us that other people had also come to him with similar plans. *Hajji* Bashar, the district administrator of Keshkinakhud, shared our opinions and was ready to cooperate. "We will undertake every effort we can," *Mullah* Mohammad Omar told us. He thought that we were obliged to solve the problems of the people to the very best of our ability, and that everything else must be left to God.

"In the end everything that happens depends on God," he said. "I will consult some of the *Ulema*' and we will persuade *Mawlawi Saheb* Pasanai. Then let's see what we can do."

All the meetings and consultations we held took place in the four to six weeks after the first discussion in my house with Abdul Qudus and Neda Mohammad.

The founding meeting of what became known as 'the *Taliban*' was held in the late autumn of 1994. Some forty to fifty people had gathered at the white mosque in Sangisar. *Mawlawi Saheb* Abdul Samad, *Mullah* Mohammad Omar Akhund, *Mullah* Abdul Sattar Akhund and *Mullah* Sher Mohammad Malang all spoke, outlining their responsibilities.

The respected *Mawlawi* Abdul Samad was designated the *Taliban*'s *Amir*, and *Mullah* Mohammad Omar was its commander. *Mullah* Mohammad Omar took an oath from everyone present. Each man swore on the *Qur'an* to stand by him, and to fight against corruption and the criminals. No written articles of association, no logo and no name for the movement was agreed on or established during the meeting.

The *shari'a* would be our guiding law and would be implemented by us. We would prosecute vice and foster virtue, and would stop those who were bleeding the land. Soon after the meeting, we established our own checkpoint at Hawz-e Mudat along the Herat-Kandahar highway, and we immediately began to implement the *shari'a* in the surrounding area.

We sent out groups of people to the nearby villages to let them know who we were, and to collect bread and sour milk from the houses. *Mullah* Masoom was in charge of managing the collection and of informing the people. Many of the *Taliban* were well known in the area and respected, and people were eager to help.

The next night the BBC announced the birth of a new movement in Afghanistan, and that the *Taliban* in Sangisar had started it. According to the BBC report, the *Taliban* wanted to cleanse the region of the illegal armed groups that were robbing the people. Members of the *Taliban* had not issued any official announcement or press statement about their objectives; they hadn't even given any interviews. The media immediately started coining names for the movement, though, like "the movement of the *Taliban*", "the Islamic Movement of the *Taliban*", "the *Taliban* faction", or just simply "the movement". Even though the *Taliban* had now taken shape and were an undeniable fact, I was still worried.

I was worried about the old commanders. They would stand against us and their men would not join what was to become a national movement. We had to find some way to include them among our ranks.

9/11 AND ITS AFTERMATH

It was around seven or eight in the evening and I was at home waiting for dinner to be served when Rahmatullah rushed into the house. He seemed worried, and turned to me with a pale face: "Zaeef *Saheb*, have you seen the news on TV?"

"No. What happened?" I replied.

"Turn on the TV. You need to see what is happening in the United States," he said. "America is on fire."

I didn't own a television at the time; the embassy had a set which was used for media monitoring, but I kept myself personally informed through press clippings and reports about current events happening around the world.

Rahmatullah was the brother of Ahmed Rateb Popal, who lived in the house across from mine, and was Popolzai, the same tribe as Hamid Karzai. He and I went over to Rahmat Faqir's house. Many people had gathered, including colleagues from the embassy, and we watched as one of the towers of the World Trade Center in New York City burned. There was fire and large clouds of black smoke billowing up from the building. A second airplane hit the other tower soon afterwards. It smashed into the building like a bullet, with fire and debris shooting out of the tower on all sides. People who were caught above the fire threw themselves from the sky-high buildings, falling to the ground like stones. The scene was horrific, and I stared at the pictures in disbelief.

My mind raced as I looked at the screen and considered the probable repercussions of the attack. At that very moment, I knew that Afghanistan and its poverty-stricken people would ultimately suffer for what had just taken place in America. The United States would seek revenge, and they would turn to our troubled country.

The thought brought tears to my eyes, but those sitting with me in the room looked at me with genuine surprise and asked me why I was sad. To be honest, some of them were overjoyed, offering congratulations and shaking each other's hands for the events that we had just witnessed.

This happiness and jubilation worried me even more; I was anxious about the future. How could they be so superficial, finding joy in an event for a moment, but oblivious to its impact on the days to come?

I turned to the others, asking them, "Who do you think the United States and the world will blame for what has just happened? Who will face their anger?"

They said that they didn't know who would be blamed and that they didn't know why they should care. To them, America was our enemy, a country that had imposed sanctions on our country and one that had attacked us with missiles. The image on their screens – a symbol of that power burning on its own soil – was a reason for celebration.

I didn't talk with them for long time, but I felt the need to share what I believed to be true.

Drying my eyes, I spoke: "I don't want to convince you of anything, or change what you think is right, but I tell you now that you will remember this moment, here in this room with your colleagues, because we will have to pay the price for what has happened today. The United States will blame Osama bin Laden, a guest of Afghanistan as you all know. An American attack on Afghanistan is more than likely given the fear and sorrow of that country today. America might strike soon.

"Bin Laden is America's 'enemy number one' and has been blamed for major and minor incidents in the past. For America, blaming and incriminating a prominent figure of the Islamic world will give them the opportunity to interfere in Muslim countries with the support of the rest of the world. Osama bin Laden is the perfect scapegoat to allow America to pursue its wider agenda. America also needs to cover up its mistakes and failures; it will use individuals like Osama to mislead the world. I fear that he will claim responsibility for the attack and will give Americans the proof they need, whether he was involved or not. Osama's mouth is not easily controlled. And America does not tolerate such events in silence or without taking action."

I reminded them of the Second World War, when the Japanese air force launched a surprise attack on the US Navy at Pearl Harbor. The Navy suffered greatly in the attack, with heavy casualties, and America was swift to retaliate. Without hesitation, the United States attacked

Japan by dropping two nuclear bombs – 'Little Boy' and 'Fat Man' – on Hiroshima and Nagasaki, and tens of thousands of civilians burned in the hellfire of the bombs. I told them that I was sure that America would invade our country with equal vigour. The Islamic Emirate of Afghanistan was already a thorn in America's side, and now the world would join her. That, I told them, was the reason for my tears.

Those with me didn't share my worries, though, and insisted that most of what I said was wrong. They quoted a Pashtun proverb back to me: "look where the attacks happened and look where the war now takes place". They thought America was too far away to retaliate. I returned to my house, anxious about what would happen in the coming months.

*

When I first arrived in Guantànamo there was only one camp consisting of eight blocks and a separate confinement ward. There were forty-eight cells, two walking sites, four simple bathrooms and twenty-four cells in the confinement ward. We were issued with red coloured cloth made out of thick material that gave some prisoners a rash. Every prisoner was given two blankets, two water bottles, two towels, a small plastic carpet, a toothbrush and toothpaste, one holy *Qur'an* and a mask. A common punishment was for all these items except the plastic carpet to be taken away.

When the second camp was built and the general who had been in charge was replaced, the conditions for us changed. We were divided into categories and the punishments got worse. The number of cells increased to three hundred, the *Qur'ans* were taken away, we were shaved again and prisoners were increasingly abused during interrogations.

The name of the new general was Miller; he was later transferred to Iraq and took over Abu Ghraib prison there. He established Camp Echo, a very dark and lonely place. There were different places for detention within Camp Echo, one of which was a cage inside an average room with a bathroom in front of it. The room and doors were operated by remote-control and prisoners were monitored 24/7 with video cameras. Inside the room you could not tell whether it was night or day, and several brothers who were detained in these cells suffered from psychiatric disorders afterwards.

No one could hear you when you were screaming inside and were waving a hand in front of the cameras to get the attention of the guards. No books, notebooks or any other items were allowed and the prisoner was left alone living with the four walls that surrounded him.

Many prisoners suffered from psychiatric disorders after a few years in Guantánamo. Ahmad, who was from the west and had migrated to Britain, had been in Pakistan for religious studies when he was detained. He had been my neighbour in the Kandahar prison, where he was among the group of people who were wearing heavy metal chains all the time. Finally he broke down and started to suffer from some psychiatric disorders because of the difficult situation in detention. But instead of being helped he was punished over and over again and I remember him fainting several times. His condition got worse when he came to Guantánamo. At some point he was brought to the cage next to mine; all night long he would recite the holy *Qur'an* and poems. He would proclaim over and over again that the *Mehdi* (Peace Be Upon Him) would return this year. He was consoling himself. One day he hit a soldier with his food plate. He was transferred to Camp Echo and spent three years there.

Ahmad was well-educated but the detention made him lose his mind. The soldiers were well aware that he was suffering from the very final stages of depression, but he was still abused and not helped. There were numerous people who suffered from psychiatric disorders, like Dr. Ayman, Tariq or Abdul Rahman. The mad and psychotic are forgiven in front of almighty *Allah*, but not by the American soldiers.

I was detained in cage fifteen of Delta block and cage eight of Gold block in Camp Delta till the beginning of 2003. I was later moved to cage 37 in Cube block. From my cage there I could see the ocean and ships passing by, but after a short while I was brought to a separate set of cages for detention where I spent a lot of time.

In the beginning we were allowed to shower once a week and could walk in one of the exercise courts for fifteen minutes with hands bound.

The time was later extended to thirty minutes, twice a week. Our clothes were changed weekly. For a long time we could not trim our beard or clip our nails. Later this too also changed and we could use nail clippers and razors once a week.

Military food rations were replaced by freshly cooked food for breakfast and dinner, and the following year lunch was also provided fresh. The soldiers who handed out the food decided how much each prisoner would get served but it was cooked in a manner that made it tasteless. It was served in small quantities and we were often hungry. Fresh fruit was served three times a day, which felt like a big privilege.

We were allowed to pray five times a day and even the night prayer was announced. The soldiers played a tape for the *Azzan* and would imitate it themselves, but still we relied on the sun for the proper time. Later we were even permitted to pray in congregation. Praying in separate detention rooms was more difficult. Often there was no way to judge what time it was, and prisoners had to pray whenever they thought was appropriate.

When the third camp was built, our circumstances deteriorated. We were served less food, the quality worsened and punishment increased. Cube block was an example: newly made, the living conditions were very hard. Prisoners were left to live in open cages in their underwear no matter what the season, not being able to cover themselves even for prayers. Very little food was served and the soldiers would abuse the prisoners. The toilet was visible to all and the cages weren't big enough for prisoners to lie down to sleep.

In the winter it was very cold; prisoners would jump up and down just to get warm. One of the worst things was when the toilets became blocked. The smell of dirty water and faecal matter would blanket the whole block. We were not given toilet paper or water to clean ourselves after using the toilet; only our hands could be used, but could not be washed afterwards. The prisoner had to use those same hands to eat his food with afterwards. This is how those who claim to defend human rights made us live.

Prisoners were made to live in Cube block for one to five months at a time. Those who could not control themselves stayed for longer. A separate block was built for psychiatric patients; most of the prisoners detained there were suffering from severe depression and wanted to kill themselves. At the time I was there, there would be suicide attempts even on a daily basis. They were chained afterwards and given injections of barbiturates to calm them down; many of them became addicted to the injections.

But there was also violence among the prisoners. Some of the prisoners were believed by others to be spies and to be cooperating with the Americans; they were scolded and at times abused. Other prisoners would spit on them and they would ask to be transferred somewhere else. Many of them tried to hang themselves in their cell and then got transferred to the psychiatric ward, which itself made things worse for them.

Some of the spies were Afghan, and a number of them changed their religion and abandoned Islam. They would abuse the name of *Allah* and the holy *Qur'an* that was then taken away from them. There were people from Iraq and Yemen among them. Prisoners would be careful and suspicious when one of those people was placed in the cage next to them and would thank *Allah* when they were transferred elsewhere. All this happened in Camp Delta; the group of disbelievers even wore crosses around their neck and they grew in number each day. Many believed that this was a plot of the Americans to change our minds to abandon Islam.

Two more camps were built; one was a good place with facilities and better living conditions. The other was another place for punishment. Camp Five was far away from the other camps, but word about this place soon spread, and even the interrogators told us that it was the worst place to live.

In reality, the conditions in Camp Five were not good, but the brothers could tolerate them. The rooms had no fresh air and no window, so there was no sunlight coming in. Each room was monitored with a video camera; there was a kind of cement-made bed, toilet and tap. The walls were made of concrete and the doors were remote-controlled. Only a *Qur'an* was allowed in these cells. Food was served through a small window in the door, but we were not allowed to face the window while the food was handed over. Often during the process food would be spilled on the floor, but no new food was provided. Walking outside in the sunshine once a week was a privilege. Medical treatment was only provided in severe cases and never seemed to cure their illnesses.

Mullah Fazl was detained in Camp Five; he was suffering from a gastric disease and so asked for treatment for over one year but was only transferred to the hospital after he went on hunger strike and lost consciousness.

The conditions were extremely severe. The American soldiers often lied and deceived us, and there were many cases of abuse. Each brother who spent time in Camp Five looked like a skeleton when he was released; it was painful to look at their thin bodies. When Abu Haris returned from the camp, I did not recognize him; there was no resemblance between the man who had been taken away and the body that was returned. I was so scared by his appearance that sometimes I would even dream of him and would wake up screaming. May Almighty *Allah* release all Muslim brothers in good health and save them from the hands of the pagans and cruel people. Camp Five was often called Grave Five; it was like a grave for the living.

NO GOOD MEN AMONG THE LIVING
AMERICA, THE TALIBAN, AND THE WAR THROUGH AFGHAN EYES

Anand Gopal

The best reporting about war refuses to stick to the script. Michael Herr's *Dispatches* hit the spot – John le Carré reckoned it 'the best book on men and war I have read in our time' – because it told the story of the Vietnam War as it was, at grunt level, not as American military commanders wanted, and pretended, it to be.

In *No Good Men Among the Living* (2014), which was a finalist for the Pulitzer Prize for general non-fiction, **Anand Gopal** attempted something similar. Sceptical about President Bush's 'good' versus 'evil' and 'you're either with us or against us' narrative, he did what every good reporter does: 'I learned the language, grew a beard, and hit the road like a local, using shared taxis and motorcycles.' He took the time and made the effort, in other words, to understand what was really happening in Afghanistan, not what our leaders wanted us to believe.

Through the lives and voices of three Afghans – a Taliban commander, a US-backed warlord and a village housewife – he tells the devastating story of how America got it so wrong in Afghanistan. This is visceral reporting which packs a mighty punch.

1
The Last Days of Vice and Virtue

Early in the morning on September 11, 2001, deep amid the jagged heights of the Hindu Kush, something terrible took place. When teenager Noor Ahmed arrived that day in Gayawa to buy firewood, he knew it immediately: there was no call to prayer. Almost every village in Afghanistan has a mosque, and normally you can hear the muezzin's tinny song just before dawn, signaling the start of a new day. But for the first time that he could remember, there was not a sound. The entire place seemed lifeless.

He walked down a narrow goat trail, toward low houses with enclosures of mud brick, and saw that the gates of many of them had been left open. The smell of burning rubber hung in the air. Near a creek, something brown lying in the yellow grass caught his eye, and he stopped to look at it. It was a disfigured body, caked in dried blood. Noor Ahmed took a few steps back and ran to the mosque, but it was empty. He knocked on the door of a neighboring home. It, too, was empty. He tried another one. Empty. Then he came upon an old mud schoolhouse, its front gate ajar, and stopped to listen. Stepping inside, he walked through a long yard strewn with disassembled auto parts and empty motor oil canisters. Finally, when he pushed his way through the front door, he saw them huddled in the corner: men and women, toddlers and teenagers, more than a dozen in total, clutching each other, crammed into a single room.

"Everyone else is dead," one said. "If you don't get out of here, they'll kill you, too."

In wartime Afghanistan, secrets are slippery things. The Taliban had planned a surprise attack on Gayawa, but the villagers had known for days that the raid was coming, and those who could had hired cars or donkeys and moved their families down into the valley. But this had been a hard, dry, unhappy summer. Times were not good and many villagers could not afford to leave, even though they knew what might await them. Of those who stayed, only the few hiding in the schoolhouse, where the Taliban soldiers never thought to look, escaped untouched. The rest met an unknown fate.

Back then, Gayawa was near the epicenter of a brutal, grinding war between the government of Afghanistan, controlled by the Taliban, and a band of rebel warlords known as the Northern Alliance. In their drive to crush the resistance, government troops waged a Shermanesque campaign, burning down houses and schools, destroying lush grape fields that had for generations yielded raisins renowned throughout South Asia, and setting whole communities in flight. In the region surrounding Gayawa, the Taliban enforced a blockade, allowing neither food nor supplies to enter. Those who attempted to breach the cordon were shot.

America's war had yet to begin, but on that September 11, Afghans had already been fighting for more than two decades. The troubles dated to 1979, when the Soviet Union invaded a largely peaceful country and ushered in a decade-long occupation that left it one of the most war-ravaged nations on Earth. The Russians withdrew in defeat in 1989, and in their wake scores of anti-Soviet resistance groups turned their guns on each other, unleashing a civil war that killed tens of thousands more and reduced to rubble what little infrastructure the country still had. Rival gangs robbed travelers at gunpoint and plucked women and boys off the streets with impunity.

In 1994, a fanatical band of religious students – the Taliban – emerged to sweep aside these warring factions and put an end to the civil war. On a fierce platform of law and order, they forcibly disarmed and disbanded many of the militias that had been terrorizing the populace and brought nearly 90 percent of the country under their control. For the first time in more than a decade, peace took root in much of the land. Criminality and warlordism vanished, and the streets became safe from rape and abduction.

In the process, however, the Taliban instituted a regime of draconian purity the likes of which the world had never witnessed. Moral and spiritual decay had dragged the country into civil war, the Taliban believed, and a puritanical version of Islamic law offered the only hope for salvation. All music, film, and photography – which the Taliban regarded as gateway drugs to pornography and licentiousness – were banned. They caged up women in their homes, executed adulterers, and whipped men of flagging faith. They prohibited, with only a few exceptions, all female education and employment. They outlawed the teaching of secular subjects in school. In many cities, roaming packs of religious police under the authority of the Ministry for the Prevention of Vice and Promotion of Virtue saw to it that no one missed the mandatory five-times-a-day prayer. All men were required to wear a fist-length beard and were beaten and jailed unless they complied.

A land of Old Testament rules, the Taliban's Afghanistan was brutal and vindictive. Relatives of murder victims were invited to gun down the accused; thieves had their hands lopped off; and obscurantist religious clerics, often semiliterate, decided matters of jurisprudence. If it were possible to distill the zeitgeist into a single devastating moment, it would be the Taliban's infamous demolition of two massive fifteen-hundred-year-old Buddha sculptures. Among South Asia's great archaeological treasures, the statues were brought tumbling down in an effort to rid the country of "false idols."

Yet Taliban rule did not go unchallenged. Remnants of some of the defeated militias fled to the mountains north of Kabul, Afghanistan's capital, where they regrouped in 1996 to form the Northern Alliance. For the next five years, Taliban troops fought a bloody campaign to subdue the north, meting out the greatest punishment to villages along the front line, like Gayawa.

Years later, I visited Gayawa to try to understand the Afghan world as it had appeared on the eve of 9/11. Some of the Taliban's old, rotting observation posts were still standing, and many houses remained abandoned. Memories of those war years lingered, and the rancor echoed in conversation after conversation. "The Taliban were evil. They were tormentors," Noor Ahmed told me. After finding those survivors in the schoolhouse on the morning of September 11, he had fled the area, returning only months later after a new government had assumed power. "They weren't humans. The laws you and I abide by, they didn't mean anything to them."

As I met more villagers in the area, I found that many of their stories centered on a particular roving Taliban unit, a feared team of disciplinarians who journeyed from village to village demanding taxes and household firearms. "Their leader was a tall man named Mullah Cable," said Nasir, a local. "We heard his name on the radio. He traveled a lot. He would search your house looking for weapons, and when you swore you didn't have anything, he'd bring out his whip, a cable. That's where his name comes from. He was a clever man – I don't know where he was from, but he was very smart. He was one of the first to use a whip on us like that. After a while, all the Talibs started carrying whips."

Mullah Cable. The very name spoke of the strange language that Afghans had acquired in decades of war. No one in Gayawa knew quite what had become of him. "When the Americans invaded," Nasir said, "all those Taliban vanished like ghosts."

I first saw Mullah Cable on an early winter evening in Kabul, the hour of dueling muezzins, dozens of them crooning from their minarets. It was 2009, and more than one hundred thousand foreign soldiers were on Afghan soil battling an increasingly powerful Taliban insurgency. When I approached him, he was pacing uncomfortably in a park, hands in his pockets, his eyes shifty, a black turban stuffed into his pocket. Tall and lanky, he stood with his shoulders hunched, as if he were carrying some dangerous secret. He wore glasses, unusual for an Afghan. Tattoos flowed down his arms and henna dye covered his fingernails. When he smiled, gold teeth glistened. Only his thick, spongy beard and a missing eye, a battlefield injury, placed him unmistakably among his Taliban comrades. Even without such telltale marks, though, as an Afghan you can never truly hide – a cousin, or an old war buddy, or a tribal chieftain somewhere would know how to find you. So I had tracked him down, and after months of effort I finally convinced him to speak to me.

"I don't come here often," he said. "Kabul is a strange place. I'm a village guy. I need the open spaces and fields to be able to think." As the typical Kabul evening smog settled in, commuters headed home, many with their faces wrapped in handkerchiefs. Toyota Corolla station wagons and minivan taxis, with arms and heads poking out, rattled by. A Ford Ranger police truck passed us, making Mullah Cable nervous. He had slipped in from the surrounding countryside and was worried about being noticed. We took shelter in a taxi, moving slowly through the darkening streets as we spoke in the back.

Almost a decade after battling the Northern Alliance, he was still fighting – now against the Americans. Though he didn't mention it, I later learned that the band of guerrillas under his command in the province of Wardak, a few dozen miles southwest of Kabul, had assassinated members of the US-backed Afghan government, kidnapped policemen, and deployed suicide bombers. On numerous occasions, they had attacked American soldiers. He fought, he told me, for "holy jihad," to rid his country of foreigners and to reinstate the Taliban regime.

This much I had expected, but he also surprised me. He admitted to not having received a single day's worth of religious instruction in his life. He could read only with great difficulty. Maps were a mystery to him, and despite his best efforts he could not locate the United States. In fact, growing up he had only the foggiest notion of America's existence. He cared little for, and understood little of, international politics. He had no opinions about events in the Middle East or the Arab-Israeli conflict. And even though he had been a Taliban commander in the 1990s, after the American-led invasion of Afghanistan in 2001 he had quit the movement and for a time actually supported the new US-backed government.

This is what fascinated me most: How did such a person end up declaring war on America? Nor was he alone. It turned out that thousands of Talibs like him had given up the fighter's life after 2001, but something had brought most of them back to the battlefield just a few years later. I wanted to learn his story. At first he was skeptical. "I don't understand why it matters," he said. "My story isn't very special. I think you won't find it interesting." I assured him that I would, and for a year we met regularly in the backs of taxis, in drowsy dark offices in Kabul, or out in the countryside. In his tale I found a history of America's war on terror itself, the first grand global experiment of the twenty-first century, and a glimpse of how he and thousands like him came to define themselves under this new paradigm – how they came to be our enemy.

As with so many Afghans, the beginning was hazy. He could not state where exactly he had been born, although he believed it was somewhere on the squalid outskirts of Kabul. Nor did he know when he was born, so he wasn't sure if he was three or five when the Russians invaded in 1979. That war had unfolded mostly in the countryside, and people in Kabul spoke of it the way they spoke of foreign countries, as something far off and vaguely interesting. But the Russian retreat, followed by the outbreak of civil war in 1992, brought the conflict home to the capital, and eventually he enlisted in a local militia. It was an "aimless life," as he put it, until the Taliban swept into power in 1996, inspiring thousands of young men to rally to their cause. He was one of them.

The Taliban provided a welcome home for unsettled youths like him who were repulsed by the chaos. In their regimented order he found a sense of purpose, a communion with something greater. "You have to understand," he explained, "we felt like we were the most powerful people in the world. Everyone was talking about the Taliban. The whole world knew about the Taliban. We brought good to this country. We brought security. Before we came, even a trip to buy groceries was a gamble. People stole, people raped, and no one could say anything.

"Under our government, you could sleep with the doors open. You could leave your keys in your car, return after a month, and no one would've touched it."

On the battlefield against the Northern Alliance rebels, he had risen quickly in the ranks, first leading a few dozen men, then heading a fifty-man unit, and finally establishing himself as one of the top commanders on the front line. By 2001, he was directing a force of a hundred or so fighters tasked with trekking through the mountains near Gayawa, hunting for rebel sympathizers. He was also chief of police for a district north of Kabul, occasional director of military transportation and logistics, and the sole authority responsible for disarming the population in any newly conquered territories. It was in this last duty that he acquired his nom de guerre, one that, in those days at least, he had carried proudly.

For five years, the fighting between his Taliban forces and the Northern Alliance ground on. For every insurgent hamlet put down, it felt as if another sprang up in its place. Then, on September 9, 2001, in the first suicide strike in Afghan history, a pair of young Arab men posing as journalists assassinated Ahmed Shah Massoud, the legendary leader of the Alliance. Rebel forces were thrown into disarray. For the first time, Mullah Cable could sense the prospect of total victory. On September 10, he and other Taliban commanders launched an offensive across the entire front line. By the morning of the eleventh, they had swept into the strategic village of Gayawa.

"We were on the verge of something great," he recalled, "but everything changed after the planes hit. That was the biggest mistake that ever happened to us."

EARTH AND ASHES
Atiq Rahimi

If there is some small consolation to be derived from Afghanistan's enduring tragedies, it is that they have inspired no end of human creativity and, in exceptional cases, some literary masterpieces.

Atiq Rahimi (1962–), a French-Afghan writer, photographer, film director and soap opera guru, fled Afghanistan after the Soviet invasion, relocating first to Pakistan, then, from 1985, to France, which became his home. After several years working in television documentaries, he published his first book, *Earth and Ashes* in 2000, an immediate international bestseller which he later turned into a prizewinning film. His second novel, his first written in French, published in English as *The Patience Stone*, won the 2012 Prix Goncourt, France's most prestigious literary award.

A work of hallucinatory power and intensity, delivered in characteristically spare prose, *Earth and Ashes* conveys the devastation of war through the lives of an old man and his grandson. Together they wait... and wait... and wait – for what? – in this Beckettian homage transposed to the blasted landscapes of Afghanistan.

The foreman, sitting in his chair again, starts to speak, slowly and carefully.

'Murad is down the mine. It's his shift now. Would you like tea?'

In a quavering voice, you reply, 'God protect you, sir.'

The foreman calls to the man who led you inside and sends him for two cups of tea.

You are relieved that Murad isn't available right away. It'll give you some time to come up with coherent answers and words of comfort. Maybe the foreman can help you. You ask, 'When will he be off work?'

'At about eight this evening.'

Eight this evening? Shahmard will be returning at six. Where will you go till eight? What will you do? Could you spend the night here? And what about Yassin?

'Good brother, Murad is fine. He has received news of the incident that has stricken his family. May God absolve them and give their souls peace...'

You don't hear the rest of the foreman's words. Murad has received news? You repeat the words to yourself a few times. As if you don't understand what they mean. Or you didn't hear correctly. After all, at your age one grows hard of hearing and misunderstands.

You ask loudly, 'He has received news?'

'Yes, brother, he knows.'

Then why didn't he return to the village? No, it can't be your Murad. It must be another Murad. After all, your son's not the only one with that name. In this very mine there are probably ten men with his name. The foreman hasn't understood that you're looking for Murad, son of Dastaguir. He must also be hard of hearing. Start again.

'I'm talking about Murad, son of Dastaguir, from Abqul.'

'That's right, brother, I'm referring to him, too.'

'My child Murad learned that his mother, his wife and his brother have died and he ...'

'Yes, brother. He even heard about you, that you ... May God protect you.'

'No, I'm alive. His own son's alive too...'

'Praise God...'

Why praise God? If only Yassin and Dastaguir had died as well! That way a father wouldn't have had to witness the frailty of his son, and a son the helplessness of his father. What has become of Murad? Something must have happened to him. The mine has collapsed and he has been entombed in coal. Swear to God, foreman, tell the truth. What has happened to Murad?

Your eyes flit about. They seek an answer from every object: from the worm-eaten table; from the portrait in which the foreman is immortalized; from the pen lying lifelessly on the paper; from the ground that trembles under your feet; from the roof that is collapsing; from the window that will never be opened again; from the hill that has devoured your child; from the coal that has blackened his bones...

'What has happened to Murad?' you ask in a loud voice.
　'Nothing, thank God, he's fine.'
　'Then why didn't he come to the village?'
　'I didn't allow him to.'
　The bundle of apples falls from your knees to the ground. Once more, your eyes search the room before fixing on the dirty lines of the foreman's face. Once more, your mind fills with questions – and with hate.
　Who does this foreman think he is? What does he take himself to be? You're Murad's father. Who is he? He has taken Murad from you. There is no longer any Murad. Your Murad's gone...

The foreman's gruff voice echoes around the room:
　'He would have gone. But I didn't let him. Had I, he would have been killed as well...'

What of it? Death would have been better than dishonour!

The servant brings two cups of tea and gives one to you and the other to the foreman. They begin a conversation. You can't hear what they're saying.
　With trembling hands you hold the cup on your knees. But your legs are trembling too. A few drops of tea spill on to your knees. They don't burn you. No, they do burn you, but you don't feel it. You're already burning within. Within, a fire burns that is more fierce than the tea. A fire stoked by the questions of friends and enemies, relatives and strangers:
　'What happened?'
　'Did you see Murad?'

'Did you speak to him?
'What did you tell him?'
'What did he do?
'What did he say?'

And how will you answer them? With silence. You saw your son. Your son has heard about everything. But he didn't come for his dead mother, wife and brother. Murad has lost all his integrity, he has become shameless...

Your hands tremble. You put the cup on the table. You know that your sorrow has taken shape now. It has become a bomb. It will explode and it will destroy you too – like Fateh the guard. Mirza Qadir does indeed know all about sorrow. Your chest collapses like an old house, an empty house ... Murad has vacated his place inside you. What does it matter if an abandoned house collapses?

'Your tea will get cold, brother.'
   'It's not important.'

The foreman continues:
   'Until two days ago Murad wasn't doing well. He wouldn't go near bread or water. He withdrew to a corner of his room. He didn't move. He didn't sleep. One night he went out of his quarters completely naked. He joined the group of miners who spend the night beating their chests in repentance around a fire. At dawn he began to run around and around the fire and then he threw himself into the flames. His companions came to his aid and pulled him out...'

Slowly you open your clenched fists. Your shoulders, drawn up to your ears, relax. You know Murad. Murad isn't one to remain calm. He either burns or causes others to burn. He either destroys or is destroyed. He didn't set fire to others this time, he burned himself. He didn't cause destruction, he was destroyed... But why didn't he come back and burn together with his mother's corpse? If Murad were Dastaguir's Murad, he would have returned to the village, he would have beaten his chest beside his lost ones, not around a fire... They told him that you too were dead. The day when you do die – and you will die, you won't live eternally – what will he do? Will he see you have a proper burial? Will he lower your coffin into a grave? No, without shroud or coffin your body will fester under the sun... This Murad isn't your Murad. Murad has sacrificed his soul to the rocks, the fire, the coal, to this man sitting before you, whose hot breath stinks of soot.

'Murad is our best worker,' the foreman says. 'Next week we'll be sending him on a literacy course. He'll learn to read and write. One day he'll hold an important post. We're sending him because he's a model mine worker who earns respect for being an enlightened, hard-working youth who's committed to the revolution...'

You don't hear the rest of the foreman's words. You think of Mirza Qadir. Like him you must choose whether to stay or leave. If you see Murad now, what will you say to him?

'Salaam.'

'Salaam.'

'You've heard?'

'I've heard.'

'My condolences.'

'Condolences to you too.'

And after that? Nothing.

'Goodbye.'

'Bye.'

No, you have nothing else to share with each other. Not a word, not a tear, not a sigh.

You pick up the bundle resting on your knees. You no longer want to give it to Murad. The apple-blossom scarf smells of your wife. You stand and say to the foreman, 'I am going. Please tell Murad that his father came, that he's alive, that Yassin, his son, is alive. With your permission...'

Goodbye Murad. Head bowed, you walk out of the room. The air has grown thicker, heavier and darker. You glance at the hilltop. It seems bigger and blacker... The men coming down the hillside have faces that are even more tired and even more black. You don't want to look at these faces, the way you did when you first arrived at the mine. What if Murad were among them?

You head towards the gate of the mine. You have only taken a few steps when a shout stops you:

'Father!'

The voice is unfamiliar, thank God. You recognize the foreman's servant hurrying stealthily to your side.

'Father! What I say stays between us. They told Murad that it was the mujahiddeen and the rebels who killed his family... in retaliation for his working here at the mine. They terrified him. Murad doesn't know you're alive.'

You are now even more hopeless and forlorn. You glance back at the foreman's building and grab the servant by the arm.

'Take me to my child!'

'It's not possible, father! Your son is working at the bottom of the mine. If the foreman knew, he'd kill me. Go, father! I'll tell him that you came.'

The servant wants you to release him. Confused, you place your bundle on the ground. You explore your pockets. You take out your box of naswar, hand it to the servant and request that he give it to Murad. He grabs the box and rushes away.

Murad will recognize your box of naswar. After all, he gave it to you himself, the first time he was paid. As soon as he sees the box, he'll know you're alive. If he comes after you, you'll know Murad is your Murad. If he doesn't, you will have no Murad anymore. Go, get Yassin and return to the village. Wait there a few days.

You quicken your step towards the exit of the mine. You reach the gate. Without waiting for Shahmard, you walk towards the hills. A sob constricts your throat. You close your eyes and weep quietly within. Dastaguir, be strong! A man doesn't weep. Why not?! Let your heart's sorrow overflow!

You wind around the side of the first hill. You want naswar. You have none. Maybe the box of naswar is already in Murad's hands.

You slow your pace. You stop. You bend down. You take a pinch of grey earth between your fingertips and place it under your tongue. Then you continue on... Your hands are clasped behind your back, holding tightly the bundle you tied from the apple-blossom scarf.

PARWANA
RECIPES AND STORIES FROM AN AFGHAN KITCHEN
Durkhanai Ayubi

It often feels that Afghanistan has been reduced in the Western mind to a tragic trio of war, poverty and suffering. There is rather more to the country than that. As **Durkhanai Ayubi** (1985–), the Afghan-Australian restaurateur and food writer argues: 'For too long the dominant narrative surrounding Afghanistan has been trapped in the idea of its conquest, taming and manipulation by those who seek to control it. Images of violence and catastrophe almost always prevail.'

Parwana offers something much more heartening for the soul: a beautiful, life-enhancing, colour-filled celebration of food as an expression of 'a universal desire to connect, irrespective of perceived differences'.

Ayubi's story is that of so many Afghans. Her parents fled Afghanistan for Australia in 1985, midway through the Soviet occupation. In 2009 the family restaurant Parwana opened its doors in Adelaide. Here is the world of succulent curries and rice dishes, soups and pastas, chutneys and pickles, from the classic national dish of Kabuli Pulao, an aromatic rice dish with lamb or chicken bejewelled with carrots and raisins, to Haft Mewa or 'Seven Fruits', a naturally sweet fruit-and-nut-laden compote made once a year to mark the Nowroz New Year.

The writing in *Parwana* is as delicious and mouth-watering as the recipes it contains, teeming with an exiled family's memories of home and Afghanistan's rich traditions of hospitality. It won the Guild of Food Writers Award in 2021. The British food writer Diana Henry said it stole her heart.

History on the menu

It is from this long and intertwined history that the cuisine of Afghanistan and the culture surrounding it emerged. Alongside the emperors, religions and artefacts that crisscrossed the Silk Road into Afghanistan came a panoply of impressive culinary offerings from across the globe. From India came the variety of dahls and the prized spices, so intensely sought after throughout the West, including chillies, turmeric, saffron, cumin, cinnamon, cloves, nutmeg and pepper. These spices, apportioned in delicate amounts, became a mainstay of Afghan cooking – seared daily into meats and curries, and baked into rice dishes and vegetables. Special mixes of four different spices, named chaar masalah and often unique to each household, form the flavour base of sauces and palaws, giving rise to the gentle and fragrant aromas typical of Afghan cooking. From the ancient shared history with Persia came the coriander, mint and other green herbs that are now so prevalent in Afghan cuisine. From China and Mongolia came a tradition of hand-rolled noodles, known as aush, and dumplings, adapted to reflect the milder Afghan palate and stuffed with natively grown vegetables such as gandana. From Turkey and the Middle East came the sweet floral notes of rose water and syrup-drenched nutty desserts.

And from the lands of Afghanistan itself – a region home to some of the earliest known examples of domestication of livestock and irrigation to create arable pasture – comes the liberal use of dairy and a diet inclusive of meat such as goat, beef and lamb. The country has a widely varied topography, creating the right conditions for a plethora of crops to thrive. Its warmer plains have the conditions conducive for wheat, corn, rice and barley – all staples that form the basis of the Afghan diet; these are milled and baked into hot naans or used to create the rice dishes that form the centrepiece of Afghan dining. Other areas sit high above sea level in fertile valleys at the base of the mountain ranges, where the pure mountain waters that gush down in winter and spring are redirected as needed to cultivate fruit and nut orchards. Afghanistan grows pistachios, almonds, pine nuts, grapes, melons, plums, apricots, cherries, figs, mulberries and pomegranates. These have long been enjoyed fresh, or dried as snacks to serve with tea, and have been worked assiduously into the cuisine; they adorn rice dishes like jewels or are infused into sauces and curries, adding base notes of flavour and an undeniable element of beauty and artistry.

Inseparable from Afghan food is the style that encapsulates it. The way in which food is enjoyed reflects the gregarious spirit that underpins the ritual of eating in Afghan custom. Food is rarely served as individual portions, but piled copiously onto large platters from which everyone helps themselves. And a meal rarely consists of a single dish – but an array of dishes spread out, from which smaller portions all placed together on a plate make a full meal. Alongside main dishes, such as rices, curries, meats or dumplings, sits an assortment of accompaniments – pickles, preserves, chutneys, fresh vegetables, hot naans or yoghurts – to add bursts of acidic citrus flavour, freshness and texture. This feeling of generosity often begins long before and continues long after the meal is served. Food is hardly ever prepared in isolation, more usually with others. And the highest tenet of eating in Afghanistan, perhaps its holy grail, is the hospitality that surrounds it. Unexpected guests are treated with the utmost care and attention; even those who have very little to share will ensure their guests are always treated to the best.

Aside from the offering of food, the belief in hospitality is embedded in a spirit of servitude – the place of the guest in a home is equated to near-divinity, and the role of the host is to ensure the visitor leaves with a sense of dignity perhaps even greater than when they arrived. Given the long history of Afghanistan at the heart of the Silk Road – a place where many guests proclaimed themselves messengers of divinity, or were merchants and traders with riches to share, it is easy to see why the custom of hospitality has become so deeply engrained in the genetics of Afghans.

Just like the forging together of many cultures in Afghanistan, the intermingling of local and introduced ingredients and the arising customs surrounding food have created a cuisine that is simultaneously familiar and unique. Such culinary transmutation is an act of creativity analogous to our constant human evolution, making Afghan cuisine emblematic of a story into which we have all been written.

*

The recipes in this chapter have been chosen for their reflection of the shared ancient history that has given rise to Afghan cuisine, and of the congenial spirit that underlies the culture of food in the region.

THE RITUAL OF NOWROZ

Among the first few recipes in the chapter are some dishes usually prepared to commemorate Nowroz, a New Year celebration that is significant throughout Afghanistan, Iran and across Central Asia.

The Nowroz festival coincides with the spring equinox in March and, just like the full circle of the seasons, it is symbolic of rebirth. Predating Islam, Nowroz is an ancient celebration that traces its roots to Zoroastrianism, the spiritual homeland of which is said to be Balkh, Afghanistan. The colour associated with Nowroz is green, reflecting the Zoroastrian tradition of marking the spring equinox and celebrating the new life it brings.

Afghan communities around the world celebrate Nowroz with general festivities in the lead-up to the day, including the preparation of specific dishes at home, such as haft mewa, sabzi and kolcheh Nowrozi, which are all included in this chapter. In my parents' youth, it was a time for picnics, sweets and flying kites. As a child, my mother recalls making an annual trip with her family to Mazar-e Sharif in the north of the country to a festival known as Meleh Gule Sorkh. There, the desert plains would be transformed into fields of red tulips, heralding the start of spring.

CHAAR MASALAH
'Four Spices'

Makes 1 cup

Chaar masalah translates as 'four spices', but rather than literally meaning a blend of four spices, it generally refers to a mix of multiple spices, which can be used as a flavour base for many different dishes. The spices used vary from one region to the next, and even from one household to the next, but usually include a selection of warm spices such as cumin, coriander, cardamom, pepper, cinnamon, turmeric, saffron and nutmeg.

Chaar masalah is similar in concept to the garam masalah, meaning 'hot spices', of Mughal origin that is used extensively in traditional Indian cooking. However, compared to that of some of its South Asian neighbours, Afghan cuisine is milder, and chilli is generally added fresh to taste, rather than being used in powdered form in a spice mix.

The chaar masalah recipe given here is the one used in our kitchen at Parwana, and it will be referred to in recipes throughout this book. The choice and proportion of spices in the blend has been fine-tuned over the years to create a delicate balance of warmth, flavour and fragrance, designed to bring out the best natural qualities of the ingredients to which it is added – but it can of course be adapted to suit your own tastes.

4 cinnamon sticks
8 dried bay leaves
7 brown cardamom pods
1½ tablespoons green cardamom pods
1½ tablespoons cumin seeds
2 tablespoons coriander seeds
2 teaspoons cloves

Dry-roast all the ingredients in a non-stick frying pan over low heat for 3 minutes, or until fragrant. Keep a close eye on them and shake the pan frequently so they don't burn. Set aside to cool completely.

Once cooled, transfer to a spice grinder or mortar and pestle, and grind to a fine powder.

Store chaar masalah in a tightly sealed jar, where it will keep for up to 6 months. But note that the potency of the mix corresponds to its freshness, so it's best used within a few weeks of being made.

HAFT MEWA
'Seven Fruits'

Serves 6

Haft mewa literally translates as 'seven fruits' and is a type of compote comprising a selection of dried fruit and nuts, steeped in water until their flavours and natural sweetness emerge and combine. Traditionally, it is made once a year to mark the ritual of Nowroz.

Despite the translation, haft mewa can and often does include more than seven different fruits and nuts. Different families use different ingredients because the recipe is flexible enough to vary according to personal preference and taste.

This recipe is one my mother grew up with, and which we continue to make here in Australia. It includes two types of dried apricots: those widely available in supermarkets, and a specific type of Afghan dried apricot that is dehydrated and a little sour, which can be found in Afghan and Persian grocery shops. Sinjid, also known as dried Russian olives, are also available from Afghan and Persian grocers.

Start this recipe two days ahead of serving to allow time for the flavours to develop.

100 g (3½ oz) almonds
100 g (3½ oz) walnuts
100 g (½ cup) pistachios
300 g (2¼ cups) sultanas
100 g (3½ oz) black raisins
100 g (3½ oz) whole dried apricots
100 g (½ cup) whole dried sour apricots, with seeds
100 g (3½ oz) sinjid (dried Russian olive)
3 litres (12 cups) boiling water

Soak each variety of nut separately in bowls of hot water for at least 30 minutes to help with peeling off the skin. Once the skins are slightly softened, drain the nuts and use your fingers to rub off the skins, dropping the skinned nuts into a very large heatproof container that has a lid.

Add all the dried fruit to the nuts and mix well, then pour in the boiling water, place the lid on top and set aside to cool. Refrigerate for 2 days to let the flavours fully develop.

Serve chilled, ladling some syrup into each bowl. Haft mewa will keep refrigerated in an airtight container for up to a week.

OUT OF THE ASHES
THE REMARKABLE RISE AND RISE OF THE AFGHANISTAN CRICKET TEAM

Tim Albone

Let it never be said that Afghans do not take their cricket seriously. Afghan cricketers and cricket fans bow to no one in their love of the game. Hard-hitting and courageous, the national team – which was granted Test status by the International Cricket Council (ICC) in June 2017 – is the darling of World Cups, admired for the players' exuberant style, infectiously positive approach and the ability to rise above a uniquely unpromising environment to compete at the highest level internationally.

In **Tim Albone**, a film-maker and former war correspondent in Afghanistan, the team has found its energetic champion and storyteller. 'I was fed up of writing about war and death, the country was so much more than that,' he explains. 'I wanted to do a film that showed the other side of the country. The beauty, the madness, the humour, the resilience, the enterprise, the people.' And out of the documentary grew this book, based on Albone's experiences travelling with the team for two years. It is the story, above all, of Taj Malik (1975–), a cricket-mad Afghan who dreamt of producing, in the words of Mike Atherton, the former England cricket captain, 'a team that might make the world sit up and take notice'. In this Malik gloriously succeeded, another testament to the art of defying the impossible.

7
HERO OF AFGHANISTAN
Jersey, May 2008– Part 3

The build-up to the semi-final against Nepal is tense. Both teams are desperate to win. Victory is essential to keep the World Cup dream alive, as the two losing semi-finalists will remain in Division Five. Added to this, the two have history. Afghanistan beat Nepal in the third-place play-off match in the 2006 ACC Trophy and Nepal are out for revenge.

Cricket was first played in Nepal in the 1920s. In the 1940s a federation was formed to promote the game among an aristocracy who had learnt to play it while being schooled in England and India. After Nepal joined the ICC in 1988 the game started spreading and gained a following among all social classes. They are taking the tournament seriously. For Jersey they have appointed a top quality coach in Roy Dias, a Sri Lankan, and the first of his countrymen to hit a thousand Test runs. He has a lot more experience than Taj, both as a player and as a coach, but even he is feeling the pressure.

On the bus to the game the players are quiet and nervous. They know Nepal are a good team with some exceptionally talented players. In particular they are worried about the main strike bowler, Meheboob Alam. In an early match against Mozambique he had taken a ten-wicket haul to win the match single-handed.

Things get better once they arrive at the ground. For once the rain has stopped and the day is clear. The wicket is drier than it has been and occasionally the sun even breaks out of the clouds, warming the sparse crowd that has gathered to see this vital qualifier. Massoud has dressed up for the occasion. Gone is the Inter Milan football shirt, he's wearing a smart, neatly pressed, beige shalwar kameez underneath a suit jacket. He looks regal and distinguished.

Afghanistan win the toss and elect to bat. They feel, with the unpredictability of the Jersey climate, that it might rain later, and they much prefer to bat on a dry wicket. Despite the wicket being dry the outfield is very heavy, as it has been all tournament. This will make runs harder to come by so the Afghans expect a low-scoring contest.

They start safely and in the first 40 minutes they make slow but steady progress. Karim posts 18 and, backed up by Ahmad Shah, Afghanistan reach 26 for no wicket. When Karim is bowled though, the batting starts to wobble. Noor Ali, who comes in next, is out for a golden duck and Ahmad Shah heads back to the pavilion shortly afterwards as Afghanistan slump from 26 for one to 29 for three. Nowroz, who comes in at No. 4, gets an edge and is caught in the slips for seven. Thankfully the rest of the middle-order avert disaster: the next four batsman, Asghar, Nabi, Raees and Sami, steady the ship, adding 99 runs between them. Nabi top scores with 48. Finally, Afghanistan's tail collapses and they go from 119 for five, to 142 all out.

Taj is worried that they don't have enough runs on the board, but Nepal's batting line-up proves even more fragile. The bowlers tear through the innings – benefitting from the drier conditions by really making the ball zip through. Dawlat leads the haul with three for 18, ably supported by Hamid with two for 12, Hasti two for 13 and Nabi two for 15. Nepal are all out for 105. Afghanistan have bowled themselves into the final by a margin of 37 runs.

After the final wicket falls, Taj oscillates between tears, smiles and hysterical laughter – back-slapping his colleagues and anyone else who comes near him. More than anything he is visibly relieved and declares it to be the proudest moment of his life.

Afghanistan have qualified for Division Four. By getting through to the final they have cleared the first obstacle on the way to the World Cup. But Taj knows that after all the claims and boasts he has made, they also need to win the final against Jersey.

The day of the final is fine and sunny and a crowd of around a thousand, the largest of the tournament, turns out – largely because the host nation has made it through. Jersey come into the match unbeaten. Peter Kirsten, their tough, no-nonsense coach who played for South Africa, has instilled a level of professionalism in them that few, if any, of the other teams at this level can match. And no one would claim that Afghanistan are even close to that standard. This professionalism, coupled with strong team spirit, some experienced players and home advantage compensate for the fact that they are not the most naturally talented team. They are extremely tough opponents.

Jersey's Australian captain, Matthew Hague, played grade cricket in Melbourne and Ryan Driver, their towering medium-pace bowler, played county cricket for Worcestershire and Lancashire. The Jersey players are all employed in jobs that the Afghan players can only dream of – as financial advisors and civil servants as well as accountants and teachers. For them cricket is a part-time passion – for Taj and his team it is the focus of their lives.

Before the game, undoubtedly the biggest in the nation's history, Nowroz gathers all the players on the grass around him and delivers a rousing captain's speech. He tells them that the most important thing to remember is discipline. Even if they lose they must do so in a dignified way, so that they will be remembered as a credit to the country they love. The one thing he really emphasises, he thinks successfully, is not to get angry and lose control. Nowroz reminds the players of their days playing in the dusty refugee camps of Pakistan and how far they have come. He finishes by asking them to visualise the joy of holding the trophy in their arms as they touch down in Kabul Airport.

The speech seems to work – when they go on to field they play the game of their lives. The match starts like a dream for Afghanistan. With a mesmerising display of fielding and bowling, they skittle Jersey out for 80 runs in 39 overs. Jersey are powerless to resist the pace and ferocity of the bowling attack. Hamid is the pick of the bowlers with four wickets. He destroys Jersey's middle order giving up just 27 runs in 9.5 overs. Hasti also returns impressive figures, taking three for 17 in ten overs. Afghanistan's bowlers have again swung the tie in their favour.

When Karim and Ahmad Shah open the batting, scoring ten runs off the first over, victory looks all but assured. They only need 70 runs from 49 overs and with all their wickets in hand they don't need to rush. But predictably Karim has other ideas. He wants to score runs and he also wants to get Man of the Match and win the final for Afghanistan. To do that he has to be on strike.

In the second over Ahmad Shah hits a shot, goes to run and then checks himself, realising he doesn't have enough time to make it. Karim though doesn't seem to care and keeps running towards the striker's end. He hurtles down the crease screaming at Ahmad Shah to swap places. Ahmad Shah remains rooted to the spot, he knows to run is suicide. The throw comes in from the fielder and the bowler breaks the wickets.

For a moment there is total silence across the field. The crowd and the players are transfixed and Taj stands mouth open, completely still and aghast. This is the calm before the storm. When the umpire raises his finger to send Karim back to the pavilion, the insults begin to fly.

Karim curses Ahmad Shah and screams at Taj, asking him why he put him to bat with a bisexual? As he reaches the boundary he flings his bat through the air and it clatters to the ground. The crowd takes a collective gasp as Karim stomps through to the changing room, ripping off his pads and gloves and throwing them about as he does so.

The looks on the faces of the spectators say it all: this just isn't cricket. The only saving grace is that most of them don't understand Karim's foul-mouthed Pashtu tirade. They are shocked enough that he threw his bat away as he stormed off the pitch. His colourful language would have sent them over the edge.

Taj is particularly upset: not only does the run-out put the match in jeopardy, but he is also upset for his favourite brother. Taj thinks that Ahmad Shah should have taken the fall for Karim. His fury at the not-out batsman leads him to pronounce that if Afghanistan lose, Ahmad Shah will never play for the team again.

On his day Karim is very good. In Peshawar he would routinely hit hundreds with knocks of style and panache. He is the least fearless and most uninhibited of the Afghan players at the crease. He loves to pull the ball – stepping easily into wayward or loose deliveries. However, he hasn't really found his best form in Jersey yet – scoring 47, 11, 62, 22 and 18 in the previous games and he had hoped to make a mark in the final. Now he is out for three and the team is wobbling in a game that should be a formality.

Karim's outburst has a negative effect on the other players. Nowroz has been trying to get the team to play with patience, to relax and not to panic. But all that has changed now. It seems Karim had failed to remember his captain's advice and the rest of the team are sent reeling by his astonishing outburst. From being ten runs for no wicket in the first over they rapidly collapse to 42 for 7. It is another disaster in the making. The situation is not helped as Karim loudly announces to whoever will listen that if he was still in, they would have won by now.

When Ahmad Shah is out he is greeted by silence in the pavilion and he sits away from his teammates, ignored for the rest of the innings. Emal Pasarly, the Pashtu BBC correspondent, is not surprised at the unfolding disaster. He says that this behaviour is typical of Afghanistan, because they are hot-headed and impatient. They had been cruising and now they have thrown it all away, with Karim's outburst serving as the catalyst. This, Emal felt, is all too common. In Kabul, he says, the interest in the match is intense. Although there is no TV coverage at home, Emal is relaying a ball-by-ball commentary and thousands have again crowded into the capital's Internet cafes to keep up with the score. Rumour has it the BBC website has already received over a million hits during the match.

Less than an hour ago these Internet cafes had been full of happy, excited fans – potential converts to the cause of cricket in Afghanistan. Now the atmosphere has changed – people are edgy or disappointed. This isn't what they expected from cricket.

On the boundary Mohammad Nabi moans that it isn't Jersey who's getting them out, they are getting themselves out. Karim continues his unhelpful comments but now Nowroz gives him short shrift and tells him to shut up. Inside the dressing room there is bewilderment and unbearable tension. Sherzada Massoud lies on a bench: he can't face watching the match and is shell-shocked by the turn of events. He hasn't moved for the last hour, as the Afghanistan players, their wickets falling, stumble in and out of the room.

Back outside, Taj is a nervous wreck. He strides back and forth bizarrely kitted out in a puffa jacket and tartan cap, which he has somehow acquired during the tournament, chain smoking and visibly shaking with anger as he sees his dreams being crushed by the unpredictability of sport. Sometimes he hates the game. Although his team are through to the next stage of the qualifying competition Taj is very competitive and can't bear the thought of losing the final. He had also promised his mother that he would bring the winners' trophy back, so they just have to win.

Coaches normally go out of their way to manage their supporters' expectations. They talk of never underestimating the opposition, of the difficulties in the unusual playing conditions, of the possibility of injuries, anything to avoid looking complacent or looking like a fool if the team loses. This kind of behaviour just isn't Taj's style – in his dealings with the media he lets the dramatic side of his personality do the talking – it's high theatre with big claims and emotional language. Before he left for Jersey he said he would throw himself in the Atlantic if they didn't win the tournament, he talked of scoring 400 runs against Japan and also bragged that his team was capable of beating England.

He is now reaping what he has sowed. The pressure that he has heaped on his own shoulders and those of his team is beginning to tell. He has told the world how brilliant his team is and now, if they fail to win, he will look like a fool. In the eyes of the Afghan public, defeat for such a brilliant team could only possibly come about because of poor coaching decisions. Their defeat would be seen as his failure.

With seven wickets down, Hasti Gul, the elder of Taj's two brothers, is in next. Although he classes himself as an all-rounder he is not really a batsman. Hasti's scores in the tournament so far have been one, a duck and one. He had come into the game in bad form but his bowling against Jersey was impressive – ten overs, 3 wickets for 17 runs. He decides not to wear a protective helmet but strides on to the pitch in an Afghan baseball cap – allowing the fielders to see the intense look of determination on his face as he takes his guard from the umpire.

Asghar, Afghanistan's last specialist batsman, is at the other end. But not for long. He is soon out, lbw for ten. His innings has taken 65 balls and lasted an hour and a half. He has batted exactly as Taj wanted but has not managed to see the game out for Afghanistan. As he trudges off the pitch he removes his helmet, and the Afghan flag he uses as a bandana is drenched in sweat. Asghar's despair is compounded by the knowledge that he is the last recognised batsman and now the tail is exposed to the Jersey bowlers. The situation now looks very bleak as Afghanistan find themselves eight men down for 62 runs – still needing 19 runs to win. Only Dawlat and Hamid are left to bat.

The decision is made to send in Dawlat, the fast bowler, to join Hasti Gul. With the bat he looks awkward and clumsy, he is tall – a few inches over six feet – and he looks like an adult playing with a child's bat. At the crease he hunches over it and shuffles uncomfortably. Hasti Gul knows that if the Afghans are going to win he will have to score the runs.

On the pitch Hasti looks and acts like a man possessed. His determination and focus transform him into a proper batsman: he judges every ball perfectly and nudges Afghanistan closer and closer to the total. As his confidence grows he unleashes two massive sixes: one over long on and one over deep square leg. When he clips another ball to fine leg, pushing the score to 80 the players flood the pitch thinking they've won. But as the umpires and match referees fight to impose order it dawns on them that they have to score one more run to win. Four balls later the run comes. Hasti has scored a patient unbeaten 29 off 40 balls. His highest score, by some way, and the most important innings anyone has played during the tournament.

Once again the players flood onto the pitch. Hasti and Dawlat grab a stump each. Taj's tear-stained face, showing all the strain of the previous week, is red and his voice hoarse and cracked. Finally, he thinks, the country with nothing, the country marked by tragedy has achieved something. We have played a game foreign to us, in a foreign land, against a foreign team, with more experience, more money and a better infrastructure and we have won. My team from Afghanistan has won its first competition and is on to the next qualification stage in the World Cup.

Players fall to the ground all over the pitch; they drop face first as if they are fainting. They kiss the grass, sob and thank Allah. Five Afghan immigrants now resident in Luton and who have flown in for the final, charge onto the pitch carrying the Afghan flag. Exhaustion and the emotion of it all cause Hasti to drop to his knees. Players help take his gloves off and his hat is soon lost in the melee. Taj charges towards him and embraces him, kissing him on the cheek and calling him his hero and shows him that he has changed the entry in his mobile phone book from 'Hasti Gul' to 'Hero of Afghanistan'.

The players hoist Hasti onto their shoulders and cries of 'Allah Akbar' soon bellow out. Dawlat is also hoisted up and he waves a stump in the air. The players cry that today Allah has shown his hand, how else could this nation riven with war and desperately poor, win? It is all Allah's will.

Geoffrey Boycott, the former England captain, arrives to present the trophy and the Man of the Match award. Before the presentation he comes over to the players to congratulate them. Taj is overjoyed to meet him and tells him he is a cricketing legend. Boycott responds enthusiastically about what an exciting match he has just seen. Although the Afghans are the antithesis of Boycott as a player – they are fast, furious and cavalier – whereas Boycott would occupy the crease for hours and methodically, calmly eke out a score, both are outsiders and seem to have a common bond. Although it was a low-scoring game, he says it was very exciting, he keeps repeating the word 'exciting' as if he can hardly believe such a low scoring game can be so exhilarating.

During the presentation Boycott turns to the Afghans and makes a speech. He says that considering where they have come from, what they have achieved in Jersey is remarkable. There is genuine warmth in Boycott's words and he seems honestly impressed by the Afghans. He has understood the sacrifices, the hardship, the effort and the skill that has gone into winning this tournament. As an ex-cricketer who played at the very highest level, he can see how much the players have invested emotionally and he can tell how much victory means to them.

Hasti Gul, unsurprisingly, wins Man of the Match. As the trophy is presented, Sherzada Massoud takes off his watch and in a grand gesture places it around Hasti's wrist. Cricket might be a team sport but it is clear who the hero is. After victory, Karim is quick to forgive Ahmad Shah; he doesn't apologise for his tirade but the two are quickly talking again. The ICC issues Karim with an official warning for his behaviour.

On the coach back to the hotel Hasti can't stop grinning. When they get back to the hotel the team celebrates with a swim in the hotel pool.

Despite the victory, there are murmurings of discontent among the squad. They are unhappy with the guidance they received from Taj and feel he lacked the calmness and maturity to help them through the pressurised situation. They have won, but they have been lucky. Despite the victory, Taj's future looks more and more uncertain.

BUZKASHI
GAME AND POWER IN AFGHANISTAN

G. Whitney Azoy

Football and cricket are all very well as popular imports but one sport in Afghanistan towers above all others. Buzkashi – literally 'goat pulling' – symbolises the (male-dominated) national character and culture. To call it rough and tumble misses the point altogether. This is a free-for-all, no-holds-barred contest on horseback in which individual riders or teams compete to drop the decapitated and dehooved carcase of a calf or goat on a target on the ground. Broken bones and bloody gashes to the head are par for the course, barely cause for comment.

As **G. Whitney Azoy**, an American former diplomat, humanitarian worker, journalist and film-maker writes, 'leaders are men who can seize control by means foul and fair and then fight off their rivals. The Buzkashi rider does the same.' The sport originated among the nomadic Asian tribes who swept west in a series of migrations beginning a thousand years ago and was a full-blooded test of a warrior's prowess and courage. Often played on Fridays, the Muslim holy day, a game of buzkashi can attract thousands of passionate spectators and, like so many things in Afghanistan, is not for the faint-hearted.

Under a cold winter sky the landscape of northern Afghanistan stretches towards a bleak horizon. Here on one rim of the Central Asian steppes, the hard ground runs – grey, yellow, and brown – in an empty latitudinal band below the Hindu Kush. It is less countryside than wasteland: flat with only an occasional low rise, and, even at this time of year, bone dry more often than not. A number of rivers tumble ambitiously northwards from the mountains, but most falter well short of the Russian frontier. Wherever water flows, generations of men have dug fragile irrigation networks, marked now by groves of leafless trees and rows of frozen earth. But these delicate canal patterns, however elaborate in construction and vital for livelihood, exist as exceptions which prove a starkly arid rule: For the farmers and herders who live here, water and well watered land are critically scarce resources. Beyond a last outlying mud hut, the featureless steppes begin again, desolate and only somewhat less dusty on account of a recent cold rain. And not far from the village, on marginal ground, hundreds of horsemen gather over the mutilated carcass of a calf.

The dead calf is hard for an outsider to see. Unless the earth is still really moist, great clouds of dust hide much of the central action. Powerful men on powerful horses mass with one another in a mayhem of frantic movement: pushing and shoving and changing position and trying to grasp the carcass, headless and hoofless, from the ground. The men are now yelling past one another at the top of their lungs and now urging their horses onwards with an incongruously soft hiss. The horses respond: lurching and rearing, sometimes kicking and biting, and forcing their way towards the center where the carcass lies. Only the best horses and men ever penetrate that far, and only the very best dominate the center for more than an instant: Tosh Palawan, for instance, on the famous *kashka* of Mohammed Hafiz Khan or old Habib on the great roan stallion of Hajji Gulistan. Such horses and, by extension, their riders are said to be able to "stand over the calf until sunset if they feel like it" and so, indeed, to "control the buzkashi."

For most competitors, however, the chance is momentary. In the midst of dust and noise and sweat, the calf comes underfoot. The horse, if well trained, feels the bulk below, braces for an instant, and drops its near shoulder. Clenching his whip between his teeth and cocking one foot behind the saddle, the rider leans and stretches an arm towards the ground. Metal stirrups graze his head, and unshod hooves batter his fingers. Lunging half blind in the melee, he manages to grab hold of the carcass briefly, but, as another saying goes, "Every calf has four legs," and other riders quickly wrench it away. Nothing stands still. The calf is trampled, dragged, tugged, lifted, and lost again as one competitor after another tries to gain sole control. Eventually, one horse and rider take the carcass free and clear and let it fall in uncontested triumph. Their victory, however, results in no more than a momentary pause. Already a new play cycle is underway: the increasingly mangled calf carcass on the ground and the mass of horsemen gathering around it. Hour after hour the wild scene shifts back and forth across an unbounded field. There are winners and losers. Some men never win; no man wins for long. What makes the difference between success and failure? Fate, they say, is always a crucial factor. It would be foolish, indeed vaguely sacrilegious, to argue otherwise. In the world of a buzkashi game, however, a world both volatile and violent, one acknowledges luck, but puts his trust in that other ingredient: power.

Once again, the "great game" is underway in earnest, but only alien superpowers could perceive the situation in even ambiguously playful terms. The Afghan perspective is that of a buzkashi carcass: "Like a goat between two lions," mused Amir Abdur Rahman, who in 1901 was the last khan of Kabul to die of natural causes with his authority still intact.[13] For those whose shouq interest is buzkashi, world reaction to the Russian initiative has presented one immediately familiar feature. Who better than the horsemen would understand the principle of Olympic boycott? The first half of 1980 resounded with rhetorical speculation on the link between play and politics. Now the Moscow tooi has come and gone. Some guests accepted its invitations, others did not. Level of competition, fairness of adjudication, adequacy of accommodation – all these issues have been debated back and forth by rival factions, just as in buzkashi. It is a remarkable irony that the ambiguous relationship between the 1980 Olympics and world politics would perhaps be most readily appreciated among back country traditionalists in the very nation whose misfortune prompted the issue.

---

[13] Of the ten men who have subsequently ruled – or tried to rule – from Kabul, five have been assassinated (Habibullah in 1919, Nadir Shah in 1933, Mohammed Daoud in 1978, Noor Mohammed Taraki in 1979, and Hafizullah Amin in 1979), three were exiled (Amanullah in 1929, Inayatullah after three days in 1929, and Mohammed Zahir in 1973), one was executed by more or less legitimate authority (Bacha-i-Saqao in 1929), and one, Babrak Karmal, is still in power, but only as a Soviet client.

For the Afghans themselves, authority is now more than ever an obsessive problem. With political ties always in flux, individuals rise and fall in lonely arcs. Success is transient; failure trips at its heels. Whole lifetimes are perceived as ephemeral. Their accomplishments, like the conquests of Alexander, Chingiz Khan, the British Raj, and – who knows – perhaps someday the Russians, recede in time until even the vital names themselves merge in legend and finally disappear. This philosophical perspective has few adherents, however, and does little to ease the compulsive quest for authority. Virtually all men participate in the process; some are briefly successful; but none can hold the political calf forever. It eludes the grasp and falls to the ground where another cycle starts. Only the sufi stands aside, and few share his sense of deviant clarity.

Most men, instead, are like Habib, who at nearly 70 has been a buzkashi chapandaz for half a century, and now knows no other way of life – at whatever level of game. One day late in April, 1977, we sat on a carpet which his sons had spread by the streambed next to their village, far from town. Spring in northern Afghanistan is as idyllic as it is brief, and this particular afternoon seemed almost magical. For once the stream fairly gurgled, and its valley and even the steppe beyond shimmered in generous green. Both water and color would dwindle within a month, but it was hardly a moment for harsh prospects. Instead we sprawled in a sun too expansively warm for the questionnaire I had prepared. Its structure seemed too much like business, and Habib began to regale me instead with one anecdote after another.

Most dealt, at least at the outset, with his own buzkashi exploits: often heroic, but never really boastful and occasionally quite comic. Inevitably those stories led into life beyond buzkashi: from the details of his relationship with some horse owner khan, to an estimate of the khan himself; from the disruption of a tooi, to its political circumstances.

From narrative to narrative, the cast of characters varied with Habib himself as their only common link. For a while he had ridden the horse of such and such a khan, but then had switched to another patron, and then another. He spoke repeatedly of his family, particularly of his father, but otherwise the ties in his life had come and gone. Gradually there emerged from the stories his own sense of social persona: a man inclined towards fellowship but ultimately alone, loyal by nature but forced into opportunism. Above all, he said, he had to be wary. Even at his age, there was no respite from vigilance. It was like that spring day, he said, beautiful and peaceful, but dangerous and certain to change. You could never take it easy, never relax.

The afternoon waned and we both felt an early chill. Habib had kept a quilted winter cloak tucked in a ball behind him, but now he hunched forward and wrapped it across his shoulders. For a lost moment he stared at his fingers, turned them over and back, and then slowly began to trace the bit of intricate carpet between us. Before I left for town, he told one last story.

*

It was in the month of *Dalw* [February] and I was on my way to the tooi of Hajji Latif in Ishkamish. You remember, Whitney, you were there. Two strangers passed me on the way and asked me where I was going.

I told them, "To the buzkashi of Hajji Latif."

Then one of them said, "You must know, *baba* ['old man'], that not far from here lives the famous chapandaz Habib."

"Habib?" I said, "Habib? I have never heard of this man."

"Oh, baba," they laughed at me, "How is it that you are so ill-informed? Are you the sort of man who has never been abroad in the world?"

"This Habib," I asked them, "is he about my age?"

"Send your children to school, baba, since you are too old yourself," one man said. "Habib is young and vigorous, not an old man like you."

"How big is he?" I asked.

"Habib, were he but here with us, would make two or three of you, baba. Habib is a man who could move you over a mountain."

I thought to myself how times had changed and asked them if their village had a khan whose guest house I could use to pass the night.

"Hajji Jura Khan has a grand guest house and Habib has stayed there, but you, baba, had better find a place in the mosque where no one will trouble you."

They went their way, and I told them nothing. You remember the buzkashi, Whitney? You remember that one calf I took when the salem was 800 afghanis and Ghafour never even reached it? I did well, did I not? And yet, you know, it is different now. My father died last year. He was 96. Now I am alone with only my own sons. Every year the policeman comes and asks me to play in Kabul. Every year I play. But now I feel old, and my telpak [the chapandaz cap] is loose on my head. My head, I think, has lost some of its meat. I feel old and alone, but what can I do? All my life I have played. How can I stop?

WAR GARDENS
A JOURNEY THROUGH CONFLICT IN SEARCH OF CALM

Lalage Snow

Afghans love their gardens. While Babur may have been one of the country's most famous gardeners back in the sixteenth century – the restored Babur's Gardens remains one of Kabul's most popular family attractions – there is no shortage of green fingers among the nation's men and women.

War Gardens pays tribute to them as **Lalage Snow,** a freelance war correspondent, photographer and film-maker, travels from Kabul's royal gardens and their heroically loyal centenarian gardener to the British soldiers and sometime gardeners of Camp Bastion in Helmand. Snow also goes beyond Afghanistan's borders to report from divided Jerusalem and Ukraine, where gardens and their gardeners still manage to flourish in the depths of war. Her heartening narrative, supported by ravishing photography, testifies to the healing qualities of these verdant spaces in the toughest corners of our planet. In the midst of untold grief and suffering, these gardens are oases for the soul.

The ruins seem to rise slowly out of a thick layer of city smog and dust three kilometres ahead. The wide, asphalted and modern motorway is arrow-straight and sits at odds with the mud-wattle, higgledy-piggledy buildings flanking it.

The taxi pulls over next to a crumbling stone wall and a sign tells me that the National Museum of Afghanistan is just over the road, but it is the iron and steel skeleton bare to the elements next to it that we are destined for. Its smashed-up, hollow window frames smudged black with burned-out sadness; a massive crumbling neoclassical façade and columns improbably supporting the remains of a jagged roof. Beyond it are the sure, immovable mountains.

A small, sandbagged Afghan army checkpoint covered in camouflage netting and messy concertinas of razor wire sits at the foot of the palace. A tatty Afghan flag, undisturbed by any breeze, hangs limp. We walk across a vacant area of scrub beneath it. Another sign reassures us that the area has been cleared of landmines – ubiquitous annotations of the violence of former front lines.

A group of teenage street children are kicking a football to each other and on seeing me, a foreigner, quickly abandon their game to crowd around asking for *baksheesh*; money. Without the charm or 'cuteness' of prepubescence, they are wild and unruly. One tries to grab onto my trouser pockets and shouts. Another is missing the lower part of his arm – presumably lost before the de-mining initiative. His amputated stump is crudely – although not recently – scarred, and for no reason other than to shock, he hits me with it and laughs when I flinch. The subversion of normalcy is disconcerting but Zia, my friend and fixer, looms his full six-foot-something over them, growling.

Life is so fragile here. These are children of the dust, who will live loitering in a half-life where the future is short and brutal, where limbs are snatched by mines planted long before they were even born.

Zia ushers me ahead, still looming over the teenagers like a bear and I climb up to the crumbling ruins.

The Afghan soldiers yawn out of their camouflaged shadows. While Zia explains why we are here through a chicken wire gate fence, I stand back and take in the palace – my favourite place in the whole city.

The ground floor is a loggia of some forty heavy arches built out of pale stone and arranged in a horseshoe shape. The upper floors are comprised of two galleries of Corinthian columns precariously holding up the fragile ceiling or soaring into a roofless sky.

Built in the 1920s by the reformer King Amanullah, Darulaman Palace was originally intended to house the parliament and secretariat and sat in the middle of a luxurious parkland of exotic trees Amanullah had brought home from state visits to Europe. In the intervening years it has suffered the slings and arrows of Afghanistan's outrageous misfortune. Corroded, burned and looted, the palace is a physical metaphor for the country and home only to stray dogs, scorpions, snakes and an Afghan army lookout.

But it is not that history we have come to see. It is the improbable garden in the ruined palace courtyard. It is a wild and scruffy patchwork of marigolds and maize fronds, beans and begonias crammed in together as unlikely flower bed fellows. And this is what Nicki had stumbled across a few days previously.

A man comes to greet us. '*Salaam wailekum,*' he says, and I see that he has few teeth. His face is as gnarled as a walnut, and when he strokes his wispy white beard, listening to Zia introducing us both, the veins running over the back of his hands are like wood grain. Despite the warmth of the afternoon, he is wearing at least four layers; his blue shirt and olive-green V-neck jumper are tucked into his brown *shalwar kameez* trousers. Over the bright green nylon jacket that had once been part of a boiler suit and which I take to be his 'official' work uniform, he wears an oversized pinstripe waistcoat with large and useful pockets I imagine to be full of string and secateurs.

The sunlight is making me squint and a bead of sweat trickles down my back beneath my heavy camera rucksack. My headscarf has trapped hot air in its folds and I suddenly feel a little faint. I fan my face with my hand and the old man takes his cue and leads us to the shade at the back of the courtyard where we sit on the stone steps beneath the arches.

'His name is Mohammed Kabir,' Zia says as I pull out my notebook.

Defeated by the heat, I ask a lazy non-question. 'Tell me about your garden.'

He peers at me. 'Well what do you want to know? It's here for you to see.'

'Let's start at the beginning.'

Kabir tells his story in a voice which, although thinned by age, is even and unwavering.

He was born in Charikar, a small town around sixty-five kilometres north of Kabul and the capital of Parwan province. It is nestled in a green valley at the foothills of the Hindu Kush and has been host to many a bloody battle over the years. Today it bustles with life and commerce and just gets on with things. When I last drove through, its main drag of leafy trees and shops selling everything from kitchen goods to tinned foods to plastic toys and buckets, half reminded me of a seaside town in southern Europe – minus the American military checkpoint and the sea.

'I am 105 years old,' Kabir says. I look at him dubiously and ask Zia to clarify this. It might seem pedantic, but ironing out personal details is key to deciphering an often confused narrative. In a country where around seventy per cent of the population is illiterate, where birth certificates were, until recently, an afterthought, where years roll into each other only to be defined by who was in power, where fact and fiction are at best contradictory but mostly just blurred, it is not uncommon for an interviewee to give a date of birth and describe a childhood clearly set years before this – and stubbornly argue if you point this out to be technically impossible.

There is a short exchange between the two men and I doodle a snail in my notebook next to his age.

'I think he is telling the truth,' Zia turns to me in mumbled *sotto voce*. 'He didn't change his story once.'

'I am a gardener for Kabul municipality and look after the army's garden here,' Kabir begins and goes on to explain that the soldiers based here subsist off a small kitchen garden where a few edible crops are grown: beans, potatoes and okra. It makes sense; the Afghan army has always preferred a (recently slaughtered) lamb stew over the processed, dehydrated rations issued to foreign soldiers. Colonel Shirin Shah, the gardening base commander I met in Helmand two years ago, pops into my head and I realise that, as this is a nation of farmers and gardeners, it is in no way surprising that the army lives off the land.

'But what about the flowers?' I point at the messy square of colour in the middle of the courtyard.

'Well,' he says, 'I just decided to bring some seeds from my home and plant them in the courtyard. The soldiers helped me to dig and water. I am an old man,' he reminds me.

I ask him why he would make a garden in the ruins of a forgotten palace where only the military and the ghosts will see it. He looks at me as if I've asked him to count up to three.

'Everyone needs a garden. This is our soil. When you work with it, things grow. It's nature, life. I am a poor man, sometimes my family and I only eat once a day, but I can live without food; I couldn't live without seeing green leaves and flowers. They come from heaven. Each one,' he insists, 'is a symbol of paradise. I have a flower in my garden at home and have counted seventy colours in its petals; tell me that it doesn't come from heaven!' he exclaims.

He pauses to look at his oasis shimmering beneath ribbons of heat and I follow his gaze, thinking of Babur's earthly heaven and of Eden and the tree of life and everything that followed. As if reading my mind, he says softly, 'I feel like I'm in paradise when I garden.'

Water, he explains, is his biggest problem. I nod; not only are the ruins situated on a mound, they are at the foothills of barren mountains. But it is not this which is the root of his problems. It is Washington.

'Washington has built a military base near here and they have stolen our water.' Kabir becomes animated and I try not to smile. It is true that there is a NATO base a kilometre or so away from the palace – there are many dotted around the city, most of which have disrupted city life one way or another. As support for international troop presence wanes, the bases have increasingly become the scapegoat for a multitude of municipal problems.

In a culture driven by rumour, conjecture (and an unerring belief that Afghanistan is actually the centre of the world), conspiracies concerning the true motive for outsiders being in the country abound. The CIA is considered to be actively funding the Taliban along with Pakistan and Iran (perhaps not so surprising a theory given the CIA's support of the mujahidin against the Soviets); the British are in Helmand to avenge their defeat in the Battle of Maiwand in the second Anglo-Afghan war; Western governments are directly invested in the continuation of opium production; the war is just a huge cover-up while Afghanistan's mineral wealth is exploited by the international community; if America itself is not responsible for 9/11, then it is either the Israeli or Pakistani intelligence services. Or Iran. Although some theories have their feet in fact, most are wildly inaccurate.

That outsiders are to blame for the depletion of water levels in Kabul city is an axiom for Kabir. And to him 'Washington' is as good a collective noun for all foreigners as it gets. It is also a reflection of how poorly the international community understands Afghan public opinion. But fortunately for him, the Afghan soldiers at the palace have a well from which they help him draw water.

I ask him what else he loves about his garden and he hugs his knees like a schoolboy, smiling proudly.

Zia translates: 'It makes him very sad to see this palace in ruins but since he came back to work here, he's tried to make it look like it used to.'

'What does he mean "like it used to"?' I ask. The palace has been in ruins for years.

After a few minutes of discussion Zia says, 'When the gardens were first started.'

I don't understand the reference and start flicking back through my notebook, looking for this vital bit of information I appear to have missed.

Finding none, I ask for clarification.

The story is remarkable. Kabir first started working in the newly built European palace as a gardener when he was a teenager alongside his father and uncle.

'When the gardens were built, they looked like this. It was different then.' He picks up a stick and begins to sketch an outline map in the dirt. 'They were all the way over there, and there and behind us there' – he points to the furthest points we can see – 'so you had different areas for the trees, different areas for flowers, different areas for shade and water. There was a pathway here' – he draws a straight line – 'which separated the flower beds, and there were different types of apples and apricots here and here. The king had been travelling and brought back different species from Germany, France, Italy, England – all over. We needed to use donkeys, horses and even elephants to move the big things around,' he says.

I am a little sceptical at the mention of elephants – they are not indigenous to Afghanistan – and it sounds like a tale of fancy. However if it is true, Kabir is a living, breathing window into a version of Afghanistan few would believe ever existed.

'It was a very modern garden for the time. But it was a different era then,' he sighs a little forlornly.

In a career spanning over half a century, Kabir continued to work as government employee in various guises. His preferred job was in the palace gardens. With a wistful gaze he describes his favourite memory, 'The king's mother was very kind to me. She used to come and sit in the shade beneath the apricot trees with us and chat and smile.'

I find this dubious and imagine the story to be the imaginings of an old man. With my journalistic hat on I want to press him for more details, to pick holes and find flaws in his story. But I stop. For him, it is a real memory and it makes him happy. Happier than remembering a brutal time of war which seems never to end, so who am I to take that away? Instead I ask him to describe the weather and what was in bloom during the afternoon in the garden with the king's mother.

'Oh, sunny. It was always sunny then,' he says simply, 'everything bloomed.'

The sun, trapped in the courtyard of the palace, has created an inferno and I am wilting again. But when we stand in the courtyard garden I feel cool and protected from the heat. It is in no way reminiscent of the formal gardens the palace would have been used to – in the middle of the ruins it looks rather like an unkempt toupee, but as he points out the areas of zinnia, miscanthus, maize, cosmos and coleus, I see that he has tried to maintain structure. He moves between each plant like a teacher in a playground, chastising and praising each in turn.

'Since starting this garden I feel I am getting younger. Every tree, every plant, every flower gives me energy.'

I ask him what he will do if and when the palace is restored.

He shrugs. 'My garden will be destroyed. But still,' he goes on, 'I feel younger and more powerful here. People say I look younger too.' And he shows us his beard, which he is convinced is darkening the more he gardens.

Before we leave I ask the soldiers if I can wander around the ruins. I turn back into the palace and make for the cool, dark interior. It is so vast I feel like I'm Alice in Wonderland – albeit a very ruined Wonderland.

The ceiling has collapsed on one side and shafts of sharp sunlight score the shadows on another. In front of me are the remains of a grand spiral staircase, the banister of which has long since been looted. I climb up to the second floor where there is more light – and a lot more rubble. A collapsed floor gapes like an open wound of steel and stone. It is as still as a grave, but soft toots from traffic and the faint tinkle of bicycle bells reminds me that the city is still breathing.

Scrawled parachutes, helicopters and tanks with captions in French and English describe the recent history of Canadian, British and American special forces whose date-stamped litany of graffiti is a signature to the official end of the Taliban's regime.

This close, the ruins are somehow even more forlorn, and I am reminded of Stalin's maxim 'a million deaths are a statistic, one is a tragedy'. So it is with buildings. From a distance, ruined buildings are in a way more digestible but the absence of any attempt to clear the rubble renders the palace frozen in time. Nobility and grandeur lingers here, and it is easy to imagine the elegant men and women in Edwardian dress perambulating along the galleries, perhaps protecting themselves from the sun with silk umbrellas.

I take another flight of precipitous stairs to the top floor where the wind and dust are masters of the world. It is silent there and ethereal. I scramble over to what was once a dining room and survey Kabul through the remains of a window. The long, straight highway bustles on, mutely carving the open horizon, ferrying toy cars and antlike people.

I scramble over to the other side of the long gallery overlooking the courtyard and rest on a balustrade. From that great height the garden below is the size of a postage stamp but an emerald in a vast canvas of tan and devastation. The acoustics of the courtyard mean that I can hear echoes of Kabir, Zia and the soldiers, still pottering in the garden. They are laughing easily. The garden really does make people happy, even when everything else is unravelling.

'Lali-Lali?' Zia has seen me up near the clouds and his voice echoes. 'Shall we go go?'

Reluctantly I drag myself away from the ruins and back to earth. I ask the soldiers what they make of the garden. One of them is picking the petals off the bright orange head of a marigold like a love sick poet and explains that in the evenings they sit and drink tea here. 'It's good to have greenery around. Green is happiness, green is peace. Who doesn't like that?'

*

The water is perfectly blue – a crystal of tourmaline shining out from a dull rock. At its shore frolic young Afghans. They wait impatiently and loudly for their turn in the back of one of three speedboats which make a loop around the lake at top speed. Couples and young families clamber into blue pedalos for a more sedate experience. On the sandy strip of beach, wiry horses are raced within an inch of their lives by young men eager to show off a native equine prowess. Larger groups and families recline on semi-private, raised platforms with urns of green tea and mounds of kebab and *naan* from one of the many *chai khonas* (tea houses) or eateries catering to day-trippers.

I am in a taxi driving along the edge of Qargha Lake. Built on the outskirts of Kabul in the 1930s the reservoir was converted to recreational use in the 1950s.

The car continues on a road heading away from the resorts and, turning off up a steep dirt track, it stops at a blast wall chicane. I pay the driver and weave through the concrete maze to an enormous steel door which clicks open immediately. A few uniformed guards point me towards the basement of the house, but before I reach the door a smartly dressed man with salt-and-pepper hair and a neatly trimmed moustache steps out to greet me.

'Dr Zabi Mojadidi,' he says kindly. 'Come. Where shall we sit?'

'Outside,' I suggest, 'in the garden.'

He leads me outside to a paved patio. It is the first of a number of terraces and covered in potted cacti and geraniums. The second is a lawn flanked by colourful flower beds and the third, a vegetable patch.

We sit beneath a parasol at a table fashioned out of a tree trunk in another patio in the middle of the grassy terrace. He points at some boulders next to us. 'These were unearthed when we were building the house. The workmen were going to smash them up to make gravel, but I like them just as they are.'

He rubs the edge of the table and reiterates his love of recycling nature. 'Sadly we had to dig up quite a few old trees for the building work so I tried to replace what I'd disposed of. They were going to throw this one away, but why trash something if you can make something out of it?'

He managed to save the oldest tree of all – a walnut which he guesses is around 150 years old. 'It used to fruit abundantly, but this year I don't know, we've hardly had any walnuts – maybe fifty or so. I need to research what might be troubling it.'

The vegetable patches are bigger than I had first thought, more kitchen garden than cottage garden and abundant with cauliflowers, basil, spinach and rhubarb which are all plump, succulent and healthy. He and his wife brought many of the seeds from America.

In the early nineties, Mojadidi left for Virginia (he had been a scholarship student at Virginia Tech in the sixties and seventies) and remained there for eleven years. He returned to Afghanistan in 2004 to work as an engineer with a privately owned company, and in 2009 he was persuaded by old cohorts and allies to take on the mantle of governor of Kabul.

'I thought it would be a good opportunity to help rebuild the city, but I soon realised that the role was merely symbolic and I couldn't do what I wanted without abusing the system. So I quit.'

He continued to work as a structural engineer however, and tells me that the house and this garden is the product of his own hard work and determination not to walk the well-trodden path of corruption and abuse of power.

Using a traditional Afghan design, updated to suit modern living, he built his new home and then set to work on the garden.

It is by far the brightest and most manicured garden I have seen so far. With its patio for barbecuing, outside lights, parasol for shade, it is also the most American. But there are water channels, and I ask Mojadidi if he was influenced in some way by the Mughal tradition.

'Maybe subconsciously,' he says. 'But I love the sound of water and when we have guests we sit and listen to it. It's pleasing for the ear. It *is* an Afghan garden, through and through.'

Babur's gardens were divided along fault lines of shade, fruit, beauty and water – an earthly paradise. Mojadidi's garden contains all of those elements – they are just laid out in a slightly different way and with a different colour palette.

I ask him if he was here during a recent Taliban attack on a hotel near the lake and he nods.

'Were you afraid?'

'No. I've got good security up here' – he points out the sentry posts – 'and the lake is an extra buffer. That's why I'm out here – not just the better air.'

As a former governor of Kabul, a political activist who is outspoken against different political parties and the ISI (the Pakistani intelligence service), *and* as the son of a former president, Mojadidi has every reason to need extra security. He is followed by his enemies when he leaves his house, and is often threatened.

'They did the same with my father when he criticised the Soviets. He was incarcerated for five years. People don't like it when you speak out.'

I ask which is his favourite area of the garden.

'This one,' he says pulling his right knee across his left and smiling, 'It's right in the middle of everything. I love sitting here when the moon rises. My wife always jokes that I love the moon and the garden more than I love her. It is not true. It is the moon that reminds me of her when she is away.'

THE FAVOURED DAUGHTER
ONE WOMAN'S FIGHT TO LEAD AFGHANISTAN INTO THE FUTURE

Fawzia Koofi

> While senior politicians fled from Kabul in the summer of 2021, none more ignominiously than President Ashraf Ghani, **Fawzia Koofi** (1975–), a trailblazing former member and deputy speaker of parliament, candidate for president, women's rights activist and Nobel Peace Prize nominee, was surely one of the bravest among the many who stayed – as long as she could. Left to die in the sun the day she was born by parents who had been hoping for a boy, Koofi has spent her life breaking barriers, defying expectations and surviving assassination attempts. At the time of writing she continues her advocacy for women in exile with her two daughters. *The Favoured Daughter* is a tough read, an eye-opening memoir which provides an undaunted insight into the unspeakable challenges faced by Afghan women on a daily basis and especially under Taliban rule.

SEPTEMBER 2010

The morning I wrote the letter that begins Chapter 1, I was due to attend a political meeting in Badakhshan, the province of Northern Afghanistan that I represent as a member of the Afghan parliament. Badakhshan is the northernmost province of Afghanistan, bordering both China and Takjikistan.

It is also one of the poorest, wildest, most remote, and culturally conservative provinces in all of Afghanistan.

Badakhshan has the highest rate of maternal mortality and child mortality in the entire world, due in part to its inaccessibility and crippling poverty, but also in part to a culture that sometimes puts tradition ahead of women's health. A man will rarely seek hospital treatment for his wife unless it's clear she won't survive otherwise. With childbirth, this often means a woman may undergo three or four days of agonizing labor. By the time she reaches a hospital – often on the back of a donkey after traveling over rocky mountain tracks – it is usually too late to save both mother and child.

On the day I wrote the letter I was warned not to travel because there had been a credible threat that the Taliban planned to kill me by planting an improvised explosive device (a roadside bomb) underneath my car. The Taliban dislike women holding such powerful positions in government as I do, and they dislike my public criticisms even more.

They often try to kill me.

Recently they have tried even harder than usual to murder me, threatening my home, tracking my journeys to work so they can lay a bomb as my car passes, even firing on a convoy of police vehicles that was supposed to protect me. One recent gun attack on my car lasted for 30 minutes, killing two policemen. I stayed inside the vehicle, not knowing if I would be alive or dead when it was over.

I know the Taliban and those others who seek to silence me for speaking out against corruption and bad leadership in my country will not be happy until I am dead.

But on this day I ignored the threat. I have ignored countless similar threats, because if I didn't, I could not do my job.

But I felt the threat. I always feel it. That's the very nature of threat, and those who threaten know that.

I awoke my eldest daughter, Shaharzad, who is twelve, at 6:00 A.M. and told her that if I didn't come home from this trip in a few days, she was to read the letter to her ten-year-old younger sister, Shuhra. Shaharzad's eyes, full of questions, met mine. I placed my finger to her lips and kissed her and her sleeping sister on the forehead as I quietly left the room and closed the door.

I regularly tear myself away from my children to do my work, despite knowing I might well be murdered. But my job is to represent the poorest people of my nation. That purpose, along with raising my two beautiful daughters, is what I live for. I could not on that day, and will not ever, let my people down.

Dear Shuhra and Shaharzad,

Today I am going on political business to Faizabad and Darwaz. I hope I will come back soon and see you again, but I have to say that perhaps I will not.

There have been threats to kill me on this trip. Maybe this time these people will be successful in doing that.

As your mother it causes me such bitter pain to tell you this. But please understand I would willingly sacrifice my life if it meant a peaceful Afghanistan and a better future for the children of this country.

I live this life so that you – my precious girls – will be free to live your lives and to dream all of your dreams.

If I am killed and I don't see you again, I want you to remember a few things for me.

First, don't forget me.

Because you are young and have yet to finish all your studies and can live independently, I want you to stay with your aunt Khadija. She loves you so much and she will take care of you for me.

You have my authority to spend all the money I have in the bank. But use it wisely and use it for your studies. Focus on your education. A girl needs an education if she is to excel in this man's world.

After you graduate from eighth grade, I want you to continue your studies abroad. I want you to be familiar with universal values. The world is a big, beautiful, wonderful place and it is yours to explore.

Be brave. Don't be afraid of anything in life.

All of us human beings will die one day. Maybe today is the day I will die. But if I do, please know it was for a purpose.

Don't die without achieving something. Take pride in trying to help people, and in trying to make our country and our world a better place.

I kiss you both. I love you.

Your mother

A DREAM FOR A WAR-TORN NATION

Let me share with you a memory.

Two years ago I went to one of the villages in Badakhshan in order to hear the problems of the people and to find out what I could do to help them. On the way the weather became dark and we had to spend the night in one of the houses in the village. The family that we spent the night with was one of the richest families of what was a very poor village. The house owner guided us toward his home, and the young people of the village had lined up on the both sides of the road to welcome us. After greeting them we went on toward our host's house.

A beautiful young woman, about 30 years old, wearing ragged clothes and a red scarf came out of the house to welcome us. I greeted the woman and she bent to kiss my hands. I was embarrassed. I did not expect the young and beautiful woman to respect me in that way. I hadn't done anything for this woman or for her village, so I didn't allow her to kiss my hands. The woman, who seemed unhappy and worried, invited us into the living room. The room was small and dark. It took a while for my eyes to adjust to the darkness. When they did I noticed she was heavily pregnant.

The woman brought us green tea, dried mulberries, and walnuts. I asked her how many children she had. She replied that she had five children and was now seven months pregnant.

I was worried about the woman because she did not look right. She left the room again and came back with a big plate of sweet Afghan rice pudding that she had made for us. She spread out a cloth and then put the big wooden bowl of rice on it.

Dinner was a good time for me to try and engage her in conversation in order to get more information. I started by talking about the weather. I said: "It's summer but your village is high in the mountains and the weather still feels cold; in winter it must be very cold here." The shy woman replied: "Yes, in winter we have a lot of snow, we can't even get out of the house it snows so heavily." I asked her: "How do you work then? Is someone helping you with the house work?"

She replied: "No one helps me. I wake up at four in the morning. I clear the snow until the doors of the stable are accessible, then I feed the cows and other animals. After that I prepare dough and bake bread in the tandoor oven. Then I clean the house."

"But you are heavily pregnant," I said. "Do you still do all this on your own even when pregnant?"

"Yes," she replied. She seemed surprised that I was surprised by her answer.

I told her I didn't think she looked well and that I was worried about her. She told me she felt very ill: "I work all day and at night I cannot move because I am in so much pain."

I asked her why she didn't see a doctor. She told me that it wasn't possible because the hospital was far away.

I told her that I would talk to her husband on her behalf and tell him he must take her.

She replied: "If my husband takes me to the hospital then we would have to sell a goat or a sheep in order to pay for my treatment. He would never agree to that. On top of that, how would we get there? The hospital is three days' walking and we don't have a donkey or horse."

I told her that her life should be more important than a goat or a sheep. If she is healthy she can take care of the whole family, but if she is sick then she can't look after anyone.

She shook her head and smiled a slow, wistful smile of sadness: "If I die then my husband will marry somebody else, but the whole family is fed by the milk of the goats and the meat from the sheep. If we lose a goat or sheep then who will feed this family? From where will this family get food then?"

I have never forgotten this poor woman. And I doubt she is alive today. Her multiple pregnancies, her poor diet, her exhaustion, her lack of access to a doctor. Any one of these things could have killed her.

There are hundreds of thousands of women like her across Afghanistan.

Her attitude was typical of many. The typical Afghan woman does not fear death and wants to keep her family happy and satisfied at any cost.

Brave and kind, she is ready to sacrifice herself for the sake of others, but what does she get in return? Normally very little. And a husband who puts the cost of a goat or a sheep above his wife's life.

When I remember this woman, tears come to my eyes and I feel more compelled than ever to help all those others like her.

I have a dream that one day all the humans in Afghanistan will have equal rights. Afghan girls have talent, skill, and the capacity to be educated. They should be given every opportunity to be educated and literate, and to participate fully in the political and social future of the country.

I dream that the culture of ethnic division disappears in Afghanistan. I hope also that the Islamic values that have shaped our history and our culture are kept safe from false and wrong interpretations.

The Afghan people are the main victims of terrorism worldwide, but Afghanistan is also known to the world as the main producer of terrorists. I hope that with active diplomacy and good representation we will be able to change this understanding.

Afghanistan is traditionally a poor country but we have great resources. I hope our untapped mineral wealth can be used to combat poverty and give our country importance.

Afghanistan as a nation has witnessed great struggles. We have never accepted invasion nor been colonized or conquered. That is something we Afghans are proud of. We are warriors by nature. But this does not mean that the doors of globalization and global opportunities and cooperation should be closed for Afghanistan.

I dream that one day Afghanistan will be a nation free from the shackles of poverty. I dream it will no longer be labeled the worst place in the world for a woman or a child to be born.

Since 2001 and the fall of the Taliban billions of dollars of aid money have been spent in Afghanistan. I am grateful for every penny of it, but unfortunately much of it has been wasted or misdirected, or fell into the wrong hands, such as those of corrupt local politicians or American contracting companies who took great profits but built poor quality roads and new hospitals without proper plumbing.

Despite their good intentions some of the decisions taken by the United Nations and the international community have proved only mixed successes. At a meeting in Geneva in 2002 it was decided that the United States would train the newly formed Afghan National Army, Germany would be responsible for the police, Italy would look after the justice system, Britain would take counter narcotics, and Japan would focus on disarming illegal groups. This so-called Five Pillar approach had at its heart the issue of security, yet almost ten years after Operation Enduring Freedom began Afghanistan is still far from stable.

A large part of the problem is that for far too long Afghanistan's leaders have acted like the country is theirs to do with as they please. They forget that there's a whole nation of people living here – real people, good people, with families and businesses and children and dreams for their future. Instead Afghanistan has been run like the personal fiefdom of a few powerful men. Their agenda has generally been entirely selfish.

In the case of the Soviets, Afghanistan was as a stepping stone in their ambitions for empire, as they jealously eyed Pakistan's warm-water ports. Afghanistan lay in the way, and as such was largely an inconvenience to be subjugated as part of a greater game.

Then the mujahideen cloaked themselves in nationalism. They were the liberating heroes of our nation and while all Afghans are proud of their long and tenacious victory over the Soviets, the mujahideen's grasp for personal power turned into civil war and nearly destroyed my country. It was their infighting and the chaos that followed it that opened the door for the Taliban.

The Taliban strove for a kind of great backward leap, propelling Afghanistan into a medieval era of Islamic conservatism and hyperbole barely seen in the history of the world or in Islam.

Little, if any, thought was given to the ambitions, hopes, and welfare of ordinary Afghans. Ironically, it was perhaps the Soviets who got closest, building hospitals and learning institutions to improve people's lives. But that was about a hegemonic pacification as a means of achieving a larger strategic goal, not the enrichment and development for the greater good of a diverse people who call Afghanistan home.

Ordinary Afghans, be they Pashtu, Takjiks, Hazaras, Uzbeks, Aimak, Turkmen, or Baluch, have hopes for this country. Unfortunately for far too long they have had leaders who are only interested in serving themselves, and in many ways that is still true to this day.

The average Afghan politician has the attitude that once they come to power their office and authority is a personal plaything, whether it is giving influential jobs to friends and relatives who are completely unqualified for the position, or enriching themselves through bribes and outright theft. The last thing on their minds is the welfare and happiness of the people they are supposed to represent.

Nepotism is rampant in Afghanistan's political system. Family and friends are incredibly important in my country, just as they rightly are everywhere. However, our politicians have yet to realize that public office is about public service, not giving your nearest and dearest key positions in the administration. It is wrong, even when such appointments are well intended, for example: "I need someone I can trust. Well, who better than my cousin/ nephew/old family friend?" It is not the way to run an effective government and is a catalyst for worse corruption. The new staff does not bring the desire to serve their nation with them. Instead, their loyalty lies with the person who hired them. Decisions are taken on the basis of what's best for each other, not what's best for the people.

Accountability and transparency break down, and the fundamentals of good government are cast aside.

Sadly, while most Afghans dislike the way our government runs, many are accepting of it. Expectations of political leaders are low, and all too often dissenting voices can be bought off with a job, a contract, or maybe just cash. And if they can't be bought off? Well, sadly my country is a dangerous place. People die here all the time, and very few of the murders are ever solved. Much is written in the world media about the kidnapping of foreign aid workers, a rare but very unfortunate occurrence. These people have come only to help us and my heart weeps every time one of them lays down their life for a country that isn't even theirs. But what the media do not report is how commonly Afghans are kidnapped. Every rich businessman in our country knows someone who has been kidnapped for ransom. Even small children are not safe from the kidnap gangs who want their parents' money. Therefore most of the Afghan business people who hold dual passports have fled the country, creating a massive brain drain.

And that won't change until the system changes, and by that I mean the people whose job it is to run the country must start to do things for the right reasons. A person should be involved in public service only if they truly want to serve the public. If all our politicians and government officials were to adopt this mindset, there's no limit to what could be achieved. The billions of dollars of aid and development money that has been poured into Afghanistan would go where it is actually needed. The contract to do the work would be performed by the contractor best able to perform the service, not the one who pays the biggest bribe. The police and army would be solely loyal to their uniform and to the nation it represents, not to a corrupt boss. Local governors would diligently and honestly collect taxes and duties and deliver them to the central treasury. The central government in turn would see that the money gets spent wisely and efficiently on the ministries and projects the politicians have designated. And the politicians are beholden to listen to, and act upon, the wishes of their constituents.

I don't wish to sound politically naive at this point. All governments have their problems. But the best governments have mechanisms for improvement. That requires parliamentary inquiries where the members are free and willing to investigate and present their findings in an honest way. It requires a judiciary that can act independent of influence, and has the teeth to fight off any corrupting pressure. It requires a police force disciplined and proud enough to refuse committing petty larceny, and bold enough to investigate any level of criminal activity, no matter who is implicated.

So where does one start in a country that has the dubious honor of being rated one of the top three most corrupt countries in the world according to Transparency International's World Corruption Index? I believe it has to begin with the opposition. Only when there is the political will to listen to the people and act on their behalf with honesty and integrity can things begin to improve in Afghanistan. This is my personal opinion, but it is one formed by talking to hundreds, maybe thousands, of ordinary people. Many Afghans have given up hope, or maybe resigned themselves to never having an honest government. They have been fed a diet of rubbish politics for 30 years, so it's no wonder the political health of this nation has suffered. As a country we are politically malnourished, and our growth has been stunted as a consequence. This is beginning to change, though. There is a rare breed of politicians who are listening to the electorate and acting with honesty and integrity. And in doing so they are winning the respect and trust of the people.

So much of Afghanistan's success as a democracy hinges on two things. The first is education. All people, all children, both boys and girls, must receive a decent, affordable education. They need it for their personal future, but they also need it to make informed decisions about the future of their country. The second is security. There needs to be law and order so that ordinary Afghan families can build their lives safely and in peace. And when it comes time to elect a government they need to feel safe both during the act of voting and in the knowledge that their vote actually counts. Afghans generally want the opportunity to elect their leaders. They don't, however, yet know what it means to have free and fair elections.

If a genuinely democratic government can be established then I hope that given time, all aspects of government, including the security forces, will form the backbone of a stable, free, and just society. There is something of a chicken and egg argument here. Does security produce better government? Or does good governance produce security? The answer is probably both.

And what about the Taliban, who stand for both and neither at the same time?

As I write this book, the world's powers are talking about withdrawal from Afghanistan. In my view, they are planning to withdraw before the job is finished and while war and conflict still blight our land. This conflict could at any point explode on an international scale. The warning that the great Ahmed Shah Massoud gave the West that terrorism would come to its shores is more relevant than ever. Unless our international friends start to work on a wider regional approach to tackle the Taliban issue, then the dangers to the world remain.

Recently, there have been many talks about Taliban reconciliation and reintegration into the government. Much of this process has been led by the international community and its purpose is to serve the agenda of withdrawing their troops as quickly as possible. But that is a mistake. It is another short-term quick fix that will do nothing to solve the world's problems, only store them up and make them worse for another day.

The Taliban will argue that their form of conservative Islam is the only form of government Afghanistan needs, and that they alone can bring stability to the country. But they've proven through their interpretation of education and healthcare policy that at least half the population suffers greatly under their rule. And their views on security and justice bear no resemblance to what most people want or expect. Should they be given a political voice? I suppose under the type of democratic system I believe in everybody has a say in politics. But that is the point – politics is about talking, reasoning, and persuading. It is hard to see how the Taliban will ever sit in a parliament alongside female politicians like me. I have just won a second term in the parliament and received even more votes than I did the first time. Like my father before me I am proud to say I am known as an honest politician who is not afraid to speak out when needed. I believe the Afghan public now sees me as a politician first and a woman second. This is something I am extremely proud of.

Yet the Taliban will never accept this and they make regular attempts on my life and on the lives of many other intellectuals, opponents, and friends of the West. Are these people who will ever understand or respect what democracy means? I doubt it.

Will they sit in debates with us and try to reach a common ground? Will they support new legislation or ideas put forward by me or other women? The answer is no. And it is naive of the international community to think this is possible. So much has been done in recent years to support and enhance the overall progress of Afghan women; bringing the Taliban back into the government will undo all of that.

As I drive through Kabul, I always smile when I see the beautiful sight of little girls dressed in the school uniform of black shalwar kameez and white head scarves. Within the past decade, hundreds of thousands of little girls, including my own daughters, have gained the opportunity to be educated. This not only gives them the chance of a future but also improves the future economic and physical health of their families. This in turn helps our entire nation grow stronger and powerful. If the Taliban returns, these little girls will once again be forced back indoors and silenced underneath their burqas and a set of arcane laws that accord women fewer rights than dogs. Our nation will once again slide backwards into darkness. To allow this to happen would be a betrayal of the highest order.

In October 2010, I won a second term in the parliament. I had not let my people down and, despite widespread fraud and cheating on the part of some of my opponents, I got even more votes than I did the first time.

I was also thrilled that my elder sister Qandigul (known as Maryam to her family) was elected as an MP. She is the sister who was beaten by the mujahideen the night my mother refused to show them where my father's weapons were hidden. She was illiterate and did not attend school as a child (I was the only female member of my family allowed to do so). But after she married and had children, she watched as I gained my education and saw what I had achieved. She too wanted to serve our country and do something important with her life, so she decided to educate herself. She started by going to night school to take computer and literacy classes and a few years later she graduated with a university degree. Now she is an MP like me and the latest member of the Koofis to take her place in the family business of politics. I am immensely proud of her achievements and I know she will work hard in her new role.

During the latest elections, there were even more threats on my life: gunmen trailing my car, roadside bombs laid along my route, warnings that I would be kidnapped. On the day of voting, two people were arrested who admitted that they had planned to kidnap me, take me to a different district, and then kill me. It was reported that they had links to other local politicians, but the politicians denied any involvement. One of the men has since been released while the other remains in custody. I cannot explain why one of these men was released without charge after admitting his evil project. I can only say that due to my outspokenness, I cannot always rely on our national security forces as much as I would like. Often I don't know who my would-be assassins are, whether they wear civilian clothes or official uniforms. At times in Kabul, I have had my car pulled off the road and been intimidated by our national intelligence forces, always without reason or explanation. This has become such a daily part of my life now. I will not say I am used to it – no one can ever get used to such threats – but I have learned to live with it.

Like my father, I am not afraid to speak out on difficult issues when needed. I have proven that I can deliver services and direct funds to those in need. Of course, the people I represent are still among the world's poorest and much work still needs to be done.

But I know I have improved their lives by bringing them roads, schools, jobs, and mosques. Recently I championed the building of a series of women's mosques in some remote and very conservative villages.

The mosques are a place to pray, and no man would deny his wife the chance to leave home for an hour a day to worship God. Sometimes it is the only opportunity these women have to get out of their homes. The mosques will make other services accessible to women. In these centers of religion, women can now get advice on nutrition and hygiene or take literacy classes. Just one building like this can transform the dynamics of a poor village almost overnight.

Today I am probably the best known of all the female politicians in Afghanistan and am extremely popular with the public, both men and women. My supporters have suggested I run for president. I will not lie and say that the role of leading my nation is not something I would love to do. Of course I would. Name me a serious politician anywhere in the world who wouldn't want the top job if offered it. And I know it is a job I am capable of doing well. But in truth, I do not think the time is right. I don't think my country is ready to accept a woman in this role. Of course, I hope this will change one day. Until recently, no one thought a black man could be president of the United States but it happened. Other Islamic countries have had female heads of state. Megawati Sukarnoputri was president of Indonesia from 2001 to 2004; Begum Khaleda Zia was the first female prime minister of Bangladesh; in neighboring Pakistan, Benazir Bhutto was also prime minister and was on the verge of being elected president when she was killed. I think about my early political heroines, Margaret Thatcher and Indira Gandhi. They are women who are remembered not for their gender but for their policies and their strength as leaders. And I know it could one day be possible in Afghanistan.

For far too long politics in my country has been conducted at the end of a gun. It has had more to do with who's got the most soldiers or the best tanks. It hasn't been about policy, plans, or reforms. But it must be in the future.

These changes will take time. But while these changes germinate, take root, and grow, so too will the economy. A stable Afghanistan will sprout opportunities for its people. Whether it is the farmer who can use better and safer roads to get to market, the budding entrepreneur building an import-export business, or the hundreds of thousands of Afghans living abroad, many of them highly educated, the building blocks for a better future will begin to present themselves.

I don't wish to understate the challenges that lie ahead for my country. There are so many problems we must overcome. Afghanistan is awash with corruption, flawed religious extremism, and a river of money from the sea of opium poppies grown on our farmland. But through the generations of suffering this land has endured, there is a strength and resolve in the people that has never been broken. I believe and pray that the time is approaching for all Afghans to put aside the past and look to the future. After so many years of war and oppression we are left with virtually nothing. The only choice we have is to rebuild, and I believe that's what the majority of my countrymen and women genuinely want. They just need the framework to do it.

And if we can achieve that, my darling daughters, then perhaps someday your children's children will grow up free in a proud, successful, Islamic republic that has taken its rightful place in the developed world.

This is what I live for. And what I know I will die for.

If this should happen, my darling daughters, then know that every word in this book was written for you.

I want and need you, and all the boys and girls of Afghanistan, to understand. My dreams for this nation will live on in you.

And if the Taliban does not succeed in killing me? Well Shuhra, maybe I will try and beat you to the post of first female president of Afghanistan. And maybe we will form a new dynasty of powerful Islamic female leaders.

I know as I write these final words my mother is most definitely smiling in heaven.

THE PEARL THAT BROKE ITS SHELL

Nadia Hashimi

Nadia Hashimi (1977–) is not your average novelist and *The Pearl That Broke Its Shell* is anything but your average novel. Daughter of Afghan exiles in the US and a paediatrician educated in New York, she became the first Afghan-American woman to run for Congress as a Democratic candidate in 2017. By that time it seemed there was nothing Hashimi could not do. She had just published the last of a trio of international bestsellers, translated into seventeen languages, one appearing every year from 2014. They don't shrink from taking on big issues such as forced migration, misogyny, colonialism and drug addiction. *The Pearl That Broke Its Shell*, her debut novel, confronts the tortured history of gender relations in Afghanistan as two young women, separated by a century, adopt the ancient custom of *bacha posh*, dressing and living as boys, to enable them to shop in the market, escort their sisters to school and provide for the family. But how long can it last?

RAHIMA

"WE WOULDN'T BE THE FIRST. It's been done before."

"You're listening to that lunatic Shaima and that story about your precious grandmother."

"It wasn't my grandmother. It was—"

"I don't care. All I know is that woman makes my head ache."

"Arif-jan, I think it would be wise for us to consider this. For everyone's sake."

"And what good will come of it? You see everyone else who has done it? They all have to change back in a few years. It doesn't help anything."

"But, Arif-*jan*, she could *do* things. She could go to the store. She could walk her sisters to school."

"Do what you want. I'm going out."

I listened carefully from the hallway, just a few feet from the bedroom we all shared. Our kitchen was behind the sitting room, a few pots and a gas burner. Our home was spacious, built in a time when my grandfather's family had more. Now these walls were bare and cracking and looked more like those of our neighbors.

When I heard Padar-*jan* strain to get up, I quickly tiptoed off, my bare toes silent on the carpet. When I was sure he was gone, I came back to the living room to find my mother lost in thought.

"Madar-*jan*?"

"Eh? Oh. Yes, *bachem*. What is it?"

"What were you and Padar-*jan* talking about?"

She looked at me and bit her lip.

"Sit down," she said. I sat cross-legged in front of her, careful that the hem of my skirt reached over my knees and covered my calves. "You remember the story your *khala* Shaima told the other night?"

"The one about our great-great-great-great . . ."

"You're worse than your father, sometimes. Yes, that one. I think it is time we change something for you. I think it would be best if we let you be a son to your father."

"A son?"

"It's simple and it's done all the time, Rahima-*jan*. Just think how happy that would make him! And you could do so many things that your sisters wouldn't be able to do."

She knew how to pique my interest. I cocked my head to the side and waited for her to go on.

"We could change your clothes and we'll give you a new name. You'll be able to run to the store any time we need anything. You could go to school without worrying about the boys bothering you. You could play games. How does that sound?"

It sounded like a dream to me! I thought of the neighbors' sons. Jameel. Faheem. Bashir. My eyes widened at the thought of being able to kick a ball around in the street as they did.

Madar-*jan* wasn't thinking of the boys in the street. She was thinking of our empty cupboard. She was thinking of Padar-*jan* and how much he had changed. We were lucky when he brought home some money from an odd job here or there. Every once in a while, his mind focused enough that he was able to tinker with an old engine and breathe life back into it. His small earnings were spent, unevenly, on his medicine and keeping us clothed and fed. The more Madar-*jan* thought about it, the more she realized how desperate our situation was becoming.

"Come with me. There's no reason to delay anything. Your father is taking more and more . . . medicine these days. Your *khala* Shaima is right. We need to do something or we're going to be in real trouble."

We girls were nervous about getting sick. We worried that if we did, we would have to take the same medicine that Padar-*jan* took. It made him do funny things, behave in funny ways. Mostly he just wanted to lie about the house and sleep. Sometimes he said things that didn't make sense. And he never remembered anything we said. It was worse when he didn't take his medicine.

He had broken nearly everything in the house that could be broken. The dishes and glasses survived only because he lacked the energy to pull them from the cabinet. Anything within reach had already been thrown against a wall and smashed to pieces. A ceramic urn. A glass plate that Madar-*jan* had received as a gift. They were casualties of the war inside Padar-*jan*'s head.

Padar-*jan* had fought with the *mujahideen* for years, shooting at the Russian troops that bombarded our town with rockets. When the Soviets finally slinked back to their collapsing country, Padar-*jan* came home and prayed that life would return to normal, though few people could recall such a time. That was 1989.

In that year, he returned home to his parents, who barely recognized him as the seventeen-year-old boy who had left home with a gun slung over his shoulder in the name of God and his country. His mother and father hurriedly arranged a marriage for him. At twenty-four years old, he was long overdue and they thought a wife and children would bring him back to normal, but Padar-*jan*, just like the rest of the country, had forgotten what normal was.

Madar-*jan* was barely eighteen when they were wed. I imagine she must have been as terrified on her wedding night as I was on mine. Sometimes I wonder why she did not warn me, but I suppose those are not things women should speak of.

As the country planned for new beginnings, so did my parents. My sister Shahla came first, followed by Parwin and me. Then came Rohila and Sitara. We were all a year apart and close enough in age that only our mother could tell us apart once we were walking. But with one daughter after another, Madar-*jan* did not become the wife that Padar-*jan* expected. Even more sorely disappointed was my grandmother, who had respectably borne five sons and only one daughter.

Things fell apart at home, just as they did across the country when Russia left. While the Afghan warriors turned their guns and rockets on each other, Padar-*jan* tried to settle into life at home. He tried to work alongside his father as a carpenter but a man who had been taught only to destroy found it hard to create. Loud sounds jarred him. He grew frustrated and drifted back to the warlord, Abdul Khaliq, he had fought under.

Warlords were Afghanistan's new aristocracy. Allegiance to a man with local clout meant a better life. It meant an income when there otherwise would be none. It wasn't long before Padar-*jan* had oiled his machine gun, slung it over his shoulder and gone off to fight again, this time in Abdul Khaliq's name. He returned home every so often. When he returned the first time and found that Madar-*jan* had given birth to yet another girl, me, he walked out again and returned to the killing fields with fresh anger.

Madar-*jan* was left behind with a houseful of girls and only her bitter in-laws to turn to. We lived in a small two-room house, part of the family's compound. War pushed families together. Two of my uncles were killed in the fighting. My uncle's wife died giving birth to her sixth child. Until he could remarry two months later, his children were cared for by my mother and my other aunts. We should have felt like one big family. We should have been kind to each other. But there was resentment. There was anger. There was jealousy. There was, as there would be in the rest of the country, civil war.

Madar-*jan*'s family lived a few kilometers away, but they might as well have been on the other side of the Hindu Kush mountains. They had given their daughter to Padar-*jan* and did not want to interfere in her relationship with her new family. Madar-*jan*'s deformed sister, Shaima, was the exception.

Deformities were not easily forgiven, so Khala Shaima steeled herself to resist the name-calling, the ridiculing, the gawking. Older than Madar-*jan* by nearly ten years, our aunt would tell us things that no one else would say. She would tell us about the war, how the warlords controlled everything and conquered without mercy, even attacking women in the most shameful way of all. Usually Madar-*jan* hushed her older sister with a pleading look. We were young, after all, and it wasn't Khala Shaima who would have to quiet our night terrors. Sometimes Khala Shaima forgot we were children and told us so much that we sat wide-eyed, frightened of our own father.

When Padar-*jan* came home, we cowered. His moods ranged from jubilant to foul but there was no predicting where on the spectrum he would be or when he would make an appearance. Madar-*jan* was lonely and welcomed her sister's visits, even if her mother-in-law griped about them. My grandmother made sure to report to her son just how many times Khala Shaima had come to visit while he was away, clucking her tongue in disapproval and inciting his wrath. It was her way of showing Madar-*jan* that she was in control of our home, even if it sat fifty feet away from the main house.

Everyone wanted control but it was hard to get. The only one who seemed to have any was Abdul Khaliq Khan, the warlord. He and his militia were able to gain control of our town and the neighboring towns, having pushed back their rivals. We were north of Kabul and hadn't seen any fighting in about four years but from what we heard, Kabul was besieged. People in our town shook their heads in dismay at the news but our homes were already pockmarked and turned to rubble. It was time for the privileged in Kabul to taste what we had survived.

Those were ugly times. I can only imagine what my father must have seen from the time he was just a teenage boy. Like so many others, he numbed himself to the ugliness with the "medicine" that Madar-*jan* referred to. He clouded his mind with the opium that Abdul Khaliq kept around, as crucial to his men's ability to wage war as the ammunition strapped to their backs.

Madar-*jan* grew weary of our father but all she could do was look after us girls. Khala Shaima brought her some concoction that she took so she wouldn't have any more children after me. I don't know what the medicine was, but it worked for six years. When Madar-*jan* felt her belly stretch again, she prayed and prayed and did all the things that Khala Shaima told her to do. Nothing worked. Disappointed and fearful, she named our youngest sister Sitara and dreaded the day that Padar-*jan* would come home to find out she had brought yet another daughter into his home.

Then came the Taliban. They were just another faction in the civil war but they gained in strength and their regime crept across the country. It didn't affect us much until we were pulled out of school, windows were blackened and music was banned. Madar-*jan* sighed but carried on, her daily routine largely unaffected by the new codes.

When word got out that our town had fallen to the Taliban, Abdul Khaliq brought his men home to fight back—and to defend his honor as a warlord. There were weeks of explosions, crying, burying, and then the men came home, victorious. Our town was again our own.

Padar-*jan* stayed home for a few months. He spent time with his brothers, tried to help his father recover some business and even helped some of the neighbors to rebuild their homes. Things were going well until the day that a young boy came knocking on our door with a message for Padar-*jan*. The next morning, Padar-*jan* oiled his machine gun, donned his *pakol* hat and headed back out to rejoin the war.

He came back here and there but his mood swings were worse with each visit. We saw him only two or three days at a time and we were children, too young to understand the rage he brought home. He was not the same person at all. Even Bibi-*jan*, my grandmother, would cry after his visits, saying she had lost another son to the war.

It was my cousin Siddiq who told us about the news. He had heard from our grandfather.

"Amrika. That's who. They came and they're bombing the Taliban. They have the biggest guns, the biggest rockets! And their soldiers are so strong!"

"Why didn't Amrika come before?" Shahla had asked. She was nearly twelve years old then. Wise enough to come up with questions that made us look at her with admiration.

Siddiq was ten but had the confidence of a boy twice his age. His father had been killed years ago and he grew up under our grandfather's wing. He was the man of his house.

"Because the Taliban bombed Amrika. Now they're angry and they're bombing them back."

Our grandfather entered the courtyard and overheard our conversation.

"Siddiq-*jan*, what are you telling your cousins?"

"I was just telling them about Amrika, Boba-*jan*. That they're firing rockets at the Taliban!"

"Padar-*jan*," Shahla asked timidly, "did the Taliban destroy many homes in Amrika?"

"No, *bachem*. Someone attacked a building in Amrika. Now they are angry and they've come after him and his people."

"Just one building?"

"Yes."

We were silent. It sounded like good news. A big, powerful country had come to our rescue! Our people had an ally in the war against the Taliban!

But Boba-*jan* could see in Shahla's eyes that there was something that puzzled her and he knew just what it was. Why would Amrika be so upset after just one building was attacked? Half our country had crumbled under the Taliban. We were all thinking the same thing.

If only Amrika would have been upset about that too.

A NIGHT IN THE EMPEROR'S GARDEN
A TRUE STORY OF HOPE AND RESILIENCE IN AFGHANISTAN

Qais Akbar Omar

> It is difficult, if not impossible, to imagine staging Shakespeare's *Love's Labours Lost* in Kabul under the Taliban. What a difference a decade or two makes. Back in 2005, the Taliban had been forced from power and there was a widespread feeling, certainly in the major cities such as Kabul, Herat and Mazar-i-Sharif, that anything was possible. So why not give Shakespeare a go, never mind that it had been thirty years since men and women had shared a stage in Afghanistan and that there were few Afghan actors who had ever trodden the boards. So much for the challenges.
>
> In *A Night in the Emperor's Garden*, **Qais Akbar Omar** (1982–), author of the acclaimed memoir *A Fort of Nine Towers*, tells the unlikely and heart-warming story of how a sundry cast including a housewife, policewoman and street child came together and made dramatic history in Kabul.

PERFORMANCE
Kabul, 31 August 2005

Opening night. Corinne was anxious and did not know what to expect. For the first time, all of the actors arrived at the Foundation on time. They all used one dressing room and put on their costumes quietly. The men went in first, and when they were finished, the women used it. They had come a long way from the days when the girls would not look at the boys. They had decided themselves that they all wanted to be together in one room. No one wasted time chatting, or using the bathroom, or drinking tea, or eating, or smoking, or arguing about unimportant issues. Everyone had a script in hand and was going over their lines. They all looked nervous.

The garden of the Foundation filled up as soon as the doors opened. Foreigners were offered the seats in the first row. Afghans filled the other seats, all talking to one another. About a hundred chairs had been set out in a semi-circle around the playing area. Within minutes, they were filled.

Mustafa Haidari, who worked at the Foundation, was the one who always solved everyone's problems. Anything that anyone needed, Mustafa would make it appear or happen. Now he was racing around with other Foundation staff locating additional chairs as people continued to pour in. Corinne watched everything from behind a window facing the courtyard. With all the seats filled, some of the later arrivals settled on the carpets in the playing area, not understanding that this was where the actors would be appearing shortly. One man tried to set a chair between the *takht* of the King of Kabul and the tent of the Princess of Herat. Mustafa was there to redirect him.

The ever-increasing audience was the kind of problem that any theater impresario anywhere could only dream about. In the end, no one ever really knew how many were in the audience. Estimates that appeared in the media in the days that followed varied. One suggested four hundred, others fewer. There was no way of obtaining an exact count. The garden, though, was densely packed with people, and the excitement that they generated was intense.

The time to begin was approaching. Once the actors were in their costumes and the girls had finished putting on their makeup, Corinne joined everyone in the dressing room. She wore an ankle-length, dark blue Afghan dress covered in elaborate embroidery. With her dark hair and eyes, she could easily have been taken as an Afghan woman. She asked everyone to hold hands, close their eyes and take a deep breath.

"Open your eyes," she said after a moment. "Everyone say '*Merde*!' in one loud voice."

They did, even though they did not know what it meant.

"What is '*Merde*'?" Nabi asked.

She smiled. "It is French, it means 'shit'."

"So we are now supposed to do a shitty performance?" Nabi asked incredulously.

"No, no, it is just a French tradition," Corinne reassured him. "We always say it before a performance."

"A weird tradition!" the actors exclaimed in a rare moment of total agreement.

The boys left to take their positions in a garden shed out of the sight of the audience. Everyone waited for the play to begin. Then it was 5:00 pm. Time to start.

*

The king and his nobles made their first appearance. As they entered, the audience immediately quieted. As they did, a donkey on the street outside the Foundation started braying loudly. Shah Mohammed had no choice but to say his opening lines. The audience broke out laughing as he tried to outshout the donkey. The other actors forced their jaws into a locked position to keep their composure. Finally, the donkey stopped, and Shah Mohammed looked triumphant, as if he had won a competition. Nabi, now as Sherzad, was the second actor to speak. A low rumble of approval rose from the Afghans as he took center stage. Here they were seeing Bulbul in real life.

The first joke came about two minutes into the script when Aref, now as Sohrab, suddenly realizes that the vow he has casually made to study for three years with the king also included a provision that he could not talk to women during that period. Somehow, he had missed that point. The look on Aref's face as he digested this unexpected news sent a wave of tentative laughter through the Afghans. They seemed undecided on whether they were meant to laugh out loud. But from that moment, they understood that the show was going to be funny. The foreigners, not understanding Dari, had no idea what Aref had said. However, they could tell from his face that it had been something humorous. They responded with the twitters of polite guests showing approval.

A few minutes later, the girls entered. A buzz went through the crowd. History was being made as women and men stood together on stage. For the Afghan men in the audience, especially the younger ones, seeing women like this was a rare experience, and something close to a thrill.

The audience, though, was also reacting to the girls' costumes, which looked rich and regal in the early evening light. The girls walked with dignity and grace as the swirls of fabric swept around them. Shahla Nawabi sat to one side scrutinizing the costumes, and nodding her approval.

Saba Sahar led the girls in at a stately pace, her artfully applied makeup completely intact, as she had always said it would be.

For those who had seen the production take shape, and been aware of the sometimes fractious rehearsals, nothing was more surprising than seeing Breshna moving with feminine airs and graces she had never before revealed. She was every inch a noble-woman, her tough policewoman's persona nowhere to be seen. The delicate way that she moved her hands, the shyness with which she smiled, the charm that she projected through her character were utterly unexpected. She had kept her mastery of the craft of acting as much a secret as her detective work.

No one in the cast was more transformed than Marina. Where was the giggling, frightened girl who had choked on her lines only a week before in rehearsal? Who was this elegant woman who moved with total assurance and spoke with the sophistication of someone ten years older? As the performance progressed, she seemed to grow into the role, exuding the self-confidence bordering on hauteur that Shakespeare had intended.

The first moments the women were on stage were very formal, as the Princess of Herat explained her mission. She had come to settle an old financial dispute between her father in Herat and the King of Kabul. While that was going on, the boys tried hard not to reveal their immediate interest in the girls.

The verbal interplay between the king and the princess went smoothly, with more quiet ripples of Afghan laughter, especially as the women accompanying the princess confided their opinions of the men to one another. Then the banter between the men and women began with Aref, as Sohrab, addressing Marina, as Senober:

SOHRAB
Did not I see you dance in Kunduz once?

SENOBER
Did not I see you dance in Kunduz once?

SOHRAB
I know I did.

SENOBER
How needless was it then to ask the question!

The laughter from the Afghans in the audience was becoming more confident, more robust. Perhaps it was the inclusion of a reference to the northern Afghan city of Kunduz. Perhaps it was the unexpected snapback from Marina to Aref's question. By the next scene, Aref's Sohrab was already trying to set up a secret rendezvous with Marina's Senober, with the help of Parwin's character, Fatima. The audience was eagerly waiting for their next funny line.

As the madcap efforts of the men to communicate with the women unobserved mounted, the shyness in the audience eased. At one point, Aref sought a hiding place by climbing a tree. Nabi then took refuge behind the same tree. Faisal ran around like a cat being chased by a dog, and ended up under the very same tree. Though he pulled a branch to cover his face, the rest of his body was plainly visible. And Shah Mohammed's serious-minded King of Kabul, when caught with amorous intentions of his own, first looked to his right and then to his left, then raced towards a flight of stairs.

Once the boys had discovered each other's schemes and decided to pursue the girls, the King of Kabul gave the battle cry: "Soldiers to the field!"

Big laugh.

While the laughs were one way to track the audience's interest, a look at their faces showed how intently they were engrossed in the story as it was unfolding. They all gave the appearance of being totally engaged, even the foreigners. They had been given a printed program that included a scene-by-scene synopsis in English. Many of them said later that while the synopsis was welcome, they had had no trouble following the story because of the clarity of the acting.

For one of the foreigners, though, one moment in the play brought a wrenching jolt. As the four noblewomen sat in front of their tent, their manservant, Kabir, served them tea in cups without handles. David instantly recognized the cups as his. He nearly jumped out of his seat and screamed, "Those are mine!" After the last performance, they were returned with thanks, and intact.

*

The show continued. Not one line was forgotten, which had been Corinne's biggest concern. Neither Kabir nor Parwin showed any hesitation or difficulty in remembering anything. Later, both said that running the entire show straight through had made things easier for them, instead of doing only a scene at a time, as in rehearsals.

The only distractions came from a few ringing mobile phones in the audience, the honking of the cars and buses from outside, the noise of military helicopters passing overhead and a child who wandered across the stage.

Midway through the performance, a nearby mosque called for evening prayers at sunset. A small number of men in the audience got up from where they were sitting. They went to the one end of the courtyard to an open area behind some tall rose bushes where there were no seats, as the roses blocked view. The men laid their head scarves out on the stone pavement, said their evening prayers, then headed back to their seats.

This created a problem as some of them came back through the playing area and climbed over the foreigners in the first row and the Afghans who had not prayed. When they got back to their chairs, a few found that their seats had been taken by others who had been standing at the back. The praying men whispered to the seat-grabbers in a threatening tone and demanded that the new arrivals get up.

In a country where some men stop to pray as soon as they hear the *azan* even if they are standing by the side of the road with traffic whizzing past them, it was not out of the ordinary for these men to break away from the performance for a few minutes to fulfill their religious obligations. Nor was it unusual that many other men chose not to pray at that time, but to wait until later, after the performance had ended.

*

As the early evening sunlight faded, a pair of floodlights that had been set up in the garden added a different quality to the light. It made the fabrics in the costumes, which had been eye-filling in the daylight, visually sumptuous.

Meanwhile, the kerosene lamps in the houses on the small mountain behind the Foundation were being lit. Their soft glow filled the windows of the countless mud-brick dwellings that perched in rows up the mountain. Youngsters were standing on their roofs, looking down into the Foundation's garden, trying to see what was going on. A couple of boys were flying kites over the audience's heads. The kids slowly disappeared as the darkness deepened. The lights in the houses twinkled like stars.

*

In due course it was time for the boys to appear as Indians, shirtless and wearing only *dhotis*, long panels of white cotton cloth wrapped around their waists then pulled through their legs. On their foreheads were red dots made with lipstick that they had rifled in a mad scramble through Breshna's handbag. No one had remembered to buy proper *bindi* powder from the Sikh shops that sold such things to Kabul's tiny Hindu community.

Nabi was the first to enter. The audience had not expected anything like this. Laughter erupted that only grew as Nabi started singing a well-known Bollywood song that everyone had heard for years, "Hey Ninee Gori, Hey Ninee Gori."

No sooner had he finished, than Faisal appeared, followed by Shah Mohammed and then Aref. Each one sang an equally well-known tune.

All but Aref had good singing voices. The actors joked that Aref "does not have an ant's talent as a singer." That only made his song funnier. Everyone laughed at him more than the other boys because of how he tortured a song "that even babies can sing," as Afghans say.

The audience were out of their seats clapping, cheering, screaming. The sudden switch to Urdu had brought it all home. The Afghans no longer felt they had to be polite; they were having too much fun. The play was now about them. Not about Shakespeare. Not about kings. Not about princesses. Not about Taliban rules. This was the new Afghanistan, and it was happening right there in front of them, as comically-clad men sang outrageously funny songs to women seated with them on a stage, laughing themselves silly.

The foreigners, who probably did not know Urdu any more than they knew Dari, could not help but be caught up in the wildly joyous excitement all around them. They clapped and cheered with everyone else. The ten minutes or so that it took to play that scene was a living definition of euphoria.

For reasons only he knew, Faisal had come on in that the scene wearing a black T-shirt along with his *dhoti*. He wore the shirt inside out, but it was still possible to read the words "Pizza Hut" in reverse. It looked awful. Someone in the audience jokingly shouted in boisterous Afghan style, "Where is your tray of pizza?" It brought an extra guffaw, but not one the actors really wanted.

After the show, Faisal explained that he did not want the audience to see the large, ugly scars that he bore from the shrapnel wounds he had suffered on the night his five friends were killed. He wanted to be handsome. Understood. So, for the remaining performances, he found a way to tie his *dhoti* around his neck so that it not only covered the scars, but made his character look even funnier.

Now the actors could do no wrong. In the scene that followed, the boys one at a time chased the girls around the garden, and the audience went wild again, especially when Nabi chased Breshna. For many of the Afghans, it was Bulbul and Gul Chera as written by Shakespeare. Most of the Afghans who came to see the play thought their pairing had been deliberate.

Before the scene was over, four noble couples were poised to become four pairs of lovers. Actually, there were five couples. Parwin's Fatima and Kabir's Sikander appeared to have developed an interest in each other as well. Though both were middle-aged, they had begun to act like teenagers, giving hints with their eyes of their growing interest in each other. That made everyone smile.

From the back of the audience, Corinne sat quietly watching the actors and feeling proud.

*

The same Mustafa Haidari who solved everyone's problems at the Foundation now entered the play briefly to resolve the issue of the vow taken by the four young nobles. Looking severe and handsome as a messenger from Herat, he arrived unexpectedly and ominously to announce that the father of the princess had died. The women must return home.

The sudden somber moment, so typical of Indian movies, provided a gentle transition out of the high jinks of the previous scenes and led to the parting of the couples as they agreed to meet again after one year. In the meantime, the women set tasks for the men. Marina, for instance, demanded that Aref take his wit to hospitals to cheer the sick, much to Aref's dismay.

*

Saba's Princess was never more riveting to watch than in her last scene as she dictates terms to the men. The smitten King of Kabul begs her to accept him.

HAROON, KING OF KABUL
Now, at the latest minute of the hour,
Grant us your loves.

PRINCESS OF HERAT
A time, methinks, too short
To make a world-without-end bargain in.

Her self-assured presence allowed no arguments. Several Afghan women in the audience could be seen to be nodding in approval. That is exactly what Corinne had wanted. That is every director's dream, to resonate with the audience. As Saba prepared to leave, the princess briefly takes the king's hand in hers. It was the first and only time that a man and a woman touched during the play. She initiated the action. It was unforced, and, in the end, unremarkable, because the actors had prepared the way for this moment so well. With that touch, one more small piece of Afghan history was made.

A moment later, the princess offered one of the best-known exit lines in all of Shakespeare.

PRINCESS OF HERAT
So now, you that way: we this way.

With wistful looks at the boys, the girls gathered up their skirts, and strolled out of the king's garden, leaving dented hearts full of promises and expectations. The audience did not wait for them to go. They jumped to their feet, clapping, cheering, shouting.

The boys tried to make their exit as directed from the side of the stage away from the girls, but the audience surrounded them. Both the boys and the girls returned to the stage. After bowing for several minutes, they sat down on the carpet-covered *takht* platform.

Nabi started playing the harmonium and singing a famous Afghan folk song. Everyone in the cast joined him, swaying from side to side. Many in the audience sang along. Corinne jumped to her feet and clapped along with everyone else. The moment had been unplanned, and was all the more powerful because of that.

*

More bows, more applause, and the actors ran off to their dressing room in the Foundation's old mansion. Before long, however, they were back in the garden greeting friends and relatives. The girls still wore their costumes, because everyone wanted to have their photos taken with them in their beautiful outfits.

Marina, who on so many days during rehearsals had never been far from a giggle, stood solemnly as several young men asked to be photographed with her. Their requests were formal; her response was pure *noblesse oblige* as she allowed them to stand next to her while someone focused the camera and snapped. All those appearances at film festivals had taught her how to maintain her composure while being admired and ogled.

As soon as the cameras had been put away, though, and the eager young men had left, she smiled again. It would not have looked decent for a young Afghan woman to be seen smiling in a photograph with men she did not know. Some boundaries had been crossed that night; others remained in place.

Parwin's husband, Tawab, was standing off to the side, basking in the glow of his wife's success. Dressed in a light-colored Western-style suit, he waited while Parwin and the other actors received the plaudits of the audience. Though few of the actors had met him, they immediately figured out who he was. His son and daughter, who stood next to him as enthralled as he was, had become the mascots of the production. The cast members introduced themselves, and congratulated him for Parwin's performance.

As the crowd thinned, the cast and their relatives moved into one of the Foundation's large rooms, where food had been set out on a long cloth laid on the floor, and Afghan *rabab* music was spreading its twangy joy from a CD player. Everyone settled themselves on *toshaks* as they ate and talked about the evening. Corinne was exuberant. Nabi had a look of contentment that had not often been seen from him. And the interpreter was happy that his job was nearly over.

*

That night, Afghan television networks such as TOLO TV and Afghan National Television talked about the play during and after the evening news, which made many people curious about what was happening at the Foundation. The next evening, nearly a thousand people stood in the street wanting to be in the audience. Though the Foundation had greatly increased the number of seats from the night before, there were still not nearly enough.

Corinne was concerned that a riot outside the gate could cause problems for the actors. She went to the entrance, and tried to stop the incoming flow. "Tell them they cannot come in," she told the doorkeeper in her most commanding voice. "We have no seats left. We are full. Tell them to please come back tomorrow night," she implored.

The doorkeeper, a pleasant middle-aged man, smiled, but people kept pushing past him, with a couple of hundred more well-dressed Afghans, both men and women, still in the street trying to get in. Finally, the thick wooden door to the Foundation was eased shut, to shouts of disapproval from those outside. They continued to mill around for some time, though, expecting that the doors would open after a while and let more in. To the regret of all, they did not.

*

At the first performance, most of the Afghans in the audience were men. When they saw that there was nothing anti-Islamic or un-Islamic in the play, they came back on subsequent evenings and brought their wives and daughters to see it.

Just before the third performance was to begin, several women in *burqas* led by a young man entered the garden. They made their way down the stairway that led from the entrance to the grass, then found a place to sit in a far corner. They sat there quietly, pulling the *burqas* away from their faces whenever Marina came on stage. They hung on her every word. Their eyes filled with laughter at her many jokes, but they never made a sound. They looked at each other and shared their joy, but only among themselves. They were Marina's mother and sisters, led by one of her brothers. Their pride in Marina was plainly evident. As soon as the performance ended, they glided back up the staircase, and out the door.

From one performance to the next, Marina had been finding new depth in her role as Senober. She finally understood what it meant to do theater. The lines that had once so terrified her now propelled her into an immediate rapport with her audience.

"I love theater," she said to the interpreter after the fourth performance. "As much as I enjoy the poetry of Shakespeare, I enjoy the reactions of the audience more. Shakespeare's lines and the audience are interlinked. The more I say my lines with confidence, the more the audience applaud me. They probably think I put those words together. Poor Shakespeare! He wrote this beautiful play and people like me get credit for it. He should be known worldwide. Do people know who he is?"

"Maybe some do," the interpreter said with a hint of a smile.

THE WASTED VIGIL
Nadeem Aslam

Nadeem Aslam (1966–) wasted little time beginning his literary career. He published his first short story in a Pakistani newspaper at the tender age of thirteen. A year later, after a childhood in Pakistan, he moved to Britain, where his first novel, *Season of the Rainbirds*, appeared in 1993, winning the praise of Salman Rushdie among others. Among Aslam's many admirers is the Irish writer, critic and poet Colm Tóibín, who considers him 'one of the most exciting and serious British novelists writing now'.

The Wasted Vigil is set in Afghanistan, a country Aslam had never visited before embarking on this challenging novel, laced with beauty and brutality. The central trio of characters are British, Russian and American, symbols perhaps of the three countries who have done so much in recent years to shape the history of Afghanistan for better and worse.

Her mind is a haunted house.
The woman named Lara looks up at an imagined noise. Folding away the letter she has been rereading, she moves towards the window with its high view of the garden. Out there the dawn sky is filling up with light though a few of last night's stars are still visible.

She turns after a while and crosses over to the circular mirror leaning against the far wall. Bringing it to the centre of the room she places it face up on the floor, gently, soundlessly, a kindness towards her host who is asleep in an adjoining room. In the mirror she ignores her own image, examining the reflection of the ceiling instead, lit by the pale early light.

The mirror is large – if it was water she could dive and disappear into it without touching the sides. On the wide ceiling are hundreds of books, each held in place by an iron nail hammered through it. A spike driven through the pages of history, a spike through the pages of love, a spike through the sacred. Kneeling on the dusty floor at the mirror's edge she tries to read the titles. The words are reversed but that is easier than looking up for entire minutes would be.

There is no sound except her own slow breathing and, from outside, the breeze trailing its rippling robes through the overgrown garden.

She slides the mirror along the floor as though visiting another section of a library.

The books are all up there, the large ones as well as those that are no thicker than the walls of the human heart. Occasionally one of them falls by itself in an interior because its hold has weakened, or it may be brought down when desired with the judicious tapping of a bamboo pole.

A native of the faraway St Petersburg, what a long journey she has made to be here, this land that Alexander the Great had passed through on his unicorn, an area of fabled orchards and thick mulberry forests, of pomegranates that appear in the border decorations of Persian manuscripts written one thousand years ago.

Her host's name is Marcus Caldwell, an Englishman who has spent most of his life here in Afghanistan, having married an Afghan woman. He is seventy years old and his white beard and deliberate movements recall a prophet, a prophet in wreckage. She hasn't been here for many days so there is hesitancy in her still regarding Marcus's missing left hand. The skin cup he could make with the palms of his hands is broken in half. She had asked late one evening, delicately, but he seemed unwilling to be drawn on the subject. In any case no explanations are needed in this country. It would be no surprise if the trees and vines of Afghanistan suspended their growth one day, fearful that if their roots were to lengthen they might come into contact with a landmine buried near by.

She lifts her hand to her face and inhales the scent of sandalwood deposited onto the fingers by the mirror's frame. The wood of a living sandal tree has no fragrance, Marcus said the other day, the perfume materialising only after the cutting down.

Like the soul vacating the body after death, she thinks.

Marcus is aware of her presence regardless of where she is in the house. She fell ill almost immediately upon arrival four days ago, succumbing to the various exhaustions of her journey towards him, and he has cared for her since then, having been utterly alone before that for many months. From the descriptions she had been given of him, she said out of her fever the first afternoon, she had expected an ascetic dressed in bark and leaf and accompanied by a deer of the wilderness.

She said that a quarter of a century ago her brother had entered Afghanistan as a soldier with the Soviet Army, and that he was one of the ones who never returned home. She has visited Afghanistan twice before in the intervening decades but there has been proof neither of life nor of death, until perhaps now. She is here this time because she has learnt that Marcus's daughter might have known the young Soviet man.

He told her his daughter, Zameen, was no longer alive.

'Did she ever mention anything?' she asked.

'She was taken from this house in 1980, when she was seventeen years old. I never saw her again.'

'Did anyone else?'

'She died in 1986, I believe. She had become a mother by then – a little boy who disappeared around the time she died. She and an American man were in love, and I know all this from him.'

This was on the first day. She then drifted into a long sleep.

From the various plants in the garden he derived an ointment for the deeply bruised base of her neck, the skin there almost black above the right shoulder, as though some of the world's darkness had attempted to enter her there. He wished pomegranates were in season as their liquid is a great antiseptic. When the bus broke down during the journey, she said, all passengers had disembarked and she had found herself falling asleep on a verge. There then came three blows to her body with a tyre iron in quick succession, the disbelief and pain making her cry out. She was lying down with her feet pointed towards the west, towards the adored city of Mecca a thousand miles away, a disrespect she was unaware of, and one of the passengers had taken it upon himself to correct and punish her.

Her real mistake was to have chosen to travel swaddled up like the women from this country, thinking it would be safer. Perhaps if her face had been somewhat exposed, the colour of her hair visible, she would have been forgiven as a foreigner. Everyone, on the other hand, had the right to make an example of an unwise Afghan woman, even a boy young enough to be her son.

Marcus opens a book. The early morning light is entering at a low angle from the window. The fibres of the page throw their elongated shadows across the words, so much so that they make the text difficult to read. He tilts the page to make it catch the light evenly, the texture of the paper disappearing.

Within the pages he finds a small pressed leaf, perfect but for a flake missing at the centre as though chewed off by a silkworm. The hole runs all the way through the pages also, where he had pulled out the iron nail to gain access to the words.

He has given her only the purest water when she has been thirsty. This country has always been a hub of things moving from one point of the compass to another, religion and myth, works of art, caravans of bundled Chinese silk flowing past camels loaded with glass from ancient Rome or pearls from the Gulf. The ogre whose activities created one of Afghanistan's deserts was slain by Aristotle. And now Comanche helicopters bring sizeable crates of bottled water for America's Special Forces teams that are operating in the region, the hunt for terrorists continuing out there. Caches of this water are unloaded at various agreed locations in the hills and deserts, but two winters ago a consignment must have broken its netting – it fell from the sky and came apart in an explosion close to Marcus's house, a blast at whose core lay water not fire, the noise bringing him to the window to find the side of the house dripping wet and hundreds of the gleaming transparent bottles floating on the lake in front of the house. A moment later another roped bundle landed on the lake and sank out of sight. Perhaps it broke up and released the bottles, or did it catch on something down there and is still being held? Water buried inside water. He skimmed many of the bottles from the surface before they could disperse and found others over the coming days and weeks, split or whole, scattered in the long grasses of his neglected orchard.

He lowers his pale blue eyes to the book.

It is a poet's diwan, the most noble of matters, dealt with in the most noble of words. As always the first two pages of verse are enclosed within illuminated borders, an intricate embroidery in ink. Last night she clipped his fingernails, which he normally just files off on any available abrasive surface. When she leaves she should take a volume from the impaled library. Perhaps everyone who comes here should be given one so that no matter where they are in the world they can recognise each other. Kin. A fellowship of wounds. They are intensely solitary here. The house stands on the edge of a small lake; and though damaged in the wars, it still conveys the impression of being finely carved, the impression of being weightless. At the back is the half-circle formed by the overgrown garden and orchard. Shifting zones of birdsong, of scent. A path lined with Persian lilac trees curves away out of sight, the branches still hung with last year's berries, avoided by birds as they are toxic.

The ground begins to rise back there gradually until it reaches the sky. The broad chalk line of permanent snow up there, thirteen thousand feet high, is the mighty range of mountains containing the cave labyrinths of Tora Bora.

At the front of the house, a mile along the edge of the lake, is the village that takes its name from the lake. Usha. Teardrop. Thirty miles farther is the city of Jalalabad. Because Lara is Russian, Marcus's immediate fear regarding her illness was that she had been fed a poison during the hours she had spent waiting for him in Usha, her country having precipitated much of present-day Afghanistan's destruction by invading in 1979.

In the darkness soon after four a.m. one night, Lara had got out of bed. Accompanied by candlelight she went into the various rooms of the house, moving under that sheath of books, needing movement after the countless hours of being still. She avoided the room where Marcus was but entered others, looking, enclosed within the sphere of yellow light from the flame in her hand. Somewhere very far away a muezzin had begun the call to the prayers of dawn, defined by Islam as the moment when a black thread can just be distinguished from a white one without artificial light.

When enough light began to enter the house, she placed mirrors on the floor to look at the books overhead, though not all of them had been nailed with the titles facing out, and any number of them were in languages she did not possess.

Some years ago, at a point when the Taliban could have raided the house any day, Marcus's wife had nailed the books overhead in these rooms and corridors. Original thought was heresy to the Taliban and they would have burned the books. And this was the only way that suggested itself to the woman, she whose mental deterioration was complete by then, to save them, to put them out of harm's reach.

Lara imagined stretching a fishing net at waist level, imagined going to the room directly above and banging her feet until all the books were dislodged and caught without further harm in the net. Marcus said the deep rumble of the B52s had shaken loose every book from one side of a corridor when Tora Bora began to be bombed day and night up there in 2001. The intermittent rain in the whole house had intensified during those weeks in fact.

The Englishman said he had bought the house more than forty years ago, just before he married his wife Qatrina, who like him was a doctor. 'I used to say she brought me Afghanistan in her dowry,' he said. The house was built by an old master calligrapher and painter in the last years of the nineteenth century. He belonged to what was almost the final generation of Muslim artists to be trained in the style of the incomparable Bihzad. When the six-roomed building was complete, the master – who had painted images on the walls of each room – brought to it the woman he wished to make his companion for life. Beginning on the ground floor, each of the first five rooms was dedicated to one of the five senses, and as the courtship slowly progressed over the following weeks, the couple went from one to the next.

The first was dedicated to the sense of sight, and on the walls, among other things, Subha in a dancerly gesture presented her eye to a rogue in the forest.

Allah created through the spoken word, read the inscription above the door that led to the interior about hearing. Here the walls showed singers and musical gatherings, a lute with a songbird sitting on its neck – teaching perhaps, perhaps learning.

From there they moved to the faculty of smell, where angels bent down towards the feet of humans, to ascertain from the odour whether these feet had ever walked towards a mosque. Others leaned towards bellies, to check for fasting during the holy month of Ramadan.

In the room about the sense of touch, there was a likeness of Muhammad with his hand plunged in a jar. He was someone who would not shake hands with women, so in order to make a pact he would put his hand in a vessel containing water and withdraw it, and then the woman would put her hand into the water.

Then it was on to taste, and from that room they ascended to the highest place in the house: it contained and combined all that had gone before – an interior dedicated to love, the ultimate human wonder, and that was where she said yes.

The imagery was there on the walls still but, out of fear of the Taliban, all depictions of living things had been smeared with mud by Marcus. Even an ant on a pebble had been daubed. It was as though all life had been returned to dust. Consolation of a kind could be had from the fact that most of the rest of the images had survived – the inanimate things, the trees and the skies, the streams. And since the demise of the Taliban, Marcus had begun slowly to remove the swirled covering of mud. The highest room stands completely revealed now.

Marcus took Lara to one corner and pointed to the foliage painted there. When she looked closely she saw that a chameleon was sitting perfectly camouflaged on a leaf. She leaned closer to that lovely fiction and touched it. 'The Taliban would even burn a treasured family letter because the stamp showed a butterfly,' said Marcus. 'But I missed this, and so did they.'

Roaming the house at night, her shadow trembling in accordance with the candle flame, Lara had entered the topmost room. The walls were originally a delicate faded gold, painted with scenes of lovers either in an embrace or travelling towards each other through forest and meadow. They were badly damaged by bullets. When the Taliban came to the house they had proceeded to annihilate anything they considered unIslamic within it. What they had heard about this room had enraged them the most. This they wanted to blow up, even though the lovers had been made to disappear behind a veil of earth by Marcus.

Lara's eyes moved across the shattered skin of the walls, the light picking up hints of gold here and there. This country was one of the greatest tragedies of the age. Torn to pieces by the many hands of war, by the various hatreds and failings of the world. Two million deaths over the past quarter-century. Several of the lovers on the walls were on their own because of the obliterating impact of the bullets – nothing but a gash or a terrible ripping away where the corresponding man or woman used to be. A shredded limb, a lost eye.

A sound originating in one of the other rooms startled her where she stood, her heart speeding up at the possibilities.

It was not a thief, she reassured herself, nor a Taliban fighter looking for somewhere to hide. Nor an Arab, Pakistani, Uzbek, Chechen, Indonesian terrorist – seed sprouted from the blood-soaked soil of Muslim countries. On the run since the autumn of 2001, al-Qaeda appeared to be regrouping, to kidnap foreigners, organise suicide bombings, and behead those it deemed traitors, those it suspected of informing the Americans.

'What fool drew this?' the Tsar had demanded to know of a fortress that a student at the Academy of Military Engineering in St Petersburg had drawn inadvertently without doors. The young man was Fyodor Dostoevsky, and Lara wished this house was similarly devoid of entrances as she slowly moved along the corridor, the drops of molten wax sliding down the side of the red candle in her hand.

No one came near the house, Marcus had told her, because the area around the lake is said to contain the djinn. Lake wind, mountain wind, orchard wind collide in the vicinity, but to the Muslims the air is also lastingly alive with the good and bad invisible tribes of the universe. If that was not sufficient, a ghost said to be that of his daughter Zameen had appeared in one of the rooms the day the Taliban came here, the apparition putting them to flight.

After the sound, she was aware of the completeness of the night's silence.

Perhaps Marcus, fumbling, had dropped an object. The word 'lame' described what happened when a foot or leg became damaged or was missing, but she could think of no specific term for when an arm or hand became unavailable, though the body was just as out of balance.

She entered a room and stopped when she saw the book that had detached itself from the ceiling and fallen with the thump she had heard. The disturbed dust of the floor was still in movement around it.

She picked it up and, setting the candle down, wrested out the nail. Opening the book on the floor she began to read, sitting chin-on-knee beside it.

Tell the earth-thieves
To plant no more orchards of death
Beneath this star of ours
Or the fruit will eat them up.

In the garden Marcus opens his eyes, feeling as though someone has drawn near and blocked his sunlight, but there is no one. Letters and messages, and visits, are received from the departed. And so occasionally, and for a fraction of a second, it is not strange to expect such a thing from those who have died. It lasts the shortest of durations and then the mind recalls the facts, remembers that some absences are more absolute than others.

It was in the darkness of the night, in 1980, that the band of Soviet soldiers had broken into the house to pick up Zameen. The cold touch of a gun at his temple was what awoke Marcus. The darkness was crosshatched with the silver beams of several flashlights. Qatrina, beside him, came out of her sleep on hearing his sounds of confusion. In those initial moments of perplexity she thought this might be a repeat of what had happened the previous week, when a patient was brought to the house in the middle of the night, the victim of a Soviet chemical weapon from the day before, his body already rotting when he was discovered in a field an hour after the attack, his fingers still looped with the rosary he had been holding. He must have been in unimaginable pain, and though he couldn't speak the stare from him was so strong it verged on sound.

The couple were not allowed to switch on the light but there appeared to be about ten soldiers. From their voices Marcus could tell they were in their teens or early twenties. He wondered if they were deserters, frightened young boys running away from the Soviet Army, running away from the Soviet Union. People from East Germany, even from as far away as Cuba, came to Kabul and then defected to the West. His mind was jolted out of this consideration when they asked for his daughter by name.

Qatrina's grip on his forearm tightened. There had been reports of Soviet soldiers landing their helicopter to abduct a girl and flying away with her, parents or lovers following the trail of her clothing across the landscape and finally coming across her naked bone-punctured body, where she had been thrown out of the helicopter after the men had been sated.

Two of the soldiers could speak a broken Pashto and they were asking for Zameen and would give no explanation as to how they knew her or why they had come for her. There followed moments of rancour and violence towards Marcus and Qatrina. The men had searched the house before waking them, and had been unable to locate the girl.

A soldier stayed with them while the others spread out through the house once again, their voices low: it was a time of war and they always had to be alert to the possible presence of rebels near by. Some were searching the garden and the orchard, others Marcus's perfume factory which stood beyond the garden, a voice drifting up now and then. There was great urgency in them, and Marcus thought of the night the previous year when the Soviet Army had entered Kabul, the Spetsnaz commandos running through the corridors of the Presidential Palace looking for the president, whom they immediately put to death when they found him.

Marcus and Qatrina managed to engage the Pashto-speaking soldier in a conversation.

'Your daughter is sympathetic to the insurgency. Her name is on the list we have been given by an insider.'

'There must be some mistake,' Marcus said through the cut mouth.

'Then where is she at this hour? We are here as part of a big operation in Usha tonight, to capture those who attacked the school earlier this month. We'll make them pay for the twenty-seven lives we lost.'

The sun was beginning to rise outside when someone came in and said Zameen had been apprehended.

The lapis lazuli of their land was always desired by the world, brushed by Cleopatra onto her eyelids, employed by Michelangelo to paint the blues on the ceiling of the Sistine Chapel, and, from the look of certain sections of the sky above Marcus and Qatrina as they came out into the garden, it could have been Afghanistan's heights that were mined for lapis lazuli, not its depths.

The couple searched their surroundings and then went into Usha, trying to understand what had happened.

Hours later, as dusk began to fall, Qatrina stood beside an acacia tree, holding with both hands the clothesline tied around the trunk. Marcus thought it was for balance, but then saw that the section of the rope between her hands was tinted indigo, where one of Zameen's dresses had once seeped colour into it, the dress she must have been wearing when they captured her because it was missing from her room.

He led her back to the house, the perfume from the acacia clinging to her. The djinn were supposed to live in the scent of acacia blossom, making themselves visible only to the young in order to entrap them in otherworldly love.

CYANIDE CAN BE EXTRACTED from apricots, Casa knows. He had distilled it at a jihad training camp, injected it into the bodies of creatures. The memory comes to him as he walks past a flowering tree at the edge of a street in Jalalabad city centre, the flowers still not finished emptying themselves of scent this late in the afternoon. An ant travels up the trunk at the speed of a spark along a fuse wire.

Pencils. Lemons. Corn syrup. Dye. As he walks through the street he knows he could fabricate explosives from many things on the carts and in the shops around him. Sugar. Coffee. Paint. He even knows how to make a bomb out of his urine.

Three international military patrol vehicles go by containing khaki-clad soldiers, a clamorous knot developing in the traffic because all others have to make way for them. There are women and blacks among the soldiers, an attempt, Nabi Khan says, by the USA-led Western world to humiliate Muslims by having sows and apes be their new monarchs.

Word has come that the explosion outside the school has delighted the Taliban, al-Qaeda, and the covert grouping of Pakistani military officers led by Fedalla. They have promised further help.

Casa himself has never attended a school, just various religious institutions. Attached to a number of which there was a military training camp. At about ten he had wanted permission to fight in Bosnia but he was told it was too far for someone so young. And the response was the same at eleven when he wanted to pursue martyrdom in Chechnya. By then he had been holding a Kalashnikov for three years. He knew the finger on the trigger was steadier during exhalation as opposed to during inhalation. He knew how to strip and clean the rifle blindfolded, and he could do it in sixty seconds. He had fired it from moving vehicles and had fired it in the darkness, had fired it after running for an hour to simulate the banging heartbeat of a battle. He was proud of the fact that it was a Soviet gun. The Koran told of Daud, the raw youth with no weapons or armour who had used Jaloot's own sword to slay him, Jaloot the giant whom the Christians call Goliath, having felled him with a sling first; and so the Afghans had used captured Soviet weapons as the instruments of the evil Godless empire's own destruction. The Koran being a guidance for all time, this method continues to be relevant. Of the sixty-six Tomahawk missiles fired at Afghanistan's training camps in the 1990s, across thousands of miles from an American warship in the Arabian Sea, a number had failed to detonate – and these had been sold by al-Qaeda to the Chinese for millions of dollars.

Casa was present at a camp at the exact moment the missiles landed. He had been bowing before Allah and had just raised his forehead from the prayer mat. The needle of the small compass fitted at the head of the mat – to allow the faithful to always find the direction of Mecca – had started to spin at great speed just as it did in lightning storms. He was severely injured but Allah had spared his life, having better plans for him.

Because no true Muslim should shrink from killing in cold blood, his jihad training had included slitting the throats of sheep and horses while reciting the verse from the holy Koran which gives permission to massacre prisoners of war: *It is not for the Prophet to have captives until he has spread fear of slaughter in the land.* In the laboratories of the camps, stocked with labelled drums of various acids, acetones, cellulose, wood composite and aluminium powder, he had learned to mix methyl nitrate, had hit a small drop of it with a hammer to see it shatter the hammer. He blew up a car with a sack of fertiliser and ammonium nitrate fuel oil, the burning chassis travelling in an arc through the air to land a hundred yards away. He crumbled a boulder with twenty pounds of US-made C-4, and, for comparison, others with C-1, C-2, and C-3, and also with Czech Semtex. He knew the Americans were trying to get back from the Afghans the Semtex they had supplied for use in the Soviet jihad, so dangerous was the substance. During all this he chanted the sacred words of the Koran. *I will instil terror in the hearts of the Infidels, strike off their heads, and strike off from them every fingertip.*

The faces of women are on display around him but he keeps his eyes off them as he walks. Nowadays he doesn't think of such matters but at one time he had dreamed of a wife, preferably one of the thousands upon thousands of Bosnian women who had been raped by the Serbs, many of them becoming pregnant so that the Bosnian men banished them. These men couldn't contemplate raising a child who was half enemy. But Casa and his brothers at the camps and madrassas had felt it their duty to marry these women, and raise their children to become jihadis, who could go on to slaughter the Serbs whose blood they shared.

He arrives at the crossroads where someone is to pick him up. To take him to Nabi Khan at the poppy farm. There they'll get ready and wait. Tonight, under cover of darkness, he and four others are going to Usha.

IN CITY OF GOD St Augustine records his belief that the peacock's flesh has the God-given property of resisting putrefaction after death. Marcus withdraws his hand from deep within the bird's breast, having plunged the scissors into the topiary figure to snip at a branch. He is in the shattered glasshouse to the west of the house, most of its panes missing. The candle flame shudders as he turns around, suddenly aware of the three men standing at the lake's edge. He walks to the house where Lara sits reading by lamp at the kitchen table.

'Stay in here, Lara,' he says to her without stepping in. 'But could I please have the light for a moment?'

She stands up perhaps too fast. In a moment of vertigo she has experienced before with the books in this house, she feels as though the things printed on the paper would drain away through the hole in the centre of the page. From the door she sees him disappear along the curved path, catching the last hint of his greyed blue jacket amid the rustle of the long grasses.

She is in darkness. She switches on the cell phone she brought with her from St Petersburg, though there is no signal for it here. In the silver haze of its light she goes out and moves along the path until she can see him in the distance, talking to the three figures near the tree split in two by Qatrina's despondent love for her countrymen.

She stands there and then David arrives from his day in Jalalabad, the beams of the car scattering on the low foliage. He gets out and joins the group, a voice from there drifting towards her whenever the wind spins around – she realises she has begun to recognise the voices of these two men.

'The doctor in Usha is away for a few days,' David walks up and tells her. 'One of the old men out there got injured last week but the wound he thought was healing is suddenly giving him trouble today. He's hoping Marcus can help.'

They will not come into the house, she knows, afraid of the ghost of the perfume maker's daughter. Of the Buddha, the suffering stone that had bled gold, that had been granted life by bullets.

'I'll get more light, to make it easier for Marcus.'

When she had appeared at Usha and asked for Marcus, she was mistakenly brought to the current doctor's house, and his young daughter – the teacher at the one-roomed school Gul Rasool has permitted in Usha to please the United States – had lovingly taken charge of her. Before leaving for Russia she intends to visit the girl.

She follows David towards the lake, bringing a hurricane lamp and a flashlight. All things considered, the Afghans she has met have been helpful and kind towards her – with the exceptions of the boy who attacked her with the tyre iron, and the guide she had hired to bring her from Kabul to Usha, who had absconded with most of her money one night.

Marcus is leaning towards the bloody shoulder of the man sitting on a tree stump, and now with a sound of astonishment he extracts a piece of paper from within the gash. It is blood-soaked and folded tight to the size of a coin. The man attempts an explanation while Marcus tries to spread it to its full size: what appear to be verses of the Koran are written on the paper. As she doesn't understand the language the aged man is speaking, Marcus explains,

'It is a talisman. Given to him by someone at the mosque to make the wound heal. Instead of just wearing it around his neck he has inserted it *into* the wound, thinking it'll speed up the process! That is why the bleeding won't stop.'

She can smell the injury, the small percentage of blood in the air.

The man takes the paper from Marcus's hands and begins to fold it again, both of them shaking their heads at each other and talking very fast – he obviously wishes to slot the holy words back under his skin.

The three strangers steal glances at her from time to time, their faces lovely to her, the beard of one fox-orange with henna, the eyes of another an uncontainable grape-blue. And Islam and its love of flowers! They have helped themselves to a pink rose from somewhere and are passing it between themselves.

One of the men, his skin the colour of violins in this light, says something in her direction. She realises it is '*Rus.*'

Russia.

She nods.

'*Rus*,' the man says again, grinning. And he makes a comment which elicits an identical reaction of surprise from David and Marcus. They ask him questions and soon the other visitors begin to contribute – a discussion with many gestures.

'What are they saying?' she asks, smiling. Old timers. Perhaps one of them had visited Russia in the past. She tells herself to restrain the expression on her face – her guide had told her that she smiles too much for a woman. One of the men shakes the rose in his hand, thrusts it at the others.

The talk continues and then she hears one of the men clearly and carefully utter the name Benedikt, syllable by syllable.

She is suddenly numb.

'What did he just say?'

'Nothing,' David replies but she catches him exchange a glance with Marcus.

'Didn't he say Benedikt?'

'No, no.'

A man is now drawing a shape on the dust between his feet. A lobed oblong with a stalk. An oak leaf? Like the one she has, like the one Benedikt carried with him. Or is she mistaken? It could just as easily be a quick map of Afghanistan.

David quickly rubs away the drawing with his hand, avoiding her eye, while Marcus pretends busyness, the face determinedly turned away from her.

'They are just talking about a visit to Russia,' Marcus says to her at last. 'The Afghans are great travellers. Farming the valleys of California or journeying across the Australian deserts for trade.'

'There is more than one Giovanni Khan in the Italian villages that their fathers saw in the battle heat of the Second World War,' David adds; and, turning to Marcus, says, 'Now, we must try to persuade him to keep the paper in the layers of the bandage and not in the wound itself…'

She can't help but feel shut out. There is a profound uneasiness around them. Even the air and light feel different to her, and after standing at the edge of the group for a while she walks back to the house. Not sure what has just happened.

AFGHAN RUMOUR BAZAAR
SECRET SUB-CULTURES, HIDDEN WORLDS AND THE EVERYDAY LIFE OF THE ABSURD

Nushin Arbabzadah

'Why are imams telling us about nail polish?' **Nushin Arbabzadah** wonders in this very original, extremely funny and unexpectedly revealing study of Afghan society and culture. It doesn't take long to realise that Arbabzadah, a journalist, cultural critic, author and lecturer at UCLA in Los Angeles, delights in diving headlong into taboos that lesser writers would do everything possible to avoid.

Mini-chapters on 'Gay Afghans', 'Child Rape: Speaking Out', 'The Trials of Transvestitism' and 'The All-New, Same-Old Taliban?' suggest both that she is a fearless commentator who likes to provoke and that this is not a book for the government iconoclasts in Kabul. She takes in everything from sex and soap operas to drugs and diplomacy in a narrative that gallops along with wit and wisdom. Hilarious cameos run through *Afghan Rumour Bazaar* like staccato bursts of machine-gun fire. Her account of an encounter with the BBC's diversity team for a job interview, to take just one example, is completely priceless.

Gay Afghans

The first time he slept with a man, Hamid Nilofar was a young Afghan with little experience of life outside the city of Kabul. His lover, an older Pakistani man, happened to be just the right type – educated, mature and well-mannered. The young gay Afghan met the older man by accident. Hamid, like most Afghans, had family in Pakistan and while visiting his sister there, one day he went for a stroll in a nearby public park. The other man just happened to be there, walking towards Hamid from the opposite direction. In his brutally honest memoirs, *Passing Through a Nightmare,* Hamid writes about other, equally restless lone men, purposelessly wandering about the park. He suspected that they, too, were looking for that forbidden love with another man.

The older man held the young Afghan's gaze as he walked towards him, getting closer and closer. He stopped when he reached Hamid and struck up a conversation. Soon after, intuition kicked in and the two men sought privacy on a bench hidden away from public view. The older man complimented Hamid on his beautiful eyes and asked for permission to touch and kiss them. He cautiously stroked Hamid's face, and carefully watched the young man's reaction. Far from being appalled, Hamid was flattered and already melting. He soon found himself holding hands with and being kissed and caressed by the older man. One thing led to another and for Hamid, this first experience of gay love felt just right. It was, after all, the realization of what he had dreamed about since puberty. "I feel sorry for all those men who die without ever having realized their dream of love with another man," Hamid writes in his memoirs. Such men do exist in Afghanistan. More than often they are married and have children, leading a perfectly "respectable" life on the surface. But secretly, they yearn for this other love – the one that dare not speak its name.

Officially, Afghanistan is a strictly heterosexual, family-based society where sex outside the legal bounds of marriage is a crime punishable by imprisonment. But behind the clean-cut surface of respectability, there's a foggy underworld of chaotic sexuality with no clear rules and boundaries to protect the vulnerable, including gay men. "We fall in love easily and give our heart and soul but only to be betrayed and ridiculed," writes one gay blogger from Kabul. He gives an example of the kind of fear and loathing existence that is part and parcel of being gay and Afghan. The blogger's ex-boyfriend, who turned out to be an intelligence officer, finished their relationship with an action that reeked of self-hatred bordering on sadism. Upon ending the affair, the intelligence officer gave his ex's name and telephone number to all his male acquaintances, encouraging these random men to approach the former boyfriend for sex. Needless to say, the emotional damage of such cruelty can be irreparable and yet it is a piece of cake by comparison with the danger to one's life that can accompany such forced public outing of a gay man. After all, if an Afghan man is outed as a homosexual (sometimes it's enough to just be labeled gay), he is considered a disgrace to his family and runs the risk of becoming a victim of "honor killing." Family is king in Afghanistan – a mini mafia structure that rules over life and death, providing protection for those who comply with its rules and punishing those who dare to stray. To be gay and Afghan means to live life in perpetual fear of discovery and betrayal, a paranoid existence spent in continuous terror of forced outing.

In addition to such soul-crushing anxieties, there's the tyranny of a conformist society with a stubborn image of the ideal manhood to which every male is expected to aspire. This ideal is represented by the figure of the strong and powerful patriarch. To get married and have children is not enough to live up to this ideal. A man has to be tough and masculine, rich and powerful. More importantly, he has to father many sons and raise them as obedient foot-soldiers under his command. That's the kind of man who is envied in Afghan society. (The warlords, with their big bellies and long beards are all but a contemporary reincarnation of this traditional model of brutish, militant masculinity.) Needless to say, far from aspiring to this ideal, gay Afghan men dread the prospect of wedding, dodging the barrage of questions and postponing marriage as long as possible. For Hamid Nilofar, the first openly gay Afghan man, leading the fake, pretend life of a married heterosexual man was simply out of question. He fled Afghanistan, and endured years of horrific hardship in Iran and Turkey in order to escape the tyranny of Afghan conformism. It's a conformism where married life is forced upon everyone, young boys and girls, homosexual men and lesbian women as well as those who simply have no interest in sexuality or in leading a typical Afghan family life. Many Afghans don't flee because of politics, they flee their society and escape their culture, Hamid writes in his memoirs after meeting teenage runaway boys who fled Afghanistan to avoid marriage.

Hamid finally settled in Canada where he wrote his pioneering memoirs. It was there in Canada that he met online the man he would have become had he not fled Afghanistan. This other man, also gay, had succumbed to society, marrying and fathering four children. "What bitter life it is to have just one longing and to never, not even for a day, have this longing fulfilled," wrote the other man from an office in Kabul. For Hamid, these words were enough to clarify which one of the two had made the right decision.

Afghanistan's Accidental Gay Pride

If you are gay and proud, Afghanistan is quite likely the last place on earth to show it publicly. How, then, are we supposed to make sense of the conspicuous appearance of the rainbow-cultured gay pride symbols all over the streets of Kabul and other urban centers?

The pioneer Afghan Pajhwok news agency took it upon itself to investigate this unusual sociocultural phenomenon, sending a reporter to interview drivers who had decorated their cars with gay pride stickers and rear banners. After all, these Chinese-made car accessories had suddenly become popular, available in any garage supplying vehicle parts.

Even more remarkably, Afghan drivers seemed to have little concern about using their cars to openly advertise being gay and proud of it. In a country where social conservatism sometimes results in gay men sharing their life with their partner of choice and an arranged wife so as to keep up appearances, there was certainly something very unusual about this apparently new openness.

Needless to say, Pajhwok's reporter soon discovered that Afghans who had decorated their cars with the rainbow symbol had no idea what it stood for. For them it was just the newest car fashion accessory but, on learning of its meaning in the west, drivers immediately started removing it.

The rainbow stickers had first arrived on secondhand cars imported from Canada. Afghans had simply assumed that the color combination was the latest fashion fad in the West, and duly adopted it. Had it not been for the news agency's interest, the gay pride symbol would have continued to flourish in Afghanistan. Uprooted from its original cultural environment and landing in the country by sheer accident, it would have led an existence devoid of any meaning aside from showing that, like everywhere else in the world, Afghan men loved their cars.

But since Afghanistan is no longer an isolated country, imported symbols are bound to be recognized and decoded not only by globetrotting members of the middle class but also the many expatriate internationals and returnee Afghans. Once informed about the symbol's meaning, the stickers were removed en masse. One commentator even expressed the hope that the embarrassing incident would serve as cautionary tale, warning Afghans against their tendency to blindly follow fashions imported from elsewhere.

The confusion that had allowed for the gay-pride car accessories to become coveted goods in Afghan garages is not restricted to the symbol itself. Judging by the way homosexuality is debated in the public sphere, the term itself is understood incorrectly. It is usually used as a synonym for what would be described in Europe and North America as pedophilia. Hence, on the rare occasions when Afghan writers dare to publicly tackle problems related to sexuality, we encounter the local terms *hamjins baazi* (homosexuality) and *bacha baazi* (pedophilia) used interchangeably, as if they both deal with the same phenomenon. There seems to be little awareness of the fact that in liberal democracies of the west the term strictly refers to relationships between consenting adults.

Given that Afghanistan is an exceedingly conservative society, it is astonishing that articles openly discussing homosexuality actually exist. The content of such articles is often surprising. Hence, in what – by Afghan standards – is a frank and almost judgment-free article, one writer establishes that it is the country's social conditions that contribute to unorthodox practices. Blaming strict gender segregation, the author points out that since desire is natural to humankind, its suppression is bound to make it resurface in a different guise: "For example, monks and those who renounce worldly pleasures quite often tend to be fat, with big bellies. Their desire has resurfaced as greed for food."

Following this rather strange line of argument, the reader is then confronted with a curious assessment: if necessary, relations with underage persons should be conducted with girls rather than boys because even if they are physically immature, the female anatomy still renders girls more natural partners.

A recurrent theme in all such debates is a juxtaposition of European countries' treatment of the hijab with their attitude towards homosexuality. Authors are genuinely puzzled that France has banned the hijab, which in their view is a religious obligation, but protects the rights of homosexuals – which they say is banned by all religions. Such articles as a rule make generous use of question and exclamation marks. These loud orthographic markers, in turn, echo the profound divide that separates the Afghans' traditional society from the liberal markets from whence secondhand cars make their journey across continents, sometimes complete with dangerously loaded but misunderstood ornamental accessories.

The Trials of Transvestitism

"Take off your *chador*," the police officer orders an Afghan cross-dresser in a video that has been shared endlessly on social networking websites.

"Take off your wig!" Beneath the shiny black locks, the head is revealed as male with receding, closely cropped hair.

He's also wearing a scarlet short-sleeved *shalwar kamiz* – sexy but traditional female attire. The feminine look is accentuated by large sparkling bangles and see-through embroidery.

The victim's ordeal goes on for what seems like eternity as he endures humiliating comments and laughter from the police officers.

"Please have mercy, don't make fun of me," he whispers.

"Boy! Face the camera," they shout, forcing him to remove the fake breasts from inside his top. The breasts turn out to be a pair of socks filled with dough.

"Dough to make the breasts feel softy-soft," an officer shouts amid laughter. Male cross-dressing is familiar enough in Afghanistan for the locals to have coined a special term. The word is *ezak* – a vague but deeply derogatory noun referring to anything from a eunuch or a hermaphrodite to a transvestite or a male homosexual.

Following the discovery of the dough, a barrage of questions ensues in the video. "Why are you dressed like this? Where did you put the makeup on? What is all this about? What have you two been up to?"

This final question is addressed to a shy young man leaning away but standing next to the transvestite. The two were arrested together. "I was shopping for clothes," the cross-dresser whispers, taking off the bangles. He is trying to tell the officers that his dressing up is just a silly, harmless game.

"Put the bangles back on," a police officer orders. The victim reluctantly obeys, his eyes filled with tears.

"Please, officer, we haven't committed a crime," the victim's companion pleads, turning away from the camera.

Like most of the sensationalist Afghan news that is spread online, the video gives no information about the date, the source, or the victim's fate following the arrest. The clip made the rounds, creating lively debate before people tired of it.

My immediate reaction was to regard it as a clear example of ignorance breeding cruelty. From the officers' tone it was evident that they felt proud of the arrest, believing they had protected ordinary families from a couple of "dangerous perverts." But the officers' pride was also mixed with utter bewilderment. This confusion was neatly summed up in the video's title: "A man dressed as a woman – but why?" The title cried out for explanation and the numerous comments left by viewers revealed a wide range of interpretations, including political paranoia, with some viewers suspecting that the cross-dresser was in reality a suicide bomber trained by the Pakistani ISI to infiltrate Kabul disguised as a woman.

There was also a more sober reaction, with commentators criticizing the police for wasting their time on mundane incidents while the threat of terrorism was all too real. A few comments interpreted the cross-dressing as a sign of cultural anarchy, a symbol of Afghans straying from the path of Islam. A couple of people demanded the cross-dresser should be executed, while others said that even though the cross-dresser was misguided they still felt sorry for him.

Amid such voices of confusion, and at times outright cruelty, it was heartening to read comments expressing anger at the police's humiliation of the victim: "The man has committed no crime. Cross-dressing is a psychological condition. What he needs is treatment rather than public humiliation."

Others recalled their own encounters with transvestites:

"During the Taliban, we had an *ezak* in our neighborhood. His brothers used to hit him for acting like a female and finally killed him."

"I am worried about this man's future. His family is bound to kill him because of the shame he has brought on them. To protect this unfortunate person, people should stop sharing this video."

It was the presence of these voices of sanity among Afghans themselves that encouraged me to write this article. It showed that people are beginning to realize the importance of psychology in making a society more humane. This is vitally needed but much neglected in Afghanistan. Students are often discouraged by their own families from pursuing their interest in psychology. "Do you really want to end up a doctor to the crazies?" is the usual reaction. The prejudice is widespread, even inside the medical community.

The result is a nation deeply in need of psychological treatment but left with little choice but to turn to "traditional treatments," which include chaining patients to the walls of saintly shrines or depriving them of food and drink for long periods. Amid such dark despair, the sane voices of compassion that appeared alongside the aggressive comments offered a glimmer of hope because they showed that Afghans are beginning to understand that transvestites are not criminals.

It is true that different cultures create distinctive personality traits, but as the case of the unlucky Afghan transvestite revealed, such non-standard but deeply felt psychological needs are universal, with transvestites from the dusty roads of Kabul to the sparkling clubs of New York feeling the same urge to dress up as women with or without society's approval.

Becoming Professionally Afghan

In 2004, I applied for a job as a chief sub-editor for BBC Monitoring's Afghan desk and was asked for an interview. Needless to say, given that Afghans were involved in this enterprise, a surreal scenario was bound to unfold. The unfolding occurred during the second interview stage which involved a team-building exercise dreamed up by the HR office. Personifying the UK's equal opportunity laws, HR included two people of Asian and African origins, one woman of size and a wheelchair-bound colleague. Seated on plastic chairs against bare walls, the diversity group watched us in action. We were three Afghans and one Iranian; two women and two older, middle-aged men. The exercise's purpose was to exam our teamwork abilities. Communication, after all, was key to the job we had applied for. The idea, to sum up, was to show that we could work together efficiently.

As the exercise began, the Afghan man in our group launched into a vicious attack against everybody else, gleefully pointing out our faults and mistakes, sometimes telling us plainly that we were ignorant. Given the excitement on his face, he enjoyed this mini-jihad against his fellow competitors. I recalled a poem by Pazhwak, a famous Afghan poet and diplomat. It was about Alexander the Great's bewilderment with the Afghans under his rule. In the poem, which is a letter to his mother, Alexander says something to the effect of, "if you put four Afghans in room together with a non-Afghan in presence, they soon start fighting each other." He then adds, "They are very patriotic but as soon as they smell the soil of their country in each other, they start a war." This was exactly what was happening in the small HR room of BBC Monitoring.

Ten minutes into the performance, the diversity team collectively let its hair down, bursting into laugher and taking pleasure in our tragicomic performance. Looking back, I am not surprised they let themselves relax. I later learned that the HR-team had nothing to lose because they were already facing the sack due to BBC cost-cutting. Besides, no-one could accuse them of discrimination or racism; they had all minorities in their group, big people, disabled people, dark-skinned people. If we had raised objection, it would have been us to face the accusation of discrimination. Be that as it may, the team had a field day of free comedy with us. They left the room without a word, shaking their heads in disbelief. The four of us shared a taxi, acting as if the attack that was obviously for the benefit of the non-Afghan observers, had not taken place and we were all good friends. We even invited each other to tea and future meetings and in a strange and unfathomable way, we really meant it when we said, "Yes, let's stay in touch." As the taxi reached the train station, referring to the HR team building game, the Afghan man exclaimed, "Ah, the British. Strange people! They don't cut your throat with a sharp knife. They do it subtly, with a piece of cotton."

In team-building workshops on the ground in Afghanistan, Afghans tearing each other apart is a regular occurrence. One trainer in Kabul confided in me her own experience of such an exercise. "I asked my class to write anonymous feedback notes about the strengths and weaknesses of their fellow workshop mates. When I opened the notes, I couldn't believe my eyes. They all, men and women alike, were ripping each other into pieces. It was unbelievable. I had to clarify that this was not what feedback was about." The non-Afghan trainers are often appalled at this inter-Afghan hostility but they keep mum for fear of being accused of racism. But the truth is that underneath the surface of the Afghans' polite conformism there lurks a strong spirit of ruthless rivalry. The country is poor and economically unproductive with trade the only financially worthwhile activity. Everybody is basically a business man or woman and the resources being limited, life becomes all about the survival of the ruthless and the beautiful. An Afghan saying sums up the competitiveness, "No-one wants to be a fifty-cent in Afghanistan, everyone wants to be nothing less than a dollar note!"

I got the job and joined my new Afghan team. Recounting the embarrassing episode of my fellow Afghan's aggressive competition in a game that was about cooperation, my colleague, a disillusioned but highly informed man, told me the following story.

In the 1980s Afghan and Polish exiles occasionally held joint, anti-Soviet protests in London. But while the Polish protestors stood out for their organization, having people allocated to distinct roles (banner holders, refreshment providers, and people who simply stood in the crowd in solidarity) the Afghan protesters found themselves in chaotic disarray. The crux of the problem was that no-one in the Afghan protest group wanted to be a mere banner-holder, a nothing of a standing protestor. Everybody wanted to be the keynote speaker. "You see, that is why the mujahedin divided into so many splinter groups. When you split from your group, you have the chance to become a leader yourself, running your own group. Everybody in Afghanistan wants to be nothing less than a leader." With this simple logic, my colleague solved the mystery of the endless internal splits that had ultimately brought down both the communists and the mujahedin. Understanding Afghan politics can be sometimes as simple as this. Sometimes there is no need for complex theories, or to use an American phrase, there is no need to over-think it.

Malalai Joya: The Darling of Western Liberal Left

Malalai Joya is the undisputed darling of the liberal left in Europe and North America. Her devotees include wealthy liberals, idealist students, anarchists and the occasional intellectual star – Noam Chomsky, for example. To her fans, Joya represents the Afghan face of leftist anti-militarism. There are many people in the world who hate the United States but few of them have carved a career for themselves out of their contempt for Washington. Joya has made anti-Americanism her profession and her products range from ghost-written biographies to posters to lecture shows conspicuous for the use of crude language and display of photographs of injured Afghan babies. In sum, she is best-known for her categorical rejection of the US intervention in Afghanistan and it is this wholesale nature of her repudiation that is unfair. After all, without US intervention, Joya would not have been able to own a passport, let alone travel abroad. Equally, without the international community's interference, there would not have been the 2003 Loya Jerga where she first gained international fame. Joya's anti-US military rhetoric resonates with the leftist circles of the West who are her chief audience, and Joya's celebrity status reached a climax when she appeared alongside Noam Chomsky in Boston. Back home in Afghanistan, though, she has become irrelevant.

But to understand Joya's contradictory views, we need to look at how her career began and developed. Let's go back to the constitutional Loya Jerga of 2003 when Joya first became famous. At the time, she was an independent voice and had the audacity to make a relevant, but politically explosive comment. She said that the inclusion of war criminals threatened to undermine the assembly's legitimacy, that Afghans risked missing out on a historical chance for justice. Morally, she was absolutely right; but the truth was that, after two decades of violence, it was inevitable that the leaders that had emerged owed their power to war.

The international community had to work with what was there – and what was there was war leaders with dubious human rights records. To exclude them from the assembly was unreasonable because it would have driven them to start a new war front. Including them in the assembly meant that the Taliban remained the sole insurgents while the former mujahedin stopped fighting and began a new government. It was a morally flawed but pragmatic solution. Joya was driven by a burning desire for justice – pragmatism has never been her strength.

Joya's outspoken comment took the assembly by surprise. It was up to the assembly leader, Sebghatullah Mojaddedi, to diffuse the situation because he was older and more experienced. But Mojaddedi took offence and ordered Joya to leave the assembly. He then changed his mind and struck a gentler note, "Come back, child, you owe us an apology." But it was too late: the old man had lost the young woman. And with that, Joya lost a chance to fully develop her potential and work on the kind of constructive and reconciliatory politics that Afghanistan needed.

Since then, Joya's career as MP has been marked by repeats of that crucial early scene of her, a young woman, confronting old jihadi men. The location shifted from the Loya Jerga tent to parliament, but Joya and her jihadi nemesis remained stuck in an endless cycle of accusation and counter-accusation. The Afghan audiences found the confrontations first interesting, then amusing and finally lost interest in them altogether. By then, Joya was ousted from parliament, but her career abroad was beginning to flourish. Her book tour of the US, where she met Chomsky, was part of this development.

The tragedy of Joya is that she was spotted by the international media and a clandestine radical leftist Afghan organization at a time when Afghan democracy was in its infancy. At the time, Afghan human rights groups had not yet developed fully to give Joya the kind of support she needed. Isolated and vulnerable, she became an easy prey and was picked up by a group whose politics were steeped in the anti-imperialist revolutionary world of the 1960s and 70s ideological battles. Joya has served as a respectable front for a group that otherwise has little backing in Afghanistan. Joya's recurrent reference to "warlords in the pay of the US" are all about the group's bitterness that Washington allied itself with the group's Islamists rivals in the 1980s, enabling them to defeat the left. The alliance was abandoned between 1992 and 2001, but resumed fully with the 2001 intervention. Little wonder, then, that the group felt doubly betrayed by Washington.

But Joya's sudden fame in the West offered the group an unexpected chance to turn the tables and use Joya's popularity abroad to give her legitimacy to attack the group's jihadi nemesis in parliament. Joya's confrontations often came out of the blue. During a session about trade, Joya raised her hand but instead of asking questions about trade, she questioned the mujahedin's legitimacy. The speaker cautioned her that her comments were irrelevant because the session was about trade, but the damage was done and the session disrupted. Joya's disruptions of parliament eerily resembled similar incidents of leftwing versus rightwing fights that interrupted parliament in the 1960s. The resemblance is natural because the parties involved were the same old leftist comrades versus rightwing Islamist brothers. Joya has become simply a new player in an old political dynamic.

This also explained the intensity of the jihadis' reaction to Joya. After all, criticizing warlords was nothing unusual by 2007. But Joya was re-opening old wounds. Her repeated reference to the internal wars of the

1990s was the group's message that the jihadi victory was not complete since they had failed to cement it through establishing a solid state.

Needless to say, such nuances have been lost on the western media who presented Joya's provocations as a woman's struggle for rights and democracy. The thought that her disruption of parliament was evidence of an anti-democratic attitude on her part did not occur to them. After all, in the simplistic world of western politics, a young woman fighting bearded old men simply cannot be wrong.

'THE PLANE HIT THE TOWER AND ALL OUR LIVES CHANGED'

Bilal Sarwary

Few can have managed the transition from Afghan carpet-seller in exile to high-profile journalist on the ground as brilliantly as **Bilal Sarwary**, who exchanged hotel haggling for a life of international reporting in the immediate aftermath of al-Qaeda's 9/11 attacks on the US in 2001. For the next two decades he worked indefatigably with Western media, covering Afghanistan and its interminable war for the BBC. In 2010, he graduated as an independent scholar from Middlebury College in Vermont, specialising in the links between war, drugs and terrorism. His thesis was entitled *Farcification of Taliban*. All that changed in 2021, when the West pulled the plug, the Ashraf Ghani government collapsed and the Taliban took over. Sarwary managed to escape during the lethal chaos at Kabul Airport, a life-shattering wrench which he later described as 'the most painful journey in my life'. Today he lives in exile again. '*It has broken me from within,*' he wrote of covering the latest collapse of Afghanistan and the Taliban take-over.

In 2001, I was a carpet salesman at the Pearl Continental Hotel in Peshawar, Pakistan, having yet another unremarkable day at work.

I'll never forget glancing up at the TV in a brief moment between sales, only to witness firsthand the dramatic footage as a passenger plane careered into the World Trade Center in New York. Then the second plane, and another at the Pentagon. None of our lives would ever be the same.

International attention immediately focused on Afghanistan where the ruling Taliban were accused of providing a sanctuary for the attack's prime suspects – Osama Bin Laden and his al-Qaeda movement.

Only the next day, there were suddenly hundreds of foreign media crews crowding the hotel's lobby, desperate for anyone who could speak English to assist them as a translator as they crossed the nearby border into Afghanistan. I took up that offer and I haven't stopped since.

Within hours, people were lining up again outside barber shops to have their beards trimmed. Rhythmic Afghan music filled the streets, filling the vacuum left by explosions. Afghanistan was born again that morning.

From that moment onwards, I was intimately involved in observing the lives of ordinary Afghans firsthand, as they transitioned back to normality, no longer as a translator but as a journalist in my own right. From covering Tora Bora in the East to the Shai Koat battle in Paktia, I had seen the Taliban toppled.

Their fighters vanished into the mountainous rural areas, and their leadership fled to Pakistan. In retrospect, it is clear to me that this was a missed opportunity, a time when the US should have sat down with the Taliban to discuss a peace deal. I saw a genuine willingness amongst the rank-and-file of the Taliban to lay down their arms, and resume their lives. But the Americans didn't want that. From my reporting, it seemed to me and many other Afghans that their motivation was revenge after 9/11.

The ensuing years were a catalogue of errors.

Poor and innocent Afghan villagers were bombed and detained. The Afghan government's willingness to allow foreigners to drive the war effort created a gulf between it and the people. I remember clearly an incident where the Americans had mistakenly arrested and detained a taxi driver named Sayed Abasin on the highway between Kabul and Gardez. His father, Mr Roshan, was elderly and a legendary employee of Ariana airlines. After we exposed the error, Mr Abasin was eventually freed. But others were not so connected and not so lucky.

The Americans persisted with a heavy-handed approach, causing excess loss of life among ordinary Afghans. In a clear attempt to minimise American casualties, they prioritised bombs and drones over the use of ground troops. Trust for the Americans continued to erode and hopes for peace talks faded.

The year 2003 was the turning point. It was when the insurgents started to strike back with a renewed strength. I remember one day very clearly – it was the day that a huge truck bomb pierced the heart of Kabul, shaking the city and shattering windows. I was one of the first journalists on the scene and I'm still traumatised by what I found. It was my first experience of witnessing what would become the new normal, an imposed fact of life – carnage, flesh, and dead corpses littering the blood-splattered ground.

Ordinary Afghans came to see the sky as a source of fear. Gone were the days of gazing at the sunrise, sunset or the stars as a source of inspiration. On one trip to the lush green Arghandab river valley, close to the city of Kandahar, I arrived eager to see the country's most famous pomegranates. But when I arrived, it was the blood of its residents, not the fruit, that was flowing. What I saw was a microcosm of what has happened in so many rural areas in Afghanistan.

It was also during this period (between 2001 to 2010) that Afghanistan's 9/11 generation – young Afghans who had been granted opportunities to study overseas in India, Malaysia, the US, and Europe – came back to join the country's effort to rebuild. This new generation had hopes of being part of a great national rejuvenation. Instead, they found themselves confronted by new challenges. They returned to see newly empowered warlords enlisted by the Americans. And they saw that corruption was rife. When a country's reality drifts too far from its ideals, day-to-day pragmatism becomes a person's primary driver. A culture of impunity started to prevail.

Our country's landscape is deceptive.

It is easy to be struck by its beautiful valleys, sharp peaks, winding rivers, and little hamlets. But what presents as a peaceful image hasn't provided ordinary Afghans with any peace. You can't find peace without safety in your own home.

People often overlook the human cost for the Taliban – there are widows, fathers who have lost their sons, and young people crippled by war on the other side too. When I asked this father of the Taliban fighter what he wanted, his eyes filled with tears and he said: "I want an end to the fighting. Enough is enough. I know the pain of losing a son. I know Afghanistan must have a peace process, must have a ceasefire."

When the Americans recently commenced negotiations with the Taliban in Doha, we were initially overwhelmed with hope. The country was pining for a comprehensive and permanent ceasefire and the negotiations were seen as the only pathway through. I, like so many millions of Afghans, had not seen peace in my country in my lifetime.

One of my former classmates is a member of the Taliban and we are the same age. Over the last 20 years, we have continued to talk despite the fact that he's adhering to a different ideology. But recently, I saw him at a wedding and I could see how his attitude had hardened and soured. I saw and felt how this conflict has really divided Afghans. When we met, we could barely converse. He wasn't the guy that I remember from our days in Peshawar, playing cricket and stuffing our faces with juicy oranges.

How could I know that all these years later I would find him on the other side? His story is also one of deep personal loss. His brother, father, and uncle were killed in a raid that was based on false intelligence and petty local rivalries. Separated as we are, I can't help but hope for a future of national reconciliation.

But that seems a distant possibility now. I covered the regional capitals falling to the Taliban in recent weeks, with massive surrenders where no one put up a fight. But I didn't think they could make it into Kabul and take over the city.

Then I was told that my life was in danger.

I took two changes of clothes and was taken to an undisclosed location with my wife, my baby daughter and my parents. This is a city I know intimately – every inch of it. I belong to this city and it's unbelievable to think no place was safe for me.

I thought about my daughter Sola – her name means "peace" – and it was simply devastating to think the future we had hoped for her was now in tatters. As I left for the airport, I was reminded that for the second time in my life, I was leaving Afghanistan behind. When I got there, memories from years of work came back to overwhelm me – trips I had taken with officials or as a journalist heading to the front lines of the war.

Then I saw all these people, all these families lining up to flee. A generation of Afghans burying their dreams and aspirations.

But this time I wasn't there to cover the story. I was there to join them.

CONTEMPORARY AFGHAN POETRY

'Poetry,' the Afghan poet Masood Khalili writes in the foreword to this anthology, 'is as important to us as the air we breathe and the water we drink.'

Afghanistan, like Iran, is a nation of poets. It is a country where someone without much education would think nothing of reeling off a *ghazal* – a rhyming love ode – by Hafiz, the fourteenth-century giant of Persian poetry, learnt by heart as a rite of passage. Poetry is not something locked away in schools and universities and unopened books, as is so often the case in the West. It is a living, breathing aspect of daily life, an essential part of the vocabulary of everyday language and communication. This is as true for an overeducated professor in Kabul or Herat, who may be a master of formal poetry, with its intricately crafted *ghazals* and *rubaiyat* quatrains, as it is for an uneducated woman in the mountains, who will invariably have a clutch of sharp-tongued *landays*, stinging two-line verses, often sung, at her command. Poetry is everywhere and by everyone.

Today's poetry from and about Afghanistan confronts the harrowing situation in which millions of men, women and children in the country find themselves. Poets here deal with war and terrorism, bloodshed and destitution on the grandest scale. They write under fear of persecution and death, 'When terrorists are drinking your blood with / their iron straw', in the words of Samay Hamed, a doctor, poet and founder of Afghan PEN. They also tackle love, loss and longing – perhaps for an absent lover, for a moment of peace in the raging conflict, or simply for something better. Anything, surely, would be better than this.

The poetry by Afghan women can be especially devastating. Who could not be moved by the piercing despair of Roya (we only know her first name; poetry can be a matter of life and death for women here, and some writers remain anonymous), whose poem 'Not an Afghan Woman' is a lacerating *cri de coeur* and an indictment of the patriarchy.

I would love to be anything in nature
But not a woman
Not an Afghan woman.

Some of the poets featured here have paid for their verse with their lives. One of the most notorious cases was Nadia Anjuman, a twenty-five-year-old poet and rising star who in 2005 was beaten to her death by her husband, Farid Ahmad Majid Neia, who considered her poetry a disgrace to the family's reputation. Under pressure from the tribal elders of Herat – a famously cultured city of which the fifteenth-century poet Alisher Navoiy wrote, 'In Herat if you stretch out your feet you are sure to kick a poet' – Anjuman's father agreed to forgive Neia for the murder. The court then pronounced her death a suicide and Neia was released after a month behind bars. The shock of his son-in-law's release, at the brazen injustice of it, reportedly killed Anjuman's father. Nadia died before she could see her second volume of poetry published. Its title? *Yek Sabad Delhore, An Abundance of Worry*. In 2007, Nadia's complete works were published in the original Dari by the Iranian Burnt Books Foundation.

Little known outside Afghanistan, the *landay* is folk verse at its pithiest. 'Like a cry coming from the heart, a lightning flash, a flame, the *landay* captures the attention by its brevity and rhythm,' wrote Sayd Bahodine Majrouh, one of the greatest Afghan poets of the twentieth century, assassinated in the Pakistani city of Peshawar in 1988. The *landay* may be beautiful or bawdy, it may express the full force of a woman's fury, her contempt for a cowardly husband, her lust for a young lover, or despair with a father who has forced her into an unsuitable marriage.

You sold me to an old man, father.
May God destroy your home; I was your daughter.

As another woman puts it:

Making love to an old man
is like fucking a shrivelled cornstalk black with mould.

A *landay* may mournfully mark the death of a loved one or celebrate an abiding love of Afghanistan. Short in stature, its range is as wide as the country's mountain-framed skies.

Rahila Muska was another young Afghan woman who paid with her life for her poetry. A teenager from Gereshk in the southern province and Taliban stronghold of Helmand, her real name was Zarmina. In 2010, her brothers beat her savagely after finding her writing poems – another supposed disgrace to a family's reputation. She doused herself with heating oil and set herself on fire. She died later in hospital, leaving little behind. Her life had barely begun. Today she is remembered in a tragically prophetic *landay*, one of the many she used to love sharing with her fellow poets over the phone.

I call. You're stone.
One day you'll look and find I'm gone.

Who would be an Afghan woman?

Is it any wonder they often excoriate their menfolk in verse? Should we be surprised that Afghan women, in the words of Somaya Ramish's brilliant, brutal, bullet-filled verse, 'Load Poems Like Guns'? Writing from exile in the West, the poet Bahar Saied pours scorn on supposedly religious men obsessed with forcing women to wear the veil.

You men of God! Cast your eyes from my face.
go and hide your weakness of self –
veil, veil your withering faith.

Flicking two fingers up at censorious Afghan men, she celebrates her own sexuality and sensuality in a culture where merely writing about this taboo can be tantamount to a death sentence.

Come and carve me, my body is yours
carve me in your heart in the night of dreams
come and carve me until morning
with beautiful touch and kiss.

Although much of contemporary Afghan poetry can be shattering – a case of literature reflecting the society around it – there is still space here for beauty, joy, love and celebration. Women and men alike rise to the occasion with poems plunging into the thrills of romance and sexual desire, such as these lines by the modernist poet Partaw Naderi:

I kissed her –
her whole body shivered
Like a branch of almond blossom in the wind
Like the moon, like a star
  trembling on the water
I kissed her –
her whole body shivered…

Reza Mohammadi is transfixed by the 'two bewitching rubies' of his lover's eyes, an unnamed girl invites a boy to slide his hand inside her bra to 'Stroke a red and ripening pomegranate of Kandahar', and Roya Zamani Hareva warns an unknown man – a lover? – he will be 'lost with ecstasy in the waves of my hair'.

Afghanistan is a country that is grievously wounded. Yet the following pages demonstrate, in the most heartfelt and eloquent fashion, that no matter how terrible the turmoil, the poets' words, like the ruby red wine in the classical verse of Attar, Saadi, Rumi and Hafiz, continue to flow like a raging, effervescent torrent.

Four poems by Khalilullah Khalili
(1907–87), former poet laureate of Afghanistan
Translated by G. Whitney Azoy and Masood Khalili

To Rumi

Tonight I'm no more than a handful of thorns.
Burn them. Pour my ashes across the sky.
Tonight I broke every snare and chain,
Freed myself for you to hunt me down.
Tonight I'm a broken bell, dropped from a late caravan.
Ring my song, to keep the camels going.
Tonight you're a free eagle, and I'm broken wings.
Gather me up, fly me up to the heavens.
Tonight I'm a lifeless flame, a heart with dead hopes.
But I'm entirely yours. Set me alight.

Vengeful Magicians

These champions of spite and malice are at it again
Putting new spins on the same old chicanery.
Every single day these vengeful magicians
Promise us peace-making but keep on making war.

Neither Lions Nor Foxes

How long will you persist with sword and dagger?
How long with artifice and cunning?
One is fit for lions, the other for foxes.
So: Be fully human and free from both.

Hope's Candle

Dark wilderness makes you feel like a voiceless orphan,
But in the desert's heat, pain can turn to song.
There's an oasis. If you want to reach it,
Don't let the candle of hope slip from your palm.

*

Sayd Bahodine Majrouh

The Trial of the Lovers

Translated from the Pashto into French; translated from the French by Marjolijn de Jager

When he arrived, it had all been played out.
The turmoil had abated. The crowd was slowly breaking up.

To one side stood a few religious dignitaries with sombre beards, their turbans and black robes enveloping them in an aura even more funereal than usual.

The Voyager reached the centre of the square.
Half buried beneath a mound of stones lay a young woman and a young man, covered in mud and blood.

*

Nadia Anjuman

Poison
Translated by Diana Arterian and Martina Omar

That night . . .
the scorpions gathered in secret
for a fierce exchange
    that went on for some time
The subject: *Injecting poison into bodies of knowledge!*
Choosing that poison
    They could not reach a verdict
Suddenly, from the group
the most hideous of them all
opened his mouth, his tongue like a sword
    and spoke:
    The night is passing—no time for delay
When our prey close their eyes
rise and find a point to sting
I have inherited
an ancient jar of deadly venom from my ancestors
Now I am the generous one who will pass it on . . .

Daughter of Afghanistan
Translated by Adeeba Talukder and Aria Fani

I've no desire to open my mouth. What will I recite?
I who will remain despised by my age, whether or not I recite

How will I sing of honey? It's turned to poison on my tongue –
curses upon the fist of the tyrant who crushed my mouth
Bless this world with no one to share my grief
whether I weep or laugh, whether I live or die

I and this prison: my longing cornered to nothing.
I was borne of futility, born only to be silenced.

Heart! I know Spring has passed, and its joy too
but how could I fly with these ripped-off wings?

Though silent all this time, I've listened closely:
my heart still whispers her songs, births new ones for her every moment

One day I'll smash this cage, its very solitude
I'll drink the wine of joy, sing the way a bird should in springtime.

Though a delicate-limbed tree, I won't shudder with every breeze
I am a daughter of Afghan – I'll sound my *faghan*,* weave it to eternity

* A *faghan* is a cry, an expression of regret and pain.

*

Roya

But Not an Afghan Woman

I would love to be anything in this world
but not a woman
I could be a parrot
I could be a female sheep
I could be a deer or
a sparrow living in a tree
But not an Afghan woman.
I could be a Turkish lady
With a kind brother to take my hand
I could be Tajik

or I could be Iranian
or I could be an Arab
With a husband to tell me
I am beautiful
But I am an Afghan woman.
When there is need
I stand beside it
When there is risk
I stand in front
When there is sorrow
I grab it
When there are rights
I stand behind them
Might is right and
I am a woman
Always alone
Always an example of weakness
My shoulders are heavy
with the weight of pains.
When I want to talk
My tongue is blamed
My voice causes pain
Crazy ears can't tolerate me
My hands are useless
I can't do anything with
My foolish legs
I walk with
No destination.
Until what time must I accept to suffer?
When will nature announce my release?
Where is Justice's house?
Who wrote my destiny?
Tell him

Tell him
Tell him
I would love to be anything in nature
But not a woman
Not an Afghan woman.

*

Roya Sharifi

Those Bleeding Tulips
Translated by Farzana Marie

They gave no quarter in those freezing nights,
only darkness, filled with laments.
First they crushed the heart's defenses,
then tore limb from every limb of tree and leaf
and gardens blooming tulips in the spring:
they marked them all for summary destruction
(amazingly in the commotion a bird broke free).
As the locust-army marched en masse on rows of wheat
without cause except for ignorance
and blind to the horizon of our history,
they filled their laps with slaughtered innocents.
Don't speak of the zeal of those bleeding tulips;
their destroyers' slogans were all Islam and liberation
but they came in anything but peace.
And now the world thinks it knows us
by the famous 'valor' of the Afghan nation.

*

Reza Mohammadi

Album
Translated by Hamid Kabir with the Poetry Translation Workshop

Your hand plays with your hair.
Your hair plays across your face.
Your eyes are two bewitching rubies,
rubies my heart longs to play with.
The next picture has you sat beside me,
two children playing 'ghosts'.
Sometimes our hands grip.
Sometimes our arms touch.

In the next picture, you say to yourself,
'Perhaps we weren't ever meant to play together'.
But I say, 'It wasn't us, it was god,
playing with our destiny'.
Next: two birds in two cages, playing with seeds.
Children in a game of hide and seek,
people playing 'house'.
And next, when you're taken away
everything dies: life, its bustle, playing.
In the next, when you're with me again,
rivers want to play with valleys,
perfumes want to play with colours.
My eyes want to follow you like a playful gazelle.
In the next picture, your fingers run through your hair.
Your hair plays across your face.

Illegal Immigrant
Translated by Hamid Kabir with Nick Laird

it is possible
the sun has risen
and over the mountains
the clouds are there still,
that winds are driving
and families arriving
and there is the sound of a party
sound of dancing, chanting,
and glasses smashing,
the laughter exploding
in every minute and people
and happiness and also
me, with my big heart,
in a ship or strapped under
the truck, I am crossing
the border and moment
by moment am entering
with glory England

To Love
Translated by Hamid Kabir with Nick Laird

We don't wake together. I come to
in an empty room by the sea long after
you've woken and opened the window
and showered and dressed and left.

Your day is a street which leads
to a road that reaches a building,
then leads to an avenue, lastly,
caught in the grid of the city.

My day is a corridor that runs
through my veins and is closed
neatly with copper buttons.
We make our own ways home.

You wear your purple dress
to match the colour of the clocks
and I slip on my patu.
A good time for green tea.

Meals bring each together,
as does the TV, the news, the computer.
I love you like the fire loves the stove.
You love me like the stove loves firewood.

Later on we clutch each other and dream our separate dreams.

*

Shakila Azizzada

Kabul
Translated by Zuzanna Olszewska with Mimi Khalvati

If my heart beats
for Kabul,
it's for the slopes of Bala Hissar,
holding my dead
in its foothills.

Though not one, not one
of those wretched hearts
ever beat for me.

If my heart grieves
for Kabul,
it's for Leyla's sighs of
'Oh, dear God!'
and my grandmother's heart
set pounding.

It's for Golnar's eyes
scanning the paths
from dawn to dusk, spring to autumn,
staring so long
that all the roads fall apart
and in my teenage nightmares
side roads
suddenly shed their skins.

If my heart trembles
for Kabul,
it's for the slow step of summer noons,
siestas in my father's house which,
heavy with mid-day sleep,
still weighs on my ribs.
For the playful Angel of the Right Shoulder
who keeps forgetting
to ward away stray bullets.

It's for the hawker's cry
of the vegetable seller doing his rounds,
lost in my neighbours' troubled dreams,
that my heart's trembling.

The Bridal Veil
Translated by Zuzanna Olszewska with Mimi Khalvati

I've hung my wedding dress
on a hook of white memories,
my gaze like silk on his shoulders.

I've torn my heart from his chest
which still smells of my milk.

He'd wake,
his fingers pulsing on my neck,
the same old clamour of lust in his arms.

I've torn my heart away
but my eyes are filled with him,
his back, broad and resplendent
in a bridegroom's shawl.

I won't remind myself
that, with the next breath,
he'll take off her veil.

I won't count
his breaths.

*

Partaw Naderi
(1953–), President of Afghan PEN

The Bloody Epitaph
Translated by Yama Yari with Sarah Maguire

This palm tree has no hope of spring
This palm tree blossoms
with a hundred wounds
    the daily wounds of a thousand tragedies
    the nightly wounds of a thousand calamities
This palm tree is a bloody epitaph
at the crossroads of the century

*

Here, by the river,
    a river of blood and tears -
the roots of this palm tree
are congealed with disaster
are knotted with the blind roots of time

*

Here, the sky
unwinds its bloody cloth
from barren red clouds
to shroud the shattered lid of a coffin
    a broken mirror of rain
This palm tree has no hope of spring

*

This palm tree has no hope of spring
This palm tree is starred
with a hundred bruises
    from the whip of the north wind
My palm!
    My only tree!
        My spring!
Many years have passed
since the bird of blossoms
flew away from your desiccated branches
Butterflies abandon you
My heart is broken

Kabul,
November, 1989

On a Colourful Morning
Translated by Yama Yari with the poet Sarah Maguire

I kissed her –
her whole body shivered
Like a branch of almond blossom in the wind
Like the moon, like a star
    trembling on the water
I kissed her –
her whole body shivered
Her cheeks showed one colour
her gaze revealed another
And the sun rose from her tender heart
And the thousand-and-one nights of waiting
ended
And on a colourful morning

I shared a bed
>with the meaning of love

July 2002
Peshawar City

*

Samay Hamed

When you have no political power

When you have no political power
Make new jokes on warlords
and say to your shadow in silence
When terrorists are drinking your blood with
their iron straw
Write new poems with red pens
When you have no political power to
challenge corrupt dinosaurs
Borrow money from your friend
and buy a bottle of forgetfulness Wesley
When you got drunk,
stand on a chair like statue of a hero and
shout:
I will change this country!
Spit on the dark poster of the sky and shout
louder:
You bastard night! Where have you hidden
the sunflower of dreams?
Show me your diamond teeth to break them!
When you have no political power
Sit down on your broken shoulder like a
destroyed monument

And watch the window TV
with its boring four-season daily soup!

*

Masood Khalili
Translated by Robert Darr

Persian Honey

Where Her lovely scent, where the dawn's fragrance?
Where Her light, where the radiance of sun and moon?

Alas! Old age exposes the ruins of the body's shelter.
Where are grip and hand, strength of arm and waist?

The decrepit royal falcon is for little birds a branch of hope;
Where is that hunter with signs of majesty head to foot?

The outspread night affords passage to the desert camels;
Say, O camel-driver, where is there hope for the dawn?

O Beloved, come! Don't anguish over the danger-filled night;
On the path of love, where is there night time without danger?

Send from me to the great masters, Hafiz and Rumi:
"Where are flames to ignite the harvest of my love?"

The venom of separation has made my existence bitter;
Where is that Persian honey and those lips full of sugar?

Death of a Child

O death! Many chambers of the heart you've scarred!
In many hearts and eyes you've kindled simmering fires!
My precious, heart-warming child of endearing charm
you have taken from me and hidden beneath the earth!

Your Narcissus Eyes

It's from your wine-hued eyes that the town is drunk!
Ah, for your fragrance which gutted the price of amber!

Last evening as the townsfolk gazed at your lunar face,
the great joy of seeing you made them moon worshippers.

Should you strive to stride through the great bazaar's gateway,
your bold pace will have the market turning to wine-worship.

When parting your robe to reveal your lovely stature,
Pleiades and the moon joined Venus to settle at your feet!

One worshipper caught a whiff of your musk-like breath
and severed ties to the temple, the mosque, and the idol house.

When the rumor of your Love spread across the madrassa,
Helpless was Plato and the books of philosophy were shut.

Just a glance like Layla's from your narcissus eyes
freed Majnoon from sorrow, lament, and anguished cries.

Dawn's Seeker

Be like the seed awaiting its own sprouting!
Be like the rosebud preparing to blossom!
In dark night's deep and somber blackness,
be it your desire to seek out dawn's light!

The Text of Hate

A clamour arose when one of the Taliban, citing verses about 'enemies', broke the tavern's gate and shattered the jar of wine and its full cups.

He is ignorant of the wise words of God-inspired authorities; from a devil's text he shouts a stream of concocted litanies.

While he curses and maligns the Hindu and the Christian, they both remain a thousand times more honourable than him!

The windows to knowledge have been shuttered to women and girls; bound are their eyes and mouths! Bound their fine words of renown!

Take note of the vain, ignorant fool who argues without insight that God created women to be lacking in honour and might!

Tell that ignorant fool that the peerless, Divine One bestowed upon women strength and creative will!

To women God sent down verses of majesty and honour! To you He stressed the duties of ablution and charity.

What entered you from Satan was supreme ignorance, whereas God bestowed on women true beauty of character!

*

Bahar Saied
Translated by Bashir Sakhwaraz

He kissed me once and stole my lips
and robbed me from sleep
I am scared if he touches my body
my patience will be invaded.

I have come to you to taste your body
my lips fall on yours, tasting your mouth
with my fingers I tear off your shirt
I taste the nakedness of your chest.
I am inhaling the perfume of your breath
and touching your body with my breast
tasting the burning of your body on mine.

Come and carve me, my body is yours
carve me in your heart in the night of dreams
come and carve me until morning
with beautiful touch and kiss.

I love the buttons on your collar
which ask me to open them
and throw myself on you.

*

Farangiz Sowgand
Translated by Adeeba Talukder and Aria Fani

Just to herself, she laughs for an hour
the passing breath of a prostitute

Then, shivering, she screams out loud
the frightened grief of a prostitute.

For a moment she gazes in the mirror:
she isn't there. And then she is
hidden in dust
dust of the world of a prostitute.

Every night, every day, every hour
held in sturdy arms
she weeps the tears of a prostitute.

Turns into a scorpion,
stings herself, cries
then imagines a cure for a prostitute

Death, busy
playing somewhere in the city
laughs in the wet eyes of a prostitute

With autumn's passing, another story
remains unspoken:
I've spent my birthday
spent with the grief of a prostitute.

*

Somaya Ramish

Load Poems Like Guns
Translated by Farzana Marie

Load poems like guns —
war's geography calls you
to arms.
The enemy has no signs,
counter-signs,
colors
signals
symbols!
Load poems like guns —
each moment is loaded
with bombs
bullets
blasts
death-sounds —
death and war
don't follow rules
you can make your pages into white flags
a thousand times
but swallow your words, say no more.
Load your poems —
your body —
your thoughts —
like guns.
The schoolhouses of war
rise up within you.
Maybe you
are next.

EXTENDED COPYRIGHT

We are grateful to the following for permission to reproduce copyright material:

HUDŪD AL-ĀLAM: Extract from *The Regions of the World: A Persian Geography*, translated by Vladimir Minorsky, The E.J.W. Gibb Memorial Trust, copyright © 1937. Reprinted by permission.

TIM ALBONE: Extract from *Out of the Ashes*, Virgin Books, copyright © Tim Albone, 2011. Reprinted by permission of The Random House Group Limited.

SVETLANA ALEXIEVICH: Extract from *Boys in Zinc*, translated by Andrew Bromfield, Penguin Classics, 2017, copyright © Svetlana Alexievich 1989. Reprinted by permission of Penguin Books Limited.

MOHAMMED IBN JARIR AL TABARI: Extracts from *The History of Al Tabari, Vol XXIII, The Zenith of the Marwanid House*, translated by Martin Hinds, State University of New York Press, 1990. Reprinted by permission of the publisher.

SHAYKH AL-ISLĀM ABŪ BAKR ʿABD ALLĀH AL-WĀʿIZ: Extracts from *Faḍāʾil-i Balkh, Or The Merits of Balkh: Annotated Translation with Commentary and Introduction of the Oldest Surviving History of Balkh in Afghanistan*, translated by Arezou Azad and Edmund Herzig with Ali Mir-Ansari, The E.J.W. Gibb Memorial Trust, copyright © 2021. Reprinted by permission.

KHWAJA ABDULLAH ANSARI: Extracts from *The Book of Wisdom*, translated by Victor Danner, The Society for Promoting Christian Knowledge, 1979. Reprinted by permission of the publisher through PLSClear.

NUSHIN ARBABZADAH: Extracts from *Afghan Rumour Bazaar: Secret Sub-Cultures, Hidden Worlds and the Everyday Life of the Absurd*, Hurst Publishers, 2013, copyright © Nushin Arbabzadah, 2013. Reprinted by permission of the publisher.

NADEEM ASLAM: Extract from *The Wasted Vigil*, Faber & Faber Ltd, 2008, copyright © Nadeem Aslam, 2008. Reprinted by permission of the publisher and The Wylie Agency (UK) Limited.

FARID AL DIN ATTAR: Poems "Since there is no one to be our companion in Love My heart's on fire, O wine-bringer;" "I got drunk at the tavern last night;" "What's being in Love? Abandoning life" and "You're of our tradition if you've donned the belt of infidelity", translated by Kenneth Avery and Ali Alizadeh in *Fifty Poems of Attar*, re:Press, 2007. Reprinted by permission of the publisher.

DURKHANAI AYUBI: Extract from *Parwana: Recipes and Stories from an Afghan Kitchen*, Murdoch Books, 2020. Reprinted by permission of Murdoch Books, a division of Allen & Unwin Pty Ltd.

G. WHITNEY AZOY: Extracts from *Buzkashi: Game and Power in Afghanistan*, Waveland Press, Inc., copyright © 2012. Reprinted by permission of Waveland Press, Inc. All rights reserved.

RABIA BALKHI: from Ilahi-Nama, translated by Munazza Ebtikar, https://ajammc.com/2021/08/16/rabia-balkhi-afghanistan-poet/ copyright © Munazza Ebtikar. Reprinted by kind permission of the translator.

RABIA BALKHI: Poems "His love has caught me once again–;" "My hope's that God will make you fall in love;" "I'm drunk with love to know my love is here tonight" and "The garden shows so many flowers, as though" translated by Dick Davis in *The Mirror of My Heart: A Thousand Years of Persian Poetry by Women*, Mage Publishers, 2020. Reprinted by permission of the publisher.

IBN BATTUTA: Extracts from *The Travels of Ibn Battuta*, translated with revisions and notes from the Arabic text by C. Defrémery and B. R. Sanguinetti, by H.A.R. Gibb and C.F. Beckingham, Hakluyt Society/Taylor & Francis. Reprinted by permission of David Higham Associates.

CONTEMPORARY AFGHAN POETRY:
Nadia Anjuman: 'Poison', translated by Diana Arterian and Martina Omar, https://www.asymptotejournal.com/poetry/nadia-anjuman-dark-flower/; and 'Daughter of Afghanistan', translated by Adeeba Talukder and Aria Fani, https://www.pbs.org/wgbh/pages/frontline/tehranbureau/2012/03/poetry-daughters-of-afghanistan-literary-voices-of-change.html.

Shakila Azizzada: 'Kabul', translated by Zuzanna Olszewska with the poet Mimi Khalvati. First published in *Poems* (Poetry Translation Centre, 2012); 'The Bridal Veil', translated by Zuzanna Olszewska with the poet Mimi Khalvati. First published in Poems (Poetry Translation Centre, 2012).

Samay Hamid: 'When you have no political power', from the collection 'Writing with Eraser', https://pen-international.org/news/three-poems-by-samay-hamed.

Khalilullah Khalili: four poems, reprinted with the permission of Masood Khalili.

Masood Khalili: 'Persian Honey', 'Death of a Child', 'Your Narcissus Eyes', 'Dawn's Seeker', 'The Text of Hate'; all poems translated by Robert Darr and reproduced with the permission of Masood Khalili.

Sayd Bahodine Majrouh: 'The Trial of the Lovers', reprinted by permission of The Other Press.

Reza Mohammadi: 'Album', translated by Hamid Kabir with the Poetry Translation Centre workshop; 'Illegal immigrant', translated by Hamid Kabir with the poet Nick Laird. First published in *Poems* (Poetry Translation Centre, 2012); 'To Love', translated by Hamid Kabir with the poet Nick Laird. First published in *Poems* (Poetry Translation Centre, 2012).

Partaw Naderi: 'The Bloody Epitaph', translated by Yama Yari with the poet Sarah Maguire. First published in *Poems* (Poetry Translation Centre, 2012); 'On a Colourful Morning', translated by Yama Yari with the poet Sarah Maguire. First published in *Poems* (Poetry Translation Centre, 2012).

Somaya Ramish: 'Load Poems Like Guns', 2015, translated by Farzana Marie, reprinted with the permission of Somaya Ramish, Farzana Marie and Holy Cow! Press.

Roya: 'But Not an Afghan Woman', by Roya: from the Afghan Women's Writing Project https://awwproject.org/2010/03/but-not-an-afghan-woman/.

Bahar Saied: 'He kissed me once and stole my lips', translated by Bashir Sakhwaraz, https://pentransmissions.com/2014/06/19/the-erotic-and-revolutionary-poetry-of-afghanistan/.

Roya Sharifi: 'Those Bleeding Tulips', translated by Farzana Marie; published in *Load Poems Like Guns: Women's Poetry from Herat*, Afghanistan, Holy Cow! Press, 2015); reprinted with the permission of Roya Sharifi, Farzana Marie and Holy Cow! Press.

Farangiz Sowgand: *'Just to herself, she laughs for an hour'*, translated by Adeeba Talukder and Aria Fani, https://www.pbs.org/wgbh/pages/frontline/tehranbureau/2012/03/poetry-daughters-of-afghanistan-literary-voices-of-change.html.

WILLIAM DALRYMPLE: Extract from *Return of a King: The Battle for Afghanistan*, Bloomsbury Publishing Plc, 2013, copyright © William Dalrymple, 2013. Reprinted by kind permission of the publisher.

ARTYOM BOROVIK: Extract from *The Hidden War: A Russian Journalist's Account of the Soviet War in Afghanistan*, 2001, reprinted by permission of The Grove Press.

DIODORUS OF SICILY: *Diodorus of Sicily*, Book 17, Chapter 82, translated by C. H. Oldfather. Vol. 4–8. Harvard University Press; William Heinemann, Ltd. 1989. Licensed under a Creative Commons Attribution-ShareAlike 3.0 United States License.

NANCY HATCH DUPREE: Extract from *An Historical Guide to Afghanistan*, The Afghan Tourist Organization, 1977, pp. 395–402. Reprinted by kind permission of the Estate for the author.

SIR HENRY MORTIMER DURAND: from "The Amir Abdur Rahman Khan", Proceedings of the Central Asian Society, delivered 06/11/1907. Reprinted by permission from Royal Society for Asian Affairs (RSAA).

JASON ELLIOT: Extract from *An Unexpected Light: Travels in Afghanistan*, Picador, 1999, copyright © Jason Elliot, 1999. Reprinted by permission of the publisher through PLSClear.

E.M. FORSTER: Extract from *Abinger Harvest*, 1935. Reprinted by permission of Peters, Fraser & Dunlop (www.petersfraserdunlop.com) on behalf of the Estate of E.M. Forster.

CHARLES GAMMELL: Extract from *Herat: Pearl of Khorasan*, Hurst, 2016. Reprinted by permission of the publisher.

FAROOKHA GAUHARI: Extract from *Searching for Saleem: An Afghan Woman's Odyssey*, University of Nebraska Press, 1996.

AMITAV GHOSH: Extract from *The Man Behind the Mosque*, https://www.amitavghosh.com/essays/mosque.html, copyright © Amitav Ghosh, 2003. Reprinted by permission of The Wylie Agency (UK) Limited.

ANAND GOPAL: "The Last Days of Vice and Virtue" from *No Good Men Among the Living: America, The Taliban, and the War Through Afghan Eyes*, copyright © Anand Gopal, 2014. Reprinted by permission of Henry Holt and Company. All Rights Reserved.

HAFIZ: from the poem "Call me and I will come" by Hafiz, adapted by Richard Jeffrey Newman in *Selections from Saadi's Gulistan*, Global Scholarly Publications, 2004. Reprinted by kind permission of Richard Jeffrey Newman.

HAFIZ: Poems "My friend, hold back your heart from enemies;" "Last night she brought me wine, and sat beside my pillow" and "Sweet lips and silver ears - that's idol's elegance" translated by Dick Davis in *Faces of Love: Hafez and the Poets of Shiraz*, Penguin Classics, 2014. Reprinted by permission of Mage Publishers.

HAFIZ: Poems "Someone Should Start Laughingfashes" and "The Great Secret" rendered by Daniel Ladinsky in *I Heard God Laughing: Poems of Hope and Joy*, copyright © Daniel Ladinsky, 2006. All rights reserved. www.danielladinsky.com.

NADIA HASHIMI: Extract 3 from *The Pearl That Broke Its Shell*, HarperCollins, 2014, copyright © Nadia Hashimi, 2014. Reprinted by permission of HarperCollins Publishers;

HERODOTUS: *Herodotus Histories*, Book 3, Chapter 102, Book 4, Chapter 204, translated and edited by A.D. Godley. Harvard University Press. 1920. Licensed under a Creative Commons Attribution-ShareAlike 3.0 United States License.

FRANK HOLT: Extracts from *Into the Land of Bones: Alexander the Great in Afghanistan*, University of California Press 2005, copyright © The Regents of the University of California, 2005, 2012. Reprinted by permission of the University of California Press.

KHALED HOSSEINI: Extract from *The Kite Runner*, Bloomsbury Publishing Plc, 2018, copyright © Khaled Hosseini, 2018. Reprinted by kind permission of the publisher.

HUGH KENNEDY: Extract from *The Great Arab Conquests: How the Spread of Islam Changed The World We Live In*, Orion, 2008, copyright © Hugh Kennedy, 2007. Reprinted by permission of the publisher through PLSClear.

KHWANDAMIR: Extract from *Universal History Habib al Siyar, Habibu's-Siyar. Tome three, The reign of the Mongol and the Turk* translated and edited by W.M. Thackston, Harvard University, 1994. Reprinted by kind permission of the translator.

DAVID KILCULLEN & GREG MILLS: Extract from *The Ledger: Accounting for Failure in Afghanistan*, Hurst, 2021, copyright © David Kilcullen and Greg Mills, 2021. Reprinted by permission of the publisher.

FAWZIA KOOFI: Extracts from *The Favoured Daughter: One Woman's Fight to Lead Afghanistan into the Future*, Palgrave Macmillan, 2012. Reprinted by permission of Michel Lafon Publishing.

CHRISTINA LAMB: Extract from *The Sewing Circles of Herat*, HarperCollins, 2002, copyright © Christina Lamb, 2002. Reprinted by permission of HarperCollins Publishers Ltd.

PETER LEVI: Extract from *The Light Garden of the Angel King*, HarperCollins, 1972, copyright © Peter Levi, 1972. Reprinted by permission of Eland Publishing Ltd.

JUSTIN MAROZZI: 'Lunch with the FT' interview with Ahmad Shah Massoud, *Financial Times*, 21–22/12/1996, copyright © Financial Times/FT.com. Reprinted under licence from the Financial Times. All Rights Reserved.

S. A. MOUSAVI: Extract from *The Hazaras of Afghanistan: An Historical, Cultural, Economic and Political Study*, Routledge, 2006, copyright © Sayed Askar Mousavi, 1998. Reprinted by permission of Taylor and Francis Group, LLC, a division of Informa plc.

ALISHER NAVOIY: Poems "I ached to see your body so…" and "The one who was to come that night…" translated by Andrew Staniland with Aidakhon Bumatova, https://www.andrewstaniland.co.uk. Reprinted by kind permission of Andrew Staniland.

ERIC NEWBY: Extract from *A Short Walk in the Hindu Kush*, HarperCollins, 2010, copyright © Eric Newby, 1958. Reprinted by permission of HarperCollins Publishers Ltd.

QAIS AKBAR OMAR: Extract from *A Night in the Emperor's Garden: A True Story of Hope and Resilience in Afghanistan*, Haus Publishing, 2015. Reprinted by permission of the publisher.

PLINY THE ELDER: Extract from *The Natural History*, Book 6, Chapter 23, ed. John Bostock, M.D., F.R.S. H.T. Riley, Esq., B.A. Taylor and Francis, 1855. Licensed under a Creative Commons Attribution-ShareAlike 3.0 United States License.

HOMEIRA QADERI: Extract from *Dancing in the Mosque: An Afghan Mother's Letters to Her Son*, translated by Zaman Stanizai, Fourth Estate, copyright © Homeira Qaderi. Reprinted by permission of HarperCollins Publishers Ltd.

ATIQ RAHIMI: Extract from *Earth and Ashes*, 2002, reprinted by permission of The Random House Group Limited.

AHMED RASHID: Extract from *Taliban: The Power of Militant Islam in Afghanistan and Beyond*, I.B. Tauris, Bloomsbury Publishing Plc, copyright © Ahmed Rashid, 2022. Reprinted by kind permission of the publisher.

RUMI: Poems "Like This;" "Only Breath;" "The Many Wines;" "Dervish at the Door;" "A Moment of Happiness" and "Five Things to Say", translated by Coleman Barks in *The Essential Rumi*, HarperCollins, 1995, copyright © Coleman Barks, 1995. Reprinted by permission of Michael Meller Literary Agency.

CHRIS SANDS & FAZELMINALLAH QAZIZAI: Extract from *Night Letters: Gulbuddin Hekmatyar and the Afghan Islamists who Changed the World*, Hurst Publishers, 2019, copyright © Chris Sands and Fazelminallah Qazizai, 2019. Reprinted by permission of the publisher.

BILAL SARWARY: Extract from 'The Plane Hit the Tower and all our Lives Changed', https://www.bbc.co.uk/news/world-south-asia-58071592, 25 August 2021; reprinted with the permission of Bilal Sarwary and the British Broadcasting Corporation.

ÅSNE SEIERSTAD: Extract from *The Bookseller of Kabul*, translated by Ingrid Christophersen, Virago, 2004, copyright © Åsne Seierstad, 2002, translation copyright © Ingrid Christophersen, 2003. Reprinted by permission of the publisher through PLSClear.

SAADI SHIRAZI: from *Bustan, The Orchard* and poetry from *Delphi Collected Works of Saadi*, translated by A. Hart Edwards, Delphi Classics, 2019.

SAADI SHIRAZI: Poems "Love's Secret;" "Sweeter than these lips I have not heard anyone speak" and "No one can come between us tonight" from *Sa'di in Love: The Lyrical Verses of Persia's Master Poet* translated by Homa Katouzian, I.B. Tauris, Bloomsbury Publishing Plc, 2016, copyright © Homa Katouzian, 2016. Reprinted by permission of the publisher.

SAADI SHIRAZI: from "The Rose Garden" translated by Richard Jeffrey Newman in *Selections from Saadi's Gulistan*, Global Scholarly Publications, 2004. Reprinted by kind permission of Richard Jeffrey Newman.

LALAGE SNOW: Extract from *War Gardens: A Journey Through Conflict in Search of Calm*, Quercus, 2018, copyright © Lalage Snow, 2018. Reprinted by permission of the publisher through PLSClear.

RORY STEWART: Extract from *The Places In Between*, Picador, 2005, copyright © Rory Stewart, 2004, 2014. Reprinted by permission of the publisher through PLSClear.

STRABO: Extract from *The Geography of Strabo*, Book 11, Chapter 11, ed. H. L. Jones, Harvard University Press; William Heinemann, Ltd. 1924. Licensed under a Creative Commons Attribution-ShareAlike 3.0 United States License.

ALEX STRICK VAN LINSCHOTEN, FELIX KUEHN and CONTRIBUTORS: Poems "I am an Afghan mujahid;" "Trenches;" "Afghanistan is the home of Afghans; "I live in flames" and "Afghans bring me to tears" from *Poetry of the Taliban*, Hurst, 2012, copyright © 2012. Reprinted by permission of the publisher.

GORDON WHITTERIDGE: Extracts from *Charles Masson of Afghanistan: Explorer, Archaeologist, Numismatist and Intelligence Agent*, Orchid Press Inc, 2023, pp.74–79, 85–86. Reprinted by kind permission of Orchid Press.

LAWRENCE WRIGHT: Extract from *The Looming Tower*, Penguin, 2007, copyright © Lawrence Wright, 2006. Reprinted by permission of Penguin Books Limited.

ABDUL SALAAM ZAEEF: Extracts from *My Life with the Taliban*, Hurst Publishers, 2011, copyright © Abdul Salaam Zaeef, 2013. Reprinted by permission of the publisher.

EDWARD ZELLEM: 18 proverbs from *Zarbul Masalha: 151 Afghan Dari Proverbs*, Cultures Direct Press, 2015; and 18 proverbs from *Mataluna: 151 Afghan Pashto Proverbs*, Cultures Direct Press, 2019. Reprinted by kind permission of Captain Edward Zellem, U.S. Navy.

Every effort has been made to trace copyright holders and to obtain their permission for the use of copyright material. The publisher apologies for any errors or omissions in the above list and would be grateful if notified of any corrections that should be incorporated in future reprints or editions of the book.